Priestess and professor, Margot Christina Shaunessy, her DNA engineered by mastermind industrialist Johnstone Warren, endeavors to spread her benign vision of liberation in a wordfreedom before embodying a malignant malware form of his.

Failed painter, Dark Mor enlisted
by Warren, through his old friend, James Korner, to paint a portrait of Christina, falls under her spell. Together they find themselves on a harrowing pursuit of redemption and enlightenment.

Mor has never forgotten or forgiven friend and nemesis, Korner for the tragic death of his wife. Now, years later, Korner returns to enlist Mor
to paint a portrait of wisdom deva, Christina, a key to initiating Warren's evil virus and to recovering lost treasure listed in an ancient trove of scrolls and codices.

The quest for art and treasure expands to a journey into the heart of awareness in this taut and sophisticated thriller.

Never before has a book of letters offered such enticing debate in abc's of a b'ng'c'ng a y'eye a peering it still in a wordfreedom in the first place indivisible in'visibility of any individual. Or. Y'or you appearing of it
now awhile az's'eX y'all. As'z'any understanding spelling of abc's a k'no'wing D"NA'eye'll int'word twisting in two appearing a pairing azs'eX.

PAINTING CHRISTINA

WYLY'EM

MOORE ART INC

PAINTING CHRISTINA

Published by Moore Art
wylyemart.com

Book design by Mary C. Moore

Library of Congress Cataloging-In Publication Data (TK)

ISBN: 978-098-5686-093 (hardcover)

ISBN: TK (paperback)

ISBN: TK (e-book)

Edition: December 2017 Merry Christmas Dad

10 9 8 7 6 5 4 3 2 1

TO CHRISTINA

Dear Reader / a Re'y"e'a'dhi'or / aR'eye a to perceive it or na
Welcome y'all to a k'new wayeve

Novel Painting Christina is written in an 'alternating alternative form between action or debate. A debate of any reader merely a peering it as audio visual mean and means or appearing of it any meaning'ful of memory alone.

A debate or dialectic logical manner of speaking now of a y. A y or. A y or a y na. You now az's'ex. A y now az's'eX. A y eye merely a peering it. Or.

Appearing of it in memory z's'ex's ting. Awhile now.

A y eye merely a peering it. Now appearing captivated at attention merely in word memory of it. It a b c's of a b'ng c'ng still in the first place indivisible invisibility in a wordfreedom awareness of it.

That this dialectic may release any readers attention from any in word captivity is a potential 'debatable' reward. For you dear reader simply acquiring a taste for it. Indivisible invisibility in visibility of the dialectic debating any in'formation of it as'king of it y perceived ar'king of it now.

Y'or y now az's'eX.

That is the debate raging caj'in in the novel before you cherished reader as'z well s'z'any life lived merely in name alone. We all in h'our turning may not be able to az's'ex ex'plain the question of why beyond the obvious way of function of it, a y now z's'ex. Ex's ting in formation. Awhile now.

Yet we all may turn to debate why or why not. A y'or y na. This debate or dialectic offers opportunity to place any eyez z z'at attention in a b c's in a wordfreedom moment by momentum by merely a peering it alternating with the alter'native of anybody now appearing out of it in wordsz' as'z'anybody in name alone.

Any reader now picking up this sublime quest of questioning a Y may find themselves engaged merely a peering it with letters as a mean formal means sound still untouched in a wordfreedom without meaning to appear of it. In other words'z any wondering readers may find themselves still in the first place indivisible invisibility in a wordfreedom awareness now a k'no'ing out of it as'z'any appearance of it. This awareness still of a complete liberation is a 'debatable' reward reading absorbing the Y'or y na dialectic debate introduced by Margot Christina Shaughnessy on p. 31.

Due to the 'debatable' infinite potential of this liberation in a wordfreedom awareness of merely a peering it at any page the author yours truly in blood & bone feels necessity to offer some TIPS for reading the dialectic as it appears alternating now and again with normal literal letter'll action of the story.

TIP 1: You and you alone awesome reader as'king of it y are the twin tween macro-micro cosmic mean & as'z'any means for the story to unfold before eyez z z'a merely a peering it now out letter'all'y y'all int'word a twis'ting in two appearing a pairing in a memory as'z'any twin tween a meaningful of it. Now by turning a k'no'wing d'na'eye'll out of it in two any scant meager measly thin'king of it a y appearing a pairing in formation az's'ex y'all .

In other words'z'a a pre-semantic audio visual flow of the text is y'all twin tween mean means of any meaningful memory of it az's'words. Metaphorically cutting & gutting y'all up.

The dialectic debate is in the classic specific logical argument in the G.W.F. Hegel mode of thesis antithesis synthesis. Thesis of a y eye merely a peering it. Or antithesis of a y eye now az's'ex'et'ting duplicating in a dubious duplicity appearing out of it a twin tween awhile now of it. Synthesis in a wordfreedom awareness of a y now az's'ex. Awareness of a y eye merely a peering it now out az's'ex's ting in formation appearing of it awhile now. A space in time.

TIP 2. Realize any indifference or apathy to this debate due to ignore'ance of it now as cause or ka's of any appearing by a k'no'wing out of it. Thus apathy or indifference naturally accrues as'king of it y a k'no'wing understanding of the spelling of a b c's. Beware of turning at attention into a meager scant chintzy thin'king of it.

A turning of it into a craft carrying away attention. Int'word a twis'ting in two appearing a pairing of it in memory. Mem mind or y. Yet a twisted in two anybody at attention captivated merely in any name alone. Thus the Y'or y na dialectic offers moment by momentum alternating alter'natives in a wordfreedom memory freedom indivisible invisibility as that awareness of it.

Why? Why now ignore what you are already k'no'wing? Thats'z'a real debate. Why still ignore what we all already turn into any k'no'wing out of it?

TIP 3: Avoid eye freeze. Relax stretch out be entertained by the 'debatable' action s'z'any ex'cite'ment az's'ex'periencing of it. Then put it in a higher gear eyez z z'a rolling over way'eves of it hitting patches of the dialectic. Roll with the flow. The peh'ss'y w'hole point of view of you keeps circling a b'lack'g'round. The'sis consistent repeated for sake of hammering with sheer love that w'hole point of view of you of a y eye'am is is it. You're still it.

It is a debatable acquired taste like free jazz & anchovies. Y'all that I'm saying from the bottom of my heart to the top of the ka's'mic chakra inches above the head is Ye'ei'ow'zz'a baby cakes ey'e'a sum goo she"na.

Ma'ng,

Wyly Em

PS. The following pages offer debatably the alter'native awareness of a Y'or you yet in the first place still indivisible invisibility. Alternating as eX appearing a pairing in visibility produced understanding the in word spelling of a b c's of a b'ng c'ng now by a k'no'wing out a D'NA'eye'll of it. As'ex y'all. Thatsz the meat and greet of the dialectic debate between a y eye merely a peering it or appearing of it by a pairing supernaturally as'z'any thoth'tsz of it. Az's'ex y'all. Az's'ex's ting debatably in formation. Just us we all learned as though two az's'ex per eye in c'ng(experiencing) sensorial worlds from the point of view of you of y'or you now az's'ex'et'ting duplicating in word appearing phonographically by any k'no no no'wing out int'word a twis'ting in two appearing a pairing beside the point. Of view of you of y'or you now az's'ex y'all. Debatably a now k'no'wn unk'no'wn. Az's'eX. Like y'sz. As'z y'all pick up on the debate of it or D'NA'eye'll of it find yourself lost in that peh'ss'y w'hole pow pow power of potential infinite still from that central point of view c.c.c. seer sight see'n now merely a peering in plain ordinary sight as'z'any in formation of it a in word deceit. She'e'na still virgin or merely a b'lack mirror see'as womb for'ma'sz'ex'et'ting duplicating now complicit in h'our k'no no no'wing out of it. By that simple twist of fate faith family fame or in'famy. Of h'our own D'NA'eye'll. That will we all a wheel of good or bad medicine. D'NA'cid creatingsustain-ingdestroying it'self. A being completely complete completion. . . c.c.c. . . yet a being center centered centrality of it awareness of it aten'cion by now bi nary appearing a pairing of it yet indivisible invisibility. Now debatably in visibility. Yet as'z'any in'formation of it a deceit. As'z'any or eve're'y'body. A b'lack'g'round mer'cy supersonic peh'ss'y w'hole body. Y? y? Y? Y'all gotta laugh y'or azs'of'f finding out y y'all been chasin' tail so long!?! Still y'all must if only because you can. Or not. That'sz the debate. A y'or y na? Moment to momentum attention may be paid to it. It a b'ng c'ng merely mirrored in a b c's. Share the moment to momentum of it. Awhile now. . .taste awareness yet in the first place indivisible invisibility as'z'any individual

* * *

az's ex'ample tastings of the Y dialectic debate of "a Y'or you still in the first place indivisible invisibility debatably now az's ex's ting in'formation . . . "Following the supersonic trail of the monotheistic priests in word exodus from a being still in the first place indivisible invisibility now out of it as thoughts inked on papyrus scrolls in the new phonographic language of 22 letter alphabeta code. Out inked as m"ark of the covenant letter'all'y y'all now a b c's of a b'ng c'ng in word information. Awhile now. Awhile now of moments or millenium." . . . "She had in that blink of eye a're'y'alized invisibility now a k'no'wing out of it a being anybody. Out now in her eyez z z a peering it. A b'ng c'ng turning a b c's into a k'no'wing out of it any appearing of it awhile now merely mirrored in word." . . . "Christina az's'ex'pressed her breath. Oh scientist where is eve'll now?" . . . "a y az's ex . . . az'sex . . . she could smell testoserone in the air . . . around the Korner . . . what she knew about him . . . nice guy for a psychotic killer." . . . 'Y'or Y Now Az's'eX' was the shorter title of the article written in the dialectic or practise of speaking with intent of ex'pressing merely why you're you or me appearing in word memory in a b c's out of a b'ng c'ng still in the first place. . . . A chuckle passed her lips. The double entendre of a y as ex or sex, so quickly turned geometry to psychometry. G-motion to e-motion. . . . A'sz int'word a twis'ta fate faith or family. eLaws reminding why she now appeared to be other y'sz in any mirror or reflected in the cunning stare of recent aquaintance James Korner." . . . " A y'll of Eve'll. Her will put that knife in my hand as surely as it had put her in his, she thought with a shudder. . . . Eve'll of eve're'y bodhi. . . . She now laughed out loud at the double entendre. The sheer duplicity of it a peering it still in the first place now out of it as thoughts appearing of it in her eyez z z'ion eve'n't now in'formation in mind or y's'z'any memory thinking about it. . . . Of a b'ng c'ng still indivisible in'visibility in'for'ma'sz in word in her eyez z z'a peering it at any or eve're'ybody appearing of it to disappear in it . . . fade back to one indivisible b'lack'g'round turning into or out of any or eve're'y'body. . . . "In word of it. Finally she now a're'y'all'eye'zed a denial of k'no no no'wing a b c's of a b'ng c'ng now out int'word in'formation of anybody anywhere anytime still a y eye a peering it in the first place. . . . Yet immortal while in denial of it. Of a being still in the first place. . . . Same'e same still denial in a b c's of a b'ng c'ng now the real e-motional e'go trip. A k'no no no'wing out of it y'all along the long or short wily w'h'ile of it out and about in word in formation now flashing through her eyez z z of eve're'y'body. . . . "Find yourself still she now told herself. Still a being free of any mere or y na mirrored you y'll DNA in that simple int'word a twis'ting in two one fate. Of mirror appearing of it in word in any information asz thoughtsz of a being now out of it in word. . . . As'k'ey"es on Sanskrit Hebrew Aramaic Greek and Latin in for'ma'sz that letter'all'y y'all approach or reproachment as'z z z'leep black into that one black peh'ss'y w'hole of it out in her eyez z z'of eve're'y'body." . . . "Only those valuing or surely desiring in a wordfreedom or liberation will be drawn out to it. . . . It seems slavery can be addictive. Genetically neuronically chemically addictive. . . . We all a wheel turning a b'lack'g'round echo into or out of one appearing of it. A b c's in word in formation of a b'ng c'ng now as'z'anybody ignoring a b'ng still indivisible invisibility." . . . "we all a wheel turning churning burning mirror'el'y in supersonic superimposed bio'cog'neuroninic cellular felt fields of you in D'NAy'll feeling a being that alone . . . feeling a black'g'round echoing that in a b c's of a b'ng cing still in the first place indivisible invisibility of a b'ng that alone. . . . She now found herself in visibility a peering it out mirrored in word mind memory. In word speaking y'or y now without appearing az's ex. As ex's ting alone in formation at aten'shunned. Y'or y now in the'or'y of man'as mind or y in word mirror'el'y function of fun'ny'a'ction of a twis'ting the na't away." . . . "Could more letters qualify to reveal the gravity of it as'ka's mic quantum quandry, a black peh'ss'y w'hole body b'lack'g'round creating sustaining or destroying of it simultaneously? You die now. In word death. A death merely supernaturally now as a k'no'wing of birth." . . . " . . . gave her the cajones to suggest in the or y a being in theory of man'as mind or y you're you now merely appearing supernaturally by duplicating in word as'z'any thoth'tsz of it . . . as'z'any universe . . . that verse of you ni'q appearing as'z'any being biologically y'all born az's'ex . . . y'all still remain that indivisible invisibility. Of a Y, that yod iota referred to as'z'anybody that I am is is. It is as that, that I am thinking this, she thought with a sly smile. . . . "duplication as'z'any thoughtsz of man a being in theory the or y of man'as mind or y you're you. Now a k'now'ing mere mirror duplicating duplication as'z'any thoughtsz yet in visibility of any eye a peering it now out in formation. In a b c's of a b'ng c'ng in time now az's ex, a k'now'n un'k'now'n. . . . A k'no'wing out of it a cunning duplicity of appearing a pairing of it . . . a subject in a space in time awile now of objective objectivity. That a Y az's eX"y'all. . . . What a hoot, she now thought, that I am as awareness complete completely free freed in a wordfreedom. . . . now then . . . falling as'z z z'leep from that giant step off a ledge in time as'k'now a kurving a b'lack'g'round echoing complete roles of d"ark'ness to be played as'z'any fool. As'z'any fool fooled by any a na y denial of a being indivisible invisibility. A Y in time now to get it on aw'h'ile. In'for'ma'sz a cunning act az's eX. . . . . She now laughed to herself at the witchy'ness of that crafty in word spell. The spelling of a b c's asz a b'ng c'ng in formation. What a why a y eye stew she stirred. A y eye a peering it out in for'ma'sz appearing awhile now. In for'ma'sz a wily wile. A cunning crafty deceit of that duplicity az's ex. X's ting int'word information of a twis'ting in two. . . . appearing a pairing . . .as'z'any wordship crafty craft a say'ling out in her eyez z z'of eve're'y'body. . . . Thus she now understood the vehement denial of merely a peering it now necessary to mirror it in word into any appearing of it. . . . Christina realized the paradox of a b'ng c'ng out in her eyez z z'of eve're'y'body now a k'no'wing out of it a denial a're'y'dhi'a'ting out of a y eye b'ng c'ng merely a peering it. . . . merely supernaturally as'z'any thoth'tsz of it. . . . She now k'new that with the arrogance of her colleagues' ignore'ance of it, the k'ey"e of it, a're'y'all'eye'zing directly merely a peering it would remain hidden. By their own complicity. Hidden from them another ten million years. With out eyes merely to see or ears to hear, without valuing liberation now eve'na while a k'no'wing a denial of it, they might or must remain ignoring their freedom for a million zillion years or more to come. . . . A stillness of anybody of any religion now a k'no'wing a b'ng c'ng of that Great God'ess'e to be found letter'all'y y'all in the word she mused. . . . Then that academ'y wall arises. Ignore'ance as'z'any k'no no no'wing of it with eve're'y breath . . .

as'z'any k'no'wing out of it with intent at aten'cion of a binary reenforcing any false peh'ss'y'ence az's ex. A y subject subjective subjectivity debatably complete awareness of that b'ng"lack" instilling intent of a b'ng c'ng a gain of it. Awhile now. . . . Chasing that tail as well as a being of that tail chased, she understood plenty, she thought. A being now out in her eyez z z'a k'no'wing of it a virgin or a womb? The re'y"e y'all y'oni source of any mirror y'na bodhi's of k'no'wer's the'or'eyez'ng a peh'ss'y'en'tific theory issuing from that mouth or'is out to a dog eat dog'matic academia awaiting to get conceptual designing A.I. hooks set. A man with or without womb. Man'o man'as mind or y. Y? Why az's"ex'per eye en'c'ing? Y X's tingin formation as'z'anybody? . . . She found in the scroll something not lost so much much as waiting to be rediscovered with a message for the eve'r'ey present far more impactful than silver or gold. A message of liberation. A liberation now while still living on with our day to day moment to momentum roles. . . . es'ka'roles playing out in time. . . . Still a being of that first ma'tter in the first place now a mirrored k'no'wing out of it as'z'any matter of a b c's of a b'ng c'ng still in the first place in a wordfreedom now. Awareness in a wordfreedom foreve"rey'body. . . .The scroll 99 percent pure copper . . . tantalized her enigmatic mind . . . Perhaps following the money could lead to its true design or be a ruse to stir interest, a disguise as temptation to touch the untouchable . . . to have to hold that indivisible invisibility of anything . . . That true design, that indivisible in'visibility of any meaning could only be discerned by those with eyes to see. Otherwise, she thought, the meaning as words would remain unclear as the nature of the people involved transmitting it. . . . A door opened. Christina saw a great rode leading to a palace shimmering amidst lush gardens . . . below glistened forty foot hammered brass gates trimmed with pure gold. She found herself on to an ancient yet timeless code playing out in eve're'y human voice echoing a b'lack'g'round the whorl'd'ing of it us we all a wheel of fortune fate faith and family. . . . The whole point of a peh'ss'y w'hole c'ng the pow pow power potential of it in her eyez z z'of eve'll fell upon her eyez z z'a field of view . . . She'e'na felt his field of D'ark'ness falling upon her eyez z z'a like a moonless night in country. She said it. She would recognize him then meeting him now. . . . A mirror'ed as'king of it y as'ka's'all body a pairing out a la que"en que' of that in which appearing out of it in her eyeyz z z of eve'll'y'ears supersonically in her eyez z z'a'ringing it out in word. A Y az's'eX. Y'all asz'eX'hodos way'eve eyez z z'in a're'y"ez z z'a're'y'all. Information awhile now. . . . A'y eye in y'all asz'za seer now a k'no'wing out of it int'word or out of that a b'lack'g'round of a b'ng complete role of d"ark'ness. Or'e y'es'peh ark of the covenant. The supersonic supernatural e'sp'ar'king of it y aggreement a chord free a're'y'nge'ment a re'y"e'all go'a'ld'en y urge energy as'z'any thoth'tsz of it. A singular Great God'ess'e to be. Letter'all'y y'all set free of any in word captivity. . . . of'ten a b'ng c'ng now out of it as'z'any thoth'tsz of it in word captivity. A binary captivity by a being y na re'y'eas'z z z'ap'ping echoing a y as'ex's ting in formation. Of'ten in denial of a k'no'wing out of a being still in the first place. Now a k'no'wing out of it in word as'z'any information. . . Or . . . or . . . or a're'y"e gold ore go el da. The a're'y'all go'a'l'don body in a wordfreedom. The az's'exodus of mirror'or y slavery. In word she'e'na now held the k'ey"e a peering it still a being c'ng in the first place indivisible in'visibility as'z'anybody now in plain sight. Yet a peering it."

page 31 Christina introduces dialectic to Dark Mor . . . "In that I am practising a new dialectic just let me carry on as though making sense. In that dialectic using the classic Hegelian trinity of thesis antithesis synthesis a y poses as ex. Thesis y now antithesis as'ex's ting out in formation. Thus any antithesis of a y now as'ex still a y being the whole point of view of you of y you're you in the first place. Thus synthesis that awareness of the indivisible invisibility of any individual or any a na y'or y now as'ex y'all." She tossed another hook. Mor stuck it deep in his lower lip. . . . "Had me or you? Now it seems we all a wheel turning into or out of a k'no'wing of it any memory. A living of it mirrored as thoughtsz in the'or'y a b c's of a b'ng c'ng as'z'any mere in word memory of me or you. A y being still in the first place now out as'word dividing us. . . . He knew she now instantly knew he knew that she knew of it. Of a b'ng c'ng still in the first place indivisible invisibility now out of it or a b'lack'g'round echoing a peh'ss'y whole power. Now az's ex. . . . Shrugging she picked back up on the thread Mor sensed would lead back to awareness of a blackness. Of a prior state of a b'ng c'ng indivisible in'visibility. A b'ng c'ng in a state of it now in a wordfreedom still a b'ng'lack instilling intent to be a gain of it. Out in her eyez z z'a peh'ss'y w'hole power and if that don't float your boat what will he wondered. Y'or y speak dialectic offers an in word debatable awareness of a state of a y being supernaturally that macromicro ka's mic mean means meaningful of eve're'y'body as'z'any wayeve function. A b c's wayeve supersonic sound function of a fun'ny'a'ction ma'king of it a y eye merely a peering it now out int'word a twis'ting in two appearing a pairing of it. . . . A man'as mind or y memory mean between. Between greater or lesser possibilities of a being. A being twin tween macromicro ka's mic a'ten bi'na'rey. As above so below. The b'lack'ness causal x body of infinite potential instilled with intent of k'no no no'wing ignoring y. Instilled with intent of projecting a negation of any now k'no'wing of it. K'no no no'wing disregard of why, y'or you still in the first place indivisible in'visibility. As'z'any in formation of it is a deceit. . . ."Of eve're'y'body." He heard the words coming from his mouth as though from another's mind. He felt the dialectic flooding his in word field like a tsunami disappearing his sense of a being a y az's'ex's ting in formation. In formation merely mirrored in word. Now attention remained in her'him'it indivisible in anybody out of a being in visibility. Invisibility in visibility. He now felt disappeared in her'him'it as'ka's mic overmind or memory. Mor felt form as indefinite moment after momentum merely defined awhile now in word. Beyond that in word definition he drown formless in her eyez z z. He resisted panicking by focusing on his breath. . . . "Now we all a wheel turn in her eyez z z'a ma'sz nature of a b'lack'g'round echoing eve're'y'body supersonically supernaturally superimposed as'z'any thoth'tsz of it. It indivisible invisibility now a y eye of anybody merely a peering it out as'ex's ting by k'no'wing out of it in word in formation. As'z'anybody. As'z'anybody as thoth'tsz of it appearing a pairing in any role of loop'dy loops. Now turning a b'lack'g'round echo of it as'k'no'wing out of it a b'ng c'ng by a b c's in wordsz of a denial. A projection of thoth'tsz in a b c's of a b'ng c'ng of any or eve're'y'body." She now seemed to be testing him. He flashed on Korner setting him up. Maybe slipping a drug in his coffee? Some unseen influence seemed altering his consciousness. Pulling him into or out of some in word vortex. He thought for a split second but merely spoke what came to mind. "Kinda like an in word consensus of ignorance?" . . . he liked that she got right on to the point. That point of anybody appearing of it in the first place out of the soaking darkness. He'd found most preferred finding themselves . . . somehow out beside it. A b'ng c'ng now as though beside the point. She was funny that way. In her eyez z z'a pointing out of him. A being still in the first place. . . . Perhaps for the first time in his life he felt at home in the first place now with k'now'ing another human being. . . . Soon enough though we all grow weary now then finding ourselves falling as'z z z'leep into a black'g'round indivisible invisibility. Only then now awak'h'ening yet playing out roles. Or rolls now turning into or out any or eve're'y'body merely mirrored in word. . . . "That put on of any in word masked captivity of a living merely in name bound to wear thin on anybody after awhile now. Naturally we all turn black'g'round. Turn a b'lack into or out of any or eve're'y'body appearing a gain of it. . . . "The d'ark'ness now in her eyez z z'of eve're'y'body merely a peering it out in word appearing of it awhile as'z'anybody. Out of a b c's of a b'ng c'ng still in the first place. . . . a singular being still indivisible invisibility now instilled with b'lack intent to be a gain of it. It yet completely complete completion. . . . c.c.c. . . . now a b'lack'ness inciting appearing a pairing of it awhile now yet as'z'any appearance of it must be a deceit. . . . Any being appearing of it out awhile now still in visibility of a b'ng c'ng a slight slice of a meager thin'king of it. . . . A now to be perceived ar'king of it out in her eyez z z'leeping a wayeve re'y"e as'z'a b'lack'g'round body. . . .a b'lack mirror se'as body . . . in her eyez z z'a mirror'se'a. . . . The d"ark'n'ess'e now to be perceived ar'king of it. . . . c.c.c. . . . in her eyez z z'a eve"re'y'body merely a peering it out in word appearing of it awhile now as'z'anybody. Out of a b c's of a b'ng c'ng still in the first place now turning out of it. A b'lack'ness instilling intent to be a gain of it merely supernaturally as'z'any thoth'tsz of it. A Great God'ess'e to be letter'all'y y'all in a word. . . . That predjudice against the d'ark reflects the neurosis and psychosis of anyone living in near complete denial of it without realizing y. A y that I am speaking of it in the first place. A y being now that as'k'as mic memory of a k'no'wing out of it. A being still in the first place. Now that indivisible invisibility as'king of it y now turning a b'lack'g'round supersonic echo instilling intent hear a gain of it. Awhile now. As'z'any in formation of it is a deceit. A y'or y your you now appearing a pairing az's'ex'eting duplicating an ending by denial, by D'NA'eye'll of it yet indivisible. . . . Now by that simple twis'ting int'word in two . . . . a con spiralling . . . a D'NA'eye'll . . . I'll . . . I will we all a wheel . . . churning yearning burning . . .denial of a being still completely complete completion . . . c.c.c. . . in the first place. Out of that completion it cannot be a gain . . . yet it appears by h'our own complicity. . . . H'our k'no'wing denial of it . . . it seems we all a wheel must turn into or out of it till finding y'or y now az's'ex y'all or as'z'any scant skinny thin'king of it y now az's'ex y'all. . . . "Please continue. In that I am appearing confused may be due to a certain double entendre that I am picking up in your words." He found the dialectic a dichotomy splitting a b c's off a b'ng c'ng of indivisible invisibility from any in word information of it. Revealing without now a k'no'wing out of it in word there is no information of it. The dialectic set up a debate between awareness of a y eye merely a peering it or now as'king of it y a k'no'wing out of it in word thoughts appearing of it. It a b'ng c'ng as though now out in a b c's cunning wordship craft of a ka's mic'ro wayeve b'lack'g'round indivisible body echoing any hearing of a language now in the dialectic debate cancelling itself out of any information of it. Revealing a being still in the first place indivisible invisibility. Invisibility before falling as'z z z'leep understanding any in word spelling of a b c's in forming it out in visibility awhile now. . . . Mor could only observe this crazy flow of energy in formation in words as though vomitting up or down a glut of a b c's of a b'ng c'ng gushing out in word information. He felt it all now a b'lack'g'round him a k'no'wing out of it without realizing why except as a b'ng c'ng in her eyez z z'a present presence. She smiled back from across the table. . . . "as though projecting out of it a b'ng c'ng lacking of it instilling intent of any a na y body to be of it a gain. Thus a y eye being complete in the first place a peering it out now a b'lack'g'round turning into a k'now'ing out instilled with intent of intentionally disregarding a being complete to begin with." The supernatural supersonic p'sy'lent buzz of the dialectic seemed to settle down. His stomach no longer lifting into his throat Mor felt a deep relaxation coming over him. . . . "Complete encirclement d"ark'n'esse of a being now to be perceived as black. As'king of it y a desire of eve'll. A wayeve will to turn into or out of it a gain. . . . "Projecting it. Ignoring it is a positive negating projection of it. A positive negativity in any mirror mind or y memory wayeve function of a being anybody as out in word though'tsz of it projects indivisible consciousness as a b'lack'g'round k'no no no'wing out of it any denial of it. . . ."

"Thoth? You said thoth?"

"Thoth'tsz of a Great God'esse to be now letter'all'y y'all in word. Thus any in word being. . ."

"A being of a duplicity now in word information of a b c's letter'all'y y'all supernaturally appearing of it. A being now a mind mirrored memory in a supernatural duplicate superimposed in word of a b'ng c'ng as'z'any thoth'tsz of it appearing by the grace of a God'esse. To be letter'all'y y'all phonographically appearing of it merely a peering it out of a b c's.

Now he found himself within her eyez z z'azz'leeping superimposed as'z'any thoth'tsz of a b'ng c'ng directly across the table. Praise God and pass the whiskey he mused. And by now he could use a drink.

She'e'na left that h'OO'ka out there on the table. Mor took to staring at his hands now holding the sugar shaker. It seemed the 'Y'or y na' debate divided az's'eX. Y'all as'ex's ting of it as'z'any information. Awhile now. A wily twis'ting twisted sisters he mused. Of a mean means meaningful of memory. Of a cobra and a vulture. As'z two strands of D'NA'eye'll he thought.

. . . she'e'na a wayeve waved an index finger with the wide eyes of a school girl. Then Mor felt kneck hairs standing out as a denial of kali ma'sz ef'ang. Still a b c's of a b'ng c'ng it informing it int'word a D'NA'y'll. A twis'ting in two sisters. We'd"ja'tah"ne'ba'ty. The name slid into his narrative from an ancient muse.

Out of it in her eyez z z'of eve'll. A wayeve will we all a wheel of eve're'y'body now turning a y eye int'word as'king of it y a k'no'wing out of it appearing as'ka's mic da y na light igniting any personic person appearing as'z'z'a superimposed supersonic ignore'ance of it.

Chapter 1

James Korner stepped to the edge. Below him, the sheer cliff face fell some hundred feet to a scattering of partially buried boulders giving on to chaparral thickets and a river valley stretching out for miles. A wisp of smoke drifted from a tiny cabin he spotted through a pair of binoculars. Wind flattened his graying hair as he kicked a cluster of stones over the side, watching them clatter in a free fall.

Hearing their hollow echo was as though now knowing that desire of death coming from above, falling on him like stone. He had felt that weight, waiting on death since leaving San Francisco, driving north to find an old friend, Dark Mor, with a new scheme to right some old wrongs. Getting reaquainted meant falling back through layers of ghosts haunting him since the war. Though which war was still a question up for grabs as he had found himself in several while losing some parts of himself in others. He sauntered over to his dark brown Mark IV Lincoln town car sitting under a stand of fir trees, layered with dust from miles of unpaved road leading up to the four thousand foot descent into the West Fork Valley. Korner pulled a dented Altoids tin from his pocket. He gave it a long look before putting it back.

He slid behind the wheel of the Lincoln, steering it back onto the road that snaked down the mountain. Korner took the curves hard, g-forces throwing him against the shoulder harness as the Lincoln rocked, a rooster tail of dust clouding off behind.

He turned on the road leading through a stone arch with a wrought iron winged "V" swinging on rusty chains overhead. A brown-skinned man in a high peaked cowboy hat stood by the open steel gate. Korner pumped the brake as he pulled up. He noticed the vaquero's thin lips set in a taught line as he stepped out from the car. Road dust that flared behind smoking tires settled in his lungs as he stepped forward to shake the hand of the stranger. He thought the Lincoln looked at home covered in the rough country road matching his dusted denim and muddy boots. Korner took a breath of air a tad too fresh for him, road dust caking his throat called for that smokey tang of meat burning over an open fire with tequila shots for company.

"Buenos dias, senor. Que pasa, amigo? Como estas?" Korner saw in the deeply lined face of the vaquero reflections of that war south of the border. Around the eyes he detected that sadness of centuries being worked over by certain other interested parties. He resisted the urge to embrace him a companero amigo. The mestizo drew Korner out of his white-bread soul bubble, breaking open into the field, in country.

"Puede usted decirme donde un hombre, Dark Mor?"

A shirtless young native, wearing cut-off levis, dreadlocks, arms labeled with prison tattoos pulled alongside him on a high sprung trail bike. He gave him a sly smile that said to Korner, el mano would be pleased to shake his hand or slit his throat, no difference. He recognized himself on tortillas and puro vida.

"We speak gringo here, pendejo. Who you looking for?" he asked.

"An old amigo-conoce usted a mi amigo-un Dark Mor? No tengo el gusto de conocerte."

"Mi llamo es Paco. Who you, hoss? The fuck you want?"

"James Korner. Me and Darkie boy go back a long ways, before you were a gleam in your daddy's eye."

Paco grinned. He pulled a machete from the fringed leather scabbard that hung from his belt.

"You have a branch hanging from your fender. Allow me to cut it off, permitame."

"No me importa nada. Put away your blade, bucko, and tell me where to find my amigo. Inmediatamente."

"Okay hombre, follow me. Vamos!" Paco pumped the starter on his bike and sped down the road.

Korner shifted his gaze to the vaquero, shrugged, slipped back behind the wheel, and slammed down the accelerator. He went a quarter mile before jarred, bouncing over a low hump of earth mounded across the road. The impact from the water bar rattled his teeth. He cursed the boy and floored the accelerator, watching the speedometer climb to seventy. Still far ahead of him, the dirt bike poured back a dusty challenge. Korner eased off the gas pedal, catching himself taking Paco's bait so early in the game. He knew the Darkness had been hiding here for awhile. He wasn't going anywhere fast. Moss draped oaks and steel fence posts flashed in his peripheral vision. Korner chewed his lip as the Lincoln ate the road along with brake pads burning.

The stench of hot iron friction eating asbestos made him look for conical hats and elephant grass. Anyone who had survived a war lived with those memory triggers waiting to fire off. It could be road dust or open fecal decay mixed with damp earth filling the nostrils. Korner's mind flashed back to rubber tree plantations, rice paddies, opium fields, and burning hootches turning into desert, hot winds, digging sand out of eyeballs. He recalled the odor of phosphorous jellied gas sizzling bare flesh echoed in the continued ringing in his ears from the sound of heavy artillery thundering in the night. Or maybe it was just the rock'n'roll that ravaged his hearing.

As the years turned away he came to find slightly ravaged country a suitable environment for his own ravaged soul. Being in any comfort zone too long made him completely bonkers. He found that mundane world a walking death by minutiae. Nothing trivial or mundane in war, then every act vital, edged with that mettalic taste layered on his tongue. The fat city life had threatened to infect him with a softness, a comfort level that deadened his nerves in a death by inches. Coming long after forgetting being alive in the first place.

That sound of his boots pounding the earth had once made Korner cocky. Now he wondered whose steps he heard. Maybe they. Them. They dogged him with ghosts of the men he'd killed. Friggin Darkness. We kill for your freedom. We kill and kill 'em all. Let God sort it out. Feeling his years, no longer young, his edge had begun to turn dull. Now, vestiges of his youthful fire stirred in anticipation of his meeting with Mor. Kick ass and don't take any names, only ears, he mused.

He loved the open country but stopping to think about it, the neon whore of the city ever beckoned. She called him home every time, bought, sold, and paid for, a sold soul the only one he could trust. Out in the open land, sea, or sky he needed to keep moving, usually with one hand on the wheel and the other on a weapon. His only salvation was in movement, wheels turning, churning, yearning for wings in the sky joining the sun racing with the stars.

Wind tore through the open windows, whipping up the collar of his cambric shirt, flattening the peak of brown hair high on his forehead, and watering his eyes. He saw a bend in the road ahead and slowed. Open pasture gave way to a forest of oak, and madrone studded with shining oblong leaves. Fifty yards from the road in the shade of overhanging trees, he saw a maybe seven-point buck moving in shifting shadows as a red-tail hawk screamed out of the canopy, soaring towards him then twenty feet overhead. He sensed warning in the flight pattern of the hawk. As he made the bend a large ball of feathers slammed the windshield. Head jerking, his hand slipped from the wheel. The heavy Lincoln fishtailed in the loose gravel, spinning 180 degrees.

Having collided with a turkey vulture, Korner looked through greasy residue on his windshield, catching a glimpse of knobby tires as the dirt bike came whining back around. Flaring dreads as he bounced on the bike seat, Paco almost lost his balance skidding around the stalled Lincoln. A fly buzzing a bull. He pulled it out in a trail of dust, smiled a backward glance, cranked the throttle, and zipped down the road. Korner chuckled as he whipped the Lincoln around to continue his chasing the macho hustler rustler.

He never saw the drop off. All four tires left the ground as he plunged over the edge into a deep washout lined with razor-edged bottle rock, blowing out the front tires. Korner heaved against the shoulder harness, bloodying his nose as he smacked the steering wheel. Paco had set him up good. Seems he would have to wait a bit longer to meet the Darkness.

Holding a handkerchief to his nose, Korner popped a CD into the slot while a considering his next move. The sweetness of Gina Morales poured out of the speakers. He buzzed the seat back and put his boots across the dash. He thought about that night he recorded it at Ted's, a small after-hours club on Chicago's South Side, The haunting quality of her voice still chilled his spine. Songs from that night fell away as another voice reverberated along with Gina, that of Mor's. "Darky boy," he thought out loud. Just living that sheltered rock'n'roll life. He listened to the duet merge for that brief moment inside sorrow and longing. Five years later, the recording still caused a catch in his throat. Still burned instantly through layers of armour surrounding his heart.

On the edge of their voices he picked up on the sound of a helicopter blading the sky. Suddenly Korner regretted not having a weapon on him. He thought about jumping out of the car but he couldn't break away from Gina's voice. The helicopter came in fast, hammering the treetops. Korner cranked up the volume. Gina silky and smoldering as the blades slapped the air over the mountain ridge, held him to her breast. Helicopters brought good guys and bad. For a moment he wondered whether to be relieved or worried.

Korner knew they spotted him by the change in their rpms. They came in hard on the ridge line, the pilot hitting that spot in the blade revolution where they spanked the earth. The sound of something nasty, like Gina when she got funky, drilled into his chest. The black helicopter with dark tinted windows came into view. He saw her sleek and ominous with one bay door open. A bushy-haired jock, beefy in camouflage pants, white T shirt crossed with 9mms, and legs kicked out on the struts hunkered down with an M-16 across his lap. Big, dumb, and got a gun, Korner thought.

He saw the bull-jock's eyes, brush mustache, and the hoop of gold in his left earlobe as the chopper circled the Lincoln in a lazy arc. His dazzling eyes flashed Korner back to the flower children that had wilted away after the Summer of Love. That summer they shined so bright that you could see through them to a place where God's finger touched the earth, leaving a few skin flakes getting multitudes blessedly bombed. Love then flowed on a street called Haight. He liked the neighborhood better after the shine turned dull, when junkies and meth heads prowled the streets, preying on the vulnerable. For Korner at that time San Francisco felt more like Chicago with a freaky edge.

The helicopter passed over low enough that the breeze from the blades whipped Korner's hair as he poked his head out the car window. The chopper cowboy jumped from the skids and approached. Korner kept smiling as he scanned the helicopter for markings. He found none. The black machine, silhouetted against the open sky, hovered in a lazy arc, circling the crippled Lincoln, blasting rocks and brush. Korner, one arm still on the leather seat, pulled out his Altoids tin. He popped the lid, knuckle-size rocks glistening in the light. He offered the largest to the cowboy who grinned and winked at the nugget of pure Bolivian flake laying like dry snow in his open palm. Without a word the cowboy rejoined the helicopter, raising the M-16 as he lifted off and sailed over the mountain ridge, swallowed back into that blue sky. Korner wondered if he would repay his generosity by calling a tow truck.

The tranquility of Gina's voice returned Korner smiling with the knowledge Mor would soon join her. Musically, they had made love on Ted's tiny and smoky spot lit dance floor. The whole romantic deal made him sick, all candy, hearts and flowers. Their marriage could not have lasted.

"You were wrong for her," Korner said aloud. "Weak bastard with your whining love. I wanted to eat her soul. No man could have drained Gina like me, bucko."

Darkie man had painted her, did her, and sang with her on stage, he thought as the jealousy that drove him to the only option, the betrayal that left Gina dead, curdled in his gut. Knowing she gone chilled him still.

☼

Dark Mor buttoned up his long sleeve plaid shirt against the morning chill. Sinewy arms flexed as he gripped the heavy worm-drive saw. Carbide steel tore through wood as yellow sawdust peppered his heavy beard to match sun-bleached hair. He saw dawn breaking over the horizon with shafts of morning light finding the building site scattered with six-inch thick logs stripped of their bark and smooth as bone. He hitched up the leather tool belt, slung with hammer and chisel, dragging on his waist. Standing on the elevated framing surrounded by the logs, sunlight pooling an array of power tools juiced by a gas generator he stretched out his arms to embrace the spirit of a new day. The generator cacophony seemed to him, providing some validation for a man's mind lost or found so insignificant in that vast forest turning around its billions year old planetary god el Sol. He found man or mind invisible turning in fields of planets stars and galaxies.

Paco gave out a "Ye-haa!" above the drone of the generator and the rattle of his dirt bike. He roared into the building site, letting the knobby rear tire of the bike slide sideways with a spray of dirt clods.

"You're late, amigo," Mor said.

Paco swung a dusty boot over the high sprung bike frame and let out another scream.

"Hey muchacho, that's the problem with being a tight-ass gringo. You don't know how to relax and enjoy your days."

"My mother, god rest her soul, was crazy. She would look at me with these huge black eyes."

"Oh, by the way, you got a visitor. Says his name is Korner."

He dropped his tool belt on the deck of the cabin and flicked off the generator, catching a reflection of himself in the chrome gas cap as he bent over. Clouds gathered in the reflection.

"Where?" He shook himself and raked fingers through his hair.

"The pendejo tried to run me down with his stinkin' Lincoln. He took a header into the washout. Last I saw him he had his feet up on the dash."

"I'll get him, you stay."

"Come on, muchacho. We take the man together. You familia. Check out your drawing of Rachel. Only familia could do such a beautiful thing. You caught her soul."

"She is a portal to a greater longing."

"And being my sister, one you must never enter."

He shot Paco a friendly slap across his back as they jumped into the pickup. The four-wheel drive truck eased along the road with caterpillar speed.

"What is it about this pendejo?" Paco shouted over the growl of the V-8 engine digging in low up the steep grade.

"He's no toy soldier," Mor barked back. "He trained with the Army and saw action in Vietnam, Nicaragua,Afghanistan, any place they wanted someone to stir the shit."

"He looking for trouble or something?"

"You know, trouble knows him. I knew him before his mercenary days."

"What was he like when he got back from the war?"

"The same James except with a new lust added to his usual sex, drugs, and rock 'n roll."

"Yah, what's that?"

"Blood, amigo, blood. You've seen the scar on my chest," Mor yelled over the roar of an engine running at high r.p.m. in low gear. "I've seen you starin' at it. He gave it to me."

"The man shot you. That explains somethin'" Paco laughed.

Chapter 2

Mor eased off the accelerator near the top of the grade, letting the truck crawl to the crest of the slide. He shut down the ignition, locked the E-brake before jumping out tossing a wheel block behind the front tire. In the sudden quiet he caught strains of Gina singing the song he loved most,

"Someday if all my prayers are answered

And maybe you'll

Be there."

Paco leaned on the truck's horn. "Man is a killer. Got to let him know we're here."

Music poured from the busted Lincoln. Mor skidded down the slide, rocks breaking loose to hammer the top of the car, one leaving a crack in the glass of the Lincoln's sun roof.

No one stirred. He reached the taillights and saw a head lying back on the seat. He slid along the side panel, easing over to the front door. Gina Morales sang. Gina in her sweetness about the bitterness of loss as Korner stretched out with his feet on the dashboard. Mor reached out a hand to check for a pulse when one eye opened.

"Remember this one?" Korner hit a select button. After a moment of silence, Gina floated back with an old Gatemouth Brown tune, 'Here I Go Again.' Another voice joined hers on the CD, "Here I go again, Doin' those same old things I used to do."

"Where did you get that?" he asked.

"The lady gave me a copy from that night she pulled you on stage. Nice pipes," Korner chided as he removed dried blood from a nostril with a flick of his thumb.

Korner's ease made Mor ill at ease. Paco slid down the bank, setting off a stream of gravel. Korner lifted his boots from the dash and planted them on the ground. He stood, stretched and punched the deep blue sky. Mor saw the mustache. It meant Korner had been stateside for a while. He always stayed clean-shaven when abroad. He clenched his fist and hit Korner in the mouth, then the gut. His bulk crunched into the dusty Lincoln.

"Bienvenides," Korner managed, grasping breath as he pushed back up against the Lincoln.

Mor hit him again with the same combination. Blood streamed from a nostril as he fell against the car still staying on his feet.. Korner should have stayed away, gone to ground in any other country but this one, he thought. His knucles burned as he shook out a fist.

"I hate to tell you, brother, but that's all the fight you've got. Invite me up to the house for a beer and we'll do some talking. Bleeding in the sun ain't what I had in mind for a reunion." Korner offered with a smile, blood leaking from his gums as he pushed away from the Mark IV.

He shook out a cigarette and held it in clenched teeth, rubbing at his new bruise. "I can see where country living might be hard on a man," he said, hawking a glob of mucous and blood.

"Ain't no way to winch this piece of Detroit iron out of here without ripping off the oil pan," Paco offered, surveying the blown tires with long brown fingers. His forearms rippled and veined as he pushed himself to his feet. He wore a faded denim work shirt with sleeves hacked off at the shoulders to expose a prison inked tattoo of a branding iron and a rose.

Mor looked back over his shoulder at Korner grinning at him like dinner in a cage. The throb from his bruised fist brought his focus back to Korner's mayhem, the pain, the grins, Gina pouring out of the disabled car.

"We need a snatch block. We can tie off to that fir," he offered.

"The block is back at the main house," Paco replied, slapping a pair of leather gloves against a knee.

"We'll take the truck." Mor looked over at Korner.

"All of us," said Korner. "Darkie man and me can keep busy lying about how nice it is to see each other again," he added with a grin.

Paco climbed the bank, the purchase of his boots sending more stones down to whang off the crippled Lincoln.

Mor saw an opportunity to lay more blows. Korner faced him with a knowing smile, dangling cigarette, feet spread beneath a slouched posture. "Come on. You want to take another shot? Go ahead. I ate my heart like a piece of cold meat when Gina died."

"I'm done with blame. Gina is part of the past I live every day. Comes with having a conscience, messy stuff for people in your line of work." Mor felt his eyes squint as they fell over Korner. He cocked his head to look sideways, imagining the man on his back with a lily on his chest.

He pointed to the truck on the road above. The two men scrambled up the sliding rock to join Paco. Mor vaulted off the bank into the bed as Korner eased up, stepping on the rear bumper, pulling himself up by the tailgate. Slapping the top of the cab as Paco dropped it into low, he looked back at Korner slouching down in the truck bed. They eased down the logging road with the engine acting as an rpm brake.

He stretched with his back against the cab, the metal warming through his shirt. Korner leaned against the tailgate with his legs stretched out. Mor needed time to clear his mind about who was guilty for Gina's death. He favored Korner over himself but as usual his confidence tended to slip.

"I've found you a new model," Korner said with a smile, one eye scrunched as cigarette smoke curled around his face. Sun brought a gray pallor to his skin, as if the accumulated toxins of a larcenous life were leaching out.

"I don't paint," Mor replied, loud enough to be heard over the truck engine. He could feel irritation heating his blood. Korner could only be trouble at this time in his life. Then again, trouble could be a woman.

"Building houses in the sticks for rich pricks. Nice career move." Korner pulled out his flask as he jolted with the truck. Mor declined the offered shot and Korner rattled on with the truck. "I'm here to keep my promise."

Mor glowered at the man. Here he was again, he thought spinning out plots and plans where other people get hurt. Here comes mayhem a knocking on my door, he thought. Do I open it or not?

"This is an opportunity for you to reenter the world and start painting again. Come down to the city, meet some people, and see how it feels. What have you to lose?" Korner continued, his tone growing more confident.

Mor felt he was stumbling onto a stage, forgetting his lines. Korner spoke again.

"Remember the painting you gave me, the one you made me promise not to sell?"

He knew the painting, the last thing he had done over five years ago. A rare creation that poured through him like a living supernal fire. Descending through neuron pigment and brush.

"I have it hanging in a special place in my house in San Francisco. An acquaintance of mine happens to be a prof at Stanford University and wants to meet you. That's thee Stanford, hot shot. She says the painting has a visionary quality. This is for you, man. This is way too huge for us not to set aside the past." He field stripped the cigarette butt, flicked shreds of tobacco from his fingertips, and watched Mor's face as tiny brown threads zipped into the wind.

He wanted to grab Korner by the neck and throw him from the truck. Paco sang along with the radio in the cab rocking with the terrain.

"Get back to painting before you're too old to hold a brush. You talked years ago about a Madonna series that would cool a man's gonads. How was it? 'Make them forget who they think they are so they can remember,' oh hell, I forget, " Korner offered with a wink. Stabbing a pinkie finger into one ear he scanned the tree canopy. He watched a spotted hawk launch from a snag. "That's how this woman talks. She said she recognized a moment in the painting she'd been waiting for."

"What's her name?" Mor asked.

"Christina."

☼

A cloud drifted across the sun as the wrecker from town trussed up the Lincoln. Mor thought the battered car an apt metaphor for his friendship with Korner, and the bad puns on his name. Watching James Korner drive away, he wanted to chase after him and tell him the hell with Christina. He was done with painting and had no need for any hundreds mile trip into the urban wasteland to confirm what he knew. He had found a home on the Flying V, with clean air breaking over distant ridges and peaks. The idea of leaving his sanctuary gave him a wave of nausea.

His steel-toe boots would not move. How could he let himself get involved with Korner again? Anger at his agreement to meet Christina gripped his muscles and he hurtled a long-handled chisel at the logs stacked on the cabin deck. It whacked off a splinter, falling between the two short pieces wedged underneath.

Paco looked up from stacking rocks. Saying nothing, he went back to his work. Soon he started in on another song. Mor tried to pick up the worm-drive but found his hand shaking and vision blurred. He needed to escape the dread seeping into his thoughts. He marched to his truck, unbuckled his leather tool bags and hoisted them into a steel box mounted on the bed, then jumped into the cab, gunned the motor and jammed down the hill. He wanted to catch Korner at the main gate and pound his fists into the man. Instead he bounced over the chuckholes and waterbars to his tiny cabin.

Mor kicked open the door. In one corner stood a cabinet, an old army cot that kept him above the spiders and scorpions, and a squat wood burning stove on a layer of flat river stones. He pulled a bottle of Jose Cuervo Especial tequila from the cabinet and carried the bottle to a faded armchair on the side porch. He looked at the sweep of tree-covered valley wedged by smoky ridges joined at the horizon by an ancient lake. His anger dissipated with the hazy clouds as they drifted, torn by the ridge edges. The sun broke through. A spotted hawk spread his wings overhead. The hawk glided in a lazy turn toward Konocti, the weathered volcano standing watch just above the lake water.

He looked at the bottle nestled in his arm. The silver paper seal was cracked along the ridge of the cap but unbroken. He lurched out of the chair and replaced the tequila in its niche. Another day straight and sober, yet not a better man for either condition, he thought as Christina came to mind. Trouble could be a bottle or a woman.

☼

Stanford philosophy professor Christina Shaughnessy adjusted the jeweler's loop on its flexible arm poised over the light table littered with transparencies of scroll fragments. Thick red corkscrew locks clipped in a pile on the top of her head bobbed as she bent to slide the film over the luminous surface. Two-thousand-year-old Aramaic script came into focus. The ink lines, grainy yet so familiar against the texture of animal hyde, revealed more than words. In her eyes the reconstructed fragments identified characteristics of an individual hand. Connecting the form of letters with a body that lived and died breathed energy back into matters of a long lost day in the life. A day as any filled with hunger, anticipation, touch. Hand to brush. Inked hairs to hyde, parchment or papyrus. That day now revisited once more through her reading. Reaching out, she traced their contour, realizing now the point of view then, same now appearing before eyes. Hers or theirs. Did she move into theirs' or did they move into her, she wondered with a smile.

Paying attention. Seeing grainy letters reminded her of the three years absence from the field. Absence from the heat and grit. Absence from laying hands straightaway touching on thousands years out of touch. Merging with kindred mind reflecting as though'tsz of a being of that indivisible in'visibility of any individual. An immortality of awareness of a being now as though in formation glyphically. Phonographically. Or personically in the sound of her voicing it now. Then as now. Buried from human touch over centuries and millenia. She recalled the gidiness they all felt connecting Hebrew script to more ancient Egyptian hieroglyphs. They had slipped the bonds of tradition. Broken their father's idols. Touch of mind or y man with or without womb as mind still aware of a being in the first place. Or the last place. Her then sunburned and lean on the last dig in the Wadi Qumran, near the northwest end of the Dead Sea. The camraderie. Her mates jubilent with direct knowing touching connecting Jerusalem with Akhetaten. Following the supersonic trail of the Monotheist warrior priests' in word exodus from a being still in the first place indivisible invisibility now out of it as thoughts inked on papyrus scrolls in the new language of 22 letter alphabeta code. Out inked as a m'ark of the covenant letter'all'y y'all now a b'ng c'ng out in word in formation. Awhile. Awhile of moments or millenium.

That night. Leaving comrades and comfort for late hour street she remembered the invincible feeling realizing knowing something lost to 99 and 9 tenths percent of people now on the planet. Now knowing a re'y'ality out in the same ignore'ance ignored by most everyone. Ignored around now knowing it.

Compromised by leaving the apartment at a late hour. Traveling alone. Cautious but also brave. Excavating in the wilder places had toughened her in ways that surprised even her. She certainly had her share of harassment, the usual obscene gestures, getting groped in crowds. Then that Israeli army sergeant starting to unbutton her blouse until convincing him she would meet him later. She could still smell his aftershave.

That night. She flexed her fingers feeling the flow. Jerusalem as a man stepping from the shadows, attacking her with a knife. Never losing her grip she fought him, drawing his blood with her fingernails as he dragged her into an alley. She rolled her neck recalling the back of his hand slamming her head when she tried to get away. Dazed by his blows she woke pinned down under the weight of him breathing hard, deep in her crotch. The weight of him on her. The stink of him. She still felt that transfer of power when hearing the knife clatter loose by her side, finding that bone handle in her grip, stabbing him in the back again and again. She remembered pushing off his dead as'z weight as he slid out of her then sticking him good in the belly six times before coming to her senses.

Rubbing a thumb across her fingertips she recalled the slipperiness of his blood. Seeing the man bleeding out, her piercing scream as she fled, echoed in her mind still.

Christina thought about her return stateside, busying distracting herself with work and teaching. Hiding from the rape with codeine, walking the streets at night in an opiate haze, she found herself offering her violated body to strangers in need of companionship. A year hazed by. She detoxed but never really came down. You are the same but you're not, she thought. Still learning and burning from the rape, she repeated her vow to remember no man, no him could ever really violate her. She knew. A're'y'alized in her awareness of a being asharee'ram shari'reshu, bodiless even amidst bodies. She had in that blink of a y eye a're'y'alized invisibility now k'now'ing out of it a being anybody. Out now in her"eyez z z a peering it. A b'ng c'ng turning into k'now'ing out of it any appearing of it awhile merely mirrored in word. Mirrored in any mind or memory as though'tsz of it in formation. Still her neuronic cellular e-motional body disconnected or became incoherent to her over mind. Or y else suffer to begin with? Temper. Temper. Temper. A're'y'all gaining coherence of overstanding any understanding ramped her fortitude of a being still completely free in first personic person that eye of I a'm'emory is is a being c'ng still in the first place.

People might and did call her crazy but she knew she had the 'bona fides'. Extraordinary direct experience. Along with teaching from a qualified master with scriptural authority to fully comprehend and bear witness in that incomprehensible complete freedom merely realizing a being free of attention captivated in word. Information awhile . . .the words bounced back and forth in her memory, her mind or y. Her thoughts . . .a being of any being . . .in word mirrored out in her'eyez z z' any appearing of it as though'tsz written and spoken in formation . . .she now was a muse she amused with a chuckle. In the or y of man as mind or y memory of a being of that as'ka's mic causal y potential . . .a being of mean centrality . . . a being twined tween micro or macro, any mere . . .a na y mirror duplicating . . .a y na now . . .she'e now thought . . .you or me . . .me'm or y weaving as'z z z dream of awakening . . . as'z z z'leep out . . .a y as'ex . . . as'z though't'sz of it appearing a pairing of a being still indivisible . . .those thoughts of appearing out . . . x . . .X . . .a un' known . . .man with or without womb . . . man as mind or y . . .as'ex is ting now woman. . .as'z thoth'tsz of a God'ess'e to be letter'all'y y'all a woman as mind or y me . . .or you while still that indivisible in'visibility of any individual . . .her'him'it in a y eye a peering it out of a b'ng c'ng in word . . .only potentially victim or predator of eve're'y man in her'eyez z z'a ma'sz mass of eve'll . . .out in her'eyez z z'a will . . .out in her'eyez z z' any urge y . . . out in her'eyez z z'energy.

Christina expressed her breath. Oh scientist where is eve'll now? She genuflected her spine drawing cerebrospinal fluid up from her perineum into her brain, putting pressure on the crystals of her pineal gland, activating the singular eye of a mind or a'y. Now a being still in the first place. A b'ng c'ng out in her'eyez z z. She closed her eyes. The innerscreen of consciousness played an incomprehensible x'plotting y'plotting rainbow shimmering color patterning in'formation from that a x m meeting point. That center centered centrality . . . of a being c'ng y'all that now k'now'ing out of it anybody in word . . . she'now let awareness of it fall b'lack down to the second chakra . . .wheel . . .we'll . . .we all will turning . . .of prostatic ganglion x'siting . . .y as'z ex . . .as'ex . . .she could smell testoserone in the air . . .around the Korner . . . what she knew about him . . . nice guy for a psychotic killer. Killing her softly. She let awareness drift back to singular focus of the 'pinecone', the pineal gland in the center of her head . . .let chips fall where they may . . .they, the y. She would challenge any of her illustrious colleagues to produce equivilant bona fides in their respective fields.

She had recently published a paper in La Vie Philosophique, "Ancient Knowledge and the Revelation of in the'or'y of A Being C'ng of That True Indivisible In'visibility A'Re'y'as'on Y Now Appearing A's Thoughtsz Out Awhile As'z eX's ting In'formation in Man' as Mind 'or Y." AKaRe'y'asz'eX's ting.

'Y'or Y Now As'eX' was the shorter title of the article written in a dialectic or practise of speaking with intent of ex'pressing merely why you're you or me appearing in word memory out of a b'ng c'ng in the first place. Her paper, based on her direct a're'y'all'eye'zation, unfolded what she now referred to as the three y's man'as'ex. Or y you're; you as'ex. A chuckle passed her lips. The double entendre of a y as ex or sex, so quickly turned geometry to psychometry. G-motion to E-motion. Turned any mirrored y na or you now letter'all'y y'all into seduction under irresistable laws of attraction and repulsion. A polarity created by merely as'z though'tsz breaking open the complete d"ark'en'ess'e. A perceived turning to be. Any beginning by ending the loopy de loop with opening mouth to release tale of two siddhis. That singular pow pow power appearing out of it int'word a twis'ting in two formation out as'ex's ting. eLaws out in her'eyez z z' a're'y'all'ization could still succumb too. A'sz int'word a twis'ta fate faith and family. eLaws reminding why she now appeared to be other y'sz in any mirror or reflected in the cunning eye stare of recent aquaintance James Korner.

Seeing that wolf's eye stare in her'eyez z z of a mind's eye, she booted up the 'y as ex' paper on her laptop. It offered cool detached type face without the experience, the's ex per eye in seeing magnetic predation in 3D blood and bone around the man Korner. Trouble is a man she thought, brushing back an errant curl. In her eye'za refocusing outwardly in words trailing across the screen. Reading digital ink, a hand instinctually reached for a scrap of 2+ thousand year old goat hyde she'e'now carried since Jerusalem. Fingernails dug into sweat softened hyde as she now flashed on the sound of a thin scream dying on deserted streets. The taste of sweat mingling with tears as meaty fingers closed over her mouth. Heart knocking in her ribs. She had tried to carry the stink of his breath and the slick of his blood along with the scrap of scroll till eve'll prevailed. In her'eye a will. Now that irony of a terror being eve'll, a being c'ng out in her'eyez z z.

Of eve're'ybody's will tasted delicious becoming aware of that awareness that eve'll is in her'e'yez z z. Is eve's will of eve're'ybody as'z a way'eve'na a're'y'all in her'eyez z z'a while being raped. Out in her"eyez z z of eve re'y body. Out in her"eye z z z a wily wile. Out in her"eyez z z a deadly duplicity. She'e'na now out in her"eyez z z'a fingers digging into hyde. A b'ng c'ng in the first place now k'now'ing out of it a place to hide a second or two.

Sweat popped out on her brow. A heart raced with recalling Jerusalem. Jerusalem. Washed, showered, flooded bathed with blood shed in centuries screaming by in the name of vanity of my brothers and sisters. My encounter, she now thought, would not register any more in that regard than my choked faint scream deadened by ancient stone stacked walls of a deserted dark alley. A y'll of Eve'll. Her will put that knife in my hand as surely as it had put her in his, she thought with a shudder. How quickly the blade slipped into the belly. Soft belly. Guts'za. His blood . . .her blood. Eve'll of eve're'y bodhi . . .in her"e re ye . . .in her"e'ye re ye dhi'a'ting. . .out of it in her"eyez z z . . a're'y asz from a y eye of her'him'it.

. . .Energy experienced directly and periodically y'all . . .all y for'ma'sz potential in her"eyez z z'ap'ping . . .out from a b'ng c'ng in her"eyez z z . . .out of it in her"eyez z z of eve're'y body thinking of anybody, she now thought . . .y'all would for'eve're include a y . . . A Y all . . .all Ya . . .blood in the all'ey . . . his blood her'him'it blood y . . .y . . . .y you're; you she now flashed, then black again indivisible in'visibility reading a laptop screen. ". . . as'z z z'leep b'l'ack'g'round into one indivisible in'visibility of any individual as'ex experiencing singularity of a un'consciousness, a state ancients recognized as the'e primary singular indivisible black body or bodhi . . .eve're'y bodhi, bo . . .bo . . .ba . . .being dhi . . .buddhi . . .buddha . . .being to perceive by, for, in . . .to, from, of eve'll, in her"eyez z z a'way'eve of will in first matter . . .in her e'yez z z'a caring carrier wayeve will . . .of a being be'am'ing any urge, out in her'eyez z z' energy . . .a'zen Y erg . . .any desire . . .any wave e.g.g"o motion is out in her"eyez z z a peering it out na you now she na . . .wily con she us en'ess'e to be she'e'na asz though'tsz of us na . . .as'z thoughts of a b'ng now not . . . denied denying a y'll for . . .ma'asz eve'll . . .a y now k'no no no'w'ing out of it a denying of y you're; you asz though'tsa'z'z'ex's ting in formation . . .of man'as mind or y ". . .of his blood her blood.

Jerusalem qualified in her"eye, sanctified in her"eye'zza blood as a bridge over in her"eyez z z'on of eve'sz now horizon. A nexus from apparent a pairing, y as'z x, back to black w'hole bodhi singularity eve'n'a w'h'ile awake. A y eye of a b'ng c'ng a peering it indivisible in'visibility. Out of it in her"eyez z z' a w'h'ile. Out in her'eyez z z a b'ng craft. Out in her'eyez z z' a witch'y'ness. She now laughed out loud at the double entendre. The sheer duplicity of it a peering it still in the first place now out of it appearing of it in her"eyez z z'ion eve'n'a now in'formation in mind or y's'z'any memory of think'ing about it. Y'all thought in her'eyez z z a thought as'z though'tsz of y you're; you now of eve'll. Of a b'ng c'ng still indivisible in'visibility in'forma'sz in word in her"e'yez z z'a will to appear to be born to die. Out in her'eyez z z' a peering it at any or eve're'ybody appearing of it to disappear in it . . .fade back to one indivisible black'g'round turning into or out of any or eve're'ybody. A b'ng c'ng merely mirrored living now out supernaturally as thoth'tsz of letter'all'y y'all born in word in formation.

Shrotram she had. Scriptural authority enabled absorption in her'eyez z z in'visibility into living now aware of awareness of a b'ng c'ng immortality a k'now'ing out of it a death. In word of it. Finally y'all she now a're'y'all'eye'zed a denial of k'no no no'wing out of it a being c'ng now out int'word in'formation of anything anybody anywhere anytime still a y eye a peering it in the first place. That indivisible in'visibilty in sight of divine awareness. Yet immortal while in that denial of it. Of a being still in the first place. Paramamsamya. Sam'e same still denial of a being c'ng now the real e-motional e'go trip. A k'no no no'wing out of it y'all along the long or short wily while of it out and about in word in formation now flashing through her'eyez z z' of eve're'ybody.

Paid dues. Paid attention to a being c'ng still a y eye of her'him'it a peering it from above. Play out the role or roll but exit the green room. Find yourself still she now told herself. Still a being free of any mere or y na mirrored you y'll DNA in that simple int'word a tw'is' ting in two a fate. Of mirror appearing of it in word in any information asz thoughtsz of a being now out of it in word. Scholastically she learned to find the in word key to resolving merely appearing of it only asz two disappear y'all while still indivisible in'visibility of it a y eye a peering it. Out in her'eye'z'za supersonic in word way'eve found in the ABBC code threaded thru y'all permutations of language. As'k'ey"e's to the highway. As'k'ey"es on Sanskrit, Hebrew, Aramaic, Greek, and Latin in for'ma'sz that letter'all'y y'all approach or hieroglyphic reproachment as'z z z'leep black into that one black peh'ss'y w'hole of it out in her"eye'z z z'of'eve're'y body. A reY'a'ten or y A'ten with intent or attention of appearing by a being y na you now a're'y a bi'na'rey radiating a w'h'ile. Appearing now as though'tsz of it out in space bi'o'logically in'cellular e-motionally felt fields feeling determined as though in word in formation of a ka's mic memory intelligence consciousness. The con in her'eyez z z of appearing out a pairing she us now to be any mirrored y na body.

She'e now brought attention back out to her laptop which coincidently played a similar loop. She also knew ignorance as k' no no no'wing out of it any positive negation of it. A polarity of any opening of the complete d"ark now providing potential polarity of endings. Positive negativity. Intentional disregard of a being c'ng still indivisible in'visibility. Thus any ignoring body by a being still a y eye now mirrored as'ka's mic potential k'no'wing of it must be repelled by her transmission of that same positive polarity of knowing y unless the intent is a're'y'versed from ignoring y, y you're you by embracing, actively seeking discerning a being c'ng drawn out of it. Only those valuing or desiring in a wordfreedom or liberation will be drawn out to it. A being c'ng same polarity repels it. Repels a're'y'alizing of it. It seems slavery can be addictive. Genetically, neuronically, chemically addictive. She watched it play on in Y'or Y Speak dialectic projecting from the screen of her laptop. . . . "In that we all a wheel turning is the' e turn'i'ty. Eve're'y way'eve roll or role is completely complete e'lectro-magnetic one directional loop. It takes consciousness int'word hair fire desire to break out a move in a're'y'verse of it. We all turning black'g'round into or out of it one appearing of it. A b c's in word in formation of a b'ng c'ng now as'z anybody forgetting a being still indivisible in'visibility.

"Of any a na y mere or y na complete roll or role as'ka's all y causal y d"ark'ness. Macro-micro mean as'ka's mic bliss. That d ark is a covenant with the go'a'd of any energy wave function of fun'ny'action ka'mic ka's all y y'all still merely in word appearing of it out in'formation. Invisibility Y now denial projection as though'tsz Z'ayin eX's ting in'formation. Thus the singularity of a being c'ng in'still that indivisible in'visibility of a being a're'y'mains hidden in a be"am'ing a re'y'all still a being awareness experienced experiencing complete black'g'round inclusive blackness of a un'consciousness. Of one invisibility invincible you na'turally not now y'll d'na denial of d"ark en y ess'e to be with intent of appearing under quantum gravity of aw'h'ile the'n disappearing. . . . .Gravitas Vitae . . . . .intentional disregard is deadly straight away. . . . .Y you're; you k'no no no 'ing y'll d'na merely now appearing awhile. In awhile a cunning deceitful play . . . .we all turning churning burning mirror el y in supersonic superimposed bio cog'na'neuronic cellular felt fields of you y'll DNA feeling a being that alone. . . . . feeling a black'g'round that of a being still in the first place that indivisible invisibility of a being that alone." Alone in a being eye of the herhimit. Indivisible in'visibility a peering from above. That thought stopped her in her tracks. She now found herself in'visibility a peering it out mirrored in word mind memory. In word speaking y'or y now without appearing as ex. A's ex's ting alone information of aten shunned. Y'or y now in the'or'y of man'as mind in word mirror el'y function of fun'ny'action of a twis'ting the na't away.

Christina's in word attention moved back to the screen. . . ."of that a Y y'all by a b'ng c'ng a y eye a peering it now out of it appearing a pairing Y as'z ex. X, a twis'ting in two one known unknown as'z death is one known unknown . . . ." she considered with a slight grimace. What intrigued her about the artist Dark Mor. Would he be a man of black humor. Surely liberation turned that in word wheel as though in a're'y'verse ending any beginning merely in word as sound means for'ma'sz appearing of it . . . a supersonic in'for'ma'ing of any image imagined in word now merely mirror'ed or a y a peering it out in ka's mic memory. Me or you now the Dark'ness. Hey boy who you be? Or maybe he a boring oaf who just got lucky with a brush she now chuckled.

" . . . . Could mere letters qualify to reveal the gravity of it as'ka's mic quantum quandary, a black peh'ss'y w'hole bodhi black'g'round creating sustaining and destroying of it simultaneously. You die now. In word death. Death merely now as a k'now'ing of birth. Mirror el y. She'e'na, prima materia, funny that way out in her'eyez z z of eve"re'ybody mere mirror mur'ic acids created function of a being c'ng dissolving creation . . . . creative dissolution . . .positive negativity. . . . .any appearance of it in formation in awhile must now after awhile fade back to one black of a black'g'round mirroring da y na light. Eve'na're'y still these in word thoughtsz she wondered. Somehow letters, those crazy squigglies n'eve'r'e quite qualified or quantified as'z concept of that inconceivably aware of a being c'ng a peering it in that awareness of it.

Piled on or under that bridge black'g'round to that black w'hole singularity, her university credentials and following of students, along with continuing study of ancient Hebrew, Greek, and Sanskrit scripture, gave her the cajones to suggest in the or y a being in theory of man as mind or y you're; you now merely appearing by duplicating as'z in word supernaturally y'all as'z'any thothtsz of it. In that indivisible in'visibility of a being c'ng a peering it at we all in turn'ing black'g'round out of it appearing of it as'z'any universe, . . . that verse of you ni'q appearing as'z any being bio'logically born as eX'u'all still remain that indivisible invisibility. Of a Y, that yod iota referred to as'z'anybody that I am is is. It is as'z that, that I am thinking this, she thought with a sly smile.

Christina's fingers played along the edge of her laptop as she continued reading the 'Y' paper "...... duplication as'z though'tsz man a being in theory the or y of man as mind or y you're; you now is mere mirror duplicating duplication as'z thoughtsz yet invisibility of any eye a peering it now out in'formation. In a b c's of a being c'ng in time as'ex', a known unknown. A being still in the first place indivisible invisibility. A subject now in a being c'ng in time as'king of it a kurving aw'h'ile in space. A k'no no no'wing out of it a cunning duplicity of appearing of it in a being now in a space in time of objective objectivity. That a Y as eX'u'all." In other words y'all a's sexual, she reflected with a grin. What a hoot, she now thought, that I am as awareness complete, completely free freed in a wordfreedom. Yet, as any mere fool, that I am, me in na'me appearing of it to be a being in my mind, or y, by memory in images informed by that in word imaginary spell, that spelling of ABBC. In a being Any B'ng C'ng that, I am information as'z'any mere mirrored y na now appearing appearance in timespace, falling. Falling as'z z z'leep from that giant step off a ledge in time a kurving a black'g'round in complete roles of d"ark'ness to be played as'z'any fool. Any fool fooled by a na y denial of a being indivisible in'visibility. A Y as now time to get it on for awhile. Informa'sz a cunning act as eX.

She now laughed to herself at the 'witchy' ness of that crafty in word spell, the a b c's spelling of a b'ng c'ng. What a why a y eye stew she stirred. A y eye a peering it out infor'ma'sz appearing a while. Infor'ma'sz a wily wile, a cunning craft'y deceit of that duplicity as'ex. X's ting int'word information of a twis'ting of fate. The indivisible invisibility of a y eye of yod a peering it as'ex's ting. As a being now one k'now n'a, one complete k'urve of time, complete d"ark'en'ess'e, one to be perceived turning into an y thin'king of it turning into anything in her'eyez z z'a wayeve of mirror function. The crafty craft say'ling out in her"eyez z z of eve re'y body. Function a y'll d'na. Thus she now understood the vehement denial of that proposal of mere a peering it of a y eye being c'ng now mirroring a b c's appearing out in word. Immutability of a being still immortal now only as thoughtsz of it not. Christina realized the paradox of a being c'ng out in her"eyez z z of eve re'ybody now a k'no no no'wing out of it a denial a're'y'dhi'a'ting out of a y eye being c'ng merely a peering it. Thus colleagues' polite ridicule now rolled off the black'g'round k'no no no'wing of it out in her'eyez z z. She now knew that with the arrogance of their ignorance of it, the key, are'y'alizing directly of a being that y'all along, would remain hidden from them a million more years. With out eyes to see or ears to hear, with out valuing liberation now eve'na while k'now'ing a denial of it, they might or must remain ignoring their freedom for a million zillion years or more to come.

Christina had found clues to confirm and reaffirm merely a peering it that a're'y'al'eye'zation of it. Now then still a being that revealed in scroll fragments uncovered over 70 years near the

Dead Sea. These scraps numbered in tens of thousands. Still in her'eyez z z, no matter the content, they remained primarily letters in formation. A's to be seen from the same timeless point of view of them that applied the ink in the first place. Still a being in the first place of the first person that I am is is writing of it now she flashed. Thus as paleographer the concern remained a're'y'alizing a being that then as now. In that she now was, is, and as eve'r'e'y body will be of that awareness of that I am is is. No need to define, imagine, or project or reflect a being other y'sz. Merely a're'y'all'eye'zing a being in any a peering it still that indivisible invisibility of anybody appearing out of it.

The scrolls also showed in her'eyez z z the multi-hued complexion of orginal Israel along with the development early pre-Christian doctrine. There were many sects of Judhaism. Essenes and soon to be Christians. Jerusalem city of peace washed in blood. Especially at the time of J.C. and that growing rivalry with Rome. A gathering of a hot whirlwind to stir the western world. But in her'eyez z z'a inquiry went inside in a wordfreedom as well as outside religious dogma, relying on complete realization of it by intuitively a're'y'all'eye'zing'ing a being c'ng still in any a peering it. A stillness of anybody now k'now'ing a b'ng c'ng of that which any religion purports to seek she now mused. In that sense of a're'y'al'eye'zation she now had the biggest advantage a woman had over male counterparts. In her'eyez z z'a intuiting a torus. An electro-magnetic roll or role int'word a twis'ting in two roiling in'formation black'g"round in word she now recognizing y you're; you eve're'y body in the first place in first superson'ic awareness that I am is is now for'eve'r'ey in her"eyez z z' a will a peering it out of any or eve're'y body with intent of appearing of it out and about raising hell or y na. That seemed the only answer to y or y na she now thought stretching her legs.

Then that academ'y wall goes up ignoring y'all now by any k'now'ing out of it with intent at aten'cion of a binary reenforcing any false science based on that as"eX." As though one unknown known objective objectivity. The subject subjectivity of the Quantum, 99 and 99 tenths percent of a'Re'y'al'l'ity still that invisibility of a being c'ng a peering it now appearing of it out in word awhile. A y'll d'na denial. A positive negativity with intent of intentionally disregarding human singularity in favor of a being c'ng merely mirrored out. A b c's in word living a wily while asz thoughtsz born. Now awhile in time space finding out in word definite separateness in isolation of such that she found it a towering of in word babel. Academic tower of in word eX'position. As'eX posing of a being y y'all. A babel of mere mirror'age mirage of in word in formation. A being as'z though'tsz reflecting by mere mirrored intent still a being c'ng indivisible in'visibility. Awareness of that asz though k'no no no'w'ing a b c's now out in word. Reflecting a black'g'round. A denial int'word infor'ma'ing a b'ng complex supersonic in word mirage. Awakening stimulating receptors on the dendrons, billion plus trees of neurons, set up to be zapped from a'n'y A'xo'n. She laughed hard out loud that that tower made of bricks of human speech must be struck. Destroyed by the e've're'y in word force that caused it to be built out of a b'ng c'ng still in the first place. Eve're'y body now that iconoclastic binary lightning synapse between the mouth of man'as mind and the tail. That tale of peh'us'sy'"en'ce with pun intended, she mused. Chasing that tail, as well as a being of that tail chased, she understood plenty, she thought. A being now out in her'eyez z z'a k'now'ing of it a virgin or a womb? The real y"on'i source of ana'y mere mirror y'na bodhi's of knower's the or'i'zing scientific theory issuing from that mouth. Out to a dog eat dogmatic academia awaiting to get their conceptual designing A. I. hooks set. Man with or without a womb. Man o man'as mind or y. Y? Why eX per eye en c'ing? Y X'is ting in formation as'z'any body ?

Thoughts turned to her Irish Catholic father, Matthew and her mother Sarah, descendant from Sephardic Jews. Matthew working on the Manhatten Project, meeting Sarah thirty years later, after Hiroshima and Nagasaki were incinerated. He never talked about his work until that one late Thanksgiving evening after a few whiskies she remembered him confessing about being exposed to radiation. How he feared her being born undersize might be a defect from that exposure. Then Sarah being so self assured she would be fine, giving her the name Margot, the pearl shining through the blackness of his fear. Pops guilt from having abandoned his Catholic faith, giving her the middle name Christina. She recalled him telling that night, several years since Sarah's passing, how he wanted her to have a healing impact on a society slightly mad from the release of atomic power. When she had asked him the following morning what he meant, he merely looked away with a sad smile. Now she would be left to resolve the irony of their Judeo-Christian union.

The phone on her desk jangled, bringing her out of the reverie.

"Korner here. This a good time?"

"I am busy," Christina replied curtly. There was something too cunning about this man. The unnerving glint in his eyes, she thought.

"I've located the artist."

She flashed on the painting she had seen at Korner's house. The one he enjoyed showing off. The image left in her'eye a see'ng of a lost memory.

"He'll be in tomorrow. Should I have him drop by your office?"

"No, the cafe in the student union at noon. I will know him when he comes in."

Christina hung up. She wondered about Korner when she first met him looking for a translator of the Copper Scroll. A copper Scroll. That copper scroll kept scrolling in her inner pineal 'pinecone' eye along with myriad Dead Sea scrolls. These numerous scrolled animal hydes marked with ink relaying words on esoteric wisdom and ancient history stood in stark contrast to that single rolled sheet of hammered copper listing caches of gold and silver. Copper now black as night.

She now looked out the window opposite her desk. Thoughts of the Copper Scroll pulled her'eye into a grander scale of time. Time of immeasurable centuries millennia light years collapsing in coalescence of awareness of a being in that as'ka's mic memory of it. She now had these recurring dreams of copper snakes writhing into winged discs soaring over a golden calf.

She found in the Scroll something not lost so much as waiting to be rediscovered with a message for the ever present, a message far more important than silver and gold. A message of liberation. Liberation now while still living on with our day to day, moment to moment roles . . . es'ka'roles playing out awhile now in time. Roles turning around eve're'y body in awhile still a being stillness of a y eye of her'him'it. Still a being of that first matter in the first place now a mirrored k'now'ing out of it asz any matter of a b'ng c'ng in word informa'ing in any place. A b'ng c'ng still in the first place in a wordfreedom now. Awareness in a wordfreedom forever.

From her desk she watched tree branches sweep the blue sky, recalling deserts of spiny acacias, reeking with the musk of camel urine, and sand, sand, sand permeating y'all. The grit of it grinding away any information not carved in stone.

Korner's digitally remastered copy of the Copper Scroll, compared to the blackened, wrinkled, and sliced up reality in a museum, had chilled her blood. She had never seen anything like it. Naturally, that put Korner into her court. It seemed as though Korner's came from the original copy that she surmised crossed the desert in the Exodus from Egypt thirty three hundred years ago.

The scroll, 99 percent pure copper, already hundreds of years old when it was buried during the time of the Essenes and still, likely a copy of the original, tantalized her enigmatic mind. Other scholars had translated lists of material wealth but she felt there must be more to it. Perhaps following the money could lead to its true design or be a ruse, a disguise as temptation to touch to have and to hold that indivisible in'visibility of anything out appearing disappearing in that blink in her'eyez z z of eve're'y'body. That true design, that indivisible in'visibility of any meaning could only be discerned by those with eyes to see. Otherwise, she thought the meaning as words would remain unclear as the nature of the people involved. Added to this was the confusion over translation and the whims of scribes recording languages where words were often pronounced several ways for different meanings, first syllables switched with last, or even several meanings given to words with the same spelling and pronunciation. The lack of vowels in the written form added to the arbitrary nature of the whole affair. Only when heard, she considered, are vowels of ancient semitic languages known, ka now en. Languages, languages, langue lingua linguam, echoed in her head as she pressed tongue against cheek. That Shem, she thought, that oldest son of Noah, no ah ka now a hay known as ar ka man, this first son speaking as Arab jew caucasian befuddling translation. Even though the words were written in one alphabet, she found a bewildering array'all of cultural layers of various languages within a b c's of that one tongue of a being c'ee'ng a peering it still in the first place. At this now or later a k'nowing out of it any or eve're'ybody.

Once, pondering hieroglyphs carved into red sandstone on a wall in the hypostyle hall of a 3800-year-old temple in Edfu on the Upper Nile, she had recognized a Hebrew letter among the pictographs. The temple had to be at least 500 years old before the development of the Hebrew alphabet. Further research led to a cursive form of hieroglyphic writing, where she recognized more Hebrew letters. A door had opened. Christina saw a great road leading to a palace in lush gardens guarding a sun temple running to the horizon. Sixty foot pylons, bedecked with banners, rose above. Below them glistened forty foot hammered brass gates trimmed with pure gold. She found herself onto an ancient timeless code playing out in eve"re'y human voice echoing black'g'round the whorl'd. Into that letter"all'y y'all towering hurricane of emotion building behind the weir, the ka's mic gate. The y na-gate opening or holding back an y infinite reserve of potential energy for let'ting in her'eyez z z'ion, all y y'all ways of eve"re'y bodhi, wayeves unda"el'a'ting to the horizon. In any event of eve's en'ting in formation, that en'y urge energy, played her vocal chords vibrating the life force breath, a b c's of a being c'ng in eve're'y supersonic wayeve out in her'eyez z z. Casting awareness out of it from any mirror mind or mem'or'y y na now around k'now'ing out of it as'ex'et'ting duplicating a mirror duplication of she'e na appeared. Then a black g"round overstanding any understanding in her"eyez z z a'way of eve. Out in her"e yez z z'ion a wave of ka's mic memory disappearing any mere mirrored y na trace of a being c'ee'ng still indivisible in'visibility in the first place. In the proverbial blink of'ten a being binary by her"ey'e'z'za a na re'y radiating intent intentionally y'all disregarding a being still in the first place indivisible in'visibility of any individual she'e'na appearing disappearing. Margot Christina Shaughnessy moved supersonically beyond mirror superimposition of a being c'ng in name alone. In mirror mind or y memory her"eyez z z at attention liberated from in word captivity flew free of any duplicity. Or y na. Now. Why not play the role of C.S. as it served its purpose?

Like most scholars, C.S. had assumed that the temple mentioned in the Copper Scroll belonged to Solomon until she deciphered a name that had been transliterated into Greek, the letters interspersed in the first four columns of the Scroll. There that name blazoned across in her'eye'z' z inner screen. AKHENATEN. Ahkenaten, now as'king of it awakhening the heretic pharaoh. A being still in the first place. A aten being c'ng still a peering it in the first place. Awakhen now as'king of it any k'now'ing out of it. A being still in the first place. This could mean that the treasure was Egypt. a'Re'y'al'eye"zing a y eye of A'ten being c'ng a peering it still in the first place. The sheer weight of it waiting for'ma'sz appearing of it now completely as'eX posed crushed the breath out of her body. Slowly she now inhaled to offset the still beating heart. The whole point of a peh'ss'y w'hole c'ng the pow pow power potential of it in her'eyez z z of eve'll fell upon her'eye z z z'a field of view. That as'king of it commanding her yet at her command. That as'ka'ing of it a y'll. As'ka's y'all a b'ng'lack'n'esse of it now to be a gain. She'e'na felt his field of D'ark'ness falling upon her'eyez z z'a like a moonless night in country. She said it. She would recognize him then meeting him now.

A mirrored as'king of it as'ka's y'all bodhi a pairing out a la que"en que' of that in which appearing out of it in her'eyez z z of eve'll'y'ears supersonically her'eye'z z'a'ring"in'g it out in word. A Y eye'zas'z e'X. Y'all asz'eX'hodos way'eve e'yez z z in a're'y'all. Information awhile. Only still awhile of a b'ng c'ng now a peering it out in a b c's awhile. A'y eye in y'all asz'za see'r now a k'now'ing out of it asz'any appearing of it in word int'word or out of that a black'g'round of a b'ng complete role of d"ark'ness. That to be perceived ark now a k'now'ing of it black'g'round the a y eye of her'him'it holding up the l'amp'latitude flattening of it as'ex'planing the roll or role. Or'e ye's'peh ark of the covenant. The supersonic supernatural s'par'king agreement a chord free a're'y'nge'ment a re'y'all go'a'l'd'en y urge energy a'sz thoth'tsz of it. A singular Go'a'd esse to be. Letter'all'y y'all set free of any in word captivity. In a wordfreed'om'us in the firsta'h"om'e of'ten a being c'ee'ng now out of it as'z'any thoth'tsz of it in word captivity. A binary captivity by a being y na re'y'as'z z'a'p'ping echo'ing y'a's ex's ting in formation. Of'ten in denial of k'now'ing out of a being still in the first place. Now a k'nowing out of it in word asz'any in form'aton.

Or . . . or . . . or a're'y ore gold ore go el da. The real go'a'l'd'en"y'body in a wordfreedom. The exodus of mirror y slavery. In word she'e'na now held the ke'y. Her inner screen translated all words sa so si peh'eh si as silent supersonic sounded sound mean means meaning which a're'y veiled el que ve of the one who sees a le da see'r'eye surveying that hiding hidden within y'all word da sa for ma'sz now in a wordfreedom awareness of liberation.

She'e'na her'me'asz'thoth'tsz of it searched the a'ka's'ic a're'y'chord to find a list of Herod the Great's ma'terial treasure scattered around Judea and concentrated near the Temple Mount. A y eye on the Scroll pointed out a point of view of you of a y in word. A'wayeve of a b c's of a b'ng c'ng a peering it of a greater mystery that promised to reverberate the core of the three main religions of the western world along with the complete peh'ss'y w'hole consciousness of man'as mind. Or a y eyez z z'a now turning a black'g'round a're'y'dhi'a'ting a k'now'ing it out of a y eye in for'ma'ss a're'y'al'eye"zing'ing it. A being c'ng a peering it in the first place. A peering it from above as'z below. The'understanding of us. To the core or y care carrier wayeve of y'all's humanity and peh'science or a're'y'ligion. Still a being in the first place that indivisible in'visibility alone. Indivisible in'visibility of any individual. Feeling it. Feeding it. It of a being still in the first place now out of it a'sz'z'any supernatural supersonic thoth'tsz of'ten appearing bi'nary being y'all alone. A y eye of her'him'it. Freed of a being eve're'y'body appearing of it. A being still indivisible invisibility awareness of that I am. Is is. All she needed was the time to plot out what or why in the or y the scroll a're'y'veiled it. Her'him'it she mused with a sly grin. A b'ng c'ng of it y'all along she laughed like the crazy chronus woman she'e'na of'ten found herself to be. A bi'na re'y. A's be't'ween a being twin appearing of it twined y'll d'na. Still a being that indivisible now as'king of it a k'no no no'wing out of it a ka's all'y a body. A la que"en que' of that in which. As'z'king of it a'la queen. At aten'cion of her'eyez z z' of eve'll. Adam a la'Eve. The guarding of e'don. The'e as'ex'o'dus into el'and fun'ction of mirrored in word captivity. The g'OO'da la'b'OO'ka. A b c's in word captivity in'formation of a y eye a peering it out as'ex's ting. She'e'na k'new to let the dialectic flow to its logical conclusion.

Then she'e'na now turned around that Korner. He had asked her about the Sicarri, a sect of radical Jewish freedom fighters. Zealots in almost continuous rebellion against the Romans for 70 years. To the death they defended Solomon's Temple against the Roman legions. His eyes took on a strange cast when she told how, being overrun by Roman Legions at Masada, Herrod's stronghold, the Sicarri committed mass suicide using their sicas, short daggers made for carrying out assasination. She thought this seemed obscure knowledge for someone like Korner. It meant his search focused on Judea. She could keep it there by feeding his friend, Dark Mor, tantalizing bits of disinformation.

☼

Mor awoke the next morning before sunrise. He took fresh clothes from the neatly stacked pile on a wooden crate, stepping naked on to the moonlit porch. The cold air chilled the damp sweat on his chest and back. He pulled on shirt and trousers. Moonlight bathed the valley as miles below lights twinkled from buildings scattered around the prehistoric lake. San Francisco and Stanford seemed a lifetime away. The fluid rustle of rushing creek offset the howl of a coyote echoing from the ridge above.

He started his pickup, easing down a driveway not much more than a cattle trail. After fifteen miles of bone-jarring dirt road, he hit two lanes of asphalt that ran ten miles to the main highway. The highway left a chain of three lakes, hooking up with the four-lane 101 corridor, and from there less than three hours, depending on traffic, to the Golden Gate Bridge and San Francisco. An hour's drive south from there would put him at the Stanford University campus, a place he'd once heard called the Farm.

Dawn glowed fiery purple-orange as he hit thickening traffic on the 101. At the crest of a hill overlooking the Valley of the Moon, he pulled over and stepped out of the truck. Torn cottony clouds slunk over distant low mountain ridges, vineyards rolling out in waves over the hills below. He stepped over a drainage ditch to a fence line, finding himself watching a braquero pruning last year's sucker whips shooting off from the mother gnarl, endless rows of brainy heads shot with axon like whips laid over their wood and wire trellis rolling out to the horizon. He stretched his spine and watched the rhythm of the man's hands as they danced, mano a mano, veins thick with blood. The man sang to the gnarl to convert the blood of the earth, "la sangre del tierre" to the blood of the vine. He wondered how many heads the man trimmed before breakfast.

Mor knew it wasn't too late to turn around even as he felt the urban witchcraft of San Francisco, already drawing him back in. Chill shuddered his spine and he climbed back into the truck. He laid his head back, drifting to Haight-Ashbury daze. At that time he'd been successful hiding from himself until Korner showed again with some crystal powder. Only after snorting a line, did Korner tell him it was c four, a plastic explosive. The after-effects almost drove him to madness. Hysterical blindness alternated with visions that left him questioning the possibility of a return to sanity. Still, his mind now drifted back to the mayhem.

Opening a door to another dimension. That cosmic dimension activated by a sweeping a're'y'all of warm cool blue light. Permeating parameters. Pervasive blue light filling completely the entire bio field of view, of me or you, eyes open or closed, the indivisible invisibility now in visibility yet still indivisible.. A cool warm blue absorbing any in word mirror definition of anything or anybody appearing a pairing between betwixt macro-micro ka's mic being. A being still in the first place unwound from that simple twist of fate y'll d'na. D'na mirrored a while as thoughts of a y being other y'sz than that centrality point of view of you of y the observer observing observation that I am, he thinking thoughts of it now, thinning out in waves to reveal a silhouette, the a being now appearing in a mirrored being as ex. X expanding to a being craft sailing black mirror seas from some first inner space Pa'roo'ma of motionless, formless, timeless heart. He found himself lost in the awareness of a being still in the first place now out turning a black'g'round into a k'now'ing out of that. A being see'ng in the eye merely a peering it supernaturally. Found himself as a mere mirrored point of view observing this in word craft of colored light banking luminous waves churning indivisible in'visibility black and blue mirror seas. A see'ng"as a field of electro-magnetic view purely as thoughts of it. A singular being of that. Y'all that appeared of it int'word a twis'ting in two formation before his eyes.

"Paint that out of your head," Korner had said.

Mor remembered that cold warehouse, hands numbed as he worked the paint, using a timeless formula to finish the work with layers of a green-gold glaze for luminescence. He knew the glaze gave that certain depth to the form, but Korner said the surface looked like he had smeared it with liquid shit. He laughed with the memory of Korner's blatant indifference to the subtle nuances of painting. The paint just needed time to cure. But that was just another thing in the way of making that dollar, for once the canvas was finished, Korner always had a buyer waiting, just as Mor had another vision waiting.

Then he returned to the vision in his mind's eye to see naked bodies writhing in dance on a broad flat beach set with canvas pavilions snapping in the wind. As he approached a healer in white robe attended a man, prostrate and twisting in violent convulsions on the sand. The healer laid a pan of steaming milk before him. As the man shook, a flat serpent emerged from his mouth. The healer smashed the serpent's head with a rock before pulling the parasite on out.

He moved past the tents toward seas open to the horizon. Others en mass appeared to disappear towards that horizon, waters stretching to it rippling with giant, submerged shapes. One burst the surface in a spray of jeweled light. Giant as a whale but not a whale, it swam through water and sand to rise up before him. The creature rose on up to perch on its caudal fin, raining down showers of shells clattering off ribbons of seaweed, and bursts of saltwater crystals. He feared the great mouth would swallow him as it opened to speak an intuitive language, he understood without hearing as waves rolling out merging and re emerging out in formation. His mind now impressed with a cosmic creed, he found himself joining robed dancers blowing conch shells as they accompanied the creature back to the sea.

"Well now, good thing I'm here for you, brother," Korner had said as he brought more materials and a cheap electric space heater.

The third vision came after Roxx, a creature of the night, moved into the warehouse. She disliked Korner from their first meeting and refused to tell him her name or even speak to him. "That man has no soul," she told him. Korner said she smelled, but Mor found her enticing. Roxx was about sex. He met her in the fog on the Golden Gate Bridge, one foot on the railing and looking to the water below. She told him, she had been waiting for him. Her lips quivered when she spoke from the corner of her mouth as they walked back to the warehouse. She shared his food and his bed, staying with him as the visions went on.

Even with traffic picking up out on the highway the third vision layered into his visual field just as it had that night in sexual union with Roxx. His inner eye opened to a tortoise circling overhead. Drawing closer, its flat belly projected shafts of light from clusters of tiny windows. The turtle's head with neck extended turned back on itself as a curving lingam, a phallus head biting after its tail with the shell, now yoni vulva releasing herds of four legged beasts. This metamorphosis would be set to canvass featuring Roxx as a naked Olympia, enticing, legs spread leading to that primal allure.

Even Korner started taking second looks at Roxx after seeing the painting.

In the fourth vision, he found himself the still vortex eye of a mean storm, supersonic velocity tore in formation round this his still point of view. A cyclone of dust filled with shards of sparking orange fire turned all around him churning with creatures great and small, ancient reptilian bodies crushed in tusked jaws. Torn corpses strew the turning wheel, children turning to crones and dust, while he, the center eye of the vortex remained motionless changeless seeing. A being unseen. The serenity of a being still in the first place now in getting the point was inversely proportional to the distress of a pairing as ex being in as though out beside it. Now ex et'ting in formation around k'now'ing projecting any appearance outside the motionless pivot point on which this fury turned. We all turning into or out of this maelstrom of the crushing stormy karmic wheel of fortune or misfortune. That wheel, that we all turn into one churning yearning burning spinning race with death the only known unknown. Indivisible a being in'visibility as anybody of a pairing as ex's ting in formation around this wheel of time storm rolling roles to keep anybody busy being busy. Pay no attention now one as two being twixt that, a being still that attention in the first place, observing the ma're y g'round life as life able t'wis tingk'ing to be t'wo go go going around chasing our tail, our tale, our stare'y ay'sz out x'et ting in formation by now turning around k'now'ing that un'o'known in that in word race of any race a's ex's ting t'wix't appearing as such only to disappear, still all while knowing that one unknown. Death as any way'eve e.g.g. motion.

Finding himself calm but Korner would give him no peace. As his moods lifted, Korner would be there with some hard drugs and hard women to bring him back down. Korner turned him around into a coca crystal eater screwing into endless tomorrows. The Dark'ness black'g'round. In and out. Appearing disappearing black'g'round in or out of it.

The visions metaphorically dissolved his birth linneage, his mere in word mirrored notion of who he appeared to be. They completely reabsorbed him her'e it. The Dark'ness in'visibility priority prior in word awakhening a being now k'now'ing in formation beneath delivery truck delivering. Delivering awareness of rusted steel sprung and muffled motion. Death rust passing overhead. Indivisible Dark'ness now k'now'ing in word a being appearing awhile out of it still in the first place indivisible in'visibility. Herhimit one now turning around twisting over-riding ka's mic memory k'now'ing, ka now a being cee'ng go go gaining, realization to the any situation. In his case, now tortured by all the war imagery transferred from Korner's memory, painting out the horror with the brush, brushing with the destiny filling multi visionary in'visibility just as in a being that cosmic awareness. Aware from or for the first time of a being still in the first place. A where awareness is. A being still in the first place.

The horror, the bloody bomboraszcloth slaughter of innocence or innocents frequenting the planet turning into that vast cosmic sea. Why if only shocking anybody into realizing why a being still in the first place. In any in word captivity. Macromicro ka's mic slice in'visibility. Now completely invisible. H'earth plan'et'ting moons solar system galaxy mere dust grain in a shite sea storm of dust grains still aware. A where? A being still in the first place that attention. Aten bi na re'y paying, playing out every role I've ever known, Mor thought. Paying in pain'ting.

He turned to stare at eighteen wheels wheeling in turning in turning in turning black'g'round the Darkness supersonically into vision five. Five flew a being at supersonic attention now ka's mic seas ser se'er out as'ex's ting in formation into the solar system at large to see it as of such in that cosmic context of how much that I am is is that capability, that macromicro ka's mic mean capacity to see above as below in word letter'ally to comprehend it. The ka's mic'ro wayeve black'g'round radiating. A's that grandeur of planetary magnitude stretches the light body to invisibility glory before a being swept up into zero zee row row row of the go go go too as two a place, a body of experience. That as eX body. X're'y body.

Mor as a man of consciousness. A being man as mind. Or y memory realized now, how one cannot really fancy A being God till a's'ex expanding still a being in the first place awareness supersonically well beyond h'earth's atmosphere. Into the cosmic body of the Lord. Shiva. Parvati. Lord as two polarity of a being a's Creator. Sustained in word by now a being still in the first place. Destroyer. Her'e now Kali Ma'sz z z eN n wwwwww n"da"ing. A's being that that atmosphere that compresses that squeezes that crushes time to a point where it just ain't fun being a being functioning anymore, functioning thinking that I am he thought with a chuckle blinking from a passing truck horn. He stretched his body feeling arthritic pain where words and numbers disappeared all together. A body? What is a body. Where is a body? Any body? A being where? Still in the first place. Dark realized in word letter'ally he remained just as that a being still complete completely in the first place. Indivisible in'visibility out in her'eye of eve're'ybody. A supernatural supersonic body superimposed as thoughts of it in a memory. His memory kept fading back to that ka's mic black'g'round. Still in the Dark of it.

A nay'body may keep appearing disappearing, yet somehow, not that awareness of it, a being still in the first place that I am is is remains observer observing, overstanding understanding as such as that whatever that is that I am thinking to be he thought. Mor could still recall, stretched out now in his pick up truck parked along side one of life's busy highways, Jupiter's churning red eye and Saturn's brilliant rings fanning its massive body. He could disappear himself back black'g'round into a being c'ng a mere a peering out in word now mirroring out of it anybody awhile of a b'ng c'ng now out in word appearing that cosmic black mirror seas awareness. Mostly ignoring out of it 100 percent cosmic eye of a being c'ng a peering now out of it in favor of appearing any mirrored in word letter'al artifice of a being now k'now'ing out of it anything in any name alone. Could these planetary bodies accompaning our supersonic h'earth play'g'round be any lesser gods than Zeus and Chronos, celestial wanderers, grand parents of the children of the Sun. They swallowed him crushed into their grandeur as dust he appeared to disappear as their magnitude in that awareness that that I am is is a being stuff enough to fill vast space into a being still in the first place that singing supersonic singularity in infinite way esse. Plan e ts disappeared his self, his conceit. At least till returning in significance by forgetting a being that awareness that that I am is is significant to me remembering that this time. Or not. Then why not?

Perhaps viewed as specks from afar, as ink on paper, in 3D waking now around k'now'ing in word objective consciousness, we all in turn manage to reduce our grandure of grand gods accompaning us every day and night to mere objects mirrored in word, idea a's balls floating in empty space, separated in miles millions of space filled with quantum gravity of death the known unknown pulling it together or blowing it apart for your a being as ex's ting information now awhile longer. Or not.

Mor laughed out loud at the memory of Korner after seeing this painting, talking of nothing but the future of aviation and outer space flight which of course was fueled by copious amounts of cocaine.

The memory of that moment put Mor on to the sixth vision that marked the space in time for awareness of the return of that a being cee'ng by herhimit turning black'g'round black or blue into that cosmic singular a being. Paying attention to a being still in the first place that being. Now k'now'ing finding himself a being alone in that a being's eye. That eye expanding, opening ever wider till he felt as though he'd been a being seeing the world through a pin hole. Now his vision, his seeing awareness of any being in that a being's eye, any mere mirror horizon line of sight arked back to black or blue'sz'g"round indivisible invisibility of that complete d"ark always back to the rear to the're ar'e y radiating that Mr. re y a're we all wheel in turning in word. Wherever he turned, the impenetrable blackness always remained to the rear byond in'visibility event horizon on that any shifting periphery. His point of attention remained a being that arrow out, the eros, the e'x, unknown infinite potential projected, now black'g'round k'now'ing o'ne ka's mic now 'n' x re y vision. That being beamed x re'y as'z z z'ap'ping that cosmic synapse light a'cross X's ting of cosmic mem or y, great mind or y still that overstanding status being that free standing the e star'e eht now out x in time mere mirror mirroring her cosmic memory way of eve re y function strobing her super ca're carrying carrier way of eve her for'ma'sz energy. That a being beamed herhimit's ex re y'as unknown infinite potential a'sz z z'ap'ping a's though'tsz reflecting 100 thousand+ photo receptors echoing light in sound ways of eve re y' body asz z z'er kali ma ma'sz z z'apping a being beaming that cosmic synapse electric fire as'z z z'leep over mom'ent by mom'ent her"e eve'nt horiz z zi on. Her sound way of mere mirror function stretching from black to black or blue over that brief interlude of a being in'visibilty, of re'lation, her memory of me or you now y asz x, x'eting, x'acting, x's ting duplicating in formation x-panding in the or y mind of that cosmic being a kurving now time around occurrance of any wa'y by appearing a pairing as'z z z'ex y'all.

Mor realized at some point that point of view turned from any a na y cosmic overstanding by her"e mere mirror wave function, her en y urge turned into ma'sz z z understanding in the eye of the home boy. Now a mere mirrored micro cosmic counterpoint mirror'ly appearing awhile still being that indivisible invisibility of any individual, he thought of himself as mere artist. In that way, her way in being beaming him, he remained herhimit in the eye of the artist, in seeing realizing a being still in the first place awareness of that a being. Now a bald as'z naked singularity even downgraded to average american white man. His son. Her son. H'our sun. H'our'us . H'our i zion. The e I hill of her ka re care carrying carrier wayeve in any mere mirror mirroring you or me now in the event of appearing merely to disappear. Black into that cosmic macro micro way'eve of her conning h'our's black or blue"g'round into appearing out now awhile only as too or two twis'ting one into disappearing black into her un'a'consciousness cosmic memory.

He could gauge the time of day by the increase of traffic zooming the highway. With only a brief glance at the road he drifted on away back into his seventh vision to Union Square near the epicenter of the 1906 San Francisco earthquake. Standing there at a bus stop after work at 4 A.M., orange flames reared up dancing before his eyes. The flames so real he reached a hand out to touch even as they receded within that space in time as of such a being re re veee al'ing re'veiling reality geo logos world in word spoken in visual array ar ray ng pyros amis spiraling in two arms too form that unfinished potential as Great Pyramid peh y ra mi ida eya roiling into out X of that unknown now known as such as yet unseen in any see'ng that awareness. That I am is is now still remembering boarding the city bus and riding to the beach even while a being c'ee'ng here sitting behind a steering wheel along lost highways.

He gripped that steering wheel as Roxx came to him in his mind clear as that day she left him readying the illuminatus canvas. He had been so consumed by the painting he did not remember whether she had quit the warehouse in morning or afternoon. Finding her gone, he had confronted Korner as he carried the last canvass from the rented warehouse. He said he hoped she jumped off the bridge. Mor then wanted to plunge a broken palette knife into Korner's neck.

He remembered staggering out of the warehouse and taking a cab to the Haight-Ashbury Free Clinic. There a young intern while being oriented by a colleague spent over an hour listening to him, he realized later, because he made a good test case for paranoid psychosomatic hysterical blindness, and clinical depression. The prescribed tranquilizers had left him feeling empty. Korner had booked when the last of the vision canvases were gone. With a few bucks in his pocket, he took a city bus to the ocean, and hitchhiked north to Humboldt County where pot growers reaping the benefits of the high-dollar market, had the money to pay a carpenter to build their dream homes. More than twenty years slipped away before he reconnected with Korner in Chicago, recovering his desire to paint with the coming of Gina. That moment had been too brief, ending abruptly with her murder.

Mor awoke from his reverie, fired up the truck and drove out of the open vineyard country. Traffic eventually thickened as he reached the south end of the valley and the sprawl of residential and industrial Santa Rosa. He had that feeling there was only one more chance to paint, to turn out the worm of unexpressed dreams eating away at his gut. Maybe his last chance. He goosed the accelerator, rolling down 101 with thoughts of how Christina would look. He tried mousy to vivacious, stout to skinny, and mannish to feminine. He wanted to think of her as physically unappealing. He still had passion for a woman's body but carried too many scars from past relationships. The scar tissue kept him from attachments. Mor wondered what had drawn Christina to the painting.

Forty-five minutes later, passing down a steep grade and through a tunnel led out to scudding clouds pierced by oxide red bridge towers, sailboats afloat on the silvery bay waters, and in the distance, the San Francisco skyline. He drove into crowded bridge traffic, a congested toll plaza, and the crush of city traffic. The salt air laden with smog felt heavy in his lungs after the high mountain air he'd left behind.

His spirit lifted crossing the Presidio with its rolling lawns and pungent eucalyptus. After passing through Golden Gate Park, he hit the flat suburban west side sprawl with treeless avenue monotonous with blank stucco row houses.

After twenty minutes of stoplights and cross traffic he merged on another highway. The country to the west opened. Low ridges of the coastal Montara Mountains yielded to county parks and redwood preserves. No stoplights till he hit the Sand Hill exit on the north edge of the Stanford campus. The peninsula once swept with hundreds of sand dune hills lay now flattened by freeways surging with, to his eyes, wage slavery. Y'all slippen' into darkness.

He'd been to Stanford before. A trustee from the university purchased one of the 7-vision paintings from Kornor's agent. Invited for a tour of the campus, he had been unmoved by the grassy sanctuary of fields, reeking of eucalyptus, and rolling with its faux Romanesque and Mission Revival architecture. It was all too pretty for him at that time.

Parking in the visitor's lot, he walked under a vine-covered arch supported by short columns. Students with smart phones screening their smart purpose swarmed the grounds. With two hours before his meeting with Christina, he found a sunny spot on well-manicured grass and stretched out. Within a few moments he fell asleep.

He dreamed of the campus deserted. The lawn turned to sand as he started trudging across, feet sinking in the sea of loose grains. Finally he reached a path on the other side guarded by a spotted leopard and black cougar. The leopard seemed oblivious to him as the black cougar slunk forward with a low growl to butt his head against his leg. A woman appeared. He asked her to call off the cougar before bared canines sank into his flesh. The woman stared, shook her head, and vanished. He pushed on. The cougar gone, he found he held a book with careworn cover. Inside the cover he found a string of beads with an eye and pyramid talisman. Down the path he came to people carrying books with similar covers. In the center, the teacher appeared in a scarlet robe. He recognized in the awareness of that being, that pervasive bliss generating sorrow in that cunning duplicity of memory, of me or you magnificent acharya, great teacher still a being that all love supreme. That awareness of him being him, Dark Mor, himself as well as all the others gathered round. One bio-field. One singular duplicity. One single cunning, keen, creative deceit. That deceit of a denial.

He woke in the familiar world. Students milled past, paying him no mind or wondering why. He contemplated his dream for a while, finally standing with a long stretch while letting eyes scan for parat param puedendum. Old habits die hard he thought, heading for his appointment with Christina Shaughnessy.

He reached the cafe at 11:27. The pre-lunch crowd growing, he paid for a cup of coffee and grabbed a table near the entrance. Soon the place buzzed with young students, muted somewhat by the presence of graying faculty. He saw her entering the room with the movements of a dancer. Her aura electric she now met his gaze. Mor felt that wide open hillbilly grin coming on to his face. Christina beamed back in recognition. He gave her a slight wave as she approached.

"Mr. Dark Mor?" She asked, walking over with a smile and an open hand.

Standing Mor rocked the table catching a tipping sugar dispenser with one hand as he shook hers.

"I will get a cup and join you."

She picked up a tray and walked to three large silver urns at the end of the food line. The students deferred to her, parting in a wave as she passed, steaming teapot tossing a vapor trail off behind. She slid a cup of black coffee off the tray placing it in front of him.

"Thought you might like another," she said, shrugging off a flat shoulder bag.

"Thanks. I've only been waiting a little while," he managed lamely, clearing his throat.

As their eyes met, he realized that idiot hick smile still lifted the corners of his mouth. He let his eyes drift away to the colors dancing off backpacks, T-shirts, and jackets. He searched the room before coming back to her eyes. His gaze glanced off, catching on silk blouse, open at the collar, revealing a hint of black lace underneath.

"I appreciate you coming on short notice, Dark. I love your name. So ominous yet intriguing. What is it like wearing such a name?" she asked, crinkling the corners of her eyes.

"It's a variation on 'the boy named Sue' syndrome. My mother was, well crazy with a wicked sense of humor. Like she knew. She knew it would be my burden and my redemption," he replied, his eyes staying with hers. "Then in a way it's more prosaic than poetic. She worshipped this war hero general named Douglas, which it turns out is Galic for Darkness."

"There certainly is plenty to intrigue in the dark. It seems fate or destiny is her'e playing her hand. Interesting."

"My mother was crazy. She'd look at me with these huge black eyes," he started before catching himself.

"You have the look of meeting someone you did not expect," she replied, gathering a fistful of thick curls, fixing them on top of her head with a silver clasp.

"I guess I expected the mousy librarian type but you're, well, different," he returned, squeezing a lip between his teeth feeling his mouth running ahead of his thought.

"With my head connected to the rest of my body?" she asked, bringing her tea to her lips and gazing back through the steam.

"I mean, you're all there in a kinda wild way." he replied feeling color rise in his cheeks. He quickly looked away to a neon pink backpack being shrugged off by a skinny blond, its padded straps pulling her crimson T-shirt tight against her chest.

Christina sat up and cleared her throat. "I love your name because, well, you might say that I am seeking the darkness. In my field of metaphysics, the supernatural is the normal. The black body we all turn into as'z z'leep into a un consciousness is the supernatural eve re' y body. A re'y body of eve," she left that hook out there with a pause. In her"eve re'y body. A re'yz z z'apping eve're'y thing with a being out in her"eyez z z'inging intention. Finding himself instantly pervaded by her influence. In her"eyez z zap'ping a power. Any sane man would make a quick exit while it was still possible. But then he flashed on being a bit of a sucker for black lace.

"Mad Meg or Ma're'y Poppins. You had me the moment you said you loved my name. It seems most don't. The bias against the darkness is unbelievable. It can be I admit a tough road being Dark Mor. Then I must confess to a bewitchment down in Laguna Beach a few years ago. A witch initiated me in black body awareness. Got me so charged I couldn't take a crap for a week. Excuse any vulgarity on my part although there is no excuse for me being a vulgar painter that I am now." He offered with that hillbilly grin.

"In that I am practising a new dialectic just let me carry on as though making sense. In that dialectic using the classic Hegelian trinity of thesis antithesis synthesis a y poses as'ex . Thesis y now antithesis as'ex's ting out in formation. Thus any x's ting antithesis of a y still a being the whole point of view of you of y you're; you of a being in the first place. Synthesis awareness of a y being still indivisible invisibility of any individual or any a na y body now." she tossed another hook. Mor stuck it deep into his lower lip.

"Reckon a cat like Hegel be jumping a way over my head. But lay it on me. Like I said you . . ."

"Had me or you? Now it seems we all turn into or out of a k'now'ing of it any memory. A living of it mirrored as thoughtsz in the'or'y a b c's of a being c'ng as'z'any mere in word memory of me or you. A y being still in the first place now out as'word dividing us."

"As'ex?" Mor now found words coming thru that cosmic channel. This could be a gas he mused. Her eyes'izzled with a silent laughter. He knew she now instantly knew he knew that she knew of it. Of a b'ng c'ng still in the first place indivisible invisibility now out of it or a black'g'round echoing into a peh'ss'y w'hole power. Now as'ex. The source or y of her eyesz'ap'ped his breath till Mor felt himself passing out. Instinctively he spilled some hot coffee on the back of his hand jolting his attention back into his body. She smiled without seeming to notice while at the same time turning off the radiation gaze still a peering it at him. Shrugging she picked back up on the thread Mor sensed would lead back to awareness of a blackness. Of a prior state of a b'ng c'ng indivisible invisibility. A b'ng c'ng in a state of it now in a wordfreedom still a b'ng'lack'ness's now to be a gain. Out in her eyesz'zzazz a peh'ess'y w'hole power and if that don't float your boat what will he wondered.

"Y'or y speak dialectic offers an in word debatable awareness of a state of a being supernaturally that macromicro ka's mic mean means meaning of a eve're'y'body asz'any wayeve function. A b c's wayeve supersonic sound function of a fun'ny'a'ction ma'king of it a y eye merely a peering it now out int'word a twis'ting in two appearing of it." She'e now caught his attention. For ma's way of funny action defined his crazy notions of himself growing up merely a peering it suddenly appearing of it. Ma gave him back over to the darkness at two after initially suddenly awakening in word silent awareness of a being run over by a '51 Chevy panel delivery truck. After'words she put a dis'spelling on him back to an indivisible blackness calling him Dark Mor. Christina seemed to read his thoughts with a curious frown.

"A state of being recognized by a y or y now speak manner of speaking understanding a b c's over mind. A prior y state to it as'z'any in word captivity. A y eye merely a peering it. As'z y'or y now az's'ex. In that over mind any in word wayeve or means is a being mirrored by supersonic sound function echoing a're'y'flecting touch as'z'any touching of it. Now a black'g'round turning as'king of it a k'now'ing out in her"eyez z z'leep in two of eve're'y body. Ar'king of it any appearing a pairing of it now a k'now'ing out a y da y na light. A y'll d'na. A d'na'eye'll a peering it out ar'king of it as'k'no no no'wing appearing of it. Now out in her"eyez z z as'ka's mic sun. A per'son'ic twis'ting y'll d'na. Out in her"eye'z z a black mirror see'as shining that black'g'round d'ark'as perceived in two of eve're'y'body. In a deadly duplicity of any roll or role of a re'y'all radiating in her"eyez z z'a con fusion of a hard con. She now a peering it then appearing of it us en'ess'e. A b c's of a b'ng c'ng now int'word turning in two formation now a k'now'ing out in her'eyez z z'azz of eve're'y'body is recognized as the'e primary causal bodhi. Well . . . of eve're'y body." She added with out a trace of irony. Just warmth. He felt her radiance across the table. It seemed to suspend his attention now in one indivisible moment the'na k'no'wing out of it. She now had opened a door in a space in time. A passage in a wordfreedom awareness of a being still in the first place unborn. He felt the transition in his gut. That feeling of a free falling out in a wordfreedom.

"She"e'na funny that way. That wayeve re'y'body asz in da y na light. A manifestation of man'as mind or y memory. Macro-micro ka's mic memory of a b'ng c'ng on a h'or'eye'z zion." Her voice carried a supersonic silent buzz that suspended his thoughts. It left his will to flee melting in the fire of her intelligence. He felt himself drawn out of his body to a center slightly above his head. Through this center she now turned pouring into his mind a k'now'ing of it. "Y you are a man. A man'as mind or y memory mean between. Between the greater or lesser possibilities of a being. A being twin macromicro ka's mic a'ten bi na re'y. A's above so below. The black darkness causal x bodhi of infinite potential with intent of ignoring y. Y you're; you awareness of a being in the first place."

"Eve're'y body." He heard the words coming from his mouth as though from another's mind. He felt the dialectic flooding over his in word field like a tsunami disappearing his sense of a being a y as'ex's ting in formation. In formation merely mirrored in word. Now attention remained in her'him'it indivisible in anybody out of a being in'visibility. Invisibility in'visibility. He felt disappeared in her'him'it as'ka's mic over mind or y memory. Mor felt form as indefinite moment after moment merely defined awhile in word. Beyond that in word definition he drown formless in her'eyez z z. He resisted panicking by focusing on his breath.

"Now we all turn in her'eyez z z a ma'sz nature a black'g'round echoing of eve re'y body into or out of one indivisible in'visibility of a y eye of any body merely a peering it out as ex's ting in word in formation as'z' any body. Anybody as though appearing of it in any roll or role of loopy loops now turning a black'g'round echo of it as'k'now'ing a being c'ee'ng by a b c's in wordsz of a denial. A projection of thoth'tsz of a being c'ng of any or eve're'y body." She now seemed to be testing him. He flashed on Korner setting him up. Maybe slipping a drug in his coffee. Some unseen influence seemed to be alternating in his consciousness. Pulling him into or out of some in word vortex. He thought for a split second of fleeing the scene but merely spoke what came to mind.

"Kinda like an in word consensus of ignorance?"Though disturbed by her he liked that she got right onto the point. That point of why a being in out of the Dark'ness. That point of anybody appearing of it in the first place out of the darkness. He'd found most preferred finding themselves already appearing of it somehow out beside it. A being now as though beside the point. She was funny that way. In her eyez z z'a pointing out of him. A being still in the first place. Someone now willing to not only acknowledge the elephant in every room but get right up on it. Hell, turning black into it. Perhaps for the first time in his life he felt at home in the first place now with k'now'ing another human being. Who in their right mind embraces the darkness, he wondered. Except of course one named that or eve're'y body of a being turning into or out of a black'g'round echoing in her"eyez z z'a micro waving or radiating a complete d"ark'ness. He felt electromagnetic loops radiating turning into or out of a black'g'round by d'na y'll light of a ka's mic sun turning into we all a being as'king of it y turning churning burning into one wheel of fortune. She for sure had him for a spin of that wheel.

"There must be a deliberate disregard of eve're'y body of a being that black body singularity in order for'ma'sz appearing of it out a pairing. There must be that in word intention as though'tsz in me or you a memory of most anyone desiring appearing of it a gain out now awhile in a space in time. That ka's mic mirror mind or y memory reflecting in her"eyez z z'leeping in two a black'g'round echoing one appearing out of it capturing y'all h'our attention while awake.

Soon enough though we all grow weary falling as'z z z'leep in a turning black'g'round indivisible invisibility. Only awakhening yet playing roles now turning into anybody merely mirrored in word. Mirrored out of a b'ng c'ng in a na'me alone. Hi my na'me is Mary Poppins." She gave with an exaggerated mannerism. Mor broke out with a laugh at her antics. "That put on of any in word masked captivity bound to wear thin on anybody after awhile. Then naturally anybody must fall as'z z z'leep black into a being still in the first place indivisible in'visibility of any individual. Into a singular being still indivisible in'visibility now with intention aw'akhening aten. Awakhening a binary being. A being still in the first place indivisible now a pairing appearing supernaturally as'z thoth'tsz of a b'ng c'ng out of the first place awhile. As'z'any thoth'tsz of it as'ka'sz mic da y na light igniting ignore'ance of it. Ignoring a k'no no no'wing denial out of it. A y'll dna. Appearing bi na re'ye'sz turning a black'g'round amplatitudes or wayeve re'y thin'king of it flattening. A y as'z ex planing a being versus a being in her'e yez z z' of eve'll in complete rolls or roles of d"ark'ness. A dhi ark of the covenant with as'king of it a'kh"et aten. A'kh duplicating a'ten. Awakhen aten now at aten'cion of a b c's. Any being appearing of it out in awhile still in'visibility of a being c'ng a slight slice of a meager thin'king of it. A dhi ark'n'ess'e. A now to be perceived ar'king of it out in her"eyez z z'leeping a wayeve re'y"e asz'a black'g'round body. A r'ey'all as ka'sing supersonically a being now k'nowing out of a y her'him'it a freestanding e'ye star'e y"e of y'all radiating in formation or na na. By a being y now in a potential diversity. Understanding alphabeta binary letter code int'word a twis'ting a black'g'round echoing of it now with in word intent. A playing out letter'all'y y'all a b c's revealing a b'ng c'ng still in the first place. A b c's now ending xyz'ee'z z z'a k'nowing out roles of that black mirror see'as ka's mic mic'ro wayeve black'g'round. A're'y'diating a're'y'diation out in her"e yez z z of eve'will. We all turning into or out of a being still in the first place."

"A black'g'round echoing one being a being still in the first place appearing of it out now awhile a k'nowing in wordsz a being out a's a y eye x's ting in formation of it out in her"eyez z z' a peering it now. A being c'ng as eve're"y body?" Whose words he wondered kept coming out of his mouth. It seemed like a fully formed Medusa snaked supersonically through his in word mind. A wayeve will. In her"eyez z z of eve'll. Still it was his way to remain silent merely observing himself typically flailing about incoherent.

"The indivisible in visibility of a darkness becoming a black'g"round of it turning out by da y na light in a y eye of her'him'it y'sz dom'us in the first place now with the hard con she us en'ess'e. To be en'y'e'ye na now en'dhi'ing it as'z'za a b'lack' being to perceive a gain by a k'nowing out of it. Turning out of a y eye as'z ex's ting turning out now a k'no'wing of it in word. In formation infor'ma'sz awhile. A wily while in her"eye a b'ng cunning in word craft. A gain in a y eye a peering it now k'now'ing be'aming eve're'y body as though'tsz in forming into anybody or any measly thin'king of it," she replied studying him with a look of curiosity. Her words befuddled his head but the warmth of her. The radiance of her'him'it in her'eyez z z'ion of it melted his fears.

"The d'ark'ness now in her'eyez z z' of eve're'y body merely a peering it out in word appearing of it awhile as anybody. Out of a b c's of a being c'ng still in the first place now turning out of it a k'no'wing a b'lack'g'round potential to be a gain. A b c's of a b'ng c'ng now any mere mirrored in a word y potential. Why thank you ma'am. I do believe you be the first person that made me really appreciate my name. What it means. Darkness. As a mean means of turning black'g'round it. Can't tell you how many times that I thought about changing it. Somehow I just never could. Now. Right now I'm feeling the reason for carrying that shady handle was to lead me to you." Mor stiffened his face to keep tears from coming into his eyes. He flashed on how many times having to do it facing scorn derision and anger coming from total strangers. It seemed assuming his name cast a shadow that brought out insecurities in others. Even before learning his name. Hearing it. People taking his name as some kind of threat. Like 'how dare you call yourself that'. Like calling yourself evil. It blew his mind the prejudice against a part of life instrumental as light. No light without the darkness. The turning into or out of it. "You make me realize now the purpose of my name, hell a being of anybody on the planet in the first place."

"That prejudice against the dark reflects the neurosis and psychosis of anyone living in near complete denial of it with out realizing y. A y that I am speaking of it in the first place. A y being that aska's mic memory of a now k'now'ing out of it. A being in the first place. Now that indivisible invisibility as'king of it y now' turning a b'lack"g'round intent of a being a gain. A y'or y you're you now appearing a pairing of it by a denial ending of it as a positive ne'gating negativity. A're'y'flects that as'ka's mic memory of a being you now merely mirrored turning a b'lack'g'round echo into a k'no'wing in word thoughtsz of a b'ng c'ng in a gain now k'now'ing out of it anybody anytime anywhere. You now a b c's of a being c'ng denied in wordsz'a. In formation as thoughtsz of a y eye being c'ng a peering it still in the first place now appearing of it out understanding any in word spelling of any memory of it. As though projected by you now k'now'ing out of it a being in any name alone. You now as though denying a being of you by turning in wordsz'a y now k'no no no'wing out any thin'king of it. If that ain't a recipe for neurosis then do you know what is?" she asked with a certain sadness around her eyes. "It seems the more you seek to know it, the more you must deny it. Mem or y of it in'visibility of a b'ng c'ng not eve'r'eye in formation." Mor felt something twisted now unwinding out in the double entendre as'ex'pressed in her voice. Its sound seemed a wave rippling out of her'eyez z z'on it. A wave of eve'll. A will in a're'y'all of a b c's informing his mind into any thin'king of it. A merely appearing of it now as thoughtsz projecting supersonically out in anybody int'word as ex's ting in a twis'ting in t'wo. Appearing a pairing in formation y'll d'na. A b'ng c'ng in denial of it is the name of the game. Denial of a being still completely complete in the first place. Out of that completion it cannot be a gain. A b'ng completely indivisible in'visibility. Does not mean we all still will turn into or out of it whatʼeve'r'ey'e'asz z zion of it. That denial is necessity of now k'no'wing out of it any scant thin'king of it. A k'no no no'wing of it in a b c's of a b'ng c'ng still indivisible in'visibility. Now turning it into in word formation supernaturally as thoth'tsz of me or you in word appearing a pairing in memory of a being in that first place." Christina paused as though reading perplexity in his expression.

"Please continue. In that I am appearing confused may be due to a certain double entendre that I'm picking up in your words." He found the dialectic a dichotomy splitting a b c's of a being c'ng of indivisible invisibility from any in word information of it. The double entendre pointed out the deceit of a being c'ng now out in a b c's any in word in formation of it. Yet without now k'no'wing out of it in word there is no information of it. The dialectic set up a debate between awareness of a y eye a peering it or now as'king of it a k'no'wing out of it as in word thoughts of appearing of it. It a b'ng c'ng as though now out in a cunning craft of a wordship with in'ka's mic'ro wave black'g'round indivisible body echoing any hearing a language now in the y dialectic debate cancelling itself out of any information of it. Revealing a being still in the first place indivisible invisibility. Invisibility before falling as'z z z'leep understanding any in word spelling of a b c's in forming it out in'visibility awhile. Before thinking in wordsz of a b'ng c'ng appearing of it out as a mirror function echoing sound wayeves out in her'eyez z z'z azz eve're'y body. A being y eye a'wayeve re y a'z'z'a peering it out in word a b'ng c'ng still in the first place. Now that I'm finding myself listening h'earing it in her"eyez z z'a wayeve're'y black'g'round body echoing in formation of it. Letter'all'y y'all in word a b c's in formation of a b'ng c'ng in awhile. Mor could only observe this crazy flow of energy in formation in words as though vomitting up or down a glut of a b'ng c'ng gushing out in word information. A ka'ma'ing from above as well as below. He felt it all a black'g'round him now a k'no'wing out of it without realizing why except as a b'ng c'ng in her'eye z z z'azz a present presence. She smiled back from across the table. Mor blinked with imagining her leaping into his mind. A'shrieking kali ma. The hairs razing on the back of his neck forewarned of danger. Still he felt a great kindness in her'eyez z z of a being indivisible in'visibility. She gave a slight nod before continuing speaking the cryptic dialectic debate thesis antithesis synthesis of a y eye merely a peering it or now as'ex's ting appearing of it information awhile. Then a disappearing b'lack'g'round complete d"ark'ness now with intent to turn as two k'now a b'ng a gain.

"As'ka's mic'ro wayeveing a black'g'round a're'y'dhi'ation out in her"eyez z z'i'on eve're'ybody now as'kurving e turn'ing y'all as'king of it a k'no'wing out of it any a na y'or eve're'y body is causally y'all by mere mirror function of mind or y memory reflecting in word any appearing of it out as x's ting by denial of a being completely in the first place complete. Complete. A completion in d'na'eye'll now as though a k'nowing out of it projecting in'completion. A being b'lack' is a being completely complete still in the first place as though projecting out of it a being lacking of it instilling intent of any a na y body to be of it a gain. Thus a y eye being complete in the first place a peering it out now a black'g'round k'now'ing out of it with intent of intentionally disregarding a being complete in the first place." The supernatural supersonic p'sy'lent buzz of the dialectic seemed to settle down. His stomach no longer lifting into his throat Mor felt a deep relaxation coming over him.

"Complete encirclement d"ark'ness of a being now to be perceived as b'lack'. As'king of it a de'sire of eve'll. Of any or eve're'ybody as though lacking of it necessitates ignoring a being full up completely in the first place? Sounds like a recipe for a disaster. A disaster we all in turn bring upon ourselves by our own ignoring of it." In a flash of insight he found a certain calm no longer ignoring himself out of a b c's of a b'ng c'ng still in the first place.

"Projecting it. Ignoring it is a positive projection of negating it. Positive negativity in any mirror mind or y memory wayeve function of a being anybody as out in word though'tsz of it projects indivisible consciousness a b'lack'g'round k'no no no'wing out of it any denial of it. A denial y'll d'na in a being that still singular singularity of a y eye now out in her'eyez z z of eve're'y body is in one int'word a t'wis'ting in two a black'g"round echo of it. Anybody a pairing of it in a supernatural mirage of any in word mirrored infor'ma'ing appearance of it. Merely a peering it out in her"eyez z z' as thought waves. E supernatural electromagnetic sound pulses as'z'any thoth'tsz of it infor'ma'ing appearance of anybody anything anywhere." She paused with a quizzical look in her eye. Mor, somewhat familiar to all things Egyptian recognized Thoth as god of art of a being c'ng letter'all'y as knowledge science and writing. He also had been initiated by a shaman into the native way of perceiving all creation as body of the great grandfathermother.

Thoughtsz of it as a being now as thoth'tsz of it. A God esse. A God to be letter'all'y anybody in name alone. The supernatural wayeve're'y eye of thoth'tsz of the whorl'd. The pyramis eye vision now having him insight. Swallowing him w'hole offered further of it as'ex'per'eye' en"cing it thru an eye of anybody as'king of it y. A y eye a peering it out now aska's mic memory in a b c's of a b'ng c'ng out of it in word. That experience piquing his interest some years before led to more study of the history of it. It as thoughtsz of it. Now a k'nowing out of it supernaturally as thoth'tsz. Some thought America's USA a reborn Egyptian civilization. For him the whole universe. He knew the entire polytheism of Egyptian gods rested on a re'ye of a b'ng c'ng freestanding in a wordfreedom a peering it from above as below still one p'sy'lent singing singular indivisible principal principle of a b'ng c'ng still in the first place, a're;Ye'aten. He knew about it. Something told him now with Christina he would become it. A b'ng c'ng from a singular point of view.

"Thoth. You said thoth?"

"Thoth'tsz of a God esse to be now of letters. Thus any in word being . . ."

"A being of a duplicity in word information of a b c's letter'all'y appearing of it. A being now a mind mirrored supernatural duplicate in word of a b'ng c'ng as thoth'tsz of it by the grace of a God esse. To be letter'all'y y'all phonographically appearing of it merely a peering it out of a b c's."

"A God esse. To be art of a being letter'all'y y'all appearing of it in wordsz out in her'eyez z z'leeping a wayeve 're'y in'for'ma'sz in'formation." She had now touched on the supernatural. He touched by her'eyez z z'leep into the macrocosm of ka's mic overmind. A great mind he knew intimately as a being saved by it at two y'ears young. Only as one too appear a pairing later learning a b c's as in word thoughtsz of a be'tween. A twin now then out of it. As other y'sz than it. Now finding himself touched of a black'g"round echo by her as mother nature touched him in sun rain and wind out there where a God lost his shoes. Now he found himself within her'eye'z z z'azz'leeping superimposed as thoth'tsz of a b'ng c'ng directly across the table. Praise the gods and pass the whiskey he mused. And by now he could use a drink.

"In that we all appear of it as though turning in wordsz into any mirror appearance or effect of it. As in word though'tsz echoing out in her'eyez z z' a black'g"round a're'y'dhi'a'ting in the or y of mind or y memory complete loops of electromagnetic d"ark'n'esse. Perceived now to be ar'king as'king of it any k'no'wing out of it."

Now that of a blackground absorbed a b'ng c'ng of him just prior to his sudden in word awakening saving his life as'z two a k'no'wing of a truck running over. Him now a k'no'wing in recognition. A're'y"cognition now of a being still in the first place mirrored out in word as though'tsz of any meager thin'king of anybody appearing of it out in name alone. All that flashed in his mind or memory turning in a wordfreedom a peering it back to black. A blackness of a b'ng c'ng prior to his first in word memory awakening a split second space in time now under that delivery truck. The sheer miracle of it now came to mind. How was it possible to move blindly to that perilous place to begin with he wondered. Why the set up necessitating a supernatural supersonic in word awareness superimposing itself instantaneously. Saving his a life before now any k'nowing out of it. Yet there it was and now still is complete. A're'y'cognizing of it now of him in a b c's as a b'ng c'ng there. Personically. Su personically came as answer. Su asti ka. A'kh it is well. We'll is it a'kh. Him a turning out in her"eyez z z'ion of it. Indivisible invisbility su personic'ka's blackness of that of a being c'ng as'z' any scant thin'king of it in a eve're'y body. Now he remembered it in the same way we all in turn remember a deep'a'sz z z'leep un'two un'winding a un con she'us n'ess'e. As only on awakening is a recall of a b'ng c'ng that way possible. As'z z z'leeping out or b'lack into the wayeve a b c's of a b'ng c'ng indivisible. A'Re'y'called now out of that. A black body by a being c'ng out in wordsz of anybody as'k'no'wing any appearing of it from a merely mirrored a peering it out. Or a y eyez z z' a peering it out int'word a twis'ting in two now mirrored the'n echoing that black'g'round sound wayeves of a supernatural voice within anybody. In a're'y'calling that first memory he found himself an indivisible black mirror se'e'as bio fields'z z' any wayeve function now turning out of it a k'nowing d'na'eye'll in word in forming any chintzy thin'king of it supernaturally superficially y'all right before his eyes. Now still k'no no no'wing it out in word he found himself alternating in a wordfreedom there as awareness of it indivisible in'visibility of any individual. Christina gave him beseeching eyes as though she hesitated to continue. He recognized that swinging far out on the limb with a veritable stranger. Mor gestured with a nod and a slight flick of fingers for her to continue. At the same time he adjusted his position to absorb the solvent of the dialectic debate of it without losing breakfast or his mind along the wayeves rippling out in her'eyez z z'ap'ping'ting. He felt weightless. A for'ma'sz eve're'y'body. Any potential movement impossible when a body dissolves itself black'g'round now any knowing of it with out word in forming it. It seemed that dialectic debate stirred his awareness of a black'g'round invisibility. She now had his attention swept away in her'eye'z z z'azz a voice echoing out information of a cosmic black'g'round potential appearing supersonically as thoth'tsz of it now.

"Me or you in memory merely duped by that apparent in word mirror duplicity of a being c'ng still in the first place a peering it out now a k'now'ing of it awhile. A b'ng c'ng a wily deceit of it out in her'eyez z z a peering it in word. She'e'na funny that wayeve of eve're'ybody. As'ka's mic ka'mic. Let objectivity of quantum science follow laws of general theory completely black'g"round to find a being still in the first place. Indivisible in'visibility in a wordfreedom. As'z'any or eve're'y body periodically turns black as though h'our eye'sz z'a're'y'turning over that zygomatic boney horizon into the black of the head. A re'y turning again now out over that horizon int'word in sight of anyone gazing it out as'z'any eyez z z. Now finding himself lost in a being c'ng mirrored in that complete kurvey'e k'nowing role or roll of indivisible a y eye potential. Any laws y'all melt back instantly into a being still in the first place a peering it out in her'eyez z z' of eve're'ybody. A're'y'dhi'a'ting in formation as'z z' any potential indivisible black mirror see'as see'ng. Out in her"eye of eve're'ybody turning black into or out of a being still that complete d"ark'ness of a black'g"round beginning any ending of it in the first place. A b'ng c'ng turning black into or appearing out of it in da y na light of d'na'eye'll."

Now Dark Mor found himself out in her"e'ye'sz a black indivisible invisibility. A peering it out of it in her"eyez z z' a wayeve appearing of it anybody in its fun'ny'a'ction function. She'e'na funny that way. That awayeve a're'y'all. As'z z z'leep in a black'g'round now turning out a k'now'ing of it anybody any thin'king any where in a b c's of a b'ng c'ng still of that singular indivisible subjective awareness. That e've're y body same awareness of such that we all in turning a black'g"round of it now a k'no'wing of it still by a y eye being c'ng merely a peering it out of any a na y mirrored y na you now appearing of it in word. As'word he was able to cleave it or define it supernaturally as'z'any thoth'tsz of a being out of it in the first place. Y'all a's any a na y a's ex's ting in word objectivity. In that sense any k'no no no'wing denial of the singular darkness is now as thoth'tsz supernaturally projecting that a known as'z'any un'known. A dying merely supernaturally as thoth'tsz in a b c's of a b'ng c'ng now born. Anybody now turning out of or black into one a k'no'wing out of it any role of a being c'ng as thoth'tsz of it born. Appearing to live merely anybody of it a y eye a peering it now out mirrored supernaturally as'k'no'wing thoth'tsz of a God esse to be letter'ally a b c's g'eez us appearing of it in wordsz'a still in the first place awareness in a wordfreedom indivisible in'visibilty. A b'ng c'ng now superimposed out t'word a t'wis'ting in two in formation by a k'no no no'wing d'na'eye'll of its indivisible invisibility. A y eye a peering it out in word as'ex's ting appearing of it in name alone. Of such was the debate of the y dialectic tearing lose looszing'ing him in a great overmind. Mor blinked. Finding himself still in her'eyez z z of eve'll. She'e'na sliding her hips tight to the plastic molded chair with a hypnotic stare of entreaty.

"In that awareness of a b'ng c'ng y'all times and places merely a peering it now out in wordsz mirroring of that infinite in any a d'na y'll potential of the Darkness. The sacred KRYST'y'all gee'sz us pressured by the gravity weight of waiting on death. Any a na y eye in formation merely awhile of it appearing in word. As'ka'y'gee kali ma'ss of it out in her'eyez z z of eve'll. A peh'ss'y w'hole universal black eve're'y body covered by ignition of da y na light igniting ignore'ance of it projected supersonically supernaturally superimposed as'z'any thoth'tsz of it out in her'eyez z z'i'on. A crossing out in her'eye'of'eve'll ways. In her'eyez z z'azz wayeves eye re y dhi'ating eve're'ye'sz'zazz z in'formation in word." She'e'na paused. Staring deep into his eyes she seemed to swallow him whole. Mor could not or would not resist. Still his survival instincts held their position.

"Did Korner tell you I was half Jewish and half shiksa, as well as being a librarian-type professor?"

For a moment Mor found himself stumbling into normal. Or a version of it before the debate now raging the caj'in him. Now it seemed up for grabs between the dark'ness or a while of it out in her'eyez z z. In her'eve'rey"e'body completion absorbed his sense of one somehow. Some way incomplete. Dumbfounded by her words he found himself now in a wordfreedom awareness completely bodiless amidst bodies. A na y invisibility in visibility. A y eye merely a peering it. Or it appearing in a word or two. As'words they seemed somehow a cutting into bits anybody as'ex'peh'ressed a'while out of her'eve'll peh'ess'y whole body. Or a ba"by of it. Pull yourself together dawg. Y'all just met. A voice addressed to a center of him broke his train of thoughtsz'a open into a b'ng c'ng still at attention now just inches above his head. Just beyond the range of his in word comprehension.

"He only mentioned scrolls from holy roller land. I guess that's the connection," he replied, furrowing his eyebrows as he spoke. Momentarily his attention diverted to the pink backpack slouched on the nearby table as the blond pulled her long hair back into a ponytail through an elastic tie. A gold stud flickered in her ear lobe. "Then I suppose you have to mention the 'Dr.D.' word. Sometimes, if I'm feeling contrary, I'll introduce myself as De'ath, that's Mr. De Aath. Hard to imagine a Jewish girl named Christina, sounds like it came from the shiksa half." He turned b'lack in her eyes.

"It is actually Margot Christina, the pearl in black velvet. My mother, a Sephardic Jew, died when I was very young. Dad was Irish Catholic. Despite all the guilt he carried from his work decades before on the Manhattan Project, he had more guilt from not raising me in the Catholic Church. After my mother passed, he asked me to use my middle name. If I asked why, he merely looked off. So you see that I am too having a name for redemption, a Jewish girl in Catholic perdition. You might like to know both our names refer to a darkness. That now turning into any k'now'ing of a black'g"round macromicro mean means meaningfullness quantum bodhi of a unified field of view of you of yod iota. The w'holy blissful Darkness of the Great Soul, the Kryst, for Christ's sake," she returned with a slight lilt of her head without a trace of irony. "Think about it Dark, we all appear turning into or out of one a known indivisible un'known experienced directly and periodically as'z' z z z'leep black into a un'consciousness. A b'lack body con of eve're'ybody exprienced directly over a third of h'our lives. As'z'z'za mode'l . . ." Dark in the dark. The debate ignited in him awareness of a b'ng c'ng a peering it in the first place now out of a singular b'lack eye of eve're'ybody or yourself supernaturally appearing as'z'any thoth'tsz of it in word in'formation with a pow pow power. A peh'ess'y whole power. Brahmayonim. A b'ng g'ee'sz z ze us as a pure indivisible invisibility darkness b'lack'body with peh're'y'ssure to be a gain. Out in her'eyez z z of eve'll. A will way'eve wheel race turning churning burning. We all he mused crushed in a wily cruel cunning craft a'say'ling out over it in her'eyez z z'azz'z'any b'lack' mirror se'e'as anybody of a seer. Anybody of a b'ng c'ng a peering it out in wordsz'. As'z'z'any information of it. As"z a singular mode. A model of o'ne indivisible invisibility. A un'consciousness of that one eye that I am is is. A y eye a peering it now a hard con'sci'ous'n'ess'e awareness at aten'cion captivated in a b c's of a being c'ng. A now as'king of it y any k'now'ing out of it anybody supernaturally as a un"con"she'us thotht'sz'z"z appearing of it. A u'na you now still of a b'ng c'ng turning it in't'word a t'wisting in two y'sz now as'ex's ting information of a knowing out of it a b'ng c'ng a un'known. Still with the primary b'lack' body intention instilled of waking up a b'ng c'ng a gain. Mor's attention caught up now a un'k'now'ing it out in her'eyez z z a'way'eve're'y a're'y'dhi'a'ting. ". . . of a memory without in word information. A b'ng c'ng still knowing out of it a blackness indivisible from any man'as mind memory. And if a man without womb now out of it raising a little hell," she added with a mock frown. "The ancient wisdom keepers recognized that eye of a being invisibility in visibility in any eye a peering it now out of it in her'eyez z z of eve're'ybody. Now the black'g'round as'king of it a k'no'wing bodhi of a being to perceive of it out in wordsz understanding the power of da y na light igniting it with a positive negation of merely a peering it now int'word a t'wis'ting in two a denial of it. Appearing a pairing of it. As'ex. A 0 as a twis'ting in't'a 8."

She'e'na left that h"OO"ka out there on the table. Mor took to starring at his hands now holding the sugar shaker. It seemed the a y debate divided as'ex. Y'all as'ex's ting of it as'z'any information. Awhile. A wily twis'ting twisted sisters he mused. Of a mean means. Of a cobra and a vulture. As'z two strands of d'na'eye'll he thought.

"Any in word body of a b'ng c'ng still in the first place now a twis'ting in two the first last and only primary peh'ess'y w'hole body. Could it now be we all still turn into or out of that as'king of it a k'no'wing out of it a'su asti'ka man's"ka's mic black'g"round? In that I am saying to my students, why not? Why not a're'y'al'eye'ze awareness of a being supernaturally still in a wordfreedom awareness in the first place? Any one or eve're'y one is a knowing out of it experienced directly asz z z'leep black into a un consciousness. Trust first hand experience over a being merely mirrored as thoughts of any measly thin'king of it in wordsz in the'or'y. Imagine yourself still free indivisible in'visibility in a wordfreedom awareness of anybody. Awareness of a free being merely mirrored supernaturally as thoth'tsz in a b c's of a b'ng c'ng in the first place now superimposed in wordsz turning out a k'no'wing any role or roll of that complete d"ark'ness bodhi. As thoth'tsz of it as'ka me'ing black'g"round and around in the e'turn'all'y y'all experienced directly and periodically black as eve're'y body. Or neither black white or any hue of man'as mind yet complete. A na y eve'r to be a gain."

"Supernatural? Why the heck not?" Mor offered having found himself now in that state of mind. He thought find yourself right now indivisible in'visibility free in a wordfreedom from any a na y mirrored in word memory as though a y now as'ex's ting in formation. Pick up on a b c's in the first place now still indivisible in'visibility of anythin'king of anybody is a being c'ng free now, free forever. Use it as a model he told himself of a free being. In a wordfreedom to expand beyond boundaries of any mirrored mirage self concept. Find yourself dawg indivisible in'visibilty. Now merely turning int'word a k'nowing out of it that supersonic'a ka's mic micro wayeve black'g"round echoing a mirror se'e'as body mirrored into anyone see'ng it appearing a pairing as though two. Is this singular ka'man experience not a gift, a model he wondered of anybody turning out of and black'g'round into one eve're'y body? A model to help realize it's a being c'ng still that indivisible indivisibility he wondered. An awareness of it as'z'any in word in for'mation of it as'z the first time now in that first su'per'sonic person that I am is is in the first place. Merely superimposed as thoughtsz of a being c'ng out in any a na y in word information of it. A being mirrored in any a na y na'me.

"Who are we all turning black into or now out of?" she asked giving him an amused smile. "Your name could just as well refer to that small daily routine death as'z z z'leep black into un'consciousness so essential to life. Any role or roll of a being still eve'r'a complete d"ark'ness. As'z'any encirclement of a y'or you now as'ex planed flattened out or opened up in awhile must return to a k'urveing or finding her'him;it complete yet closing a black'g"round into one complete d"ark. D'ark?"

"Huh? Sorry as I am that feeling of falling as'z z z'leep back into you black Margot." Mor's heart skipped a beat with words leaving his mouth faster than they pulsed in his pea brain.

"Realizing a being of such singular indivisible invisibility is powerful liberating subjective awareness now energy of awhile ignited by ignoring it. In essense any intent incites objective k'no no no'w'ing. . . " she'e"na wayeved waved an index finger with wide eyes of a school girl. Then Mor felt kneck hairs standing out as a denial of kali ma'sz f'ang. Still a b c's of a b'ng c'ng it informing it int'word a d'na'y'll. A twis'ting in two sisters. We'd'ja'tah"ne'ba't'y. The name slid into his narrative from an ancient muse. ". . . incites inflames researchers researching in chasing tail or tale of their own role. Or roll e'turn all'y y'all asz'z z a race in that encircling complete d"ark' of it. Out of it in her'eye of eve'll. A wayeve will we all wheel of eve're'ybody now turning a y eye t'word as'king of it y a k'nowing out of it appearing as'ka's mic da y na light igniting any person appearing as'z'za superimposed supersonic ignore'ance of it. It a b'lack' mirror se'e'as body a peering out da y na light sol'ar'ey'ez z z'a't'i'on now out in her'eye of eve're'ybody k'now'ing out of it.

"Pay attention my D"ark'a'rtist. As'z 'any stinkin thin'king of it. About it is as'z'any thoth'tsz of a projected denial of it. A purely subjective state is uncrossing that eve'nt as'ex'hodos horizon. A're"y'turning black . . . " She'e'na paused at black. Catching his attention in that split second before its initial in word awakening beneath that panel truck backing overhead. She'e now turning his attention black in that sheer un'crossing of the event horizon. The event of falling as'z z z'leep off a ledge of k'now a b c's of a b'ng c'ng now out at aten'cion in word captivity. Mor now found himself a dopey dope duped in a duplicity of objectivity. We all he thought now a wheel turning a black'g"round a y eye as'ex's ting out into one singular indivisible black peh'ss'y'n'sah w'hole pow wow power of b'ng'lack'in'g subjectivity with a gee's us weight of intent of a b'ng a gain a waiting death.

"A dhi'a'th"ema perceived echoing wayeves. As'ka's mic mic'ro wayeves black'g'round a're'y'dhi'a'ting it. You may not cross the event horizon without falling into any understanding of it. It' a y overstanding a're'ye a peering it from above as'z below. Ove a b'ng c'ng now falling as'z z z'leep off that a ledged'ly as'ka y now. Appearing now k'now'ing disappearing. Time now appearing disappearing as in a while a space in time. A Y'll d'na. Still you're a b'ng c'ng invisibility without a trace of anybody as'ex's ting out in word in formation. You a're"y'e a peering it now know'ing out of it supernaturally appearing as'z'any thoth'tsz of it out in word in her"eyez z z'ion eve'll. In her'eyez z z'a wayeve will of a b'ng'lack instilling desire to be a gain now then appearing disappearing. A b'ng still in the first place indivisible in'visibility y'all along. Still merely a b c's of a b'ng c'ng out in her'eyez z z'i'on of eve're'ybody.

"Now a y'll midnight to four a. m. h'our melatonin levels at their highest. A y eye consciousness reaches the long stretched out delta length, you have a proverbial toe in the water. Then you may surf or fish that long long wave on the cool ultrviolet edge of a being in'visibility, the edge of appearing a pairing y as'z ex. . . oops got a class coming up. So much for the small talk. I have seen the catalog from a series of your vision paintings. Korner showed it to me the day I went to see the painting."

The sudden shift of her focus caught Mor from falling completely under her spell. The spell he recognized coming from the supernatural as'king of it y a ka's mic over mind. That subtle sublime overwhelming overstanding any scant understanding any thin'king of it. He paying attention to it now but often, more often than not, ignoring it in favor of all the personal crap. She'e now had him in a serious 'buzz' of high gamma goochie . . .oh babycakes y'all gettin' orgasm in the center of the brain.

From that cosmic center only inches above his head stimulated now by her voice, he felt its synapse, its fire zapping ignition of his pea brain. She was giving him head with her mind. Supernaturally as'z'any thoth'tsz zapping directly to the center of his head. Head to head. For a moment he swore he smelled hair burning "I painted and Korner commissioned the hype for the catalog." He responded as though on cue be'coming aware of his fate or fortune brought into him by merely painting a dream.

"You must have given Korner the words. He got all his t's crossed, metaphysically speaking," she replied, stretching both hands behind her neck.

"He got the i's dotted, too." Mor replied as he stretched his legs, trying to relax, "Now, shiksa? That's like calling a fat man Tiny, ain't it?"

"Like a left handed compliment. Like calling God a's z z man," she replied with emphasis, letting her tongue play past bared teeth,

"He's not?"

"That is one theory, but it's probably bupkis, or bullcrap. We all should realize it by now turning periodically black'g"round into or out her"eyez z z'azz of eve're'y body. Eve re y thing is her"eye'sz z'za first for'ma'sz'zamatter. Y'all that matters. In her'eyez z z. A mother d'nature. That eye ama'sz eve, ma she'en'a"a're'ye. Ma'sz'za'y'eye of eve"re'ybody be'am'ing projecting in her'eye as'z'any thoth'tsz. Of a god ess'e el et'te'ra re'ye a b'lack' mirror seas. A're'y'e'flecting the in word stuff, letter'all'y y'all a denial y'll d'na t'wis'ting int'word infor'ma'ing the ma'terial whorld in for'ma'sz peh'ss'y'n'c'ng energy out of her'eyez z z of a peh'ess'y whole black eve're'ybody.

"Y'all out in her"eye of eve'll way of eve're'y wayeve function of fun'ny'action of e'gg motion is nothing a na y thing is but in word prima materia g'ee's us x'et'ting from the spacious womb of the'e Sacred Feminine. Still y'all mother na'ture. Eve'na're'y now man with or without womb. Eve're'ybody now a man as mind or ey'e potential now projected out around k'now'ing thoughtsz of awareness of a being c'ng asz'za'na'ybody. His body, his desires, now nothing but herself, Kali Ma," she said, then laughed, and pressed the tips of her fingers into a steeple that she laid alongside her nose giving him what he thought as coy. "You Dark man got me started. Hearing y'all this, you be probably thinking, 'maybe Ma wasn't so crazy after y'all'" She gave him coy such that his heart skipped, catching him way off balance. He knew she had him in the palm of her hand or the be'am'ing of her voice.

"You're welcome to any patriarchal residue I have in my bag of tricks, just don't take my blue suede steel-toe boots. I remember getting whipped real good in a wrestling match for a championship of our weight class in high school. Didn't matter he was three years older. I knew from that moment I wasn't long for that macho dick-swinging world."

"Korner's world."

"Being a painter seemed to get me off that hook and still get me off, metaphorically speaking of course," he added with a grin.

Coins rattled into cash register drawers as coffee grinders hacked beans. A short stack of books replaced the pink backpack, the ponytail transformed to stray black hairs popping out of a knit cap, with silver disk earrings instead of gold studs. She right she left.

"I love your work. There is such presence in it, a connection with those who have eyes to see. Do you know the meaning of the painting you gave to Korner?" she asked, stirring her tea. "Remember I have read the catalog."

"Never really tried to put it into words. That image is pure imagination. In other words I have no idea what it means. Korner gave it the title 'Adam and Eve.' In those days I lived on psychedelics that induced an overwhelming spiritual imaginary dimension. Any thought as there in that state is as you say thoth'tsz of a god esse to be on the edge of any potential ka's mic memory. In that state all creation is a wordless body of a god taken to be described literally in a word. Yet imagination goes far beyond word. Why a painting out of it can't be defined in word. Still it is in word that we all turn to communicate. Thus any painting is bound to be related to in such a way. Like the man said, there are many mansions, many dimensions, many universes in the house of gee'sz us. At that time, in that intensity of painting and drugs, I or eye a peered at some incredible rooms. Really at some point art seemed to be inhabiting me more than in that I am it. The brush held me. I tried to use the drugs as a tool to focus the brush through the inner eye, to paint what was traveling through my head, me as cosmic memory purely coming from within or without of a being still in the first place that now out of it information of some cosmic e'motions. In between Korner always had the best coke. In return I gave him the weirdness in my head, conversations with alien elders and travel to distant civilizations of which ours is but a poor mockery. Mostly fantasy dribble, but real to me as any experience in outward 3D space time," he offered, finishing the sentence with open hands pushing on the edge of the table.

"Are you familiar with the Kabala or Tarot?" she asked, fingering a length of gold neck chain that lay against her chest.

"I'm a former painter, present carpenter. Mysticism was an interest of mine until I found building homes more financially rewarding. Something about that level on the reality spectrum-thing," he replied with a shrug, masking the inner fire fine tuning his attention..

"Spoken like a true iconoclast. You have the great fortune of being born in the West in the modern atomic computer era. Perfect set up for a rising internet iconoclast. Kabala is a word associated with mystical tradition systems and secret societies like the Freemasons. KaBaL'a is in essence a function. A function as'ka's or cause of a ba. A b'ng'lack as'king of it y eye a being a gain." She now paused a'gain to let the word import sink in. A gain of the b'lack' body. There again Mor found himself moment by momentum alternating black invisibility within visibility of any a peering it now a k'now'ing of it out appearing of it in word. He a being informed now as'z'any denial as'k'no no no'wing it out of a y eye a peering it out in word informing any appearing of it by its as'ka's mic mirror wayeve memory function. It now seemed he remembered a b c's in visibility by denying that ask'no'wing invisibility of a b'ng c'ng. Now out of it in word information. Awhile till disappearing a'gain as'z z z'leep into an indivisible black'g'round of it. Dark Mor now found his way black. Home in the first place indivisible in'visibility of anybody anything any time any where. That awareness sent a shudder up his spine. He gripped the table to keep from passing out.

"Letter'all'y y'all in the pure sense, Kabala is chasing tail." she gave with a wink. "Ka Ba La. A fun'ny'action function of a b'ng c'ng a peering now out of it a wayeve of a b c's. Ask'a no'wing in wordsz sound echoing as'ka's micro wayeve black'g'round information of it. As'Ka'mic. As'Ka's of it. A being as'ka's of any potential cause from above as below. Ove a ba a being now a b'lack' body with intent of a y eye a peering it in the first place now supernaturally out of it as'z'any thoth'tsz of a b'ng c'ng as'king of it a la que"en que' of that in which it appears out in her'eyez z z. Into or out of her'eyez z z of eve're'y'body a gain in word. Th'er"e eve're y bodhi a's individual es"el'ves, a way of wayeve function of will. A great go'a'd energy. Kabala, A y eye the ka's mic eye b'y'all of w'ax. Asz. In her'eye away of eve'll." Mor felt that wayeve out in her'eyez z z'a crashing his bioelectric field of view. As'ka's'ing a breaking up of his idols of de'sire.

"Ka's ba. Ka boom. Ka ba'by el"ectrick'city. Gee'sz us gimme the spark. The synapse. The fire from the mouth of the dragon burning my hair." Mor replied feeling still dumbfounded by her speech he let his mesmerized mind speak freely. Funny, he thought this y speak dialectic debate reminded him of other in word conversations. Understanding of it aska's mic overmind.

"Normally I associate the phrase 'y'all' with a southerner. Korner mentioned that you're from the East. Y'all seem to be firing up some old memory like donkeys and camels and pyramids and ancient codes. But I dig your metaphysical take on the darkness, which naturally to many means evil but now you're telling me is merely mother nature's mirror body. Kali ma's cunning duplicity of any appearing of it awhile. Y'or our body of anybody. Out in her'eye a peering it now a'wayeves of eve will. In for'ma's s a wily will of eve're'y body. Hell ya, I can dig it as the big black body picture. But I still gotta tell you, between us it seems very personal. As'z"z' ex, y'all," he rambled on intoxicated by the piter-pater of his heart pea brain. She'e now. In her'eye a wayeve will got it going merely a peering it b'lack' he mused. "Tell me more of this metaphysical darkness. That darn darkness has haunted me my whole life. Haunted me till becoming superstitious as anybody about the dark. As y'all might imagine with a name like mine it created a lot of confusion in my life," he offered with a wink. And a blink as he felt his attention irresistably drawn and absorbed into the black peh'ss'y wholeness expanding out from the center of her eyes.

"Call it 'you speak'. Y'or y now speaking in the first place. A dialectic practice of debating speaking as'ex or y. As'ex planing it or a y eye merely a peering it. Rather like You Tube as'z you to be of it. A y eye now as t'word two now as'k'no'wing out of it to be anybody anything. A na y as'ex's ting. Or a y now as in word thoughtsz in a b c's of a being c'ng. A y eye still a peering it in the first place now a k'no'wing out of it as'ex's ting supernaturally as'z'any thoth'tsz of it.

"In that I am just coming on out with it. You as'ex." Once again Mor's neck hairs bristled with a mixed signal. It couldn't be good but then. He knew on opening his eyes today. Out in da y light igniting it is a good day to die. That and the black lace thing he thought. "Never rule out y you're you as'z'z ex," she gave back with a wink. Mor felt the change in temperature and pressure as the nearly tangible darkness out in her'eyez z z of a peh'ss'ye'n'c'ng a whole'n'ess'e. A now to be. A're'y'dhi'a'ting spinning a'sex'panding out from the center of her eyes and the center of her chest hit him like a tidal wayeve flooding a blissful black whole ab'sorbing any metaphoric shelter. "Thing is, and please do not take this personally y'all as'ex is the inevitable combination, eve'n on a purely phonic way of sandhi. A joining of purpose or intent of a y as'ex posing out of it in her'eye of eve're'y body. Y'all. In a'Y'or y' speak debate find Y and all inseparable. In that I am warning you the dialectic is a habit forming un'formation of it. A liberating of it in word picking up on thesis of a y eye merely a peering it. Or captivating attention of it in word antithesis of it as'ex's ting out in formation awhile. In for'ma'ing a na y'or y speaking in word states avoid the void of any mere a y being mirrored as'ex's ting asz though information. Realize a Y'z domus is in the first place a being indivisble invisibility. Thus ANY mere mirrored information of it must now be a k'no no no'wing denial projection of it a y'll d'na. A denial of it as'z'any thoth'tsz of a y eye awareness of her'me's herhimit yod or you still a being alone in the first place."

"A b"lack indivisible invisibility. Or y not now a being mere or y in memory." Mor gave back with a grin. He felt some visceral movement in his gut as though an old identity changing into a whole new day. The profundity of the new dialectic offered the freedom of dissolving any in word defined boundaries to a being of him. Of her'him'it. A freestanding of a y eye a peering it da y na light igniting ignore'ance of it now as'king of it a k'no'wing out from above. As below.

Is this DMT the spirit molecule pulsing directly into and out of the center of his brain he wondered while getting that familiar peh'ssy'ka'delic metallic taste in his mouth. Time could only be now a complete cosmic moment shimmering with infinite potential of any long or short in word while of it. That wily craft carried away any attention paid to it. Any in word awareness of a b'ng c'ng of it now a memory k'no'wing out of it as thoughtsz of it appearing now out as'ex's ting. Still with any appearing brought a pairing off opposites eros thanatos ending beginning. Any complete roll x planed or flattened out now awhile neccesary infor'ma'ss feeling felt fields of view, of you not with a guilt or guile of gee's us now under peh're'y'ssure as'ex's ting with gravity weight of waiting death playing out any roles quickly rolling black up periodically in complete loops of d"ark'ness fired by awakhening asz two twis'ting into da y na light. . . .y now the light of d"ark or d"ark of light . . .out in her'eyez z z'a wayeves of eve"re'y body. . . She was right about it becoming habit forming. The dialectic unfolded in word blowing debatatable holes in the web spell of anybody asex's ting supernaturally as'z'any thoth'tsz of it in'formation. A b'ng c'ng now as'z'any in word k'no'wing out of it thoth'tsz of a y eye of her'him'it merely a peering it alone still indivisible in'visibility. Supernaturally finding a being that ka's mic indivisible invisibility he would keep firing, letting any without churn his do nat pass go torus bionic supersonic electro-magnetic recog'na'tive body especially in the presence of this in her'eye of a professor.

"You have that breakthru look about you now. You be digging a Y'or y speak. It can blow it y'all up. In that w'ay'eve that I am is is a dynamite. Gonna blow y'all black into one smithereen"

"Or y na?"Mor felt himself in that quiet space beyond words and speech. Still he found himself grinning like that village idiot he no doubt was.

"Your name calls out that inevitable darkness a're"y'all 'joining the loop'y purpose y'or y. Y now with all. Y'all per pose of a free standing. Never been able to separate it since getting on to a Y'or y speak. Y'all. Out in her'eye of eve're'y body. The now time el esse Quantum. The Quantum of a naY mirror seas potential of any y na you ni Unified Field of View, of You, experienced by y'all a's y'all. The key to darkness is "'d"ark. D'hi roll of any role we all as'z'any thoth'tsz in turning into it play it or it plays us. A na y being y by now a's too a b'ng c'ng a's t'word a twis'ting black'g"round in word memory of me or you you'ni' fied. A functioning by, you guessed it, a being y'on'i with the Quantum energy of any erge'ent karma with gravity weight waiting a'sz z too die black into one black'g"round. One ka's mic black'g"round turning man'as mind or y into any ka's mic memory loop. En'ting or en'ding is beginning. Denying it is knowing it."

"Then in that I am knowing you now is denying you?" He found the words merely spoke themselves.

"Good one. Any thoughts of me appearing before you now are in word projections of any idea of me or you. Projections as thoughtsz of memory out in her'eye of eve're'y body. Y'all now turning into or out a k'no'wing of it. In the black now headed into the re'd, the re'deception. The union of these two symbolized by the caduceus is the re union of you ni on. Neon of one still merely appearing a pairing as two in the indiscriminating man'as mind. Or y now of choosing a being twin between serpents. Ignoring the tail trying to get a head y'll d'na. A denial of a being still a singular serpent gripping its curved ka'smic micro wayeve blackg"round tail by a being y now opening mouth as organ of speech to release that supersonic tale. One y now out as'ex's ting in awhile. Appearing a pairing as'z z t'word twis'ting wrapping in helixes around the pole'ar'e'ty like DNA. Y'll d'na. Near complete Denial. Near complete d'na y'ell wayeve're'y eye function of fun'ny'action. Out in her'eye a cunning in word appearing of it. Appearing a pairing. That snake, that's na ke, ke na, canna't. Thus we all in turn must chase our tail. The tale of h'our tail runs through many many loops. The possibilities are really infinite. E turn all'y y'all in any roles or rolls. In near complete denial. Re'freshed periodically as'z z z'leep black into a un'consciousness." She paused finding him staring intensely into her'eye'z za. He felt transported out in the'm. Out in a memory word craft now appearing naked. Stripped of pretension of a being anybody in particular. The sheer exhileration rushed his spine. That shit eating grin spreading. He resisted the urge to jump on the table and do a little dance.

"That mere near denial of you now as thoth'tsz of it out in awhile appearing in e or gee's us or'y energy motion still a being c'ng motionless pi'vo't'y'all point of view, of you now as thoth'tsz of the eye star'e ye'or you. Of a y eye view. Point is of you denied is any mere mirrored y na you now as'ex. The e subject not. A y eye of you a peering it. Denied now by a being c'ng a y'll appearing a pairing as'z z a field of view. Of you now that felt feeling of a being a'field alone without as'ex eve'r'e knowing y. With out a'x ka'ing y. Why? Why? Why?" Mor felt himself out in her'eye a movement in word. Sound waves of her voice broke his heart open like an egg. She now used tonal modulations to break up the shell of him supernaturally supersonically as thoth'tsz in formation. Now in'visibility he found a b'ng c'ng free in the first place at last.

"Chasing that tail. You just told my life story or most any man's. The queen bitch of de'nial is in her'eye? Kali Ma'sz. That's how I see ma, my ma, shrieking, wild hair streaming snakes, eyes in a cunning evil arch. When I took the runover by the delivery panel truck, the overmind activated my attention in a way that instantly, in that blink of eye, I, a mere toddler, chasing a ball, or whatever, awoke opened my eyes fully aware of the world, its machinery, truck carriage, exhaust system, drive differential, as seen laying flat on your back with darkening of your skies, actually I have zilch how I got there, finding myself being run over stilled by the voice of God or the Uber Mensch. The overmind still stilling me under a moving truck carriage passing inches above layered with hot rust, road dust, and air compressed by the weight of death. Shite that just don't look all that good. Especially with a voice in your head telling 'be still'. That a hearing first words of a voice of that inner attention of a being still saved the boy in a life or death situation before a boy even new that I am having a life or death. That's how it started for me. First words heard a hearing of an inner voice. A sheer miracle of which a being still mute two year old could utter not. Then after words I saw. I recognized for the first time the evil menace that was my ma. From the heighths of sheer miracle now falling back into the pit of Kali ma. The shock later caused a mumble in my speech. She scared the shit out of me then but now I'm feeling fear goes both ways. She feared losing me. Back then I thought she wanted to bite my head off and eat it. Two years old, the Darkness filled by the voice of light, of reason, of a now knowing y. Then assailed by a psychotic shrew ma that the boy is seeing, recognizing for the very first time. That's the kick. Y'all don't recognize your own mother or anybody for several years. A being of that indivisible we all in turn see hear smell taste touch nada till having words to define it. A personic being purely a wayeve eye function with attention of any intention. Now y'all these years later realizing that I am finding myself still indivisible invisibility of a supersonic being." The words seemed to open him up into a new being still in the first place now a k'now'ing black'g'round of that. A blackness indivisible invisibility out in her'eye of eve're'y'asz z za supersonic body. Any in formation or idea of identity evaporated like dream as'z z z'leeping black into indivisible invisibility.

"There that I am awoken by the voice of the over mind fully aware as activated survival awareness of a truck passing perilous over me. Now I see it as y'all the overlife intervening at the same time offering me a window black at any time now as'z z z'leeping beyond the role of me. A role of complete d'arkness that develops as'z'anybody over y'ears a h'earing it in word merely as though'tsz of a b'ng c'ng now out of it in na'me alone. Before that. A being anybody not recognizing it by denying it defining it or k'no'wing of it a being. Now simply a being c'ng by a y e'ye a peering it alone. After mirror el y function duplicating it as thoth'tsz of that. A being still alone indivisible in the first place. Now a k'no'wing wayeve functioning out of it in a complete mute memory that could recall awareness before the awakening. Or y a me for the first time out in memory. Once the truck passed over me jumping up and running back to mama. To tell her the great good knews. Running back across a vacant lot. Unscathed. Seeing her obliviously sweeping aimlessly at the edge of the drive. For the first time knowing what she looked like scared the living shite out of me. Plus you're completely mute at that age. You ain't saying shite.

"Me ma lived on the edge of sanity and incoherent screaming rants under the best of conditions. Though having full visual cognition, unfortunately zero audio. By the time I reached her, running across the backside of that vacant lot, my sister had told her what happened. Ma freaked into kali ma. My first up close visual of my mother is the demonic kali ma devouring her own children. Their blood dripping from her gums. Thereafter my relation to her was primarily fear. Now my father. The day after the incident I observed him from the street, coming home from work typically totally ignoring me in a rush to get any calls. How I knew this is complete mystery as I had no conscious memory of him prior to that moment. Now I was able to read subtle expressions on his face. How y'all that awareness came to me I haven't a clue till now.

"This time he stopped when he saw me. His grin, like seeing me for the first time. It lit up the whole street. In that moment I saw him for the first time. But I never saw that grin again. Only the sorrow of a junkie. Then he pulled from his coat pocket a red and blue yo-yo covered with white stars. That was the only thing he ever gave me. You see, he was a junkie. Why he always ignored me coming home from work. He was anxious getting to his calls from his connections. Thing was I could remember his typical demeanor coming home from times before the incident. The over mind allowed me that memory. He o.d'd when I was in high school. Sorry, I didn't mean to run on. Its just that always astonishes me, every time I recall a being at that level of inward awareness before having learned any words. That over mind instantly filled in word what would take me many years to learn. It was a miracle I couldn't communicate until now. That y'or y dialectic is breaking up my in word spell. Now listening to you I'm finding myself struck dumb in much the same way. I can feel it. I can feel the difference in my father's moods but I couldn't describe him so completely objectively as I might seeing him now. Plus memories bear the patina of time."

"Plus y'all got that portentous handle. The Darkness, messenger of Death," she swatted his hand in mock disapproval. "That overmind, that above, as ka's y chakra is mere inches above the head. The ka's mic, permeates y'all from above as below, in front, behind, to the right, to the left, projecting it as thoth'tsz y'all as'ex's ting in a black'g"round. A b'lack'g'round as'z' any roles of complete d'ark'n'ess'e. To be now a turning into or out of it supernaturally y'all as thoth'tsz of it holding polarity in the left hand. Da y eye star'e"ye'or y now light igniting ignore'ance of it on the right. Shining that black'g'round the 8th wheel will we all of intelligence of transparency. As'ka's mic memory will from above the head. Activating the pineal gland serves to consciously access this ka's mic energy. The only intelligence center outside the body capable as'king of it a ka's mic synapse zapping the brain. Flowing down through 7 centers of the central nervous system as'z' any ka's all y causeless mirror potential. A black'g"round supersonically supernaturally as thoth'tsz in a i energy doughnut or do not."

"Do not pass go. Do not collect 200 dollars?" he replied with a grin.

"Why yes. A mono poly of one mirrored as many. One indivisible invisibility now as'ka's mic memory of a b'ng c'ng now ask'no'wing out of it a time turning black'g'around powered by one thoth'tsz of a being a gain. Letter'all'y y'all now with in word intent of mirroring it supersonically y'all echoing as'k'as micro wayeve black'g'round a're'y'dhi'a'ting invisibility of you now t'word a twis'ting in two a d'na y'll. A denial of invisibility appearing a b'ng c'ng mirrored supernaturally y'all superimposed as'z'any in word thoth'tsz of it appearing out in formation. A y'or you now understanding the spelling of it as'ex's ting in formation."

"Y'or y you're you. . . Not only are you mute at that age but deaf as well. The function is there but without any in word recall. Echoing of that black'g"round passes freely off or thru at attention indivisible. Oh my gosh. That attention still indivisible." Mor felt more wall slipping away. Christina studied his face with a bemused smile. In that blink of eye he realized a being still indivisible at attention in the first place.

"Similarly the function of sight informing any meager in word thin'king of it is learned per'sonically in sound. As'z awareness of a b c's int'word a twis'ting in two appearing a pairing of it in word mem'or'y. A sonar that keeps y'all from bumping into solid things till learning to see it echoing a black'g'round of now a k'no'wing out of it in word. An echoing out of it supersonically as thoth'tsz. A supersonic god'esse to be letter'all'y y'all creating any scant thin'king of it in word. There is only that indivisible supersonic ka'mic ka's mic ka's all'y y'all. A mirror se'e'as'ka's all'y y'all a black'g"round. Still indivisible without learning t'word recognizing its wayeve echoing it as a mere in word supernatural superimposed reflection as thoth'tsz of it. Projected by a peh'ss'y w'hole power mean means of a being still in the first place. A y now meaningful as'ka's mic memory a k'no'wing out of it any mere or y appearing of it as'ex's ting in formation. Thus we all turn in word into living supernaturally merely supersonically mirrored as thoth'tsz of a b'ng c'ng now k'no'wing out of it superimposed as a b'ng born "

"Y. Or me." Christina met his eyes with a knowing ironic smile. Somehow in that passing moment he felt a're'y joined with in her'eyez z z for a mirrored e'turn'ity as'king of it. The turning of time now a black'g"round of a being c'ng out in her'eye of eve're'ybody. Black. Indivisible. Invisibility. Still she'e'now continued in word as too enchant his attention. At awareness of a y eye of her'him'it a peering it out at that ma're'y g'round. Aska's microwayeve b'lack'g'round a're'y'dhi'a'ting it. Information awhile.

"Each center with its own mode of intelligence. Ironically the first chakra at the perineum, the pelvic floor pivot for the base of the spinal column is center point of administrative intelligence. H'our bodhi, any bodhi is an instrument of consciousness administrated from below as above. The ka's mic energy flowing into or out of y'all that meaning full of matter as'z'any body."

"Agent above. Agent below. I can dig that set up. Right now I'm feeling that above zapping my brain. Or as y'all that matters moving up from my balls to my bra . . ." He caught himself getting personal but she merely smiled.

"Cerebrospinal fluid travels in a loop. It turns out to be a rather loopy world after y'all. Above as below. We all turning into a talking bodhi. A bo or ba plus dhi a's instument of consciousness with puposeful intent in the wayeve function beyond you as'z' z'eXxx y boogaloo ba'y be. Bring it up into the heart, the a re'y'all chakra collecting intell from the three centers below. Your sex, drugs, and rock'n'roll centers. Through elevated emotions we all may turn into higher consciousness. A being of singular luminous uniting intelligence of transparency open flowing in the wayeve out of it with a y eye of function of de'sire from above. Ove ab a being c'ng da' sire of a se'er, " she finished with a wide open gaze. The talk of desire stirred below in his gut as well as his heart and above.

"Back in the day, we fashioned ourselves yogi's when in fact we were bhogies, enjoyers of the fruits. Pleasure seekers in that rather nihilistic rock'n'roll way of "whoopee we're all gonna die". Live for today. We all in turning around knew that happiness as pursuit was y'all bogus with ole Dr. D. a being that y'all as too well of a known unknown. Now y'all got me doing that." Mor laughed but could not stop the flow in words'z'z'a pouring out his pie hole. "It seems there is a fine line between libertine or liberty. No?" Mor kept laughing, in spite of himself remembered as the shallow fool that drifted into the Haight Ashbury with Quaaludes in his hair. Now he felt downright garrulous after years of relative silence of the human tongue. Especially fired up in realizing a being c'ng in his'z z'eye'zaz'z'a seer. A one who sees now, not merely as thoughts thinking that I am beside the point. He'a y eye a peering it at attention indivisible in the first place.

'The code. Ka Ba La function of a y eye merely a peering it or a y eye on it now as'king of it a k'no'wing mirror function. A'wayeve of it appearing out in her'eye of eve're'ybody. Thatsz the fun'ny'action. A wile of any appearing of it as'z' any mirror being. We all turning captivated out of it in her'eye of eve'll. A will we all turning yearning burning of it. It. Merely supernaturally appearing as'z'any thoth'tsz of it."

"The're'ye code of a're;Y'asz'z z'aten?" This question now caught her'eye at attention. In fact Mor merely let his memory speak for itself. Her in word locution located and released thoughts from his subconscious with a spontaneity to which he happily succumbed. She'e now looked back as though seeing him for the first time.

" A re'Y'a'sz'z z'a'ten. The mystery of the first time in the first place. A now as'king of it y. As'ka's y'all now turning a're'y'all in complete d'ark'ness. Out in her'eye d''arking completely black'g'round as'ka'no no no'wing a positive negation out of it merely a peering it. Now as'king of a la que''en que' of that in which appearing of it. Voila. She'e na. Gate. Of it. It of the first time still in the first place. Interesting that some burned out country carpenter would be aware of it." She now had him by the short and curlies. On that score I am knowing more than a few so called Egyptologists he thought that have not gotten on to it. They a being too busy rummaging in past history to find themselves now aware of awareness of a being as'king of it 'y''zz'z z z'a no no no'wing out of it. Out in her'eye of eve're'ybody. A b'lack' mirror se'e'as body indivisible invisibility of it. It still in the first place. The vision of a y eye illuminatus a peering it now in his'zzeye'szapped his vision. Holy of holies'z'za any a peering out of it. Appearing out in denial of it still it. It a y eye of a b c's merely a peering it. It. A fullness filling over from above. Ove ab. Of. A b'ng c'ng still timeless'n'ess'e now to be any first time now merely mirrored out. A k'no'wing out of it in word as thoughtsz in formation of a're'y'membering of it as'zz' any informing of then. We all may turn now into the'n only supernaturally as thoth'tsz of it as'z'z'any in word wayeve personic fun'ny'action of it as'z'za any mere or y memory of it now a chintzy thin'king of a being by now nary a being still in the first place."

"'Be still' a b'ng still. Now those words echo literally the first words'za heard by me. Those words saved my life before I even new I had a life. Those words coming from within my own head opened my eyes if not my ears. Funny there was still no sound track in the action of first sight of seeing in recognition of it. The ignition of recognition with out sound echoing it in my ears. Reckon in a way my life's been y'all gravy surviving getting run over and nearly killed as a two year old. Guess that's what I am getting for now a daring of it as t'word twis'ting black'g'round into any appearing out of it." Though recalling the near fatal awakening most days of his life he'd completely failed to appreciate the sheer silence of it. Is it possible now that we all must in turn learn an in word hearing as well as recognition of anything seen he wondered. The dialectic debate stirred a turmoil in his mind causing old memories to surface. A part of him sought to flee but it seemed she now had hypnotized him with any understanding a b c's in word spelling of it.

"A mere or y. Y'or y speak dialectic offers letter'all'y y'all a y eye mean a peering it as means of breaking out of captivity of the in word meaningful spell as'z'z'any x's ting of it appearing out in formation. Now the same in word mean means of casting the spell of any appearing out of it in the first place may now break it as well. Now alternating moment by moment between a being merely a peering it or appearing of it. It as'ka's a y'asz'z a're'y'flecting out of it now k'nowing of it appearing in word as'z'z'any thoth'tsz. Informing it a're y'all 'asz now k'no no no'wing out of it any information of a b'ng c'ng in the first place." She let that hook lay out there awhile. Mor's spinal fluid rushed his brain pulsing in her'eye wayeves. Out in her'eye of eve're'y waves projecting information as 3D color mandalas on his inner screen. Y THOTH'Tsz of it merely out mirrored in a y eye a peering it out echoing the black'g'round of it. He found himself absorbed by now a k'now'ing denial of finding himself a being c'ng now mirrored as thoth'tsz. Asz awareness of a god or god'esse to be go go goading him as'z t'word a twis'ting in two any in word information of it. He flexed a face sure that it expressed more than could ever be imagined. A wonderment of finding home now in a being still in the first place. That a being c'ng now in a wayeve eyeing home after too long wandering in nostalgia for a beloved. Now irrecoverable yet still haunting in the ringing in his ears. She now always there playing on his senses. Merely forgotten from time to time.

"As'z'any thoth'tsz of a b'ng c'ng that indivisible a y eye of a herhimit merely a peering it from above yod you a pair now as though a'ten binary. Now a'ten by nary being a found objectivity any knowing of it must be a denying out of it. A y'll d'na. A denial as positive negation of it now appearing in any k'no no no'wing out of it supernaturally as'z'any thoth'tsz. A y eye a peering it now a y potential of a b'ng c'ng asz'ex's ting in'formation. In a word out appearing phonographically now awhile. That is the spelling of it. The crafty re'ading of it we all turn into a b'ng c'ng out in her'eye wayeve re'y body." Now he found bait on the hook. The craftiness read in her'eyez z z now sobered him up from any school boy fantasies. She'e'na could no doubt eat his lunch. For a moment she'e now continuing in word lost his attention. He took a deep breath and stretched his spine before tuning her frequency back in.

" . . . can only be passed orally by the human voice organ of speech, using a pramana, an ancient sanskrit audiovisual supersonic methodology. Or in ordinary speech spoken in a y dialectic debate between awareness of a y eye merely a peering it or it appearing out of it in word as'ex's ting information as'z'anybody anything any time. Thus the spelling of it continues. What is y'all too rare is a serious fool to go against any current spelling of thoth'tsz of it. That I am that fool yet initiated in a timeless unbroken oral lineage dispelling it is, well, significant. In that I am now purporting to infuse ma'sz value and enthusiasm for a dispelling of it. For a liberty. . . "

"Or a death?"

"The code also communicates in 3D audiovisual color cubes. A whorlding of them into a round by peh're'ssure of gee's us rounded out understanding gravity weight of waiting on death.From that subjective point of view of you of y as'z a being c'ng in which the know'ledge is merely any imaginary line between realizing a being still in the first place or now as'king of it in'ka'now'ing out of it that ka's mic being that eye am is is as'z'any reader reading it or speaker speaking about it. Or a denying of it as'z'any thoth'tsz from above it yet supporting it from below. Indivisible in'visibility yet projecting it as'z any a na y thoth'tsz of it by in word means. As now any supernatural thoth'tsz in a re'y'all simultaneously source and goal. Thoth'tsz of a god esse to be letter'all'y y'all of eve're'ybody out in word with mirror intent of polarity a pairing it now awhile. As t'word appearing by endings of it as though a pairing a positive negativity. Still indivisible as a y eye a peering it out now as'z'any thoth'tsz projecting projection as any potential appearing objectivity," she added with a chuckle. "Awhile in the craft spinning out a duplicity tales of woe on the go go go. So iconoclastic one, you see now before you a k'now'ing e'mergence of a b'ng c'ng still ancient sacred in the first place. Out now in any k'now'ing of it merely mirrored appearing in a modern secular in word appearance. Any body still a being that as'ka's mic memory of'ten aten bi na re'y radiating as thoth'tsz out of a being in Pa'roo'Ma Parama paramount in the first place. Thoth'tsz in word craft radiating supersonically a black'g"round echoing out in her'eyez z z the black peh'ss'y w'hole mirror se'e'as. Anybody'as'z'any meager thin'king of it any where"

A sailing out of it in her"eyez z z. A craft. A wily'ship of a while. A space in time of indivisible invisibility parama y or y na now as'king of it. A y? Now as'ka're'y'z'ee thoth'tsz of it. Now. Mor found himself at attention spun into invisibility. Indivisible a peering it of a g'ray-blue light. Still aware of a being be"am'ing that light source or y out of awareness of a y eye merely a peering it. A y eye of her'him'it in any a na y word spell spun of such a craft that re'absorbed re'flections of any mirrored imagining of it. It imagination of a being c'ng out in any na'me alone. Imagined as'z'any thoth'tsz of a being a ba'by any n'ding of it. A b'ng c'ng"go'ing out as'z in her'eyez z z of eve're'ybody. As'z z z electricomagnetic wayeves as'ex's ting universes of it. Invisibility of a black'g"round of you ni now versus a being c'ng . . . merely a peering it out now ask'ing of it y appearing supernaturally as'z'any thoth'tsz of it . . . . .

"Earth to Dark," Christina's voice brought him black into that spell paying attention to another field of view of you now unfolding before him.

"It's called the World Wide Web, I believe." he mused while scratching his head.

"Is that where you were off to. Just getting on without any device?" She asked with a frown.

"Your Y'or y now dialectic has put me on line and I a'in't never been."

"You have never been online? Trying to tell me you are a virgin?"

"Hey I work and live in the mountains. No wi-fi less y'all got a satellite dish and I don't even have electricity. Besides a y dialectic debate seems debatable to anybody anywhere. Once y'all get on to it it gets on to y y you're you letter'all'y a being in the first place."

"Still cannot believe y'all'sz an internet virgin."

"Hey now, I've looked over a few shoulders."

"The web being primarily in word offers a global platform'a'sz proliferation of the dialectic. Just needs the right catalyst to fire up the debate. It is a way certainly but you will not need a computer to log on as'ka's of yall right above you or anybody. As'ka's mic consciousness now a mere inches above as'z zynapse'e'ing your head or any body's head. If you ever try to explain your painting, explain why it is what it is then y'all can appreciate the difficulty using words to access a wordless place. Y dialectic offers thesis of a y eye of a b'ng c'ng merely a peering it still in the first place to antithesis of y as'ex drugs and rock'n'roll. Az's'ex'planing or flattening out a denial of the roll of complete d"ark'ness. A kno no no'wing out of a y eye a peering it out now as'ex's ting without realizing y" Cracking up with laughter, she now pulled the bag on her lap and extracted a card case. She took out a pen and wrote four letters, I H V H, on the back of a business card, inserting it in a small hardcover book. She handed it to him with an oblique smile.

"You see immediately in a Y eye a peering it now int'word a twis'ting in two of it a pairing H'ay'eVe'H'ay.The sheer duplicity of a n'a y eye merely mirrored as'z'z z"a y na wayeve function. Yod HayAndHay. You SoAndSo. This is in the'or'y of any mem or y na mirror as'k'eye to Tarot. A how h'our phonographic alphabeta supersonically or visually transmits a triple analogy of forma'sz'z'sound mean means meaning full of it. It awareness revealing in a wordfreedom a being c'ng of a y eye as hidden in turning black'g'round k'no no no'wing out a denial of invisibility in visibility of it now as'k'now'a'lege. An imaginary line between merely a peering it or. A b'ng c'ng now out of it in visibility mirrored in word phonographically or supersonically as'z'any thoth'tsz supenaturally superimposed infor'ma'sz sound wayeves mean of any meaning. Like the man said the medium is the message or messenger. A mean as'z'any means of any meaning. Any man with or without womb as a mind or y memory mirroring a y eye a peering it out now as'ex. The mean of it merely a peering it out now as means of it as'ka's no'win'g any mirrored appearing of it in word and meaning full of it in formation. It awareness of a b'ng c'ng still in the first place.

"A triplicity of a y eye seer sight see'ng of anybody mirrored supernaturally in word as thoth'tsz of a magus imagining imagination. A y now understanding the spelling of a b'ng c'ng now in word a's ex's ting. In a being c'ng a peering in it y'all that I am calling it the fourth book. Bible, Torah, Koran, Tarot," she now offered. "Tarot is a 3D cubic supersonic b'OO'ka de'lOOka of mere 22 picture cards or planes and edges in space centering on a being c'ng as'z' z z'a cubic TAT. That'sz a being in the first place that awareness of that first person that I am is is. Or'a y eye a peering out in any in word memory. As'z that a bOOka is a bo being oo-egg's ting as'ka's in'formation. As'ka's mic k'eye of you na now a k'nowing out of it as'z'z'any universe. It corresponds to the fourth religion in the West. Now a god'esse to be or a na re'y to be in word thoth'tsz of a peh'ss'y"en'c'e power of art in letters and numbers in'formation. The other books offer information already understanding spelling of it in word. Tarot offers letter'all'y y'all a wayeve of breaking out of it or into a wordfreedom overstanding awareness of a y eye merely a peering it at that spelling still indivisible invisibility in the first place. They the y a're y'e na k'eye's asz the y a're'ye in y'all'sz the ology. The logos, el o go's a's thoth'tsz. Thoth'tsz in for'ma's'aY'eye"of'ten"aten shee'na bi na re'y."

Mor shuffled his feet, "I find your words have left me quite stunned. I may have to sit here awhile to let it sink in. But why is it my feet want to get walking? Shall I grab us another cup?"

"That is okay. My class is in a few minutes. I want you walk over with me and talk about a painting," she said. "For me."

The girl in knit-cap raked long fingers down the back of her neck and tables from the lunch rush cleared, chairs and dishes scattered in the background.

"That painting. Where did you find the image?" she asked, as her fingers padded the top of her bag, nails pared short and unpolished. One ring on her pinky finger glinted with amethyst.

"In a dream. When I woke, I started sketching, much like automatic writing. The image developed itself, really" he replied with a shrug.

"It is very different from the usual versions I have seen—the bizarre shape of Adam and Eve, the elongated features, swollen torsos, and spindly legs. Very Egyptian and unique to one dynasty, that of Pharaoh Ahkenaten and Queen Nefertiti," she said, scanning his face.

"I recognize the queen's name. Are you saying she's Eve and Ahk-what's his name is Adam?"

Christina studied him for a long moment before answering. "You hit the nail, carpenter. The Bible, Koran, Torah, y'all name one patriarch. This patriarch either is or is in my humble opinion connected to the reign of Egypt's only monotheistic pharaoh or at least debatedly that. Some scholars insist Akhenaten was an atheist. Still his brief reign with his building the tower of Babel, the world's greatest city of Akhetaten led to the invention of alphabeta. That phonographic portable time machine generated and yet maintains the spell of the bOOka. To the victor go the spoils. Written scripture, foundation of y'all western religion impossible without that alphabeta, portable, easily assimilated, carried out of Egypt in the Exodus of Atenian Priests, Aten- A b'ng c'ng still in the first place as'key'e to the whole alphabeta. A y eye of a being c'ng a peering still now as'king of it a la que"en que' appearing anybody anything any time any where. Y'all out of it in a supersonic supernatural craft. A macro micro as'ka's mic crafty body appearing awhile out in da y light igniting ignore'ance of it a y eye a peering out in her eye of eve'll of eve're'ybody. It sorta drops the apple on your doorstep." She added with a laugh. "The peh'ss'y whole point of view of you or me memory of a y eye a peering out now is in herhimit's eye of any or eve're'ybody k'now'ing out anything'king of it. It of a b'ng c'ng still indivisible in the first place.

"Thus I believe it was at this brief millisecond of history our generations now were conceived, in a city that rose to glory and turned to dust in less than two decades. By unraveling this monotheistic in word enigma we all in turn may resolve our present ethno-theo-logical and cultural divide, with that as'ka's mic synapse as'z z z'leep black into our head. Into a right brain free of any inword captivity to grasp the k'eye merely a peering it. It still indivisible in'visibility. H'our purpose. H'our pose aska'as mic freestanding memory intelligence consciousness awareness of a being c'ng still in the first place remains to be a see'ng merely a peering out now. As'k'nowing anybody anything any time any where." She'e now gave him a wink to break the intensity of the gaze out in her'eye sweeping his attention black'g'round a singular formless wordless black d"ark'ness as'z z z'leep into eve're'ybody. Then returning out in that blink of eye of herhimit now.

"That a being the case then now in her'e'ye find a being still in the first place the k'ey'e to the highway," Mor added lamely. He glanced at one thumb, the nail torn down the center from an old construction wound whose jagged edges were packed with grit and pine sap. His manhood called for some show of bravado while a being now out of it stewed in her intelligence. Say something, he thought. "Still that sounds like a, well A B'ee'ga key eye'" he added, digging himself in a little deeper.

"It is for the coming generation, the millenials, to realize and appreciate the full implications. There is still too much inherited prejudice in the world. It will take this generation and on into the next to kick off this binding tribe'onation'o gender binary bias that holds us back from complete awareness of a b'ng c'ng a peering out now supernaturally appearing in word as'z'anybody. You are a visual artist. I am giving you audiovisual clues connected to twenty-two letters chosen from a cursive form of thousands of hieroglyphs. These are the k'ey'es to the highway. Do a painting for me."

"I haven't picked up a brush in five years. Any decent draughtsman could do the job for you following the key symbols in this her"e book," he replied, studying an open page.

"Korner waxes near poetic about your visions. I hope this project will help you return to painting if you are willing to take the chance," she replied, gathering her materials together.

"I had the 'burning bush' vision of the Illuminatus, the uncapped pyramid, the eternal flame, the eye of eyes, at a bus stop on Geary and Powell at four AM in the heart of San Francisco. Or it had me. You know what? Big deal. I still had to pay for the bus ride."

"We can meet after my lecture, in my office near the quad. The number is on the card," she said, getting to her feet.

"Only if you let me do a sketch of you," he replied.

"Come to the class. It is an introductory talk that will give you perspective on who I am and what I am about. There is no text. The students are the text. They must find themselves before getting lost in another book."

"You cannot exist, for then I would have to let you go."

"Excuse me?"

"All I could think of to say. Show me the way to your classroom."

CHAPTER 3

From the glass cupola on the roof of his house in Pacific Heights, Korner listened to the mournful foghorns. Thick gray fog rolled through the Golden Gate, blanketing his view of the Bay to match his mood. How did the line go? "Dealing friends never ends." The business was never personal, just business. Using Mor did not trouble Korner. Or at least didn't seem to slow him down much A man made his own decisions, even those that promised destruction. Always collateral damage. What are friends for. Just don't get thinking they wouldn't do the same to you. He'd watched that civil facade fall too many times. When push came to blasting away. "Bidness is bidness," his father used to say. Let the chips fall as they always will.

Gray mornings like this, neutralized his captain's perch atop his panorama of the Golden Gate. Golden thoughts filled his head. San Francisco, after all, was built on the frenzy of gold. He thought how the Yerba Buena wild mint harbor quickly disappeared in the crush of such a crazy mix of miners, gamblers, grifters, and whores, swelling this little 'ol spit of sand waste to a wanna be city of thirty thousand in one year. The RUSH. Letting that crystal rock melt into neurons firing in the night. He could smell that gold.

Korner thought gold. Dreamed gold. He remembered a plan to dredge the Bay and reclaim the residual gold washed down from all the hydraulic mining in the Sierras, when high-pressure hoses washed away mountains of earth in the search for gold. The end of the rush. Bald ass greed stripped of all romance, all fun. Greed mechanized. Weaponized. Strip her. Make love, Make war. Rape. Skin. Gut. Pulverize bones. So much dust. So much dirt washed down, that he'd walked on islands of it formed at the confluence of the Sacramento and San Joaquin rivers. Having a power launch berthed less than a mile from his crib gave him access to hundreds of miles of inland waterways or a head out on the big pond.

The gold he sought carried the allure of antiquity. Nothing turned a woman on like old money honey. He thought how gold never tarnished but the wasted mountains of lives sure as hell did. Tarnished trashed lives. Gold still can't melt into your neurons like mamacita Coca. After the rush. As all bones turned to dust, the gold remained the same bitch.

His current benefactor, Johnstone Warren, told him some about the Copper Scroll, a treasure list he described as ingots, earrings, crowns studded with rubies and sapphires and emeralds, jugs, platters, flasks, garments, basins, cups, bowls, and vessels of gold coins, enough to sink the gold standard of entire countries. Thoughts of the treasure spurred a powerful lust in him.

The phone sang.

"Have you made the arrangements?"

"I found him where you said he'd be," Korner replied. "Excuse me, Rakitin, I know this business. I do not need any damn helicopter escort. They didn't even call a tow for my car."

"Those orders don't issue from me, you know I'm only Mr Warren's go boy," Rakitin said.

"A rather ironic tone for a boy," Korner chuckled. "He's meeting the woman."

"Keep us informed. Time is growing short."

☼

Mor admired Christina's rapid gait. Her movements so languid yet compact. It gave her a bounce as they walked the path bordered by blown, clipped and edged lawn. He watched her greet passing students, her curls dancing in the wind, eyes shining brighter as each one passed. The sheer magnitude of her personality reminded him how far he had retreated from the social cultural whirl. Awhirl of a world ghosting him while vivifying her. They climbed broad steps to the lecture hall, large enough he figured to accommodate some hundreds. At least a dozen students had attached themselves to her as she swept to the podium. He hung to the back, swallowed by milling students. Eavesdropping on a conversation between a white student with extreme facial piercings talking to a black with Rasta dreads and rainbow tie-dyed T shirt, he took a seat in the rear of the hall.

"They call her la voisé. The voice," the pierced man informed his friend.

"I heard she had Tantric sex with an Indian mystic. That's how she got her power."

"He gave her the straight shot," the pierced man replied with a smirk. Mor wanted to slap his snotty, ring infested face. The feelings for a woman he just met caught him off balance. Whoa dawg.

The hall lights dimmed, quieting the buzz of the audience. Christina stepped to the podium.

"We all in turning around on this planet look in outer space for aliens but are there any creatures more alienated than us a human being right here?" she asked.

Mor studied the audience, a hip Euro-Mandarin-Latino-Arabic-Judeo-Creole gumbo. They breathed together as he thought he saw the walls pulse with them. Korner had been right about Christina. She definitely expanded.

"Obviously there is a knowing of anything. Not so obviously a knowing as a denial of a thing. A k'no no no'wing denial of the very awareness of any k'nowing out of it in the first place. Thus saying you know it may be a positive negation of it. It in this case is awareness of a being of that knower of any and y'all knowing." she continued. "Our purpose here of knowing is picking up on a being of that knower. A discernment of a being of the whole point of you knowing anything. A point of view of you as an eye being at attention merely a peering it. It as awareness of any seer still completely baffles any typical comprehension of it. Like knowing the unknown. Seeing the unseen. The same for feeling it, fielding it, bio fielding it, projecting it now k'now'ing it out as supersonic waves of thoughts of it is as though a being c'ng in denial of it. A denial of it, indivisible invisibility of any individual, by a now k'nowing it into appearing a pairing in memory of me or you. That indivisible individual now denied by turning around k'no no no'wing it as though a being of anything else.

"Thus knowing may hurt, at least for awhile yet paying attention to awareness of a being in the first place, complete completely pervading any field of view, of you, heals any heart by merely picking up on a being still in any felt feeling feel'da you. You. You. You." She concluded by pulling some students up on the stage, a dozen more streamed up to join them. Taking seats on chairs behind her, Christina spun to touch their fingers.

Her movement seemed to stream with his thoughts. Fragments of her talk pierced his reverie, one he'd found himself in since first meeting her. Hearing of it as a b'ing c'ng out in word in her eye dialectic debate between a mere a peering it or it appearing by a know'ing denial of it. Not since Gina had he felt in her"eye such electricity. Again from a woman on stage. He wondered what Freud would make of that.

"Whatever is known, written, or thought information is mortal, limited, and full of misery, and needs to be rejected as oneself. Find yourself by rejecting merely knowing denial of yourself. Those words are not mine, but they recognize the need for discrimination within the domain of a being still in the first place. A being of oneself. A mean of any meaning between the real and unreal, between a Y and a Y as's'eX. A's sz'zex y'all. Za'za"zex y'all. As ex's ting."

Mor could see Korner smile to himself. Whatever scheme Korner was cooking up, he planned on him being hooked on Christina. The crowd obviously got off on her. A man wearing a knit beret near the front laughed in steady bursts. Others like a delicate Asian woman remained implacable except for an occasional quick smile.

"So we all turn here to study metaphysics as if regular physics ain't enough to chew on," she said. "The official title of this class is 'Theory of Knowledge,' though more correctly we all in turning into it be the knowledge out in her"eye of eve're'y body projecting a knowing out of it as merely a positive negation of it. It as mere though'tsz of a being in the first place. Awareness of any eye a peering in the first place still anybody now appearing out of it. Out of it as though'tsz around k'no no no'wing of it as merely a being in theory. A being c'ng mirrored as in word mem or y in the or y of man as mind or y mem or y of a being of me or you. A being still in the first place alone indivisible. A being alone indivisible merely appearing mirrored a pairing of me or you out in word as thought'sz of a being c'ng it. A being c'ng still in the first place now k'now'ing out of it in a memory. A being c'ng appearing out of it merely mirrored in word a's anybody. Any a na y or y now k'no no no'wing a being. A being as though now denying itself k'now'ing anybody anything any time any where. A Y denial of a being still in the first place first person present singular awareness of that that I am speaking the dialectic debate of a y now k'now'ing it as'ex's ting in the first place. Now y'all may begin to comprehend the problem around k'now'ing out of it anything or anybody.

"Why? Why y'all the talk talk talk? Why any language in the first place beyond the obvious function defining it as'word dividing the indivisible merely as thoughts of it. Of a being c'ng still alone in the first place indivisible. Now a's in word though'tsz of a k'no no no'wing out of it. Y'all sliced and diced. Fried and dried. A supernatural mistake of a being c'ng merely a peering still in the first place. Now appearing completely out of it typically as trivial thoughts of it. Come on people. We all in turn can do better than settling for mere appearing awhile out in word." For a moment Mor saw sparks beaming from her'eyes. A supernatural mis take of a being c'ng of it. A being cosmic. Electromagnetic field of view. Of you or me. A're'y'all of eve're'ybody Mor mused. More and more he found typical thoughts displaced by the y eye dialectic debate raging like a wildfire. A turning of it black'g'round incinerating that typical mindless ignoring out of it without realizing it. It a being c'ng in any eye merely a peering it. Mor resisted an urge to hollar a ye'e'z'z'ow as he turned his attention black out in her'eye of eve will. A wayeve will of funny'action. She'e now funny that way. That wayeve of informing any situation.

"A b'ng c'ng still in the first place. Ancient. Yet new indeed eve'n from of old. Y'all may now think of a b'ng c'ng merely mirrored out in your memory keyed on an arbitrary name. Welcome to discovering a greater side to y'all of a being anybody. Any name. Hi my na me is. It seems we all introduce ourselves as a being na'ta. Some anybody appearing around k'no no no'wing out of it as'z a na me. A projecting of it as mere thought'sz of a na me now k'now'ing out of it as a denying of it. Her I am. That a na me of it. It a b'ng c'ng a peering still in the first place. Indivisible invisibility." Christina paused. A hush passed over the audience.

"Now out in any eye merely a peering appears in word thoughts of any a na y k'now'ing out of it. Out now in her eye of eve're'ybody. Y'all now a ka'smic eve're'y body will as a positive negation of a b'ng c'ng still in the first place. Any a na y body that a b'lack' body mirrored y na y'all now appearing by echoing sound wayeves supersonically as ka's micro wayeve black'g'round. Appearing out in word in formation understanding the spelling of it. What I am saying to y'all in words'z'za is that our attention is captivated understanding any in word spelling out of it. Now a b'ng captive at attention fixated on a name k'now'ing out of it more names. More in word denial of it. It indivisible in'visibility. Any. Any appearing of it is a mirror deceit of in word memory. Appearing of it awhile.

"This supersonic supernatural mis take of awareness of a y eye b'ng c'ng merely a peering it. Still completely indivisibible invisibility of any. Any a na y individual." She'e now paused to turn her gaze around the room. Rapt would not be too strong a word for their attention caught in the revelation of anybody now a na y you are a re'y'all being c'ng of a y eye peering out of anybody. Still Mor was aware of the peh'ss'y whole power of ignore'ance of it ignited by da y light. The cosmic sol. Ar'ey'e system. A bi na re'y body appearing a pairing out in awhile. A wily a while of which most of these students once out of ear range will quickly succumb. Anybody being carried away in its craft. A cunning crafty uncanny mirror deceit of any long or short term memory. Mor imagined himself a grizzled vet. A failed warrior crispped from the inside out by drugs sex and a rocky role of a painter turned carpenter. Toss in a few near death experiences. A decade of supernatural visions along with influence of native shamans not to mention a na me of da Dark'ness had now set him up for a date with the great unknown cast out in her eye of eve'll. Now a professor professing of it.

He found many of these students young privileged softbellies. Their arrogance and inflated self importance would offset Christina's brahmavidya flame thrower singing their in word minds.

"In that I am now teaching y'all the a b c's of it. Of it a b'ng c'ng still in the first place. Now appearing out of it by a na re'ye'szz'zap'ping a k'no no no'wing out of it any in word in formation of it. Awhile. Any appearing of it from a star to a scar merely a wily while of ma'sz d'nature. Yet still a being c'ng in the first place. Anybody. A na y body merely a b'ng c'ng still in the first place now mirrored in word memory turning into or out of it ask'now'ing it a's out in any na me alone. So arbitrary yet accepted as self evident while that as'ka's mic awareness that I am offering y'all likely quickly denied. A denial of it now out in word a's mere thought'sz of a b'ng c'ng still in the first place. In the first place. Out in word by sheer denial of a b'ng c'ng still indivisible. Out in word supernaturally as though'tsz of a being still alone indivisible invisibility in the first place now merely appearing mirrored out in word k'no no no'wing out of it any a na y denial of it.

"That is the a b c's of any in word captivity. A b'ng c'ng alone still in the first place may appear out of it only merely mirrored in word a's thought'sz of it. Keep an eye on the a b c's. They will set you free or wrap y'all in word chains.

"Fully one half. One right hemisphere of our brain still remains word free. That'sz the old brain. The timeless free brain. Free awareness of any in word captivity. Free of any in word duplicity as'z'any thought'sz in man'as mirror in word mind or y y'all arbitrary ambiguous memory of a b'ng c'ng still in the first place. Now aska's of it a k'now'ing appearing out of it in a duplicity of a b'ng c'ng of me or you in memory. Out of it in memory.

"Free free freed at last thank god'all'mighty. Freedom now. Freedom foreve'r'eybody.Now y'all k'now y a b'ng c'ng alone indivisible still in the first place. Any appearing of a b'ng c'ng out and moving about is mere in word mirrored duplicity of a b'ng c'ng still in. Still indivisible. A b'ng c'ng still in the first place. A y we all turn attention now around k'now'ing that. That a b'ng c'ng still at attention. Y speak dialectic reverses polarity from a being still in the first place now at attention k'now'ing out as x's ting to any now k'nowing of it a b'ng c'ng still in the first place y'sz dom us. Y speak dialectic reveals a b'ng c'ng still in the first place at attention. A'ten bi na re'y radiating sheer duplicity yod hayvavhay a'ska'ing of it a y mem or y. Y a being you yod iota that awareness that I am is is. That a where e'na y esse to be still in the first person present singing singular supernaturally supersonically superimposed in word as thought'sz of a y b'ng c'ng out as'ex's ting in'formation. A b'ng c'ng still in the first place alone indivisible in'visibility of any individual. A b'ng c'ng a peering it in the first place appearing out as anybody now recognition of a b'ng c'ng as a mere mirrored duplicate. Y speak about y'or y you;re you now appearing out as anybody." Christina paused to let her words sink in. Mor kept finding himself disappearing black'g'round of a b'ng c'ng in'visibility out in her"eye of eve re'y body. Finding himself lost in the richness of a being supernatural while appearing of it a being quite normal. Normal out in that neurosis of ignoring it still in the first place y'all while appearing out of it a second or two. Thus finding himself bewildered by her subjectivity he now saw Christina as mini-kryst. Y'all black whole body reabsorbing his sense of a being in any shape or form. But then he'd been dissolved throughout a lifetime of a being referred to as the Darkness. Of k'now'ing that impenetrable darkness that any potential membrane between him or it in memory stayed pretty porus. Eve'n the sound wayeves of Christina's voice echoed in his mind more as a symphony. A harmonious or agreeable mingling of sounds playing black'g'round the medium of his body as instrument of consciousness.

Reminding him of a b'ng c'ng a y eye a peering out the d"ark of a covenant. A perceived agreement with a letter'all god understanding any in word in formation supernaturally as thoth'tsz of it. A supersonic wayeve appearing of it out in her'eye of eve're'ybody merely a peering still it. A'Y eye. A why the eye hell'o you're; you in the first place. In the first place is a h"ome. A y's dom'us of a being now that as'ka's mic k'nower as'k'nowing out and about of it. As'ka's y'all. As ka's mic cause now of k'nowing anything or anybody. A b'lack'ness body of intent of a b"ng c'ng a gain. A gain. Mor paid attention to it. D"ark of it turning black'g'round into appearing any roll or role playing. A playing out of his role painting Christina.

"Any k'nowing is tripartite of a Y. A prior'y. Awareness of a b'ng c'ng cogitating merely a peering it or secondly a peering at it or last but least appearing it in a wor'd'ship of it. In the beginning is the word. The word'ship of it carrying anybody's attention letter'all'y away. That word'ship or worship captivity sets sail at an early age. Y'all may think a b'ng atheistic or nihilistic. Y'all set sail on that same wor'd'ship of it.

"Y'sz a b'ng c'ng of a singular ba'se supporting a pairing of it symbolizing it as'ex'et'ting duplicating information of it merely a peering it now as'ka's a k'no'wing out of it in word. A b'ng c'ng merely a peering it now as'ka's of eve're'ybody a k'no'no'no'wing out of it a peering at it. Finally." She'e now paused for a deep breath while scanning the room. "There is a knowing of appearing it. A wor'd'ship of it. It now as'ka's Y of it a dhi"monic singular craft of good and eve'll. A craft of go'o'd letter'all'y ar't and eve will of any wayeve letter'all'y y'all of him supernaturally projecting as thoth'tsz of a b'ng c'ng in word in'formation now k'no'wing it out in her'eye of eve're'y'body. Y'all now riding that wayeve out in a y eye of herhimit merely a peering from above as below." As painter Mor appreciated the allegory of it. A eye star'e"ye merely a peering it. Singular. Indivisible invisibility now a y eye star'e"ye of eve'r"eybody in verses or roles of complete d"ark'ness. Paint that out of your head, the man said. The bliss a're'y'ab'sorbing y'all sorrow merely that bliss denied in any now k'no'wing out of it

"Any knowledge untouched wordfree requires awareness of in word memory to precipitate ka'r'ma or action of it with a're'y'action. The in'wor'd'ship built on sound wayeves echoing black'g'round h'our mouth as organ of speech. Ahhooma." She gave a long sound that picked up and reverberated an ambient buzz in the hall. Waves of it continued for several seconds like tuning to a near subsonic frequency of the building itself. Christina repeated it several times like playing the building as an instrument.

"This sound Om'a covers the complete vocal range from air playing wayeves of h'our vocal chords from throat to as'ex"et'ting lips'a. Realize it. Become more aware of it vivifying y'all life with eve're'y breath taken. So Oma reveals in its utterence that k'nowledge of the vital breath as a complete sound untouched wordfree. A're'y'leased as'za full spectrum asz'sound packed in a singular sound of a b'ng merely breathing it. That'sz'a a prior'y wordfree knowledge as indivisible awareness now as'ka's of it pra'na life force. A p'ss'y whole power force transmitted autonomically neuronically subconsciously ask'arma action of a're'y'action. Ask'nowing a're'y'e's of any knowledge beyond perceiving learning it now. That is it. It, ka's mic memory intelligence consciousness that awareness paying attention comes from you a being a re'y'all as the point of view, of you a being still in the first place now a k'nowing out of it in formation as thought'sz of it. A being now k'nowing that ka'smic being. Pays or plays out from in the first place a y eye being be'am'ing you. Complete completely alone a being indivisible. Y'all never add to it nor take anything away from it. You are a re'y'all of it, the subject objectifying merely mirrored in word memory by a being c'ng of y the very subjective knowledge is. Thus we all may in turn seek awareness of it in awhile still projecting any denial of it. Now pick up on the paradox of k'now'ing it in awhile as thought'sz of missing it.

"We all may in turn find in word final liberation now k'now'ing it moment by moment or ignore it lifetime by lifetime. Metaphysically the loop, the quantum loop continues ad infinitum ad nauseum. Birth and death, beginning and end are a simultaneous point of you. Most will not get that, being covered by the event of either or. Birth or Death. They share a common gravity of the weight of waiting now for the event of either. Nine months. You could die much quicker. The long term memory of previous lives generally stays in the subtle luminous counterpart dream bodhi. The sheer gravity of y'all those lives still easily and instantly offset by realizing that awareness of a b'ng c'ng still alone indivisible in the first place.

"Look for that crack in the ka's mic egg. Anyone may get flashes, dreams, visions of past lives. Most will remain mostly ignorant of the past and for good reason. Ignorance implies intent. Causality. The ka's mic unified black field bo'dhi is by intent of intentional disregard of it in complete d"ark"n'ess'e, blinded by the complete role we all in turn play and pay. Realize that now y'all k'now'ing learning and earning serves one purpose. Paying attention. Paying and playing attention to a y eye of a b'ng c'ng merely a peering it. A breathing a breath of it still in the first place. The arrows of now a k'now'ing a being indivisible in'visibility of appearing out in awhile flows in one direction. Away from it now ask'a'ing y a being in the first place.

Ka's mic electromagnetic loops flow in a reverse torus a swelling doughnut of electromagnetic waves of multiple amplatitudes flattening quantum loops out full of quantum gravity moment by moment weight of waiting as'z too die or be born. She'e'na, ma re y g"round of eve re y being a loop, any mere mirror beginning is ending. Endings as'z thought'sz breaking open that continuous loop creates the polarity of positive negativity of now turning around beginning by a being still in the first place merely mirrored out of y a's a na y k'no no no'wing it.

"The eros arrow of time moves in a continuous loop'y e turn all y y'all. The turning naturally reverses direction in turning y'all into or out of that black'g'round of a being now projecting a k'now'ing it out of a b'ng c'ng in her"e eye of eve're'y body. Thus the ending of any life returns to a beginning depending on planetary polarity or in any event merely mirrored a's birth or death. Polarity shifts yet that arrow does not till it appears as though it does coming black'g'round or merely realizing, re"versing, retelling that eye star'e'y' e of that tale of chasing tail. A living now in a present k'now'ing out of it turning into a future unknown frees the mind or y of past memory.

"Any in word memory. Of a moment or a lifetime n'eve'r eve'r enters that wordfree old right brain. Anybody has in sight of a b'ng c'ng merely a peering a constantly refreshed untouched wordfree awareness. Of it now still knowing out the unknown. A turning now by the ending of it. By k'no no no'wing en'd'ing. By projecting as thought'sz of it a denial of one as'ka'ing a y now any en'dhi'ing of it. A b'ng c'ng opening any big mouth. The loop opens as though too appear in a pair of endings spiraling into one now as though'tsz of it int'word twis'ting into any race against another. In a being any a na y body appearing out of a black'g'round that race of man as mind or y memory turns into or out a y eye of anybody merely a peering it in the first place.

"Enjoy your time here. Soak it up. Outside of this class you may find its subject of now k'now'ing a b'ng c'ng in word information of it still indivisible in'visibility likely will not play well to the general public. The general must perpetuate that race war by ignoring its own tail. In that I am going to say, contrary to common wisdom, talk about it freely, enthusiastically with anyone. Feel the repulsion to it. Realize ignorance is k'no'wing of it. Ignoring a being y by knowing it. That is a positive negation of it. It, a being still in the first place now turned out of it by k'no no no'wing a denial of it is of the same polarity and thus like poles repel. That natural repulsion to realization of a being of that awareness serves to remind us our lives are predicated on ignoring it. Ignore'ance of a being in the first place in favor of playing out any mere mirrored roles of a y eye merely a peering it. A peering out of it complete roles or rolls of d'ark'ness. Out of that as'ka's all body role of d'ark'ness we all turn now k'no'wing of it appearing as though'tsz of a b'ng c'ng out k'now'ing other y's'z'z'z'.

"In the long run most will succumb to a being as thoughtsz swept away in that x sighting role. The rush. The k'rush. The energy of life and death will sweep away conscious awareness of a b'ng c'ng still in the first place now out of it by y'all k'now'ing anybody or anything understanding the in word spell. The spelling of a b c's turning out concepts, defining, as'word thoughtsz seemingly dividing the indivisible then trying to explain any roll of y or how to put it, put old Humpty back together again. Remember Humpty Dumpty, that egg'as potential slash exponential rested on a wall, a division, a's'word to cleave the indivisible as though beginning as t'word in forming ending's of it.

"Astrophysics tells we all no longer turn around the center of the Universe. If no still center then how now a k'nowing any turning of it in the first place? Our great plan"et h'earth is now reduced to invisibility of a cosmic dust particle. Thus we all appear to turn around a b'ng c'ng invisbility to become, y'all guessed it, a still invisibility center of the universe. Observer observing observation must always function from that still center centered centrality of a b'ng c'ng merely a peering in the first place. That still point of view of you necessary to be able to observe the e or g'ee's us motion. You a re; y'all still of a y eye star'e'y"e in'g out from any centrality point of view, of y you are a re; y a'sz abstract principal principle of a one thing. Of a y eye of a b'ng c'ng merely a peering y. A y that is worth looking into." Christina paused the dance and leaned the palm of one hand against the podium, waving off any more words with the other.

The audience murmured. Mor smiled at the enthusiasm for her shaman showmanship. Christina drank water from a glass on the podium letting silence settle on the room like a light blanket over an electrical field.

"As too many of us live long, hard, painful lives a by nary clue as to who what or why we all turn into or out of or really are should promote a knowing of a b'ng c'ng in the first place. Now a k'no'wing out our a b c's before understanding their in word spelling mitigates suffering that falling as'z'any thoughtsz of it. Or you may now know it a lifetime without realizing it. A're'alizing awareness of it is sa'y'me same as awareness of denying it. It a b'ng c'ng merely a peering it. It is picking up on a b c's complete now as'k'a's of k'no'wing of it a b'lackness with in word intent to appear a gain. From a b'ng lack to a gain. Of it. A completion of a complete d'ark'ness ."

With the utterence of that word she'e now caught him in her'eye of eve're'y'body. Several heads turned his way. The D'ark'ness no longer a mere imaginary thing'king of it before him. Now his'zz eye's'z z'a merely a peering it now as'king of it in'k'no no no'wing'ing out of it anybody anything any where any time mirrored in word as'z'any thoth'tsz of it. The rush of it. A wayeve of it out in her'eye'z z z'a crushing him a black'g'round in'visibility. A mere a peering it. Yet now as'k'no'wing out of it supersonically supernaturally superimposed a b c's in word mean'z'az'z z'any in formation of it. Out of it in her'eye of eve'll of a'wayeve's fun'ny'a'ction function a la que"en que' appearing anybody anything any where any time. A mere mirrored denial of now k'no'wing of it. She'e na funny that way'eve'll ka'li ma'sz z z'our're'y"e. A black'g'round as'ka's all'y y'all we all will of a wheel turning in a race. A groove of ma'shee'na. A ma'She'e'na so funny that way'eve'll cunning cruel deceit of any appearing of it out in her'eye still in the first place. Indivisible in'visibility of any individual. Mor let his attention follow the dialectic train to its natural conclusion. Indivisible in'visibility of a b'ng c'ng yet in the first place. Now you k'now you're'y'e a b c's of it he mused.

"A b c's y'all a're'ye a peering now as'k'no'wing appearing of it in word in formation carries attention along the by wayeve of it. Sheer horror or tribulation of mind or y as ex'perience in any bioneuroniccellular electromagnetic felt field of you sinks attention as though, merely as thoughtsz hardwired by hard times in the mire or mirror y na now as'z'ex's ting. As'ex'et'ting information awhile. You or yod as thoth'tsz on a slice of exo'dus't. A thin slice or sliver of a b'ng c'ng in'visibility of it appearing now awhile. Appearing of any say'l'ing the in word craft out in her"e ye'sz z z'on eve'n't of any in word spell. A spell of eve'll a'crossing the imaginary eve'n't horizon of it merely a peering it or a peering out now. As'z'any k'no no no'wing out of it a b c's turning a'cross it in a word'ship say'ling on out of it appearing by a denial of it. Denial y'll d'na in that simple twis'ting t'word in formation of fate faith and family. In this class we all will turn in word black'g'round into a b'ng c'ng more aware moment by moment. Of that indivisible in'visibility awareness of a still b'ng c'ng at attention of that one singular eye of any knower knowing knowledge of it. With intent of realizing or denying a being of that as'ka's all'y'as'ka's mic memory of y'all along. A y eye of a b'ng c'ng merely a peering it. Now ask'nowing embracing along with denying it. Either way it is y'et a peering of a y eye. A y'et'ting a duplicating of it as'ex'y'all. A y eye of you;re'ye of you. A b'ng c'ng yet in the first place. Out of it in her'eye still a b'ng c'ng in this still first place. Y'all will learn in word discrimination between a b'ng c'ng out twin'ed around roles or rolls to be played of a beginning by ending or on the one hand polarizing that of a b'ng c'ng now merely as'z'any though'tsz of it born to death or still a y eye am that of a first supersonic person. A being in the first place. Still immortal center centered centrality stillness of it. Only in form'a'sz z z'ep tepi. Ma'sz'da first time now in for'ma'sz z'a first matter still any a na y hey'ting. For'ma'sz z z'sound mean. That's'za y'or y now speak of a being in the first place a dialectic debate y'all will pick up on. This dialectic or practised debate of speaking merely of a y. Or a y na now as'z z'ex's ting supernaturally asz thoth'tsz of a being k'now'ing it out in formation. The dialectic debate is an in word key to breaking up or out of the in word captivity of any x's ting. Liberating attention paid merely to any x's ting." Christina leaned into a pause, letting her head fall. She now had raised the stakes supernaturally as'z'any thoth'tsz. A body of a god'esse to be c'ng letter'ally appearing of it in word. She'e'na looked up humming. A humming mic'ed out and harmonized by the audience swelling till Mor swore hearing a glass pane crack. She now was free moving with a cordless headset. A master of body language and the's'way of tao Mor mused. He wanted to dance in her'eye. For a split second he considered joining her on stage.

"The study of metaphysics, the special spacial ma"shee'na's'k'no no no'wing out of it appearing now as'z thoth offers a supernatural d'na'ture to anybody anything any where any time. Tearing away at the indivisible now supernaturally in visibility mirrored by in word knowledge of turning into k'no no no'w'ing or denying out as'ex'et'ting thothtsz. A body of god'esse to be anybody. A na y body projection. A body of a positive negation of it. Or image'nary felt biocogent field of you now merely as'z thoth'tsz of anybody touching a black'g'round. As'ka's mic'ro wayeve of eve're'ybody turning into or out of a black'g'round. Experienced by y'all directly and periodically as'z z z'leep black into it. A complete roll or role of d"ark'ness." She now gazing straight away him. More heads turned his way.

"You be touching of any touch supernaturally possible by as thoth'tsz of it with polarity on the one hand projecting a touching positive in word negativity. Producing merely supernaturally as thoth'tsz of her'me'as a y eye of herhimit. A'n indivisible in'visibility in a b'ng c'ng merely a peering out now k'now'ing out of it a b'ka'm'ing black'g'round into or out of it. Thus any touch touching of it always now as'k'no'wing instantaneously denial y'll d'na of a being. A projected projection as'z'any supernatural thoth'tsz of it. A b'ng still indivisible throughout any synapse of mind or y memory. Any touch a touching untouched wordfree memoryfree awareness of it. It a y eye merely a peering it.

"Or y now knowledge as awareness of a being now k'nower of k'nowing out of it any such knowledge. A being still in the first place. In the'or'y of ka's mic memory any appearing out of it now awhile is in a craft of s'kill'ing deadly daring guile and deception required in forma'szz any e'gg's'za gee's us motion of it out in her"e ye a wayeye a peering out as'king of it a la que"en que' appearing a black mirror in word see'as'z z za'any hatching of another tale from the mouths of ba'be's.

"Eve're'y body of her'eye of mother nature of a b'ng c'ng indivisible in'visibility now our self anybody as'ex's ting by appearing as thoth. A god esse to be letter'ally out supersonically supernaturally superimposed about still a being the one indivisible invisibility of any individual. A y eye of herhimit a peering. A yod within or you without. As'z z zs'you in name alone. Indivisible. Sailing off as'z'any thoth'tsz. In'formation as that eve'll crafty booty body of self deception. That one awareness of a being as mirrored memory of a being hidden as un'oreflecting a're'y'flection in y'all'sz a b c'sz'a. Seer of a being the indivisible in'visibility of now any k'no no no'wing out of it any mirror in word image may be reflected merely supernaturally supersonically as thothtsz of it. Thus whatever appears reflected is any a na y, a not you or you now merely as'z'any thoth'tsz of a being still in the first place now k'now'ing out of it any in formation.

"Thus the excellence of this enquiry centers on the omnipresent and indivisible d'nature as'z super'nature without the twist t'word a y'll d'na denial of y you're; you. Just as you would not be hearing these words if you were not already echoing them out in her'eye". . . Mor was hearing her words playing sound waves into his energy field dissolving in word biocellular-neuronic chemical synchronicities. He was stone cold floored, in love with her. Still a b c's out in her'eye of herhimit potential of any in word appearing of it merely a peering. The dialectic steady snaked through his body as an electromagnetic touching felt field in for'ma'sz she'e"na.

" . . . paying attention, along with tuition, you do not need to find completion at any point in life because you, the peh'ss'y whole point of view of you merely a peering it. It a're'y'all ity al're'y'adhi'y eye of a b'ng c'ng always complete. Completely untouched wordfree awareness of it. Any. Any a na y looking for completion must be y'll d'na denial of it. A denial of freedom.

"Completely free freed freedom of a b'ng c'ng in a still point of view of you as'z a complete seer of it eve'n"a now with out yet completing this course. You now k'now'ing out of that will never be more or less of it. This truth is of awareness of a being still indivisible invisibility. Now eve're'ybody as'k'no'wing out of it any complexity. Now eve're'ybody with the p'lexus of a b'ng c'ng twis'ting int'word it as'z'ex y'all. A y eye of you're;ye of you a being still is any a n'a y eve'r'e y a're'y'dhi'a'ting you now merely k'now'ing out of it as thoth'tsz of projecting projection of eve're y bodhi complex. A y now black eye mirror a're'y'all body. Space is n"eve're'y complex by a twist of it a peering now as'z z z'any appearing of it in awhile. A wiley cunning con of your own denial, just us a man being c'ng as'z'any man or y'll d'na of it. Man always man with or without a womb as mind or y any in word memory of a b c's. The y'or y of that's our quest and our question m'ark, whatever hook or role it may take. It the'y of a b'ng c'ng y'all informing it. Infor'ma'ss'z z z ex siting y'all.

"How do you know it? What is the wayeve of function of now as'k'no no no"wing out of it in the first place. Is it in essence gathering of it or denying of it. Denying it, ignoring a being completely complete completion wherein nothing may be added or subtracted. Or a being lacking? A being any b'lack'ness of it now to be a gain of it? And if you were that how would you know it? What do you know is why. Of what purpose do you know. Do you know why? Do you know y? Y you're you? Or merely project any mirrored y na now? Knowledge of a real thing'y'thing knowledge must embrace that y of a b'ng c'ng now informing it k'no'wing out of it that y'as'z'dom. A d'ome. A h'ome. A sound place of a b'ng c'ng a peering it in the first place now appearing out of any knowing or projecting of it as'z'any thoth'tsz of that feeling, that fielding of a b'ng c'ng alone.

"Now that I am k'nowing that asking of it who in this room, this campus, this state, this nation, this world cannot or has not felt that feeling of a being alone. Go ahead and raise your hand if you have never felt or do not know that feeling of a being alone. Anyone?" Christina scanned the group with hands on her hips.

"In that feeling y'all realizing it directly by a being indivisible in the first place. Alone. No feeling more universal than now k'now'ing of it a feeling of b'ng c'ng alone. Right now in this room anyone may still feel it in word. Alone. Now a turning black'g'round find it indivisible. What then seems to be desparate separate separation from a being alone is a y eye merely a peering mirrored out in memory as'z'any other y'sz. Ignoring a being indivisible in the first place now with intent of intentional in word disregard of that. That a b'ng c'ng as felt in word to be y'all alone in formation. Y'all alone the wayeve function of k'no no no'wing out of it any appearing in man'as mind or y memory. That's'sz a y eye of a b'ng c'ng merely a peering alone. We all turning black'g'round will learn to cultivate feeling that as'z z'a fielding that of you of a view of a being still in the first place. Y'all alone indivisible in'visibility is go'a'ld'en or'e y. Y the wiseman, the y as man'as mind or y, grieves not. At best celebrate elevation of that as'z z z'a a feeling of awareness of it. The go'a'lden indivisible or'e y"e egg of g'ee's'z us. Feel it. The peh'ss'y whole as'ex'p'ress'ed eye on it merely a peering now as'ex'et'ting t'word t'wis'ting in formationout on a b'all. Field of view of you of y you're;y"e on you. The go'a'lden or'e y"e merely a peering unified field. Of view of you of a y eye potential a peering out in the or y d'na of you a y'll. Now as'ka'no no no'wing out of it any mere mirrored memory of a y'll d'na. A denial. You not now as'ex. You no mo'e". She paused.

Mor could hear the words but they began dissolving black into it. Herhimit as'z'sound wayeves. Peh'ss'y'l'ent. Supersonic wayeves as'z'any thoth'tsz of it. He found his attention drifting black'g'round to the wordfree untouched visual world. From his perspective, the sound of her words blended with the salmon colored silk of her blouse and light glinting off the curls of her hair. Starting with the contours of her body, he saw a shimmering play into the audience like the waves of a mirage, everything connected in one conscious undifferentiated presence of a being still in the first place. Seeing the g'loss of it a'gain. He noticed other heads turning to see if neighbors experienced a similar black'g'round revelation. A b'ng c'ng in complete d"ark'ness'e now to be a ware n'esse. Now a we'ar to be. From deep in his gut he felt something tear loose. An old egotistic phantom ripped from his belly with a raucous wayeve of laughter.

He realized his outburst came at that pregnant pause that MargoChristina had been working throughout. Now more heads turned his way. He locked on her'eye'sz'za. She'e'na let go a peal of laughter that recaptured the hall's attention.

"What was it Shakespeare wrote about this earth horr'or movie, this good bad as'ka's mic dream? 'The we all turning churning burning. A black'g'round c'ng. A tale told by an idiot, full of sound and fury, signifying nothing.' A sig'ni'f'y'ing of the fu'ny'a'ction function of it out in her'eye of eve'll. We all turning into or out of a b'ng c'ng out in word in formation. . . Awhile now."

Christina gazed his way. He jerked his thumb to outside. She'e'na nodded back.

He hustled out of the auditorium to the parking lot for the box easel and drawing board in his truck. The lost magic had returned. He wanted to search for Christina with his crayons. He wanted to find her in the kinder garden of feeling fielding a being in love still in the first place alone.

He made his way to her office after asking directions from two students and a custodian, a middle age Latino with thin mustache, pressed olive green Dickies and red suspenders, the only one who seemed to speak his language. Still he found it easier to go from the jungle to the city than the reverse. Where Ma Na'ture taught hard eternal, cyclic truths, the city was always up for grabs, indulgent in its wasteful wasting power grid he mused. Just as plugging in turns on the power. Power tore from her guts. Ma'sz nature. Mor raised his hand to knock on her office door. Doubts crept into his head. Christina was a woman of significance who had answered her calling. The challenge of drawing her put a burn to his gut. He would hate to make a fool of himself if the sketch went poorly. The blood sank to his feet. As he turned to leave, she came gliding down the hall, her face flushed to vermilion around the cheeks and brow, eyes sparkling, her smile, lips parted to clean white teeth.

"Hello there. I see you brought your equipment. Come on in," she said, pulling keys from her shoulder bag. Mor studied her hands. They were of good proportion to her arms and torso. He had learned caution around women with large hands, which he associated with some form of aggression. He figured a woman like margoChristina to be aggressive to maintain their position in such a competitive world.

Her expansive nature overcame his fears. She had none of the pretentiousness he had found so distracting in academics. The comfortable hodgepodge of books, sketchpads, and piles of loose-leaf papers stacked about her office, further assured him.

"Not what you expected?"

"More of an art studio than a prof's office." Pen and ink and charcoal sketches of ruins, and figures in various classic poses were tacked on the walls. "Are these yours?"

"They are."

"Very good. You should be drawing my portrait."

"I have never been good at faces. Some of these are arch sites I have worked and visited. Study of philosophy, for me, requires a valid outward expression of this business of inner reflection. A person can become very clever with words without penetrating their inner revelation. 'I take no more account of the wind from their mouths, which caused their words, than of the wind which issued from their lower regions,' to quote Leonardo. In Yiddish we say, hakn a tshaynik, prattle like a teapot." She settled into a chair behind her desk. "Set up your easel over there and we can talk while you work."

As he set up, Christina pointed to the light table.

"These are transparencies of Dead Sea scroll fragments. It is easier on my eyes than the computer," she said, nodding to a laptop. "My mother being Jewish, I carry an innate fascination with the Yids."

"That's why you mentioned Kabala?"

"We are here in the heart of academia where y'all knowing is biased by objectivìty. Comprehending that subject awareness of a b'ng c'ng out of it fills up to the brim any objectivity in word as'zany thothtsz of it in formation. Comprehending that untouched wordfree freed freedom of a y eye merely a peering it. Merely becoming aware of a being still in the first place. Indisible invisibility of anybody. A y eye b'ng c'ng a peering of that awareness t'word t'wis'ting memory of it into a cunning validation of the mirage of any appearing of it. Appearing now as'king of it any k'no'wing out of it in word. Information awhile.

"That knowing out of it seems to require a mystical experience beyond or outside accepted logical constraints. Well it seems that is any ordinary wayeve function of mere mirrored supersonic supernatural appearing of it as'z'any thoth'tsz. A god'esse of eve're'y'body. We all turning black'g'round it periodically as'z z z'leep black indivisible in'visibility of it directly experience it asz bliss. A bliss now denied as'z sorrow.

"Somehow there seems to be that mystic veil covering layer between wisdom and 'isdom, between subjectivity and objectivity," she offered, raking back some ever errant strands of her auburn curls. "between a peering it or appearing of it. Most cultures of the Near East had books of wisdom. They realized the foolishness of living a life merely as though born to a name alone. They are to be found in the Bible, Job being one and, of course, Proverbs as well as Ecclesiastes. There are two in the Dead Sea Scrolls. I worked on one called, 'The Book of Secrets.' Any philosopher worth his tenure knows the biggest secret is the truth of his or her own self. Yet where and when is it ever talked or written. 99 and 99 percent is a k'no'wing ignoring of it. A b c's of a b'ng c'ng now anybody appearing of it in wordsz in ignore"ance of any k'no'wing it. Of still awareness that subject of a being that I am is is denied on and on ad infinitum ad nauseum," she added with a mischievous grin.

"Hey, I would'nt have it any other way. It's on, of, to, for, from, or about that subject of a being that I am thirsting. You could pee it directly into my mouth. Not to be the lewd and crude as's w'hole artist. Seriously your words give my brain and my heart a serious hand job. I hope y'all don't take this the wrong way but my brain listening hearing ringing with the sound of your voice has been in one long orgasm."

The room settled with a layer of quiet as Mor prepared his drawing materials. He looked up. Her eyes probed his. He could feel her as a molten spring spilling crashing over flooding his sense of identity.

"All true revelations are self-revelations? Revelations of a being of that awareness that I am is is, of which you speak?" he asked as he kneaded a wad of rubber eraser. Working the wad renewed his confidence. A man picking up his tools, stretching out, sharpening, tuning. Preparing for a task of pure love creativity. Drawing on it. His inward being expressed now without word. Drawing on the wordfreedom of right brain awareness. She now had her spoken word. He had his silence in sight. His of line, design, proportion, shading. All she now had pored into him he would pour back into her eyez z z. Into the drawing of it. Into a merging of a being c'ng out in her eyez z z'i'on a being now him. Herhimit. Make a little love get down tonite played into his mind.

Mor warmed up a square stick of hard pastel sharpening it on a piece of sandpaper. He would begin in loose focus. Pouncing some pastel powder on the fresh sheet before drawing with his left hand. In the cross over duplicity that seems to thread through life, favoring the literal right hand, he now sought balance on the left. He found that symmetry divide of L-mode or R mode had been predominated for way too long by the subdominate in word spell. Now a busting out of it by a dialectic debate raging in word to break that spelling of a b c's wide open.

El or a'R'e ye. As function of it or merely a being c'ng a peering it in the first place? He wondered awhile still awareness of a being c'ng primarily in sight. Are we all turning into or out of a being c'ng still in the first place? Embracing or denying in word any formation of it in memory? His field of view focused on the paper on the drawing board with one eye. A peering it at her eyez z z' with the other. "Just let your head fall until your chin rests on your chest, then slowly rotate it 360 degrees in a complete layed over loop."

"Is this to get perspective?"

"Ma'am if you don't mind my saying but that I'm on fire from you. Yes ma'am, in that I'm trying for perspective, purpose, elevation, mind and heart." Words kept getting out as he gave attention primarily to a visual non verbal a'R'e'ye of it in ar't'is't mode. Art being c'ng out in that singular eye. A y eye of that I am seeing drawing. Of a hand merely tracing eye. Feeling that field of view merely following eyez z' on you or out of me. We all turning into or out of are'y'all of it. Or are we all still turning not? Of a b'ng c'ng still in the first place? A b'ng of him c'ng watching in her'eyez z z' a head turning rotating. Muscles cording. The snake eye a peering it out in her'eyez z z. She'e now the temptress he mused.

"Loosens you up. Now turn slightly slowly to your left. Good. Throw your shoulders back.

Is that what you are looking for in the painting, a visual philosopher's stone to transmute base metal?" he asked, watching the pastel crayon dancing over the tooth of rag paper.

Christina responded with a Gioconda smile to break Leonardo's heart.

☼

Light faded into dusk as he sketched Christina. He leaned back in his chair and looked with first one eye closed, then the other. "Interesting that we always say eye of the artist. Not eyes'za. Could it be that attention stays indivisible starring out of one eye or two? That paying attention affords me a being c'ng indivisible from you? That love shared as thoth'tsz of it indivisible awareness means we all turn into or out of an in'visibility? Of it. A being c'ng now dividing it merely as a k'no'wing out of it in word. Any mere in word definition of it still indivisible awareness of a b c's?

"The Dark'ness so quickly absorbs the light of a y dialectic debate. Of it." she now replied with a straight poker face.

"Absorbed? It has burnt me up." At least any residual dross of me he thought. Or you. In one love. In any live portrait Mor found intimacy with anyone that he drew. It seems that seeing in a wordfreedom favors picking up in'visibility that still indivisible. As'words divide it as'z'any thoth'tsz of it, he mused on the supernatural status of any appearing of it. Of that awareness of any seer see'ng of it remaining quite indivisible. Indivisible from any seer see'ng out of any point of view of you now a peering it out into any in word appearing of it supersonically as'z'any thoth'tsz of it in'formation. He now thought of it as'z'any thoth'tsz of a God esse to be letter'ally a b c's appearing out of it in word'sza. Now out of any eyez z z'a k'no'wing it as other y'sz'a mere idea. Of a b'ng c'ng a peering out in any mirror now finding that indivisible divided as'k'no'wing of it appearing me he mused with amusement. "Me finding now that I am mirrored knowing out of it as'z'any me'mory as thoth'tsz of a being other wise by the power . . ."

"A peh'ss'y w'hole power." Christina interjected with that ironic smile.

"P'ss'y'n'c'ng whole power in her'eyez z z a peering it out in word spelling of it as'z'any thoth'tsz appearing of it." Mor found himself at attention of a b"lack eye of a God esse to be letter'all'y y'all a creator creation of a b c's of a b'ng c'ng a gain of it out in word as'z' any appearing of it in any name alone. It still in a wordfreedom indivisible in'visibility. Now at attention it seemed a're'y'all of supernatural supersonic's'word by its definition cleaving any artist seer off in a cunning uncanny duplicity that as thoth'tsz letter'all'y divides us as'word. As'word sound wayeve function of eL'eft brain he'misphere. A sphere'y'e b'all race of man'as'z z z'any memory enclosed by a surface eve're'y point of which is equidistant from the center point of view of you of a y eye b'all c'ng a peering it. Now as'z'any a peering it out in word's'za appearing of it in formation now awhile. Yet in fact we all turn around continuing still in the first place as awareness of a b'ng c'ng in a wordfreedom indivisible in'visibility. A b c's of a being still c'ng any e'g'g's ting motion of. He thought he'd choke on the in word information poring into his mind. Or a y her'eyez z z'i'on it. She'e'na had loosed some in word store of y'sz domus. A b'ng c'ng h'ome for this home'or boy.

"Why did you give up painting?" she asked.

"A long story. I won't bore you with the details."

"Somehow I doubt it's boring. The painting at Korner's home shows there are some interesting images stirring in your head. Why not let some more out?"

"I was responsible for a death." Echoing in his head the words sounded hollow and disembodied. Outside the window, a flag snapped in the wind and eucalyptus trees shone black against the purpling sky. Mor smelled a sour odor coming off his body as a silence rang the room. He tried to read her but the shadows had deepened. Her thoughts seemed suspended beyond the room's boundaries.

"Perhaps you better explain."

"Guilt by association is still guilt," Mor offered with a heavy sigh.

"Are you talking about your marriage?" she asked, still maintaining her pose while picking up a transparency from her desk.

"My marriage, love, hate, and destiny. The killing of my wife was the result of the influence of James Korner. He brought you and I together and if he repeats his past, he'll tear us apart."

"Rather ominous warnings about a friend."

"Korner is the worst of friends. I get involved with him to satisfy a longing for adventure, even knowing the adventure can turn fatal or maybe because it can."

"Sounds like a reasonable motive."

"Innocent people like my wife get hurt. Gina was the price I paid for following Korner. Now I'm stuck with him again to resolve the devastation. I know Korner and he ain't after ageless wisdom."

"He hired me to translate the Copper Scroll. He wants the gold of Herod the Great, the one who restored Solomon's temple," she said. "Herod had his wife, her brother, grandfather, and mother, and his own sons put to death. His passions were fierce and ungovernable."

"A perfect match for Korner. Where is this treasure?" he asked, resurfacing the wedge-point pastel crayon on a square of sandpaper.

"The Romans looted the treasure in 70 CE, including an immense seven-branch candelabra and possibly the Arc of the Covenant. Three and a half centuries later, Visigoths sacked Rome and pillaged the entire wealth of the Eternal City. Much of Herod's treasure is believed to have ended up in France where the Visigoths established mountain sanctuaries. Treasure hunters from Knights Templar to Nazis have searched in vain ever since.

"Forget the scholarship, you're helping Korner find buried treasure, quite a come down from the altruistic seeker of truth you present to your students. Where are your ethics, lady?" he asked half in jest, tossing the crayon in a box and shoving the easel drawer shut.

"Your friend brought me high def reproductions of the complete Copper Scroll, digitally restored by Electricite de France to its original sheen, no less. I saw it as bait. Now in that I am curious about you. When the lines are drawn, whose side will you be standing on? It seems there is no love lost between you and Korner. He told me you were still angry about something he did. What is in it for you?"

"See, the thing is I've known James since we were teen agers running wild around the Windy City. I know of his roots. I've known his people. People who adopted him to work on their failing farm. Well-intentioned losers but still solid farm stock, a country cultural pool that would pretty much dry up and disappear from following generations.

"His folks went belly up. Lost the farm. Moved to a hardscabble edge of the city. Then his Ma dies and Pops gets all drank up in the bottle. James drifts to the criminal side of town. See James is completely different stock. I've done some research, basically I learned that James has some good old jew boy in him but on the criminal Meyer Lansky side of town.

"Ours' was a marriage made in weed. But what happened, less than a week after we met, I run into him at a south-side blues club. We were underaged but always managed to get fake id's. Anyway, James is all worked over like a bad step-child, black eye, broken nose, head wrapped in a bandage, I says, "Gee'z, didja get the license number of the truck?" sort of thing. Turns out he was shaggin' the wife of some local wise guy. Got caught with his pants down. Told me the dude fired a round between his legs. That was the real beginning of our relationship. Maybe it was the blows to his head, brought out the psycho in him.

"That was the summer before he went to Nam. August 1st, he shot me. We'd been out poachin' deer. James still had some country boy in him. Naturally he acted all upset like it was all some terrible mishap. Took me a year to recover, missed my heart by an inch. I realized then that he could be or could have been my executioner. Except for your ma you'll never have a closer relation than with your executioner.

"See, men have this unspoken bond, the brotherhood of the warrior and all men were warriors at one time or another. Some of the most nondescript meek Marvins out there were real killers in a past loop. Still y'all warriors fall in time, the best with their mocassin's on. Most times this bond is invisible, struck in some mystic battle from another lifetime where friends now may have been enemies then. All men potential executioners executing each other. If there is other incarnations of our situation, like me appearing here with you. Somehow I'm feeling like I've known you a real long time." Mor felt his heart race with his words.

"I felt that, the moment I layed eyes on the painting, your painting of Adam and Eve at James Korner's house. Tell me more about this jew boy Korner," she replied with a curious expression.

"So James went off to the war. Actually in the beginning, he was doing okay. Flying solo, a single engine prop Cessna, dropping smoke bomb markers to signal jets where to drop their napalm bomb loads of greased fire. He was in and out while everything on the ground was still there. Just before a shitstorm of burning jellied gas, enhanced with phosphorous to make it burn hot enough to melt flesh into bones, got launched on basically unsuspecting civilians. Then James flying above it all in his little two-seater bird got knocked down by a farmer with a homade shotgun. Now he's on the ground, seeing up close and personal what exploding jellied gas does to human beings.

"Some mamasans, out cutting sugarcane, got caught in this hellfire. A local surgeon in a field tent recruited James to help hold the poor women, what was left of them, as legs and arms were amputated. He told me one had her breasts melted into her ribs. The worst part, he said, was the dignity these people showed, despite the pain. We spent many hours talking of this. He made me do drawings, from his memories and my imagination till their anguish became seared on the paper and in my mind.

"Eventually James made it back in a prisoner exchange but instead of coming home he gets reassigned for combat just in time to find himself in a little mud and stick village called Mai Lai. He would never talk to me about it but I read the report from the investigation that came out a year or so later. It made me appreciate his state of mind.

"I already had some inkling on that psycho state of mind from my mother who was a certified bi-polar schizophrenic. Sometimes she'd look at me hard with dead pan eyes and say the darndest things like, "you ain't shit boy!" or "you ain't never gonna get away with it!" I knew from growing up around her that Korner was then and is now psychotic.

"But I'm just an idiot on a fool's errand. I guess in my heart what I really hoped to find was a muse to fire up my passion to paint. Funny, that word is so close to pain. I can't guarantee that the story won't end with Korner taking the cash and leaving a trail of bodies behind." He saw her now studying him. A silent pause echoed his breathing. Then she spoke.

"On that I am without any guarantee that will not happen but can raise the stakes with some ancient intact papyri. A virtual and e've're y existing treasure trove of our ancestry. And when I say h'our, I mean IndoEuroSemeticEgyptian with the essence, the quintessence of y'all in it. A time machine of a b c's ma's'king a being c'ng as'king of it now a k'now'ing out of a ka's mic being. Trust me, Dark. That I am about to tell you will show why getting involved with Korner one more time is worth the risk."

"Go ahead. I still think you're being reckless or downright stupid." He pulled the drawer open and retrieved the stick he'd just tossed in. He moved the pastel quickly over the surface of the drawing, dancing over highlights, getting down in the shadowy recesses.

"Earlier you mentioned the burning bush in reference to your vision of the illuminatus."

"I call it that because of the flames. I saw fire, tongues of flame appeared before my eyes, in the middle of Geary Boulevard in the concrete heart of San Francisco. That's why I call it the 'burning bush,' even though there was no bush. Instead I saw a pyramid. The flame moved from the foreground until it capped the pyramid, surging with a roiling helix sea of eyeballs. Later I tried to describe it to a friend and 'burning bush' just got tagged on it. Words can only betray, only belittle the astonishment I felt at the time. You don't have a vision like that, so much as the vision has you. "as'king of it a k'no'wing of ants"" He finished with several slaps of a chamois and a few swipes of a sponge blender over the pastel. Then he brought up the highlights, stabbing with a rubber eraser. "Ants. We all seem to turn into living out ant lives. Yet as'king of it. Revealed in a vision having you then. Having you now every day for the rest of your life."

"Perhaps, there was a bush in your vision. The 'burning bush' as the Great Pyramid in the Moses story. Certain papyrii stolen from a pharaoh's tomb less than 100 years ago reveal the potential identity of everyone from Noah, Abraham, Moses, and Aaron, even Adam and Eve. It seems the bible is Egyptology revised to disguise as mere shepherds certain pharonic EgyptoIndoEuropeanSemetic ancestors. A shepherd as'king of it with monotheistic warrior priests in an Exodus from Egypt. The w'ay out now az's'ex's ting as'z thoth'tsz of a singular Great God esse to be letter'all'y y'all a b c's of a b'ng c'ng now as'king of it a k'no'wing d"na'eye'll of it. Now a k'no'wing out of it a chintzy chislin' thin'king of anybody. Azs'exodus attention now captivated int'word a twis'ting in two a k'no'wing d'na'eye'll of it. At attention merely a peering it now as'king of it out in word captivity appearing of it a slave. Their disguise came eight centuries later in Babylonian captivity as the Babylonians hated all things Egyptian. Biblical scribes revised their ancestory as Mesopotamian."

"As'king of it. This wouldn't be pharaoh Akh-what's his name?" Mor continued to work the highlights with the eraser, cleaning it with a pull like gray taffy, kneading out the pastel residue.

"No, but maybe his son or half brother, Tutankhamen. I am talking about the real treasure of King Tut. Papyrus scrolls of sacred revelations handed down to me from my maternal grandmother. Grandmama's father, fifth Earl of Carnarvon, financed the excavation of Tutankhamen's tomb in the early nineteen twenties. She got to tag along to the Valley of the Kings with her father and the American, Howard Carter. They made a premature and illicit foray into the tomb two months before the official opening. They chiseled a mouse hole, just big enough for them to slide in. Later they replaced the mortar and stones, even using a duplicate wooden stamp to impress the unsuspecting. It was a put up job but I think enough money changed hands and people were willing to look the other way. Of course two-month-old mortar would not look the same as the thirty-two-hundred-year-old mortar, but they pulled off one of the biggest frauds in history by covering their handiwork with artifacts from the antechamber. You can see the pile in old black and white photos. It worked because they were able to keep the experts out until the entire passageway was cleared and every trace of their activity was obliterated." Christina leaned back, lacing her fingers behind her head. Mor felt the hairs on his arms stand up.

"The papyri they found, might well have changed the course of nations, but they were never produced and probably would have been denounced at that time. A young girl's innocence and later the bond of mother to daughter protected them. Worth more than the gold and precious stones, the papyri remain hidden."

"You have them?" His throat clotted as he attempted speech.

"Written in hieratic, a cursive form of hieroglyphs. No one could read the script back in the day. I had kept them in a safe in the City, until someone broke in and stole them a week ago."

"So you're saying you have proof?"

"Archeological proof. With this Hebraic-hieroglyphic reconciliation, and names of certain pharaohs carved in stone stelae and cartouches we can recognize the patriarchs, Abraham, Moses, and Aaron."

"They weren't shepherds?"

"Shepherd kings. Pharaohs. Now you see why I want Korner to hunt down the missing papyri."

"This talk of pharaohs is intriguing. I want to know more. I'm feeling like my life has been meaningless until now. I mean, screw Korner. Use him and abuse him. I've seriously thought about killing that bastard myself. He's consumed by greed and power over people's lives. Part of that cancer that eats away at so much of this country but don't get me started. Hell, yes. I'm your man. Whatever I can do."

He returned to the image coming up on his drawing board. They sat in the muted light of the room, letting the quiet take the place of conversation. Christina's breathing became his breathing, Mor's heart beating in rhythm with hers. He retraced the contour of her eyes the bones of her cheeks down to the tip of her nose, then along the moist flesh of her lips. He stroked Christina's chin down to the unlined flesh of her elongated neck.

"Have you ever known somebody for a brief time only to lose them," she asked. "And not regret what little time you had together?"

He heard her voice but could not see where it came from. The words repeated till he realized she spoke to him from inches away. When she touched his shoulder, he felt current passing from her fingertips to the back of his hand squeezing the hunk of eraser.

He reached up and cupped the back of her head, drawing her lips to his. Christina stiffened. She jerked free, balled her fist, and punched him. The blow left him stunned with blurred vision. By the time his head cleared, she had gone.

☼

Wind knifed into Korner when he stepped from the Lincoln at the firing range. He pulled at his heavy wool overcoat, smiling at how only a few miles could separate hot and cold in Northern California. The rawness was a welcome distraction from his troubled thoughts. Dragging his fingers over the stubble on his jaw, he felt fleshiness puffing on bone. The years had piled on. Time for one last job.

A man had to do certain things in life despite any misgivings, like letting Warren play him for a chump. Johnstone Warren, his employer and founder of Messing Technologies, dangled the Copper Scroll to him as a diversion. When he dug for Warren's real intentions, placing cold cash in the right hands for information, the shock at what he found left him reeling like a drunk. Warren had designed a personal final solution in a word. Something about a word beginning the world and a word ending the world. He didn't know how such a thing was possible but now he had to figure which side to choose and was there a side to choose.

Korner rummaged through the trunk for a worn canvas satchel with stuffed side pockets and frayed shoulder strap. For those non-lethal engagements, he had the Taser. The pistol held a compressed air cartridge and could fire fifty thousand volts into the victim, causing involuntary muscular convulsions. Not a lot of convincing was required with the Taser. He thought of using the weapon on Christina in a little low voltage foreplay.

He hoped an hour blowing holes in paper targets at the range would settle his mind. From the satchel, he pulled a nickel-plated Colt Python.357 that fit his hand like a glove. It had the report he needed to clear his head and the cordite stench to settle his nerves. Thinking about the end of days made him wonder what he really gave a flying fart about. He was a family of one and friends were negotiable. Money was always funny, and he needed plenty drugs to keep going strong. The checkered grip of a pistol held a high position on his list, a good whore. Maybe, most of all, the fan of a card hand on the the tips of his fingers.

Why the cards, he wondered, beyond passing time. Thoughts of Colleen, the new girl at Zina's brothel, baby cakes. Her tight, small body, with a trace of baby fat, heaving with pleasure against the handcuffs and ropes Korner enjoyed using. Colleen was the perfect whore who enjoyed matching him kink for kink.

He held his stance and fired the heavy weapon. Young Asian toughs on either side emptied numerous clips from their Glocks. You gotta love automatics, he thought, especially when you be making the bullets. Salutations, Warren, you old devil, POW, POW......POW.

These damn paintings. POW.... POW... the paintings were the umbilicus joining him and Mor, Warren buying one of Mor's vision paintings. So now, it's gotta be him and the slice of professor to do the dirty painting...POW..POW..POWPOWPOW. Should he have to choose between saving himself or Mor, well, he'd made that decision the night Gina died. For now, he needed the Darkness to get next to the Professor and the key she held to the Scrolls. Korner knew he was not one of her biggest fans. She was also an unknown piece to the expanding Warren puzzle. He may have come on too strong with his questions about the Sicarri. Christina seemed to get suspicious at his intelligence. As if metaphysics were beyond his comprehension. Money was money, gold was gold, their higher meanings for those not relentless enough to make the score. He squeezed off another round, felt the Python recoil with the blast of gunpowder, and watched another slug rip thru the paper target. Burnt powder, sweat and gun oil made him smile. He slouched out of his firing stance, letting the weight of the weapon drag his arms down.

If a man stood before him instead of paper, the lead would rip his flesh, the hydrostatic charge letting loose a tidal wave in his bloodstream. All the voodoo around Warren and his last word meant nothing if he could be killed like any other man.

☼

A crescent moon glowed above the tree line as Mor headed for his truck. Despite the shock of her blow, he still tasted her lips. He knew she'd get inside him long before he could get inside her. He wondered if she was attached, or interested in his guilt stained offerings. Would he regret it if she was. He knew he wanted her too much to pursue her.

He stowed the box easel and drawing board with the sketch of Christina in the pickup. He should have given it to her, but then things got a bit awkward at the end. She'd started a hunger in him that could only be satiated one way, if not with an exchange of bodily fluids, with pain and paint. This picture book might have some ideas but he'd rather paint her than Fools and Priestesses.

Mor drove from the Stanford campus to a gas station. He found a pay phone, slipped a couple coins, and dialed.

"Korner. What is?"

"Is what is."

"Cryptic fucker. How about we meet for dinner, Toraya Sushi on Fillmore off Pine? I'll be there in forty five minutes."

The receiver went dead. Mor looked at the telephone with a frown. Same old Korner, talking like every conversation was monitored. He finessed through San Francisco traffic till finding the restaurant. The sushi bar ran the length of a narrow room with a few tables in the back. Only a handful of people occupied the bar as he pulled up a stool.

"A couple of Sapporas, Ike," Korner called from the entrance. One hand hit the bar with a slap, the other curling around Mor's shoulders, fingers digging into his flesh. Korner wore a red Gortex windbreaker over a black and white print shirt unbuttoned to his sternum. A St. Christopher's medal on a gold chain glimmered as it bounced off his broad chest. He dropped his overcoat on a hook. Tan canvas drawstring pants and leather Topsiders gave the impression that he had just stepped off a schooner.

"Make mine ice water," Mor said when the two bottles of Japanese beer appeared.

"No way, old friend. Tonight we drink for old times and new." Korner was feeling the juice, letting his body dip and flow like the old days in Chicago. Mor dipped to catch his uppercut. Bellies bumped with hugs as cheeks got slapped.

Mor blew off his sobriety with a shrug. The decision had a higher purpose, relating to art and breaking through the inertia of hiding for too many years. Bullshit. He needed a drink.

Their voices gained volume. He and Korner moved from beer to hot sake.

"How was the gig with Christina?" Korner asked with his worst wise-guy smile. He stretched with his back to the bar, arms spread, fingers tapping the polished edge. Light popped and sparked off ruby serpent's eyes set in a gold ring circling one finger.

"A moment happened and I kissed her." He pointed to his cheek. "She gave me this bruise."

"Smooth, man. She's not the kind of chick to jump." Korner pushed off the bar and pivoted on the stool while gunning his sake.

"Christina isn't any kind of chick. There's real soul there, mon."

"Here we go with the Madonna shit. Smarts or not, the bitch pisses and farts like us other mortals," he retorted, tossing some bills on the bar.

"Fuck off, Korner. Is there any woman you can fake respect for?"

"Not one. Near as I can figure, women have the world by the short and curlies, especially when they are a fine piece of ass. Christina has permanent residence in cloud coo-coo land. She wants to be a goddess."

Mor headed on out the front door. Outside, chill fog wrapped its shroud around him. Foghorns moaned as he jammed his hands into his coat pockets stomping his feet on the hard pavement. Maybe he had idealized Gina. When she died, he never finished mourning her. Was he now mixing those feelings with those for Christina. Only one afternoon with her. Was she that one woman as all women, Madonna and goddess and savior, yet still so human?

He watched Korner through the steamy window as he settled the bill and slipped on his coat. He paused to talk with a red-haired man sitting at the bar near the door, huddled over a drink. They exchanged words as Korner started for the street. He turned, grabbed the man by the back of his jacket, and jerked him to the floor. He gave him a couple shots with his feet. The man stayed down.

Outside, Korner stood on the curb and pulled on a pair of leather gloves. "Son of bitch has been tailing me for two days."

"He a cop?"

"No, private stooge."

"He must be on you for good reason."

"Who knows?" Korner replied. "Come on. Get over your hissy fit and I'll show you my new pad."

Chapter 4

Stepan Rakitin stood with a phone while gazing out a window in the Pyramid on Montgomery street, a 900 foot tall icon piercing the San Francisco skyline. Through a vent above his head came the sound of wind shivering the 200 foot aluminum spire capping Johnstone Warren's lean pyramid. Nearby Warren observed Rakitin's erect posture, forehead nearly touching the glass with the tips of his shoes a foot back from the steep angle of the walls.

Stephan Makarovich Rakitin held the telephone receiver from his ear. Rakitin brushed at the sleeve of his tailored suit jacket, the starched cuffs of his Egyptian cotton shirt, pinned with gold cufflinks in the shape of eagles. He stood a few feet from Warren in the penthouse office.

"Who is that fool, Stepan?" asked Warren, stretched out in a wheel chair reconfigured to accomodate his nearly inert prone form. He remained paralyzed with the exception of his left forearm, wrist, and fingers. When speech failed him, he reverted to an optically controlled word processor both displaying and voicing his dialogue on a large overhead screen. He now thought of himself as machine. Ma shee'na. Out in her'eye of eve're'ybody of Kali ma'ss with her fang tearing her children in time to pieces. Soon he would be mere microscopic nanoengineered viral storming bits of it. Of it in her'eye way of eve re y'body asz z za ma'ss body. Ma re'y'as'z z z g'round in pigments that I am imagining her immortalized colored by my design.

Rakitin cupped his hand over the receiver. "Our watchdog on James. Seems Korner sucker punched and kicked the crap out of him."

"Tell him to go back to spying on adulterous husbands. I could do a better job on Korner from here," Warren replied, rapping his wheelchair with a cane. Beyond the angled windows, the steel trusses of the Bay Bridge were partly erased by incoming fog.

"How long have you been in my employ?"

"Coming on fifteen years." Rakitin glanced over at Warren's emaciated body framed by the wrinkled city on seven hills. Like Jerusalem. Like Rome. Like her, ma'ss nature stretched out as the peninsula below touching bay waters reaching the sea.

"Long enough to know that I am not crazy," Warren said, adding emphasis to his words with raps of the cane. "My great grandfather, Jacobe, was a son of a butcher. In seven generations the Warren family has carved out a pretty good slice. Sure we all turn out to have a few bones and skulls in the closet. It's a big closet. Full of Brotherhoods of Templars and Masons and that popular lore. Allegiances. Allegiances, often must cross geopolitical lines, shadow governments. Cost of doing business. The Warren boys never flaunted their power.

"Jacobe's eldest son made his stake in Yerba Buena, where we sit right now. This was the edge of the original shoreline, where the San Francisco dream began. Our Trading Company had to circumnavigate national boundaries and of course there was opium and the China trade, and Chinese labor and whores to blame for the sudden appearance of the drug.

"'Old Brains' Halleck designed the original Warren Block built on this site to withstand earthquake and fire. Good thing too," he cackled. "'Old Brains' designed four stories of iron and stone, built on a raft of redwood logs sunk in the mud. Just below our feet men smelted ingots of gold from the Sierras in the brick-lined basement. They cached it all deep in the ground in an iron-sheathed vault. The place got the name Golgotha after the building withstood the nineteen oh eight earthquake and fire. A hundred million dollars in gold resting in her vault, disappeared after the dust settled from the quake and fire. They found the city leveled, the vault empty. Looters were blamed." Warren rasped, pausing to sip fluid from a straw.

"By the nineteen fifties, this Block was full of rats and trash, footings riddled with dry rot. San Francisco Bay's harbor now pushed back by blocks filled with sunken ships and former hills. When the Warren Block was finally turned into a parking lot, the place was a wasteland of bohemians.

"Remember the European Messing partners had no interest in the site. Their interests were on the East Coast and Europe. Only I was drawn to it, like a magnet. The history, fire and gold. So we all turned the starter on the Pyramid in sixty nine," Warren stopped to catch a labored breath. "Son of a bitch, digging 30 feet past the old vault, I found a cavity where all that lost bullion had fallen. The Bank of America claimed half of the gold which they then used the to erect their black granite monstrosity, that is still seventy four feet shorter than the Pyramid.

"Such are the ways of the great mystery. You see my own body, or whoever gets stuck with it when I pass," he cackled, letting out a string of muffled farts. "Here it is ravaged by a cancer created by the merger of toxic petrochemicals and pharmaceuticals. What I have designed here is a fast acting bromide of sorts for the mind. Radiation treatments have accelerated my conception, my solution in dissolution. After all, I'm only saving man from the impending crises of microbial retribution."

Now he lay upon his pile. His gaunt frame, shriveled on a steel wheelchair, chrome rails extended to accommodate his prone position. At his feet, within the panorama of heaven, ocean, bridges, and skyline, people invisibility lost in the vastness of the scale. He knew the volk carried their weight or fell under it. He also knew pumps maintained his breathing, steadily lifting and lowering his emaciated figure. Of a Ma cheen. As'Kali ma'ss body. A black singular body of itself creating devouring shrinking stretching reabsorbing anybody out in her'eye. Of eve're'ybody'sz'anybody. As subsumed subsuming all black'g"round into or out in her'eye now on him or it dissolving any and all appearance of it black still one singular black 'g"round body of awareness. A b'lack' with intent of a b'ng c'ng a gain.

"I'll end the tyranny of the in word spell by setting loose a self-replicating biovirtuocerebral virus to scatter every spoken and written language black into one wordfreedom thoughtfree awareness of a being c'ng now a gain turning a black'g'round echoing n any k'no'wing of it still invisibility. D"ark informing it. eNcirclement of it. Of such rolls or roles any appearing of it as anyone imagined image a're'y'dhi'a'ting out in her'eye of eve're'y'body. Kali ma as'z z z'Isis meri with the cool fire now of not knowing the knower y'll DNA. In her'eyez z afire. A lightning synapse now zapping the entire tower of rable babal. Humanity will be purged and the heavens praised."

"Korner will do his part?" Rakitin asked, moving to adjust various i v's running around his charges frail body.

"I think our James will follow his self-interest, no matter what havoc he may cause. The damaged professor and that lost painter are essential to my plans, but I figure you have some image waiting to substitute, Mao doing a goat or some such bloody rot. I can only try and make it irresistible to Korner, the Professor, the painter. Offer them an opportunity doing what they love most in life, only a piece of the puzzle at a time. Contact our James and only bleed him for information if, well, necessary."

☼

The three-story townhouse jutted out of the steep incline of Divisidero Avenue. Korner and Mor entered a paneled foyer, floored in a herringbone pattern of polished oak. A spiral staircase led to the upper stories. "I had to fight city hall, my man. Everything is hysterical in this San Francisco, and I don't mean historical. She ain't much, there's lot bigger joints in this neck of town, but I call her home," he laughed, stepping across the foyer and spreading two heavy pocket doors to reveal a high ceiling drawing room with the far wall of steel and glass continuing up two full stories of welded I-beam framework covered in several coats of gloss black paint. The room, floored with the same herringbone pattern as the foyer, was empty of furniture. "Yah, they didn't like all the steel taking over. But, she's my building, at least for a while, and I need steel, almost more than gold," Korner said as he strode up the stairs to an open air deck sparkling with a view, falling away to the north, the Marina and the gray chop of the Bay. Cold air brought Mor's hand to his cheek.

"I love how this town sits on the edge of the Pacific, just waiting to break loose and float on out to sea. We gotta go sailing. I've got access to a sloop and a power launch berthed down there." Korner spread his arms as though giving his approval of the vista as he pointed to a breakwater, a mile below, spangled with lights. He turned suddenly, the wind rearranging his hair.

"Follow me to the stars." He motioned to a narrow iron stairway. They clambered up to a flat roof with duck board walkway leading to a glass cupola. At their feet, city lights shimmered off to bay and ocean.

"No heat, but I've got tequila to put fire in your belly." A light rain tapped across the cupola as Korner took two drinking glasses from the small wood bar. He hunched as he poured, the red windbreaker taut across his shoulders. Mor stared at his back.

"To the future," he proposed, turning with an upraised glass. They settled into wicker armchairs.

"I told you about the professor. They don't make them like that anymore. Remember the women on Lake Geneva? Oh my living god, those Playboy bunnies. A man rarely scores like that."

"What have you got in mind, amigo?"

"A gig along the lines of the Ratnick brothers. Taking down the assholes."

Before Mor had left Chicago for the coast, Korner returned stateside from Vietnam. "I was doing my apprenticeship for being a drunk, putting away half-pints of Johnny Walker Red for breakfast, trying to wash away the bad ju-ju in my head,"Korner recalled as he swigged the tequila. "We hooked up at Buddie's, remember T-Bone was laying it down that night. We got good and drunked up. Talked you into driving my sixty two Caddy ragtop out to farm country. Remember?"

"Hell yes, I remember. I was scared shitless. I knew you had a serious death wish after Nam and enough booze in your blood. But then, I was right there with you. And the Ratnicks, come on. J.Q. and J.D., what a couple slime balls,"

"J.Q. had just finished kicking that little doggy to death with those pointy cowboy boots in the yard. Man, that set my teeth on edge. I could hardly wait to send that motha packing."

"All I remember is you running back, tossing a hand grenade and J.D. running from the barn with a pump shotgun, then you pushing me down me flooring it with my hand, us tearing off, windshield exploding," Mor replied as he held his glass up for a refill. "It was a helluva rush,"

"You needed a taste of being in the line of fire. Being moral is easy when you can pay or taxpay others to do the killing."

"For a few days I actually admired your bravado until I talked to Cheri Lynn, that teeny-bopper you were doing. That tartess had been lured away from your loving embrace by the Ratnick brothers' dope and promise of stardom on the porno screen. Seems jealousy was the real reason, not taking down bad guys. I finally had to admit you were mad."

"Unlike you? I never claimed to be a saint. By the way, putting the moves on the Professor was bad form, Dark bhud'dy."

"What's with this house?" Mor asked .

"I always swore I'd own no more than could fit in an army issue duffel bag. Still holds true. The house and boats, even the car belongs to the company I work for, Messing Technologies."

"Sounds German."

"I'm going to let you in on a little secret. Growing up when and where we did, you know, we were all aglow, the strongest and most righteous country in the world. We conquered evil in the greatest of wars. We believed. Even when I first enlisted, I felt proud to do my patriotic duty for our ongoing crusade to save democracy from the evil commies. Funny, I had those World War Two images playing in my head, the ones with parades of upturned raptured faces of the liberated in Europe. But after getting shot down, I found out, that's not the way it really was at all. We were there not to save but to kill. Kill every man, woman, child, and buffalo. The evil we fought in Europe had infected our body politic. We traded our democratic ideals for their more advanced chemical technology."

"So, can't lick 'em, join 'em?" Mor asked, wincing from another slug of tequila.

"I saved you, Darkey boy. I saved you from getting chewed up in that meat grinder. I never had a choice. They made that choice for me that day I saved you," Korner replied.

"Well, I guess I'm just one ungrateful son of a bitch. What about Gina? Did you save me from her as well?"

"Now you getting dirty. A part of me died with her," Korner answered with hanging head. When he looked up, his eyes were rimmed with tears.

"Christina fits into your plans somewhere. Don't try that bullshit about getting me back to painting or searching for truth. She knows you're a treasure hunter," Mor said shifting forward, the cane chair creaking with his weight.

"You're a loser afraid of what's in his own head. Don't tell me the Copper Scroll hasn't got you in a burn. Ancient treasure, a shot at the big score. See the possibilities or you might as well pull up the dirt blanket right now," Korner replied, letting tears fall shamelessly.

☼

Street-sweepers churned the curbside debris in the cold morning as Mor stretched his stiff muscles. He found his pickup parked outside Korner's house. He drove down Divisadero Avenue to the Bay and connections to the Golden Gate Bridge. By the time his head cleared from last night's drinking, he had crossed the bridge, and was heading north to the open country.

Reaching Santa Rosa he took the College exit off Highway 101, a few blocks west on an industrial parkway, to a local art supply outlet. He bought sable brushes, a sixteen by twenty inch stretched canvas, and tubes of oil colors for another run at painting. Buying the materials was easy, using them was another matter, he flashed. Leonardo Da Vinci called painting the granddaughter of nature and kin of God, born of all visible things brought forth from her womb of wombs. Not too much pressure, he mused. Maybe God painted the world with a red sable brush.

The sketch of Christina Shaughnessy clipped in his box easel sat on the seat beside him. He wanted to wait until he got to his cabin, where he would have perspective on its merit and his buried passion.

Korner was right about Christina. Her infectious intelligence put a steady buzz in his brain. Incomprehensible Morse code dots and dashes warned of danger, but, he wrote those off as the influence of the City's seven hills, the sweet sirens. Now he'd found his visions in her still maintained their power. He drove Highway 101, in his mind painting nude Roxx in the South of Market warehouse in parallel time with turning wheels.

As he had drifted into sleep in Korner's house, last night, he observed his head replicating into a vast sea of heads ever growing smaller to the horizon. He woke to sunlight, seeing the pyramid and eye traced in the plaster texture of the ceiling. He hoped the sanctuary of his cabin would help fade the dream.

Mor's truck rolled in under the Flying V archway. A mile further on he passed the original hacienda built by George Washington Vanwater in 1880. Armed with Winchesters and Colts, Vanwater had fought a bandit named "Blackie" Dan White and his killer sidekick "Wylykie" Joe for rights to the original homestead. He extended his holdings, buying out ex-Confederate soldiers homesick for their Southern roots. He had seen a photograph of their forlorn faces sitting with rifles across bony knees on the very porch he now passed. In the shadows of their eyes were the distant battlegrounds of Chickamauga, Antietam, and Shiloh. Canvas packs, filled with hardtack and black powder slung over tattered army shirts of butternut gray.

He wanted to blast on through a gateway of time and roll into a world of tattooed laughing braves, Black Bart, grizzled miners, outlaw half-breeds in a dogfight for nuggets, nookie, and dying with your boots on. Bring it on up to date with washtubs of iced longneck Corona, fifths of Quervo, with lime and salt. Marfil papers rolled around sticky ganja, pig meat roasting in a pit dug by three-hundred-pound men juiced on steroids, cocaine, and Jack Daniels, as fiddlers played to big-busted gals shaking their moneymakers. Once again, it seemed Korner had colonized his mind.

Five miles of tortured dirt road brought him back to his one-room cabin. Water laughed over rocks, Yellowthroats trilled to unseen mates in broad oak canopies, as wind ripped through the broken hills. Time here was counted in decades and millennia, unhampered by the Rolex-measured fragments of the urban world. He eased the pickup across a ford in the creek to stow his easel, drawing board, and art supplies inside the cabin.

Several years ago Mor had drifted into the tiny town of Lago Norte to escape his mourning over Gina. The annual Wild West celebration was going full tilt boogie. Mock dance hall women struted in tight bodices, hair dressed with ostrich plumes amongst gingham sunbonnets tied under the more conservative chins. Men postured with hog leg pistols strapped against fringed buckskin, and bat-winged chaps. There was a good crowd of broad Buckaroo hats, and jangling spurs. A smattering of stoic Indians drifted around, sombreros cocked to shadow tired eyes. He had set out his easel, offering to draw anyone interested in sitting for a portrait. Matriarch, Thelma Greer, with every day of her ninety-one years etched on her face, sat for a sketch, and introduced him to her brother, Merle Vanwater. Merle, lean as prairie grass and watchful under a gray Stetson, needed a carpenter. He had offered Mor a home on his Flying V Ranch, a twelve-foot trailer infested with a family of wood rats big as squirrels, and recently ransacked by a hungry black bear. He had accepted, building his own cabin from materials scavenged from outbuildings and a bone-pile of windows big as sheets of plywood, salvaged from a grand hotel that had defined the locale during the stagecoach era. Carpentry work on a rustic development accessed by an airstrip came soon after.

Compared to the manicured university landscape, the valley stretching below for miles seemed wild though abraded by a century of logging and cattle ranching. Mor hiked the mile to his thinking spot near the traces of a prehistoric native village. He favored one among the silent impressions that may have been the sweat lodge. A haunting laughter teased him as he tried to return to a world lost to his white-bread roots.

He stretched out on a flat-topped boulder, closed his eyes, and listened to the water gurgling from a spring. He imagined the village alive, huts of thatched tules and basket granaries bulging with acorns. Wood smoke drifting over hunters bearing deerskin quivers of obsidian-tipped arrows. Women swayed in a grinding song, stone pestles rising and falling in unison. All thrived with the songs and laughter of naked people. He imagined they were still there, hidden in minerals, plants, and currents of air and water.

Maybe when the machines ran out of fuel, and steel wheels are lost on broken highways, eaten away by rust, the seed of the original people would drift back and reclaim their land. Paco and his kin belonged here. Mor wasn't sure, where he belonged. The peace he hoped for in this undeveloped land eluded him, still. He needed to make noise with machines to drive out nagging questions of his own validity.

He slid off the boulder, hiked back to his cabin, and loaded the steel box with carpentry tools on his pickup. He would exhaust himself in the remaining daylight. He drove two miles to a hidden lake surrounded by custom built log homes. Reaching the latest, he rolled out a hundred-foot orange extension cord, and fired up the generator. Its racket broke the even flow of natural sounds like an attack of bad temper. Mor buckled on his tool belt, shoving a sixteen-ounce framing hammer into one of its deep pockets. As he slipped two honed long-handled steel chisels through leather loops, packed a 30-foot 'fatboy' steel tape measure into a center pocket, jamming a speed square and flat carpenter pencils into side pockets thoughts of the owners of these second homes came to mind. They all seemed to be part of some syndicate flying in on occassion to hunt and fish. In all the days working on this site he'd never met any of them. The weight of his tool bags served as analgesic for the pain in his heart stirred by a loneliness of absentee ownership of these log castles in the sky while children huddled in rented shacks hard by the highway miles below.

He set up electric and gas powered chain saws, a lightweight circular saw, along with the worm-drive saw. As he hoisted the weight he thought of that turning worm. Shafted by a shaft turning and turning that raised thread, like a worm, wrapped around it in an endless screw meshing with a worm wheel, a toothed wheel gearing tearing wood flesh at e-powered forty-four thousand r.p.m.. That turning worm made it go round wherever the worm went. A clever mind, he thought, must work long hours to devise such an endless screw. Like wage slaves indentured to inflated rents.

Worms and wood danced in Mor's mind. Wormwood, artemisia, sage and wisdom, and crazed painters knocking back absinthe, infused with its oils. Vincent Van Gough, drunk on absinthe and stoned on Moroccan tobacco, slicing the lobe off his left ear and sending it as a gift to a brothel. The scream of the worm-drive played reveille to an inner in word world permeated with Christina and her scrolls and philosophy, a wormhole into which he was irrevocably drawn. He flashed on her as tree of knowledge with roots deep into the earth, arms raised to the heavens bore the sensual fruit, connected with a wisdom being a cosmic being. He wanted to realize her as cosmic prima materia, freedom beyond the graven womb. But this he could only do so long before longing prevailed. For now, he wanted to just drift on thoughts of her.

Mor, in his steel-toed boots and heavy tool bag, laughed at his folly. He looked down at the log. In a blink, the earth fell away. He found himself, log in his arms, flashing on what a nothing speck in the cosmos it all was. Him, the forest, the mountains, the planet, the system all disappeared in a starry sea. He set the log down and picked up the worm drive. The torque of the worm still whipped his arm.

He flashed on worms, wood, and iron nails hammered through bones and flesh. Wooden coffins with their lids nailed shut sunk in pits of earth as worms transfigured the body—ashes to ashes, dust to dust. Luther nailed his ninety-five theses on the door of the church at

Wittenberg to protest how the remission of sins was being sold. Holy Roman Emperor Charles V had him brought to Worms, Germany, on the charge of heresy. His reward was worms and dust. Stanford's board of regents waited to judge Christina. She seemed to him too wild and unfettered for a university prof but then he was an art school drop out. He found her manner baffling him in a way that recalled old demons still knawing away on the edges of his sanity.

Mor believed his world was just one memory, one glimpse, one snatch of a much larger unseen influencing life. He turned off the generator and packed his tools. The denial he developed over the last five years had unraveled. He must take another run at the brush. Did he fear who he would be without the disguise of his indifference. Hell ya, he did. It, that worm turning in his head, made him tremble.

He reached his cabin, shucked his clothes, and grabbed a towel hanging on a line. Buck naked, Mor ambled down the trail to the creek, wanting to paint his skin different colors.. Below the shallow ford, a deep pool offered a natural bath. Diving into icy water shocked his brain into cold reverence such that for a split second he thought he might not make it back out. Then, adrenaline flooding in, he found himself quickly hauling out. Goose pimples covered his flesh. as the chill shivered his spine.

Cold had settled in the creek bed as dusk fell. He grabbed his towel and ran back to the cabin to shake the chill. Bursting inside he grabbed a blanket, huddling in a fetal position till the rampant shivers rattling his bones finally subsided. What doesn't kill you, he thought. He slipped into dry clean clothes and grabbed the gold bottle in the cabinet. The liquor burned as it slid down his throat. He took another drink and set the bottle down. Now the madman living upstairs in his head had been invited down. He picked up the easel by its leather handle, kicked out the adjustable legs, and set it in the middle of the room.

He reached for a box of kitchen matches to light the kerosene lamp. He took two thick candles from a battered steamer trunk, once Gina's. He hoped the dim light would mask the rawness of painting after so long a break.

Mor gathered tubes of paint, fist-sized bottles of oil and turpentine, along with the sable brushes. He added a palette knife with broken tip and the tequila. He saved the blank canvas for last. Adjusting the easel for height he sat on a milk crate, and pulled out a thin wooden palette. The kerosene lamp along with the two candles flickered on the cabinet's chipped top, lighting the empty canvas with a golden hue.

Cold in the cabin stiffening his fingers, he kindled a fire in the wood stove, retrieving logs from the porch. Smoke escaped before he shut the stove's metal door, acrid fumes blended with kerosene, turpentine, and tequila. With the fire stoked, he went back to the easel and canvas. There was the sketch of Christina on his drawing board and one of Gina, done when they first met. The two women had the same curly hair, high cheekbones, protruding bird eyes, and full lips. He took another pull on the Cuervo. He let the sketch of Gina fall, bringing Christina to the front. He held the stretched canvas for a moment, then laid it on the floor beside him, selecting tubes of umber, crimson, and turquoise, squeezing a nub of each on the wood palette. He splashed turpentine in the Mason jar, dipped the large flat brush, loading it with color, then splattering it to meld in free random patterns across the blank canvas. He brushed in more turpentine, watching pale rivulets racing over the canvas as he turned it in his hand. He damped off the residual, and began drawing into the wet paint with a sable brush.

He swigged from the tequila. Gina loomed from the drawing. He shook off the memory, letting his fingers define the shapes of Christina's eyes and lips. He drank more tequila and reinforced the partially blurred areas with the loaded sable brush, working quickly with the large flat brush to fill in shadow around eyes, and grab paint runs in the dark under nostrils, knocking high lights back out with a rag, offsetting it in the blackness at corners of the mouth.

Colors bled as he continued laying darks in shadow under brow and chin. Pigments ran exploding in solvent ruptures down a slender neck. Mor dipped the flat brush in the spirits, flicking pure colors to rupture and fuse over the canvass, tracking purplish solvent tears.

Dropping the brush, he carried the tequila to the porch, where he collapsed into the armchair. The chair had a missing leg, replaced by a tin pot wedged under a rock. A metallic squeak punctuated the shifting of his weight, before vanishing in the wind.

☼

He woke to the scream of a hawk. His head lay back against the sun-bleached fabric of the armchair. Overhead he saw the giant star Betelgeuse in the constellation of Orion, a speck of light, he'd read to be, six hundred million miles across. The tequila bottle rested between his feet. What was the nature of an awareness that could fill such incomprehensible space? He drank for an answer.

☼

Two hundred miles to the south, Christina held up a pair of binoculars, focusing on Betelgeuse, the name a corruption of the Arabic yod al jauza, the hand of the Central One, Yod, Yod heyvavhey, familiar star in her eyez z'a star'ey"e ing back. A mystery echo of a light coming indivisible from her eyez z zazz'a peering it. At a 1500-year-old light seen now that beginning its journey in the early Middle Ages. She now translated the light waves into Byzantine intrigue with a rise of Greek Orthodox Christianity. The West returning to its Eastern and African roots. Christina pondered how the birth of Mohammed counter-balanced the renaissance of the church of Saint Peter in Constantinople. The clash of the peaceful followers of Abraham countered the genocidal nature of the Lion. Father Abraham, shepherd or king, she wondered. Monotheism. One the is m. The e singular m'em or y. The e, k'ey'e in 4ma'sz sight seer see'ng of it. A re'y'all'eye'zinging a singular indivisible memory of a being still in the first place. Now turning out of it any k'now'ing that as'za being y . . . b'y . . . by . . . ba'by she mused.

Christina pondered the battle lines drawn to crash against Jerusalem's gates. A building of that dome over Herod's pillaged temple mount. She now knew a real homeland lay beyond the Lavant, Greece or Mesopotamia to the Nile, the black and red lands, and the lineage of New Kingdom pharaohs who carried the scepter of the shepherd's crook along with the bull's flail crossing two lands in equal arms. Shepherd kings. The procession of the Mir'age's, bull, ram, fishes, man, lion man'as mind'or y memory. She gently pressed a fingernail into the top of her skull to leave a subtle impression in the field of her awareness. Then, taking a long slow breath, drawing from the base of her spine, flexing it forward on its tail pivot, she squeezed her abdominal muscles to draw cerebral-spinal fluid up her spine into her brain. She followed its flow with her awareness moving to the impression on the top of her scalp. The pressure of spinal fluid squeezed against the crystals of her pineal gland created a magnetic pizo-electric field drawing in a current synapse from the 8th chakra, inches above her head. She tapped the'e as'ka's mic memory. As ka as'z z z cause y'all overstanding any mirrored understanding of it.

Christina chuckled at the seemingly now casual approach to tapping that ka's mic over mind'or y memory. The fact was this discipline came hard years in the making. Years in recovery from Jerusalem. From the incident. That encounter cast her eye on a do or die dillemma. Succumb to victimhood or conquer that devouring sense of isolation and alienation from herself out of it in her eye of eve're'y body. This recovery included a crippling codeine habit that had put her eye on the street, saved only by a university tenure. She now still served on probation with full censure waiting in the wings. Some did call it in her eye'sz'any crazy lady. Wild and crazy. They did not now know her to be a murderer as well. Still they might see in her eye'sz'za Kali Ma. A mother who devours her own children in relentless crushing jaws of time. A PARANTAKALI. A supreme end time engendered by showing a're'y'all of it out in her'eye z z z'a merely a peering it. Or it appearing of it by now a k'no'wing out of it supernaturally as'z'any thoth'tsz of it. A b'ng c'ng out in word in'formation of it.

Still wondering is it better to kill or be killed. Now she knew neither to be true. If you think you kill or are killed you know not the truth. She recalled these words of Lord Death from Kathopanisad. Finding them true now hammered on the anvil of samsara. Suffering it seems promotes a desire for it in a way with gravity weight of that waiting of death. Of that supersonic gravity of appearing as t'word any disappearing in a're'y'all"eye'zation of the situation of a being c'ng merely awareness of a peering it. A being still in the first place. It took a few blows to the in word head as'z'any thoth'tsz now in for'ma'sz any h'ay'ting of it in'formation.

Christina resisted using subtle body seduction on certain members of the board of regents. She now already skated on a thin ice of dharma. Of law with blood already on her hands. His blood now her blood. She surrendered to the melatonin released from the pineal 'pinecone' gland, re'entering the y'all soaking singular d"ark'ness as'z z z'leep black'g"round turning into her'eye of eve"re'y body. A first supersonic person singular presence a being c'ng in a y eye by now out as'ex's ting supernaturally as'z thoth'tsz in'formation.

In'forming it as'ka's mic da y na light igniting'asz z'any now ask'no'no no'wing as'ka's micro wayeve re'y"e black'g'round echoing as'z'z any intent of a b'ng c'ng a gain. A gain in word. Information awhile. A merely in a wordfreedom untouched awareness of it appearing awhile in a y eye of a b'ng c'ng merely a peering it in the first place. Now a peh'ss'y w'hole power out of it in her eyez'z'azz of eve're'y'body at attention of anybody anything any time now any where. A power that commands us yet is at h'our command. A power not to be trifled with. She'e'na mess with no stinking board. She'e'na a're'y"e verse of the in word con'senses with a y eye dialectic debate set t'word a raging of the ca'ge'in breaking open any in word captivity of attention. Freed now merely in a wordfreedom awareness of it as'k'no'wing out anything anybody etc.. In a word freedom now of any k'no'wing out of in word memory. Of mem mind or y. Of an in word mind. Or. Or a y eye merely freely a peering it still in a wordfreedom.

A y eye merely a peering it. Or it as'z'any thoth'tsz of any intent'ion as'kabala function as'king of it as'ka's of a b'ng c'ng a wayeve're'y"e function supersonically appearing out of it anything or anybody ignited by ignoring it. Positively negating it awhile. She'e'na permeating that negation as thoughtsz of a projecting ot it a being still as ka's mic. The"e'g'g 's ting now awhile be'guiled in the"e gg's'ting craft of her eve're'y body. A quantum unified you na now a field, . . . YOU NOT NOW . . . positive negation igniting that felt e'lectrical feel'd of LOVE SUPREME blissful blackness. Kry'st y'all mighty. KRY'ST Y'ALL MIGHTY as'Ka's all y bodhi. Ka'li bodhi. Ka as'z cause y'all still potential virgin eve'n'a while appearing a pairing in da y na light as'z ex'u'all. Y'zs now other y's ex. Black bodhi cause in effect a w'h'ile, a cunning lie. Ka lie. Kali ma'sz z z.

Her eyes opened. Glancing at her phone she had been out relatively 45 minutes. Y'sz'eX. Y sex? Beyond the obvious, she wondered still tasting the artist, the Dark'ness on her lips. It freaked her how quickly her transcendence from the energy of her 2nd chakra had been breached. She regretted over-reacting to his kiss. Perhaps Jerusalem still chilled her blood. She did not doubt, had a knife been in her hand, Dark would have bled for his transgression. Strangely enough, she wanted to see him again and soon.

☼

Mor found no solace in the painting so he tried with the tequila. Naturally the alcohol only loosened an inherited madness waiting to devour him. He flashed on how 'the poppie jones' had ravaged his junkie father.

He launched himself back into the cabin. The place seemed to rock like a boat. The kerosene lamp still burned, the candles melted out into wax puddles. Light tightened his vision squeezing into a continuous red band as air compressed with heavy fumes of turpentine, kerosene, and melting wax. Mor, gripping the drawing board under his arm, grabbed the box easel by its leather handle. Jerking it forward, turpentine crashed to the floor. Stumbling against the cabinet, he knocked over the lamp exploding into the pool of turpentine. He stared transfixed by the spreading flames till searing heat forced him back out the open door still clutching the easel along with the drawing board. Out in the cool darkness, mesmerized, he watched flames crawl across the canvas, turning lips to a snarl and eyes to black holes.

Jumping off the porch he leaned against the bed of his pickup, watching his home burn. Flames licked at a black moonless sky. The near-empty tequila bottle dangled from his hand, the easel and his drawing board with the sketches of the two women tossed in the truck bed. Mor took one last pull and heaved the bottle into the conflagration.

The tinder-dry walls collapsed, bringing down charred and flaming broken rafters. Wind flattened a wall of smoke, singeing his lungs. Turning away, he saw the fire in his eyes reflected in the truck window. Heat cooked his backside. He hauled himself into the cab and drove. The ride to the highway gave him time to consider the consequences of his actions. The cabin was no great loss compared to the threat to his mental stability. He needed someone warm and friendly. Punching it up to Drive and heading south, he imagined the soft smile painting Christina Shaughnessy.

☼

In the early morning mist, only the tips of the Golden Gate Bridge towers were visible as Mor drove out from the Robin Williams tunnel. With the cabin burned, his crossing the 'Gate' signaled a return. San Francisco embodying home as much as any place he'd known. The bridge spanned spirit with form, a now shrouded nexus linking two poles of the gate way of two worlds.

Parking his truck on the north side, he walked the bridge wearing a black leather jacket against the chill. The light Sunday morning traffic breached the fog, shuddering the expansion joints as he neared the north tower. He glanced down two hundred feet to an outflow of seven rivers ripping into currents meeting incoming ocean tides. He neared the spot he had once witnessed a suicide jump. Here the power of dissolution of rivers and memories exerted its strongest diffusion. The abyss merely waited to be lept. He realized that day of the suicide the bridge became a passageway for him, between living and dying. He'd been peering over the railing that day when a bound figure launched from a tower alcove overhead. His gaze seemed suspended in time as the balled figure dropped, disappearing into the current with hardly a splash. He remembered staring somehow expecting the jumper to pop back up on the surface. Later he saw a photograph in a newspaper of a male jumper wearing goggles just before launching with hands cuffed behind. Obviously the man wasn't taking any chances that his survival instinct might prevail. He recalled the black hair matting the jumpers shoulders and forearms, imagining him scrubbing it under a shower. Now to be combed by riptides and sharks'teeth.

Iron bridge spanning the Golden Gate. Iron, the end of a star's nuclear fusion. Traveling crane decapitated an ironworker, before bridge construction was completed. Mor knew his name but not that of the suicide he had witnessed. Was that another death he tasted in the salty air? And whose?

Mor remembered walking the bridge early every day after witnessing the jumper, talking to the bridge cops, and toll collectors. He had read everything he could find about its superb design in making tons of iron seem to float in space. He'd read how so much was theoretical about the engineering in that pre-computer era, that the designer, fired before construction began, continued to have doubts about its structural integrity long after the bridge was built, and furthered his calculations till the day he died. He imagined the engineer buried in an apartment full of leather bound inked ledgers needed then to make the calculations.

He learned the towers of the bridge, seven hundred feet above the water, were actually a honeycomb of steel cells. In meeting and interviewing some of the maintenance crew, he gained an opportunity to see the bridge from different perspectives. In the course of their permanent painting job the boys gave him a ride on an antiquated elevator the size of a refrigerator to access the upper reaches of the towers. There was no room inside the elevator so he had rode on top. He fingered the scar from that ride, when a protruding bolt had ripped through his jacket on the descent.

Looking at the tower, now, he imagined men breathing unventilated lead fumes inside those cramped cells, buckering up white-hot rivets. No welding. Rivets heated red hot and tossed up from the deck. Headed with pneumatic hammers held with muscle gut and bone. Each tower with over six hundred thousand of them white-hot iron nails thick as Buddha's thumb. Millions in the whole bridge, hammered with the lives of iron-willed men. Men who often found themselves worked out of a job. Left with out enough coin to pay the bridge toll. The maintenance crew had allowed Mor to stand in the crow's nest at the top of the tower's thousands of tons of steel, and watch salt-heavy mists hurtle by at freight train speed. The city had vanished in the mist as had, seven hundred feet below, churning waters ripping back into their source. Mother ocean. Tearing in to meet and eat her children.

Shortly after the elevator ride, he had a terrifying dream of a colossal god devouring the bridge with people dropping off like fleas. The god's mouth swallowed him in gray as he walked the ruined bridge into the misty abyss.

Now he once again entered the City, his country refuge reduced to ashes. He tasted smoke as he thought of Christina. Her awareness mocked his delirium. His clothes, stained with paint and ash, reeked of wood smoke and road dust. He needed to get clear with Korner before he attempted to see her. The image of the canvas devoured by the flames provoked a pain in his gut. Layers of fog slowly withdrew, revealing a smoky orange sun.

He stopped to watch a cargo ship stacked with steel containers pass under the arched span. The perspective lines of the bridge truss and girders zigzagged back to where he stood. The top of the truss formed a shelf that extended several feet beyond and under the rail of the walkway. A body could jump over the rail with plenty of room to stand before making the last jump several hundred feet to the water. A two-inch pipe ran the center of the ledge with inline valves, a water line used for high-pressure washing to prep surfaces for the international orange paint applied 24-7 as a barrier to the constant corrosion of the salt air and fog. The brink of the ledge was reinforced with two I-beams four inches thick, with three inches between them and the truss. A black purse sat wedged in the space.

Cars and trucks, pounding over the roadbed, shook the railing as he leaned over for a closer look. From the position of the purse, whoever had been standing there was another jumper for the statistics. He thought twice, then leaped over and snagged the purse by its dangling strap. He almost slipped off the damp shelf, just managing to get back over the railing before a Bridge cop peddled up on a bicycle. Mor, heart pounding, jammed the purse inside his jacket.

"What the hell you doin' buddy! Wha the frick?"

"How's it going?" Mor offered with a sheepish smile. Still breathing hard.

"I seen a few jump off but I never seen anyone jump back up." the patrol man replied lifting his cap to scratch the top of his head.

"Oh that, dropped my bag when I leaned over to look at that container ship," Mor said pointing off.

"Musta been damn important to risk becoming instant fish bait."

"Might say its all I got left in the world."

"Well hold on to it, Things always look better when the fog lifts." the cop said. He wore a uniform short sleeve shirt that bulged tight over broad muscles and dark aviator sunglasses. He carried a 9mm automatic pistol and a nightstick on a web belt. He showed no sign of moving as he looked him over. Mor started walking toward the parking lot. The bag felt like a slab of contraband wedged under his armpit as the man in blue rode along side of him.

"Anyone go off lately?" he asked, taking in the city skyline floating in the morning haze a mile distant.

"Yeah, a few days ago."

"I guess a few hundred have jumped."

"Try a hundred times a few hundred. We get about two a week."

Chapter 5

Korner woke. He'd had the dream again. The dream of meeting the green man in Vietnam still chilled his blood. He remembered too well, that night, the stench of tropic decay mixed with salty air off the south China Sea, breezes rattling an outcropping of banana trees, as he sat alone around a low fire. He was enroute to the DMZ to engage with NVA regulars in a real war instead of the dirty guerrilla body count in this Quang Ngai Province, when business had sidetracked him. People of this province were a coarser and fiercer bunch than the more intellectual revolutionaries he'd met in the Iron Triangle. He knew they had been fighting here thirty years for independence.

H.Q. gave the all clear for the sector. He and a platoon of GIs were bivouacked within a perimeter of electronic sensors set to detect as much as a mosquito fart. They had been sampling some his latest inventory, hypnotized by some tracer fire to the north but otherwise enjoying a rare quiet evening. The others had retired while he gazed transfixed at the stars.

The next thing he remembered an overwhelming sickening stink growing as cold bony fingers grazed the back of his neck reaching inside his shirt, squeezing his belly. There, beside him, an amphibious creature smiled with yellow teeth, rancid breath, and rubbery green skin. "Charlie coming." he said with a hoarse growl. His hooded eyes ate into Korner until finally he broke the grip and radioed a nearby gunboat that lit the plain. Twenty NVA regulars were tagged in the firefight that ensued.

"We were dog meat till you came along," he said now to no one in particular.

The green man seemed to live just at the edge of his awareness like a second skin, too close ever for comfort. Korner still wore his Saigon bracelet, a loop of welded Huey rotor chain dangling around his wrist for protection, if not against, then for the green man.

☼

Christina Shaughnessy removed the plastic lid from the take-out cup of herb tea, cursing her decision to quit caffeine. She pulled back her auburn hair as she stared at the transparency on the light table through the jeweler's loop. She thought of the Dark one, and wondered what demons danced in his head. Her lips remembered the pressure of his unexpected kiss, her knuckles burning from the punch.

Eve're'y man she had known confused her, even her father. Matthew had waited until he was on his deathbed to tell her about his initiation into Johnstone Warren's world order.

"Brutish but brilliant. Less human, more like a manufactured being made of silicon and oilstone. We were twenty eight years behind the German chemical and rocket engineers at the end of World War Two. Warren's a realist. Those Nazis would enlist with the Russians, their avowed enemies, just to have a government to fund their programs. It's a ruthless, dog eat dog world, sweetheart. We recruited them. Do I regret my affiliation with Warren? Nobody then could have foreseen the growth of the cancer from pursuing those damned Nazis and the National Security State we've become. What happens, when we tried to save democracy by unleashing a nuclear holocaust. Just don't confuse ideology or morality with money. You say your prayers for old dad. I'm heading on upstairs." Then he died. Christina felt his soul merge with hers.

She knew Warren had engineered Matthew's exposure to radiation when he was with the Manhattan Project decades before her birth. The experiment was an attempt to accelerate the human capacity for morphogenesis, the power to alter structures in the evolution of an organism. She, now understanding this capacity as epigenetics, self switching genes on off or off on, wondered at her rapid expansion of consciousness. An expansion made possible by an intent of living in the present future orientation free of long term memory neutralized by the radiation. Allowing her eyez z z'azz finding free a b'ng c'ng in the eve're'y radiating a un'k'no'wn A peh'ss'y w'hole power of a knowing out of any a na y mirrored y na now infinite peh'ss'y'en'ce potential in a space in time now anybody etc.. Amazing the possibilities when not casting out as thoughtsz of past history to blockade the road ahead. As'king of it now as'z'any measly whithered lac'king thin king of it. Asz? She cultivated the motto 'leave it as two dis'a'pairing in the rear view of you mirrored'. Christina stayed abreast of Warren's scientific research through an old friend of her father's. She learned about his interest in a bewildering multidisciplinary maze of genetics, quantum physics, bioacoustics, electrochemistry, brain-wave entrainment and nano technology.

She knew, her father's first wife died in pregnancy, possibly due to the fetus being formed soon after his irradiation. Thirty years later he met Sarah and Christina was born. She was in grade school when she first remembered meeting Warren. He was a frequent caller and seemed always to have some hold over dad.

She looked at the transparency. The mysteries refused translation. That mystery is now ahead of her. Might as well go running and flush the chemical desire for the Darkness with adrenaline, she thought. Christina needed adrenaline to offset effects of upgraded metabolites of melatonin or seratonin jetting from her overactive pinecone. Her first eye on a being still in the first place. An eye she kept out to James Korner and the Dark man bearing down. Now she needed to charge up survival instincts.

☼

Mor hustled from the Bridge back to his truck. He jumped inside for a break from the wind that wanted to dismember him for spending too much time suspended in the vortex between land and sea. He drove south across Crissy Field and the Presidio on Doyle Drive. He sailed along the last open road running along bay waters before turning on to the trashy neon motel row of Lombard Street.

Korner's house jutted out above the commercial chaos and crowds of tourists, waiting for whatever is next on their agenda. He imagined his old amigo Cohiba in hand, perched in his glass tower, surveying the harbor and the berths of the elite Saint Francis Yacht Club. Missing Divisidero, he caught horns as he slowed to search for a street sign. He looked along Pierce Street into Cow Hollow, an area that hadn't seen any cattle grazing for one hundred fifty years.

A block above Lombard, he found rows of white canvas fair pavilions. They were pitched in the middle of Union Street over several blocks. Parking, he walked around to check out the faire. Vans jammed the street as artisans unloaded wares from coats, and silk hats, rustic furniture, photographs, jewelry, tables laden with leather goods reeking of neetsfoot oil alongside blown glassware mounted on recycled brass instruments. All the stuff you thought was cool when you bought it but wonder about when you get it home. More importantly, at every intersection, food, beer, and wine stalls with open seating. Kitty-corner to those stalls, covered stages thudded with crews setting up microphones and amplifiers for live music.

The faire energy induced in him a craving to draw. Not that he was broke. He carried his pay in his pocket. He really needed to bleed off the bad gris-gris gathering from the fire. He just hoped it had not spread to Merle's 10,000 acres of range and forest. How many paychecks would that be worth? Every dollar he carried over from one day to the next seemed like a thorn dragging on his freedom. Spend it on good times. Draw for more. Now free from the dullness of sobriety, let the good old bad times roll. Yah'ow baby cakes.

A young woman with bleach blond hair frizzing around a headset, passed by wearing a tee shirt with the fair logo, and CREW in black block letters across the shoulder.

"What's the bite for a space to draw portraits?" he asked, stretching and rubbing his eyes with a wide yawn.

"Seven hundred and fifty if I can squeeze you in. Most people reserved months ago."

"I'll pass. Have a good show." He flashed on the two hundred in his pocket, riches up north, but barely enough for a dinner date in the city.

Mor caught his reflection in the glass of a framed photograph of a cougar crouched on a rock. He hoped he wouldn't have to draw anyone that rough looking. Picking up a piece of polished carved marble, he turned it in his hand to appreciate the labor. A silver haired artist with a thick accent approached. "That's anseeent icon, bring you much good luck," he said with a smile.

"Thanks, but I'd have to buy you out, to change my luck," Mor replied.

"We could work someting out." he offered with a wink.

Mor laughed. Not wanting to take up anymore of the man's time, he moved on to check out the paintings. The art had finesse, but most painters here cultivated the decorative market. Checking out numerous canvases, he found just the right subject motif and colors for the breakfast nook or over a couch in the living room. Art with a certain charm and why not. Most folks were not borderline wack jobs like him, he thought with a shrug. Some booths were custom made and included video monitors and trac lighting streaming music for the total professional package. He felt poorer by the moment.

Then he nearly collided with a short man around his age, if better preserved, struggling with hardware to construct his homemade booth. A breeze played his wispy hair as bent to his task.

"Let me give you a hand," he offered, stepping over crates to hold the end of a galvanized pipe frame. "The name is Dark, Dark Mor, at your service."

"Johnny Sorenson," the man responded. His paintings were good size landsea'scapes, three to four feet by four to six feet, painted with a palette knife in thick untempered colors.

"How about I help you set up here? I'll draw portraits out front and get people to stop check out your work. I'll kick back twenty-five percent of my take." Mor offered, reaching up to tighten a wing nut on Johnny's pipe frame..

Sorenson, with a sideways smile, gave Mor a look like he was seeing him for the first time. His eyes were rheumy but not without humor. "Why not?" he replied as he slowly straightened. "Get your easel and we see what happens."

"Bless you, Johnny. You won't regret it." he said as he finished tightening the last wing nut. He ducked out from the pipe frame, palms stained with iron rust, heavy Bay fog rolling a chill down his spine.

From his truck, he retrieved his box easel, folding chairs in a bag, and a shoulder pack with the purse from the bridge. The little Swede hung his paintings. At one point a gust whipped through, threatening to take him air-born as he carried a canvas, arms stretched wide across its back.

By eleven AM the sun burned through the fog as knots of shoppers and partygoers began to fill the street and sidewalk. He considered drawing in public, a good distraction from her ghost haunting his private moments. Now Mor wondered just whose ghost was she. Somehow he felt Gina and Christina had merged in his heart into that one woman. That one he'd been seeking to capture in pigment since the first day picking up a crayon. On the street, a crayon in his hand created a place with no strangers, offered a portal to a shared awareness between artist and victim.

Mor set his chair to face the traffic flow. People strolled by, carefree, crippled, bouncing, dragging, and laughing, in love or hate, high and low. They came craggy or creamy, bald or hair forever, but one thing they all shared in common, they all had a face. If only one a mother could love. Now would he found that fisherman's angle on catching one of those fish swimming past?

"How you folks doing?" Mor asked a young couple as they strolled arm in arm. "How about a sketch of your beautiful woman? I promise you a souvenir that you will cherish for as long as you like," he offered. The girl fell into her boyfriend's arms. They kissed. She leaned into him, her arms thrown loosely around his neck. Her blond hair pulled into a tight bun showed dark roots down the back of her neck. Her form-fitting shades reflected his. They were dressed for jogging, he in full ash gray sweats and her in black string tank top and skimpy terry cloth shorts with white trim that set off tan sinewy legs.

Mor observed the couple with calm amusement. The girl whispered something to her boyfriend, her lips playing on his. Finally she glanced over at him.

"I don't know. I guess. Can you draw both of us together?" she demurred with a smile.

"Don't know if I can fit all that love on one sheet of paper," he chided, catching the boyfriend's eye just to confirm who was in charge.

This could be the start of a beautiful day for the rest of my life, he ventured to himself. He pulled the chairs closer, adjusted the angle of the drawing board before waving the couple to sit. From the easel box, he extracted several crayons of the darkest and richest colors. The lovers leaned into each other in a way Mor knew must be captured. His hand started moving as he watched with one eye or two. Then everytime he started that panic of failure sunk in. The early days of his drawing in public often found him succuming to this panic. Once even walking away all together. He'd learned as long as he managed to stay out of way, the drawing almost unconsciously rolled out from there. Hand merely following eye. The crayon drew on with line or shade. He blocked in some shapes, then let her rip as his eyes traced brows to cheekbones, sides of nose, corners of mouth, lips, chin, and ears poking through hair, strands tossed in the wind. He left some passages grainy, slapping the paper with a chamois to create a soft randomly blended effect on others.

Drawing on for a few moments, he learned their names, Jim and Jenny. Sweethearts from Vallejo, they had moved to San Francisco to do the City scene until they were ready for the children that they promised not to name after him. They exchanged phone numbers after agreeing that drawing did create a bond, inviting him to visit their home to see the portrait hung proudly in their den. He knew they would never see each other again, but during the drawing he was as close to them as anyone in the life.

In drawing, he found the world whole, observer merged with observed. How did it get so crazy otherwise. So broken. So shattered. He wondered, squeezing the kneaded rubber eraser for a clean edge to cut out highlights with one hand while wielding crayon to deepen the shadow, hoping with rapid motion to capture the expression of the moment. In drawing he appreciated blissful potential of a life well lived. Or poorly lived. Or typically a bitter-sweet mix. This subtle sublime joy in any sorrow eluded him as a carpenter. Sweat, blood, and screaming saws didn't lead to quiet introspection, although it did feel so good when you finished.

Mor drew for hours, a mother and child, older woman, someone's teen age daughter, and a couple freebies. Catching a break in the afternoon, he decided to call Korner. He wanted to know if he'd heard from Christina. His hair was on fire for her, his heart knocking in his chest with thoughts of her. Feeling this way he would never get enough of her. Thank the gods he could drink again. He went across the street to the Blue Light bar, whose neon glowing sign had tempted him since they opened.

A barmaid in black skirt and low cut blouse showing the tattoo of a dragon on her shoulder knifed through the crowd with a tray of tall drinks.

"Where's the telephone?" Mor asked, trying to keep eyes from sliding into her cleavage as she leaned over to deposit the drinks.

"Well, if it ain't in your pocket, it's in the back. Hey, I've been watching you out there. Want to do me?" she asked with a giggle. She balanced a tray of empties on one hand as she cleared a table with the other. She snagged a cellophane wrapper and several cocktail napkins ringed with ice sweat before she turned back to him.

"Anytime, my dear. Anytime, anywhere," he replied with a slight bow. "Find me a spare Corona and shot of tequila."

"I'll set it up on the bar," she promised, half his age and twice as sweet. No fool like an old fool, he thought.

He headed to the men's room before making the call. When you find jubilation in a bar shitter, stinking of stale beer, cleaning fluids, and crude words scrawled on the walls, you know you're there, or where. He zipped up, dropped a quarter in the pay phone, and dialed Korner. The rings went unanswered until the voice mail kicked on.

"I'm drawing portraits at the Union Street Fair and drinking in the Blue Light." He held out the receiver to record the bar sounds. "Join me or fuck off or and go fuck yourself."

He wandered back through the face crowd, the air thick with after-shave and testosterone, to find a longneck beer and shot waiting for him. Gunning the shot of tequila, he chased it with a few healthy slugs of the Corona. He watched the barmaid balancing a tray of tall Collins glasses packed with ice, sliced oranges, and candied cherries weave her way between the noisy drinkers. Mor walked over and dropped a folded twenty-dollar bill between the glasses.

"You want another?"

"Later. I'm hungry to draw. Come on out on your break."

"If the easel is still there, I might." Her hair was bobbed short, a stray curl stuck to the perspiration on her forehead. "I don't get off until six," she pouted.

"Take me home. Mine burned down."

"Then get back to work." She hoisted another tray of fresh drinks and spun into the crowd. Her stockinged thighs slipped with a shush under the short black skirt.

He drank the beer and returned to his easel. The sun that had poked out earlier lost to the fog, with stiff gusts cutting along the street to snap against the canvas pavilions. Sorenson left his display uncovered rather than fight the wicked wind that had taken out a near-by blown glass display. Mor flipped up the collar of his heavy leather jacket. His hands clenched from the damp, the earlier fire he found in drawing was banked low.

He felt dissipated in the chill air. People became a hindrance, their voices a terrible vacuous cacophony.

"Hey, mister. How much to make a picture of me and my mom?"

Mor turned, surprised he was still visible. The girl had large brown eyes, poised lips, and proud cheeks where strands of ebony hair danced across. These she brushed back by slender fingers with lacquered nails. She wore hoop earrings and a sideways ball-cap. Her lips shone with silver gloss.

"How much, mister?" she asked.

"Fifty bucks will keep me happy," he said, cracking knuckles and nodding at the mother. Her eyes smoldered above an engaging smile.

Models and artist talked. Mother was Kwasanda Nzokia, from the Sudan, and her fourteen-year-old American-born daughter named Shallahnna. Kwasanda's accent softened the edges of her words. They had a melodic flow like a filmy liquid wrapping each sound.

"Do you have a studio?" she asked, her hands stretching a black cotton scarf electric with rows of jetting yellow arrows.

"Had one until I accidentally torched it last night. Wasn't much more than orange crates and window panes," he replied without looking away from the drawing. He focused on Shallahnna first so that she would be free to move around while he finished drawing her mother.

"Without a home you come to the city," Kwasanda said more as statement than question.

"Yes, ma'am. Right now I'm living in my truck." Mor stretched the stiff muscles in his shoulders. He drew the daughter for twenty minutes before turning his attention to Kwasanda. He knew the instant he started that she was checking him out. She seemed sympathetic. Maybe too sympathetic. Seeing too much into his soul.

"Night is too cold for your truck. Here is my telephone number." Without changing her position she held out a black business card in the tips of her fingers.

"That's very kind," he replied. Shallahnna, scratching the back of her neck with lacquered nails, looked off somewhere beyond him. He kept drawing, his focus sliding from the pad to Kwasanda. Her eyes waited to take him home. They were open and he flew on in.

"I have a friend who'll put me up. He's walking behind you, but don't worry. He's not as bad as he looks," he said, as Korner loomed behind her with the collar of his leather coat turned up, hands jammed into his pockets.

Kwasanda glanced over his shoulder. Her expression changed from open warmth to apprehension, communicating a warning. Mor held her eyes for a long moment, then signed the drawing.

"He has a mean shadow," she said, coming around the easel to look at the sketch. "The portrait is very good. What do you think, Shallahnna?"

"He draws souls. I love it."

Korner spread his arms with the creak of leather. "A man would have to be born blind to miss your beauty." He slouched against a lamppost, giving a slight bow. "James Korner, and you are?"

"Kwasanda Nzokia. I wonder what your game is about." Her voice took an edge that could be cut with a palette knife.

"I'm Shallahnna," her daughter offered with enough attitude to make Mor want to kiss her. He could tell both women had read Korner's book, finding in the contents a warning of mayhem.

Korner nodded to a beefy man standing to his left, hair buzz cut, brow beaded with sweat from carrying an extra twenty pounds. "My associate, Mr. Aram Hashemi." His face, black-peppered with today's beard, gave a cruel smile that took a licentious cast as he turned to Shallahnna. "Care to join us for a drink?"

"Our religion forbids alcohol." Kwasanda managed to sound polite and insulting at the same time.

"Certainly didn't mean to offend, sugar. It's been a slice," Korner added with another slight bow. "I'll make do with your artist here."

Kwasanda leaned closer to Mor. "Call me," she whispered as she slipped money into his hand before running off to join her retreating daughter. He smelled the musk of her hair long after she was out of sight. Quick blasts of wind from the Pacific ripped through the Golden Gate and slashed at the pavilions. One not held down with sandbags lifted like a kite and crashed down on a woman selling candy popcorn. The fair was about over.

Mor followed Korner into the Blue Light bar. The noise inside had gained momentum, walls thumping with drumbeat. Boozed-up patrons slowed the trio's progress to the bar, booming bass blocked out any but the most essential thoughts. Women shook and men posed. Hashemi knocked a drink from a barmaid's tray to spill on her cotton blouse, then tripped on a barstool. He followed his misdeeds with swagger and without apology, talking with a tight grimace due to the cocaine he snorted from the back of his fist.

A man changes despite or maybe in spite of himself. Mor had watched the remnants of humanity fall from Korner as he absorbed the meaner instincts of the company who kept him. Korner called for drinks with a smack on the bar.

"Nice 'tang sitting for your Etch-A-Sketch. Nothing like a mother–daughter combo, my hairy man." Korner said as he chucked the backside of a flattened hand under Mor's chin.

"All women just tits and ass? How about a little soul there, brother?" he replied, deadpan.

"Depends if you like your sole blackened or with white sauce. You're in love with the professor, you pussy-whipped motor scooter. I've seen this act before," Korner replied, cowboy boots perched on the polished brass rail and pulling on an earlobe. A toothpick pressed into the flesh of his lip.

"You're only a bad dream, Korner. You're not real."

"As real as your punk ass. Nice purse, by the way. Thinking of a gender change?" Korner offered as he started to lift the bag from Mor's shoulder.

"Found it on the Bridge this morning. Belongs to K.L., whoever she is," Mor said as he caught the strap in his fist.

Hashemi pushed between the two men. "Yak fucking yak, like old women. Are we drinking or yaking?" He glowered, throwing his shoulders back.

Mor glared at the interruption.

"The fuck you looking at? You been glassing me since we met. Korner's friend don't make you mine."

"How old are you, Hashman?" Mor asked with an exaggerated exhalation. "I'd say twenty-eight to thirty. When I was that age, a pumped and coked-up punk like you, might have scared the shit out of me. But I grew up."

Veins popped on Hashemi's neck as his jaw tightened.

"Easy, brother, Darkster stares at everybody. It's an artist thing. Don't take him personal," Korner interjected. He turned to the bar and offered a shot of tequila to Hashemi, and another to Mor.

"I grew up in a world of baseball, hot dogs, and riding bikes in the park. That ended when JFK went down in Dallas. The dream died and what's come out of my country since then are psycho killers like this man handing us our drinks," Mor said, taking the drink with a slight nod.

Korner threw back his shot. "Us psychos have always been around. Look at the pictures of Kennedy's assassination. The Secret Service didn't react when the first bullet hit him in the throat. The car stops and he takes a hit in the head. You tell me, who's doing the shooting? Who's doing the driving? It's obvious some agents were in on the takeover. Texas, LBJ, and Bell helicopter me to Vietnam. I mean, come on. Take a good look around you, son. Good guys and bad guys don't mean nothing at the top."

"More fucking yak. Where I come from, my sister was gang raped by her husband's family, for the sin of dropping her chaldor in the marketplace. Keep your crayon rolling world,"

Hashemi growled, jabbing the back of a thin washed-out blond, causing her to spill a cherry red drink on her companion's proud clothes.

"Bastard, this shirt's Armani. Cost me two-fifty."

Hashemi grabbed a longneck bottle off the bar. Smashing it he raked the man's cheek. Blood boiled out of the lacerations.

The doorman rushed inside, biceps popping against a knit T-shirt one size too small. Mor threw his weight into the crowd and felt silk slide under his hand. Korner crashed another longneck on the head of a pony-tailed man, and caught Hashemi to drag him outside. The doorman busied himself with separating the fighting patrons.

Mor made his way to the street, the reverberating drum machine never missing a beat. He snapped together his easel, dropped the folded chairs in their bags, scooped up his pack, and fell in with Korner who carried Hashemi by the collar. He let loose with a slight shove and Hashemi did a quick shoulder roll. His eyes burned as he looked around. He walked to a table of fancy wrapped candy and flipped it with both hands. A blond woman in tight Levis and heels stood with both hands against her lips. Hashemi stepped on shattered glass and peanut brittle to pull her in close enough for his lapels to brush against her breasts.

☼

Christina's eyes twitched, going to a soft focus pouring over a plate of the Copper Scroll on her laptop. The archetypal form of the Hebrew letters had a phonetic structure akin to Sanskrit where the form of the letters echoed their essential sound. Cymatics she sighed. Forma'sz sound ways of eve'reybody. A wayeves mean means meaning'z'az'any function of a fun'ny'a'ction. Ma"asz Eve. eL eYe function of communication. Communicating what beyond the obvious she now wondered? Communicating a why as too whom. Why? Y you're;y'you in the first place now she thought.

A y you are out of it in her"eyez z zi'on eve're'y bodhi. A ma'ss world of a na y t'at'u'a're'y. Her heart beat faster starring at the letters hammered into the metal surface over twenty three hundred years ago. She now merged with the spirit of the scribe, imagining him bent over the rare metallic 99% pure copper scroll with wooden mall and stamp copying from a similar scroll already ancient at that time. Did you even know the language that you copied, she wondered. The scroll of scrolls transmitting a timeless vision awareness in a wordfreedom a b c's of a b'ng c'ng at a'ten'cion bi na re'y"e a're'y'dhi'a'ting that indivisible ka's mic b'lack' mirror se'e'as. Now a k'nowing out of it supernaturally asz'any thoth'tsz in a b c's of a b'ng c'ng still in the first place. Awareness of that promising to set man as mind or y memory now free. In a wordfreedom.Why not? Promises. Promises. Promittere. That at aten'cion of a b'ng c'ng acknowledged now still in the first place merely mirrored a k'no no no'wing it out asz thoth'tsz of it in a d'na'eye'll of it sent forth thru the ages. AWAKhEN A W/AKhEN et'A TEN. Y you are a ten bi na're'y a're'y'dhi'a'ting it as thoth'tsz of it now projecting a k'no no no'wing d'na'eye'll of a b'ng c'ng still in the first place in a wordfreedom awareness of that indivisible in'visibility. Now as'ka's mic b'ng c'ng appearing out of it mirrored in memory. Y'all merely appearing as thoughtsz in denial of a b'ng c'ng y'et indivisible invisibility of it she now mused.

A'kh'nowing of a b'ng c'ng hammered into a medium of such purity as to make it nearly the most impervious to decay. Only gold would be more so. Yet gold would be far less impervious to greed. Once rediscovered, a golden scroll would likely have been melted down for its mere monetary value. The timeless priceless value of its revelation for y'all mankind lost for pennies on a dollar. And now what of that a y eye revelation of merely a peering it she wondered. Is it time? Are people ready? Is there a value for it? Certainly the world had witnessed unprecedented global suffering and genocidal carnage in the 20th century. Was it enough to bring y'all ma'ss'z z z children around to finally a're'y'all"eye"ze why? A Y? A 'Why of such suffering in the first place. Suffering merely as thotht'sz of a God'esse letter'all'y y'all it hard wired neurologically in any hard felt feeling field of view. Of you or a y eye of a b'ng c'ng still in the first place. Was Warren's scheme necessary to complete the real mission of the scroll? Somehow she now found in herself a memory brought forth to avert his global annihillation. A memory in her eyez z z of eve're'ybody of a b'ng c'ng now as a wayeve mean means meaning of a knowing out of falling as'z z z'leep on or off that knowledge. A'Kh'nowledge of y'all a b'ng c'ng now out of that first place merely asz z z'leep into or out of a black'g'round as'king of it a k'no'wing a b'ng c'ng a gain.

Christina thought of her teacher, her acharya, Shivshankaraji, a flesh and blood firmament of ancient knowledge of a b'ng c'ng merely appearing to disappear. A b'ng c'ng advaita of a singular indivisible point of view of you of y. Of a y eye of that I am merely a peering it. She now still marveled that y'all his books were committed completely to memory. Of a b'ng completely absorbed now in any in word k'no'wing denial of it as that appearing anybody anything any time any where. Of such a b'ng c'ng now out of it turning a black'g'round echoing any knowing denial of it merged with and e'merging still a being be'am'ing on or off that knowledge. Then as'z'any thoth'tsz of it supernaturally of course a're'y'all'eye'zing that knowing out of it in her'eye of eve're'ybody. As'z'any appearing of that by a'kh'a'no no no'w'ing out of it a b c's in formation in word'sz'azz'a y'll d'na. A denial of a being still in the first place that indivisible invisibility now in t'word of that singular twis'ting in formation of fate, faith, or family. A denial of it y'll d'na. Denial as int'word a twis'ting in two turning intention of intentional disregard of a b'ng c'ng still. Now that as'ka's mic indivisible in'visibility of a b'ng c'ng as'king of it any k'now'ing out of it as thoth'tsz of it in formation. Letter'all'y y'all.

In Shivaji's revelation she found y'all in her'eyez z z'a'leep heretofore any scholarship completely upended. Turned invisibility a black'g'round. After all y y'all? Why, for what purpose had she now been turning about k'no no no'wing out of it while searching for it in those myriad untold hours. Merely mirroring herself? She now found herself lost in a mirror mind completely blown up, shattered laying in tatters y'all around. A city of the gods letter'all'y y'alls'za'zz'a words concept syntax now laying in ruin of a black'g'round in her'eyez z z'azz'a'kali ma'sz"eve'll. Yet she now remained still. Unperturbed. In a peh'ss'y w'hole center. A naked in'visibility heart of the complete d"ark'ness. The total encirclement by a b'ng c'ng point of view of you of y of a y eye a peering it in the first place. A y na now out of it merely mirrored int'word a peh'ss'y w'hole potential as'z z z'any thoth'tsz of it int'word a twis'ting in two appearing a pairing of it. As'z two twis'ting out now awhile y a pairing as ex'sting in any mirror image. The ruined city of thoughtsz, of thoth'tsz, of a God esse to be letter'all'y y'all merely falling a part black as'z z z'leep black into one indivisible invisibility of any individual of a consciousness. A hard con she us now esse to be as'z'anybody etc..

Letter'all'y y'all'sz'za hard felt field of a mirror se'e'as, a're'y'flecting out in her'eyez z z of a mercy. A while of mercy or indifference. A na'tural indifference to it as'z'anybody now ignoring it. Or'e"y"e of herhimit'sz'za a y eye star'e ye way. Herhimit eyezstare"ye'or y as'ex"et'ting duplicating any duplicity of it awhile. Playing out as'ex's ting in'formation merely supernaturally as thoth'tsz in any mirror mind or y na you ni verse. Y'all gotta be way to happy being ignorant to be indifferent to the supernature of it out in her eye'sz'zazz'any thoth'tsz of anybody anythin'king of it any time any where.

She now found in her eyez z z a eye're'y stare'y"e playing out. A y of it playing as'ex'et'ing. A duplicating in her'eyez z zi'on that indivisible black bodhi quantum black'g'round. Of it ask'urving turning, churning, yearning now in k'nowing out of it electro-magnetic loops. E loopy loops under the gravity. The weight. The waiting for that loop to end. Naturally where it begins as'ka's micro wayeve black'g'round. Exit black. Exist black appearing awhile y'll d'na. Any denial of it now the'n. Ending of it fade back to that black ka's all body of eve're'ybody. Appearing disappearing in complete d"ark'ness of e"loops. A ma re'y g'round she'ena laughed till tears streamed cheeks.

Except now, in the presence of her guru Shivshankaracharya she'e no longer waited. Was no longer weighted by the in word mirror city still turning, learning, burning a black'g"round. A B'lack'G'rounding out in her'eyez z z. In her'eyez z' a blood of his blood. In her eyez zi' on a b'ng c'ng merely in his a peering it..

The plasmic d"ark'en'ing city flowed mirror'ly a see'as a micro wayeve black'g'round of a b'ng c'ng of a y as'ex in a're'y'all out in her"eye zazz'zing'ing. A ma re'y g"round. Eve're'y bodhi of herhimit'sz'z'horisz'any eye on a line be'tween be'twixt that as'ka's mic being to perceive to see to think as'z'anybody mirrored in word supernaturally y'all asz'any thoth'tsz of a y now as'z'd na thing. Anything as a positive denial as'k'no no no'wing out of eve're'y thing. Y na now a great being c'ng awareness of Shivshankaracharya creator sustainer destroyer of y'all that still a being c'ng a y eye a peering in'visibility appearing anybody by a y mere black mirror supernatural see'as potential. With intention superimposed as thoth'tsz. Y'et Indivisible in a being c'ng a y eye of herhimit. As'z'za re'y'vealed in that singularity of a're'y'all'eye'zation of A y being that yod.That iota that ayin I am is is. Is'is ma're'y playing her ways of eve, her wayeves of pure mirror function. Still, functioning, swimming now in shark infested waters where the big ones eat the little ones, she'e'na was not looking to checking into any cave. A w'h'ile may continue now k'now'ing it yet she had just us in time slipped the bonds of in word ignore'ance of k'no no no'wing out of herself into any y na me without. AseX's ting still a're'y'all'eye'zing'ing a y. She'e now as'z'any mirror supernatural thotht'sz of a being still in the first place a're'y'turned to a race within her'eye'sz'z' on fellow rats.

Christina knew there was speculation of a more intimate relationship with her teacher. That really cracked her up. She had found herself a mere dust mote in the galactic seas consciousness of his awareness of a being c'ng still in the first place. Still she would not have ruled out sex but her study, meditation, and seva, or service, left no time let alone the energy for that desire. Her guru caused to be organized and fundraised a K thru 12 school for some 5000 native students. That was his seva beyond his function of enlightening any who came to his door and many came to his door. So many that often he would take up his robe, walking stick, and bowl, walking out in different directions, buffeted hither and yon upon her"eye wayeves. She was mere melted butter at his feet.The journey to the east had been hard on her body. Few knew how close she had come to a real psychic and biological disintegration.

The scintillating electric fire of this Brahmavidyam awareness of any knowing of it now a not knowing denial of it burned away the dross of y'all that matters'z. It really sizzled your'e grits, she mused. Christina knew a death in India in the presence of her guru more profound, more complete than any physical death. For in her'eye now the wait was over moment by moment. As'k'nowing of k'no no no'wing out of it a mere denying of herself. She'e'na was released now and forever from falling understanding its in'word spelling as'z'any thoth'tsz of it. Or still a y eye na now a peering at it. The mirror sea, that indivisible in'visibility pond of it in her'eye projecting ahead behind above below to the right to the left y'all around offered infinite potential as'z ex. Y'all as'ex.

She laughed at the way her mind wandered like an electron to a positron, like the lips of lovers, coming back around to primal desire. The fact was she had nearly burned out, the shock to her system from Jerusalem, from rape and murder caused near complete disintegration. As it was what appeared solid in Dark's eye of desire was already ash. Appearing intact but crumbling at the touch. She now knew the tragic irony of love. Should one be love or be loved? Why the desire for the body of a man in a woman of knowledge? Why is the sky blue? She might ask. The answer would be very similar. It isn't and it still isn't.

Christina changed into her running clothes and ran. She ran hard but still tasted the Dark'ness as her blood pulsed. Endorphins flooded, feet pounded, as knees churned to clear the linguistics from her head. Her work had taken her around the world, once speaking in front of ten thousand in Bombay. Career was not enough. Christina yearned for a relationship with a man where mind stirred mind, and body aroused body. Dark Mor was an obvious wrong choice. She'e'na still tasted his lips.

☼

Korner flipped the lid on his vibrating cell phone. The name R.W. McCracken lit up the screen. He didn't know what the W stood for but he gave McCracken the nickname "Whip" for his ambition and proclivity to s&m. McCracken should know better than squeezing his authority through the cell phone to try intimidating Korner.

"The mayor is not going to be happy when he finds out we tossed his girlfriend from the Bridge. You're sure he has the purse?"McCracken's voice boomed. Korner could hear him smacking his wooden fertility totem against an open palm.

"Initials and all. She called it her giggle bag, stuffed with poppers and a dildo for nights with the mayor. Kiowa had it with her the night I was at Zina's for a three-way."

"Why didn't you grab the damn thing when you had the chance?" McCracken demanded, the heat from the self-inflicted blows reddening his voice.

"Fuck-head Hashemi started knocking heads and I lost Mor in the shuffle. Not to worry, he'll show up. He wants a certain lady's number."

"Get that bag. I want the tracks covered."

Korner slipped the phone into an inside pocket and tapped the Colt nestled under his armpit. Whip might own the Portal, his Menlo Park labs with a syndicate and all, but he didn't own him. McCracken people, jumped too around him. Korner wanted to jump him with a taste of the pain Whip like to inflict on the weaker sex. He had to admit that McCracken was a wily, cunning son of a bitch. He had turned decades of public funding for the Human Genome Project into patent laws to privatize, develop, and control the new genetic-based technology. Korner collected a double paycheck, one in Johnstone Warren's service as hired hand, the other from McCracken for a touch of industrial espionage and solving unsolvable problems like Kiowa Larsen. Man says get the job done, then gets his thong in a wad when the over wrought woman suddenly takes her own life. He snuffed through his nose, threw back his shoulders, and combed fingers through his hair. He detected a faint sulphurous taste in the back of his mouth. The green beast hovered his periphery, a shadow just beyond, no matter how quickly he turned. Or he might come through a dream, appearing in Korner's face, yammering at him, showing his grotesque physique. Pinning Korner with his eyes. Freezing him with his will. Your mine, he'd harangue. You sold your yankee soul to me, he'd chide through blood stained teeth. Then he'd turn his back and walk away carrying a bullet riddled desicated corpse. Korner would know the wounds. He would recognize the bullit riddled torn face, the smile of one with flesh and muscle shot away from corners of the mouth. War without end he thought, despite years walking on, while some, like Darkie'man, seemed so sheltered in safe harbors.

He'd felt a certain kinship with Kiowa Larsen. She had weathered her share of storms.

Ambitious, the Mayor's girlfriend, assistant director of Messing's west coast research and development division, she was capable of shedding blood to protect her turf. In a late night card game, she revealed finding large amounts of money siphoned off for a certain project. She had down loaded the files, but then tried to play Korner against McCracken by holding out the disk. He called her out. They struggled on the bridge. Her silk dress and panties sliding over the flesh of her thigh and buttocks as they struggled, he remembered. Killing the woman, no. She jumped after he let her go. Her scream as she fell was triumphal, finally she was free of possession. Like Dark'ee'man said, it's only a dream. And a scheme.

Korner's main concern remained his own survival. The green beast wouldn't let him slip away that easy, he thought. Whenever feeling free, cold fingers squeezed his guts till bowels and bladder emptied like in his first kill. Liquified by the pressure of blood released under fire. Fire from his hand. Ripping flesh from bare legs of a barefoot man in black silk pajamas. Everyone has someone and some place to go. His was with a company of ghouls led by a shapeshifting lizard with yellow teeth. With Copper Scroll gold and certain desparately sought after papyri in hand, he hoped to buy a respite from this cursed demon parlayed by Christina Shaughnessy's other world influence. Maybe even start his own dynasty.

CHAPTER 6

Mor parked in an alley off Fillmore Street. He pulled out the purse, fingering the design on the flap. In the center was a stiff circle. The tip of his pocketknife sliced into the soft leather, dislodging a plastic disk the size of a quarter that generated its own heat as he turned it in his hand. That heat seemed to permeate his nervous system exciting his spine with a shiver. Information as some sort of electromagnetic cerebral code entered his psyche, an agent slipping through the screen of his thoughts into the back of his mind. Realizing that, meant he possessed a thing worth killing to acquire. Or did it now possess him? He slipped the disk into his boot and drove to Korner's house. The Lincoln sat in the driveway as he pulled in behind.

Two hours had passed since they had parted company and the lights of the city were on. He approached the front door as a disembodied voice spoke. Crazy notions of disembodied minds swirled into his as often happened when he ingested psychedelics. Then as now in the bewitchment of the Seven Sisters of this Saint Francis he found his being their being, a confluence of pirates, plunderers, demons, whores, and lovers. All Her. Kali ma screaming as she tore thru the cosmos a being of it in her"eye'z'izz'z'lin eve're'y body now obliterating everybody, every land, every globe and globular cluster of her mirror seas potential mirror el y appearing of it now awhile. Sweeping all galactic light black into her'eyez z z'ap'ping eve're'y body. Eviscerating every thin'king of it in'for'ma'sz with in her'eye'z z'a sweeping a scythe of now k'now'ing out in forma'sz'any first time. He saw in her'eye'z z zing'ing a whirl of steel blade and flesh, a's'word slicing the indivisble, turning in'visibility of it into a whorl'd'ing d'na'eye'll of it. A world, now merely mirrored potential, a crazy cunning uncanny deceit of mind of any appearance of it as thoughts in'form'aszz mirror duplication of one invisibility a supersonic idea in a being anybody out in her'eyez z'a peh'ss'y w'hole power. Her"e'yez z z'un consciousness of eze eve're'y body. Her'eyez z zazz'a supernatural con she us now to be as thoth'tsz radiating she'e'na, her eve're'y wayeve function mirroring any of us now k'now'ing it out in awhile. A space in time in her"e'yez z' eve re'y asz raining that reigning a y b'ng c'ng asz with unstoppable intent, one pressing urgency int'word merely a pairing of it as t'wo t'wis'ting in'formation appearing to be any body or any thin'king of it. A pervasive blackness black'g"round micro wayeve energy seducing to ignore it by k'no no no'wing anybody or thing in awhile. That wily a while of anybody of a being still changeless. A being in the first place still now as thought'sz out and about k'now'ing for'ma'ss a searing seething second or two. Searching. Electromagnetic black fire. Burning. Knawing away as a need a feeling a being alone now seeking turning a k'now'ing out of it someone, something other, someone somehow missing. Out there waiting in the darkness. Feeling the compression of her weight. Of waiting for her eyez z zi'on him. Any form'asz see'ng in her"e'yez. The gravity of a being see'ng in her"e'yez z. The weight of waiting for her"e ye death. He slipped off his jacket and shirt. feeling the gripping chill of dusky fog sobering his mind till Korner broke his reverie, shouting from above as he leaned over the railing of his third story deck.

"Seen this shit go down before. Dark in the dark. Darkness lost in the darkness of his mind. Or why you never know what crazy dance goin on." he howled in gales of laughter.

"Hell yes. That evil shit done most times in the broad light of day. So don't be slandering the sacred darkness of the black Christ, depraved white man," Mor poured back. He could feel that preacher fire climbing up from somewhere down below as he slipped his shirt and jacket back on. As he approached the front door, a heavy key bounced off his shoulder.

"I'm a being on the roof. You know the way."

The old-fashioned iron key hitting his clavicle left a sting as he clicked it in the lock. He adjusted the disc in his boot with one hand, pushing the door open with the other. He took the stairs two at a time until he reached the top floor. Korner stood on the deck off the bedroom holding out a cell phone. He'd exchanged the full-length leather coat for a black leather vest over white cotton Western shirt with high starched collar and snap buttons glinting with mother of pearl. Mor detected the faint odor of gun oil as he approached.

"It's your girlfriend, the professor."

"Christina?" Mor asked, his boot heels clicking on hardwood as he strode across the room.

"I am very surprised by this call, Mr. Dark Mor." Her voice raised his heart rate. "Few people have the number." He caught his breath as he turned his back on Korner's sly smile.

"Korner digs into people's lives like a depraved miner. Something to do with the company he keeps," he replied.

"He's close to certain influences that unfortunately connect you to me. How can I trust your motives are honest when he pulls such long strings?" she asked. He thought he detected a slight tone of longing or ocean rolling in background.

"I want to love you but I don't know if the world will let me."

"That's from an old Bogart movie. How's the eye?" she said with a laugh.

"A little blue around the edges but nothing I didn't deserve. I need to see you. Something is going on. I tried to paint your portrait last night and torched my digs."

"Sounds like a Korner plot."

"More like a cosmic angle. Let's talk face to face. We can see what's real and what's not."

"Come to my house, 44 Olympic Way. I'll be waiting."

" 'I am all that was, that is, and is yet to come.' "

"That's an inscription from a temple to Isis in Egypt. You do get around."

"Not really. I read it off the plaque on your desk when I drew your portrait."

***

"Oh my, my," Korner chortled as he walked over to give Mor a dig in his ribs. "We do have a woody on for the Professor." He moved to climb the stairs to his glass haven. As they reached the roof, Mor tossed Korner the phone. Chill air jumped his bones sending a shiver up his spine as he took the leather purse from his coat pocket. Korner took the bag with a smirk. "You're pathetic." His expression went flat.

"We know each other too goddamn well. I saw the signs at the bar. You get flushed when you're guilty or want something really bad. The purse belongs to Kiowa Larsen. She's the mayor's side dish who's gone missing. What'd you do, drop her off the bridge?"

"You got an unhealthy thing for the Bridge. Accuse me of murdering a woman? I hope you filled those britches with sand before you got here." Korner lifted a finger toward Mor, the Huey bracelet sliding down his wrist. Mor felt another shiver corkscrew his torso into his hips. Korner's hands were substantial from his years of pounding sandbags after Vietnam. Mor never reached past five feet nine inches and from that height Korner's six feet plus could pass for a towering menace.

He concentrated on deep breathing to keep from shivering. "Sorry if I offended your integrity, except I know the number of kills you've collected. From you."

Korner had confessed his sins to Mor soon after his return from Vietnam, a weepy, alcoholic evening of self-recrimination. The confesssions came with colored photographs of various bullit torn bodies, includung women and children. He remembered not being able to speak for several days, overwhelmed by sheer sadness. His country. His government. Her. Mother Liberty's host slaughtering the helpless. Burning babies. Murdering women and children. Even now he remained stupified wondering what could possibly justify such brutality. Murder in the name of the flag on the sleeve, good ol' Us here all pitching in or burning riot in the street. Tossing pebbles at an iron wall. Was he really any different from Korner or just lucky?

"Fucking Darkness Mor. Why didn't you have the sense to stay north?" Korner turned to the mini-bar built into the cupola, spitting in the stainless steel sink. "You're dumber than an dustbowl Oakie." He leaned on the polished wood sideboard as he turned the hot tap to full. Clouds of steam billowed behind him as he picked up an ivory handled skinning knife. Light from the bar and the steam from the sink cast a nimbus around his head. His eyes glowed like white-hot coals in the shadow.

"That shiver, that shake that rattles your bones to the very core of you? That's death knocking on the door, son." Korner pointed with the blade of the knife. He pulled out a small cutting board and began slicing limes. "I thought I'd seen it all. I was on my third tour. The first two, flying the ol Dog, the Cessna I sent you pictures of, you know. After I got shot down, and seein' corpses, burned, some still alive and screaming. From my hand, tossing those damned SDR's, those smoke rockets on some poor mamasans cutting cane. I didn't deliberately target them, but the napalm that followed my marker sure as hellfire, did. I watched, after they shot me outta my Dog. I watched, as a field doctor amputated both arms of one of those mamasans, she was burned so bad. I cried, dawg. I cried hard and I bled tears. I needed redemption. I wanted to find the real war. Go up against the NVA, the real North Vietnamese Army, get a real taste of our mission in Vietnam, a conventional war against regular communist enemy. Not just shaking the place down, killing the men and fucking the women." Korner paused with the knife, pulling out a liter bottle of Cuervo. He popped the seal and poured tequila in two water glasses, handing one to Mor while avoiding eye contact.

He slumped into a wicker chair, the Huey bracelet clicking the throat of the tequila bottle as it dangled from his wrist. "I pulled strings, but got side tracked on some supply business in one of the bloodiest provinces in the whole guerrilla theatre. Guerrilla, baby, that means anyone is your enemy. On the ground, the whole name of the game is search and destroy. We were four or five platoons and we weren't bearing gifts and goodwill. I said four or five platoons because one of the units got cut up pretty bad before I got there. They got jacked in an empty village full of booby traps set by Koreans, American ordnance, claymores and clusterfucks. One guy lost his dick. Just his dick. They were running around trying to pick up pieces of their brothers while more were going off. They were wiping brains out of their shorts." Korner slouched in the chair, giving Mor a sideways glance with raised eyebrows. He leaned his head back, free as any man in a starry glass cage.

"I didn't know when I went in the Army that I'd be witnessing the descent of man. I just wanted some good clean mano a mano fighting. I think it was the acid. I got it in my head that I needed to walk through the gates of hell to find paradise. I'd been over there nearly three years and still hadn't done what I needed to do, hadn't seen the face I needed to see.

"We choppered in from the firebase to a series of hamlets, hardly more than sticks and cook-fires along a lazy stream the color of green manure. The area was a notorious stronghold for Victor Charley, the Vietcong. I'd met Charley when I was shot down a year or so earlier. I was looking forward to going up against them. They were honorable men. I knew they'd be good fighters. Our boys, well, you know," Korner paused to refill his glass and suck on a lime.

"They were a mixed bag, conscripts without the slightest clue about geo-politics, communism, or who the real enemy was. They'd seen comrades in arms blown to pieces by US goods set by US allies. You might say they were looking for a face to kill. There was one guy, Olsen from Portland. He had a college degree but more than that, I could see in his eyes some moral resolution. Some of the others were no more than thugs looking for an excuse to release their personal dogs of war."

" 'I am all that was, that is, and is yet to come.' "

"What's that?" he asked dully. Korner poured another draught of the Cuervo. His voice had become guttural until it was indistinguishable from street noise, mixed with wind from the Pacific Ocean that rattled the glass panes against iron framework.

"Isis, she said that over 3,000 years ago. Story goes she mated with Osiris, the logos, or word. He lost his rod, too. His brother, Set, cut him up into 36 pieces. Isis found all the pieces except that one, his johnson. Still, Isis managed to immaculately conceive a son."

"Thanks for the tour of Egyptian mythology. You're tripping like you've swallowed a hit of Owsley's finest, only Owsley isn't around any more." Korner dragged himself to his feet and slipped out the Altoids tin, fumbling for a crystal rock.

"I need a camera," Mor said, reaching over to grab the tequila bottle.

"Want to take shots of the Professor? She'd look good strapped down and slung up in leather and chains," Korner chided as he played a rock of the cocaine below his lower lip with the tip of his tongue. His eyes glazed as the coke short-lined into his brain and the neuron highway. Mor tossed the bottle at Korner. He caught it in flight, laughed, and poured another glass.

"I give you the camera, you give me a straight answer. What are you going to photograph?"

"Fair enough. The Illuminatus vision I was never able to put on canvas is calling to me and I want to be ready. What speed film do you have?"

"Film? Man you do still live in the dark ages. I got one that can catch a jet on the dark side of the moon. You're losing your hold on the here and now, Darkhead, I hope Christina can help. Here's the deal. I'll give you a cell phone to go with the camera. Call me when the visions get too bright."

"So what happened?"

"Happened?"

"At the hamlet?"

"Judgment Day, brother. Like no other."

"Did you get the disk?" McCracken's words came over the speaker phone.

"Got the bag but no disk. Not to worry, I've got Mor monitored with a GPS cell. I'm giving him some leash," Korner replied as he waxed the tips of his mustache.

"What, he just happens by and grabs it? He's following you, maybe?"

"Could be Warren's boy, Rakitin, tipped him off." Korner hung up. He was not blind to his friend's connection to Warren. He didn't understand it, the fool could paint a portrait, big deal. Put that between two.38s and see how well the picture protects you. Korner went back to cleaning his Colt, rubbing the blue steel with an oil soaked rag, salt air mixed with machine oil tasting like iodine on a hot knife.

☼

Mor headed south on Highway 1 to 19th Avenue with its corner bars and residential townhouses stacked like stucco encyclopedias. San Francisco State University anchored the terminus of avenue and freeway as 19th Ave fed into 280 freeway at seventy five miles per hour. His heart raced with his wheels, the road drawing him moment by moment closer to Christina.

His mouth felt dry as he drove up her curving driveway, bordered with flowering jasmine, following the sweet fragrances to her glass and beam home perched above black water crashing the 200 foot cliff face. Mor stepped from his truck parked beneath laminated beams thick as tree trunks catching stout rafters anchored with galvanized iron brackets. He watched her through glass walls till she descended the stairs wearing a black woolen turtleneck sweater pulled down mid-thigh over cotton tights. She bounced the last few steps in a pair of Dansko sandals, heels popping on the concrete landing. Her eyes shone from the diffused lighting through a ring of curls. Her lips trembled slightly in the evening chill. He resisted the urge to lean in and touch them with his. The lady could throw a good punch.

"Nice pile of sticks y'all got here," he offered with a grin.

"A Japanese gardener built this in the nineteen fifties. He landscaped the entire lot with bonsai trees and arched bridges. I'm afraid I haven't been able to maintain his standard," she said, swinging the door open with a smile absent of any malice from their previous encounter.

"Looks immaculate to me. No dead branches or empty McDonald's bags," Mor replied as he climbed the stairs, his hand brushing hers. Entering a vestibule he doffed his dusty boots before stepping on to polished hardwood floor leading into the living room. Furnished sparingly, the room gave straight away to a view unobstructed. Flat ocean horizon filled his sight from periphery to periphery. A large hand-knot carpet shot with purple, green, and vermilion lay slightly off center. Walking across it, the colored threads popped with static electricity. He backed into a low mahogany coffee table, catching a gray ceramic vase at the neck, as a spray of carnations and daisies popped out. When he stuffed them back in, one drooped limp on its stem.

"You can feel Starship Earth move with a perspective like this," he replied, starring at walls of glass painted with ocean horizon banding spilt Milky Way.

"Let me get you something to drink. Corona with lime?" she asked, moving to a kitchen, adjoining the living room.

He handed her the purple drooping daisy.

"What's this?" she asked, brushing a curl back.

"Not a thing. I picked it off your table" he offered with a slight bow. "Call it a peace offering."

They moved to the kitchen. He focused on her hands as she opened the bottle. The tequila he drank at the bar and Korner's, had destabilized his nerves. He saw the mean shadow of him hovering over her.

"Mind if I check out your deck?" he asked.

"Not at all. I will join you." She handed Mor the beer and slid open the glass door. Sound of surf crashing rocks two hundred feet below filled the space between them.

He resisted the urge to sweep her in his arms straight away. She sensed his hunger and moved to the deck railing. The belt of Orion and the red Betelgeuse dominated the stars.

"Yod el janza, the hand of the central one," she said softly. "We are nothing. Or one thing, Yod el."

"You really live on the edge of this world," he said, licking beer traces from his upper lip.

"You mean this house?"

"This house, you. You're awake from the dream most of us still tremble in."

"Once you see the ocean, the world is never quite the same," she said, turning to him, the words having barely left her mouth. Christina ran her fingers down his face, the Braille reading of a man lost, he wondered. Pulling her to his chest, his eyes went off her shoulder out to the light years streaming in from beyond the Milky Way. She gently ran her fingers alongside his brow.

"The eye looks rough. I am not very good at one to one relationships," she warned as he leaned his head closer in. He smelled the soap and talc on her skin.

"It's possible we met for another reason other than sex." he replied, touching her lips with his.

"Is it possible for a man to have anything else on his mind?"

Christina gave him her lips and he took them. His hunger threatened to overwhelm him. She pushed him away to keep talking. He knew the chance of him taking her to bed lessened as conversation stood in for lovemaking.

"I figure you as innocent in the whole scheme that appears to be unfolding."

"Excuse me, ma'am?"

"There you go. Feigned innocence but real enough compared to your friend, Korner. His retaining me to translate the Copper Scroll set off all my alarms even though I'm pretty sure he is ignorant of its true purpose or value, and I want him to find the papyri. There's something going on with Korner's employer. You should know we are somewhat at odds," she said.

"I just fell into stupid. Who hired Korner to hire you?"

"You really don't know, who is pulling the strings?" she asked with a puzzled expression. "Johnstone Warren, industrialist and whatever else he likes to hide behind. I should tell you he was an associate of my deceased father. Your friend is his errand boy who brings me you and that painting. I wonder what that evil man wants," she said, wrapping her arms around her chest.

"I know of him. The man who stole the bomb from Uncle Albert. I tell you what he wants, a painting of a face like the Mona Lisa, except he wants the Magdalena. He wants you for the model and me the artist."

Christina stood motionless, her attention on Yod el janza. Mor put his hands on her arms and held her. Tight auburn curls dove around her like a natural extension of the firmament of stars and nebula framing them. He saw her now as cosmic androgyne, an embodiment of realization, the sacred packet of liberated quantum energy, electric fluid in velvety flux, the jewel in the lotus, the pearl in black velvet. He felt himself merged in her body extending into ocean, moon, and stars. His carnal desire evaporated in the coil of a snake unwinding from his pelvis, wheels of light transformed his spine from bone to breath, libido soaring to the third eye.

"Yod," she said, letting her eyes drift back to the heavens. "The one. You see. It's the first letter of the tetragrammaton. Y iota."

"Yod instead of God?"

"Ultimately the same awareness free of causality rather a mere potential."

"Yod hay, I am all there is."

"Was."

"And will be." he threw his head back with laughter as Christina joined him in his arms. He crushed her until he felt her ribs against his and she let out a groan.

"Sorry, it's been a long time." Gusts tore off the water, tangling her hair. She pulled from him gathering a fistful against the wind.

"Let's keep things simple until we sort this out," she said, offering her hand. "Somehow I do not see Warren as an art patron."

"Actually, he bought one of the vision paintings." Mor drained the beer and crunched the lime. Christina appraised him as she took his empty.

"Let me get you another. Did you really burn your house down?"

"Two nights ago when I tried to paint from the sketch." He kneaded his cheek. "I broke five years of sobriety and crawled into a bottle of Quervo, got shit-faced with paint on my hands."

"Did any get on the canvas?"

"Stardust fell into my veins. I went a little mad and next thing I know I'm watching flames consume my cabin, but not your sketch," he said in a raised voice as she went in for another beer.

She handed him another Corona glistening with ice sweat, topped with wedge of lime. As he took the beer, he noticed one crooked tooth on her lower jaw. Mighty Aphrodite had fallen again.

"I remember Warren's name. He bought one of my vision paintings through Korner. He told me Warren hung it over his desk. I've never met the man. Korner told me the story how Warren conceived the atom bomb from a series of Sunday lunches he had with Albert Einstein" He let his voice trail off into surf pounding rocks below. "Somebody left a note in my truck about a purse on the Golden Gate Bridge. Then low and behold, what do I find right where it was described," he said with a wave of his hands. "I'm ready to hear about what I've been dragged into. Strange has been dogging me since Korner came back on the scene."

"If you want old money, old brotherhoods invested in petrochemicals, pharmaceuticals, genetic engineering, and global banking, Warren is your man. I trust none of them, even with Rothschild in my blood. Warren in his younger days was a student of Hashkalah. He wanted to be a rabbi. He wasn't Jewish but this should be a problem? Warren went from wanting to be a rabbi to being the father of modern venture capitalists. The Warren family has embezzled kings, and countries, back to the American colonies, invested in both sides of the U. S. Civil War. But if you were to hear him say it, his rise corresponds with the fusion of a deeper understanding of ancient mysteries with the ever-widening Freemasonry tradition. He'll tell you. It's what World War Two was really about. I wonder what's in your heart, the visions, suicides, and bones clattering in the closet?"

"I'm descended from Vikings, drunk Irishmen, and mercenaries born as fodder for war," he replied, taking a long pull on the beer. "I shoulda been in that meat grinder in Vietnam but Korner saved me by giving me this," he said, pulling down his shirt to show her the scar.

"He shot you."

"You say that as a statement of fact. He still denies and I won't get into what all that denial entails," he resisted taking her in his arms.

"Maybe you're both infected with the death wish so common in men. That's why the Kabala perpetuated as a deck of playing cards. Someone knew men would turn to gambling as an alternative to war, like gladiators and the National Football League. For Warren, the world became a big crap game."

"Other than rape, burn, and pillage, we men aren't much good. Tell me, darling, what is Warren's power trip really about?" he asked, leaning back on the railing to look at the stars.

"Welcome to a world beyond the world as we know it. Warren is Korner's source for the Copper Scroll, and he encouraged Korner to have me do the translation. Only he knows the purpose. I've tracked down what I could about Warren's current project but my sources tell me the old hellhound is keeping his cards close."

Mor gazed out to the snowy track of the Milky Way cleaving the vault of sky like a starry river coursing through black firmament. Cassiopeia zigzagged past her daughter, Andromeda, to Daneb, crown of the Northern Cross. Constellations blazed out from a field of nebula storms, swirling with cosmic dust bombarded with x-rays from black holes.

"I wonder, do we really look at where we live?" he asked, rolling his neck to pop a few kinks. "Who said, 'we live in the infinity of the gods'? Where did the gods go?" Overhead Jupiter shined as bright as a mini full moon. "Once we see planets and stars as gods and goddesses, we wake from the slumber of thinking too much of it as only dust and gas in an empty vacuum. It lives. It breathes me or you."

He moved his arm across her back, drawing her close. He felt the muscles ridging off her spine, the beating of her heart, the expanding and contracting of her breath. He smelled the rosemary in her hair mixed with iodine from sea salt evaporating in the wind. She drew him out of the spell of orbits creating the mirage of solid matter, a matter of time, space mere appearance in a being c'ng out now awhile that flashed in word memory in his mind.

"Language is the trail I follow into the cave of deep time, time measured in millennia," she said. "What I discovered when I came up against the stone wall where language becomes purely oral, is that, as mankind developed alphabets, we lost touch with our inner divinity. Y'all that divine now mere in word idea as'z thoughts of a being mirrored in the'or'y of man'as mind or y memory. That spell of in word alphabeta creates a mirror duplicate of that indivisible invisibility by letter'all'y y'all appearing any form'asz . . ."

"Sound ways of eve're'y means . . . ."

" a thin slice of a being invisibility now out k'now'ing awhile in a primary indivisible wave spectrum. Her way of eve 're'y as'z'ex spectrum for'ma'sz appearing out x's ting in formation now awhile. Now a w'h'ile is an uncanny . . . "

"Cunning deception. These thoughts have been playing in my head. Thinkin' too much," he replied with a frown.

"In her'eyez z z of eve're'y body is eve'll. In her eyez z z'a will be seen any scene of it. Eve'll'ness to be a na y wayeve will or intention . . .," she touched his lips with a static charge that captivated his neuronic mind. He felt the wayeves of her eye'sz z z rippling his autonomic nervous system playing into his spine and the chakras. The wheels. The we all's he mused kissing her back in her eyezazzaz ways, in her eye seen a wile. He gave himself to it. It taking him like a flea on a dog's back he thought with a chuckle.

She now answered with their lips touching.

☼

McCracken bit down on his lower lip until he tasted blood. To the side of his desk, the stone carving of a winged man spoke a silent language. The statue, smuggled out of Iraq after the last invasion, was procured just to piss off Warren. Gazing at the ancient relic set off by the glass and chrome of his modern office, he reflected on the old geezer, the man who burned grandfather Albert, compared to his own siring the 21st Century genome project child.

R.J. remembered from abandonment and poverty, his mother and father unnamed and unknown. Adoptive parents lived above a tailor shop where the elevated trains of Chicago's North Side shook chunks of plaster from the walls. Street toughs robbed the pocket money he earned working in his father's tailor shop, until he grew into size thirteen shoes and learned to fight back. Learned the street. Learn to knock a big man on his ass.

McCracken left home. He washed dishes, pushed gravel hoppers across miles of flat industrial roofs, and hauled lumber on construction sites. He saved, and starved thru college, majoring in mixing chemicals, computers, and lite bondage as a fetish intoduced to him by an offbeat girlfriend.

He came of age with the dawn of integrated micro circuits, riding the information highway to riches, holding patents on compression software, and leading him to the edge in proteomics and nano technology. His was the largest consortium of computer technology on the West Coast, which he called Portal.

His dream. Ro'bionics. He wanted to create self-replicating living man machines from nano engineered protein building blocks. The winged stone man symbolized his pursuit. There were glitches in the process. The human genome only contained 40,000 genes, whereas a typical cell made hundreds of thousands of distinct proteins. His people were on the verge of a breakthrough when the mystery darkness came reabsorbing protein holograms like a transiting black hole. Research faltered, then sputtered to a halt.

McCracken's only competitor was Warren with his Messing labs consortium. Now the key to Warren's latest breakthrough research floating just beyond his grasp on Kiowa Larson's disc. Just as that golden ring appeared within reach, some half wit half baked artist snags it. That old man waiting for his life to end, could never understand the subtleties of twenty-first century intelligence, but he's got more lab.

McCracken thought he might live to regret hiring Korner, paying him enough to compromise his loyalty to Warren, but never knowing exactly to what side of the fence he might jump. The price of doing business with a fiend like Korner. Sure he introduced him to Zina's, letting Korner believe he was depraved, part of a subterfuge he had worked out with Larsen. He wanted Korner to believe, to keep him guessing. Leave it to a blond with fake tits to try and play him against that killer.

He recalled those nights at Zina's with her snorting cocaine, and drinking whiskey straight up. She had played a mean stick at pool, and sex. She was fun, if slightly damaged. Korner really was psycho, he reflected, rapping a fertility stick on his palm .

McCracken seethed to see that disc and get a leg up on Messing. He looked out the heavy glass windows that fronted the atrium courtyard of Portal's Menlo Park inner sanctum. His corporate logo, implied access. He envisioned his destiny to control the secrets encoded in the genetic matrix of life. To build a better mankind or kind of man. A synthetic kind of man, self replicating armies of that kind of man. Kiowa's disk held information he needed but she gave him a companionship he longed for. Now Korner had silenced her. Lifeless eyes stared back off the glass through the murky veils of his daydream.

☼

Passing lights pierced the water droplets splattering his windshield as Mor headed downtown. His thoughts turned to always getting found, drifting up and down these seven hills, once forty, counting sand dunes on the Peninsula. He got found, in that city of wasted saint, an urban body of gods and devils fire, two sides of one forged gold coin. The original barren windswept peninsular tip had remained uninhabited in those pre-Columbian centuries. The first invaders, Spanish missionary priests chose for their mission site, a more sheltered location along a stream a mile inland from ocean tinged bay. He'd read the original mission had been reduced to a saloon and stable by the time of the Gold Rush. He knew the action of the gold rush in eighteen forty nine, centered on a harbor of wharves just around the eastside. Sheltered from the Golden Gate where gold fevered crews abandoned hundreds of ships. He imagined lathered teams of mules, huffing some wooden hulk on shore for a saloon, a hotel, hell, even an insane asylum for those losing their minds in the 'rush'. An instant city arose from those wooden hulls, their sail cloth now tents for saloons and gambling parlors.

For Mor, the rush was still on. Minds still being blown. Longhaired hippies and sweet butts in patched Levis had replaced the roughneck miners and bustled madams, gold now in hallucinogens, opiates, and tetra-cannabinals. In this wind swept and fog-shrouded land, he along with countless other refugees sought the soul of a country that failed any real complete definition. Failed in a bloody quagmire 10,000 miles west across the Pacific. Failed in assassination or incorporation. Failed in other wars on race, poverty, or drugs. This second rush was on to find free love in a fairy landscape that had turned sand dunes to picnic parks, rododendron grooves, stately Redwoods, artificial lakes, or a neo classic glass conservatory, all flowing into a blue collar neighborhood teeming on a commercial street called Haight. Looking for love in the Haight. Mor knew it well. Knew it as golden gate to other dimensions. Luminous dimensions as real as the myriad rows of Victorian ginger bread alongside stucco faux mission style houses and five story apartments rolling up then down the neighborhood called Haight Ashbury. He knew her mad chemists separating out pure white crystals of lysurgic acid on the upside or dipping innocuous mushrooms in animal tranqilizers on the downer side. It was a place to meet God and the Devil mixing it up in one crazy dance of elite spiritual beings and criminal degenerates. About blissful liberation or enslavement to addiction and self annihillation.

Such was the irony, he mused, of looking for love in the Haight. When the flowers faded and the drugs hardened, that street would live up to its name. After the affluent flower children returned to college from a summer of love, the rush still on, a poorer trashier legion drifted in from thousands of miles north, east, and south.

Coincidently the degradation of the neighborhood dropping real estate values like a hippie coming down from a dose of windowpane acid, afforded the mayor's daughter the opportunity to make the proverbial real estate killing. Then there was real killing in the Haight. Mor remembered bodies turning up in basement graves. Destitute drifters lost in her maw. Drugged hippie girls raped in the spreading shadows. The Psychedelic Shop burned to the ground. Police sub-station bombed. The rush still on. On speed and downers.

He recalled the day a blue wave showed up in force along with innovative shadowless street lighting casting out many of the demons. Religion poured in from taps around the world. Mor figured all the acid had burned a hole into which a litany of gurus and would be's were drawn along with the lambs. Boomer parents feared them more than the acid which had at least the patina of good old American entrepreneur about it. This next religious wave smacked of foreign gods, of heresy, of mind control diverging from that of the great American religious institutions conventionally accepted. Mor flashed on 500 hippies, the good kind educated liberal hearts filled with back to the land hope. Mother earth in their shoes, headed out in old school buses for a farm in Tennessee. Or 1500 poor ghetto black and white taking the kool-aid in the jungle of Guiana. He been up then down these hills of ecstasy or despair enough times to know better. Or not.

He neared Market and Powell's fog smeared amber streetlights, turned north on Jones, then east on Post, entering the Saint Francis Hotel through the Geary Street parking garage. A valet in a red vest greeted him with a smile, nonchalant about parking the dusty pickup with Jags, Beamers, and Benzes

"Find a good spot for her, Jackson. She's all I got left after my pad burned down last nite," Mor gave as he stepped out.

"You gots it brother. I'll see she gets tucked in," the attendent replied with a grin.

"Gonna be a chilly evening with that fog," Mor returned before catching up with his self sworn vow not to talk inanely about the weather.

Kwasanda was right about the night too cold to sleep in his truck. Just thoughts of trying to sleep shivering in the chill put his nerves on edge. Tonight he chose the Saint Francis for its name and proximity to the site of his vision of the pyramid and the flaming eyes. There was an answer, a reassurance he hoped to find. Craved for.

Checking in at the desk, he went straight to the bar. He had no luggage, only the fresh clothes on his back after he'd showered at Christina's. The tinkle of jazz piano caught his attention and he took the three steps up to the Compass Rose lounge. The pianist shook out her fine waist length black hair as her head bobbed up from the keys just as he looked over.

He had seen too many movies of hotel lobbies with shady characters and femme fatales. The Saint Francis had that century old dark wood paneled ambience with low lit raised lounge offset from the open lobby. This may only be a movie, his role unfolding as the story projected on the blank screen. Then who was the director and would he get the girl?

Mor looked around candle lit tables in the oak paneled lounge. Through tall arched windows fronting the street, he saw a bus parked at the stop where the pyramid had once appeared, mirage flames dancing above its truncated base. Holy gnosis revealed amongst the clamor of city streets, more real to him than steel and concrete.

Notes from the Yamaha grand piano played over him like the creek rushing over the rocks below his cabin. A few guests seated around the circular bar occupied the room. Mor turned his attention to the woman at the keyboard. She picked up a chord as others scattered beneath her fingers.

He drifted over to a small table by the window. Outside, blue flashing lights zig zagged from the roof bar of a tow truck hooking up a disabled Muni bus.

"Would you mind taking our picture?" He looked from the street to a couple standing over his table.

"Excuse me?"

The pianist joined the couple.

"Hello there. Can you take a photo of us?"

"Let me at the camera. I'm Dark Mor," he offered.

"Sue Lee. Thanks for doing this," she replied, and handed him a small digital camera.

Sue lee and the couple pulled in around the piano, chandeliers in the background. Mor popped a couple of frames. Her porcelain skin, faintly rouged at the cheeks, flared in a flash-against the dark of the candlelit lounge. They took the camera and left the bar.

"Friends?"

"Actually just met. They liked my music."

"I've never heard anything quite like it, kind of an Asian cool jazz."

Sue Lee went back to her playing, shaking back her silky tresses, ends falling across her back. Flesh tones of thigh stretched out from a sequined burgundy mini skirt as her black spike heel rocked on brass pedals.

"How often do you play?" he asked.

"I'm only here on trial basis. My sound hasn't brought in the crowds."

"Saw a man here once do Frank Sinatra in a tux, smooth back-up band with a stand-up acoustic bass, martinis in long stemmed glasses. Nostalgia for the good bad old days filled the tables."

She answered Mor with a silent smile.

☼

Warren drifted off into contemplation, his wasted body slumped in the wheelchair. He dreamt of bombs, hundreds of thousands of bombs, stacked pointing out, pointing down, running to the horizon. More bombs, pointed upwards, marched endlessly left and right. On the far periphery he saw explosions, showers of blood rain thick with mangled body parts. He turned back to a board room, associates seated alongside one another running the length of both sides of the table. They were a mixed breed of faceless creatures wearing various smiling masks. A red river, flowing with slag and offal, ran beneath them. Then he smelled Rakitin's soap.

"Is that you, Stepan?"

"Yes sir. We're you sleeping?"

"I have been observing. War, you know, is no longer a winnable game. Whereas endless war against faceless terror is very profitable, complete doom is very bad for business. It is time. Time to recognize we are ready for space even if it means enslaving and killing millions. Ultimately we all turn into a liberation liberating everyone. I am not talking of space ships and colonies. Not that, I am seeing. Seeing the big picture. Recognizing the spatial nature of us as a being. The singular indivisible BLACKNESS body just us of a being cosmic. Are we all not invisibility in the vastness of ma'ss nature. Invisibility yet still aware of any appearing of a being c'ng of that. What is all this business of busi'ness. Plunder and pussy," he cackled.

"All that is holding us back is archaic crumbling attachments. Tiny grubby fingers blindly grasping for a desperate and fleeting fragment . . ." Warren hesitated as he grasp for his breathing to get back in rhythm with the pumps supporting his life systems. "Now, the true Christ prophecy will come to pass with a sword to smite and sever those ignorant unwashed that would hold us back with every wasted breath in their meaningless lives. I must lead. I must advance us at all costs. This end, this final journey, will be my legacy. Do you think those demons at Messing have any vision of liberation? Only I, Stepan. Only I have the power to execute this grand awakening. The dying white race has become coddled and lost the will to perpetuate this myth. Soon, Stepan, no more vanilla ice cream, only mocha, lemon, and strawberry. "

☼

Mor threw back the shot of tequila as Sue Lee finished her last set. They had talked briefly during her previous break. As the Buddha said, imagine everyone as once being your mother. Better to gain detachment than make a fool out of yourself. But what the hell. It wouldn't be the first time and probably not the last. Feeling no more pain from the last bruise, he still felt irrevocably drawn to that pudendum spread across the sky. Christina had ultimately refused his advances but the last parting was amicable. He would see her again. Just now, he felt an arousal dormant over the past few years.

"You have a card?" Sue Lee asked as she sat across from him. Outside, the decommissioned bus had been towed away. Others came and went.

"Join me for a drink."

"I have to meet my fiancé," she said.

"Why ask for a card?"

"Sex is not all a woman wants. She can be interested in getting to know someone."

"My apologies. I felt a certain tension between us I usually associate with mutual desire. Must be the booze."

"Are you an alcoholic as well as a sex fiend?"

"Are you a ball buster as well as a musician?"

"When I'm playing, the music gives me flashes inside people. I enjoy men with minds."

"What a concept."

"My fiancé is a neurosurgeon."

"What's that got to do with me? I'm a burned-out painter."

"I watch people and ask myself, what do they think? Do they ever wonder who they really are, what they're really about? Do they ever question or merely stumble forward with the herd? I look for a man who can think and you're there. You have the look of someone thinking about more than football and vaginas."

"Pure coincidence. I'm still stuck on the riddle, 'that I am.' "

"Now you're going into the real question. That turns me on."

Mor studied her face. So much blood rushed to his brain that it seemed to swell. Ultraviolet hues pulsed in the shadows.

"Listen to my music. Answers are everywhere," she said, slipping a CD into his hand.

Sue Lee touched his head. Static electricity arced between palm and forehead as her fingertips pressed on the top of his skull. She walked the carpeted stairs to the lobby and out through the revolving doors. He looked at the cover of the CD. Sue Lee smiled over her bare shoulder as she sat in a sequined red mini-skirt on the edge of a white baby grand. Enough of musical women, he cursed. He slipped the CD in his pocket.

He took the glass elevator that passed the rooftop of the original hotel to another thirty stories above. Opening the door he found his room had the usual bed, bath, mini-bar, and side table with a telephone. He turned on the light in the bathroom, took off his shirt and touched the scar on his chest. A year had passed before he'd fully recovered from the shock of being shot. Circumstances that evening being somewhat murky, Korner was never charged. For Mor, it was just something in the cards being dealt. Drawing saved his life in a way, for in his recovery, he rediscovered with in, a silent friend who helped heal the boy and taught the man to see. For Mor, drawing was his dhyana, his means for finding himself whole if not completely sane. For the Sanskrit, he thanked Christina. He saw a silver plate with gold foiled mints on a table. He pealed the foil, letting the chocolate melt on his tongue.

Chapter 7

Christina stayed awake, to jot some notes for the next day's lecture. She felt Dark Mor's desire but her intuition warned against such a level of involvement. She had a deep and abiding commitment to her mission expressing the inner voice, the soundless narration in a wordfreedom awareness of a being in the first place now for those k'nowing of it with y'ears to hear. She now wondered if Dark was trying to warn her or she should warn him about Warren and his scheme to use them in his game of intelligence and liberation. Were they both of the same ancient order, existing outside movements of time, mere vocal symbols in an allegorical myth like those carved into temple walls, scribed on scrolls of papyrus, and passed on through unbroken oral tradition? Meeting the Dark'ness stirred a blacked up awareness appearing of it out in her'eyez z z'i'on of eve'll. A will of we all a wheel turning yearning burning of that in word knowledge of a b'ng c'ng still in the first place. It took living the street life hard to integrate visions, e.t. encounters, mystic dreams . . . intense y'ears of fear in tearful loss to feel it, field the LOVE SUPREME shining in above. Ove a b'ng now turning a d'na'eye'll of it into k'no'wing devastating sorrow. Thus she now had bore witness to an intellectual wasteland laying high or low while still sheltered in the ivory tower estate. She now wondered is gaining intellectual objective understanding important when real spiritual a're'y'al'eye'szation came from overstanding above any understanding it below . . . is that clarity of mind almost a mistake . . . a make believe point of view . . . a pulling up short of a being c'ng merely a peering it out of it by now still a k'now'ing of a subtle denial of it . . . is this clarity of mind . . . so hard to obtain . . . in fact enemy of final liberation . . . confounding any further learning or y'earning to pay attention . . . still as int'word a being'zz'a turning churning burning now around a k'nowing out of it at attention yet na as thought'sz of na standing at it . . . it a being still in the first place or as'z'anybody appearing of it as thoth'tsz out of it . . . it still now supernaturally superimposed as'zz'any k'now'ing out int'word thoth'tsz of it appearing a pairing . . . letter'all'y y'all a God esse to be art of peh'ss'y"ence. A w'hole now k'nowing out of it as'ka's mic memory. A b c's in word mean means meaning full of denial as'z k'no'wing of it anybody of a b'ng c'ng still in the first place . . . Pa'roo'ma . . .indivisible in'visibility in a wordfreedom now with a supernatural b'lack'g'round intent of appearing of it out a'gain. . .a'gain of it out and about by sheer pow . . . pow . . . power . . . supersonic peh'ss'y w'hole power out in her"eyez z z'azz a will wayeve re'y"e a're'y'e'dhi'a'ting in'visibility still indivisible as'ka's micro wayeve black'g'round . . . that keen overstanding free status state, the eye star'e'or ey 'e a peering it. . . out now as'ex posed . . . posing appearing of it . . .as'ex . . . o'ne un'o . . . un'a known, objectified or merely duplicated as now k'now'ing out of it as'z'any thoth'tsz of it letter'all'y y'all appearing of it out in word a pairing of it a y as'ex'y'all as'ka's mic memory potential. . . macro micro wayeve black'g'round echoing as'king of it aska's mic'all'y y'all me or you.

In her eyez z z the journey started with that inner confidence that she now could bring forth from the impenetrable deepest mists of time that in word disconnect connection of it. In word that a're'y'e"awakening of de'sire from above. Ove a b'ng c'ng in reaching black untouched in a wordfreedom yet a y eye merely a peering it. A're'y'e of a b'ng c'ng in the first place of what the Egyptians called zep tepi in'for'ma'sz any first time. Every girl remembers that, she now thought of at least one memorable version of it. Yet, though that be but one memory in time zep tepi points to a b'ng c'ng still in the beginning. Still it n'eve'r'ey passes eve'n'at your eye'sz'za all out in her"eye a peering it. A b'ng c'ng a peering it out int'word a twis'ting in two a present presence in appearing a pairing moment by moment millions upon zillions of passing versions of it. Untouched passing virgins of it as mirrored in word potential that she now pondered.

Christina went into it with in her'eye on a mission wide-eyed and open-minded. After facing entrenched academic and gender bias or fear of what could only be called extreme hostility, extreme ignorance of it, she now had backed off. Backed into all the validation she needed still in a wordfreedom awareness of a y eye of a b'ng c'ng merely a peering it. It out in her"eyez z z'ap'ping'ting see'ng in him. Him see'ng in her'eye. Her'him'it. Ay eye of a b'ng c'ng of that point of view of you of a y'in her"e y'e"ang'st searching scrolls and codices in hieroglyphic and hieratic phonographic writing on papyrii, tombs, and temple walls. A b'ng c'ng of that. Akh et a'ten. A first place duplicated of'ten. A bi na re'y a're'y'e'dhi'a'ting it. A perceived feeling of that. A fielding of that supernatural supersonic radiant a're'y'e'dhi'ance of view of you of a y eye of that seer insight of a b'ng see'ng it. Or any a na y body of a being that feeling alone. A still indivisible in'visibility in the first place.

Shaking all over with laughter and pure glee, she now got it. It, the vision of the ancient sacred order yet a b'ng c'ng still in the first place. Out of it infused in the sound wayeve re'y of it in form'aszz'a mean means meaning full of the letters themselves. The a b c's of it. Out in word as'z that sound wayeve re'y'ez z z'a black body never confused without in word in'formation of it with a b'ng c'ng still in the first place. Y'et indivisible invisibility of a b'ng c'ng merely a peering it out int'word concept syntax or semantics of language phonographically recorded. Y'all now k'now'ing a b c's out in wordsz'azz'z awhile still a b'ng c'ng it. A be"am'ing of it a'sz any in word appearing the appearance of it. A mere mirrored a pair'ance of it with a b'ng c'ng asz'any mirror supernatural thoth'tsz of it out in her"e'yez z z'azz'a eve re'ybody appearing of it in wayeve patterns. A bingo bongo baby. Letter'all y y'all let her keep hitting those as'key"es she now a're'y'flected of it. A b'ng c'ng a're'y'all'ity as'king of it out in her"eyez z'a re'y'all'eye'zinging it.

* * *

Then traveling to the Middle East and the Indian Subcontinent, Margot Christina cast a breast upon the great 'Eastern Star of Ancient Wisdom'. She now anticipated that metaphorical psychic thrashing and trashing of the notions coded in the name of the 'little' Christ. Christina. Now with ovaries and womb. High Priestess, Empress, the High Noon. Eve're'ybody virgin mother as'z'z'any Ma'ss'z sound ways of eve. A'wayeves out in her'eyez z z'i'on it. Now a black wayeve're'ybody. A'n'ocean of e'motion of e wayeves. Electricomagnetic. A'Re'y aL function of function. A y eye now turned int'word a twis'ting in two a k'no'wing d'na'eye'll of it as'ka's micro wayeve blackness of the Christ. G'ee's"us. A weight of a'waiting on it.

Ove eL. Love Supreme bliss. Of a Kryst. As'Krishna, the blue black sacredness body of a b'ng c'ng a peering it out of that a y eye as'ka's micro wayeve of it. A b'ng c'ng echoing of a black'g'round. Captivated at attention in wordszazz' a y el. A space in time now the web of deceit of ma'trix. A tricky wayeves function of fun'ny'a'ction. A Ma'sz bag of tricks. A Ma's jest y of a cunning supercraft of sheer folly . . . a supernatural duplicity of Y as'eX. The Geometry of 3D. DaDhiDupe. Duplicating duplicity with a quantum gravity. The weight of gee's us death . . . the waiting . . .d'na'eye'll of eve're y now knowing out of it. The d'Nu u'ni mind as alternating alter'native man. Or y a b'ng c'ng now turning a b'lack'g'round as'king of it echoing any thin king of a k'now'ing out of it in word. Echoing a duplicity of it as'z'any measly chintzy meager thin king of it. A'sz peh'ss'y'enc'ng w'hole a pseudo dominance of the right brain by the left over thin'king of it int'word in'formation a la que"en que' mode. Still a b'ng c'ng a visual predominance primarily out in her"eyez z z'inging of a hearing brain. Supersonically informa'ing it. The old yet eve're'y nu brain. Perpetually y'all Eve re'ye of a virgin mother Empress GoD'hi'ess'e. A BoDhi. A Buddhi. A Buddha.

Now homeostasis. A ripening of the fruits of thrashing and gnashing of teeth. Of it as'z'any thoth'tsz of it dying and reborn asz zillions. The journey East nearly devoured Christina. Leaving just enough id, just enough blood and bone for Jerusalem. Why? She now thought, this stirring for the Dark man? A burning of egg'spectations flashed in her'eye. Of eve re y'body a virgin mother but Dark Mor hardly immaculate. Still with that testoserone stink she now smiled with a heart beating faster till drawing a quick breath. She now could not help letting attention drift down to her 2nd chakra. A SVADDHISTANA az's'ex'citing eggs'spectation of it.

In her'eyez z' a smile. A sva'dhi. A self perception of it. A self desire was starting a slow burn. Using breath and the contraction of abdominal muscles she now forced a peh"ssy w'hole energy back up through a heart into a brain.

The bus broke down crossing Afghanistan. She had hitched a ride with a slightly mad Pentacostal priest who tried over a thousand tortuous miles to turn her head around to his way of Christianity. But by the time they reached the Kashmir border, in her'eyez z z'inging a little Krystos completely swallowed his Christ'ism. She now found out in her'eyez z z' of e've'reybody as'ka's all'y y'all a causal still virgin awareness in a wordfreedom untouched indivisible in'visibility of any bodhi. A na y body of deeper roots'z'z za'y eye of wisdom. A wordfree'dom'us of we all in a y eye dialectic debate enraging engagement of it. Awareness of a y eye merely a peering it. Or appearing of it letter'all'y y'll information moment by momentum. As'z'any in'formation of it no matter how well stated yet completely underrated. As'king of it now any k'no'wing appearing of it out in formation of a starved stunted thin'king of it. Awhile. Once again she now found that ancient one and asked, 'do you believe in aliens and aryans?

"Why honey, in that I am an alien aryan," the ancient one had replied without a trace of irony.

Christina had doubted there were any legitimate teachers left alive in this prehistoric Indo Aryan Brahma'vidya oral tradition but let faith take her'eye through Persia and Afghanistan, to India, and mother ganga, the Ganges River, and at her headwaters, Rishikesh. Reaching there, wasted from dysentery and pentacostal'aian fever, she collapsed before a woven straw hut. Awakening, she now looked into the glowing eyes of a dark holy man in a scarlet robe.

For a few moments they didn't speak.

"Where am I," Christina had asked.

"Now that I am awakes to ask the question," he had replied with a giggle. Her whole quest resolved in his statement. She now realized it, once more. As yet now today, she might venture, that I am still a b'ng c'ng y'all in the first place. That awareness of it completely y'all that I am can eve'r'eyez z z'i'on it. Out in her'eye or ther'eye. Out in her"e'ye the a"re'y"e. Then the grand journey to the East lay in tatters at her feet. A mere mockery of obsession with y'all things ancient. A modern office in Palo Alto might have sufficed. In that I am thinking you gots to laugh along with the tears she now mused.

Everything clicked then it clacked. The dysentery had inroduced a parasite that affected her mind, which fragmented with all the languages learned. Then too quickly assimilating Sri Shivshankaraji's wielding the Sanskrit pramana. This ancient oral device removed all traces of ego. Burned the dross in the fire of BRAHMAJNANAM. A'kh'nowledge'menta of a being still in the first place. Transmitted with raz'z z'or sharp logic. Scintillating clarity. Not about it. IT. A b'ng c'ng a peering it out now as'k'no'wing of it still. Then, where are you, in'visibility of a dust mote in galactic awareness. Out in her'eyez z z'i'on a journey of it shattered into a black mirror se'e'as a're'y'flecting da y na light into a mosaic with hundreds of thousands. Scarlet robed

Sadhus chanting through phases of sun and moon riding thick chillum clouds of hashish. Freed by the decay, the putrifaction, the corrosion eating away at tradition. Or any institution of it. In formation awhile. The ancient land innoculated modernity with its myriad spiral virus parasites and its staph of worms. Still Jerusalem waited to call her'eyez z z to a fate for some of her flesh, her meat and bones. Kali ma Inja would continue in her'eye of eve're'ybody devouring years after a leaving of it out in her'eye"land.

☼

The cell phone rang, ruining the beginnings of an erotic dream that included Kwasanda, Christina, and Sue Lee. Korner spoke, making Mor grind his teeth.

"See you got checked in. I can imagine the set-up, you asleep on the covers, bathroom light on, and no woman for the Darkness."

The nickname came from high school. He had stupidly left a city bus after an angry argument with Korner, only walking a few blocks before it hit him. He a flat foot white boy in Blackstone Ranger territory on Chicago's South Side where even black cops don't go. Before Korner had showed back up with a ride, he'd earned the razor scar carried over one eyebrow.

"That night I gave you the name, remember, I knew you were as crazy as me," said Korner.

"I remember. There I was. It's dark, but then I'm white. I see this cat across the street, standing on the corner. He's full on crushed velvet overcoat, fur collar, heavy jewelry, black as that south side hood could possibly make it and darkest Africa could not beat."

"And what does my wise brother do?" Korner's voice betrayed his sarcasm.

"What else could a lone short blond punk in hard gettoe' hell outa here land, do? I kissed him. Can still smell his cologne, found out later it was french."

"And with great big lips he kissed you back?" Korner asked, not stifling a laugh.

"I kissed him on the cheek. He sliced me quick with a straight razor. You pulled up in that caddy and we got the hay outta there." Mor detected the shift in his speech patterns. He tasted that metallic flavor of psychedellia. Tie my tail to a rocket, he thought.

"Too many drugs, brudder," he mumbled as the glue of his personal ignorant world started dissolving. "Where are you anyway?"

"I'm on a schooner east of the Farallones," Korner replied. "I'm looking at starlit ocean rippling under a half moon, babycakes, but then, you have a wonderful cruise, there your own self."

Korner was gone. Mor looked at the other gold foil and the purple haze emanating in his periphery. He realized Korner or someone had dosed him. He pealed the other chocolate and slipped it on his tongue. Much too late for common sense anyway, he thought.

He recalled the flaming helix of eyes pouring out of the truncated pyramid. He imagined the precision of shaped and surfaced stones, veined with nearly invisible lines of mortar. The eye began a's point of view. A seer see'ng of a b'ng c'ng now k'now'ing in word a projection of it. A re'y eye a peering it out into appearing of one living flame shifting into a churning double helix of roiling balls of eyez z zap'ping. Eye and pyramid a re'y'velation of a b'ng c'ng still in the first place at aten'cion for those with 'eyes to see' merely a peering it.

In a blink of one of those eyes, Mor found himself heading for the parking garage. He handed the valet a ticket and a green SUV appeared.

"Your car, sir."

"Is that what I came in on?"

"Well, sir, that wasn't my shift. But have a pleasant evening."

He drove to the Marin Headlands and a high gabled New England colonial mansion, buffeted by head winds till it appeared slightly out of plumb. There was no gate or guards, the house looking deserted, along with the parking lot Mor passed on the way in.

He drew his leather jacket tight as he walked the empty house. He made a fire in an open outdoor brick fireplace, brewing tea in an iron kettle on the hob. By the time he had the mug to his lips, he looked to see vehicles arriving. A tall black man with chevron stripes on his arms and red beret joined him by the fire.

"What you doing here?" the sergeant asked around large, square teeth.

"I'm officially listed as a hand painter. But I don't paint hands, har, har. Painted a few names on doors before I was released from further government service. You guys CIA?"

"Ain't no CIA." He growled as he backed away.

Mor hunkered over his tea mug as the parking lot filled with all manner of wheel and tracked vehicles. Personnel swarmed in various uniforms. Officers parked close to the house, giving him only the lightest of recognition. A woman in a blue jumpsuit tapped him on the shoulder.

"Take these tickets. Tickets to a play, actually three tickets, two to one play and a third to something else." She offered a smile as she walked to the fireplace.

"Nice butt," he muttered under his breath. The house expanded to include a three-story atrium surrounded by concentric rings of offices and apartments, bristling with activity. He flashed on one pumped muscled hulk, wearing a black beret with white piping and gold braids on his collars. Mor read, Israeli Sky Commando in stitched red on the blue patch of his massive sleeve.

He went out the front to find a bivouac of several hundred troops with lines of tents. He wanted to find his ride and get down the road, but considering the bewilderment of vehicles, finding the SUV would be impossible.

He pushed aside the flap of a tent and entered. Women in low-cut blouses served the men food and titillation.

"Need direction?" asked a trooper in battle fatigues, combat boots, and white tee shirt.

"The saints be with you, brethren. I'm just a messenger."

"We haven't had a man in a while and you're pretty enough to fuck."

The troopers smirked at each other as they toyed with the only civilian in town. The women kept serving.

Mor ran. The troopers grabbed long coats to cover their insignias as they chased him. He chewed the "something else" ticket as he ran. He flew several feet above the ground, sailing through a windbreak of poplars, till he touched back down. The troopers were still behind him. He took flight again, landing in a closed room, flapping against the walls like a helpless bird banging into shut windows.

"You may as well sit down." A man in khaki trousers and zippered jacket motioned to a desk in the room. Shelves held stacks of books and files. He recognized a being. To his astonishment, Mor found himself pulling down shelves, kicking over boxes releasing swirls of paper in innocent fun, till a being gave him stern uncle, stopping further vandalism with a look.

"We accessed you through the chocolate, better than sending you permanently over to the other side," he offered. "Come over for your assessment."

"I'm in my non-programmable mode."

"Everyone has a program that is part of larger patterns. We represent the joining of nations into the new order, a process of 150 years, culminating shortly."

"I'm more a fan of the new chaos."

"One must subtly tend chaos like a control burn."

"Why am I burning for her?"

"We want you to mate."

☼

Mor opened his eyes to sunlight breaking through the hotel curtains. It was a dream but real enough. A low buzz came from the cell phone.

"You Mor? I need that disk. Don't move, I'll be there in five minutes." The caller finished with a click.

He frowned at the phone's tiny presence. The voice had not been Korner's. As his friend had said, "there's always somebody looking for you. Just don't know if they want to pay you or flay you." Korner's wisdom had sounded like bullshit to him until one minute ago. The KPIX local tv news had the story of Kiowa Larsen, all over the screen, painted with lurid intimations of drugs and sex and murder.

The disk felt hot when it settled inside his boot. He slipped on his leather jacket, grabbed Korner's camera and headed out. Flower vendors were opening their kiosks on Powell as he hit the street. Mor wandered Union Square, to see if anyone was following but saw only pigeons, old men bleaching in the morning sun, and au pairs pushing baby strollers. He was on a high from having the disk everyone wanted. He walked down the boulevard and found in an empty booth at the O'Farrell Cafe.

"I'll be right with you," a young woman offered. She paced the length of the counter refilling cups. "What'll it be?"

"Eggs over easy, home fries, and sourdough toast. Is there a washroom here?"

"At the back." She pointed to the doors at the rear.

Mor washed his hands at the sink as two skate punks joined him.

"Hey bitch, we want the camera. We saw you fucking with it out on the street."

"It's not mine. Belongs to a friend."

The skaters had him pinned to the stall when the door crashed in. A middle-aged man in a charcoal gray suit held a snub-nose.38 lowered at his side. He crashed the pistol on the head of one assailant, twisting the other's arms into a pair of handcuffs.

"Lieutenant Casper Richards, at your service. Be back in a moment." He dragged the punks to his unmarked squad car in front of the cafe as Mor headed back to his breakfast, the adrenaline giving him an appetite.

Richards slid into the seat across from him. "Mind if I get a coffee?"

"I'd be happy to spring for a whole pot." Mor replied as he blinked to see if he was still breathing.

"Thanks. Nice joint here. A couple years ago, a waitress got on a cook's case about some burnt eggs. They get yelling at each other, next thing, he pulls a piece and shoots her next to the pies."

"Did he kill her?"

"No, but ruined a good lemon meringue." Richards sipped at his coffee. "You're in a shit load of trouble, friend."

"How's that?"

"I got the sheet on you this morning from the federal level. You're wanted for questioning in regards to the theft of a disk containing state secrets. Somebody's doing a hell of a PR job on you, calling you 'the Darkness.' Sounds like instant terrorist to me."

"How'd you catch up with me?"

"A concerned anonymous party gave me your room number at the Saint Francis. I handle the delicate stuff. Ever since Larsen went missing, the police department has been jumpy. She stole a bucket of information from a highly classified computer base, Homeland Security and all."

"I'm not a threat."

"I got a strong feeling you have the disk or know where it is. You're being way too casual."

"Say I'm holding the disk. What do you suggest?"

"Stay away from official channels," Richards said, glancing about. "I'm telling you this unofficially on account of the orders stink. There's money and influence behind this and I want to know whose. You help me and I'll help you. Should be easy with that cool edge you're playing."

"When I lived up north, no one cared if I lived or died. Right now I've never felt more vital."

"That may not last."

"Never does. Your prisoners are getting nervous."

The skate punks banged on the windows of Richards' car to get his attention. He waved his coffee cup.

"Fuck them, they're not worth the paperwork. I want you safe until I figure out what's going down."

"I have a friend who might help," Mor replied, and pulled Kwasanda's card from his pocket. "She's on Filbert, near Larkin. I'll call her on my cell."

"Dumb move," Richards replied, grabbing the phone and grinding it under his shoe. "My nephew can trace those bastards and he's still in diapers. Let me cut the idiots loose and drop you. Stay the fuck away from any phone."

☼

Richards drove him to the Filbert Street address as promised. Mor hit the button on the intercom outside the building for the iron grate to buzz open. No one answered. He slid into a crouch on the stairs and dropped his head. If only Kwasanda would come home. He needed a home.

After a while a friendly hand shook him out of his funk. Kwasanda gave him a warm smile and unlocked the door.

"Shallahnna will be happy to see her favorite artist when she comes in from school. You should have called."

"The phone got crunched by a cop who kept me from getting crunched."

"That doesn't sound good. Are you associating with criminals?"

"Apparently the wrong ones. I don't want to bring you trouble."

"Come in and see my world."

Mor followed her up the steep staircase to the flat, resisting the urge to take her in his arms on the landing and feel her against his chest. They entered her apartment, a world of carved hardwoods covered stretched skins decorated with painted animals thundering a savannah dotted with acacia trees and spiny shrubs. Bay light played across batiks and masks from an African home he assumed to be Kwasanda's native Sudan. Deep green potted palms offset the earth colors in the room.

"My ex-husband, Charles, was in the import-export business, mostly in Africa, but also in the Middle East. "

"Incredible. Shallahnna must get a kick living in another continent here in the city. I had a teacher at the Art Institute who believed modern art was a return to the primeval. Surrealists and Picasso had a great interest in African masks. Seeing this sacred art makes me believe all art is ultimately an expression of the collective mind."

"You know, you're really full of shit."

"I know, but it's good shit."

"I hope so, for your sake. This is my idealized Africa. Not the land I came from, battered with drought, disease, and constant war. In here my Africa is safe and peaceful."

Mor followed her through the dining room into the kitchen. The portrait he'd drawn earlier, was pinned on the far wall over a walnut hutch topped with relics of carved bone and pounded brass. A framed photograph in grainy black and white showed a child staring out from the crook of a bony arm.

Kwasanda busied herself with running beans through a grinder and measuring spoons into a french press.

"In four minutes we'll have our coffee."

"That's enough time for the truth," he replied. "If you want. We can drop the serendipitous street connection."

She fumbled in the cabinet for cups and saucers. "I'm sorry to be your finder. McCracken hired me to bring you in."

"Who the hell is McCracken? What about Korner?"

"Let me give you more of the picture."

"From the moment I found that purse on the Golden Gate Bridge I've been involved but only getting pieces. Knowing Korner, he's playing two sides against his middle."

"There's no trust there. He is on both sides."

"And there is you and your daughter."

"Let me tell you some of my story. I met my husband, Charles in Khartoum, where I traced refugees from Chad, Eritrea, and Uganda to reunite them with their families. I had a talent for finding people, even if they were corpses. Sudan was in constant civil war and my work flourished until I ran out of tears. Let someone else tell the mothers their sons and daughters had died. Sorrow has its limits. Still, my mission is a global revolution focused on spiritual energy healing rather than iatrogenocide, disease induction through pharmaceutical poisonings. Africa, as well as the Americas, is becoming increasingly involved with this program.

"Charles needed someone to translate Arabic for his business and we became lovers on the promise he would take me out of Sudan. He moved us here and got involved with treasure hunting for McCracken, statues from the Middle East, anything that Johnstone Warren and Messing Technologies wanted, McCracken wanted. The last was a stone man with wings from Iraq. Charles went missing with half a million dollars. Now I'm paying off McCracken."

"He must have been the man on the phone Korner gave me. I had a call early this morning from someone who said I had to retrieve a disk or he'd put my balls in a vice."

"McCracken has had a fixation on Warren for years, and believes he mastered some crucial problems, engineering proteins, dah da dah. McCracken wants the research to engineer synthetic life forms. What more do you need? Kiowa Larsen did the theft and I'm not sure how discriminating she was in what she downloaded."

"So, guess what I'm asking, are you my savior or temptress?"

"I'm a finder. As far as I know McCracken has no interest with you personally. You can talk to him when he comes for the disk later this evening."

Mor felt the burn from the disk hidden between his boot and sock. "I'll pass it along only under the condition that you make a copy before giving this to him."

"This disk? Only McCracken and Warren have the computers to run it."

"I don't even know how to turn the damn things on," Mor replied, as he handed the disk to Kwasanda.

"Rest until he arrives."

"What about Shallahnna?"

"She's staying overnight with a friend from school."

He dozed on the sofa until the door buzzer woke him, and he heard Kwasanda's footsteps. Night had settled and the living room was in shadow save for the light from a single table lamp.

"Our situation has changed. I don't recognize these jokers. Let's get gone."

"You have the disk?" he asked, rubbing his eyes.

"I have it. We'll have to take to the roof."

The front door burst open as two men stormed the apartment. Kwasanda dashed with Mor through a back door leading up to the roof. Outside, fog blurred streetlights in gusts coming off the ocean. He heard a cat shriek and glass shatter inside, followed by curses. They leaped on the neighboring building's roof and ran down a rickety wood staircase. Kwasanda took the stairs two at a time and Mor lumbered behind.

"They're on the roof. Call Leddy and tell him to watch the street. There they go. I just saw them."

Kwasanda vaulted the railing on the last run of stairs. Mor hit heavy but managed not to lose his balance. He saw her leap over a fence twenty yards ahead. A pursuer's feet pounded after him as he tried to close the distance. He attempted a leap but a man pounced on his back and the world lost its light.

When he gained consciousness, he found himself zip-cuffed in the rear of a black sedan. A Plexiglas shield sealed him from the two men in the front seat. Mor laughed. He was free captive in the hands of his enemy, the disk away with the Sudanese. The driver steered the sedan through the night streets. He made a couple of lefts, then a quick right before he pulled into an underground garage.

Mor saw the Mark IV bear down on the sedan, high beams blinding the men in the front seat. He braced his knees against the back of the seat and waited.

Here it comes

Here it comes

Here comes your nineteenth nervous breakdown.

The Mark IV crashed with enough force to blow the airbags into the men in the front. Next thing he knew, Korner pulled him from the backseat, cutting free the plastic cuffs.

"Glad to see me?" Korner grunted, firing a couple rounds into the front tires.

"If not now, when," Mor answered, as he shook glass fragments from his hair. Korner helped him to the Mark IV, slipped behind the wheel, and spun out of the garage. Mor looked back to see the men just struggling free from the air bags before they got gone.

"How come your bags didn't inflate?" he asked Korner.

"Took them out. Can't be wheeling around with a death wish only to have dick-less safety devices fuck up the thrill," Korner replied with a tight smile.

* * *

They were on the Embarcadero, the numbers of the piers decreasing, then increasing. Korner caught most of the streetlights, those he missed, he ran.

"Do you believe in synchronicity?" Mor asked as the street flashed by. "Like fortuitous accidents?"

"Only the ones I cause. The disk, son." Korner gave him the condescending uncle routine.

"I don't have it or know where it is or what this is all about. I am only the painter. Take me to her, I will paint her. I keep falling from one woman to another "

"This is how the story goes. Johnstone Warren has billions through his company, Messing Technologies. He's gone off his nut from old age and cancer, with one last big ugly planned. You figure in on account of he bought a painting from that show years ago. He wants you to connect with Christina to make a painting, some earth mother image. She knows the signs and arcane bullshit, but she'd be damned to do it for him. My guess is he thinks this image can stop his dying.

"In the meantime, he plowed a bunch of money into research, nano technology and fucking with proteomics, whatever the fuck that is. Something to do with the study of the structures and functions of proteins, though what the hell for is beyond my head. I figure he's hedging his bets, using any resource to put life back into his stinking corpse."

Korner turned up Powell from Pier 43, grinding gears for the steep hill. He fumbled into his jacket for the flask, damning its emptiness.

"Seem to be running on empty. Check the glove compartment."

Mor found a sealed pint of Cuervo, spun off the plastic cap and passed the bottle to

Korner. The city seemed lurid and detached to him, its mystery reduced to thieves and robber barons fighting for market share, its romance sold into prostitution, till people moved without caring or sharing. Only the likes of Warren and McCracken counted the limitless wealth without seeing the bodies left in the wake. Mor saw his saint, his city, skinned and bloody.

"Much better. Warren is weird enough, then here comes McCracken. He has Kiowa Larsen planted in Messing, using her to steal Warren's research so his Portal will have all the cookies when it comes to the protein business. She has ideas of her own and not very good ones. Larsen downloads the stuff for McCracken, then tells him the price for the disk has gone seven figures. If he doesn't come across, she'll tell the press that he hired her for the espionage and goodbye to any fat government contracts."

"This is where I came in."

"Stumbled in like a juice head on a three-day bender. McCracken is tossing around buckets of cash to find Kiowa's disk and you pick it up walking across the Bridge. That my dear brother will require some explanation on your part. The truth is, that poor woman took her own life," Korner added with an expression of sadness. "I chased her down to try and save her. I knew she was distraught, getting in over her head with this dirty espionage business. She slipped out of my hands when I tried to stop her from jumping."

"From what I saw on the news, she'd been a bad girl in the party world," Mor said, while wondering why he should be reassuring to a killer.

"Warren is accelerating his design because of McCracken's shinanigans. He knows about the disk, and he knows how desperate McCracken is. He'll do about anything to get the damn thing, but mostly Warren doesn't want any flies in the ointment."

"Who dosed me in the hotel?"

"McCracken, I figure. You're an easy man to follow. He had the room tossed and when the disk didn't come up, dropped a chocolate on the pillow laced with lord knows what psychotropic drug."

"For you it's about the money."

"As long as I have my Colt and can see down the runway for take-off, I'm good to go. In the middle of this firefight, Christina is close to finishing her translation of the Copper Scroll with the location of the treasure. Warren says he knows where the booty is and his version sits on the doodad. Wouldn't that be a bitch to get your hands on?"

"Hold it, amigo. I thought Warren hired you to hire Christina to translate the Scroll. If he already knows where the treasure is, what's with Christina?"

"Plots within plots make the world go around. Confirmation, I guess, a double blind set-up to make sure the translation is correct. Plus he wants her for the model in the painting. Duh. A lot of biblical scholars have screwed up on the Scroll but Christina has her own connection to the mystery. Her interest is in the truth, like that ever filled a belly or snagged a coin."

Korner turned left on Broadway, shooting through a tunnel, across the blocks of Pacific

Heights to Fillmore. Mor caught a glimpse of the dance hall where he and Roxx had gone during a break from his painting, meeting Jerry Garcia backstage. The night was a flash of memory, twenty thousand bands ago. He turned on the Mark IV's radio. "I'm just a boy whose intentions are good," crooned a disembodied voice. "O Lord, please don't let me be misunderstood."

"You don't seem edgy," remarked Korner.

"The action, I guess, means more than longevity. I'm feeling past my petty bullshit. Meeting Christina brought me out of hibernation. Put a charge in my blood."

"I can see you have a definite glow."

Hot pink neon light flashed over Korner's face as they hit Market Street. Mor felt the roller coaster of the hills bottom out in the flat stretch heading again down to the Embarcadero.

"Do we just cruise all night?" Mor asked as he pushed radio buttons.

"Like the old days in Chicago. There's a city a man can wrap around him. North Side industry, Gold Coast, and the South Side blues. 'Hoods where no white boy ventures alone. I miss real weather, the melting summers and snowdrifts past your head in the winter. Streets aren't broken with hills, fog, raggedy hippies on Social Security, and those fucking gingerbread Victorians."

"I get it, San Francisco blows. What next?"

"We take it as it comes, whatever that turns out to be. You know me, I'm for grabbing the gold. Shooting bad guys that try to stop us," Korner added with a wink.

"I gave the disk to Kwasanda."

"Aeii, she has a deal with McCracken. We need to get it back before she gives it to him," Korner replied, casting his head down with a scrunched eye.

He popped in a CD of west Texas blues. A hard-driving version of "Goin' Down" boomed through the speakers. The music took Mor back to another night cruising Chicago's North Side. They had hustled tickets to the jazz and blues festival in Ann Arbor Michigan featuring Freddie, Miles, and Muddy. They drove all night, Mor sleeping with Korner at the wheel. He woke to find Korner drifting off with the car heading for oncoming traffic at 75 mph. He had grabbed the wheel in that split second before they crashed. Korner owed him. He wondered if his account was still in the black. or if he even remembered Mor saving his bacon.

"Got my big feet in the window," Mor growled, "and my hay ed on the ground. Goin' down, goin' down, down, down, goin' down."

"We're all going down," Korner echoed with a raspy voice.

"Whoopee, we all gonna die."

Chapter 8

Korner parked the Mark IV in the shadows of a derelict warehouse at the last of the old wharves from 'frisco's' halcyon shipping days. Scraps of paper skittered past as he cut the lights. Shadow from the car's roof line fell across the padded dashboard, city lights glowing beyond.

In the early days of living on the Flying V ranch, Mor had met an old prospector who showed him a technique to find gold nuggets without panning or slewing the black sands of Cali's sierra creeks.

He'd say, "Fools fill their noses with crank and smack, tweaking all night to rake a few grains out of a pile of black sand," then show him a nugget the size of his thumbnail. "The earth still spits it out. The bitch is that gold doesn't always make you rich, and only greed hoards it." The old sourdough had talked on about the gold rush. Gold fever. What it was like to tease wealth straight away from the earth. He'd told endless tales of 'the Rush' when prospectors, after raking in buckets of gold all day, would catch and boil a fish for dinner, only to find gold in the pot afterwards. Then the real rush of cashing in. How gold dust found it's way in and out of any and every man's pockets. Inevitably to return to its source in a rain of tears with that haunting last laugh of lust's sireen.

"What's your part?" he asked Korner. "This is outside of your usual intrigues."

"Maybe I'm trying to get next to Christina's knowledge, what the treasure represents. I've had the cars, planes, and women. I want to find out before somebody blows my shit away. Find out what all this bleedin' and blowing is really about. That's the real deal, the real high, ain't it. To be in on the know. The Darkness I know has had a taste of it. Seeing what it's all about beyond just being bloody busy being busy only to turn to dust and bust. Maybe there is something, some real gold to this philosophy business."

"My mother, you know, was a ditsy city girl with split hemispheres. People called her crazy as a loon in heat, but one thing she said stuck with me. 'What's real never turns unreal, and the unreal will never become real.' Right before saying something like, 'and that's why you ain't shit'. Now I have the Professor, a multilingual diva of wisdom, telling me the same thing. Think that's not messing with me?"

"The unresolved Oedipal conflict," Korner returned with a smirk.

"Baseball."

"What the fuck you talking about?" Korner slouched low in the seat with wrap around sunglasses and chewed on an unlit cigar.

"Must be a flashback from the drugs. I'm flashing on those long summer evenings of the Kennedy sixties, remember? Basking in the new glow of the space age. After those stale Eisenhower golf daze? Playing under lights that made the all the colors of the caps and unis more intense, the sheer joy of youth and the game. We were right and the good guys. We weren't evil. We defeated evil. Then the murder of the king, the dark curtain coming back down and the quick descent into the meat grinder of 'Nam."

Mor flashed back to playing baseball in Chicago early in his high school years while his folks were still alive. His weak father had a strong mistress in heroin, got rousted by a vice cop who said he dropped a dime on his connection. When the dealer made bail, his pops made a hot shot of strychnine on the frozen stubble of a winter cornfield. His mother committed to a psychiatric hospital saved enough of her daily allotment of Thorazine to take the big sleep shortly thereafter. As family life crumbled he found acceptance at the Chicago Art Institute. He later found the extreme mental anguish of his parent's deaths caused a crack in his psyche. He thought about how this jagged fissure opened up a brief glimpse, a flash of recognition of a being that timeless androgyne. That realization tempered with long hours of creative drawing and painting saved him from suicide.

Korner interrupted the silence. "Come on back, brother."

"You ever feel like you're lost and there's no way you can be found? That you'll just drift and wander, never picking up more than a few crumbs here and there."

"Key ryest, that is why I would never be an artist. You're too happy being miserable," Korner grumbled around his cigar.

"It just not about happiness. You just said yourself how it all turns to dust. How can anyone really be happy knowing about that little 'catch 22' comin' around any bend? Though when I get around the Professor, it feels like I swallowed a big ol' happy pill. I just wonder what we're really expecting out of all this mayhem and carnage? Like somehow it's going to all make sense by the time we get to the end of our days."

"Expecting to get the treasure and keep our guts and brains intact. Maybe your shit will stand up when some monkey is peeling your hide like a green banana. Probably not. Warren is easy to figure out, just an old fuck wanting one last wet dream. McCracken has enough screws loose to fill a hardware store. His boys in their suits and ties, hundred dollar haircuts, and spray-on tans are fighting his blood feud. You don't have a clue how ruthless they are."

"I feel more juice from the Professor than that arrogant voice on your phone." He thought of her at the podium in the lecture hall, running across campus in tee shirt and shorts. The way she looked, backlit by stars and ocean.

"She's out of this for now. The disk is more important for the moment."

Mor scrunched down in the seat. The warehouse brooded behind razor wire topped chain-link fence as Freddie railed the blues through the car radio.

"Goin' down, bro. It's all going down back into itself, back into a being of it. Our world for all its trials and tribulations is just a lite snack for him to gobble down in the middle of one those lost sleepy afternoons. The ones that all run together like raindrops on a pond," he thought out loud as he leaned his head back.

"I need the disk, whatever the fuck it is. Sleep if you can till my call comes in, we'll stay here until then."

☼

Johnstone Warren blinked in his wheelchair. Day and night his body grew more numb, he now of a being nearly inseparable from the atmosphere in the penthouse. Then again, the more it all seemed to leak away, the more he stood still at or in the attention of that awareness of a b'ng c'ng yet indivisible in'visibility. That greater uber mensch'on of it. Out in her'eye. Or his mercy might give him some reprieve from the morphine tempered pain from the PrP proteins replicating in the astrocyte cells of his 'other' brain. A're'y'leasing their neuro-toxic agents killing the neurons in the electric slime, the e'plaque of of his self-replicating nano engineered virus. A virus activated and disseminated by a denial of it. It would play on apathy or indifference that ignoring away of anything as nothing brings to the futile race of man. As mind or memory of a b c's of it out appearing in wordsz. Irony of that of a b'ng c'ng merely a peering it in the first place now out of it appearing supersonically as'z z z'any thoth'tsz of it. A God esse to be letter'all'y Wa'r're'y'na was still all too aware in word of his left brain as the sacrificial lamb whose blood would infect a D'Na y'll of it out in her'eye of eve re y'body'az'za's'word. Turn out of it a black'g'round a beaming a wayeve're'y"e echo a're'y'pli'ca'ting in any word in'formation out of her'eye'szaz'zaz'any image of it. Out now in her'eye a supersonic ping'ting as'ka's no'wing a vi're'y"us bi na re'y"e of it int'word a betwixt in two a D"Na y'll. A denial of it in any formation in word image eye ma'jik echoing any imaginings of her'me'as'zany'thoth'tsz of her'him'it. Alone indivisible invisibility. Wa'rey'na now echoed supersonically as'k'no no no'wing of it out as'z'any bi"vi're'y'us echo captivated in verbo e fields. As'ka's mic micro wayeve e personic felt neurocellularchemical fields of view of you of a y eye merely a peering it. Or. Me"m or y a bi na re'y"e a peering it at de'fence of that field. A'tor'us a tower'z z'ap'ping bi a lightning igniting z'synapse of cosmic mind. Asz'z"z'in't'word any zsimple t'wist of fate faith family. Still indivisible in'visibility as'z'any individual.

Only Albert's brain packed more packing, more glia astrocyte star cells, with as many 'stars' as the galactic 'milky way' of it in her eye on him making it, making him the ultimate incubator for a virus designed to use their e"ver'ey own destructive power. The 'other' brain, cells holding the micro neurons, would naturally contribute its cellular arsenal of toxic cytokines and proteases, oxidizing, corroding, replicating a supersonic plasmic az'z'ap'ping'ting. An electric es'lime subtle sub'line of h'our eye'szz'ion line a imaginary image a're'y'all ping'ting echo a're'y'verbo'ra'y'ting consciousness instantaneously in one unified black'g'round of it int'word a twis'ting in two a b'ng c'ng as'ex'et'ting. Duplicating. A guidance guided by da y eye light now as'king of it a k'no'wing out of that as'ka's mic memory of it a b'ng c'ng freestanding eye star'e'y'ing at attention. As'za now. Asz'ka's now'ing out of it. A Supernatural eye of Her'me's thoth'tsz of Herhimit a peering it from above as below with a polarity gripped in one hand. Da y na light a're'y"e'dhi'a'ting now out igniting a b'lack'g'round ignore'ance of it.

Outside glass windows high-rise apartments on Telegraph Hill poked up before the Bay of seven rivers flowing out. Passing an old prison island under an orange red iron bridge spanning the gate way tidal meeting to the rim of a wide open Pacific Ocean flowing into it. Warren did not need his technicians to tell him what was going on. It was in him or in it was he. A true power commanding him yet at his command. Now as'king of it a k'nowing out of it a being wide open stretching to the periphery, clear to China and beyond. Incubating his own super virus, nano technologically engineered fulfilled his dream of a're'y'versing alternating alter'native polarity. Electromagnetic wayeves travel in one direction. A'way'eve out in her'eyez z z'i'on li'on of eve're'ybody. Yet there you a're'ye yet a peering it. Still it now appearing of it out as'ex. The 'e wayeves merely echo it as'ka's mic'ro wayeve black'g'round indivisible body of her'me'as'z'any thoth'tsz of herhimit. In a wordfreedom standing still center centered centrality point of view of you of a y eye a peering it out now a supersonic mirrored k'now'ing of it into appearing anybody. Spun out of it now in DNA'y'll. A denial of it understanding the in word supersonic phonographic spelling of a b c's. A b'ng c'ng merely a peering it. That brilliance of Margot Christina engineered in for'ma'sz a're'y'e awareness played into his hands as a b'ng catalyst of a're'y'e verse'al'l of a peh'ss'y whole power polarity. She'e'na la sonoridad. Sonorizacion para'ma aten'cion. The voice of it engaging the enraging dialectic debate between awareness in a wordfreedom of a y eye merely a peering it. Or. It appearing int'word a mirrored eye y now a twis'ting a b'ng c'ng now in two appearing a pairing of it a'spiraling D'NA'eye'll of a mere supernatural for'ma'ss her'me'sz'any thoth'tsz of it. War're'y'na mused on that in the or y eye now etc. That in the or y eye of a b'ng c'ng a positive negation of it. A negation still a're'y's'pelling its positive'ty. A b'ng positively still in the first place. Now out as'z'a positive negation a k'no'wing of it as'z'any thoth'tsz of appearing of it.

Warren or War're'y'na a're'y'dhi'a'ted merely supernaturally as'z'any thoth'tsz of it. A polarity of touch. A touching of its touch. The weight of that amount of waiting on any touch touching touched of it is a quantum gravity of it. As'z'any thoth'tsz of it.

The dream came in color abstractions of awareness that alternated a alter'native between any a na y eye merely a peering it or it appearing out of it now turning into anybody as'kas no no no'wing of it causing it as'ex's ting in formation. That int'word a twisting of a b'ng c'ng in'two a complete d'ark'ness. A space in time now to be perceived ar'king complete encirclement as'z'any guard guardin guardian as'king of it a la que"en que' of that in which appears any or eve're'y'body. That dhi ark not now black or white or any hue of man'as mind. A dhi ark a'reye'dhi'a'ting of it a complete black'g'round rolls or roles playing out with a polarity on hand. Out as'ka's mic da y na light igniting ignore'ance with the weight of it. A b'ng c'ng'g'ng gee'sz"us. Ask'ing of it a weighting of its touch. A waiting spell of any touching echoing black'g'round that quantum gravity weight. Any touch of it now as'k'as no no no'wing out of it a gravity of sheer folly waiting on a b'ng c'ng now out of it.

A positive negativity of it. Of any e'wayeves polarity of a positive ignoring or negating its invisibility into any a na y memory appearing of it. Any in'formation of it a'while. Of a y'll DNA.

Following that alternating a're'y'all ity in Warren found himself merely indivisible invisibility. That a're'y'all'ity out of a being c'ng still in the first place now informed of it understanding any spelling out of it in word. As'ka's mic memory

Thus he found himself complete completely at attention in a wordfreedom untouched awareness now turning into k'now'ing a falling off a k'now ledge of it as'z z z'leep black. Into awareness of a being 'lack with an irresistable urgent energy peh's'y en'c'ng whole power to be a gain. Now a b'ng caught in any role of complete d"ark'ness of a covenant with a god esse to be letter'all'y supernaturally appearing of it awhile out in word. Out in word as'z supersonic sound wayeves. A's'word wayeve mean means meaning it into dividing any information of it. A'wayeve now as'king of it a la que"en que"'eye a peering it now int'word a twisting it a b'lack'g'round as'z 'z z'apped in her'eye'sz'z'i'on it. A"'cross of it. Of yod of you of a na y of that out in her'eye of eve' wwwayeve're'ybody.

Now a k'no'wing out of it a virus infinitely self replicating and self organizing. A perpetual echoing of it aska's micro wayeve black'g'round turning it out in her'eyez z z'i'on eve're'ybody now a b'ng c'ng any painting of it as'k'no no no'wing out of it as thoth'tsz of a supersonic ping'ting of it. A gaining and a gaining into a mega tsunami wayeve. A're'y'kurving e'ye'turn'all'y. A painting of his viraly engineered pigments of a full color spectrum. A're'y'dhi'a'ting a spectre of it a'sz ex'pectation of it appearing generated by a social and print media campaign.

An eight by ten color photograph of Christina sat on top of the afghàn covering his legs. His fingers played one corner. Out in her'eye a painting ping'ting image would be emblazoned through three D holograms induced by his virus interacting directly with human DNA. They will now deny it in her'eye. Now a k'now'ing out of it merely in word as anybody anything any where any time. Of it out in her'e y'all of eve're'ybody turning black'g'round herhimit. Casting out da y light on the other open hand. Her will. A wayeve will. Eve'll or his volition.

His a're'y'volution. He could feel the compression of air waves as Rakitin passed into the room.

"Where is my painting? Dark Mor is a painter, why is he not painting?"

"That business with the disc and the stolen files, but James has the man in tow. The chemistry between him and Ms Shaughnessy seems to be taking affect."

"Such is the nature of art and passion of desire. The painting will be their child. A changeless progeny of love that expresses that divinity, kindles that propensity for devotion coded into human DNA by the original genetic engineers, the eL'o'him. A mode eL of it. It is no coincidence humans called the engineers God. The human is a b'ng c'ng designed to be slavish. To make an efficient slave a high degree of self consciousness is necessary. As k'ey'e of a being c'ng out there are in a're'y'all of it in fact no degrees to it. You give a potential slave that self awareness and you give that slave a potential choice to now realize his freedom moment by moment. You give him the k'eye in the center of his brain. But program that slave to ignore it by turning to keeping busy. A being busy k'no'wing it all the time. Too busy working and jerking off to realize they are master of their own simple twist of fate. That twist t'word turning a black'g'round awareness in word information of a b c's of a b'ng c'ng merely a peering it in the first place indivisible invisibility of any individual."

Therefore, the engineers programed this inclination to a worship of a being rather than a're'y'al'eye'ze on awareness still of a b'ng c'ng it merely a peering it Warren reflected. Too worship their god as goad to function as slaves of a being now k'now'ing a god letter'all'y in word captivity as a busi'ness of a being busy being busy. One god best off in some faraway heavenly place sitting with his only son. "My design will play on this but the after effects will be freedom not captivity to any letter'all in word creator gods. Elohim is plural. The image coded holographically in the virus along with its mass projection will release e'go'd from in word captivity of a b'ng c'ng now busy turning black'g'around of a k'now'ing out of y'our mind. Now exposed in sight of my ping'ting echoing reverberation of ecstatic wayeves y'all will k'now that will turning black'g'round a re'y'all dissolving all in word concepts. In a b'ng c'ng still in the first place all understanding of the old spells will be broken." Rakitin watched the words as they appeared on a computer screen. Warren's lips were no longer moving. Warren raised a finger and Rakitin moved in close "Get my painting . . . ping . . . tin..."was all he managed to say as the print out continued. He watched his preprogrammed words continue. His time was short. Warren's mind's singular eye spied a skeleton walking over wasteland of dry wash and deep river canyon. Wind swept free over these treeless wastes, carrying away the last traces of man and his insanity. The sun baked away any trace of the human family and their chemistry, engineering, and capital, to an empire of dust. Warren had once tried to convince the board of directors to retool Messing Technologies as a pure research laboratory. Too much money came from government contracts, developing military weaponry for them to agree. It seems there is a lot of money to be made in killing people he mused.

☼

"What about Gina?" Korner bit off her name, sending an elbow knifing into him. Her name brought her alive. Mor could see her, plain as day, pulling up in her ruby-red Volkswagen after two hours work done on her hair, prepped for a show at sundown when the light turns from gold to violet. Her songs filling him up till he spilled back out running all over. Now, all he caught was dead air and a lump in his throat.

"Goddamn you, why wake me like that? I've tried to let her go."

"You were talking in your sleep. Remember after she died?"

Mor's mouth went dry and his fists tightened. "I ran."

"That's your way of being pissed off. Right now you got a very ugly fucker named McCracken ready to smoke anyone for the disk, including Kwasanda. Losing one woman made you waste years weeping. Another one will bust you in a thousand pieces. Time to make a stand, I'd say."

He watched digital moments tick away on the dash. He felt deep for a renewal of strength and to curb any desire to flee and hide. Korner had flushed out his gutlessness. What are friends for, he asked himself.

"We take the son of a bitch down, I 'm just confused about my role in all this."

"You've been confused about all that since the day or night we met. Look, I didn't want to go into this now, what with the commission, but," Korner shrugged and threw his hands up. "This McCracken, he's responsible for Gina. It's why I left that note in your truck."

"You."

"Yah, I wasn't gonna say anything, let you play detective, be hero for once. Catch the bad guy and paint the priestess. See? Now you see." Korner hugged him around his shoulders. "I'm trying to square things, brother."

"You're not going to kiss me, are you?" he asked, too late as Korner bussed him on the lips.

Through the open windows the air was thick, layered with baywater odors of creosote, algae, and salt decay. Korner took a pull from the tequila. He stuffed a rock from his Altoids tin under his lip, popping open a compartment under the dash that held a pair of blue steel custom-built.45 automatics.

"Fuck my boss. Take one. You'll need help where we're going."

"No guns for me."

"The world is chaos, my brother," Korner replied. He kicked the compartment shut. "There are no good or bad guys, only the smart and lucky." He had a long drink of tequila, slammed the Mark IV in gear. In the background sirens screamed by as Korner eased out then jammed, the car joining early rush hour traffic on the Bay Shore Freeway.

"They'll turn on me like pack animals when they get what they want," he said, cruising south against the crush of the northbound commuters. "Puts me in the mood for killing. We don't have much time left."

Korner pulled over to the shoulder of the freeway to retrieve the satchel from the trunk. Mor watched traffic shoot by and wondered about his friend's state of mind. Before he got far with those thoughts, Korner knifed back in, setting the bag between the bucket seats, shoved the car into gear, and drove several freeway interchanges to the Hillsborough exit before leaving the controlled traffic mayhem for the order of what Mor saw as McMansions in Bel Aire north.

"I love this old neighborhood," Korner said. Mor laughed at the irony.

"What's funny?" Korner dipped another rock and gave his lip a cowboy bulge. Flower and shade tree dappled streets, red-tiled gabled porticos with vine covered verandas passed by. They followed a winding street until the estates grew in acreage. Korner whipped into a driveway with touch-key controlled gate. He tapped the code in then eased up the brick drive.

The Mark IV came to a stop by thick columns that supported the main portico. A short man with shaved head, wearing a blue ghee, white silk shirt, and painted tie, his expression serene, stood motionless at the front door.

Reaching in the satchel, Korner slipped a derringer up his sleeve. He stepped from the Mark IV and walking with arms extended as if too embrace. Approaching, he let his arms fall back to his sides with a shrug. They conversed in low tones. Mor watched as Korner raised a hand to scratch his chin, shooting the man in the forehead. He caught the body as it crumpled in the driveway.

"McCracken ain't home. Help me with this asshole," he called.

Mor felt nauseous and light-headed, almost passing out when he stepped from the car, "I guess I don't have the stomach for this."

"Good," Korner replied. He jerked his head toward the over sized front door, and dragged the body inside.

Temple bells reverberated off the high ceilings. The few potted palms added green to the starkness of cream-colored walls, low couches and black-lacquered tables. Korner heaved the body in a closet.

"You must have the same decorator," Mor said, surprised at the casual sound of his voice. He thought about saying something appropriate to dying but only trite piddle about furnishings or the weather came to mind. Trivializing murder masked the shock, he mused. Who dies, beyond obvious falling bodies. Somehow nothing seems to disappear, at first. But then, is seeing a death a dying of the witness as well? The looming 'rub out' in that blink of eye still flashed in his mind while watching Korner carrying on like picking up dirty laundry.

"He's into a Buddhist bag and other shit. These assholes think they don't walk the same ground as us."

"They don't. So where is he? And why the shooting," he asked without mentioning the k word.

"He double crossed me on another thing, got an associate killed. It was purely a point of honor. Honor amongst the holy band of brothers is all, all... Down the road at his headquarters." Korner babbled in an over amped talking jag.

"I just saw a man die and you're talking about holy bands."

"Shit, man, this ain't just money. When our boy McCracken learns about Warren's real secret on the disk, he'll go after Christina. If you have any sand left, you can help her and Kwasanda. Maybe you've been in the woods too long and turned soft. Sometimes a man gots to buck up and take care of business. Can't be all soft with privilege of tax paying hired guns to do the killing that goes on every day. And believe me, it takes plenty killing to keep the American dream going, buddy Dark boy. I've seen plenty of it. Been up to my arm pits in it. Oughta be a law that every white boy must kill at least one brown man just as right of passage to manhood. Then none of these self righteous soft belly sons a bitches could cop an attitude against those of us they hire to do the dirty work for them."

"Unlike you, I've never killed except for a few flies. I have been nearly killed though and I must say, it's funny, I never felt a thing, one minute you're there, then there is no there, tho there is you, still. So what is the real secret to who lives and who dies?"

☼

Kwasanda Nzokia woke in a chill under a gray blanket in the backseat of her Volvo, hidden on a side street in the shabbiness of Hunter's Point. Originally an industrial shipyard, its sparse neighborhoods of rotting stucco homes were hard by the oily waters of toxic industrial spoiled Bay. She regretted leaving Dark behind but priorities dictated.

She imagined Shallahnna, walking to her class. She was stronger than Kwasanda admitted to herself. Last week, shook up from an encounter, with a gang of skinheads, while following Kiowa Larsen's trail, she discovered Shallahnna had come home with a .22 automatic.

When she met Dark Mor, Kwasanda was unprepared for the impact the spaced out artist had on her. The drawing had found her mind merging with him in a way more intimate than sex, where it's found that 'I am you and you are me'. She thought about McCracken and the spark between them that threatened but never quite erupted. Now Korner. Ten years ago, in Costa Rico, as an investigator working for a Senate subcommittee, she had interviewed an American pilot with a ranch outside of Cartago, with his own air force, including a helicopter and a C143 transport. They drove by a hanger where men were loading heavy black duffel bags. A tall stranger with wavy hair, supervising, with a Mac 10 propped on his hip, had caught her eye.

Her host stopped to exchange a few words with the man, introducing him as James Bishop. His eyes burned into hers. They had naturally found each other that evening. Worse they had found each other drunk and wanting. Ghosts drifted off.

It seemed people who associated with Korner usually ended up being burned. She burned with him that evening, and like all the men she'd known, he'd turned into that sad lonely boy before the last orgasm. Now Dark, a man who seemed somehow scorched from the inside out. From her cell she called R.J. McCracken.

"Where are you? When are you coming to me?"

"I thought you were coming to me. Then a bunch of goons show up, tear my place up. What was that all about?" she asked, patting down her hair with the phone cradled under her neck.

"Not with Korner in the mix. I just can't predict him. I needed a little more weight. Sorry for the damage. You know, I'll take care of it, but what about my package?"

"Unlike him, I plead principles and a just cause. I am coming your way, Bwana. I want to lay your egg and I'm not talking about spreading anything," she replied, shaping her nails with a file.

"You're more than human, but are you sure you're ready for such a voyage? I warn you, once you lay in my Pod, you'll never be the same."

"Maybe I need to change." Kwasanda dropped the receiver and ran for her Volvo as a sedan pulled to the curb. She jammed into reverse, slamming the sedan's driver's door as he tried to emerge. He grimaced from the impact as she sped away.

☼

Korner shut the closet door like he had just hung up an old overcoat instead of a body. He ran his fingers through his hair and looked around.

"I need to make a statement." He went to the car and returned with the satchel.

"I think your pistol already said enough. Does killing someone give you detachment from the body?" Mor asked, still dazed from his amigo's actions.

Korner grunted, unzipping side pockets for several cigarette pack size devices.

"Remote control bombs. I can blow up a car or a building in ten minutes or ten days. I'd like to see how McCracken reacts to his crib suprema reduced to smithereens. Maybe this time he'll show a little respect."

"I fear you can get respect from violence, but is it real?"

"I'll show you real. James don't fade away, he blows away."

"That include me?"

"A body in the atmosphere is no different than a fish in water. It's outside. It's inside, and in between. No real loss." Korner headed down the hallway to the pagoda in the bamboo atrium. He flipped a switch on a post and the bells stopped. "It's just a tape while the real bell is being shipped from Sumatra."

Mor drifted through the rooms behind Korner, wondering why he tried to make sense of a psycho's ravings. Scary thing if he did start making sense. He watched as Korner went about setting the miniature charges. The house was mostly ground floor, with the exception of an upstairs bedroom. In the study were two museum quality statues, a man with wings and an elephant's head on a human body with a necklace of rats. Gods that created and sustained but also destroyed their creations were his kind. Mor noticed both idols were stained with sacramental oils and leaden with fresh flowers. Someone knew the real power of an idol is that invested by the priests and worshipers. Otherwise, it's just dead stone like a museum piece. A curiosity. Seeing a phone, Mor reached out and dialed Kwasanda's cell number.

"Hey, girl."

"Where are you?"

"Me and Korner are at McCracken's house. He's setting the place to blow."

"That is most considerate of him. I'm on my way over."

"The door is open."

☼

Explosions began in the bedroom as the Volvo pulled up the drive. Mor ran towards it, the rear of the house disintegrating in a rain of fiery debris. A bullet sped past his head, splintering off a pillar. He dashed for the passenger door, seeing Kwasanda silhouetted in the window as two more shots zinged by

. "Korner's playing cat and mouse. Haven't seen anyone else come in," Mor cried. Another round cracked a spider web in the windshield, inches from his face.

The Volvo left ruts in the rolled lawn as Kwasanda wheeled the car around and headed for the street. Mor turned to see Korner emerge from the driveway, coming up fast to rear-end her with his Mark IV. She gripped the wheel, her foot to the floor. He caught Korner in the sideview mirror, wraparound shades, cowboyed out to for the run. He grinned back at Mor with thumbs up. For a split second, they were young again, blowing up the Ratnick brothers. Korner fell back as a host of squad cars and fire trucks screamed by towards the tower of smoke, just as a ball of hot cadmium orange exploded behind. They come quick in this part of town, he mused. Streets broadened as Kwasanda cruised into the quiet shade of a spreading oak.

"Nice style, lady," Mor said.

"Charles and me drove some pretty hairy roads through parts of Africa where you needed armor for protection from the bandits and landslides. We need another car."

"You know how to boost one?"

"Before my employment at the Portal, I repoed for Williams Associates in the City. I still have my touch and I'm liking that silver BMW 330 xi across the street."

Kwasanda shouldered her packsack as she slipped out of the Volvo and walked over to the sleek Beamer parked under the broad canopies of tree-lined street. She pulled out a slim shim, popping the door lock. Before jumping in, she gave Mor a wave.

"Maybe you can get in, but you'll never get this jewel started without the key," he said, sliding into the passenger seat..

"Professionals never say never." She worked an electric probe into the keyhole, and they were off.

"Now where?" he asked.

"To McCracken's headquarters."

"I need to see Christina. You have your agenda. I have mine." He watched the slanting rays of sunlight glinting off a row of polished cars parked for a lawn party sounds coming from across the street. Disembodied laughter from beyond a hedge sounded tinny and hollow to his ears still ringing with death. The landscape had turned cold with the surfeit of wealth so beyond the man in the street. He felt Kwasanda's eyes. Turning he caught her features fragmented by shadows of the oak canopy.

"Who is Christina?" Kwasanda asked. "We have to settle with McCracken, I'm trying to save our butts, and you think about another woman."

"Maybe so, but I fear for her safety as well. She's connected to Warren and that means the disk. I just don't know how."

"Are you in love?"

"What's love? Being all giddy and moronic? Although seeing a man killed today takes the some of the glow off. I mean, Korner took a life so quickly. He killed so many with a flag on his sleeve that his heart turned cold. I guess the shock shattered my sense of being somebody, any body worth others dying for. Now I don't have a head so I retreat into my heart."

Kwasanda tapped the steering wheel in thought. "Okay, give me the address."

"Take the Pacific Coast Highway. I'll recognize the street when we get there."

"Let me get this call. I'm making a slight detour," she said into her phone, as she stayed with Mor's eyes. "I know what I said, I know the risks involved." She snapped the phone shut. "My former employer. They owe me."

Kwasanda leaned over to meet his lips. He tasted the salt of a tear rolling down her cheek.

"Sorry. I don't normally lose control like that."

"Only an innocent kiss," he said.

Kwasanda drove out of the neighborhood back on to the freeway headed south. "What do you think is on the disk?"

"I don't know or care. Is it anything worth dying for? I seriously think Korner is coming unglued. I don't think he gives a damn for any Scroll, gold or no gold. He's getting old, wants to settle old scores, and die with his boots on." He watched Kwasanda's profile in the sidelight, her cornrow braids as tight against her scalp as the skin on her high cheekbones.

"McCracken stole my husband's bones, I think mostly because he wants to jump my bones. Charles was caught in the middle of an attack on an archeological dig. I went looking for him when J.R. called with news of some missing half million dollars, and now I trade my expertise for Charles' remains."

They left the freeway and headed west to Christina.

"So the ex was the reason for the tears?"

Kwasanda frowned. "I'm taking a little journey. There may be some risks and I got thinking of my daughter."

"She's a beautiful girl woman. This San Francisco is a body snatching kind of place," he said, gazing off at the passing homes and street signs. "There. Olympic Way. The house is hidden from the road behind a screen of oleander and honeysuckle."

Kwasanda parked the BMW at the top of the driveway by a hedgerow of shrubs. Sky broke through blue patches in the clouds as Christina came out the side door in slacks and a cream-colored blouse, her hair gathered in a green tie.

"I thought that was you. I was just heading for the campus."

"Forget your life, Korner's on a rampage. We came to warn you," Mor said, as he stepped out of the car. He glanced back at Kwasanda in the silver beamer as she pulled out her cell phone to answer a call.

"I see," Christina replied with a questioning frown. "Who is your friend?"

"Kwasanda Nzokia. A friend of ours." he offered with a pat on the car roof. "Kwasanda meet Christina Shaughnessy." Kwasanda gave a slight wave as she continued her conversation. He bounded up the stairs to embrace her.

"What is this madness," she said. "I had a feeling this was coming, that Korner's cork had popped, chickens coming home to roost."

"Tell me what you know, darlin'. I'm all confused between Korner and Warren, and Korner and McCracken, who I think, dosed me with a psychedelic last night and may have had something to do with my wife's murder."

Running up the steps, Kwasanda interrupted. "Harry found my car and a Mark IV was waiting for him. The driver asked where we were and when he played dumb, he said the driver had a henchman along who gave him a hard time."

"Hashemi," Mor replied. "Bad news just got worse."

"We should get to finding a safe place,"

"Time to call for back-up." He searched his pockets for the card Richards had given him. "Where are you going?" he asked as Christina ducked back inside.

"To get some papers. If I'm part of Korner and Warren's treachery, I'm fighting back. My work on the Scroll and the papyri might be good for a bluff."

He stood flat-footed as Kwasanda, engaged in another phone conversation, drummed the porch rail with her fingers. Mor began doubting his eyes as he stared at his boots with the steel toe glancing through a hole in the leather. Was he the same man who less than a week ago, felt safe and sane in his mountain sanctuary? The fire that burned down his cabin in the lost hills amplified his disintegration, his life smeared in the ash, blood, and dust on the ragged leather of his boot.

"Grow up and be a man," Kwasanda hollered as she hustled back to the car. "Stop running from yourself."

Women always seemed to turn against him. Where he looked for love, he found anger. An anger growing out of a deep inbred contempt for all things male. Nausea swept over him from the pungent smell of eucalyptus. He wanted to sprawl on his back and surrender to the vacuum of the night sky. He held his scream inside until it rattled in his guts. Kwasanda turned over the BMW, crunching gears, she drove away, leaving behind only a trace of red taillights.

The clean lines of Christina's home returned his attention, the glass walls and iron-bracketed beams protruded beyond the eaves like the prow of a ship. A ship sailing through a sea of wisteria exploding off the bow, bunches of ice plants lining the path off the deck. He concentrated on the details where concrete married wood with rings of steel. He imagined the carpenters working teak and redwood with bamboo handled flat double-cutting saws, drinking green tea, speaking in haiku and zen koans.

Reaching the entryway as Christina opened the door, he barred her exit with an arm thrust against the jamb. Bending his head to kiss her brooding lips, he caught the smell lavender. She turned from his advance, giving him instead the soft nape of her neck.

"Don't hate me," he begged.

"Dark, just try not hiding from who you are, what you're really about."

"Hiding is the best move. We have a psycho out there," he replied

"Warren does not have the Scroll translation. Your friend will not kill me because I know what is behind the words."

"Doesn't mean he won't try. Korner always had a fascination for killing things. I was his first human victim." He pulled his shirt aside and showed her the scar. "Since I survived, he's left with the quandary of me asking why he shot me. Being a coca eater makes him psychotic on a wire. I saw him kill a man only an hour ago. He's over the edge. We need someone in this sorta game. Let me use your phone."

"Go ahead," she replied with a nod of her head.

She stared after him as she slid away, letting her fingers drag lightly across his chest. Horizon of ocean and sky spread across the glass walls. He sat on cushions on the floor with the telephone, the muted crash of waves in the background.

"Its just never been about power for me. Guess I just knew I was too much of a fool to know what to do with it. Probably end up blowing out my own brains," he said with a shrug.

"I sense some violence in your psyche but I'm afraid Korner's blood lust is beyond redemption."

"That's my man Korner. He's more cold-blooded in his advancing age. I saw that this morning. To him everyone is a soldier and probably not a friend." He dialed the number. "I'm looking for Casper Richards."

"This the Darkness?" Richards' voice crackled in the receiver. "I heard about some commotion at your friends apartment, and a major explosion in a house belonging to E. J. McCracken, with a body in the ruins. Tell me these aren't connected"

"They are, I believe it's R.J., and that is why I'm calling you."

"I'm coming. Listen for a series of short blasts. Be ready to jump and go."

Mor gave him the address and cut the connection. "Take what you need and get ready to run, darling. The cavalry is coming over the hill."

"Men and their war games." Christina took a navy blue pea coat from the coat rack.

"So give it to me straight. Is there a treasure or not?"

Christina went to the bedroom and rifled through documents in her wall safe as Mor trailed behind.

"There is always treasure." She replied while filling a red leather briefcase with papers. "Sometimes, no one can claim it without starting a holy war."

"You haven't answered my question."

"Treasures get looted. I do not know for certain what remains where. The reality of my concern is not about precious metals. All of that gold is really a subterfuge. It makes the mystery more tantalizing. Keeps the search alive. It is where it starts and who is following it that counts. One clue is in treasure, the word. It is a doublet, a pair of words derived from the same original. Another word for treasure is thesaurus or book. Knowledge is the real treasure. A knowledge of anybody be'am'ing now k'now'ing denial of a ka's mic being. An immortal. A being beyond time, history, idol, imagination, or word. Or word'ship. What is realizing being that a being still in the first place worth? Though told of a being of it we all it seems remain captivated at attention of an arbitrary named in formation of it. That'sz the simple twist of fate faith and family. A denial of it now as'ka's mic eye merely a peering it to embrace any mere supernatural thoth'tsz of it appearing in word."

Mor could only stare at her eye wayeves appearing to him in such a bewildered state. He remembered once of a being c'ng teleported in dream on a ride out into the solar system. His vision of a being in sight brought attention close enough to Jupiter and Saturn that their mass completely filled his field of view and beyond the point of a being c'ng as though beside it. Outside of it. Remembering now a realization of it pervaded his awareness. The cosmic magnitude swallowed whole any mere senses of a being other than the cosmos of a cosmic being of it. Sheer planetary magnitude disappeared his awareness then quickly back to black. In a being of it now k'now'ing it out of a black'g'round projection as thoth'tsz of it. Now with intent of k'no'wing out of it intentional disregard of a being indivisible invisibility. Of it merely appearing mirrored out in word memory awhile as thotht'sz of a being any individual. Often a'ten. A bi na re'y a're'y'dhi'a'ting of it now out as'k'nowing anybody. Any a na y potential of a being c'ng out in a y eye a peering still by now as'ex's ting appearing in formation as t'word reawakening, holding that memory, that cosmic perspective from which we all turn into or out of. Appearing disappearing into one in word idea of a being in the first place. Now appearing out in k'now'ing any name of it alone. Awhile. A being still in the first place one indivisible invisibility of it appearing a macro micro cosmic mean while. A cruel cunning deceit of anybody appearing disappearing out in her'eye of eve're'y'body.

He now a're'y'all'eye'zed it merely a peering it. Y'et at attention caught up in a raging of that a y eye debate of that. Merely a peering it or appearing of it awhile of space in time now where paying attention as'k'no'wing out of it a wayeve're'y"e'function as'ex'pands to a memory of a macromicro cosmic perspective. Y'all mean meaning still invisibility of it he cogitated. From a point of view of you of a y eye merely a peering it. Awareness of it. At attention he na disappeared black out in her'eye of eve're'ybody as'z z z'leeping off any imaginary ledge of k'nowing out of it a cosmic micro'wayeve black'g'round. Echoing of it any supersonic information of a b'ng c'ng him appearing in word.

That visual artist's sensibility engaged that untouched in a wordfreedom awareness drawing on the right side of the brain. Mor's decade of powerful visions had him, kept him, burnt him up, surpassed him. A be'ng ka'm'ing a black'g'round into or out appearing anybody anything any where any time. Him now a k'nowing out of it as'z'any mere idea of himself. Christina's mirror presence, let alone the supersonic peh'ss'y'lent sound wayeves out in her'eye of an'y or eve're'ybody'sz'za voice precipitated his attention back into a micro cosmic state of indivisible infinity of a y eye potential merely a peering it now as'king of it a k'no no no'wing out of it appearing etc.. Why a be'ng c'ng otherwise, he now wondered. Why a want to be otherwise? The mere mirror suggestion from her lips reflected a being c'ng of it, a macro micro cosmic mean awareness of it meaning full from above. Ove a b'ng c'ng from that still centrality completely forever completion. She astonished him, baffled his pseudo identity, leaving him starring dumbstruck. Then why be otherwise?

"We all are conditioned by turning into or out of them. Them the m man'as mind or y memory to think of ourselves as though otherwise. Other y'sz y'all while mirror'ly supernaturally as in word thothtsz appearing to be other y's. The visions are breaking down the conditioning in your case, now a k'now'ing out of a being c'ng as the Darkness," she gave with a knowing smile. Of a y eye of her'me'szzaz'anythoth'tsz of herhimit. A Yod. A You. Or me in a memory of it. Awareness of Herhimit.

He continued merely to stare. He knew the sound of his voice could only betray his failure to sustain her eye level of consciousness. Buck up bucko, he flashed.

"Breaking it back down with drugs, a bullit, and a woman," Mor managed with a frown. "Is that why you socked me? Break down the conditioning?"

Christina laughed. "In that I am always prepared."

"You do throw a good punch. Where did you learn that?" he asked her laughter breaking the spell. He felt his confidence rushing back in with the beating of his heart.

"After an incident in Jerusalem, I took some boxing lessons at a local gym."

The sound of two short blasts from a car horn ended their conversation. He grabbed her arm and bolted for the door. Richards sat behind the wheel of a grey Chevrolet in the driveway. Mor and Christina slid into the back seat.

"Casper Richards, SFPD, at your service, ma'am," he said, shooting a backward glance at Christina. "Where's the disc, Darkness?"

"My friend took off with it a few moments ago."

"Dumb move. Lady, I hope you have your shit together better than your boyfriend," he replied as he pulled out of the driveway. Just as he was about to turn to say more, his instinct gave a short jerk to the steering wheel, just avoiding a sideswipe by the Mark IV.

Chapter 9

The Mark IV braked, making a 180-degree turn to follow Richards' sedan.

"We've got Korner and Hashemi behind us," Mor said. "They're coming fast."

Richards stepped hard on the accelerator. "Does he know that you don't have the disk?" he asked, his tires burning parallel stripes as they hit the highway.

"Korner is more concerned about gold and settling old scores however they may add up in his warped mind"

"Strap in. This may get rough." Richards growled, his bald head catching the light blazing from the Mark IV.

The heavier vehicle gave them a jolt as it rammed the rear of Richards' car. Mor turned back to see Korner grinning above the wheel.

He came up on the left, crashing into them. The lighter car slid into a skid on the shoulder. Richards wheeled back to the pavement as Korner rammed him again. The detective's expression fell into the blank look of a chess player thinking ten moves ahead.

"He's got the weight advantage but I can out run him," he muttered. He hit the straightaway along the Pacific Coast Highway, the smell of salt and diesel wafting into the sedan. Korner maneuvered for another shot, oncoming cars swerving to avoid him. Hashemi fired on the Chevy. The rear window of Richards' car shattered in chunks spraying over their backs. Korner fell back as oncoming traffic picked up.

Gunfire from the Mark IV was followed by the flat pop of a bursting front tire. The smell of burning rubber filled the car as Richards jerked the sedan to the highway's ocean side. They spun into a rollover with Mor feeling pinned in against the door. He saw the back of Richards' head gleamed with sweat as Christina's body crushed into his.

* * *

The car left the pavement, twisted metal crunching onto a field of rock heads protruding from beach sand. It rolled over twice before landing back on its tires. Christina exhaled her breath, crushed by the force of the impact as the car rolled onto the rocks. She let out a groan. The restraint of the safety harness had tore her blouse and scraped flesh from her shoulder. Dark appeared unconscious but otherwise intact from the flight off the pavement. The air, acrid with rubber and gasoline choked her as she popped the seat belt. Pushing open the rear door, she clambered out unsteadily, stumbling on the unsure footing of slippery surf stained rocks. Sea gulls scattered screaming as ocean waves hammered the sandy beach a few yards below.

Blood streamed from Richards' head leaning against the steering wheel, the driver's door dented shut. Christina smashed the window with a rock, dragging his wiry frame through the opening. The gun in his leather shoulder holster dug into the soft flesh of her armpit, making her grimace. She jerked until his legs pulled through, one shoe snagging the rough edge of the window frame. She unhooked the shoe before freeing him from the wreck.

As she turned to look for the Darkness a stone shard exploded from a bullet ricochet inches to her left.

"Get down. We're under fire," Richards wheezed. Christina dropped to her belly as the next round split the air at head level. Course rock dug into her side as she rolled toward his voice, her palms scraping against salt slime and sand grit,

"There's a tunnel under the highway just a few yards down." he managed, pushing himself to crawl across the rocky terrain.

"What about Dark?

"He'd want us to get the hell out of here."

"I am going back for him."

"Listen, lady, we move now and we might make the tunnel in one piece."

Several rounds zinged off the wrecked sedan sending sparks into patches of fog as it raced in from the sea.

"It's a good night to die," Christina cried, as a round pierced the car's gas tank, sending a burst of orange flame blazing the dark sky. She ran until the heat scalded her bare skin, then froze at the sound of his voice.

" You should know better than to look for me there in all that light."

"Too dark to die," she laughed.

A shot spun her like a dancer. She dropped to her knees but kept her head down, crawling to Dark. More shots zinged as they made their way to Richards' silhouette waving from the tunnel entrance.

"You got to bleed to believe," Dark whispered, his lips brushing her cheek and ear lobe. "Korner is toying with us. He's drawing blood to see if we've got the stomach for it."

* * *

Mor limped on a bleeding knee as he trudged with Christina through the sand. By the time they reached the tunnel entrance the shooting had stopped. They stepped through the sand to concrete, her body sliding against his. He cupped her neck, turning her mouth to his.

"Well, ain't that sweet," Richards croaked. He headed into the tunnel. The traffic on the highway meeting the crashing surf swept away the moment. A distant siren wailed as Christina followed Richards with Mor limping along behind, his pant leg plastered with blood. The figures moved to the dim light at the far end of the tunnel, traffic still thundering along overhead. Emerging, they moved into the shadows of a row of eucalyptus trees. Richards bent at the waist as Christina braced him. Mor hobbled over.

"Can you walk up the hill?" she asked.

Richards nodded in agreement. The stand of trees obstructed the view from the highway. "This is a mixed blessing. We don't want to get lost from each other in the process of losing Korner," he said, clutching at his chest.

Mor pulled the detective's cell phone from his pocket and punched in numbers.

"Where are you?" Kwasanda asked through a background of static.

"Pacific Coast Highway, a mile or so south of Half Moon Bay. Korner's gone completely off his nut. We managed to evade the assholes through a tunnel that comes out on a road heading for Woodside. You know the area?"

"Tunitas," she replied. "I had a repo there. I can be to you in a few minutes. What about Korner?"

"I heard sirens so he may have split. We're heading for cover in no condition to run if he comes after us."

"Look for me and I'll look for you."

He helped Christina and Richards scramble up the hillside. The bank of fog broke through the tree line. Richards shivered in shock. He rubbed his arms while he negotiated layers of slippery leaves and mossy rocks. Despite the terrain and their wounded condition, Mor thought the light he detected filling the sky offered hope of a new day.

They reached the shelter of a precipice. Richards lay propped against an up-thrust boulder as Christina helped Mor wrap his wounded knee with his bandanna. Early commuter traffic droned on the Pacific Coast highway just below.

Focusing on the weave of Christina's gabardine slacks torn at the knee, skin rubbed to raspberry, blood on the fringes of her torn blouse, he glanced at Richards. His shoulder knobs suspended his off-the-rack loose fitting suit, bald head glistening with sweat. The flesh below his eyes looked mottled and slack, his mouth tightly drawn in a near death rictus.

"Your friend needs immediate medical care," Christina said as a siren wailed through the pounding of surf on sand and tires on pavement. "There must be police on the scene now. Use the cell phone and tell them where we are."

"No," Richards rasped "Stay away from official channels and get to a refuge." The detective forced himself to sit. "Keep me talking. If I fade out I'm not coming back."

"Why are you helping us?" Mor asked as he slipped an arm around the shoulders of the injured man.

"I'm not. I work for them, or at least I did." Richards spit the words out with a fit of coughing. "Trust no one." His last words came with a grimace.

Kwasanda waited with the stolen BMW on the shoulder of the two-lane highway branching northeast along the creek. As Mor and Shaughnessy emerged from the tree line carrying Richards between them, she jumped from the car to help. A tired gurgle from his slumped body signaled another casualty. Mor reached for the carotid artery.

"His pulse is gone."

A tenor sax wailed from the car speakers as time seemed to stand still. Mor brought blood on his hand to his nostrils. He looked to Christina, shifting his weight to his good knee as she gripped him around his ribcage. Kwasanda's braids danced in the wind. Then the awful still moment evaporated as sun rays shot up into the sky from a patch of pink to the East as last rites for the detective.

"We leave him here," Kwasanda said as she walked toward the car. "His family will see he gets a proper burial." She motioned Dark and Christina into the back seat, slid behind the wheel and turned on to the two-lane. He gathered Christina in his arms, straightening his bleeding leg best he could.

"Somehow it seems he is still with us," Christina said as he slid his arm around her shoulders and glanced back at the detective's crumpled body.

"What's scary about seeing corpses pile up is this indifference I feel," he replied. "It makes me feel jaded somehow. Are we just ghosts drifting in and out of temporary abodes? Funny how all along I had this nagging gut feeling that Casper Richards was not who he said he was. Just the way he reacted when Christina suggested calling the law," he wondered as his eyes caught Kwasanda's.

"I can see where you might be feeling a little turned around. I suspect he too works for Warren or McCracken," she offered.

"Either way, I saw the bird." he rasped, straightening his good leg, pressing against the soft leather seat. "The sweet bird of paradise. I saw it fly when his soul passed."

Kwasanda punched the speed dial on her cell phone. "Officer down, Tunitas Creek Road in the rocks above PCH. No names, I'm only a concerned citizen." She squeezed the phone shut, putting pedal to the sleek BMW. "I have a feeling our man was a real cop at one time. I'm letting a contact on the force know. He'll handle it discreetly. Casper Richards may have been moving to the shady side of the law road but he may still have family who deserve some respect. There's a Redwood preserve up ahead. It's part of a wilderness space along that mountain ridge up there. There's a cabin you can reach from a back trail. I'll drop you guys there while I go check the status of our hunters."

"How far is the cabin from the trailhead?" he asked as his fingers gently examined Christina's shoulder. "The shot just skipped along the muscle, missing the bone. Whoever fired, and I'm afraid it was brother Korner, wanted us to know he could shoot close enough to kill. The wound will leave you with a scar," he consoled. "But you don't need stitches. It's more like a burn than a gunshot wound."

"It burns alright but I am more concerned with the bleeding on your leg," she replied.

"Give me your panties and maybe I can stop the bleeding."

Mor knew he could cut the dead silence with a knife. Tires kept chewing asphalt as Kwasanda shot a quick look back. Then they all burst out laughing.

"I really don't know where that came from. Blame Korner's influence," he replied feeling giddy from the excitement. He caught himself from babbling on in shock and nervousness. He recognized that disembodied enchantment being around passing souls. Mostly he recognized it from his own passing or near death experiences where he had passed completely out of his body, images of a life shuffling by his mind's eye like cards in a dealer's hand. As wheels turned he became more aware how everybody lives with in that whispered extended moment between living and dying. Is life but a long near death experience, he wondered.

He watched the road following the contour of the creek that snaked through rolling pastures fenced with woven wire riding for miles along crooked steel stakes. The BMW passed a blur of ranch complex with barn, hacienda with verandas surrounded by horse corrals. Christina wrapped a hand over the hole in her pea coat where the slug had cut its path.

"My briefcase blew up with the car. In it were some papers related to and explanations for the stolen papyri. Those missing papyri may be the last link in a chain of evidence going back three thousand years. Evidence that could realign global power. Of course it is all contingent on whether or not these truths will be believed. Be recognized. From my experiences in academia, it may not yet be time for this awakening. Rarer still are those who have awoken to realize being that a being still in the first place now k'nowing it as that micro macro ka's mic being. Most are still alienated by their roles of complete darkness generated by a being y'all. Now k'now'ing ignoring that overstanding any mere understanding of a being."

"Hallelujah to that, sister, I pray to the Goddess almighty that it is time. I'll give it all I got to find it, to bring it home," Kwasanda offered, slapping her hand on the dashboard.

"You think McCracken is ready to negotiate? Sounds like an empty vessel to me," Mor replied. The road humped as Kwasanda shifted gears, the needle of the tachometer a nervous thread jumping up and down around rpms.

"McCracken has no need for more deaths and Korner brings him too much heat. He must want the chase to end. Not to put a damper on the party but I should tell you Korner has been following us since the cut-off junction. I want to lose him before I leave you."

"I'd like to lose that son of a bitch down a black hole," Mor retorted.

"Yah, you got a real psycho brother there. But then we all hope to see another day." She accelerated until the Beamer was coming out of sharp curves at seventy. She hit a straightaway at one hundred ten and the world flashed as light scattered, and tires flared. Their bodies thrown together, he found his lips kissing the back of Christina's neck.

"Here we go," Kwasanda interrupted. "This road is a mean snake but we can outrun Korner."

By the time they came to a screeching halt at the trailhead, they had ascended to a world where sky seemed suspended above the ground by masts of ancient redwoods standing hundreds of feet into low lying clouds. Feeder creeks swollen by recent rain crashed as brown gravy, roiling on home to the sea a few miles distant. A patchwork of pavement from different eras melted off narrow shoulders that plunged down the bank through sheared mossy boulders. There were no painted median stripes, only hand-sized steel mile markers marching along the road disrupting the forest maze. One of the timbers rested at a forty-five degree in the crotch of an adjoining tree. Despite their speed, the weather seemed to move with them, drinking the rising sun rays in a drifting gray mass. Tires blew foamy water from rain-filled chuckholes as Kwasanda wheeled the Beamer into the cover of the trees.

"He's coming up fast," she said. "For a psycho, the man can drive."

Hardly were the words out her mouth when Korner's Lincoln tore by.

"You guys better make tracks. He won't get far before he realizes we got behind him."

"Where is the cabin?" Christina asked.

"First I have to tell there's a wild Injun, named Enoch Tuttle, living there. He's the last holdout of native autonomy and the only man who ever shot at me when I repo'd his vehicle. This trail is a back way I used to sneak into his property. Locals call this Confusion Hill. Sometimes it's hard to tell up from down. Walking up the hill can seem like down. Stay on the path until you come to a steel gate. Tell Enoch his friend from Lee Williams sent you."

"Should we give a hollar when we get close so he knows we're coming?"

"Don't worry, his pit bulls will let him know you're there," she replied as she drove away.

" 'I am all that is, that was, and is yet to come,' " Mor offered to the dense forest dwarfing them in its magnitude. He put his arm across Christina's shoulder and they started trudging down the up hill.

"Well this is a far cry from your sandstone towers," he offered. "Somehow our significance goes to zero out in this great world. So tell me. Why? Why are we still here? I mean we're really dwarfed to zilch just in these trees," he finished with an outstretched wave of his free arm.

"Careful or we may yet disappear," she replied, smiling up at him. The air was chill, giving her cheeks a vermillion glow. They paused, breath charged. Mor adjusted his arm on her shoulder. His lips turned in to meet hers. For that eternal moment captured in a kiss, he felt the world fall away. Then it poured back in a chill shower and they trudged on.

"You know it is funny in an appropriate sort of way. I mean us humans having basically two brains. Two distinct hemispheres inside our head. It can make us crazy. Always looking for the other that is not missing," she offered. They paused to kiss as mist gathered into a soft rain.

"A being that I am really getting off on you right now. If you were not bleeding to death as we speak, I would throw you down and make mad love to you right here and now but better to take a moment to gather our energies. Here, sit down. Let us see if we can do something about that bleeding." Christina put her arms around his neck as they leaned against the bark of a giant redwood towering into clouds above with its girth enveloping their bodies.

"Guess it's crazy to get personal with all this going on. But I'm getting off on you too, big time, baby, but I don't think I could come down enough to get it up." His voice seemed hollow against the massive redwood trunk. Looking up hundreds of feet to its canopy, he thought for a second they had disappeared back into a mere awareness of a being there.

"I am going to try and put a tourniquet on that knee," she said, tearing strips from her blouse. She took strands of bark and wrapped the wound, tying it with the cloth. She adjusted the pressure by twisting in a stout finger of a branch. "That is a bit too tight but let us see if it will stop the bleeding before I loosen it."

"So, tell me who we are right now. I can't go any further till I know. Are we love or lovers?" Mor reached out and pulled her in close enough to look deep into her eyes. "Tell me who I'm looking at?"

"Looking or seeing? Seeing not what you think, what you desire. I know what you are feeling, I feel it too. Still you can never see the indivisible eye of one who sees. A seer in any eyesz'za. Never really have what you desire as anyone other than the one desiring. You are me or I am you. Ironically your desire only seems as though, as thoughtsz, to move us apart. To divide as'word as'ex y z'sz zap'ping a thin'k'ing of it." Mor thought he'd heard painting as'word cutting an echo of any information of it as personic e'wayeves. Now he found any sense of it folding black jack. Of it unseen unheard in a wordfreedom untouched awareness of anybody anythin'king any time any where.

They moved at arm's length. Their eyes still locked. "I'm looking at you. You're looking at me but we cannot see in word the one who sees,"

"Only as a denial of a b'ng c'ng still indivisible in the first place."

"A na me of me. Any awareness of the a b c's of who we really are stays in a wordfreedom. It's a real hoot, all this fire and blood and lust."

"In a word. In the beginning middle end is the word."

"It's really blowing my mind with brain cum."

She laughed. "Yet still remaining ever free, untouched," she offered breathlessly as she leaned back in to kiss his lips. "but reality includes hypothermia. Best keep moving."

"Only ferns and lizards can live in the redwoods, a man once said."

Linked together, arm in arm, they ambled beneath a canopy so dense that only the fiddleback ferns competed for the path.

He pulled from Christina. "Prove me wrong, but I think Kwasanda doesn't want to give anything to Korner. We may be on our own. The whole chase seems like a set up somehow, but people keep dying."

Shafts of light fell through as the forest gave way to open country of chaparral and manzanita. The trail seemed to play out as a dog's bark and a wisp of smoke stopped them in their tracks.

"This place is definitely enchanting."

"We hope enough for Enoch Tuttle."

☼

A doe danced down the cut bank and onto the road sending Kwasanda skidding sideways down a steep grade. She pulled out of it just before hitting a series of switchbacks. She flashed on Dark and Christina and the undisturbed back trail leading to Enoch Tuttle.

She remembered years ago having been issued a repossession order on his Camaro, sending her driving to Tuttle's at midnight, pit bulls and buckshot waiting. She admired Enoch's ride as one of the funkiest 'res' cars she'd had the pleasure of hotwiring. She knew of his reputation as a native mix of gristle and hot blood and therefore not surprised he took a shot at her while she worked the ignition. Enoch chased her with amazing speed for a man an inch under five feet tall with a belly like a sumo wrestler. His levis were hacked off for length to accommodate stubby legs, barrel chest, bare to the elements, he was an apparition to scare the shit out of her. She was dialing 911 into her cell when Enoch broke out with a laugh, a meaty paw snatching her phone.

"You a sister and working for the man?" he had growled.

Over cups of black coffee, she'd offered to try working out a deal with the company. The Camaro in its 'res' condition of rusted rocker panels and torn upholstery had seemed hardly worth life or limb.

Then, coming over a rise, she saw in the rear view mirror the tree lined ridge free of Korner's stinkin' Lincoln, As the road leveled out into civilization she felt confident she'd make it. She speed dialed McCracken.

"Want to try again?"

"Kwasanda, my dear. So good of you to be in touch"

She negotiated traffic, her muscles tightening when the voice came back.

"Tired of the chase? About time to come home to papa."

"I'm taking the chance to read the disk. Get behind me on this. I need your support, papa. Heard about the fire."

"Korner is all over that. But it's not the pile of bricks that concerns me. A body was found. I haven't made an i.d. yet but I'm afraid it's my sensei."

"I'm sure he died in his boots. Anyway, I don't want to come in with him coming up behind. Then he's your problem."

"Let me talk to some people."

Chapter 10

Drizzle turned to downpour as Mor approached a steel gate fixed with case hardened iron chain threaded through a rusted steel padlock guard. Woven wire fencing topped by three strands of barbed wire ran out at opposite sides of the gate. Water droplets breaking loose as wind tightened the it against the thick links. Someone had cut a hole in the wire just large enough for him and Christina to squeeze through. Limping over a brief rise, they crossed a narrow bridge to a wasteland of wrecked cars and trucks only partly visible between a sea of thick looping blackberry canes. The path, littered with machined offal, rusted gears, axle rods, twisted remnants of rubber hoses, and giant tires bleached by years in the open sun was anything but inviting, he thought. Spiked blackberry arms seemed to be gathering in the wasted steel, rubber, and plastic back into its own source, its own earth, its own body. Piles of refuse and a mountain of black garbage bags smoldered over a sick glow from a green fire. The heavy downpour covering their scent, they surprised a stumpy-legged pit bull dancing against a short chain twenty yards ahead. Spotting the two visitors, he let out a howl. His bark seemed even more ominous by a hand-painted sign above his chain warning, "No Trespassing On Injun Land! White Trash Shot And Survivors Prosecuted."

Light showed from inside a bungalow speckled with moldy plank walls blackened with rain. Plumes of smoke drifted from the tin chimney. Two stout brown skinned men, in their early thirties, appeared, one glaring their way.

"As a white boy, I've been around enough reverse racism before and all I can say to it is, hey, 'I didn't burn your villages. I'm Irish, for Christ's sake," he muttered under his breath. The men wore their black hair long and brushed into braids. One had a wispy mustache deepening the shadow around the corners of his mouth, his eyes burning. His partner showed only mild concern colored with a slight smile to his expression.

"This is Indian land," the angry man growled. He stopped inches from Mor, rotting teeth bared.

"We're looking for Enoch Tuttle. Kwasanda, the repo princess sent us." He held the man's glare with a hard squint of his own. "I'm about two seconds from going on my butt," he whispered from the side of his mouth into Christina's ear.

"We can cut you up and toss the chunks to Butch over there. No one would be the wiser."

Christina's voice came out of the rain like a change in the weather. "Now why would you gentlemen want to do that?"

"I got this," Mor interjected just before losing his balance and toppling over. Christina caught him with an arm around his ribs with her hip thrust out.

"We are not law. We are running from the law or people who claim to be law. Where is Enoch Tuttle?" she asked, struggling to hold on to Mor's limp body.

"You're looking at him, toots."

Rain was letting up, the air carrying a damp chill, but Tuttle, shirtless to show his tattoos, stood with a staunch calm. Stubby legs gave him a low center of gravity like the pit bull that strained against his chain. His thick curly black hair seemed impervious to the water as he shook it back. He smiled with a broad grin missing two front teeth.

"Someone mention the dark princess?" he asked.

"She said you are good to your word and hated the law as much as the repo man," said Christina as she adjusted her balance.

Clouds tore open and late morning sun poured through the hole. Tiny raindrop prisms scattered diffused color as Mor stirred.

"I'd rather blow up my rides or bury 'em here in this graveyard than let them be taken by anybody, including a bank stooge." Tuttle spread his arms, dwarfish appendages compared to his bulk. "Might as well come in. We'll smoke a bowl and you can tell me the latest on the Queen of Sheba while we check out your amigo."

The angry man jumped into a primer gray Cutlass, belching a cloud of black smoke as he drove away. Tuttle walked to a rusted cast iron pumpkin, a transaxle thick with grease sweat. He hoisted the iron globe as if it were no more than a watermelon and heaved it onto a set of box springs rusting in a decaying truck bed.

"My brother Richard doesn't take a shine to white people. We've been kept out of the white man's world, except to attend his prison facilities." He wiped the grease off his hands with a sodden rag. The ground was littered with broken glass, blackened bolts, wire springs, and sharp rocks dappled with dung from the pigeons and chickens flapping about. Tuttle's bare feet had swollen toes splayed to help stabilize his three hundred plus pounds. He kicked an empty bottle into a bent tire rim with enough impact to shatter it into a spray of glass.

He ambled toward the shack waving a meaty hand to the door, a nailed up blanket of turquoise and pink horizontal stripes, sealed with grease. He bowed for Christina and Mor to enter. The interior was dimmed by similarly striped blankets tacked over the two front windows. Smoke drifted out from the iron door of a wood stove opened slightly against a smoldering oversized log. A muted television pixelated on stacked milk crates against a far wall. Tuttle directed them to a chrome rail leather couch repaired with duct tape patches, supported by cinder blocks and an overstuffed Naugahyde chair, its insides bursting out like cotton popcorn. Christina eased Mor onto the couch.

"You two look like you been in a shooting. I know the smell. Been in a few myself," Tuttle said, plopping on the couch next to him. Christina sat on the edge of the chair, her face pale in the television's popping light.

"We are reluctant outlaws. I am a professor in my normal life. Christina Shaughnessy, and this is Dark Mor," she said with an outstretched hand.

"Our mutual friend, Kwasanda Nzokia, rescued us from some bad people with guns."

"The black queen has real class, not like other repo scum I've known. The way she talks so damn continental gets me going. She even got the bank off my back." Tuttle offered a howl. "Hot damn, it's been boring lately. I can use the action."

He loaded a glass pipe with hashish that he heated with a match and crumbled between thick fingers. Mor took a long hit. He caught Tuttle smiling slyly before he laid his head back. The room spun, the air acrid with log smoke and the guarantee of mayhem. A pair of lips shone in the half-light of an adjoining room.

"Fawn, come meet some folks." Tuttle gently pulled her in. "My woman, Fawn Rave. This here is a professor and her sidekick, Dark."

"Pleasure," he mumbled, reaching to squeeze her free hand. "Fry Bread Power" was inked with a felt marker on the other that she held to her chest. Her face was oily and dotted with pimples, eyes made larger by thick applications of mascara drawn to points at the far corners like a cat, her glossed lips shaped by liner. Her glistening hair trailed down her back except for a single braid that sliced across her features. She wore open-toed sandals showing off purple lacquered nails. The raised heels exaggerated her hip movements, her butt jiggling in a tight faded denim skirt with pink ribbon lace fringe at mid-calf.

"Make us some tea, my sweet mia."

Tuttle grinned as he unleashed a head of thick, spiky hair. He loaded the pipe, took a huge toke, and passed it off to Mor, scanning his wound as he cracked some knuckles.

"Professor, how does a high-powered woman in the legit world end up getting shot at running from the law?" asked Tuttle. "The brother you met outside is young, full of heat and anger. I can imagine a lot of people who'd fire a bullet at him, but why you." He lit an unfiltered Camel as Fawn shaved a sage bundle over the stove. The leaf fragments sent up bursts of sweet smoke as they hit the hot iron. Tuttle leaned back and kicked his feet up on a scarred coffee table. "This heap is the last Indian land out of what twenty five years ago was over thirteen square miles. The tribe traded out for a casino down on the highway. Got everybody living in condos and shopping at Wallymart."

Dark hoisted his bad leg as clay packs plopped out from the heavy tread on the sole of his boot.

"You're bleeding pretty good, bro," Tuttle said, his canines catching his lower lip.

"I'm a bum. I bleed and breed, about all I'm good for. Mind if I take another hit?"

Fawn poured a baggie of dried tea into a kettle of water coming to a boil on the wood stove. Mor took another long toke on the hash pipe.

"Good shit. Afghani?" he asked, exhaling a cloud of smoke.

"Hell man, we be making better hash than those scag merchants. Those mothers cost me five years in the 'Q'. I kill any of them get around me."

"Tea's ready," Fawn said, breaking Tuttles tirade. She poured the steaming tea into a variety of jars and cups. Rain banged staccato across the corrugated tin roof in the shadows of pole rafters. Inside, the walls were covered with a patchwork of cardboard, newspaper, and fabric.

Christina sat slightly out of range from the fan of light glowing out from the muted television. Her eyes were closed, her chin slightly raised, her breath even. He watched Tuttle studying her for a long moment.

"Been in a few shoot-outs myself and caught a round or two. Better let me check out that knee. Suck 'em up and we'll have a look," he said, raking a beefy paw through his thick mane. He tapped another cigarette from a crumpled pack, firing up a kitchen match with a thumbnail.

Fawn handed Mor a tall mason jar filled to the brim with a hot brown bitter brew. He sipped at it gingerly as that sickeningly sweet odor of opium wafted in his nostrils. Christina held a cup in her lap.

"That's some nasty, bitter ass shit, man. Tastes like shrooms, and opium," Mor sputtered after a large swallow. "I'm already getting purple trails."

"People used to communicate with the realms of spirits beyond the human. Now we got cell phones but can't find our nuts with a tractor," Tuttle offered as wood smoke continued to leak out from the iron stove.

☼

Kwasanda dropped out of mountains into the traffic of the flat valley. She scanned parks, parking lots, and low-rise commercial buildings on streets with names like Middlefield and Glenwood, sailing by. This America, she thought, anchored by Neiman-Marcus and Saks West, seemed a good fit for a wannabe like R.J.. She remembered his high tech Portal in Menlo Park, when it was only a decrepit airplane hanger, a few football fields in length. She rolled on down a tree lined main thoroughfare with a grassy central esplanade. The avenue ran for several blocks of three-story chipped sandstone and red tile tech sweat shops made to blend with the architecture of their Stanford neighbor. She went another quarter mile till the thoroughfare fed into a circular three-lane drive with a single geyser of water falling in a white plume at the center.

She parked near a border of flaming red ornamental trees and took the pedestrian walk half a block to a five-story office building with open-air penthouse galleries. Kwasanda recognized part of the original airfield, now a lone strip on the edge of Portal, protected by chain link fence.

She used her company ID and optical scan to gain access to the grounds. The disk could only be read on the Portal's supercomputer, known as the Pod. Word was the design had been stolen from Messing. The rest of the rumor had it that no man had survived the Pod experience with their rational mind intact. Kwasanda had investigated and found evidence of this darker side to the Pod. The machine's developer had been committed to a local institution to get his wits redialed. She had studied the print outs and recognized in his experience, what her ancestors called Phareena, or ecstasy. Enough to make the average white man loose his mind. From what she could gather, the Pod accelerated the vibratory levels on a psycho biological level with such magnitude, such love bliss that the brain was virtually launched into permanent orbit. Kwasanda thought she had three distinct advantages over the previous researchers. One, she would be the first woman. Two, she had received initiation through her grandmother into a lineage of her tribal shamana. Reality, it seemed, is now still timeless after all this time, something easier for her African soul to acclimate to than that her modern white bread counterparts. That was number three. Naturally, the only man with the keys was R. J. McCracken.

Her heart rate accelerated as she grew closer. She could almost taste the menace in the rarefied air of the Portal's upper echelon. Just as she approached the great man's office, her cell phone rang.

"Have you missed me?" Korner's mocking voice jarred her focus.

"Like an abscessed tooth. You responsible for that murder out on Highway One last night."

"Listen sister. Believe me, it wasn't supposed to go down like that. Good help is hard to find these days. We're all driven by the unseen hands of fate. The difference between the Darkness and me is I'm willing to tempt 'em before they tempt me. He's afraid of the big picture."

"You are so completely full of shit. Your actions are preordained only by your own greed and blood lust."

"Aw, gee. Now you're hurting my feelings. My GPS shows you at the Portal. If you're about to do what I think you're about to do, don't do it."

"What, find out the truth about what's going on. Expose the lies?" she replied with a bravura that covered her increasing nausea.

"That sounds all noble, but you don't have any idea what or who you're really dealing with. The less you know the better. For you and your family."

Kwasanda slapped the phone off and tossed it in a trash can.

☼

Leather crunched in the wheelchair as Rakitin helped adjust his employer's position. In that familiar sound, Warren recalled boardroom meetings in the past, decisions affecting the fate of millions. Now the sound only signaled the passing of gas from his intestines. The board of directors had bought much of Warren's interest in Messing, but he retained the penthouse offices in the Pyramid. His eroding tissue and bone provided the essential decay needed to catalyze the virus. My body will have much more power dead than alive, he cackled to himself. He would save the fools from their own corruption. You do not put new wine in an old skin. They could never be more than ash in the wind. With the virus, they would be liberated from self-imposed bonds of ignorance and absorbed back into a cosmic undifferentiated black body first matter prima materia in the first place of first personic person of that eye. Out. In her'eye of eve re'y body with intent of now k'nowing out of it a being in her"e'turn all in one consciousness. A devious con she us na esse. A ma'ss hysteria he chuckled. That wayeve fun'ny'a'ction out of it in her'eye merely a peering it supersonically supernaturally superimposed as'z'any thoth'tsz. A letter'all god of gods. A dissolution of it a fun'da'mental process of the Great Work. A mirror deceit the name of their gods in word game. Awhile wily wordship. A craft of limitless potential now as'king of it a k'no'wing out a denial of it. A y'll DNa in forming any whorl'ding'sz'za'p'ping ting's echoing it as'ka's micro wayeve black'g'round with g'ee'sz us quantum gravity weight of any waiting to touch on a touching of it.

"Korner called at six. Ms. Shaughnessy is in company with the artist," offered Rakitin.

"What of the painting?" Warren rasped.

"They have not arrived at the studio." He replied as Warren's face turned to a deep scowl. The distant lights of the Golden Gate Bridge appeared as a narrow vein held aloft by iron threads silhouetted against a white bank of fog.

"He said he was on their trail. McCracken's agent, Kwasanda Nzokia, absconded with them and he believes she is headed for Portal. Our man, James, says Mor and Shaunnessy are secluded in the mountains."

Warren felt his temperature rise. Could anyone other than Korner screw this up?

"Hashemi intercepted calls between Korner and Nzokia. It appears they may be negotiating for the stolen disk and whatever mutual interests they may be scheming on."

"Will you too, betray me?" scrolled his thought now on the digital screen. The weakness in his plan was that it fell on the artist, a man already nearly killed several times. His rendering of a woman's face so enigmatic and beckoning could not be forced at the point of a gun. Only one force could generate the image and Warren knew nothing if not of the power of love. In the power of love he found the duplicity of hate. He was counting on hate and fate to deliver at least nine lives in the case of the Dark artist.

"Where are they?" he screened. A gift's a gift, he thought, you either have possession or not. Mor's gift came in capturing the soul of her as only a mere man can accomplish with the dexterity of heart eye and hand. As a spirit of it. Her eye c'ng in eve're'y form at least that of earth woman. A goddess. A nun. W/www wayeves out in her.'eye asz. d'Na y'll a moon. He could see in her'eye a wayeve but words did not come easy to Warren as his last hours melted away. Seemed all he could do, just to scan the swirling patterns, churning into seas of grain in the walnut burl paneling of his office. Amber wall lights shone buttery as they played over the lacquered surfaces. He felt his attention expanding the swirls to a macro cosmic scale. That brought him to Albert and those long New Jersey lunches where he first conceived the A Bomb. That cast him in the pariah pit. But then he completely accepted his role as the destroyer. He and Albert often spoke on the silent level of numbers, symbols, and the Quantum field perspective. Dark matter energy of that singular singularity of a being c'ng a peering it out as in her'eye of eve're'y body experienced directly as'z z z'leep off her'ey 'e k'urve's now a'ledge'd'ly . . . a re'y'all . . .black into one sacred singular indivisible invisibility bliss in her'eye on LOVE SUPREME darkness. Albert's Newtonian objective science having purged the gods and settled into the vacuum of a greater good wanted to deny his role of destroyer. Aware of the god'esse p'ssy'en'ce whole power Warren merely averred to a body experienced directly and periodically by eve're'y body on the planet. A black body consciousness where Quantum mechanical laws dissolved completely at the nexus of eve'nting information out of her eye of eve's n't'ing eve're'y bodhi. Or a black indivisible bodhi now crossing a horizon of in'visibility. An imaginary line between a singular indivisible darkness and any complexity of it in light of in word division of that indivisible consciousness supernaturally as thoth'tsz of it. Of it appearing out in her"eye merely a peering it. Ma'sz energy completely reabsorbed in bliss so infinitely potential still that the macro micro cosmic universe, having only potentially expanded in word for a mere trillion plus light years might be reabsorbed periodically in that blink of eye, that hood falling as'z z z'leep black into one indivisible black'g'round invisibility of any individual in one mirror breath of Brahmin a re'y"ality . . . . thus his awareness skirted this nexus at a high enough frequency yet ultra low amplitude as to synchronize cosmic activity over wide areas of the e electric fi're'y dhi'a'ting neuronal brain. He knew his body served as ultimate instrument of consciousness that he could easily expand or contract in its full macro micro cosmic potential. . . . .so much energy, most, wasted on maintaining that twis'ting X identity. Why. . . . .Uncle Albert's words came onto his inner screen . . . . "the beautiful thing we all can turn to experience . . . .the mysterious" . . . .Mr. re'y'e. . . .re'y'e dhi'a'ting . . .a's'pect'rum . .of it out in her black eye of eve re'y body.

Warren recalled Albert's demeanor with respect. . . .how sad his eyes turned when Warren told him of his inspiration for the ultimate weapon of ma'ss destruction. . . .naturally Albert was partial to Creation . . .Warren stood on the opposite side . . .his god the Destroyer . . . his process fundamentally dissolution of her eve'll craft. . .Albert even tried to stop him by appealing to the U. S. president Roosevelt and their constitutional democratic government. Warren knew even then, that that dream of the demos was playing out into a multi-national security state to be resting squarely on the destructive power of his baby, his thermo-nuclear weaponry of Ma'ss destruction. Like all great inventions, the bomb came to him fully conceived including the national security state of mind. The people, the demos, had no more chance of stopping that than the citizens of Nagasaki after his package left the plane passing over their heads he thought with a mind now seared without emotion.

"Hashimi trailed them to a shack belonging to a half-breed named Enoch Tuttle."

Nothing very remarkable, he thought. His attention flashed back to Albert's eyes when he realized his own genius had spawned such destruction. E=mc2. Warren on the dark side realized the mirror potential power as creation or destruction. What comes in time goes in time. Any X's ting in'formation potential is merely still indivisible invisibility of a Y eye appearing a pairing Y as'eX now k'now'ing any un'known. Time out awhile space. Curving mirror of intent of her will, her mirror seas way of eve will. A wayeve out in her eye of eve'll . . .that d"ark body . . .E body . . .Einstein's body y'll d'na . . .Y'll D'NA . . . that denial power of it's indivisibility . . . Albert's weakness that preoccupation with relativity . . .the appearing always still disappearing . . . still that awareness of a being in the first place. The 'old one' wordfree untouched drawing on the right side of the brain.

Albert sensed it . . .sensed him, saying "are we closer to the old one with this knowledge . . .this constant feeling of a being alone in the first place . . . the center eye of true religiousness" . . . .best when his brilliant mind receded from all language of objectivity of numbers, signs, symbols, form, for ma'ss light . . . then he would say "In this sense and only in this sense of the old one, of feeling him in touch with that of a being all, alone I, indivisible, in'visibility of a y eye of a b'ng c'ng belong now to the ranks of in word truly liberated men."

"He's known in those parts for trafficking drugs, including pscillosybin mushrooms," Rakitin interjected into Warren's thought flow.

Fruits of love, the connections crackled in his old brain. Now a k'now'ing out of the old one. Warren had stayed on top long enough to know there was always someone, some awareness of a being of that. A cosmic eye being c'ng higher above pulling strings connected to a greater power base, just as Messing Technologies intertwined with other corporations to become the beast now consuming its founders. Just as the Milky Way along with many nearby galaxies were drawn to the cosmic Zone of Avoidance where some 10,000 galaxies warped the expansion of macro cosmic spacetime gathering as a point 150 light years distant. How could he affect any concern for this insignificant crumb of earth when gamma X rays of such magnitude entrained his mind now k'now'ing macro ka'smic realms so far beyond his crumbling body on such a crumby planet. He had always intuited the unseen grander design, plan et, that E.T. macromicro aska's mic being now awhile a y eye a peering out now any mere mirrored potential with intention of a being a Y now as'eX out k'now'ing of it not. Why not ? Mushrooms or mushroom clouds. E. T. spores of it out in her black eye body of eve're'y body of LOVE SUPREME bliss could work in his favor with Mor and Christina.

☼

The last rays of sun gave in to a purpling sky. McCracken drummed his fingers on the stainless steel desktop. His office suite, decorated with antiquities, Egyptian anthropomorphic gods with heads of dogs and birds along along with Mesopotamian winged men, gave him a visceral connection to a grander view of time. As a boy, stories of the ancients served as an escape from the poverty of his young life. In dreams he discovered a vortex in time with a spirit guide that teleported his awareness of a being far beyond parameters of his stark waking reality. Though that awareness seemed to fade out in adolescence as his imagination was squared away by education, he never lost the spark of believing in the supernatural.

Then one day at the University he discovered Friedrich Nietzsche and the uber mensch, the over mind. That was the day his destiny called with the mystical spirit guide returning.

He gazed out the window at the low lying coastal mountains sawing across the horizon. He knew Nietzsche found his spirit guide hiking for hours everyday in the mountains. It struck McCracken how one must climb thousands of feet above sea level to reach higher elevations of mind, get above that soupy morass of marine layered air. Climb up into the greater mind atmospherically clearer at ever higher elevations till reaching the tree line, oxygen diminishing till bio man evaporates back into one cosmic being. Then mountain climbing became his passion.

He found the ceremonial power necessary to awaken the idols in a diminutive East Indian electrical engineer named Ramaswamy. Ram. The thought of his clipped character calling typically before daybreak, on a Saturday, brought a smile to R. J.'s lips. Ram was a gifted engineer who, covered in sacred ash, could perform traditional ceremonies, anointing and awakening ancient idols whose other world dimensions freed him from the conventional self concepts that boxed his competitors. These ceremonies with their ensuing transitions of mind to the greater timeless over mind, freeing it from biological limitations, along with Ram's brilliant engineering, led to the development of his super computer, the Pod. Unfortunately, the only three people who had attempted to operate it came out with brains so scrambled they turned into incommunicative zombies. The Pod, technological extension of the uber mensch, the over mind, the macrocosmic mind seemed to swallow whole the relative microcosmic identity of any man. It operated on them as they tried to operate it, he mused with a frown.

"Yes," he replied to an interruption from the intercom.

"Ms. Nzokia to see you."

"Good, send her on in," he replied as he straightened his jacket. Just when he needed another guinea pig to operate his baby. He was familiar with her background as a tribal shamana. Was she not a living archetype? An African woman. The womb of the cradle of mankind. A perfect match to the archetypal matrix from which he had derived his design for the Pod. Plus she had a great ass.

"Korner, that psycho son of a bitch. He killed my sensei and blew up my fucking house." he ranted to the black Sheba that loomed over him. "Fortunately there was already a fire truck in the neighborhood. Sit down, would you. I can't think with you hovering like that. You really want to go into the Pod?" he asked, stepping from behind the desk. He walked over to the full length windows, stood, and drummed the glass with his fingers. Spread out below he saw his mini empire with employees hustling about manicured green open spaces, vital, he knew for his elite minds to meditate. Meditation. Merely a being of that as a being cosmic. Man as mind memory mirror reflecting overmind. Uber mensch. Supernatural man'as mind. Protean man. He knew it as the key to unlocking the protean alpha state. Timelessness and immortality still reality. Immortal man as mind. Or y? Reality at the heart of an'y mir'r or'e mind. The real gold. The real goal of mind or y thinking of a being in the first place, he thought . There was the Y'de open door, yet, somehow the approach remained unapproachable. The mythic line, the event horizon, once crossed, no body ever returned to tell the tale. The paradox made his jaw clench. It seemed to reach that complete absorption of realization of that supernatural a y being he, R. J. must die, must disappear black into that indivisible.

"Unless there's some other way to read this disc?"

McCracken turned with the mention of the disc. He found the black princess holding a 22 auto in her right hand. He couldn't help but smirk, seeing that tiny pistol in a woman's hand, trying to intimidate him in his own sanctum.

"You're kidding, right? You threatening me, here? How far...."

She fired a round at his feet, catching a bit of the Italian leather of his loafers. The report so muted that it wouldn't pass beyond his office.

"I can and will seriously fuck up your day. I'm not so concerned for my safety, tho, having worked security for you, I do know my way around here, otherwise, I wouldn't be going into that crypt of yours. So come on, R.J., fire that bad dog up. You know you want another test dummy."

"Hey, easy, fuck sake these shoes are hand made. Let's cool down a second and consider our options. I do have the husband's ashes card."

Kwasanda gave him the sad eyed treatment. And of course he always fell for it. She would always hold the missing mother card. That and she had a great ass and lips that promised some entirely different cosmos to inhabit. Then a cell phone rang.

"Korner, you puta hijo."

"Easy, boss. I didn't do your man. Dark Mor went full-blown psychopath on me. He got hold of my gun, before I realized what the frac, he cold blooded shot your sensei. Somehow he got it in that demented paranoid artist brain thinking your man had killed his wife." Korner barked from the other end.

"What about the explosions?"

"Faulty gas lines what I heard. Fortunately there was a fire truck in your hood. On medivac. Some old fart slipped in his bathtub. And heads up for that black brat with the kinky braids. I was on her trail, trying to recover your stolen property when she got lucky and managed to give me the slip."

"And what about the disk?" McCracken asked as he let the phone go silent for a second before turning it off.

"Here is the disk," she said, tossing the item on his desk. "So, how about my husband's ashes?

"I must have known you were coming. I got them out of my safe earlier. They're in the urn there on the shelf. We'll bring them along on the way over to the Pod. It's in the old hanger. You remember the last of the original nineteen forties air strip. It's my sentimental side. You wouldn't like to fuck somewhere along the way, would you?" he asked with what felt like an almost fatherly grin.

"Oh gee. Let me think about that for a second. No." she said as she moved over to him. "I know about your proclivity for pain, somebody else's, and I would have to be the one delivering the blows." She concluded her words with a fist tightened around his cajones.

What was a man to do. He leaned in and bit her gently on the neck. He felt her flesh quiver on his lips.

"It ain't all bad, sister." he said, looking down into the pools of her eyes. "I make everything available to you. I'll call down. Get the guys to fire up the beast if you're ready? Forget about the gun. The deal has expanded. I do need a compatible user. If you're into going in, I'll roll out the red carpet. I really think women are more compatible for reasons I've explained to my technicians but they still don't understand."

"They're probably all men. Show me to the Pod."

Kwasanda and McCracken rode the elevator down to the open courtyard ringed with trees twinkling with amber diodes strung like miniature stars. For a moment, she dreamed of a different world built on love and cooperation rather than hatred and war, with the Portal as a center for art and humanities instead of exploitation and the hoarding of capital. She saw lovers young and old drifting across the plaza then blinked, realizing they were men in lab coats engaged in a discussion. Probably about engineering a man's mind or a memory in hers, she thought.

Above the hanger, the sky shimmered with carbon exhaust as nearby rush hour traffic droned. They entered through forty foot sliding doors. Standing elegantly, suspended in a web of filament, the cool warm white 3D egg shaped Pod glistened in the overhead light. She watched McCracken touch a screen setting the whole affair in motion. The Pod in free motion appeared suspended as if in a di-polar anti-magnetism floating on an electromagnetic invisible blanket right before her eyes. Kwasanda stood transfixed by the intermeshing pattern of light and shadow. McCracken signaled her to the vacuum room to suit up for her baptism. She stepped into the changing room and without bothering to close the door, stripped completely naked. She turned to face McCracken as she slowly slipped out of her panties. Standing with her legs apart, she reached over and snagged the jumpsuit from its hook.

Kwasanda followed an array of zigging lights to a console. She looked back over her shoulder with a 'whats with the lights' expression. McCracken shrugged with a smile. Kwasanda went ahead and popped the quarter size disc into the receiver. The Pod lowered as she approached. A seam in the elastic eggshell finish widened to reveal an interior somewhere between galactic and black hole. She picked up on a vibratory hum. To calm her nerves, she began to hum along in the same pitch, finding herself merging with the atmosphere of static charge that pervaded the open Pod. One synapse. In a blink she slipped inside.

The Pod enveloped her eye in a way that, much like falling asleep, instantly dissolved any sense of a being other y's. She was in the heart of it as complete awareness. She now was the heart of awareness. She thought later she would remember to think about it. Then a prick of tactile impulse awakened an abiding focus. Her fingertip was dented by a pointed shaft. Kwasanda realized she was fingering the medallion on a silver chain around her neck. The lingam-yoni. The diamond in the challis. Her focus slid away. She thought, let there be light. Beams of cool radiance spread before as digital arrays filling her, pervading her. Projecting her inner sense of a being still in the first place seeing now as k'now'ing out of a y eye singular indivisible vision see'ng insight ser seer pervasive pervading. A being of singular blue electro magnetic light penetrating even the hoods of her closed eye lids. Absorbing her'eye in it. She it. A being c'ng still in the first place.

Fractal patterns informing complex geometrical configurations translated information from wayeves of it out in her eye of eve re'y body. Wayeves of her eyes. O see'ng o'cean. Her"eye now k'now'ing out a mere mirrored seer insight see'ng on in an ocean craft a'sailing over it in her'eye upon mirror see'as. Her eye ways of eve"re' y bodhi of that mirror are'y'all. High Priestess Virgin going out of a being gaining that go'a'ld, that holy black p'ss'y whole womb. A being c'ng now a y eye merely a peering out infinite potential. Dhi Ana still immaculate virgin now appearing as Empress with do"or way of it out in her eye wayeve. Her eye wayeve function. In her"eye a fun'ny action of that black womb peh'ss'y'en'c'ng a whole bom'b born on a y eye insight of man'as mind. Ocean of motion still a Y he. Why the man with out womb as mind or y. Why then womb bom'b memory. Why? If only to lose it. 'You don't lose it '. Why me or you she wondered from her spirit guide, her totem in cast silver diamond entering the bowl challis hanging in 3D around her neck.

'You do not. You are that a y'll d'na luminous subtle body of denial. A while repository of y'all myriad possible mirrored potential lives'. Her spirit guide speaking straightaway to her inner hearing.

Lingham and yoni. Function and Freedom. Ma'ss. Kali Ma. A Na y. Y na N'ow. Time'ma"sz z z'leep black. Black. BLACK. . .BLACK . . .BLACK . . . EVE'Re y as too . . .now awhile as two being"sa'z z zapping as'z'leep, synapse electric spark now uniting one supernaturally supersonically as thoth . . .Thoth . . . .THOTH . . .a great god esse to be a great goad of that peh'ssy w'hole synapse . . . p'sy e'n'se gap . . . goad of any mouth chasing tail . . . Woman after Man after Womb'man with or now as Thoth, god esse to be letter'ally as in word thoughtsz of a being c'ng denied now k'now'ing a being in the first place without it . . .man as one great mind a y'a eye yoh complete or not now y na. Why not appear to be a pair to draw from it. For it. For Ma or Pa Peh esse'eye whole indivisible . . . .power to be as thought continued streaming her mind's eye . . . Kwasanda realized she now needed to add personically the sound of her own voice as Ohm'a . . .Oh"ma . . .Oh"mother mercy.

The egg reverberated like the crystaline ringing of a thousand synchronized bells. Fractal ringing mandalas continued to stream 3D information directly as thought form'asz'za waves flowing sparking leaping into neuro-cellular transmitters contacting receptor hairs of her pineal gland. A 3rd Eye. Her now first eye in a being c'ng still in the first place. Now out in her eye of eve're'y body. Her eye a black mirror seas a're'y'all body. Her re'y"e. HER RE'Y"E . . . HER"RE'Y"e . . . . aRe'y'flected by the mirror a're'y'flection of herhimit as her'me'sz thoth'tsz. HIM A'S THOTH . . .Ibis . . . . I a being is . . . .As go go go(a)d any letter all'y y'all in y'll d'na me. Y na me mere mirror denial of it . . .out now as k'no no NO w'ing supernaturally superimposed as of thoth. T'sz letter all y any mirrored y na. The duplicity. The mirror craft of her"eye of eve're'y body. A wiley word'ship craft. Awhile. Space craft. In wordship sailing as z z z'apping her eye mirroring a se'eas in the eye any a na y point of view of you of y. Or y na, Y Noon. A wayeve of her"eye infor'ma'ss in word of it a be"am'ing for'ma'sz z indivisible in'visibility now k'now'ing in'formation z'apping, k'zapping, ka'kurving spinning chakras wheels turning we all into ganglions of neurons firing y'z z z do me do'mus esse to be a being in the first place a's supreme end . . .time now. Why? for'ma'ss what purpose? Per her eye pose seer sight see'ng Nun . . seeing sending out in her'eye of eve"re'y"'as'z z z'leep into a body. . . .Ka's mic synapse between her mouth and his tail or his mouth and her tail. In her eye a cosmic memory of me or you . . .a'sz z z'apping sight . . .p'sy't . . .Noon . . .Nu'n . . .Nu'mer ' 'all y y'all . . . her seas see'ng y'all of wayeve function of function. . .busyiness of busy busy busy'n'ess'e then complete darkness till that warm cool blue light broke then into now k'now'ing prisms of color, patterns, forms growing cellularly dividing reforming in constant constantly fluxing flux. Eve"re ybody tempted to surrender her will, her little life to this enchanting galactic seas insight out of her eye seeing. Of a be"am'ing something. A be"am'ing out in her'eye of eve're'y bodhi. Then somebody appearing a's thoth'tsz of a being other y's, she now remembered her daughter and for a moment choked on the emotion of never seeing her or touching the touch of her again.

Then she pressed the point of her medallion, the pinprick bringing her back to her senses. If she now let up on the pressure the senses of a being swept attention away in an eve're'y increasing wayeve motion stretching her body till it threatened to tear her to pieces, her neurons expanded nearly beyond their synaptic range. Then she felt a hand lifting her out of the clutches of that a y eye merely a peering. Not now see'ng out anybody in her black peh'ss'eye whole.

☼

Mor lost himself in the patter of raindrops and the muted drum beats coming from an unseen source. Rain gods beating on his h'ear drums. Gusts of wind rattled the corrugated tin roofing sheets overhead layed across the pole rafters. The psychedelic mushrooms seeped into his perception, as jeweled fruits on lush vines appeared before his eyes, light waves, psychedelic ways of it in her'eye. A ma'ss supernatural color ways of eve. In her'eye a sublime e spectre'y e spectrum radiating superimposed over the coarseness of the room. His senses of a being any body melted into the tuck and roll leather of the couch. The room, inseparable from the cosmos at large, turned into a being of universal man as mind. Eve'rey thought a chord'ing too strings of a being in the or y playing sound around his role, art'is't'at of a being c'ng here now. A being in the first place now out of it as ex pressing imaginary pigments over his periphery. A's too the zygomatic circular horizon of eve eyeing any en'dhings'of it en"ter'eye'ing that field of view. Of you. Indivisible in'visibility appearance of that in word mirror mind or a y eye in forming it asz thoth'tsz. Supernaturally supersonically superimposed by now as'ka's mic memory as'ka's all'y cause of ignoring a k'no no no'wing projection of it. It a being still in the first place now as thoth'tsz of it out casting hooks.

Tuttle's movement to a battered chair across from Christina left irridescent trails as if his mass moved in subtle stages trailing in space. Tuttle leaned toward her, black hair veiling his eyes. She now appeared as though in a mock play having tea with the president of the university at Stanford House. The rain on the roof drowned most of what Tuttle said. He talked with the same force as his laugh, a mumbo-jumbo where drugs become medicine and sacrament. Throw in a touch of philosophy, a dash of jive with native sensibility and you had the makings for an interesting spiritual miasma. A hard con of a being. A hard con now in her ma'ss eye a con she'e na us. We all free turning of a y eye na us. A b'ng c'ng na what we all in turn think of it. It a wordfree untouched awareness. Of it.

Now Mor saw Christina as a clear lens. Tuttle the trickey purple trails playing in the glass. She laughed at his jokes, giving Mor the rest of her tea. He drank it down, swallowing the soggy mushrooms at the bottom of the cup.

Fawn Rave walked from the other room, arm bracelets tinkling. Cheap perfume wafted through sage and wood smoke. She took a seat on Tuttle's lap, the compactness of her form shifting against his mass, a bird on a gnarly stump. He whispered as she snuggled and nodded with his words. Her hair appeared as irridescent multicolored glittering strands of light trailing out over shimmering fields of luminescent color. He now k'no'wing a being c'ng out experiencing that heart felt feeling e'magic bio field of view. Of you from head to toe. Of'ten you a y eye now a bi na re'y"es wayeve'da pulses playing over the plane of Mor's vision. Her"e eve're'y mom"ent'ing in forming a macromicro mean ways of eve'll. The weight of waiting on a b'ng c'ng now out in her'eye wayeve will. Weight of eve'll. Her eye'sz'ion an imaginary cunning con. A con'she'us'n'ess"e. But then he always was a sucker for black lace. Blood rushed to his brain, making him numb below the waist. He finished the second cup of tea.

"How you doing, bro?" Tuttle asked. Something affected his speech which sounded to Mor like he was being patted on the back, just before a knife slipped between his ribs. He just replied with a nod, not bothering to attempt verbal communication in his in word dissolution condition. His condition was in. Into the interior of it. Mom'en't to mom'en'ta.

"Let me have a look at your leg before you bleed to death. You're looking a bit peaked, even for a white man."

Suddenly Tuttle loomed over him, filling his vision with sharp canines across a gap of red gum. Given a choice, Mor thought he would rather have a drunken she-bear lick the wound clean, but froze when Tuttle came at him with a buck knife dripping with blood. Fawn stood next to him, tearing cloth into strips and setting them to boil in a pot on the stove. He glanced at Christina. She met his gaze with a sympathetic smile.

"We have to stop the bleeding. Enoch assures me he's done this procedure a dozen times before," she said, leaning over to whisper in his ear. "Feel the love here, Vincent."

"That's right. I have the steady hand." Tuttle replied, letting his meaty hand tremble in Mor's face. He stropped the blade on a leather belt nailed to a post, used heat from the stove to sterilize, and finished the cleaning with a strip of cloth fished out of the boiling water. Mor let out a sigh, realizing what he thought to be blood was mere water. Christina bent to put an arm around his shoulder, the nipple of her breast, hard as a coffee bean, pressed into his flesh. Tuttle sat on the thick slab coffee table as his stout fingers deftly cut the denim away from the wound.

"It's bad. The bullet nicked an artery. I'll have to put in a couple stitches." Tuttle poured tequila on the wound as Mor grimaced. Tuttle took a swig, and offered him the bottle. If this is the end of my life, he thought, surrounded with women and helped by a stranger, filled with ecstatic love, whole world vibrating in tune with one heartbeat, I'll take the ride.

When he came back to his senses, he lay naked except for his jockey shorts on a double bed under several Mexican blankets. Christina sat in the amber light of a kerosene lamp boosted by several candles. His body pressed against hers.

"How long have I been out?" he asked through sleep-thickened lips.

"About two hours. Enoch did a pretty good job. The chunk of metal he dug out of your leg wasn't a slug of a bullet," she replied, slipping off her clothes to crawl in beside him.

"Probably a fragment from the car. I'm relieved to know Korner didn't shoot me for a second time."

Christina kissed him. He let her pour in, filling every tear and empty space. Still stoned to the bone, their edges blended naked under the blankets. Prickles of her pubic hair rubbed against his hipbone, matching his beard touching her soft cheek.

"Tuttle's tea got the blood rushing to my brain instead of pouring out my leg. That's a good thing but makes me incapable of getting an erection out of old Johnson."

"There's nothing between us. Let our minds do the penetrating," she said softly leaning in to let her curls touch his cheek.

"Sex is how men express love for a woman. Take his sexuality away and he isn't a man," he replied as she kissed him. "But y'all give brain head . . ." Mor's voice trailed off till she burst out laughing.

"Well now you be my first brain sex lover"

"No I'm serious. That Y dialectic debate ignited me. It really scintillates my p'sy k'ey"e. It's like turning a corner. Pun intended. Suddenly my attention is turned completely black around a complete d"ark'ness. That d ark of my role. Complete mom'en'ting by mom'en'ting. That was a y eye of a being of me in that split second awareness a prior'y to my initial awakening out of it in word. That's y. Y me crazy p'sy'co ma gave me da Dark name. She of y'all people understood indivisible invisibility of a being bi polarity. Polarity is an imaginary break in a complete d"ark'ness of it. It in any role always a complete ark. In ma's shrieking incoherence she realized I'd had a premature in word awakening to the wily craft of a b'ng c'ng now any a peering at it a k'no'wing out of it. After she chilled from her tantrum she stared at me for over an hour." Suddenly Mor reawakened to his first in word awakening. He realized the sheer silence of. It remained completely silent except for a pingting of it impinging on his field of awareness. Great video but negligible audio he flashed.

It seems it takes longer to learn sounds than images he imagined. Without yet k'now'ing out of it any in word echo to define it. A sound wayeve informed by a word. Just as we all turn indivisible light waves into learning a k'nowing out of it in word thought waves echoing a black'g'round of complete d"ark'ness. D"ark na necessarily black or white. Just us unbroken.We all now k'now a b'lack' with intent of a b'ng c'ng a gain. A gain of complete d"ark'ness must be its denial in any k'no no'wing out of it. Out of a black'g'round eve're'y'body as'king of it paying attention to any echoing sound wayeves turning into anybody. Anything as thoth'tsz of it in a wayeve a're'y'ting in formation cognition into any objective field of view. We all turn sound waves echoing out in her'eye a peering a black'g'round into neuronic fields of strings chords wind and drum. In other words we all learn hearing now turning around k'nowing ignore'ance projection of silent supersonics with a sliver of our audible range.

"Now y'all giving me brain head. It's amazing how the dialectic seeped into your y mind. Sometimes its turning light on. In your case Darkness its turning it off. Back to black. PARANTAKALI. Supreme end time. Fade back to black. Perhaps the situation calls for you to express your Godness, your greater self. A being of the real artist." Christina planted kisses on his chest, pulling the blanket up.

He closed his eyes to hallucinate the inner wordfree world of patterns shapes color. Then in the blink of eye he found overlaying it an in word awareness. A cobra reared up out of a swirl of colored threads, transforming from serpent, too deer, too cougar, too wolf. Wolf howled in turn becoming a woman seated on a cube of stone crowned with a crescent moon. On the lap of her blue robe, she held with delicate hands a scroll that unrolled to form a path. Mountains rose beside the path now a valley cut with a river running red to match the sky. Skeletons walked, swinging swords and scythes over a field of human appendages. Heads stared with unseeing eyes. Feet walked in the direction of a setting sun. Hands waved hello good by. He blinked, the serene face of the priestess appearing before a veil stretched between two legs, one black, one white. His field of view moved between the legs now pillars leading to a doorway. Color ranges shifted from hot reds to cool blues. He opened his eyes, letting the lamp dissipate her image. Christina lay beside him. She seemed focused beyond until she turned his way.

"Enoch saved you. He could tell you'd almost lost enough blood to lose consciousness," she said, snuggling into him.

"Figures I'd owe my life to an outlaw medicine man." He watched a bat darting in the rafters. His heart pumped such pure love with Christina that a lump swelled in his throat, tears pouring from his eyes. With any luck, the stitches would hold.

A fissure of light split the darkness. It opened up as Kwasanda found herself pulled gently from the Pod by two waiting assistants. They settled her onto a cart, driving her from the hanger to an elevator leading up to McCracken's office. She felt completely numb, arms and legs limp noodles. She could see her wiry hair wild and free alongside her face. To her amazement they drove her down the hall from the elevator right on thru double doors onto the thick carpet of his office.

McCracken stood by the windows with one hand stroking his chin. He nodded to the leather sofa and his assistants carried her over. She still felt paralyzed, letting his guys stretch her out with her head propped against a pillow. McCracken walked over, settling in a chair beside her. For a long time neither spoke.

"I gotta ask," he said, finally breaking the silence. She began to blink and move her eyes. "Are you paralyzed? Blink once for yes. Twice for no."

She blinked once. He leaned in till his face filled her field of vision. He had a quizzical expression that made her wonder what she looked like. He sat back in silence. Then like a snake shedding a skin she felt her body reawaken. Sitting up, she caught her reflection in a mirror. Most shocking, her hair, unleashed from cornrow braids, stood like she'd stuck her finger in a socket.

"You. You okay. You look, charged. I bet I could put a volt meter on you and you'd be reading two twenty."

She got up and walked over to the mirror to get a closer look. It was true. Tiny sparks jumped about her hair as she moved. She seemed immensely older but looked younger in the mirror.

"Where's my clothes? I just remembered I have to pick someone up."

"I had them brought up. They're right there, on the chair."

She walked over to the pile with her white cotton panties and brassier on top. Unzipping and slipping off the jumpsuit, she looked up to see McCracken starring back. She hesitated then stood back stark naked with her hands on her hips. He continued to stare unabashedly. A slight smile began to play across his lips.

"It's sexier with the white panties against my black flesh," she offered as she shimmied into them. "And the white lace pulled tight against my nipples," she continued, snapping the bra clasp.

McCracken's lips went dry and he ran his tongue over them. Kwasanda pulled up her levis with a few extra wiggles. She couldn't resist pulling his chain and finished dressing before he managed to say another word. As she holstered her.22 he realized she was getting ready to book.

"Wait a minute. You can't leave without debriefing."

"I'll be brief. Meet me later. I'll properly debrief you then," she said, walking over giving him a kiss and a nip on his neck.

"Where and when?"

"You got my number."

Chapter 11

His throbbing knee brought Mor moaning out of sleep. Christina woke beside him, calling for Tuttle, who came like the dawn of a hairy planet.

"Easy there, bro." He gave Mor a shard of oak. "Bite on this medicine stick. Our women use them for popping babies." He clamped down as Tuttle ripped the bandage clear of the wound. He checked the stitches for signs of infection then pulled the stick from Mor's jaw.

"No worries here. Just a reminder the dig is healing."

"Thanks. Enoch. Your name sounds biblical."

"That's right. He mediated between God and the fallen angels. They were having too much fun to go back to heaven."

"Me and the Professor do appreciate everything you've done for us. You may have saved my life. There's only one way I could repay that."

"Praise the Lord brother, I am only his humble servant. 'What you do for the least of my kin, you do for me.' " Tuttle's eyes narrowed. His lips went to a tight evil line. Mor blinked with the flash of depravity and hatred he caught in their glint.

"Don't worry, bro. It'll pass."

"What's that?"

"The pain. The pain will pass." Tuttle's eyes glittered when he said 'pain'.

"I brought tea." Christina smiled over Tuttle's burly shoulder.

"My own brew with herbs, poppies bleeding BBs of opium. The water here has a lot of iron. Suck 'em up, bro." Tuttle patted Mor's foot and left the room.

The sickly sweet smell of opium mixed with iron sulfide wafted from the clay mug. A bat fluttered in the rafters, a wood rat with eyes like glassy black beads ran the dirt floor. The critters scurrying knocked Mor's edge off as he took the steaming mug.

"This shack reminds me of some archeological digs of yore. Primitive shelters put me back in touch with myself. No pretension."

"Like your glass vessel overlooking the Pacific."

"At home I am the ocean. The house is in a Japanese American family's trust. I am only the caretaker. The status of my address and work as a professor does not have any real effect on who I am," she replied, sitting down on the bed beside him. "Except for money, prestige, and influence," she finished saying with a wink.

"Easy to get carried away by it all."

"Especially when you have hundreds of eyes locked on yours, with people tip toeing around you."

He set the mug down and took her in his arms. His hands traced the small of her back.

"You are the voice crying in my wilderness."

"You need to rest, artist. We'll see what tomorrow brings."

He pulled her body in, crushing her breasts against his chest. The opium kicked in. He surrendered to the drug, falling back in a nod to sleep until gray light filled the room. Dark opened his eyes to the jagged teeth and mean yellow eyes of a carved mask hanging on a post next to the bed. The demon had a second set of tiny jaws set between eyes with more eyes fanning up the side of its elongated forehead.

Christina came into the room, her face as fresh as if she'd returned from walking in spring sunshine. She handed him a steaming mug.

"Coffee, black as you like."

"I should get wounded more often."

The wild ends of her hair tickled his cheeks as she leaned to adjust his pillow. He brought the mug up to his nostrils.

"I knew a woman who wouldn't drink coffee. Made her too wired but she loved to inhale the aroma."

Kwasanda laughed from the doorway. "Lazarus rises. You are hard to kill." Her eyes and teeth flashed electric against her ebony skin. The leather jacket she wore was tight at the waist, billowing in a satiny sheen around her chest to conceal any side arms. Her energy set off his sense of overwhelming fatigue, his muscles slack, seemed to hang on his frame like inert clay.

She jammed her fists into jacket pockets and spun against the wall as Tuttle eased his girth past her. He wore an ironed cambric long sleeve shirt with pearl snaps, broad cuffs rolled back, straining against thick arms.

"I do wear a shirt now and then," he replied to her raised eyebrows.

"How's the ham bone?" he asked Mor.

"Painful but like you said, it'll pass." he replied, catching the glint in Tuttle's eye's.

"You should be feeling plenty below the waist with these fine women around." His breath reeked of tequila and unfiltered Camel cigarettes.

"I could use some more of that tea."

Tuttle gave him a tight eyed bulldog grin, all lips and canine teeth. "Suck 'em up, bro. Suck 'em up." He gave him a quick jab to the ribs.

As Tuttle heaved from the room Kwasanda stopped him with an embrace.

"No more tea for the Darkness. We must be going."

"Bad guys to the right, bad guys to the left," Tuttle replied with a furrowed brow.

"If our problems were only as simple. What happened to the Camaro?"

"She got trashed like all my cars, and I don't care. What you got yourself into, queenie? Let me know what's going on here."

"I don't have time to explain. I'll come back next week and we'll have a good laugh when I tell you the story."

"You going to move him when he's still half zonked?"

"He's an artist. Half is a bonus. He goes."

Christina was put in charge of getting Mor dressed, helping him button his shirt. "We'll find you a pair of pants later." She ran her fingers through a tangle of curls, dragging her head back till her cheeks caught the light. He watched until her eyes turned to meet his.

"Hold that pose. This is how I want to paint you. The angles all play in your favor."

"You know about the painting," Kwasanda said.

"I'm the painter. Know what?"

"After we leave."

Kwasanda and Christina helped him hobble to the silver BMW. One of his stitches tore when he slid into the front passenger seat. Tuttle slipped him a mason jar of the opium tea, its squared glass tucked in his coat pocket. "Only take a hit when the pain turns nasty. Keep a clear head and take care of the women." Mor avoided Tuttles eyes, mumbled a thanks, and sank in the plush leather. Doors closed, Kwasanda turned the ignition. Gravel crunched under the tires as she eased out Tuttle's littered driveway.

☼

He woke in dream, his body luminous shimmering into the field of ancestor. They were all around him. Above and below. They streamed out across rolling hills of bunch grass standing above their heads studded with the ancient motionless ones spreading canopies of acorns ripening in the grandfathers light, manna from the gods, gathered by the man with womb. They climbed an ancient volcanic cone where panchamama grandmother blew her kisses of fire to the people. Be careful, she gives she takes swallowing it all back into her. Her way. Grandmama. Pancha'ma'ma.

Enoch'e saw his angelic devilin' brothers in arms, blood, fire. He they. They he. He could see the outer world as ever subtler edges, billions of layers of cool gray imbedded with firey sparks. Galaxy upon galaxy layered in time. Layered now in his periphery. His people, his blood ran for 10,000 years over these lands. His people came from the brown land to the west across her waters. They a dharmic peace loving people. Theirs were the only tribes in North America without weapons of war. Whereas they traveled east on the path of wisdom. Other brothers traveled west on the path of conquest. Some were now AIM Souix red brothers warriors on a path with heart. Still others the white fufian comorrista conquorers without heart. They of diseased heart. No corazon. No ser compasivo. Descorazonarse.

Now he witnessed the invasion of federales soldiers in uniforms on horseback pouring over a ridge to the south. Enoch'e recognized some the green amongst the blue uniforms as those of federal agents that raided his property some years before. They came armed to the teeth. The teeth, even of their horses were bared as they came. He started down the butte cone with murder in is whole being. His heart was twisted like the white one. He wanted to kill them as they had destroyed his property earlier. He felt that collective shudder that comes from native people been so long invaded, displaced, enslaved, raped and murdered by the thousands. Millions. Crushed in steely white jaws. Now they were ready and armed to fight and slaughter the soldiers.

They began a chorus of 'Hunka hay, Harey Harey. As they moved off together in unison over the cone-side great clouds of dust stirred. By the time their party reached contact with the soldiers, others from a neighboring tribe were already engaged. Enoch'e saw one warrior with blood running from his mouth. He recognized him as Baghani, an old friend. He would get up then fall back down again. The people were now coming from all around. Many of the federales had been dismounted, pulled down by the clouds of people swarming, their horses stampeding off to the river flowing away into the distance.

Enoch'e saw his people flying all around like shadows as it got darker from all the dust and smoke from many guns blazing away.

Still he recognized it as his dream, as an electromagnetic field extending projecting in all directions from his luminous body. Then a soldier appeared beside him and he found himself swept up once more in the force of sheer hatred exerted by the greater will of the people. Those white devils had come to murder mothers and fathers, us, and it was our land, he mused. When a pistol appeared in his hand he tried to fire it before finding the chamber empty of bullets. Instead he used it as a club. By the time he raised it up, the soldier was trampled by his own stampeding horse.

Now the dust was sticky with blood mixing in from both sides of the battle. He could see the people all around crazed by it. They began taking hair from the heads of fallen soldiers. Scalping some while still alive. The women joined in singing their war song. One of the soldiers played dead as these women stripped away his uniform. But when they started cutting on him, he fought back, spinning one mother around in the air till another stabbed him repeatedly.

Enoch'e saw dead men and horses scattered all about as dust began to settle. The people now moved off to a village laid out in the valley below. They were jubilant, dancing and crying'hunka hey, hari hari'. Then he saw a very old man standing off by himself. He recognized the old one's sacredness by the light that shone all around him. Telling now the old one was his spirit guide.

A federale on horseback charged down on him. Without turning, the old one merely raised a hand. The horse soldier went up, consumed in a lightning filled cloud. When the cloud passed all that remained were skeletons crawling with worms.

Enoch'e walked with his guide to the river. Gazing into its swift current he saw more federales on horseback struggling against its ever rising waters. Finally all trace of them disappeared, submerged in the relentless flow. The old one spoke. "Take courage my son, the earth is all that lasts," he said before evaporating in the wind.

That voice, that eternal way of his people, broken and trampled by invading white devils still connected him to the earth. The earth. The mountains and the valley flowing with her, with his blood all that lasts. All blood returns to her blood. Is her blood. His blood. The brief appearance of the two leggeds so quickly covered over by that cloud of layered time, leaving only bones and worms in its wake. All her. Grandmother earth. Her body his body of luminous rays extending her ways, her waves in all directions from the center of the Grandfathers eye. Any seeing his seeing. The shaman, the ancient ones passed over to the outer land many generations before the white invasion. Passed over and back building an invisible bridge. The medicine showed him the way of this bridge to el otro lado. To the other side where few whites go and if they go they go in humility that Enoch'e recognized in Dark Mor. A humility that comes only from experiencing one's death in this death of life, many times, many ways.

Enoch'e opened his eyes to find himself stretched out on his old recliner. Traces of the luminescent field played around his waking periphery. The presence of his spirit guide also lingered in the smoke from the cigarette he lit with one hand. In that moment he saw his death mask. He laughed to himself at the foolishness of it, of all the busy busy like thousands of ants running running from the fire to the river. Even so many of his brown brothers and sisters finding themselves lost in white man business of gambling slavery and murder masked behind walls of ignorance. Even with the stench of rotting and burned flesh bodies filling the air as they work making black boxes of death, they say, "how could we know?" Drinking their own toxic chemical waters from dead rivers, wheels turning churning burning. Burning her as she consumed them dissolved in their own acid chemical soup. Corroded dying in steel and wooden cages. Now they come to shelter in his home. His land they sell to build their hotel.

Now a casino. Enslaving the minds of his own people to their busy busy way. No time to find it, their spirit crying out against their own ignorance. He would eat their still beating heart, he mused with a flicking of the ash from his cigarette.

Once they put him in their steel cages for killing a man, a federal man, a real pig who came alone at night. Wearing a mask but still the flag on the sleeve, he stole and raped his sister. Enoch'e's fists tightened, crushing his cigarette flat between his fingers. Fingers that tightened around the neck of that pig. Tightened till he crushed the wind pipe like dry bark and watched the demon fade from his wide eyes.

He thought about the dream. He'd dreamt many versions of it before, parts of it from hearing the old ones tell the stories of the killing of Custer. That great victory over the blue bellies with all their guns and steel. He knew of Custer's Civil War history along with Sheridan author of an earlier final solution of murdering native tribes to confiscate their land. Enoch'e learned much from a prison library. Then there was his story mixed in. His story came later in another war on his race by federales in green coming to steal his medicine. Medicine craved by the long hair whites. Medicine to break the spell of slavery and ignorance must be confiscated by the slavers. By their mercenaries with guns and chains. Hippie boys and girls wanting a taste of red brown soul would pay the price. A taste of the over world above, covering the rats racing down below in their steel cages, beady eyes, twiching fear, chasing their tail, ignorant that it is their tale, their story all along. Their story twisted.in need, in deed, in greed and lust for that of another. Their tiny sharp teeth gnawing brown flesh, raping his sisters.

"That was my victory, my piece of Custer, Miha," he spoke to Fawn Rave as she came to lay in his arms.

"When you kill that federale? You were talking again in your sleep. I'm afraid E'noch'e. I'm afraid those haoles bring bad spirits on us."

"Don't be afraid Miha, the white sister is shamana. I see her, I see my mascarilla. It is my time. My time to pass over to the otro lado beyond this sorrow of passing away. Fear not for me or for you. You are young. You must bring other of our peoples spirits into this world for the grandfather sees this in your seeing. He is through and through you, breathing in every breath. Touching in all you touch. When you feel most alone you deny him the least. You feel him in that feeling of being alone for he is that being. Being him being me or you," Enoch'e whispered, nuzzling his lips on her neck. "Now I must kill another white demon like I kill that bandito who rape Melodie. I find so many whites to be bad, to be degenerado, depravado. But some are good bondadoso with grandfather heart without the twist. That twist. They call it DNA. He called it ignorance, ignorates. Most of them forget the tail they chase twisting back around and around is their own. Then they turn on others. The strong ones prey on the weak. They devour, devorar like ave de rapina. Many whites come to devour so much that most is wasted.

Now is the time Grandfather cuts his hair, changes his camisa. A century but una momento in his day of 10,000 moons. We are invisible in his grandisidad. Una momento," Enoch'e offered with a kiss. He brushed a tear from her cheek. Soon there would be one less diablo walking the earth. "I will trade my life for the diablo, Miha. Such is the way of my warrior spirit, to go in my boots."

"But you no wear boots, Enoch'e," Fawn managed sniffing back tears.

"Maybe so sugar bear, but barefoot or not, I ain't shuffling to no rack When I go I take one of them diablo banditos conmigo."

***

Korner waited at the Westin hotel parking lot until he knew for certain Kwasanda had stood him up. He smelled betrayal like the body odor wafting off the unshaved Aram Hashemi in the passenger seat. The fucking audacity of the black bitch, he fumed, with her bullshit promises. He was too close to the Scroll treasure to let her slip away from him back into McCracken's camp. He surmised the power of the bullet was no help with this score.

"You're my back up. Stay down with your trap shut." Korner shifted into drive, pulling out of the hotel lot.

"Why you always rag on me?" Hashemi slumped down replied with a frown, facial hair black against his pallid complexion.

Korner shook his head. His anger at Hashemi nearly made him run the stoplight. Keener instincts made him stop before a man in a wheelchair unseen in the crowd gathered at the curb, zipped into the crosswalk.

"We do the artist and the woman or what?"

"Somebody with the intelligence of gnat's ass needn't be concerned about what is going down. Just keep watch." Korner thought, he really didn't need to mangle some poor schmuck just trying to cross a street.

He gave Hashemi a sideways look of disgust before scanning the street for any sign of her blackness. Low rise storefronts broke up into big boxes with sprawling parking lots. Once they started climbing into the hills, he watched the landscape open up to ever larger lots then estates. As it opened up he began to notice only gardeners and other workmen about, their owners likely away to swank offices and country clubs. He turned west to wind up the mountain.

The boxed flat country of Bayshore turned into wrinkled forest. Korner relaxed, letting thoughts of the Copper Scroll's treasure temper his distaste for the continued presence of Hashemi. He wanted a resolution to his connection with Darkie Mor. Man had the nerve to say he, Korner, had changed the day he shot him. Not from boy to man, but from human to the inhumane. If Mor had died in the Illinois countryside, he would have regarded his corpse the same as a doe or a buck. Sure. Maybe at the time but he could still assure all those pinhead therapists that killing a man is not the same. He could never explain why he'd pulled the trigger that day. He was in favor of blaming the Darkness. After all, his own sister had led him to a near death when he was only two years old. The guy was a born target. A spook spawned by a demoness.

Shrinks told him back then that he lacked remorse. Like he was some kind of sociopath or even psychopath. Mor said he lived as a reward for showing Korner his true nature. The best thing a friend could be, a reminder of his beastly side. Remembering that incident inevitably led to the memory of his first kill in the war. Then he had fired wildly at something unseen suddenly charging him in a brown blur tearing out from the bush, a screaming fiend in black silk pajamas. Shaken, he'd fired too low at first. Emptying a clip of small caliber rounds tearing dime size divots from the assailants bare legs, slowing him enough for Korner to slap in another clip while feeling his bowls liquidate and evacuate. Fucking shit his pants as he brought his weapon up to watch his rounds tear away 'Charley's' cheek, bared teeth close enough now to see gums packed with black wedges of opium. Naturally that memory was never as far as the stink of his own shit and the colored photos of the bullet riddled corpse he carried.

Those little slugs tore that man to pieces. Korner knew the whole skinny on that. Army brass did not want that stupid shift in weapons procurement from previous wars to such small caliber in Vietnam. So much so they sacrificed the treasure of their own by contracting an offbrand lubricating oil. Rookie drafted grunts typically put the finger to the metal. Overheating. Jam city. People, our people died because their leaders, their big Pa'tron deliberately sabotaged their guns. He'd watched some shot up when their guns jammed. Korner learned to carry his own oil. He'd been carrying his own ever since. He didn't need some piss in the pants pin head shrink putting his two bits in the mix.

Stand over the bullet riddled corpse of a sinewy brown farmer barefoot in black pyjam'mas ten thousands miles from your farmer old man just farming, the most honest labor on the entire face of the earth and you just blew half the flesh off his body. Enemy or father brother? Korner learned to see it either way. The others collateral damage. Nobody innocent in war. Boy or buck? Bucks for blood. Those are some damn nasty dogs let loose now, Korner mused. What could a sheltered home boy like the Darkness know about it anyway? And why should he care? He had never asked Darkie to return the favor of saving him from that Nam blood bath. It made his blood boil to be judged as a psychopath by those just lucky and privileged enough to miss out on the necessity of killing brown people. For country, for blood, for USA'id, he swore to himself. Show me her face, Liberty's face, he wondered about her.

Wheeling the Mark IV into Tuttle's compound, he found himself driving now through the graveyard of 1950s and 1960s motoring from Packards to Ramblers with bullet-shaped chrome grills and bumpers heavier than a Honda Civic. The lot covered with rust, paint eaten by it along with mold and moss reflected Korners mood being in the great American industrial wasteland. He definitely wanted to blow this shit up.

"E'no'chey, someone coming in a big shiny car."

Enoch stubbed out his cigarette, glancing for a second at his skinning knife on the table, before cracking his knuckles and launching himself from the recliner. Pulling the blanket aside he saw a town car pulling into his driveway.

"Who are they E'ho?" Fawn asked as she came to stand beside him.

"Behold he that ride the pale horse for he is death," he replied, sweeping the curtain aside to step out to meet his fate.

"Why she drop them in this stink pile?" Hashemi asked.

"We broke contact with Warren so she could take a look at the disk. Like I have to tell you."

An idea turned in Korner's head. He'd do the neighborhood a favor by blowing this shit off the map. He smelled freshly washed earth against the stench of spoiling grease and burning plastic. A bandy-legged pit bull popped from its doghouse, the chain rattling against the doorway as he pulled into the front yard. A squat moke barefoot in a clean cowboy shirt filled the doorway of the bungalow, feet spread and eyes narrowed. A bitch peered from the corner of a blanketed window as he stepped from the Lincoln.

"Good morning, friend. I'm looking for Kwasanda Nzokia."

"Well, first of all, we ain't friends. Second, if you can count that high, who the fuck are you?"

"Okay, you Tuttle? Eenhonc Tuttle? I'll put it to you straight amigo. Mi llama es James Korner, my associate and I have enough firepower to turn this junkyard into Hiroshima after the Enola Gay dropped its party invitation. We don't have time to dick around. Tell us where Kwasanda and the man and woman with her have gone, then we'll be down the road. Comprende?"

"First, go fuck yourself. Maybe not even then."

Hashemi left the Mark IV, taking a couple of steps toward Tuttle. He grabbed Hashemi by collar and jacket, spun him over his head in a circle, tossing him in a heap of junk. Hashemi groaned as Korner went for his Colt. He leveled the pistol at Tuttle's bulk until powerful jaws filled with sharp teeth clamped on his firing hand. He fell against the car, sliding along the polished fender as the pit bull tore on his arm. Blood ran between his fingers. Tuttle called the dog to its pen, kicking the gun across the gravel drive. He hefted a length of pipe and whacked Korner across his shoulders before he could stand. Tuttle jammed his heel in the small of Korner's back until a jolt of nerve spasms made him shake. The Indian pulled him to his feet, hitting him with two quick punches that rocked his head. Korner stumbled over rusty pipes, falling on his shredded hand. He tried to drag himself away. Tuttle struck him again across the back.

He curled into a fetal position and tugged out the hammerless .38 revolver nestled in his ankle holster. Tuttle raised the pipe for another blow as Korner turned and fired. The round hit Tuttle in the meat of his shoulder. The upraised pipe dropped. He howled, making a leap for Korner's throat. Korner squeezed off another round to split the middle of Tuttle's brow. Tuttle stopped. His eyes drifted up as he fell backward.

"Indians always lose," Korner managed. His chest heaved, the gun loose in his hand, hair plastered with sweat and blood. He rolled to his knees, rocking on his haunches until he stood to lean against the fender of the Mark IV. His forehead touched the warm surface as he set the gun on the hood.

"Come on outta there before I blow up your shit!" He fell back to rest against the windshield frame. "I'm not going to tell you again. I'm counting to five, starting at four."

A young latina opened the door flap, her arms lined with jangling bracelets.

"Bring me water and liquor pronto, señorita. Keep your hands where I can see them."

She brought him a plastic gallon jug of water and a bottle of Cuervo. Korner told her to look after Hashemi. He followed the movement of her hips. A thigh-length sweater clung to her buttocks as she walked to the body sprawled in a battered truck bed.

"There's a pipe poking through his chest. He's not breathing and his eyes are flat. I think he's dead."

"Son of a bitch got what he deserved. Your old man is in worse shape."

Korner waved to her with his gun hand, bringing her close to feel her nipples against his chest. Her eyes were wide in shock. He demanded a drink and she held the bottle to his lips. The pit bull pounded his paws against the chain link fencing of the pen. He panted hard but had not barked since the death of his keeper. Korner fired a round into its throat and the dog fell with four legs kicked out stiff.

"You drive." He shoved her behind the wheel of the Mark IV, collapsing against the closed passenger door. Reaching for the keys, she stole a furtive glance at Tuttles still body slumped on the ground.

"Hold on. I almost forgot. Hand me the bag," he said, motioning to the back seat. He watched her young bosom press against the leather seat as she stretched to retrieve the canvas satchel. Not a bad piece, maybe later. She set the bag on the seat between them.

"I didn't want to kill your boyfriend. Just how the game played out," Korner offered. He pulled two cigarette pack charges from a pocket of the satchel. "We're going to give him a fitting send-off. Toss one inside the doorway and the other in the dog cage. Make any funny moves, I'll shoot you in the butt and let you bleed out. Do what I say and you'll live to drop many bueno ninyos."

She nervously popped her chewing gum, tugging the strands of hair hanging like thin snakes on her face. Her skin felt rubbery as Korner brushed a tiny speck of debris from her cheek, leaving a red smear. She quivered in anger.

"Spit out that gum. That's a man's blood I tracked on your cheek. Two men just died, for what? Chewing gum?" Korner flounced her hair as her face burned, her mascara eyes upturned at the corners.

"Enoch has fifty cousins around here. They give you a good whipping for touching me. Only Enoch touch me, cocksucker."

"Nice mouth. Glad to see our tax dollars at work educating you breed girls," Korner said. "I never meant harm to your old man. You lost your partner and I lost mine, all the more reason to do you right now. Go set these packages like I say so can you live another hour. Don't waste your breath with the hard case routine."

Korner armed the devices by pressing a button on each. He put his head back and took a pull on the tequila with his gun hand. Fawn slipped out with the charges, set them where told, then returned to the driver's seat. Korner clubbed the gearshift into reverse with a forearm while stepping on the gas.

Tuttle's bungalow turned to a sheet of flame, the yellow tongues mesmerizing the girl wide eyed still in shock. Korner eased off the accelerator, knocking the shifter into neutral. He could see excitement in the heaving of her chest. The second charge blew lit debris on the Mark IV as Korner pushed her foot down hard on the gas pedal and knocking it into drive.

☼

Mor drank from the Mason jar of opium tea as Kwasanda's words collided in his addled brain.

"Do I look the same? The Pod seems to have transformed me in some fundamental way," she asked, drumming fingers on the steering wheel.

"Well, I wasn't going to say anything but what's with the hair and those sparks like a crazy static charge coming off you?" he asked, clicking the seat belt.

"You are positively on fire. I feel this electric field exhilarating the air all around you. " Christina replied, draping her arms on the back of his seat.

"Yes, I feel somehow more awake even in the midst of this dream. Though it moves all around me, it doesn't affect me, at all," Kwasanda answered, her eyes glowing as she focused on the road cutting through suburban sprawl.

"I hate to break the spell here, but I have this feeling Korner is still out there dogging our trail. We need to get to the bottom of all this before that crazed moefoe decides to go off again," he said, buzzing down his window.

"Okay, so where do we go from here?" Christina asked, squeezing his hand as they shot

through an intersection on a
yellow light.

They drove across town into a shabbier section somewhat blighted by occasional boarded storefronts. At a four-way stoplight, a strip mall of check cashing, grocery, liquor, and lottery attracted a crowd in hotter colors from purple spandex to chartreuse hair mousse. Homeless indigents pushed shopping carts packed and draped with black plastic sacks filled with the detritus of consumer society on its final pass. Still exiting in a shopping cart, Mor mused. In the shelter of an overpass, he saw a row of green and blue tarped tents pitched against the stained concrete wall buttressing the highway overhead. Sun stole through the clouds above East Palo Alto.

"Here we are, only a mile or two from one of the richest spots in America," Mor offered as he gazed at the 'hard by' side of town. People hustling their daily bread sliced a mean thin.

"Let's call the man and see what he has to say," Kwasanda replied, goosing the accelerator to pass a grid of commuters stacking up in an exit lane.

"So we look him up in the Yellow Pages under W for World Destroyer?" he asked, shifting his bandaged leg, blood throbbing at his wounded knee.

"I have his number in my phone. McCracken gave it to me before I went into the Pod. I think he wanted me to salt the wound from his stealing the disc and activating the pod." Kwasanda punched the auto dial on her cell phone.

Mor shot Christina a questioning look over his shoulder. She shrugged and looked off. The BMW left the Dumbarton Bridge and drove north on the east side of the Bay. Kwasanda pulled into a service station as the number rang. An attendant in an orange vest with mustaches bristling past his chin like fibrous tusks, approached the driver's side.

"Fill me super, cash," she said as a reply came on the other end of the line.

"Ms Nzokia, I'm Stephan Rakitan, Mr. Warren's chief assistant. I've been instructed to give you an address."

Mor wrote on a pad as she dictated. Kwasanda clapped the phone shut as the attendant clanked the hose nozzle back on the pump.

"Thirty-two fifty," he said as he ran a squeegee over the windshield. He slapped the wiper blades back down, trimming excess with a rag that he stuffed in his back pocket.

"I'll get the change," he offered as Kwasanda slipped him a $50 note.

"How about I trade you for directions to this address," she replied, showing him the pad with Mor's scrawl. She thanked him and pulled out of the station, the fat tires crunching an empty aluminum can.

"The man say anything about the painting?" Mor asked as he looked for some music on the radio. "Being with the both of you makes me feel like painting, just can't guarantee the stability of my mind. I say let the art make the statement. If I still got it, it will be obvious right off. What do you think, Professor?"

Railroad tracks on their left cut a swath between the warehouses and marshlands that edged the Bay. A brown pelican launched from a log floating in a stew of algae and plastic jugs, the air reeking with its bloom stench dappled with dying fish.

"What did you discover on the disc?" Christina asked as she loosened her pea coat. "You find anything relating to Warren's scheme in the pod?"

"To be honest, I can't remember anything except that I am still alive and kicking." Kwasanda changed lanes, making a right on Industrial Boulevard, following the road as it curved back to the left. "And that who I am doesn't seem at all affected by this world except there wouldn't be any world without that awareness of it now appearing in a being of me. Does that make any sense to you, Professor?"

"That is where I live. Where I am that awareness mirrored making my living moment by moment. The problem with transmitting it, that awareness of a being in the first place, is any in word talking of it is a mere denial of it. Any now k'nowing it is k'no no no'wing out a denying of it. That is why that I am speaking of it in a peculiar dialectic debate. A manner of y speaking in the first place without displacing attention for a second. Touching on it in word without pushing it away by now k'now'ing denying it in word. No degrees of separation. No degrees between the indivisible in'visibility of a being it in the first place and any appearing out of it anybody as a being of it." Christina replied still gazing out at the surroundings.

They crossed a flood control channel, thick with an oily sheen and the hot green of a slime of antifreeze. Steel arms of dock cranes, iron birds without wings, jutted over flat tar and gravel warehouse roofs.

"Then I'm not who I think I am, am I? This DNA is a twisted conceit, turning churning burning into the concept of myself as Kwasanda Nzokia having completely nothing to do with the real me, the reality of me except in my mind as thoughts, as arbitrary names in tribal memory. Does that sound crazy to you?"

"Perfectly sane. We all turn in word into that arbitrary name state of a being anybody only y'll DNA. In word denial is a being now as ka'ing y. As kurving black'g'round a y potential being mirrored in ka's mic memory appearing as'ex'uall. Y'all's"ex's ting in formation awhile. That is the dialectic debate between A Y eye merely a peering it or any Y na now appearing as thought'sz of x's ting in formation of it. What's more insane or non sane is merely living as though born in word. Assuming that mirror identity of our thoughts of a being. Superficial notions of identity as a purely functional arbitrary name. Na me. daNa me. We all in turning into or out of it come around introducing ourselves as a being in name alone. As a being in denial alone. In a being still in the first place now appearing out of it as a b'ng c'ng by na me alone.

"That is the a b c's of mere in word captivity. A b'ng c'ng a me merely mirrored in mind or y memory. In for'ma'az a b'ng c'ng y'all there is to me or you, too ka's mic memory. One indivisible moment of a being still in her"eye. A y eye being c'ng him now still. We all in turning around this earth experience ourselves way beyond mere waking as twis'ting in t'word function. Beyond the sheer folly of funny action, chasing our tales just to find they are still attached to our own butt. You must never be slave to mere ideas of a being yourself. Does not mean y'all cannot try. Or cry. "

"What is crazy to me now in this moment is that more people do not realize that very same thing. Right now, and I know I'll eventually come down, every thing around me seems only a mirage, a shimmering reflection of my own light of awareness."

"Awareness of a coming black'g'round echoing of me or you in memory as thoughts of it still paying playing out an understanding. Of it at attention in the dream body. Now that I am out of it in her eye or ma'sz natural eye of eve're'y'body merely a peering it. It is mirrored appearing asz anybody. Out mirrored on a ka's micro wayeve blackground. An instantaneous mom'en'ta mom'en'ta momentum indivisible blackness of eve're'y'body."

Kwasanda braked to a stop. Glancing back at Christina she broke out with a laugh. "We all one single black as'z body." she managed between bursts of laughter. The professor stayed dead pan as she continued.

"A d"ark'ness'e body to be now percieved. Now any as'king of it a k'no no no'wing out b'lack'ness'e of it to be now a gain. A gain of it. A'gain invisibility now appearing out in word supersonically or phonographically in formation"

"A supersonic eve're'ybody with a black as'z a way of eve'll," Kwasanda replied.

Or anything appearing of it at complete attention of d'na y light igniting ignore'ance projection of him or her or it is still a b'ng c'ng of him. The mere a b c's of it." The professor paused eyes focused on Kwasanda's reclining on a leather headrest.

"Now. A be'am'ing of it out in her'me'sz'z'y'allthoth'tsz of a eye of a herhimit. Her or him of it. A b'ng c'ng indivisible now merely emerging as'k'no'wing out thoth'tsz of it a pairing. Still a crazy fun house mirror potential. Of her'eye,a're'y'all mirror se'e'as a mercy. Dissolution." the word seemed to Mor to hang in space then shower a p'ss'y whole wayeve're'y dhi'ance turning black'g'round into or out of anything. Anybody.

So how or why can I be so concerned about what's merely appearing to be there in my mind?" she asked, her hair jetting out from her face.

"Shall'ana might be a reason?" The name slipped from his tongue.

"Beyond certain obvious extenuating circumstance. But purely in my soul mind. That indivisible black as'z soul mind. That whole black a'sz body asz a shimmering field of consciousness. Shining out in her'eye. That eye mean of this a're'y'al'ity now as'king of it a k'no'wing out of it appearing ahead or behind whereve'her re'y"e turns. Y'all out in her'eye on him or it. Still it. Eve'n when I'm black'g'round to my eye'sz a normal self, reality that eye star'e'y'e'or y e'sta'r'ey won't change come riot or ruin. A being still stillness in the eye of her'eve're'y changing mirage. Why that eye I am now a're'y'al'eye'zing it still int'word t'wisting it into a denial of it. Then why not. Either or still a being c'ng merely a peering it all along."

"Perhaps you have good reason to chose to ignore it. Crazy, as it seems, crazy be our free choice more often than not. Why choose being of such limitation beyond necessity of functioning in the moment? Especially when realizing there is a choice awareness of a b'ng c'ng in the first place. A choice made moment by moment or ignored lifetime by lifetime," Christina replied touching the back of Mor's head. "Rest assured though, this mirage of sorrow will continue to seduce. Certainly I have fallen under those so real imaginary clutches at times and places unexpected despite extensive teaching of the contrary. Anyone of us may fall back under the in word spell of their own duplicity. A duplicity of a y as'ex's ting in completely arbitrary na'me alone. Which brings me to Warren and his corporate duplicity, his cunning plan for'ma'sz mass destruction.

Listening to Christina's voice, he found himself once more slipping into her eyes'za spell. He felt momentarily bewildered by a certain double entendre in her words as if her intent were to blow his mind free of personal arbitrary identity. Pull down his mask of ideas about himself. Yet somehow he really didn't seem to mind as if he were all too weary of the compulsion for maintaining it and all the notions of any being of some nobody.

"Here is what I see with Warren and his ilk. They have recognized the nature of this mass psychosis where we all have turned away from recognizing or realizing y'all that appearing out before our eyes as a b'ng c'ng despite directly and periodically experiencing that consciousness as a singular black body. Of a b'ng c'ng in sleep. A being still in the first place that indivisible invisibility of any individual. Now that complete k'no no no'wing of it as a projection of ignoring a being still that in'visibility. As ka'ing y now a kurving of now a black'g'round of it as ka's mic memory potential leaves us open to suggestions as to what or who we all may turn into or out of becoming. Karma is a three way street. Brought over from previous cycles. Created in the moment to moment life. And most importantly the unknown factor as'eX coming into play at any time int'word twis'ting y'all around. Perhaps Warren recognizes a way to channel the nature of any forma'ss neurotic psychosis of ignoring k'now'ing it y'all along. A k'no'wing of it as a denial of it. It a ka's mic being of it's invisibility now appearing by our any in word k'no no no'wing out of it. Thus it seems the fun'da'mental process of any creation is dissolution of it in'visibility." Again Mor was struck by the double entendre. Invisibility dissolved in'visibility. If only appearing of it awhile by a mirror memory playing tricks on a mere a peering now at it.

A way denying h'our now outer natural being by using a viral infection to shift y'alls attention from a still singular focus, splitting that atom, that aten with a peculiar singular image of imagination, a notion'all'y y'all'sza nation of imagining. A sublime place captured in a face in time where we all turn attention into losing our way of function, our way of will to act now surrendered to her image. Imagined out in her'eye of eve will. Out in her'eye of a wayeve'll."

"A shimmering black mirror se'e'as in her'eye of eve're'y'body still indivisible." Kwasanda returned shifting the Beamer back into drive.

"Somehow his plan parallels the power of ma'ss destruction or ma'ss deception. Of ma as'z z'apping it out in her'eye of eve're'y bodhi by splitting the atom. Instead it is splitting the singularity of attention. He could set in motion a self perpetuating chain reaction that would unravel attention from the very in word fabric of spacetime. Unravel our peh'ss'y whole wayeve power as'ex'is'tence. Tense in awhile of any being a gain turning back to a b'ng'lack. Black to the big bang of a being a gain as'z'any in formation of it. Black into a body indivisible in'visibility of anything appearing out of now k'no'wing of it. One indivisible invisibility of a black body. A god esse to be a b'ng c'ng letter'all'y now appearing supernaturally in word. A b'ng c'ng a peering it still invisibility of a singular peh'ss'y'ence of a y eye merely a peering at it. In'visibility now k'now'ing a y eye as'ex's ting int'word t'wis'ting in formation y'll d'na. A denial of it in man as'z'any mere supernatural thoth'tsz of it in mind or y memory. A being y eye a peering still in the first place. Or a being out of it as'z'any mirrored y na? Or why not? Or why now? Merely because Warren can at least now for awhile in viraly beaming timespace back into a black'g'round of eve're'y'body. Mirror' ly a're'y'versing polarity. Reversing the direction of time now k'now'ing it as a black'g'round a y eye of herhimit. A freestanding of it merely a star'e'y"e a peering from above as below now understanding any in word spelling of it with mirror polarity on hand."

"Look." Dark pointed to a giant billboard of a frisky whiskey woman stretched out on a silver Mercedes. Once again he found himself outside their sea of estrogen. They went on with their conversation as though he were mere invisibility. But then Mor began to comprehend the distinct advantage of a b'ng c'ng invisibility in'visibility. A b'ng c'ng merely a peering it n'eve'r beyond invisibility of it still in the first place indivisible.

"Warren has plans to release a supersonic bioacoustic virus. He is going to somehow blow up these fences that help define ourselves, who we all turn around thinking of turning into. "He sees mass liberation." Kwasanda spoke as if in a trance. "That just came into my mind out from left field."

"I see pandemic meltdown," Christina replied. "Now that I am picking up on your way of thinking, on that wavelength hearing that virus turning in Warren's bio field."

"We don't need Warren's virus to break it all down," Mor exclaimed, feeling the cocktail of drugs feeding the firing of a billion s'y'na'ps'y. "It's all goin' down, goin' down, down, down."

"We all only need to turn back to black to see it for what it is. A b'ng c'ng in the first place indivisible in'visibility of anybody. Nothing in word visibility of it affects us any more than a dream affects the dreamer. Sticks and stones may break my bones but words, words are mere in word memory mirrors reflecting me as thoughts of it. A being still in the first place is unimaginable now without k'no'wing it out of a y eye a peering out at it in word. A being in me appears now only as thoth'tsz in my knowing memory. A memory being mirror words can never hurt me by merely changing in my mind," Kwasanda replied with a visceral jolting shock wave releasing with the sound of her voice. Mor felt her waves washing over and through him.

"A man once said everybody has a plan till they get hit in the mouth. That's the difference between thinking of it or feeling of it. The touch of it as any touching of it. That's where the sheer gravity of a life is felt" Mor added

She downshifted for a chuckhole in the asphalt and made another right hand turn, pulling into an alley that led to loading docks and chain-driven warehouse doors. "One thing I do know now in k'nowing all this, if the world's counting on this bunch to save it, we all are turning into serious trouble. Even mere mirrored troubles in memory."

Mor felt a hot wind through the open window. He took a swig from the Mason jar, to take off the edge of the pain. Feeling it. Kwasanda pulled behind a row of rust pocked Dumpsters spotted with tattered caution stickers.

"A famous French perfume chemist was asked where he lived to develop such intoxicating scents," he offered. "A honeydew country estate bursting with lilacs and jasmine? 'No,' he had replied, 'I formulated my fragrances in a warehouse surrounded by rusting machinery, rancid grease, and industrial wasteland.' This feels like a perfect spot for a red blooded 'merican boy like me to paint a beautiful woman against a lot of concrete and iron waste. Wasted along the most famous Bay in the world. At least in our little neck of the woods. In prehistoric time a primeval redwood forest climbed fourteen thousand feet up from this bay on the slopes of mount St. Helena. Now she just a little bump on the ridgeline fifty miles north. I've seen some ot the fossillized tree remains. They were giant sempirverens ten or fifteen feet in diameter." He broke off realizing no one was listening.

"I hope you will find inspiration here," Kwasanda said. She stepped from the car to help Christina get Mor out. "You are full of shit but it's good shit," she whispered in his ear. Blood seeped from the torn stitch. He danced on his good leg and adjusted the blanket around his waist. The sleeves of his leather jacket scrunched against the women's straining muscles as they assisted him from the car.

Shocks of brown weeds filled cracks in the asphalt driveway leading to a black metal door set into a three-story red brick building. Kwasanda began to work the door open with her pick kit till realizing it wasn't locked. They followed a hallway to a rear service elevator as the door slammed closed behind them. The atmosphere was thick with years of an industrial mustiness. Yellow light filtered through grimed overhead windows.

The elevator cage clattered along the dank shaft to the third floor. Dark let his head fall against Christina. Kwasanda pulled on the scissor gate, levering it open to a room with sixteen-foot ceilings, a bank of clean windows lining the north wall. Shafts of light streamed on a large easel set up in the middle of the open space. Against the far wall of exposed brick, he spied a king-size bed with beige down comforter and half a dozen pillows in white slipcovers. A flat desk held a telephone, computer monitor and keyboard, and a straight-back chair.

The women helped him to the high chair in front of the blank canvas of gessoed linen set up on the easel. He eased his weight onto the cushioned seat, leaning back against the leather wrapped arm and backrests. Parked next to the easel was a five-drawer oak taboret topped with a ceramic vase filled with red sable, badger, and white hog bristle brushes. Their nickel ferrules glistened on clean wood handles. He reached out to touch their smooth surface and pull open a drawer of the taboret. The top drawer held forty-milliliter paint tubes of hues, tints, and tones of red from raw umber to cadmium. He caressed the fresh labels and let his fingers run over the fullness of yellow cadmium, ochre, and Naples extra. Another drawer displayed ranges from smoky green and galvanic turquoise to deep cobalt. He left the drawers open in pyramid fashion, creating a rainbow from top to bottom. The colors were so rich and stunning he wanted to squeeze them directly into his mouth. He pulled a French vermilion from the top drawer and unscrewed the plastic cap. A nib of orange pigment rose from the threaded nozzle. Mor scraped the paint off with his pinkie and dotted the tip of his tongue, fumes of linseed oil rising.

"It's going to be okay, Painter," said Christina. "What you do will not affect who you are. Do not confuse the painter with the painting. Be the field, not the fence. You've rejected the lie in favor of the truth, and your karma has already decided whether you will succeed."

Kwasanda called for the couple's attention. "Unless you have not noticed, Warren has installed four video cameras to record the progress of the painting. I expect he will be watching and communicate with you through the computer."

Mor looked at the cameras bearing down on the canvas. "So he can see us but we can't see him."

"You don't want to see him. He is one cruddy old fart," she said with emphasis for Warren's sake.

"One of them zazen cats talked about gaining enlightenment by starring at a blank wall. Here, that I am there."

"Warren knows he cannot force you to paint. The image must come from the right place, from love, from desire, from passion," said Kwasanda, turning from the door to give him a long look.

He took another whiff of the vermilion. "How long do I have, a week?"

"Twenty-four hours," she said.

"Not too much pressure. He's talking about an image that any painter would work on until he dies, and maybe, then. I think the best approach, with eyes closed."

"Hers or yours?"

"Maybe both."

"That may be the best case," said Christina. "You can never paint 'the face I had before I was born'. That from one of your Zen cats. Timing is important component of Warren's schedule for the Apocalypse. Enlighten everyone and let God sort it out, like being his own demiurge. Toying with his creation."

"Should I paint or not?"

"Paint like you never painted before. I have to find out what has happened to Korner. Be strong for each other." Kwasanda walked into the shadow until he heard the clang and clatter of elevator doors.

"Are you a painter or a lover?" Christina asked as she slipped off the pea coat.

☼

"Puts a charge in the blood, don't you know?" Korner motioned with his pistol for his hostage to get the car on down the road. They drove the dirt lane leading to the highway while flames from the blasts whipping up in the air into black smoke receeded in the rear window.

"I'm after a treasure copped by Herod, a biblical dude so rich he built a mountaintop palace with walls eighteen feet thick going up three levels with a private villa carved into rock. Big enough for him and nine bitches. That crap-heap back there wasn't even a speck of trash along my road. I'll bet you've never even been to the other side of the damn Bay," Korner rambled. "The fat Injun take care of you? Be a shame to let all the heat bottled inside your tight unit go to waste." He drank from the tequila. "Follow this road."

They entered a series of switchbacks. Korner stuck his hand deep in her blouse, groping her breast.

"What the fuck? Touch me again and I'll crash this dog shit car."

"No, you won't. You're going to wait for the opportunity to do me right. Crash the car and you're as likely to get hurt as me."

The centrifugal force of the sharp turns threw him against the passenger door. Korner felt a stab of pain in his shoulder. That fat Indian had thrown a hell of a wallop.

"Slow down, bitch. I know where they're headed and we've got business first. What's a bright little tang like you going to do besides fall back and spread your legs? You're helping me track down the greatest treasure in history, gold and jewels every way you want. Be nice and I might cut you in for a slice. I ain't no paper tiger, darlin'."

They rounded the last curve and hit the Bay flats of freeways, stoplights, and local law enforcement. His thoughts drifted back to treasure in the burning wastes of the Sinai Desert. The past rarely interested him, a jerk-off fantasy ride for academics afraid of the world, until he learned of the Copper Scroll. He read of four hundred donkey loads of booty leaving Jerusalem every day for months, heading to Masada, Herod's desert palace. He could see long dust trails clouding trudging hooves and leather sandals, smell rank sweat from the lather of treasure-laden harnesses rubbing against crimped muscles, seventy years before Roman legions swept in. According to Warren, generations of bounty hunters had not uncovered one ingot of the gold. The treasure waited for the right man to seize it.

Warren told him about how the inscribed letters and numbers in the Copper Scroll were a code for the true location of the caches. Professor Shaughnessy could break the code with her paleography hocus-pocus. Warren made Christina sound like a priestess, not of this century or Earth. Korner learned that the treasure listed on the scrolls contained more than vast amounts of gold and silver, like two oracle stones rumored to contain magnetic properties capable of felling walls built from blocks as big as box cars. He discounted any of the theories as nonsense brought on by one tab too many of bad Mesopotamian acid.

Korner stirred. "I can take you to castles in the sky, drape you in silks, and light your eyes with rubies, sapphires, and diamonds. I can make you my queen."

"You full of shit, gringo."

"Keep talking like that and you'll slide from goddess to gash real quick." He drank from the tequila and dipped into his Altoids tin. She licked her lips and broke her cold stare.

"Coca?" The open sun they encountered after dropping out of the mountains made the packed crystal glisten.

"Probably help me drive," she mumbled.

They crossed over the 280 heading to Menlo Park and stopped at the intersection of Woodside and Middlefield. Korner rolled down the window for the breeze. He looked up at a sky turned blue enough to stick a fork in. It lifted his spirit with the promise of clear air even as streams of brown smog drifted inland.

"Hang a right," Korner said, holding a match head of powder to her nose. A glow came into her eyes as she snicked the hit. As the light changed she tromped the accelerator. The scene seemed innocuous, people in their cars, running hither and yon in their ransomed ittle boxes of dreams.

"Looks like you're going to come around to my way of thinking."

His weapon lay across his lap, the weight pressed against his leg. He watched his designated driver as he dipped out a crystal with the tip of his pinkie.

"Open your mouth. I'm going to show you the real way to do this shit."

Her glossy lips parted as he slipped his finger under her tongue.

"Let that melt into your mind, chiquita bonita."

Korner stuck the Altoids tin back into his coat pocket and hefted the Colt. He twisted his neck from side to side until he heard a pop. Good as ever to go, he thought, then pain knifed him again.

"Stay on this road for about ten miles."

They passed a shopping center anchored by a Safeway supermarket. Under the windows plastered with sale offers in numbers big as children, he stared at a plump woman in frizzy dyed hair pulling a cart free with a practiced jerk. Korner pulled a cell phone from the glove compartment and pressed a number as he scanned his booty driver's glazed eyes.

"The black queen has been and gone," McCracken's voice showed surprising calm. "You sure about that gas leak? I haven't been able to find any official report."

"I'm telling ya. Ya think you know a guy. Then he goes all psycho on ya. It puts ya in shock. Then on top of that."

"I know, the gas line blows and there's nothing to do but beat feet."

"Yeh, so, soon as you give me the Scroll translation, our ax will be ground and buried. You don't want to hold out on me. I'd to have to take your nut sack along with a few other personal items."

"You're scaring me. I might be too nervous to remember where I put those codes."

"We'll see, real quick." Korner flipped the phone shut.

Chapter 12

Johnstone Warren looked from his penthouse to the span of the Golden Gate Bridge, a distant thread stitching gray waters turning molten with the setting sun. Every myth had been bled out of a scientific world, leaving a great atomic emptiness. A conquering science had led to the starvation of a soul he pondered. Warren's initiation into an ancient order had brought the gods and their duplicity back to a life of science and engineering. He realized their craft of a b'ng c'ng now in anybody moving in space. From mosquito to planetary their crafty deceit carried the day supernaturally appearing anybody anything etc. as thoth'tsz of her'me'as un con she'e na us. Any now k'now'ing of us as eve're'y'body. In her'eye a peering it it appearing of it. His prerecorded message to Christina broadcast in a thin voice as he watched through the video monitors.

"Hearing the first personic trumpet call from a herald of the herhimitage of a b'ng c'ng still in the first place. A y eye of Pa'roo'Ma. Now a peering from above. Ove a ba'el wayeve're'y golden wings of perception a peering out now. As'king of it a k'no'wing out of it me or you mom'ent after mom'ent. Her'me'as thoth'tsz supernaturally A're'y'all a la que"en que' appearing out in her'eye of eve're'y'body. Let my last great act set loose molecular armies whose devastation will release such supersonic p'ss'y el'ence energy that no h'earth of in word man-made structures are left standing in memory. As'z'any thoth'tsz of it in'formation. A y'll D'Na int'word twis'ting whorldings of worlds will merely supernaturally as'z'any thoth'tsz of it unwind. A billions of soul will be as'z'any thoth'tsz of it spilling back into her"e black eye see'ng collecting a pool of peh'ss'y w'hole mirror power of eve're'y'body."

His plan came from the Grand Architect. The fundamental process of that plan. Dissolution of it. Of the god esse to be any deceit of it now eve'r'eybody as'z'any thoth'tsz of it appearing in the first place. Any appearing of it a while. A cunning cruel deceit of a god esse to be letter'ally any in word her'me'as'thoth'tsz of now as'king of it a k'no'wing out anybody anything etc.supernaturally and phonographically in'formation. Nothing so piece-meal as ethnic cleansing. He fathomed the debacle of familiar earth life. The twisted denial of a wily dna. The stagnation and apathy of habitual ignorance of it. Her ignoring him into a b'ng c'ng of it. Saint Luke gave him two verses to guide his handiwork through the message of her re'y"e r'ey'dhi'a'ting Christ. A touching heart of gee's'z"us. A gravity weight of waiting on the touch of any black'g'round echoing a touching of it. Her through Him recognized as Liberator of it. Fire aS'word. War. War're'y'na viraly now as'z'any k'no'wing out of it merely still a peering untouched wordfree awareness of a y eye in the first place. Pa'roo'Ma's's A w/akhen aten.

The old man coughed a thin line of spittle. No time to get excited, yet if not now, when? A bloodless life re-animated by a removed passion. ChristinaMargot Shaughnessy, his true mate, waited to become icon to split the in word world wide open dissolving it in wordfree awareness of it. Releasing in word captivity understanding any spelling of a being cee'ng'g'ng do'er wayeve're'y"e informaing it. Her"e'mitting da y light between el'egg's. Egg's ting in'es'ting. Es'se' nt'y'all from above. Of a'being cee'ng de si re'y. Peh'ssy re'y radiating p'sy"en'ce black'g'round that supersonic ring'ing peh'ss'y w'hole power tower of ba'be'ng el. The one a being great go go go'a'd of function of fun'ny'a'ction wayeve're'y'body turns a black'g'round into or out of anybody anything etc.. The gee's us gravity of it. Of that process of dissolving it struck him now between the eyes. A consensus of billions flipped in that proverbial blink of eye.

Their motto, 'keep 'em busy bein' busy' kept the demos, the unwashed distracted. Staring out alone. X's ting in formation in word n'eve're'y all eyezze'ing a being cee'ng a do'or wayof re'y'e"ality. A status quo. The state in which awareness of a b'ng c'ng a peering it now a k'no'wing out of it appearing in word. The standing of a being in which. A'sz thoth'tsz of it out in a w'h'ile'y w'h'ich'ey'e. Deceived by their own eyes stareing out in the first place now k'now'ing of it a denial of it out in her'rey. That fun'ny'a'ction function we all turning it into or out of a race of man'as mind or memory. That race of the wheel. Of fortune or mis'sed'fortune. Ka's of it y'all. Ka's y'all memory. Ka's of it y'all. Macro-micro mean means meaning it a'x ka'ng a y eye of a being c'ee'ng a do'er way out. Dhi a y eye wayeve re'y dhi'a'ting a'ten bi na re'y in her"e black eye. By mirror duplicity of split hemispheres in h'our bra'hm'in. aRe'y dhi'a'ting out int'word twis'ting eve will dupe"dupe"dupe"el'i'ca'tions. That wayeve'll twis'ting in tword anybody anything etc. appearing. Turning in word a black'g'round that ax ka in'g in word information of'ten ka's mic memory. Supernatural supersonic memory a's thoth'tsz god'esse to be letter'all'y y'all art being peh'ss'y'en'ce"e a y eye feeling felt field of view. Of g'ee's"us weight of waiting on any touch of it touching black'g'round. Of you. Y you're"y dhi'a'ten'cion. Ka's mic power to perceive dhi'na eye"ll of a being still in the first place indivisible now a's thoth'tsz merely mirrored appearing a pairing letter . . . el ett'er'ey'all'y mirrored by any a na 're'y re'y dhi'a'ting da y light. A's being in the first place now x ka'in'g k'now'ing out x's ting. X's su'per as'ti ka. A y eye of eve're'y bo'dhi being to perceive ti ta'tt'a we all will wheel turning black'g'round into one da y light a while. A wiley w'h'ile. A're"y wayeve're'y body fun'ny'a'ction function of a y eye eve're y wayeve amplatitude flattening that a'y'eye'ring of power. Pow . . . pow . . . power of her'e peh'esse'y . . . man'as mind with womb of intent intending dhi's're'y'garding still a being the black eye in the first place indivisible in'visibility. A y being in visibility of a being cee'ng go go go going let'ter'all'y her'e eve'rey body turning black'g'round mirror seas of a being still in the first place now as thoth'tsz.

Mother, ma'ss'zz'a're'y'ality deri'yved from a supernatural digital supersonic matrix. He knew words have no essential meaning beyond k'now'ing the sound. A'szz'a the sound vigorous wayeves of her'eye of eve're'y bodhi. Wayeves of her eve're'y will. Her'eye on energy wayeves. En'eye urge. Gee' us weight waiting of her"e will. A wheel turning churning burning in a y eye a peering out in word sensing of it a feeling felt field of view of you of yod. Y od? A bionic. Neuronic electromagnetic as'zsyna'p'tical cellul'ar whorl'ding. AseX's ting. Y'll d'na. A while DNA spinning black'g'round roles or rolls or rings . . . PAH's ability's . . . Macromicro mean ka's mic PTAH's abilities . . . supernatural as thoth'tsz . . . the hook . . . Hey OO Ka . . . OO . . . a hOOka . . . deL"OO'Ka's mic memory . . .ma'cromycro ka's mic mean means meaning as'k'no'wing out of it . . .iT Ta A being still in the first place indivisible in'visibility . . . E'ye egg'ss'z'is'ting in formation . . . four ma'ss'zz'a anybody or her"e eve're'y body . . . Eve're'y'll. Is eve're'y'll. . . Her blood pouring into his blood . . . Ka' racing wheel. . .Man'as mind or y memory . . .ka's mic letter'ally thoth'tsz . . .h'OO'ka mean meaning means of eye of eve're'y body turning black'g'round appearing now k'nowing it . . .it being a bing still in the first place . . . indivisible in'visibility mirrored out in word . . . any supersonic's'e X press'ion gee's'szz's'us's gravity weight waiting for'ma'ss'zz'a her'e will turning churning burning . . . kali'ma'ss'azz's of any a na y appearing a pairing polarity syna'peh'ssy . . . After a lifetime of plundering, he had a dilemma that no weapon can resolve. To see her 'e'y her face is my destiny.

" . . . you know, my Priestess, I studied Sansrit elder sister of Greek and Latin. Aristotle and Plato to the Brotherhood of Pythagoras, the keystone for Copernicus, Galileo, and Newton. It occurred to me that Newton, with his laws on motion had missed the boat on purpose. On her'e'ye pur'pose of a peering from above. Isaac avoided her 'e'y'e's . . . eL OO ka . . .as'ex ka'ing y . . . a being in the first place . . . needs beyond the obvious drugs sex and all that jazz money . . . what needs of anybody still being a being in the first place indivisible in'visibility . . . a y eye a being cee'ng the real purpose of man as mind or why. Why, why, why? aRe'y'dhi a'ting aRe'y'all'izing her 'e a y eye of eve're'y bodhi. Why then now k'nowing the urge for freedom permeating denial of it in the least of actions. Re'y'ading their w'or"ka's, I sea"arc'hed the roll or role. Ore ring'in'g'o'ing in for'ma'ss'zz'a a y eye a being c'ee'ng now k'nowing a true pre Newtonian prophet prophecy a b'ng c'ee'ng a prior'y. Numbers . . . nu now language . . . we're'y re'y'dhi'a'ting in formation of her"e wayeve re'y'all a new nu na'na wayeve're'y re'y'dhi'a'ting now k'now'ing of processing process as 'ss'zz'a syna'peh"sse'y catharsis. Technology took a few years to catch up with me. Now it has surpassed my wildest schemes. Yet. We all turn in one dhi're'y'tion away from still a re'ydhia'ting it on purpose of a b'ng c'ng a gain. A black'g'round a gain. A're'y'all turning in the wheel race black'g'round a still b'ng c'ng in the first place indivisible in'visibility.

Pur pose standing free e'star'eye staring eye of a b'ng c'ee'ng merely a peering it. A're'y'all eye'sz a final liberation still in the first place. After y'all, a G'ee'sz us Priestess. A gain of A y eye of a being still in the first place indivisible in'visibility of a y eye won't call you mine for I only know you, no you in man'as my mind of in word memory. Could now a k'nowing out of eve're'y body possess you, merely a mirrored a're'y'flection of it echoing a black'g'round. Where it does y'all go? Into what if not for'word into a black'g'round into or out of your womb are we all a're'y'turning a's ka y eye of eve're'y re'ydiant body expanding in t'word t'wis'ting. Me or You a memory now ni'no nana verse. Out in her'eye a ba by being Y, Y you're you. . . "

☼

"We're being watched," Christina whispered. She helped him prop his wounded leg on the taboret. "I have surveyed the layout. There is bathroom down the hall with hot water."

"Grab me a pillow, por favor."

Christina looked over the bed. She knelt down and pulled open a set of drawers under the mattress box.

"There's a change of clothes in here." She took out a silk toga, greenish blue like brushed-out cyan. "Too much for everyday wear." Christina pawed through the drawer until she found a white terry cloth robe.

"I love you. I mean, I really love you," Mor offered. "I keep knowing less about whatever is going on, except I love you more with each passing moment."

"Lighten up. You are projecting." She gave him a playful slap on the cheek. "I am going to have a shower and then call for food. Warren wants us to be comfortable."

"You know him, don't you?" he asked, running his fingers through the white bristles of a large hog hair brush. "Not just about him."

Christina pursed her lips tightening them against her teeth.

"I'm pantless and about out of patience. Any nastiness you're concealing has to come out now. These circles in circles are too convoluted for my bent, burnt, and fried mind. Tell me the truth, Margot Christina."

"Warren knew my father from Yale and worked with him on the Manhattan Project decades before my birth. In that I am telling you we all turn around being at war. A conflict between awareness of a b'ng c'ng merely a peering it still in the first place indivisible invisibility or now appearing by a k'nowing out of it as thotht'sz of it in a state of active denial. Thus war in War're'y'na's case reflects that conflict or split. That prehistoric split in two hemispheres of the brain engineered by genetic engineering facillitates his action.

"Warren believes he engineered my creation over decades as a weapon to win this war by breaking up any potential in word long term memory. Y'all might say that I am a product of Messing Technologies, liberated like the split atom, born to blast consciousness from its apparent prison at attention in any in word form. That engineering supernaturally y'all initiated in prehistory is now revealed in plain site of anybody of a b'ng c'ng now as'ka's all y y'all a y eye a peering out aska's mic memory in denial of it hidden in the k'no'wing projection of it y'll d'na of eve're'y body." She finished with a laugh. "In that I am dynamite, like Nietszche said. In that I am about blowing up the whorl'd'ng of d'na, y'all y'll d'na, denial of a b'ng c'ng in the first place still that now k'nowing out of it a ka's mic memory of anybody. Perhaps, in that way, War're'y'na and I do serve the same race of a b'ng c'ng a peering out now in word informing man'as mind or y memory of it. It now as'k'now'ing out of it we all a's a wheel turning in word in a race. The same X cue sa me now a memory int'word twisting into a fate of a y b'ng c'ng merely a peering out now supernaturally as thoth'tsz of it k'no'wing appearing of it out the do'or way awhile still in the first place. Parooma samyaha now as'k'no'wing out of it a supersonic whorl'd'ing of a y black eye as'ex ka'ing y a turning into or out of that wheel of fortune. A b'ng c'ng in word out a's'ex's ting in formation still indivisible in'visibility of any individual."

The Professor left the room in a wayeve washing over him as he stared at the brick walls. Trace patterns of light drifted over the surface like torn clouds sweeping the skylights above. The bricks squared the angles of his thoughts. He closed his eyes, letting a steady pulse of mental images wash over. The Illuminatus vision in a pyre'y'e am'is pyramid burned in his memory every day of his life. Something seemed to tell him instead of merely a peering at the eye on top of the pyramid, he need merely a peer it to realize or a re'y'all'eye'zz a who or why of it. A why now a y eye of a being c'ee'ng of it a peering out in word. A b'ng c'ng still in the first place. A being c'ee'ng a peering it now merely reflected out in word as'k'no'wing of it supernaturally as thoth'tsz of it informing him as he thinking of himself looking at it. Now be that a y black eye awareness of k'no'wing any or eve're'y body. That a y wayeve re'y"e re'y'ality a're'y'dhi'a'ting now supersonic or phonographic in formation of indivisible in'visibility by k'now'ing it out of that awareness that I am is is. That eye is is it.

Now still him out in he'r"ey"e a peering a're'y'dhi'a'ting in formation of the a y eye a b'ng c'ng of that as'z'any seer sight see'ng k'now'ing anybody appearing of it. It struck him how anybody still now a being c'ng a peering in the first place merely appears mirrored supernaturally as thoth'tsz of it out around k'nowing of it a while. We all now supernatural he mused. Still a b'ng c'ng of that untouched wordfree invincible invisibility. Merely a peering out supernaturally as thoth'tsz at attention of a b'ng c'ng now as'z any body appearing out mirrored in word memory. A being still stillness of that immortal immortality. A being denied, forgotten, or merely ignored now awhile in favor of k'now'ing out of it a suffering artist. Ain't that pitiful, he mused, if not so fracking funny in the absurd.

He now wanted as that immortal immortality of a being to breath life into the still image of Madonna imagined by Warren or Christina. Letting him out in her'eye now a k'now'ing of it y'all in a mirror imagination run wild racing on in an allegorical canoe gliding down a swift river. In that he found himself again seeking inspiration in its creative waters. He tossed the tube of French vermilion on the easel's paint tray. Touching the bandage on his leg, putting a fingertip of glistening blood to his lips, he tasted the saltiness of it. The ironic a're'y'dness of it. He limped over to the bed and stretched out.

Christina returned from her shower, working a thick towel through her wet hair. She had found a bottle of aloe vera gel and dabbed at the gunshot burn tattooed on her upper arm.

"Any inspiration, dreamer?"

"Preparation. Should I draw or just paint? Just trying to let it flow. That's the problem, trying. I shouldn't be trying." He played with the blood and paint on his finger. "It should flow like an in word river scrolling out from the lap of a woman wearing a crown of stars and a crescent moon under her foot. Like in Revelations."

"You said she had a veil behind her stretched between two pillars. Did she have a moon crown?"

"You're right, a crown made of a crescent and an orb, but the crown changed to stars."

"The High Priestess," she said, tossing off the towel. Stretching out on the bed beside him, she took one of his hands in hers. "She is often confused with the Empress. That's reasonable considering they are one and the same awareness, functioning letter'all'y y'all supernaturally or phonographically informing of it in word as'z'any thoth'tsz of it a peering out in different guises of her"e black eye of eve re'y body now projecting a k'no'wing of it in imaginary whorld'ings of it to be perceived in word as'ka's mic memory. War'rey'na plans to cast me out as such an archetype through which a y eye being c'ee'ng he plans now to wield the k'no'wing out of it eve're'ybody a're'y"e dhi'a'ting in word chakra wheels turning burning seer'ing into our creation. Burning it. Seer'ing it black'g'round intent of intentionally y'all na now no longer disregarding its indivisible invisibility. In that y'all will still be a b'ng c'ng a's indivisible invisibility out in her'ey'e a black pehss'y whole eye felt feeling field of you touching without de'fences. A touch of it touching on a being still in the first place invisibility without in word definition. In that the or y a re'y'e"all of a main mean. Any meaning of it in a word a means of the definite article articulated articulation of a being cee'ng indefinitely. Indivisible in'visibility. A y eye of a being c'ee'ng now nothing in word while felt feeling fielding a touch touched in her"ey'e a black'g'round be'am'ing out of it eve're'y body. Not too grandiose," she added, lifting her"e'yes to the cameras. Mor merely a peering off in space now shrugged.

"So on the one hand you got, say, Venus in tight blue jeans or on the other, Diana, cool virgin goddess of the Moon. The virgin and the harlot," he offered.

"What every man wants, y'all in one woman. Humped black'g'round still a virgin." Christina turned on the computer and tapped the keyboard. "Virgin mother or mistress wh'or"e. It's not infor'ma'sz anything but a black peh'ess'ey w'hole."

Mor could have sworn hearing black pussy hole but heard in the dialectic as brahmayonim. A source of anybody of inferior manifest brahman. A're'y"e'al'ity of it appearing out of a b'ng c'ng still in the first place. Indivisible. Peh'ss'y'h'owl. Pe'y'now. Pe'y' aten'cion out in her"e'y'e. Out in her'ey'e of eve're'y'body. A po po power. Po'tiz ess'e. Portal out of it to be appearing awhile of a potential. A b c's of it ba'by. A Being C'ee'ng G'ee's us gravity going in or out a're'y'dhi'a'ting her'e'y'e. A do'er way letter'all'y now out in word way'eve're'y'sz z z'ap'ping of it. Out or in. In or out of it. A singular direction of time now turning black'g'round out't'in out't'in out'in. As'z z z'leep into or out of a. Yo yo yo'ni el'in'g'ham. Eve're'y'presence in her'me'as'z eye'sz on thoth'tsz of it. She'e'na a whorl'ding of the dialectic pramanam. As'z a mean of sound wayeves she'e'na played the peh'ss'y'en'c'ng whole scale of any human voice. As'z'any wayeve means her'eye of eve're'y'body entrained enchanted enraptured Mor's entire field of view of you of yod h'ey'eve'y'eh. El debatir de dialecto blazed his memory. Now as'king of it any k'no'wing out of it anybody anything any time any where. Merely supernaturally as'z'any thoth'tsz of it. As'z z z'any touch of it touching. Gee's us gravity weight of waiting period on any touching of the untouched wordfree awareness of a b'ng c'ng now k'no'wing out of it a black'g'round echo of it. Any echo of a b'ng c'ng now a touching touch of it. Mor's just us picking up a learning of the sense of touch as a function of coition. A y eye as'eX. As'z'any touch now a k'no no no'wing out of it. Touching as'z'any thoth'tsz of a b'ng untouched still in the first place. Indivisible merely supernaturally as'z'any in word thoth'tsz of it touching on a touch of it. A b'ng c'ng out in word informing it at aten'cion. A bi na r'e'y'e'sz'ion of it. Imaginary line between merely a peering it or now k'no'wing out of it any a peering at it.

"A'ware'ness of a being that which is, was, and ever'ey'e will be still merely eve re'y body turning churning yearning a seer'ing black'g'round into'or'out of eve re'y thing. That black as'sz'a eye re'y. That black invisibility mirroring eve're'y body'as'z potential projection appearing out her'e'y'e a black peh'ess'ey w'hole. Y'all out in a shout. In word now k'nowing out as k'ing as'ka's mic memory superimposed supernaturally y'all as'z thoth'tsz. The hOOk'a of de lOOk'a. T'wis in t'word aX'ka'ing y a're'y'flected reflection in a be"am'ing memory as'z thoth'tsz of it in ka's mic da y na light. Her energy re'y'flecting in'visibility by peh'esse'y power. Her supersonic will power with covenant of him freestanding still. D'ark of the covenant of Herhimit. Hermes tri'y'sme'gis't'us. Herhimit po'in't'at. Po'in'ten'tial of a y eye a being c'ee'ng in a re'y verse e'star'e'y of herhimit churning burning a're'y turning into or out of it. The me'gist of us y'all aska'ma'ing black'g'round in or out of her' black e'ye peh'ess'e'y w'hole." Margot Christina held a straight face before cracking herself up with gales of laughter. Eve'na 'ass'z'a she spoke still cracking up.

"Your gift is impregnating the work with that presence," she got out with a giggle. "Just what I thought, Warren has us wired into a private chat room for any requests we all in turn might have. In that I am ordering food. How about kung pao chicken and wonton soup?"

"Add spring rolls and a pot of green tea." Mor heaved himself from the bed and hobbled over to the easel.

"Delivery boy will be here shortly. How long do you need to rest?"

"A few lifetimes. But screw that, I been asleep too long. What the hell, I'm going to break in this virgin canvass. Maybe in that I am needing what Warren wants more than he does? " He started squeezing out paint. The canvass was large enough for him to move around on.

"You know, this virgin canvass is too large for just a portrait. I'll have to do your whole body."

"Naked?"

"You can keep your ankle sox on."

"Remember Isis, the source for the Virgin Magdalene heresy of Christian lore?" the Professor spoke, stretched out naked under the terrycloth robe falling off her shoulders, propped up on pillows, one arm resting on an upraised bare knee. "She was able to impregnate herself with Osiris's, the great god king's seed even though he had lost his penis in the battle with his brother Set. That is the original mythos of Immaculate Conception of a god's only son. H'our only sun Horus or h'our eye of g'ee's us. The a're'y'diant center of h'our g'ee's us, h'our center of gravity. Sol a're'y being in radiating radiation of da y light of h'our only sun. Burns more juice in a second than entire global energy output in hundreds thousands y'ears. The unbroken ka's mic loop. D"ark ka'ma'ing black'g'round a while a're'y dhi'a'ting ka's mic memory. A ma'ss'z'a'ne'y'e name for Isis is Meri. Ass'zound like you've heard it before?"

"Virgin Mary? Ma're'y turning black'g'round into a being c'ee'ng a're'y'dhi'ansa'zz'a only son. Let me see," he replied as he stroked paint rapidly over the gessoed canvass. He blocked in essential proportions of flesh in shadow or highlight. Spreading beads of color visually mimicing patterns. Patterns out in her"eye a pairing her'me'asz'za duplicity. Her'me'as'z thoth'tsz of it. Herhimit. Now a b'ng color'ass'z'a bending blending it back with a pallette knife. "You just gots to believe." He pushed paint for another twenty minutes then rejoined her on the bed, fingers reaching out to trace the ridges of her spine. He pulled the robe up to cut the chill on her shoulders and leaned in to kiss her neck. Laying back, still in his leather jacket and jockey shorts. He laughed.

"All I need is black socks and dark shades to make old fashioned porn for the cameras." For a moment, his memory slid to a girl wearing horn-rimmed eyeglasses and the bale of hay they had coupled on under the open Illinois sky. Korner filming.

"Can you do the painting without having sex with me?" Christina turned until her cheek flattened against her shoulder. The robe fell and she stood naked. Chilled air tightened her flesh. As she stretched, muscles corded in the backs of her thighs. She walked over to a high chair positioned between the bed and the easel.

"You have the legs of a dancer." Mor commented as he spied a spiral bound sketch book and pen on the bedstand. Flipping it open he found the pen in hand moving over the paper with a mind of its own.

"Mostly from running. My father wanted me to be a dancer. Maybe he saw dance as a means to prolong my innocence."

"Tell me more about him and Warren," he asked feeling the renewal drawing on the wordfree right side of the brain. Such a seemingly simple shift of attention but one of freedom from in word captivity. He thought how despite thousands of hours drawing of still falling for that in word deceit. Now under the influence of the dialectic that spelling seemed turning it into an in word release of it.

"Johnstone Warren or War're'y'na fashions himself a scholar. War're'y'na is the name given him by certain occult masters in the black or white brotherhood. My work in the whorl'd 'ing of letters incidentally mirrored his. He and my father were part of that fraternity unleashing the terror of atomic power. Some, like my father and the man who took photographs in the plane, of the blast over Hiroshima never spoke of the bomb again. Eve'r. War're'y'na saw the bomb as an opportunity for global domination. The release of radiation over the following years was very profitable for him. His knowledge of mutation caused by exposure to radioactivity goes very deep. He used my father to create me. My father worked for Warren for forty years. There is no question in my mind Warren was feeding him various chemicals. Always testing his blood. Always under Warren's or War're'y'na's thumb."

"This fraternity or brotherhood sounds racist. Are you . . ."

"A member in good standing? We all appearing in or out of it. A singular indivisible body of we all of eve're'y'body experienced directly and periodically as'z z z'leep black into a un consciousness. A turning of it into or out of a black'g'around as'ka's mic wheel race of it y'll D'NA. A race of a mythological channel of mere supersonic in word long playing phonographic record of it as'ka's mic memory of a b'ng c'ng still in the first place now a k'no'wing out of it. A y eye of a b'ng c'ng now the e turn all'y y'all of any role or roll rota taro'ta't'ion of a complete d''ark'ness. A d''ark letter'all'y y'all encircling a black'g'round of it. A'ss'z'z z'leep black into a un' consciousness to a'wak'hen a'ten a bi na re'y in anybody now k'nowing eve're'y'body out in word for'ma'sz'a wily while. Of it out in her'eye'sz'ion a be'am'ing cunning wordship craft appearing of it out in her'e'ye on a mirror se'e'as of a being c'ee'ng merely a peering at it. A see'r'ing of that race of man'as mind or a y memory of it." Mor's in word hearing followed her'eye shifting from anybody as'ex'plaining of it into a y speak dialectic debate of a y eye being c'ee'ng merely a peering still in the first place. Or y'all the troubles of the mind appearing as'ex'plaining of anybody he flashed. Any field of view indivisible in'visibility of its seer. A b'ng c'ng a peering it now a k'no'wing out of it a'wayeve're'ybody appearing in word in formation as'z'any thoth'tsz of it he now thought. Then returned to merely a peering at the pen tracing contours of it appearing ink'as black on white plane background.

"Eve're'y'body a complete d"ark or perceived en'circlement of any roll or role played in the e mirage of a mind mirrored in word memory of a b'ng c'ng still in the first place. What you think y'all see here, this flesh, this womb man'as mind, is of such that I am conceiving out of it a fully recognizing of it now as a supersonic mirage. Superimposed by a b'lack' power of intent of a b'ng c'ng a gain. Any appearing of it now as'k'now'ing out of it a ka's mic memory in word over mind. A're'y'all'eye'zing'ing a being be'am'ing of it as'z'any thoth'tsz of it. It still now a k'no no no'wing moving out of it as'z'any denial of that motionless indivisible in'visibility center of awareness in that eye of I am is is.

"Do you not think War're'y'na shares in me a're'y'al'eye'zing'ing that awareness. Him discerning a being of it indivisible still. Now out in her'eye, ma'sz eye of d'na'ture of d"ark. Of a greater being as'king of it any d"ark'ness'e now to be perceived turning into or out of a k'no'wing out of it any or eve're'y'body. A b'ng c'ng now a complete d"ark'ness'e now to be perceived turning into or out of the first place as'z any mirrored body of it. Y'all d'na y'll of a complete d"ark turning now encircling a black'g'round of any k'no no no'wing of it out in her'ey'e of eve re'y body playing roles or rolls of d"ark. A turning into or out of a singular indivisible supersonic or phonographic black mirror see'as out in eye a peering at a mirage body. That, I am now mirror'all'y y'all appearing in word as'z'any thinking of creator thoth'tsz. Supernaturally y'all thoth'tsz of a god esse. To be letter'all'y y'all in word art a're'y'flecting it as'ka's micro wayeve black'g'round echo as'z'any thoth'tsz of it. A're'y'flection in memory of it now as'z anybody imagined idol to be worshiped and believed in." She sat on the highchair with her back to him, light glancing off the contours of her naked form. He seeing the classic figure 8 contour of shoulders waist hips divided along a boney spine. The tale of a serpent. Then turning its head Mor imagined a tongue slithering between partially closed lips. A snake eye on the tree of senses. He felt his attention drawn again to the sound of her voice.

"Thus h'our minds have not merged so much as'z remain out in her'eye of any or eve're'y body indivisible invisibility merely appearing supernaturally as'z'any thoth'tsz of it. A memory imagined a's ka's mic body of a being cee'ng merely a peering awhile. As'z'z'any in word in formation of it a wile. A cunning mean word'ship craft carrying attention off away y'll D'Na. Periodically we all a're'y'turning black'g'round into or out of eve're'y'body. A singular b'lack' body of denial of a being cee'ng complete completely indivisible in'visibility of it. A b'lack' body experienced directly and periodically as'z z z'leep black into a un consciousness of it. A wordfree untouched awareness of it now to be a b'lack' body as'k'ing of it a k'no'wing out of it a gain.

"Now out of it in word a're'y'dhi'a'ting a ka's mic micro wayeve black'g'round echoing any asking of it a k'no"wing out anybody. Alter'native appearing in word denial of it. Disappearing as'z z z'leep black into one indivisible invisibility. A being cee'ng a peering at it wordfree now out appearing of it in da y na light igniting awakhening in word understanding the spelling of overmind. A god'esse to be letter'all'y y'all informing any appearing in word merely supernaturally or phonographically as'z'any thoth'tsz of it. In the or y he is seducing me or you by our own memory mirage image of it imagined making it as'ex. Thats'za what is scary about war or War're'y'na. His taking full advantage of this phenomenon of a being anybody out as int'word a twis'ting of it as'eX's ting in formation of any or eve're'y'body in denial of its indivisible invisibility. That wile of d'na used now turning any k'nowing of it into a self replicating invisibility of a supersonic bioacoustic virus as'z'za pingting to a're'y'verse polarity of y as'ex's ting informing any uni'verse.

"Still of it." She'e'na paused with a smile. "Still full of it. Any negative x pole still a y y'll d'na. A stillness of a b'ng c'ng merely a peering it while any denial of it appearing out in word. A y we all turning into or out of it as'z'any thoth'tsz informing it with any endings of it. Any beginnings of it must start with any endings of it. For the sake of a pairing a polarity between a b'ng positive of it as'z'z'ap'ping any negative pole of it, an opening of denial k'no'wing the complete d"ark must occur. There must be occurrence of a denial of a being still indivisible in'visibility. It now as'z'any thoth'tsz of it as'k'no'wing out any in word denial of it. Pay attention to the awareness of it now as'z'any k'no'w'ing denial of it. Positively now k'no'wing it black'g'round. A where of outgoing river meeting incoming ocean. A'SYANDAMANAHA. A where understanding of it meets overstanding. Disappearing any narrow banks or de'fenses of it as'z'any bios fields of view of you of yod. Of a y. Still eye'sz'at attention in the first place find any a peering at it indivisible in'visibility from any appearing of it." Mor now found his drawing a li'ne between a peering at it or it appearing on pa'per. A uni'verse now indivisible at attention in a dhi's a're'y verse. Attention to be perceived dissolving still indivisible in'visibility of a b'ng c'ng merely a peering it in the first place."

"The pingting echoes a ka'smic micro wayeve black'g'round body. An instantaneous momenta by momentam body" Mor began to comprehend the relation of painting Christina to a pingting of Warren's virus or himself for that matter. Of himself surrendering to the d"ark'ness of his role in it. Of a singular indivisible b'lack' potential body of intent of a b'ng c'ng a 'gain'. A body indivisible merely echoing a're'y"e pingting silent sound mean awareness of it at attention of now intention of a b'ng c'ng a 'gain'. A gain merely in word awhile.

He found himself the dialectic debate dissolving in word at attention now paid in full"ness of a k'no'wing out a wordfree untouched awareness of it still in the first place. Any in word captivity of attention paid strictly to it is the weak force compared with untouchable wordfree timeless awareness of it he mused. Filling it full of any awareness of its fullness denied fully as'z completely empty of it. Empty of it. E'm' pt. y. El memoria pt. of view of you of yod that eye of I a'm'em'or'y of it denied.

Mor nearly freaked from the dialectical transpositioning of any in word meaning as mean means of a liberation of attention. He really had not fully seen his ending in the D"ark'ness of his beginning. In a b'ng c'ng merely a peering it. It now a b'lack' body of D'Na eye"ll of its indivisible invisibility. A y now b'lack' eye wayeve're'y"e out in her'eye of eve'll. A wayeve're'y"e'will. He now found himself as'k'no'wing to perceive a complete ark of the covenant with a god esse to be letter'all'y y'all anybody anything anywhere any time. Alternating with any understanding of the spelling of a b c's capturing his attention mom'ent after mom'ent. Any captivity of a crossing that eve'now'tat h'our'eye'z'on it appearing awhile. Mom'en'ta'after mom'entam'a.

"Indivisible in'visibility." Christina spoke as she continued to stretch in a yoga tai chi. Mor knew she'e'na raising the kundalini energy. SYANDAMANAHA. A where river meet ocean. The X change. The ripping tidal charge of it. He observed his hand finding alternative patterns to any in word in forming of his field of view. Finding that figure 8. The unt'word twist of 0. Zzzeero ro ro of da go go go bay'a'by.

"El otro lado. The one of the other side of it. A wordfree awareness of a freestanding of it untouched in eve're'ybody touching on it merely in word mirrorored supernaturally as'z'any her'me'as'z thoth'tsz of it. A bios of it as'ex." Mor was struck by sudden awareness of her'eye in formation as'ex. Naked as'ex y'all he flashed. She'e'na out of the b'lack'ness in her'eye of eve're'y'body.

"A y eye being merely mirrored in sight a re'y'all 'or'a y na opening endings of polarity. A positive y na'gate opening any whorl'ding eye of it y'll d'na. A wily wile of d'n'ay'll. A d'n"eye"ll of it merely a peering out now supernaturally. As'z'any thoth'tsz of opening the indivisible in the first place. That'sz'za her'me'as'z'za'thoth'tsz as'z'ex'spelling a peh'ss'y'en'ce'ng whole power. A power of denial. The electromagnetic loop of view of you of yod continues in one wayeve or another unbroken. Indivisible wordfree continuity of it. Continues a be'am'ing that a macro-micro ka's mic mean of a being found inka's mic phonographic molecular PtAH's abilities. Pt.. ah the universe of you ni or we all now merely turns black'g'round into or out of it as'ka's mic polycyclic aromatic Pt.AH's abilities. A ringing supersonically still in a being one mean of killers or lovers as'king of it a la por que"en que' appearing aska's mic memory of a being still in the first place indivisible in'visibility of anybody being of it. That of a b'ng c'ng overstanding y'all understanding of any in word spelling out of it now k'nowing anybody out in versus stlll a b'ng c'ng in the first place. The ability of anybody of a being.

"A'b'el now as int'word a twis'ting supersonic function as'eX's ting a black'g'round of it as'Ka'ing'ay'na no no no'wing out of it int'word forming one dhi'rection of it'asz'za the perceived arrow, the eros of time, now turning into or out of a k'no'wing of it as'eX with de'sire." She'e'na gave Mor that crazy scary stare he remembered so well from his ma's'z schizophrenia. But then he always was a sucker for that jelly roll. It may turn anybody or anything black'g'round into appearing disappearing as'z'za unwinding or any winding of a b'lack'round it. A black'g'round it a b'ng c'ng a gain. Pow pow power of da b'lack' X peh"re'ss'y w'hole out in her'eye of eve're'y'body. A'b'el we all c'ay'na. A y eye merely a peering it.

"It a being free standing with on the one hand a still staff or pole or polarity of it now mirrored by on the other hand da y eye light shining out into a black'g'round as'z'any complete d'ark'now'ing a y as'ex'ting int'word a twis'ting a y eye's een'dhi'ng its beginning. A b'ng c'ng a gaining of it. As'z that simple twist of fate around that se'en'ding will save us by ending or destroying us by breaking up any in word understanding of its spelling into a wordfree awareness of that mirage."

"Man, you are one bewildering piece of work. In that I am feeling his interfacing with our or y"our awareness . . . somehow. . . supernaturally superimposed like y'all say by a being of y eye a peering it. Y'our now out knowing what he's got up his evil sleeve?"

"Now out k'now'ing War're'y'na? He is a cunning crafty wily old dog in that way. In that wayeve I am knowing out of it . . ." she paused, then began pacing the room. "you knowing any appearance of it is by denial of its in'visibility. It is as though a being c'eeing with two eyes in two brains or unt'word a'twis'ting mode el's turning a black'g'round out as'king of it any k'no'wing out of it in word into and out of any or eve re'y body. Old then now new. The new turning around merely a k'no'wing mind or y y'all memory mirroring in word thoughtsz of it appearing a being of anybody in name alone. Based on such an arbitrary untword a twis'ting identity of any mode"eL of any mere mirror function of fun'ny'a'ction we all may foolishly imagine ourselves turning into it merely playing out infinite loop'y roles of it.

Money is funny. And like money as'z'any mirror wayeve function roll or role is plenty funny honey," she offered with a shrug while swiveling the chair seat as she retook her pose. "Plenty funny or plenty sad. A serious sheer folly."

"So what y'all's'za saying is that its funny when a b'ng c'ng merely as in word though'tsza about a being but sad when a being felt. The pain ting is a mirrored echo of a ping'ting. Somehow Warren's virus mimics the fundamental process understanding any in word spelling of it. In that I am y'all too often feeling a sorrow or pain of a'gain now k'no'wing a loss of losing anybody." Y'all because of any in word spelling of a b'ng c'ng merely a peering? He flashed on a shaman once telling him of the second obstacle to a man of knowledge. A clarity of mind. At the time he failed to comprehend its meaning. Now he became aware of it as a serious mean folly of any k'no'wing out of it. It seems many who pursue the way of a man of knowledge come up short as bouyant warrior clowns. Confusing a complete k'no'wing denial of it with complete real eye'szation of merely a peering it. Luckily Mor had found himself more serious than many of his counterparts. Happens when y'all meet your death at two years young. A death saving his life he mused.

"Or still if anybody is eve re'y body . . . or any rock'n'rolling loop or roles'za playing out in complete d"arks of turning around perceiving a k'no no no'wing out of it any in word breaks in the lOOpa de lOOpeh'ss' y as'ex'posing by polarity opening ka's all y causing endings of possibilities of a bios'electric synapse.

"In other words opening the pie hole to release our tale. Then it seems a sp"ark of the rush blows the mind free of detritus of long term memory predominated still by a b'ng c'ng now that indivisible silence in'visibility." Mor let the dialectic roll in and out and projecting y'all b'lack'g'round him. His in word memory spewed out a veritable litany right before his y"ears.

Y"ears of a life echoed now as'k'no'wing of it in word as sound wayeves a're'y'all out in her'eye. A b'ng c'ng now as'king of it a k'no'wing out of it into anybody appearing in memory as'z'any thoth'tsz of it still in the first place. Indivisible invisibility now supernaturally appearing as'z a god esse to be letter'all'y y'all turning b'lack'g'round intent of a b'ng c'ng a 'gain'.

Now it moved him and he appeared moving. A turning a k'now'ing out of it any awareness of a b'ng c'ng in it. A being still in the first place indivisible invisibility. Mor now found his in word identity merely mirrored by a b'ng c'ng eye of a y'or y na now as'ex'pressed out of it. Or molded under gravity weight of him felt waiting as mere supernatural thothtsz of it now separate from a b'ng c'ee'ng out in her'eye. Y'all thoth'tsz in word he thought of her'eye see'ng wordfree as that eve re'y body. Still that letter'ally a b'lack' god or go'a'd esse to be a 'gain'. Y'all without yet appearing of a b'ng c'ng in word in formation A b'ng c'ng in the first place indivisible in'visibility in first person singular presence that eye of I am is is. Or y speak of it if not by a b'ng c'ng of a y eye'z z zsee'ng in the first place he now wondered. The new dialectic took on a life of its own blowing away his self conceit like 'wind from his lower regions'.

"A predominance of any understanding of it letter'all'y y'all in word spelling casts the role or race to be unduly influenced or captivated by any in word powers that be in that misunderstanding of overmind. Or y that is the name game." She'e'na swiveled the seat in complete arks before coming back to rest in the original pose. "The great Adamic atomic g'ee's us ga'me of any da'y'a being of na"me alone. A gee's us gravity weight of waiting on a time now as'k'no'wing of it in name as anybody any where else. Any of it int'word a twisting d'na y'll now of any na'me of a b'ng c'ng a peering it now turning a k'no'wing out of it into a notional denial identity. A na me. Any identity developed merely in word memory for the sake of function requires near constant reinforcement. A near constant denial of a k'no no no'wing out of it a b'ng c'ng still in the first place." She now spun several times in the opposite direction before returning still. The pen hand kept moving filling a page then another. With the li'ne between a peering at it or it appearing drawn across the page. Drawing on a seeing not what y'all think he thought.

"One subject now a k'now'ing out of it as'z though int'word a twis'ting black'g'round disappears by simply dis'a'pairing at any single moment. Dis'a'pairing inevitably a's'zz z'leep into one turning black'g'round still a b'ng c'ng indivisible in'visibility of y'all along. A b'ng c'ng in the first or a'z z z'a last place. We all in turn all'y y'all for the most part live lives merely mirrored in word as though a b'ng c'ng appearing out of it as'z anybody in name alone. H'our now a greater being remains unknown or one indivisible known while a knowing of ignoring it. Now as thoth'tsz of a god esse to be letter'all'y y'all projecting it out in one k'no no no'wing denial of it.

"That is most unfortunate and sad though typical. A case of mere supernaturally turning a bliss into sorrow around k'no no no'wing it into any denial or existential dread. Finding now fear of death while at the same time as thoughtsz projecting it around k'no no no'wing denial of a being still in the first place immortal im'mortality. Now then falling periodically and directly black into a 'un' consciousness of it. As'z z z'leep into a 'un'known k'now'ing of a b'ng c'ng b'lack'. A b'lack' eye of eve re'y body together still a're'y"e'all of'ten awakening in formation of indivisible in'visibility with a loop'y role playing intent of it appearing out in word as thoth'tsz of it in a'gain and a'gain and a'gain. Appearing a'gain only to lose yourself in any idea of a b'ng c'ng in a y eye a peering at it now turning into any mirrored k'nowing out of it y'all as"ex's ting in na'me alone."

"So we all turn around and around this race ad infinitum ad nauseum in any role played now by turning in word into a k'now'ing projecting it as though awakening out in a mirror a pairing of it appearing awhile. Appearing now turning into a k'now'ing out as'ka's mic da'y light shining any cunning duplicity tale of chasing our own tail." Mor felt fevered by the heat of it out in her'eye of a're'y'dhi'ance. Still somehow he could not let go of last vestiges of any arbitrary denial identity seeming so long in the making. Or faking he mused while his gut burned. It burned with the implication of a being so complicit in his own deceit. Ah the troubles of the mind now laying down by him drawing on merely a peering it at invisibility of any seer in sight of wordfree awareness of it. Awareness unborn deathfree undecaying ancient.

"Surely chasing tail does seem to predominate the race of man. Or y a being now in the first place appearing out of it as'ex?" she asked without a trace of irony. Mor felt the mask of pretense dissolve right before his eyes. Now then in that blink of eye turning back into k'now'ing its reappearance with lines tracing of its fragmentation offering him a reminder of its uncanny supernatural superimposed appearance of a being indivisible in'visibility c'ee'ng in the first place. He followed her steady movement now standing aiming her zen arrow.

"Now then still of a b'ng c'ng the old indivisible in'visibility of anyone being a seer sight see'ng, or a y eye of view of you aRe;y"e 'all visual mode. Y you a're'y tis't'at awareness of a b'ng c'ng still permanent in the first place amidst of any and y'all as thoth'tsz of impermanence. Still motionless amidst any e ye'g g motion. Amidst any commotion. A y y'all god'ts'ta ask yourself y."

"A y way or the highway?" he quipped feeling a building euphoria. Thatsz when he started musing on the downhill as what goes up.

"That question a's king of it y is the quest." Now a k'now'ing of y. In her'ey'e g g'aze seemed to envelope him. Swallowed black into her'eye of a radiant peh'esse'y whole being the belly of a beast. But what the hey would he be doing anyway tonite in the forest. Then he realized his life had turned into and around exhausting himself to sleep and sleeping to be able to exhaust himself. He grabbed some grins tree climbing. Once topping out on a 150 foot sempiverins redwood in Humboldt county. Then climbed a ways up inside a 5,000 year old redwood hollowed out and blackened by ancient fire still sprouting another and another above that. That brought a visit in his dreams from the ancient one in a guise as only a twisted knarly weathered tree being could appear. In that dream he found himself inseparable from that ancient matrix. A trickey ma'sz a're'y'e"ality so quickly ignored now ask'now'ing out of it an awakening. Now it seemed that matrix regenerated that ancient one in the modern form as k'now'ing of it a seductive woman. That juxtaposition caught him gazing into a wrinkly a weathered version of Christina blackened dried and emaciated like mummy. Her voice restored her fresh form leaving him wondering which was in her'ey'ere'y'ality.

"Why appear a b'ng c'ng in the first place only turning out of it now a black'g'round of k'now'ing it then. Dust to dust? Appearing disappearing? Is there really any other question of a being cee'ng out there that does not lead black to mummy?" She let the question hang for a moment. His mummy flashed in his head. Alive she had scared him. He was pretty sure what remained of her buried in wormy earth would be no less frightening. Why quest for ma'sz being in a place infor'ma'sz still of a b'ng c'ng indivisible in'visibility of a ka's mic being. A pa'roo'ma. A pharaoh in the house. Paramaht'ma. A re'y'all eye"zze of a paramount b'ng c'ng in the first place to begin with. A why of it merely supernaturally as thothtsz put y'all's eggs' ting in that mirror seas basket? Why cling so desparately to any mirror in word appearing of it as mere supersonic thoth'tsz of a y you're you. A b'ng c'ng still in the first place? Why be merely duplicitous in duplicating an imaginary image of yourself with out realizing y you're a're'y'all eye'z'zing a being still in the first place? He now asked himself. Still a peering it at the drawing he found himself indivisible in'visibility of it.

"Ma's for'ma's? Ain't that a bitch. A're'y'e on we all a'r'ey"e'dhi'a'ting turning a black'g'round into or out of a certain addiction to desperation? To an in word sense of dhi perception of separation as'k'ing of it a y eye a peering it now a k'no'wing out of it any appearing of it as'ka's mic memory creation? Excuse the pun but y'all turn that in word familiar world around into now k'nowing it in other words out in her"e'ye. Of eve're'y'body a spectacular turning black'g'round out as'ex spectre'y'ing of it. That we all turn into our own worst enemy? Or worse best friend?"

Mor found himself troubled while at the same time relieved. Like being caught with his pants down but only by the neighbor's dog. Overwhelmingly dire were the troubles of y'all that matters in mind or . . . y'all completely free. Is that our free choice he wondered. A bliss or now turning it black'g'round a k'nowing out of it any in word sorrow. Y'all for'ma's chasing that tail in the race of man with or without womb as troubled mind. Or y'all complete. Completely invincible indivisible invisibility. That choice now seemed to him quite laughable.

"That is the simple unt'word twist of any mirror understanding a spelling of it appearing y'll d'na. That denial is the intention of any or eve're'y'body appearing out now a short while by any k'now'ing of it. Projecting it in word by a b c's powered out in her'e y'ez z z of a peh'esse'y whole of any or eve're'y'body now appearing out of it in word. Without a're'y'al'eye'zing on a b'ng c'ng still in the first place indivisible in'visibility of it.

"A denial of a y eye b'ng c'ng merely a peering at it now as'king of it a k'no'wing out any generating appearing of it. It a y eye of a b'ng c'ng now as'z'any in word thoth'tsz' of a k'no'wing out of it. As'ex'et'ting duplicating a b'ng c'ng still in the first place. Duplicating supernaturally as thoth'tsz of it appearing out of a now k'no'wing a d'na'eye'll of it. A b'ng c'ng still in the first place. A pa'roo'ma. A parama being that a macro-micro ka's mic mean means of a b'ng c'ng still center centered centrality of it. On the one hand as'kurve'ing ka's mic da y eye light. In the other polarity. A positive pole turning black'g'round a y eye potential negative projection of it out now ask'no'wing of it. A'x k'ing y kar'ey'e'ma'sz black'g'round.

"That intention of denial simply moves in one direction out of any w'ay now as'ex et'ting duplicating a'w'ay into one in word continuous d'ark to perceive duplicity turning in'for'ma'sz a short while appearing a pairing of it. The self deceit of that duplicity tricks attention out of nearly any possibility of a're'y'all'eye'zing'ing out of a y eye b'ng still c'ng merely a peering it in the first place," she now offered stretching down to touch toes then drawing an invisible bow to fire an arrow directly into his heart. In a blink she'e'na appeared beside him stroking his neck. Whispering in his ear. Touching. "Re'y'all'izing a being of that now still indivisible without turning it black'g'round as'king of it a k'no no no'wing it into a pairing as though any second takes rare consideration. Are you that rare one Dark Mor? Only a veritable fool would intentionally launch on such a path. Like pulling out toenails to scratch y'our face. Setting yourself up to be global pariah. One should hate this pointing out of our in word mirror duplicity. H'our in word captivity. It is coded in h'our being a y'll D'NA. In the beginning folks intensely grow by the eve're'y 'breath' of k'no no no'wing it. The'y ignore still a b'ng c'ng of it in the race to pick up language skills in order to fully serve in her'eyez z z a'wayeve function. Then fully cast out of it understanding the in word spelling of it playing that first supersonic role. We all turn away from picking black up on a being still that invincible perpetually in a wordfreedom awareness. Then we all must turn to hate and reject out of hand any . . . any . . . reminder of a being still in the first place it . . . become paranoid in many cases of a b'ng c'ng as'ex'posed as the fraud. Of a b'ng c'ng out in any mere in word mirrored duplicity of it. The longer playing the role the more entrenched the self deceit. As one seeking a're'y'all'eye'zation should find a repulsion to success without getting addicted to failure. Are you that fool I am dreaming of?"

"That I am or at least I think that I am. "Be still" were first words coming to my mind. As beginning of my paying attention to it in word. The word saved my life and in that I am now realizing iniiated me on a path back to a being black'g'round. A path like treading the razor's edge. A difficult way to discern a b'ng c'ng still merely a peering it out the black eye of eve're'y body now k'no'wing out of it a denial of intent of realizing it," he answered scintillated by electricity of her touch. "A path I reckon of trying to catch up with your own shadow"

"In that I am finding we all turn away from realizing it by thinking too much. Knowing thoughtsz of it are a denial of it. Any now k'no'wing out of it is a scant thin'king of yourself as though merely out beside that ancient indivisible point of view of you of y to begin or end with it as such. Any chintzy thin'king about it still in word now a k'no'wing out a d'na'eye'll of it," she spoke softly around kisses planted.

"Ain't it a bitch baby. Like chasing that tail. The faster we all turn the further out of reach it becomes," he replied with a chuckle. Finally completely comprehending the contradiction of his Dark Mor life. In one wayeve he died at 2 years young. Died from any chance of living life merely as though born. The in word voice of overmind intervened. Saving him to a life of unknown quest to resolve the quandry of denying it awhile still hearing that voice a ringing in his y'ears. That dilemma was further deepened by his Dark na'me. "My not me is Dark Mor . . . ' he muttered. Then broke up with laughter. "Just hit me that we all turn around introducing ourselves by saying 'hi my not me is Jackie Doe Black' or whatever. Right up front we all in turn offer our in word denial . . .introduce ourself to the world at large by a denial of it. By a duplicity of who we all are in the beginning middle end of taking our turn in any role playing out. Out of it now asking of it y now a k'no'wing a being of complete d"ark'ness. A b'ng c'ng of now a k'no'wing of eve're'y'body." With these last words an incredible humility washed over him. Mor now wondered if a clarity of mind might obstruct that blessing of humble pie. A slice of which extinguishing any self importance arising from that clarity offers complete freedom from judgement.

"The k'no no no'wing d'na'eye'll of who or what we all turn into or out a b'ng c'ng of it. A b'ng c'ng still in the first place. Or now out of it thinking of k'now'ing ourself out of a b'ng c'ng still etc.," she added with a k'nowing smile. She moved over top to sit beside him on the bed. Careful to avoid touching on wounded knee or the sketchbook in his hands she now stretched her legs alongside his.

"Then any k'now'ing of a b'ng c'ng is a denial of it awhile. In a paradox of any positive in word negativity of it to create a mere mirrored sit'u"ation of po po po'lar'i'eye'z'za'tion of it . . .," he mused at the sheer wayeve of functional folly in any in word mirrored life.

"Chasing tail in a race against discerning it in her'eye merely a peering it out of eve're'ybody catching on to it. A race of e"turn'all'y y'all we all a turning into and out of complete d"ark'ness. Beginning any turning around it by any endings of it. Endings now mythical mirror'age po po po'tential po'les of a being still in the first place indivisible. Create an in word break in it by opening any a na y eye pi' w'hole. A being constant constantly computing of it now as'king of it e'qui'distance from any center point of view of you of an y now k'no'wing out of it anybody anythin'king etc.."

"That tale of any in word long term memory merely goes out mirrored now a black'g'round as'king of it a k'nowing supersonically y'all into appearing or back to black into a un'k'no'wn disappearing. It goes back or forth alternating in a wordfreedom to or from there in wordsz'za being only appearing as'z thothtsz of it in any mirrored memory of y'all na now. That visual eye of a b'ng c'ng a peering it out now as thothtsz of turning a black'g'round into k'no'wing of it as'z z' anybody or anythin'king of it in a mode'el function. That a way of wayeve function hides in word a being still. Now k'no'wing out of it in her'eye of eve're'y body turning a black'g'round of it. A po po po'tencial viz'a'viz anybody appearing in name alone."

"And black'g'round and around we all keep turning a way of now a b'ng c'ng out awhile k'no'wing it or anything a t'all y'all."

"In either case of or from a being still it." She'e'na closed her eyes'z z z'sending a pulsing wayeve're'y body of information flooding his in word sensibilities. Su'Personically. A sound means of it spoken silently in wordsz'a b'ng c'ng echoing a black'g'round only between mirrored her'ring of it in word minds tuned to the eye dialectic. That eye of a b'ng c'ng merely a peering it is indivisible in'visibility impossible to see any see'ng of it. It of a being c'ng to see'as seer invisibility. A su'personic seer except as mirrored phonographically in word or as thoughtsz of it.

"Instead we all turn into mirroring in word thoughtsz of it in formation of it now out k'no'wing anybody. Now a k'nowing out of it playing out any role. Any role in that race after h'our own tale. A tale of one un'tword a twis'ting in formation of her'me'as'z'thoth'tsz of herhimit. A god'esse to be letter'all'y y'all in word memory of a singular indivisible in'visibility. Indivisible one mirrored a pairing only after y'ears of un't'word understanding the spelling of a b c's. Casting as'z thought'sz memory echoes of a b'ng c'ng in anybody a peering it out now k'now'ing of it a while. Disapearing in that blink of eye in the complete psy'lence of a seer still seeing now without any word informing the complete d"ark'ness of the race of man'as in word mind or y'all a being of it still supersonic indivisible invisibility."

"After y'all these years and tears and fears of a being still . . ."

"Invisibility. Invincibly indivisible in any mere mirrored in word visibility as thoughtsz of a being any body out and about appearing now aw'h'ile." She spoke in a sympathetic key yet he found his foolish arbitrary notions of a being of Dark Mor mocking that.

"It may come down to y'all able to laugh at yourself. Taking powerful psychedelics that capability is so essential. So right from the get critical as the shell of our pseudo named self dissolves. That dissolving offers that rare opportunity to experience a y eye b'ng c'ng merely a peering it out at infinite b'lack' potential to be a gain. Painting offered for me the perfect place to be both to observe hallucinations and develop any visual painted record of them. It took many many layers of white gessoed ground to give color a glimpse of the luminosity of that interior luminary. Eventually I had to reinforce the canvass with wooden door skin to keep y'all that gesso from cracking." Mor then hesitated finding himself yammering on outside the dialectic which seemed to have a life of its own. A life and justification of its emergence after remaining silent for so long. Mor felt he'd been set up for that fall under the truck. Awakening the voice. His incoherence from that awakening served to distract him from embarking as a youth on any thing but sheer folly. Including art. Yet he now continued drawing on it. A black ink'as appearing on a white background.

"In word we all turn in two a twis'ting int'word a b c's of a b'ng c'ng a y eye now as though see'ng turning a b'lack'g'round the race a k'nowing a b"all bearing definitions of it. Two by a twis'ting int'word of it as thoughtsz separated or circumscribed by a being y y'all as'ex's ting in formation. You indivisible one remain in'visibility now w/intention mirror'ed out as'ex's ting as y'all turning around k'no no no'w'ing any potential in word appearance of it." She gave in word information as sound waves impinging his bio-electromagnetic feeling field surging his spine. He felt y'all past history matters a smattering turning black'g'round into one indivisible unified black mirror seas field energy out in a y eye potential merely a peering at it. Ah that field of you now out in her'eyez z z. Elevation of the situation. It's a beautiful thang he felt. Then in word thoughts came vomiting out from the blood in his heart and electric synapse of a peh'ss'y whole body burning wounded knee.

"So we all in turning churning burning around that race have that option at any time of realizing finding ourself completely free," he offered looking up from the drawing. A b'ng c'ng still in the first place if so desired. But a being now of a b'lack'ness instilled with intent to be a gain of ignoring complete d"ark'ness now to be perceived awakening in word captivity . . . literally a b c's of a b'ng c'ng in the in word race by ignoring of it in'visibility. Or now turning out into k'no no no'wing a be'am'ing from that still centrality in a b'ng c'ng of it . . . which is in the ending the same positive polarity of anybody appearing of it a second or two. Mirrored in word memory of a b'ng c'ng in the first place. Now that same positive of a b'ng c'ng mirrored turning any k'now'ing out of it as though in negativity. A negation of turning away out of it from now k'now'ing a denial of it with out a're'y'al'eye'zing merely a peering it of a b'ng c'ng still it. In these thoughts he found himself now k'no'wing it positively as a dialectic debate between a peering it or it appearing in any words informing it. Feeling the heat of her naked body touching his Mor now kept talking.

"That same indivisible immortality of a b'ng c'ng in the first place mirrored as though out now turning around positively k'no no no'wing it negatively. And working hard at it eve're'y way of eve're'y day. Hard at k'nowing of it. A pairing of it by a being y'all or any mere mind mirroring in word reflection of it as thoughtsz of a memory of it a're'y'flecting y'all na now . . . as though a being y'all in na'me alone . . . we all turning into or out of the one way race of playing out our mirrored role of a being anybody as thoughts'za . . ."

"Az's'eX's ting in that race of man with or without a womb as mind. Or . . . or . . . or y. Me or you a memory of a y'll y'all still indivisible. A yo yo yod iota within word as first su'personic singular present presence. Or you now out of it. A y'or you negated now out a second or two still a b'ng c'ng in the first place one singing silent singular su'personic person duplicating in t'word a twis'ting black'g'round a mere mirrored in word duplicity . . . a y'or you as'ex y'all." She leaned over to touch his lips then laughed. Sliding off the bed she'e na walked away laughing.

"Moving around ignoring or a k'no no no'wing out of it as means of generating your gig. Playing any role still a being of indivisible in'visibility . . . same a b'ng c'ng in the first place . . . same polarity . . . a re'y'pulsion propulsion . . . Cain't go turning back to a black'n'ess of a being same polarity. But can fall as'z z z'leep black'g'round in completing a dhi ark periodically as cycles within cycles. Naturally repulsed from crossing back over that event horizon. The event of appearing out in word by crossing some imaginary line between indefinite invisibility of a b'ng c'ng and the definite defined article appearing in the word a whorl'dhi'ing of anybody y'll d'na. A b'ng c'ng now out as'king of it a k'no'wing anybody anythin'king of it etc.. Any role of it appearing now in k'now'ing out a not'me mode. Appearing by denying. Dhi na'eye'ing out in that aska's mic eye of eve're'y body a're'y'dhi'a'ting it as'z'any thoth'tsz of it projecting in forma'sz sound wayeves of her'e y"e'z'z z'ion 'eve'nt of eve're'y'body . . ." Mor now reached out for her touch. She stretched the snake of her spine turning back to him with a scary smile. He turned his gaze back to the drawing feeling a tad queasy. He felt another wayeve of the dialectic debate tearing thru. . . that option of a're'y'all'eye'zing y that I am in'visibility only appearing in a y'll. A b'ng c'ng of any eyez z z'a be'am'ing as int'word a twis'ting of it in two appearing a pairing y'll d'na . . . denial . . . that alter'native then always remains . . . alternating he now mused . . . . that means awareness of a being still in the first place completely indivisible in'visibility a're'y'mean means veritably in a wordfreedom untouched untapped. Oh my gosh. Oh my living gosh. Just considering the possibility of a're'y'al'eye'zing that potential for anybody picking up on a being still that. Awareness of it as'ka's mic being takes me back to black. Black to that unified status overstanding any understanding of that. Of a b'ng c'ng now out in a black body of a supersonic invisibility. A prior'y to awakening in ignorance of it projecting as'z'any thoth'tsz of that denial. Now a black'g'round of a k'nowing out of it a b'ng c'ng as though under that delivery truck. Which weighs some tonnage with the gravity of death. That means k'nowing now how. How that I am appearing merely as in word thoughts of imagining myself still playing a role. A roll in that race of it appearing out in her'eye of eve're'y'body. A role that takes on any in word life of its own reinforced by a ka's mic consensus of billions. Billions also playing theirs now turning in the same race. A channel of it as'k'no no no'wing of a b'ng c'ng turning into any or eve re'y body. Y'all those years and tears jerkin and joltin' playing a mere in word role still a b'ng c'ng a peering it in the first place of that indivisible in'visibility. A ringing silence had settled over the room. Mor closed his eyes a moment imagining still seeing with out any in word recognition to echo a pingting as thoth'ts'za a god esse to be letter'all'y y'all imagined as'z'any particular supernatural or phonographic duplicating of that indivisible wordfree untouched awareness of it. He found himself still su'personically blind with out any in word means of turning around k'nowing of it anything. Then in that split second person of a bng c'ng now in an in word memory of me or you now k'nowing out of it he heard her voice.

" . . . from that indivisible awareness of anybody of a b'ng c'ng still it. In the beginning is a word. A's'word to letter'all'y y'all cut it up. Any beginning is as'word of thothtsz with intent of a b'ng c'ng cut out of it in na'me alone. A mirror cut out given dimension under the pressure of gee'sz us gravity weight of waiting on her'eye way'eve're'y'body will of it as'endings of any beginnings." She'e'na strectched out again on the high chair. Mor flipped the page to begin another drawing on it. Drawing on the wordfree untouched visual awareness of the right brain. Puranaha. The ancient timefree one. A b'ng c'ng on the right side of the brain.

"Of it now as'ka'riyate polarity by ending of that indivisible supernaturally as thoth'tsz superimposed in'visibility. The hOOka d'elOOka. A b'lack'ness now to be a gain. With a vigorous in word sounding of it out in her'eye'z za wayeve echoing a pingting there is a na y beginning or ending for perpetual indivisible wordfree awareness of any a na y'body of a b'ng c'ng merely a peering at it. Now y'all still you. Of'ten in a bi na Re'y mode of su'personic visual imagining of a b'ng c'ng in a y eye a peering it as'z"artist. Are'y'e'tis't'at seer in'sight see'ng it. In that'sz y you a're'y tis't'at one visual artist of a b'ng c'ng of it a seer, the one who sees, still remaining immutable." She moved in a series of what he thought of as tai chi movement. Still mesmerized by the sound of her voice he kept drawing her in the silent wayeve're'y"ez of the eye star'e'y'e'ing from above. Ove a b'ng c'ng merely a peering it now out. She'e'na had turned his attention back to black. Black into one indivisible invisibility awareness in that split second before crossing over that a's ex's ting in word eve'nt horizon. A black line between him a peering at the white background paper or it appearing across that paper. A b'ng c'ng of that then awakening in word appearing of it by the voice. The voice of a being still. The voice delivering complete silent visual awareness of a delivery truck now passing over mere inches above. Him instantly turning from a being blind into now instantaneous complete k'nowing that machinery hidden beneath the panel truck bed. Y'ears of in word conditioning compressed in mere seconds. An instantaneousness of it. A beginning in word informing of it out of a black'g'round body. From complete indivisible invisibility of a being still in the first place now a crossing over the imaginary line between merely a peering it or a peering at it. out into k'no no no'wing then the any"a na y'body. Anything in her'e'ye re'y'dhi'a'ting supersonically out in word of it there. He now turning into her'e'ye a k'now'ing of then. A being in word mirrored out in 3D. From su'personic blindness to a being of it able to recognize complex emotions playing over the faces of ma and pa. She'e'na a voice of it a y eye now mirroring that ask"ey"e in word revelation. Taking him black'g'round into one still silence in'visibility of it now merely in formed by a turning in word that black'g'round bliss a un't'word a twisting way'eveing strands of a sorrow as only that of a bliss denied fomented. Instantaneousness of that mirror awakhening now as'z'any touching of it a'sz z z'any instantaneous ask'ing of it a y eye now turning as'ka's of it a k'no'wing out of it a'wareness of a b'ng c'ng'g'ng gee's us gravity weight of any waiting for it.

A quantum gravity weight of a b'ng c'ng a gain waiting point period of any touching touch of it. It merely mirrored int'word appearing a pairing in opposition of a k'no no no'wing out of any denial of it in supersound vigorous wayeves of her'ey'e of eve"re'y body. Her'me'as'thoth'tsz zza'herhimit a y yod iota eye ya'm first su'personic person. Indivisible invisibility. He found it her'e me's it in a being still in the first place.

"Raising h'eL on the other hand, eL'ette'r'all y y'all as though duplicating in word in that twis'ting X's ting by that cross over eL function of fun'ny'a'ction left mode to right side, right hand. K'now'ing A.I. some funny pa'per ma'sz money honey. We all in that race of the ka's mic ka'mic kar'mic wheel of fortune fate faith family may turn into thinking . . . thinking and stinking of the seer'd awareness in recognized reconstituted mirrored artificial intelligence. Y'all now lost and found in turning into any k'now'ing ka's mic intell informing developmentality of artificial notions, arbitrary ex'perimental experential names as'word for slicing and dicing her'e eve re'y body into anything merely mirrored in word asz though appearing being here'e now. A being cee'ng in for'ma'sz z'apping that nameless indivisible invisibility of any a na y one now out awhile. A wily while of y'all appearing as'ex u'all. A's thoughtsz seen or heard supersonically echoing in any mirror mind or y memory, long or short term memory. Objectified with objective intention. The sacred as though weaponized." He saw the sound of here words'za'zz sublime rippling with the fluid grace of her movement. Their meaning came in that mean of vigorous high and low frequency sound waves playing high and low amplitudes across his bio-cog'na'tive field of view of you. A y eye echoing y'all now curving a black'g'round k'now'ing defining anybody or anything. She threw him some curves.

"Zapped in eL mode crossing over into A.I. by that simple twist of art appearing official. Fate y'll d'na denial favors official right handed right-wing politicals' need of authority to validate that ambiguous ambivalent arbitrary feeling of a being now out in k'now'ing it in na'me alone. A y eye being still in the first place now out of it. A y eye being cee'ng as'ex u'all by now k'now'ing it. K'now'ing eX's ting in existential angst of denial. How would you expect to feel appearing turning now around any k'nowing projection of a being any mere mirrored in word artificial intelligence of man'as mind. Or y memory in the first place? Expect existential angst and schitzy'ness mirroring in'visibility in g'ee's us now as'ex pressed by gravity of thoughtsz of waiting on death. Appearing disappearing out in'word memory consciousness. That con she us en ess'e. That being, that a ka'smic being in'for'ma'sz now then appearing artificially y'all may become paranoid of a being now as'ex'posed. X posing you as a being any other Y'z z z nobody. That paranoia of X'poser fueled by y'all appearing merely out now a short awhile. Dis'a'pairing in that blink of eye. A y eye a'peering out of it.

"Appearing gee's us under gravity weight of waiting for crushing death in jaws of any inward spell'ing. In word separation under spell of alphabeta provokes fear alienation and war. War're'y'na wills war as means of breaking attention out in word captivity. aY eye of a being cee'ng free standing. Free. Free standing now. Free freed freedom for eve're y body. Ay eye being cee'ng now out the black eye of her"ey eve're'y body.

"Captivity y'all merely mirrored freedom. Y'all a being cee'ng now k'now'ing freedom in denial as captivity. Out a's'ex's ting now k'nowing bliss in that denial as sorrow. That is the wily while of any in word now k'now'ing it. A being realized now k'now'ing it pervading sorrow with bliss. Invigorated by k'nowing silent aRe'y'all'it'y"az'za model may find themselves. Now out k'nowing peace. May realize still being that sheer bliss by a y eye being c'ee'ng in'sight of y'all. May pick up on a being now here black peh'esse'y w'hole eye of eve're'y body.A's'ex'perienced directly and periodically as'z z z'leep black into one still silent a y eye being in un'a'consciousness. A con she us en y esse to be. Anybody being in word captivity by k'now'ing a being y na now in the a pair'ent opposition of any ending or break or opening mouth releasing tale of woe in the complete loop'y role or roll of it. We all then turn around chasing tail. We be y'all turning into rolling them bones." She rolled her arms as though drawing in a cord attached to his gut. Each roll brought her steadily closer. "Baby first thing. Open mouth. A re'y lease of tale chased.

Chased till exhaustion without now k'now'ing y y'all along. K'now'ing it. A y eye being. As thoth'tsz projecting hOOka d'elOOka. Baby doan k'now k'now'ing it racing it a tale. Tale of two siddhis. One t'wis ting in t'wo rings of power. Power of her'e'y black eye peh'ess'e'y w'hole."

"Funny. Thought y'all said pussy hole." he replied then busted a gut with laughter. Laughing till tears he caught Margot Christina's wicked smile.

"In peace of'asz'za in a peaceful mind or y memory. A being completely complete reveals sheer folly in y'aLl asz'z'a function of fun'ny'a'ction all y y'all. eL mode ka's mic mirror age mirage. A supernatural a'peer'ance asz'za thoth'tsz. The hOOka of da lOOka. Thoth'tsz her'me'is it a y eye re'flected reflection as'z thoth'tsz. eL model still Mr. a'Re'yall'it'y y'all. Any and y'all in word image . . . semantic concept connection does not transpose eve're to the old one. Herhimit thoth'tsz of god esse to letter'all'y art being in word forma'tion. Supersonic supernatural superimposed a'peering out of ay eye from above. From a being ove el. eLove. Yo"d yo"d. Y'or y.

"Power means or mean polarity direction predisposed with intention of ignoring or projecting it out as'ex's ting. A re'y'projecting being y'll D'NA. A being in denial still a being that in the first place. Now turning around k'no'wing it out in any mere mirrored in word being. Y'or you out as'eX's ting. X et'ting. It is any y na now merely superimposed as thoth'tsz duplicating with the weight or pressure of gee's us now feeling in word being alone. A being in any mirror y na'me alone. You artist must appreciate that. By feeling that a being alone, seared now in loneliness and desperation without realizing y, why that feeling of a being alone in the first place from which we all turn away. Turn away from picking up on a being still it by at the same time now k'now'ing projecting it with intent of ignoring k'now'ing it. And thus project in word fear of it as'word cutting cleaving or separating in word being defined by feeling or fielding a being alone out now in a short while of a being still indivisible eve'n"a as'z appearing eve re'y body."

"Ain't nobody else? We be y'all turning into it alone? Sounds grim when you think about it." He found himself talking in spite of his visual absorption in a being c'eer see'ng in her"eyez z z as drawing her. Drawing on her sound in word wisdom. "I'm feeling you in my eye eve re'y'as'word cleaving my de'fences. Any in word dhi fences as thoth'tsz separating into any felt field of view, of you. Of you from me." Now Mor found himself baffled. Perplexed his visual awareness braided in multicolored dimensional twis'tings turning in formation against the mirror black'g'round of his first inward eye of eve re'y body. There was nothing but to follow the braided pattern in word. In a being be'am'ing out sound ways of eve re'y body mirrored in patterns now turning into one as'king of it a k'now'ing out another in formation. Now turning a b'lack'g'round a k'nowing in for'ma'sz'any thoth'tsz of it indivisible in'visibility appearing awhile in the uncanny specter of kali ma.

"Now for ma'sz z awhile. That me or you memory will pass away with the eros arrow of time. Now and then we all may roll by playing that any imaginary role back into a natural predominance of awareness of picking up moment by moment on a being still changeless motionless centrality in the ancient timeless visual awareness or alternating denying it lifetime by lifetime. Then we all may turn into realizing human is man 'as a spectrum of mind, a mere hue, still in'visibility y'or you now any color az's'ex'u'all. Or y. Old predjudices melt off in arrival and development of new X models, Model T to mo'del aRe'y. The Mr. a.re'y of it still a being invincible immutable heart of y'all'sz paradigms, purposeful positively negated possibilities of infinite potential."

"There you go again with this bewildering double entendre. My man as mind or why, now completely out of this mind. You blow my mind darlin' but thats'z why I love you. Still it's true my sanity lies in that return to a being in'visibility visual mode where in word thoughts filter off. My mind seems to haunt me enough in dreams that it pretty much leaves me alone otherwise. At least when a being in that awareness that I am drawing or painting. Why it becomes such a compulsion. Your words'za awaken some old memory before I had this face, or at least before being aware of having it," Mor replied, shifting his weight.

"War're'y'na fancies himself a catalyst for sweeping transformation. The painting, a way of eve will, her will now y'our will programmed to percolate over 33 centuries to capture, to captivate anyone now still turning out around k'nowing d'na'eye'll of a being now that eternal moment by momentum of time. Loop'y time turning endlessly ending or entering black into one beginning. Beginning by ending. Unda'lating that way of eve will as though revealing that indivisible in'visibility of awareness in sound ways of eve, her wayeves supersonically superimposed in pigments compacted for"ma's releasing aromatic waves in her'eyez z z now a virus. A nano technologically engineered self replicating air born virus. It is purely seduction of image imagined imagining infection in the body politic as bio-accoustic virus . . ."

"You are right now interfacing with his mind aren't you?" he asked, his heart racing. He felt his breath constrict with her mention of an air born virus. Glancing down, he caught a glint of light playing off the spiral binding of the sketch book. He flashed on the spiral virus wheel turning in her eyez z z eve"re'y intent back to black. Black indivisible a being in'visibility. Instilled with intent of seer seeing a gain of it in word recognition. Yet clearing out universal long term memory moment by irreversible moment. Y'all back to black. Black in'ka'now jetting through the pen in his fingertips. Drawing now is drawing on the state of a being y'all the great and terrible draw'ers he mused, turning around k'now'ing in'ka'now flowing out in that timeless fashion. Drawing in time for a being without time. Korner once asked how he could draw for so many hours. Mor knew the secret in drawing on a being in the first place that timeless being. Any passing time merely as thoughtsz he thought now k'nowing drawing now as the'n'a.

"In that I am partly of his imagining. My being as eve're'y body being an intentional product if not of his mind, the'e in word understanding mind, above as below that uber mensch, that mahimanaha great supersonic over mind. Overseer. Any human being merely that eve re'y hue, that color, that hue and cry slice of being anybody out in theory. In the or y of me or you reflected in me'm or y memory. Me . . . or . . . you. Mirrored in word mind . . . or y. Y'or you now free of a being as thoughtsz of it. A being in the first place mirrored as'z thoughtsz of it a being out in word. The seduction in her'eyez z z a y being be'am'ing on ma'sz mass level magnifies War're'y'na's viral catalyst working still with in mere mirrored in word awareness in mind or y, which, even eve now with her, as'z in her'eyez z z'ap'ping a mirror way of instantanous self replication could as it still does infect our global consciousness in ways of a eve're'y'body as'z bio-acoustic waves that can now be turned in word k'now'ing a being verbalized. Can and must be now k'now'n in word. Still, does not mean we all in turning into appearing disappearing into or out of it now, cannot talk about it, think about it, speculate about it debate it ad infinitum ad nauseum. That is what comes to my mind in my memory is a being still now eve're'y'body k'nowing of it. Eve're'y denial of it still one indivisible mere potential memory of me or you. You, the Darkness of that I am only now knowing out in word or a being without word by touch." She finished with her gaze melting hot into his. Now then Mor realized the seduction in her'eyez z z'i'on complete in wordsz' any potential of a being of any or eve re'y body.

"You. You or me? You are me. You are that in word mind or. . .y my thoughts of me or you . . . .my heart beat knocking on my me or you memory door." He found himself in wordsz slipping from his tongue before he thought about anything. Or any eve're'y thin'king of it. He felt waves of e or g motion egging him on as'z'a thin'king of it with a heart about to burst. He blinked back tears of sheer joy to refocus his mind waves rolling out into muscles focused by drawing on the wordfree untouched awareness on the right side of the brain.

"War're'y'na's catalyst operates on the same principal principle a re'y'all a're'y'dhi'a'ting in for'ma's z z zapping zapped electro magnetic supersonic waves generated by the pressure of quantum gravity of death at anOOna in that simple twist of fate, chance, destiny, supersonically broadcasting its self replication in that sound vigorous way out in her'eyez z z of eve're'y'body. She now could go out like the splash of a bot-wing weaponized cyber 'butter' fly. Making her'eye ways self-replicating infinite potential as sound wayeves permeating y'll D'NA. As'z z z acid dissolving entire pre'existing biocog'na'tive fields. . . a're'y'versing bi-polarity . . . turning attention black'g'round . . . a un consciousness un'twisting that whorl'd'ing of it y'll D'NA . . . black into indivisible wordfreedom awareness of a being . . . a being as thoth'tsz of it in for'ma'sz now out az's'ex'et'ting duplicating a b c's of a b'ng c'ng now by turning out a k'now'ing of it a be'aming one black'g'round of it in her"eyez z z of eve're'y body . . . a're'y'versing the a y eye arrow of time as'eX's'z'eros or complete cycles of time now reckoned around a fixed point of view of you, " she shrugged. "War're'y'na's role is destroyer of whorlds by unwinding in word a long term of it aska's mic memory. Long term memory or'is of a y eye a re'y'z z z'a turning back into one black peh'esse'y whole or'is out of which, by which and black into which y'all appear or disappear a while now b'lack instilling intent to be a gain by ignoring it a being completion completely still in the first place.

"A gee'sz us gravity weighting peh're'y'ssure in waiting to die now turning a b'lack'g'round into a k'no'wing of any waiting as int'word a twis'ting in two yet that indivisible invisibility supersonically as'z'any thoth'tsz of it appearing a pairing a gain with a loss out in a word as though born to death. Drawing y'all black in a b'ng c'ng still in the first place rather than out as'ex'eting. Duplicating out of it a wayeve as'eX'hodos. The wayeve out now k'now'ing anything or anybody. A's'eX that unknown now una, now a known a re;y of'ten bi na re'y re'y'dhi'a'ting now a still complete being with intent of turning around k'now'ing lack. A being still in the first place competely complete completion. No ma'sz with out. No ma'sz'ex." She gave with a wicked smile. Mor felt the black'g'round mirror see'ng'asz z z'aturning int'word a twisting in two appearing a pairing. Felt himself one falling as though in two a black'g'round turning we all into that karmic ka'mic wheel churning supersonically in word out as thothtsz of it in for'ma'sz in her'eyez z z'a now k'nowing of it any or eve're'y body.

"Black to the beginning of any ending of the complete unbroken circle of creation a bi-polarity with now k'no'wing of it as'z'any thoth'tsz of it int'word a twisting in two ends of a b'ng c'ng in a beginning by any en'n n n'ding. The pressure of waiting between bi-polarity constitutes quantum gravity. The weight of it as'ka's a kurving a beginning now out turning a black'g'round int'words a k'now'ing of it as'z' another ending. Means of it appearing in a word. BANG BANG BANG." She mocked firing an invisible pistol. Blowing the smoke his way. "A being of awareness at aten'cion as'z'any point of you of y na now. A be'gaining gravity weight pressure of intent of any mirrored mirage y na y'all now. That gravity of that gee'sz us in that weight peh'ss'y whole pressure of a y eye of a b'ng c'ng now potential intentional waiting must turn y'all out of or back into black indivisible in'visibility.

"From weighting to die into one waiting to be mirrored as though born. In that waiting may be found a b'ng c'ng in a wordfreedom standing indivisible in'visibility. Mirrored supernaturally as thoth'tsz of a hOOka d'elOOka. Ka's means of cause by ignoring or projecting as thoth'tsz of a being completely full fullness. Now turning fullness black'g'round a lack instilling intent to be a gain of it. In a b c's now as thoth'tsz of a b'ng c'ng a k'no'wing a b'ng c'ng lacking the waiting for fulfillment arises. That waiting is weight of the gravity of anybody y'll D'NA. A being now as thoth'tsz of it in memory out k'no'wing that wily while of denial."

"The weight of waiting for fulfillment. Y'all the wily while still completely full. What a hoot." Mor felt his defenses melt away as he realized in her'eyez z z' as ka's eve're'y black'g'round singular body.

"Y'all back into one sacred black power of a peh'esse'y w'hole gee's us Kryst. A b'ng c'ng still in the first place that singular indivisble in'visibility of any individual referred in first person su'personic present a'ten'se superimposed on and on and on still a'sz that in a wordfreedom awareness that I am is is. That awareness that I am now instilled with intent in her'eyez z z'azz eve're'y body of a b'ng c'ng in word now as'z turning a black'g'round now as'king of it a k'no'wing out anybody. That a b'ng c'ng now a's ka's mic ka'mic ka's all'y y'all memory function of fun'ny'a'ction. A ka'shic memory of a b'ng c'ng now of'ten binary alternating a'ten c'ion of an y or y na gaining mirror gravity of y'all in the open end waiting for the end of y'all a being grinning gaining letter all'y y'all a'peering it out in word based memory of a being still in the first place. In other words, realizing that that I am is is we all appear turning a black into a b'ng c'ng in word appearing of it now with out turning around k'now'ing disappearing. Y'all turning into X per I en'c'ing disappearing is merely asz in word thoughtsz of a y eye of a b'ng c'ng a peering it out as'eX's ting. X'et'ting duplicating in formation as in word thoth'tsz of a b'ng c'ng still y'all in the first place indivisible in'visibility. Y'or y'all now realized as the mirror'd mirror age mirage in word idea of a b'ng c'ng out X's ting." Christina swiveled the seat with outstretched legs turning a full 360 degrees. The e motion of a b'ng c'ng in her'eyez z z captivated him in gee'sz us motion'all'y hues of man'as mind or y'all streaming back in color wayeve're'y trails. In her'eye on egg's stance drew him into her'eyez z z'azz a womb. Man'as mind or y'all a being now turning out of a black'g'round in word a k'no'wing any or eve're'y body.

"On hearing y'all that, I am for a moment finding myself lost, disappeared into the sheer sight of you. It's now as though having no past or future awareness. Only now stretching out for'ever'ey a being artist drawn into awareness of a being that c'eer see'ng in sight now turning as'k'nowing drawing you," Mor added by throwing up his hands as if expecting the pen to continue drawing on its own. It merely dropped with a PLOP onto the paper. "Okay, maybe I got a little carried away. But in that, I am actually feeling your words, the sublime sound waves of them echoing off your vocal chords vibrating my memory in her'eyez z z' in word hearing field of view of you or my projecting az's'ex per I mental memory of you."

"That me or you mem'or'y moment now may be az's'extended into h"our e'turn'ity as'king of it a no longer denying h'our a being indivisible in'visibility of now appearing disappearing or now turning that black'g'round with intent into k'nowing a gain of another moment. Now is turning out k'no'wing a long long looonng while," Christina replied with that sly scary smile.

"You are a mischievious little thang. Is there any other kind of moment? Now it seems that I am a b'ng c'ng is is merely as thoughtsz of a b c's in the middle of any big or little thing. It's only seeming as'z too pass as thoughts'z'in me or you now turning around k'nowing any or eve re'y thin king of it. Maybe we all turn into or out of that black'g'round stopping now for the moment as thoughtsz of turning a gain of it out around a k'no'wing denial y'll D'NA az's eX's ting. In formation now a peering it out awhile of a y eye of a b'ng c'ng in the first place. That interlude naturally extends now to infinity. In that now we all would or could stop as though picking up on any turning into a k'no no no'wing out of it. Denying what or why by a y eye of a b'ng c'ng still y'sz z z'apping across in War're'y'n'a's eyez z z' eve"n't horus zion line with electric fire in her'eye of eve"re'y bodhi bridging past now turning a k'no'wing out the future with out weight of waiting in her"eyez z z eve will. In her'eyeve'll ending esse to be with G'ee'sz us."

"That ain't y'all bad as'z Artman. Y you're you catching on to Y speak. Or it a being in the first place catching on to a y eye of a b'ng c'ng still you." she offered moving in close to kiss his lips. As she backed away he caught the glint of a gold necklace hung with tiny charms dancing above her chest.

"I see y'all walking around all nekid, I could start thinking about it az'sex. Y'or me or y thinking as'ex y'all." Mor chuckling reached again for the spiral sketchbook and pen he'd tossed on the bed stand. The words, his words, seemed coming from an in wordfreedom. A reflection of her mind pervading his like broad daylight pervading and disappearing the frail narrow beam of a flashlight. He uncapped the pen, putting the tip on his tongue. Saliva flowed with black ink when he touched the paper. "The"or'etically how long to infinity in a y eye of a b'ng c'ng anybody see'ng in back to black mirrors? Me a seer see'ng seen supernaturally as thoth'tsz in your eyes seeing me. Super'nature of a ping'ting . . ." Wham. It hit Mor like a fist laid upside his head. The whole scheme. A plan et h'earth a pingting of it.

"Y'all just as well feeling it." she held his gaze till her"eey'e'sz'za blazed he realized by merely reflecting it. War're'y'na'szz bioaccoustic self replicating virus generated in her"eyez z z a y'or y na dialectic. In a flash. A's'ka y'sz'za ka's mic synapse zapped his tower of ba'b'y'el. His in word supersonic electromagnetic torus field of view of you yod iota pole ar're'y radiating a black'g'round reabsorbed any in word imagining of the Dark'ness back to a black'g'round as'king of it y that free standing of a b'ng c'ng in the first place indivisible in'visibility a peering it out mirroring supernaturally as thoth'tsz. Free. Standing. A y her'him'it her'me'asz'za it. A y potential eyez z z in sight of eve're'y body.

"The instantaneousness of a b'ng c'ng in sight of a peering it may be found out opening a y eye of anybody. A still presence in the first person in the first place now a're'y'all a'peering it out of it. Now appearing of it merely mirrored in word mirror see'as y'all as'ka'ma'ing a black'g'round as'ka's'zinging any a na y now y'all k'no'wing of it supersonically a be'am'ing out of it in her'eyez z z'azz any or eve're'y body. Supernaturally superimposed as'z'any thoth'tsz of it. That indivisible black'g'round of a now a k'no'wing out of it a b'lack' se'e'as'on mirroring a gain of a being still in the first place. Awareness of it. A ware now? To be a b'lack' body instilled with intent to be a gain of it. Now to be a be'am'ing a k'no'wing out asz'z z'a any thoth'tsz of appearance as a mirage. Mirror'age thoughtsz infor'ma'sz mass a y eyez z z z' a peering it out in word. A potential of a b'ng c'ng now as'king of it y'or y na. A're'y'flected in word'as'z y'all playing out in her'eyez z z'a ma'tricks in sound vigorous tricky wayeves of mind. Or y y'all the bitch of it now turning a black'g'round k'no no no'wing out of it any or eve're'y'body as thoth'tsz of putting it out there in word. As thoth'tsz of making anybody appear merely in word in the or y. In the or y a ka's mic memory of a positive negation of it now with instilled with intent of finding a completion in any complete k'no no no'wing any limitation of it. Anybody still in her'eyez z z a'peering it out as'king of it y now a k'now'ing turning into aw'h'ile of eve"re'y bodhi. Anybody now k'nowing anything merely in the or y of memory. Awareness of a being still in the first place merely supernaturally supersonically superimposed'a as'z'za thoth'tsz of it. A Great Go'a'd esse to be perceived letter'all'y y'all art a b c's of a b'ng c'ng a'peering it out in word formation.

A'sz'any thoth'tsz of a being still in the first place indivisible in'visibility." Words'z'a'zz el ignited light wayeves of it in her'eyez z z zap'ping of that eve're'y body. A're'y e black mirror see'nas anybody a're'ye"flecting as'ex'peh'ka'trum. A she'er luminous wayeve 're'ye a're'ye'dhi'a'ting el esse to be perceived in wayeves of fun'ny'action of her'eyez z zazz'a trickery. It blew his mind into the black'g'round of it still a peering it out awak'h'ening a'ten. A bi'na're'ye. A h"OO"ka del"OO"ka. Any information of it. Merely supernaturally as'zz'any thoth'tsz of it superimposed. In me or you. Out of it as'ex y'all he flashed with a grin.

"That'z any mirrored y na y'all now deceitful means of a positive negation of it by a y eye a're'y'all a'k'urving a b'lack'g'round intent of now k'no no no'wing y'all out in word a 'gain'. Out in formation as mere mirrored thothtsz of it y'll d'na. A denial int'word a twis'ting supernaturally in formation of its indivisible in'visibility of anybody merely a'peering it out in awhile. Appearing by the sheer wiles of any time now k'now'ing out of it awhile of kali'ma'sz'ex"et'ting y'or thoth'tsz of it . . . " she paused to stretch swiveling around to meet his drawing in her gaze. She'e'na seemed to project a series of flashes that sailed past his periphery. It was as though in her'eyez z z awareness engulfed him in sound waves that then echoed back in word off his vocal cords.

"A're'Y'e'a'ten. A's thoth'tsz first principal principle of a're'y"e dhi'a'ting out of a y eye to perceive in word in'formation of a b'ng c'ng in the first place still that indivisible in'visibilty of first su'personic person singular presence. Or enough reason as t'word a twis't'at that eye of I am is is . . .or something to that tat effect.". . .The dialectic disappeared him yet in that blink of a y eye a're'y'all a peered it out him of that in her"eyez z z. In her' black eyez z z of a b'ng c'ng a'sz'ka'ma'ing a ka's mic memory black'g'round turning into or out of eve're'y body. The wayeves that flashed past now seemed to flow black into her"ey'ez z z'a drawing out of it thru his mind's eye following neuronic response y'all the way to the tips of his fingers. He played in her"e'yez z z'a playing it. A b'lack'g'round now supersonic supernatural indivisible in'visibility of anybody superimposed as a gain of a bi na re'y body or still her"eye a peering it of any or eve"re'y body. Any or eve re y body a peering it out from above. Ove a b'ng c'ng in a y eye of a herhimit her'me's'it'asz'thoth'tsz of a free standing still in the first place. On the one hand polarity. From the other held above a're'ye"dhi'an'c'ng to perceive any mirror memory. In word memory of a being a herhimit still in the first place.Indivisible invisibility of a being a peering it out in an"eye of anybody. Or her'eye a peering it above. Ove a being eve're'y body.

Radiating Y'all asz'za matter'sz'za energy goaded in word in a being art'is't'at now a k'nowing out letter'all'y y'all in word. Her"eyez z z'ion in a line wordfreedom drawing on untouched awareness of a b'ng c'ng it. In her'eyez z z' a vigor re'sounded in formation as thoth'tsz of it. As'z'any thoth'tsz of a long a'go go'a'd esse to be found yet a freestanding su'personic bliss. Awareness of a being y'all her'me'as'thoth'tsz of herhimit center caring carrier ccc wayeve function. A wayeve function of fun'ny'a'ction is is ay e'ye"star'e y"e'a with on one hand a polarity of potential positive negativity. On the other y'all as'ex're'y e star'e y"e of a y eye a'peering it out as'ex's ting of it in any complete d'ark'n'ess'e. A complete role playing out now turning a black'g'round as'king of it a k'now'ing eve're'y or anybody.

A being of awareness still now he turned int'word a twis'ting in two appearing a pairing a k'now'ing out of it a's ex's ting. Finding himself a being still in the first place that individual or that indivisible in'visibility of anybody merely a peering it. Mor realized he radiated now a black'g'round instilled with intent of turning out a k'no'wing a gain of anything thru her"eyez z z'a a b c's of a b'ng c'ng supersonically supernaturally as thoth'tsz of any or eve're'y body. Aware of a'peering it out of a'na y eye still awareness of a b'ng c'ng that indivisible invisibility a're'y'fracting now in that black mirror seas a k'nowing out of it a singing su'personic person. A freestanding still in the first place. Holding a polarity in one left hand. Now as'ka'sing a'na y eye opening with intention of a b'ng c'ng awak'h'en'ing a'ten. At aten'cion a bi na re'ye beam'ing out in word anybody anythin'king etc.. Now a k'nowing of it supernaturally as'z'any thoth'tsz of a b'ng c'ng in any or eve're'y body. Then it's now about k'now'ing freedom baby he mused. Freedom now. Freedom forever. Freedom of a're'y'all'eye'zing'ing now any k'no no no'wing out of it anybody. In'divisibility now k'now'ing of it in for'ma'asz ignoring still a b'ng c'ng that as'z'any thothtsz of it projecting out in her"eye of eve're'y body. A y eye a peering it from above. Ove a b'ng c'ee'ng. A freestanding of a b'ng c'ng eye of the herhimit. Y'all turning a black'g'round of it. A y eye of a being still c'ng in the first place. Indivisible in'visibility of any individual.

"That'sz'za y nothing or anything of a being in her'e'y'e a peering it out still in eve're'y affect or effect of it." She'e'na now moved like fluid finding interstices in free space. A free flowing electromagnetic field feeling out. Touching on any touch of it. The'n merely disappearing black'g'round into a y eye of you're'ye'al'ity as'king of it. A k'no'wing felt feelings field of view of you of y out as'ex'y'all now k'no no no'wing of it denying itself. Out in her"e'yez z z a black'g'round echoing touching touch of it a un'touchability. Of it supersonically or phonographically a b c's in word as'k'no'wn out of it now any appearing of it information. A still of it merely mirrored awhile in the first place.

Now he found himself indivisible in'visibility of drawing the fluid contours of the figure 8. A legged. Armed. Handed. A seer of a hand moving with the eye of the seer. Denying out of her"e'yez z z'azz' anybody etc. in'visibility still asz'any thoth'tsz of a god esse. A to be c'ng letter'all'y y'all a y eye out of it supernaturally as'ex's ting in any in word memory in'formation of it. Still. A're'y'e'all'it'y y'all as'king of it y ways of eve a're'y"e a being still any a na y eye of y'all merely a peering it out of it in any word. As'z'any unt'word man'ner of it as'ex y'all he mused.

Now he watched his hand executing a rapid flurry as'ex's. X's now by the hundreds. Patterning. A's'matter'ing. A shading of contours of thigh hip or nipple disappearing in light or shade patterns. As'z'ex's. Or a're'y'e'dhi'a'ting a perceived black'g'round by a na y eye'll of a y of herhimit'asz yod or y you a're"y still free standing in the first place shin'ning out in her'e'ye'zz'a'pp'ing now a corrosive breath out into her'e'ye'al black mirror seas. Supernaturally y'all as thoth'tsz reflects in word now around any k'no'wing of it in theory, in the or y of me or you. Me or you a's a kurving or occurring of a b'ng c'ng by a ka's mic memory reflection of it in her"eye will, her eve"re' y way of caring carrier wayeve will of intent, of eny urge, her'eyez z z'i'on energy. Eve'll a b'ng c'ng now appearing of it on purpose. Kali ma'sz purpose of eve will. A mission of a'd"mission. Or sub'mission. Y, y'all y you're you or me, me or you still invisible indivisibility now mirror'all'y y'all appearing as'z'any thoth'tsz'a'f'it'ting in word in that indivisible love with intent of a pairing a twis'ting in two a singular awareness of a being c'ee'ng now in me or you as'king of it y a k'no'wn as thoth'tsz of it in'ka's mic memory." Christina continued turning her"e'ye'of'eve're'y"e body in fluid motion as though drawing him in her"e motion of his drawing out of her'e'y'ez z z'i'on now.

"With y'all that feelin' it. Feeling in a wordfreedom of it. Feeling fielding LOVE SUPREMO It's pouring out of you like a wildcat Texas gusher." Mor's inner eye as'ka's mic con she us en ess'e now to be in her'ey'ez z z'i'on a'mirror'age. Aquarius Lion. A'zSphinx of it. A dhi'ev'e'ouring those unwilling or unable to a're'y'e solve the a'riddle. A re'y"e'd'nile of man'as opposite a'li'e'ye'on a polarity of supernatural memory a'ten 'cion now a bi'na're'y'e'sz'any thoth'tsz of eve"re'y bodhi. A'sz'z'a'h"OO"ka de'l"OO"ka. A're'ye a peering it out a be"am'ing. Jah o'y light igniting on the other hand. Jah sus liberation in a wordfreedom awareness el'igh'ni'ting a playing out of it any roles of d"ark'n'ess'eas'z z z'apping rock'n'roll electric synapse as'z'any thoth'tsz of it in her'e'ye her'ring out as'ex"press'uring gee's us in sound wayeves through immaculate conception imagination mirror seas potential black K'reye'stos, Jah sus Krystos, in front, behind, to the right, to the left, above, below, and PROJECTING y'all around. Projecting it now a k'no'wing it in denial of it."

Mor found himself in word melting away into one indivisible awareness of a're'y'e b'ng c'ng a peering it out awhile of now k'no'wing that ka's mic being. Then in that proverbial powerful blink of eye of it in her'e'ye of eve re'y body appearing a pairing in two hands the polarity of positive negation of that indivisible in'visibility. Y'all as'eX pressed under gravity of Gee'sz us in the eve're'y'e of a b'ng c'ng in the word a're'ye'flecting black Kryst quantum mirror see'n'as a body y'all around. A bi b'el. A b"OO"ka d'el"OO"ka. A Go'a'd esse to perceive in word function of fun'ny'a'c'tion. Of'ten a bi na'r'eye'sz body of Kryst ka'reye'zee of t'h'at mercy. The sublime profundity of the dialectic revealed the presence at'a'ten'cion gods of the good old a'nu days'z'za. The go'a'd esse to perceive letter'all'y y'all at a'ten"cion c'ng out bi na re'ye in word in'formation of it.

Odin days of war in art being man'as d'na'tural neurosis of appearing by denial of a being still in the first place that invinciple indivisible herhimit her'me's of it now a k'nowing ka's mic memory. A'sz'za thoth'tsz of it in her'me's su'personic singing silence of a b'ng c'ng in any eye indivisible in the first place in'visibility. Now as turning a black'g'round as'king of it y a k'now'ing one in t'wo t'wis'ting as'ex'et'ting duplicating duplicity. A bi na'rey'e body. A loop'y role to play in one positive direction out black'g'round negation of any now k'no'wing it. Out of it in awhile turning a black'g'round that ma're'y'e g'round. Into or out of it. Supernaturally as thoth'tsz of appearing superimposed a peering it into or out of it. It a being still motionless freestanding in the first place. A y eye star'e'y'e. We all a race turning black'g'round eve're'y'e body now a k'no'wing out of it. Projecting it y'all around by mere mirrored eye of a b'ng c'ng a peering it out supernaturally as thoth'tsz of a being still in the first place. Merely mirrored out. Superimposed in word.

Then wammobammo y'all turn 180 back to black still a b'ng c'ng in a wily while of pow pow power as'z any peh'esse'y w'hole'y a y as'exu'all. That peh'ssy cycle within the'e turn'y'all roll. That as'ka'sing ka'ma'ing a black'g'round any twenty-four h'our in da'y'eye of it. A y as'ex per eye in cee'ing turning aska's mic black'g'round now k'nowing out in her'eyez z z a singular eve're'y'e body. Any god esse to be in word as thoth'tsz of it letter'all'y y'all art of a b'ng c'ng out of it. Out in word formation supernaturally superimposed as thoth'tsz of it or a y eye herhimit. Yo yo yod iota first su'personic singular power of mouth o'si'ris or'ga'i'n of a sound presence. A b'ng c'ng in this still now supersonic supernatural superimposed out in word as that. Anybody awareness of a being he mused with a profound shudder. Turning back to black'g'round now k'nowing that awareness of a being before he k'new any in word k'nowing of a y eye b'ng c'ng in word other y'sz z z. The irony of any life beginning under tons of iron rolling over suspended on rubber encased air. The mere idea of beginning anybody by es'ending's of a being by a na re'y body a'r'e'y'e'diating a y eye ignoring still be'am'ing a b'ng c'ng in the first place brought a chuckle. There in the're'ye he found himself now a being still indivisible invisibility. A being still in the first place. Before in formed as thoughtsz of a being cee'ng born out in name alone. He seemed to be slipping loose of the noose. The self k'no no no'wing chains of thoughtsz of in word captivity broke up on the assure'y'e'ness of her'eye a'peering it out wielding the dialectic.

"Eve'll play a trickery. She'ena the corrosive breath of life. The ef'ang that tears apart any wily while as'ka ma'ing before her"eyez z z of eve're'y'ebody. In a being be"am'ing asz thoth'tsz in a're'y'e"flecting a're'y'e"flection of that a peering it out of invisibility. A being in the first place perpetually pervasive awareness of right visual 'old' timeless wordfreedom brain. A being now viraly transmitted out as'z z zsound wayeves means dissolution of any appearing out of it. We all may turn black'g'round any time in a y eye b'ng c'ng still in the first place indivisible in'visibility. Now a na y k'now'ing a're'y'all of a b'ng c'ng before any falling off a'ledged k'now a k'no'wing out letter'all'y y'all understanding the spelling of a b c's in word captivity.

"A long time coming peh'esse'y w'hole power invigorating now vigorous as'king of it 'y eye a k'no'wing going black'g'round out of a y eye as'ex et'ting duplicating by a peering it from her"eyez z z'a gam'ma way'eves. That in her'eyez z z eve're'y'e ways predominently indivisible in'visibility we all could turn in the blink of eye into or out of that black'g'round. That black'g'round of a Ma're'y g'round the race of the wheel of fortune or mis'sed fortune of a singular bliss. Bliss denied as means or pow pow power turning out in'visibility merely mirrored in word as sorrow right now a b'lack'g'round any k'no'wing it. Felt feeling any field of view of you of a y eye a peering it out now as'king of it y a k'no'wing it defined in word. A b c's of a b'ng c'ng it in word forma'tion. In her'eye of eve"re'y bodhi of a b c's letter'all'y y'all along merely mirrored in word formation. A b'ng c'ng in a black eyez z z of eve're'y'e body before beginning a peering it out in a word." Mor definitely felt the see'ng of a b'ng in her'ey'ez z zap'ping ting of it.

"BANG. BANG. BANG. SHE BANG. She'e'na a black eye a peering it out of eve're'y body instilled with intent of intentionally ignoring a b'ng c'ng still full in the first place. Fully complete d"ark'n'esse. Now to be turning a black'g'round echoing a k'nowing lack of it. Necessitating a be g'ain'ing of it. Y'all a'peering it out a're' a y eye of a b'ng c'ng a cunning deceitful craft. A wordship of a b'ng c'ng merely mirrored as mirage. Mirror age's'ex planed. A complete d"ark'ness of now turning black'g'round any role flattened out as'ex pressed peh'r esse dhi to be perceived as'z'za peh'ages of herhimit eye'star'eye b"OO"ka." The blacks of her eyez z z as'ex'panded turning y'all black'g'round till he blinked light into his a'peering it out of it.

"A y eye potential of any a peering it out. Now as'king of it y a k'no'wing out of it int'word a twis'ting in two appearing a pairing in me or you with in'ka's ka'smic memory. Drawing with in'k"as letter'all'y y'all in word. Then still now a k'no'wing out of it that indivisible invisibility. Now a y eye a peering it out in word w'ay of intending funny money action function of any mere y na black mirrored a y eye POTENTIAL now. In other words, gangster of love, War're'y'na's virus turns time in a're"y verse. A e'star'e'y'e of a peering it out a be"am"ing lack by turning now in two timing a k'no'wing of it a b'lack'g' round. As'king of it a y eye a peering it freestanding with a polarity on hand as'z'za herhimit. A polarity as'z' any a'ten bi'na're'ye a're'y'dhi'a'ting bi mere a'peering it out in word awhile, a tricky busi"ness in the b'link'ing of a y eye to perceive a deceit of any appearing of it to begin with. A y eye of a b'ng c'ng in word, back to black within a word that eye of I am is is a be"am"ing it. A be'am'ing it out now as'ka's of a k'no"w'ing denial of it. It a b'ng c'ng still in the first place."

She gave him a look of longing for her flesh. Flesh to be touched merely with the eye. The sorcerer at the source of him realized any touch of her'eyez z z meant instant death. But then he always was a sucker for it. Death that is. Still appearing of it disappearing merely a peering it.

"I gotta tell Kwasanda before we all turn black." Mor cracked himself up despite or because of the gravity of her words. The grave'ity of them pouring over the in word sadness of denying it. A tradjic mad'jic irony in iron age awareness. With that a b'ng c'ng funny awhile at the same time feeling a sharp pang of sadness. Now he was a k'nowing no home beyond awareness in a wordfreedom of a b'ng c'ng still in the first place. Finding himself a mean means of a meaning'ful of the bittersweet life we all turn out or into finding y'll d'na denying a bliss. A sweet sorrow blissfully denying it. We all turning it supersonically racing in't'word a 'twis'ting in two appearing a pairing of it in memory of me or you a peering it out of singular eyez z z.

If that iron irony don't crack y'all upside on the heayd. Try falling in love with two women, he mused. One love must be one woman. Or y na? One man as a mind with or without a womb. G'or'D. Still. He found the Professor in words as'z z zapping az'sound way'eves combing thru the tangle of him. Dark Mor'sz'z as'z'any thoth'tsz of it letter'all'y y'all imagined. Imaginary image of it. It now a k'now'ing denial of it as'z'any thothtsz'za forma'sz a ma'ss of quivering blood and guts'za. Still in her'eyes'z z z'apped by de"sire. Pa's szion of di"vine.

"War're'y'na's scheme seems to offer a magnificent adjustment for y'all man'as'z'za'yeyez z z of mind'kind. Ore'y'e. A re'y'eye verse y'all of a na e'ye star'e'y"e freestanding of a b'ng c'ng holding polarity in a closed e'left h'and. A're'ye e'light on the other hand open. A el'ef'ta e'ye star'e'ye'in'g gee'sz us still in the first place of her'me'as'z'za herhimit. A being still in the first place. Indivisible in'visibility of y'all. Supernatural supersonic uni'verse of it superimposed as'z'za'thoth'tsz. Of a h"OO"ka de'l"OO"ka's'zz'a letter'all'y y'all a'peering it out merely mirrored appearing of it in word.

"But do you put new wine in old skins? Maybe then on the other hand he is only accelerating the inevitable. Awaken a b'ng c'ng merely a peering it. Awareness of a b'ng c'ng in a wordfreedom. A b'ng c'ng still in the first place. Pa'roo'ma. PARAMASAUMYA. Same supreme a y eye a peering it out now as'king of it y a k'no'wing any atom'mic a y b'ng c'ng before you. Merely mirrored in any name y'all die supernaturally as'z'za thoth'tsz of a God'esse to be letter'all'y y'all art b'ng c'ng in a word a're'ye born to death. In the a y"eye of any in word beholder. Or while dying," she added, taking a seat back on the high chair. He saw in her 'eye now a field of wayeves. Luminous quivering fibers of awareness in formation. Awareness of a being still in the first place despite any in word a're'y'e y'all information appearing out of it.

"Call it Jah sus. Realizing Jah liberates. Liberates now in a wordfreedom eve'na'sz'za k'no no no'wing it in word. Liberates eve'na as in a denial of it. Picking up on a b'ng c'ng still that first su'personic person present singular singularity of that awareness that eye of I am is is liberation from any a na y y'all merely a'peering it out in word turning into or out of any sit'uation of it appearing. A b'ng c'ng still a freestanding. We all are still in a y eye a peering it out in that turning neuronically hard wired and fired to el"OO"ka'ing only as thoughtsz of it appearing in word. A y eye now as'z'ex'et'ting duplicating in a duplicity of me or you in memory." He saw in her"e'y'e circular circumstantial circumpherential appearance of a'peering it out a luminous egg's ting. Appearing now as'king of it a y eye k'no'wing a're'y'e'all int'word a twis'ting in two appearing a pairing in'formation of a figure 8. A're"y'e'all in'finity. The appearing of it asz'za h"OO"'ka de'l"OO"ka. One'c'ng t'was a'ten. A bi na re'ye a're'ye"dhi'a'ting now as k'no'wing out of it the'n. Then he found his hand tracing the figure 8 back into a twis'ting torus torso. Legs spread. Bent at the k'nee. Head falling on chest. Lifting of it she'e'na spoke. Her'eyez z z'azz drawing on him. A her'him'it. A're'y'e"of the'm. Any memory of it supersonically broadcast. In a y eye a'peering it out.

"Yet, when you consider h'our plight, War're'y'na or no Warren, we all are y'all still turning into a b'ng c'ng faced with this'eX death mask. Death is the specter on the face of it. That spector is the royal uraeus or sacred. As'z'p'eh'c'ting of it a torus opeh'ning of mouth as organ of speech. A ba' by opening mouth inhales and exhales first breath. The'na race is on. The chase after your tail of your tall tale begins by ending the connection of it.

"Yet we all in turning after it may find ourselves complete. A final in word liberation may be found by a're'y'all'eye'zing'ng appreciating a b c's of a b'ng c'ng now in word of the dialectic debate. Still well aware of a being c'ee'ng indivisible in'visibility in any mirror duplicity of a y na'me of it. Any tale of a b'ng c'ng merely the e've're'y same body with intent of playing out any role or roll of it. A death or disappearance comes only to the mirroring of a b'ng c'ng. A b'ng c'ng a're'y"e'flected in a're'y"e'fraction of it. It now turning out a k'no'wing of it awhile as'z'any denial of it as thoth'tsz of appearing disappearing. Still awareness of a b'ng c'ng in the first place indivisible in'visibility of any individual." In her'eyes'z'z'on it words came in hear'ing luminescent translucent sound wayeves as'z means of any meaning full of it. That indivisible love still felt. Instantaneous. In free'standing a n"eye"z z z'on us he mused. A B C'ng'G's us. Awareness of a being ga'i'n'in'g'ee'sz'zus. A pow pow power of pressure in disregard of a black peh'esse'y w'hole. As'ka's of it now a k'no'wing of a y eye of eve're'y body a'peering it out. Now as'king of it y eye spy in word any appearing of it. In word the dialectic debate raged in any memory not stifled by indifference or apathy he realized now a k'no'wing out of it. Why keep denying that y'all k'no'wing out of it he wondered.

"Death as indulgence. A warrior cannot brook any indulgence especially death. Typically we all turn to indulge in it sooner or later. It's the story of my life. A warrior will take on that invincible enemy capturing that brief moment that he succeeds with a clarity, power, and knowledge enough. Enough para un hombre de conocimiento. Who now knows a b'ng c'ng complete in the first place. A b'ng c'ng of it that cannot be added to nor taken from." Mor felt a flash of melancholy. Strange longing for something that never was. Something merely mirrored in word thoth'tsz of imagining it. Was he longing now for k'nowing longing in the first place?

"Death as we all in h'our now turning a k'nowing denial of it is also denial of liberation. Liberation may not be necessity or necessarily desired at attention captivated now in any mere mirrored memory of it turning into a k'no'wing out of it the d'na'eye'll life. Understanding the in word spelling of alphabeta anyone may turn into a thin'king of themself appearing of it born and therefore dying.

"Thinking of it born in na'me alone. Then typically indulge in the seeming futility of appearing only in awhile then quickly disappearing. An indulgence leading to apathy or indifference of epic proportion. That's a measly thin'king of it now turning any k'no no no'wing out of it a d'na'eye'll. Int'word a twis'ting in two appearing a pairing as'z'any thoth'tsz of it projecting a b'ng c'ng in na'me or denial of eve re'y body a're'y'dhi'a'ting of it. It a b'ng c'ng a peering it out in word in her'eyez z z' of eve"re'y bodhi. In that we all turn into any roll or role of it emitting complete d"ark'en'ing loops that begin to be perceived precisely by imaginary endings of it now as polarity. As'z z z'leep into a b'lack' body instilled with intent of a b c's of a b'ng c'ng a gain of it. That indivisible in'visibility of any individual by awakening of it appears in sound wayeves out in her'eye personically playing any or eve 're'y bodhi roles on and on and on ad infinitum.

"Y'alls'z heaven or hell falls under the veil of it in her'eye of eve"re'ybody a're'y"e'dhi'a'ting a black peh'ss'y whole bodhi. Sleepy black death is only a temporary analgesic until we all in h"our turn are a re'y"e born. A birth as'z'any thoth'tsz of it awakening wearing another mask. A'masking of it as'z another veil of tears. A b'lack' of it into one race b'lack'g'round the karmic wheel of samsara sorrow of a bliss denied. In that h'our role as human being we all roll e turn all'y y'all. Warren's brilliant research projects a viral 'playing' of it su'per sonically out in her'eye of eve're'y bodhi as'ex'ploiting a black body quantum gravity. A gee'sz us black'g"round micro wayeve a're'y'dhi'ation loops of a y eye a peering it at that now. It a y now as'ex-posed as a y eye a peering it. A now any overstanding overseer a peering it at that. That it is a b c's of a b'ng c'ng merely now appearing in words denied supersonically as'z'any thoth'tsz of a k'no'no'no'wing out of it understanding any spelling of it. A DNA'eye'll as'z'peh're'y'ss'ured by gravity weight of waiting to die opened a door'way'eve're'y of such an event horizon line which none scientists wanted to or dared a'bout crossing over. Yet. Still merely awareness of it turning back to black." These last words set the hairs standing on the black of Dark Mor's neck.

"Till now? Till debating Y'or Y na? Y you're you no longer waiting as'z though'tsz now int'word a twis'ting in two being"s'z z z'one into which two must die?" He continued to let words from his a unconsciousness flow out personically with the ink trailing silently across the paper.

"Then you must ask which dies? As'eX or a Y. A Y or Y now as'z'any'supernatural p'ss'y' el'n'tatthoth'tsz of it as'eX? Or Y a're'y"e'all'eye'zinging it? Indivisible invisibility of a Y eye or Y eye'Me'm mind or as'eX"eting anding duplicating of it appearing a pairing in man'as mind or Y? A y memory of it as'z'ex. Got that cowboy?" she'e now added with a stretch and twist of muscle and bone.

"Cowboy. I ain't no stinkin' cowboy but stinkin' cows have been my nearest neighbor for a spell. So, is this really about dying or propogating? 'Ay Professor?" Mor replied feeling this double sided conversation somehow going his way. "Y I am confessing y'all this talk of dissolution is turning me on to a solution of consumation to the situation."

"Wait for it." she returned still holding a facsimile of her original pose twisting on the high chair.

Her reply smacked it hard back on his court. Nothing to do but wait. The silent wordfree hold on a visual artist could easily extend to infinity, or beyond, he chuckled to himself. Silence? I'll give you the grave. "Gravety." The word slipped from his tongue with out his knowing. Christina turned to meet his gaze. He felt swept into her attention, her focus sphinx like on a beyond only conceivable by still gazing out over 10'000's'z z z of da'z z'eling y'ears. Watching. Man'as'a'lion waiting for the equinoxial alignment of man'as memory of a lion. An imaginary li'on between a peering it or a peering at it.

Asz'z a re'y'e'dhi'll of the Sphinx. A y eye of a b'ng c'ng merely a peering it. A'y'eye'star'e'y"e out of it now as'ex a un'k'no'wn of it in any dna'eye'll of it. At it. Supernaturally as'z'any mere mirrored in word thoth'tsz of it. It now a black'g'round echo of a man'as memory of a lion turning. A yearning. A burning of it. A bearing of water. A first mirror of it still in the first place. A re'y"e fraction of it. Aquarius Leo. 12,000 years a're'y'e'turn'ity as'king of it anybody appearing of it merely a peering it. A sphinx a peering it. A're'ye turning black'g'round now a k'no'wing out of it in word. The man as mind or animal. Boogie baby. Artist now drawing a muse. A'muse'ment. "Talk to me baby. You be da kine voice," Mor heard the words from his voice miles away in 3D.

"Thats'z the weight. Gravety."

"That's Dave. Grave-digger Dave. I worked with him in the largest cemetery in the South, Metarie, Lousiana, one of our poorer states with one of the coolest names. Spent a few years in the Crescent City drawing portraits on Jackson Square in the French Quarter. Got a little strung out on bad drugs and good women. Took a break to find myself working with the Black man. Something about cemeteries. Mostly bodies there were interred in crypts above ground. I worked on the crypts' cleaner van. For them that was planted in the ground, even rich cats with hermetically sealed double caskets that still leak as it them us quick enough turn to dust, debri, lengths of bone, femur here forearm there poking out of bits of wasted fabric. It was our job to prepare for an internment, clean out casket debris and compact remains to make room for a spankin new coffin. Typically a crypt contained space for several coffins so depending on size or death rate in a family determined when a space needed be cleaned out, compacted. Amazing how quickly them bones can go, back to dust. It makes gold and jewels jump out. I saw some pilferage. But there was only one real grave-digger.

"One day I went on my own out to where Dave was digging a couple graves. I'd been studying him pretty close at lunchtime when all the crews would gather in a cheesy lunch room, in other words'z the shop garage. Dave always cracked a toothless smile at me when I came around. Maybe it was my name or something of a smell of death about me. Like I was coming at him across a great divide. Certainly a racial one yet the color of skin never factored in. Dave was lookin' pretty haggard that day. It had rained hard all morning. The ground was heavy digging. So after lunch I went out and spelled that old man. I dug a man's grave six feet down into the ground. Digging that grave, in the rain and gloom of over cast sky, it felt like I was digging my own grave. Sure enough Dave took sick from working in that lousy weather but he knew there was nothing but for him to keep digging those graves till he fell in one his own self. That's'za real 'gravety'. Dave never dug another as he passed away shortly after taking sick."

"Now there is a grave story. Black man in Jim Crow era South or privileged white boy in post war segregated North. The gravity of any life of man with or without womb or why now do anything only to end the same way. That is the weight. The gravity of waiting now in awhile. Living in the constant shadow of dying. Stalked by death. A dancing with death. Appearing disappearing. A shadow that falls over and is of eve're'y body. In the cunning mirror deadly deceit of you or me appearing a pairing out as'z'ex's ting awhile with a being still in the first place. Indivisible invisibility. As'king of it y a k'no'wing out of it any appearing now only disappearing later when nobody knows. We all roll a black'g'round still now a knowing out of that anybody anythin'king of it etc.. A un'known shadowing us alternating moment after moment. Ironically science demands objectivity. Demanding any appearance of it equivalent to any denial of it. Appearance by a k'no'wing out of it anybody etc. A k'no no no"w'ing of it a y'll d'na. A d'na eye'll of a b'ng c'ng invisibility indivisible still a peering it in the first place.

"Yet science demands gravity of objectivity by a feverish fervent vigorous k'nowing denial of recognizing let alone realizing it. It now as'k'no'wing of it merely any mirror potential you now. Of y'all a being of it as that still subjective a're'y"e'ality only potentially appearing reflected as in word thoth'tsz of a're'y'fraction of immutable light. Thus any appearance offers a paradox of scientist denying themselves as'z thoth'tsz of it. To create as'z thoth'tsz of it in any in word information. Now to k'no'w out of it other y's'z'z'az'ex while still a being singular indivisible invisibility. A y eye of view of you of y you're; you or me etc.. Thus we all spin into confusing the mirror image with a still invisibility in visibility of a y eye of a b'ng c"ng merely a peering at it. Now a k'no'wing out of it into a supersonic black'g'round echo body as'z'any in word thothtsz informing of it appearing awhile. A b'ng c'ng still in the first place any seer sight see'ng in plain sight. Me or you in her black eye of eve"re'y bodhi. A womb of potential of it as'ka's mic memory. Appearing of it int'word disappearing black into one indivisible invisibility of y'all. Of you . . ."

"Or me. Me or you. Dying or propagating?" He thought as if dying to find out.

"As long as we all a're'y"e a wheel of it turning a black'g'round . . ."

"Into or out of anybody anythin'king of it etc.."

"That is the weight. The gravity of the loop . . . the role playing out like h"our planet. A plan et'ting h'ear'th. A supersonic as'ka's mic plan et'ting duplicating that h"ear'th echoing her ka's mic macro mic'ro wayeves black'g'round into or out of any or eve"re'y bodhi turning churning burning yearning of it in word. In diurnal cycles, day or night, moment after moment appearing as'z 'any thoth'tsz of it actually disappearing while merely turning into or out of a black'g'round of it. An echo of it in light or shadow of that singular indivisble in'visibility of h"our only begotten sun shining out of her black eye peh'ss'y w'hole of eve're'y womb. Invisibility sacred g'ee'sz us Kryst black eye of eve"re'ye bodhi. Offering potential gravity loops in word beginning by endings ways of eve will, her wayeve will. In her'eyez z z of eve'll a wayeve function of eve're'ye body. A y eye merely a peering it out. That eve re'ye will of we all turning into or out of it merely mirrored in word.

"Her eve'll of appearing int'word a 0 only twis'ting in two appearing a pairing as'z 8. Me or you as'ka's mic memory twis'ting in two. 0 as'z'za 8. One ze'e'ro'll twis'ting in two'twir'ling a b'lack'g'round now a k'now'ing out of it appearing disappearing black into or out of one complete d"ark'ness." Mor felt electricity raising hairs on his body. A certain exhilaration gladdened his heart now as'king of it y a k'no'wing out of it a liberation in words of the dialectic debate. A b c's of merely a peering it or now a peering it out in word. As'k'no'wing out of it information of any in word memory bringing up y'all the troubles of mind. Troubles of now anythin'king of it a k'no'wing it into appearing eve'n awhile. The crazy cruel ride in a wordship craft. An y mirrored y na in word craft of D'Na'eye'll. Any now ask'no'wing out of it anybody anything etc. appearing merely in word. Now we all in turn as'k'no'wing h'our a b c's of x y z's merely a peer it to disappear still it. Of it still he thought of it now.

"Now a death. A death is the pickle of a life. Without awareness of death everything seems trivial or so fleeting to endeavor indifference or apathy. As'z'za death becomes the teacher or guide in this impermanence as'ex's ting in any in word form then the mean means of it is'z any meaning of it. The means of death as a wayeve function as'z'z z'any motion. A E.Gg'ee'sz us kryst wayeve motion into or out of a black'g'round of it. It a b'ng c'ng still in the first place indivisible invisibility. A mean means meaninglessness beyond sheer wayeve function of function. Of business for the sake of being busy." Mor felt a chord playing out a memory in a wordfreedom awareness of a being still in the first place. Indivisible invisibility. Now an echoing ka's mic'ro wayeve black'g'round of awareness in memory ask'no'wing out of it anybody etc.. A priori. A wordfree untouched unsullied awareness of it. Of that indivisible invisibility now a black'ness prior to aw'ak'h'en'ing a gaining of it in word anybody etc. at aten'cion. Of it. A b'ng c'ng still now a peering it out into a k'no'wing of it in words'z'zz' one mirage b'lack' mirror see'as'z'zaz z'memory of it a b'ng c'ng a 'gain'. A b'lack' a 'gain'. A pingting as'z'any thoth'tsz of it had begun ringing in the black'g'round of his y''h'ear'ing of it. Mor was learning of it in that debate between mere a peering it or appearing of it. As'z similarly he had learned his a b c's in the first place while a being c'ng run over by chevy panel truck. Learned to see a b c's etc. in word informing of it. Learned to hear etc. a b c's informing it in word as'z k'no'wing out of it personically. The soundsz of it. The smell and taste of it. The touch of it. Y'all learned. A b'ng c'ng merely a peering it now out a k'no'wing of it anybody etc. appearing of it. Awhile out in her'eyez z z'a black craft'y wordship. As'eX'peh'ress''eda out in her'eyez z z a peh'ss'y w'hole. Any a peering at it. As'ex y'all.

"In a un''k''no'wing of it ending back to black. A beginning in word of a b'ng c'ng in the first place now a's'ending of it with out. A beginning knowing out of it a y now ending of it as'ex. As'ex'et'ting duplicating without a're'y'e'all'eye'zing y. An endless loop of a y eye potential means as any lifetime we all appear to turn into or out of a b'ng c'ng of a y eye now a peering out with gravity peh're'y'e'ssure of intent of intentionally ignoring of it as'z that's'z y. Blasted blasting a y eye a'peering out a wily w'h'ile. Y'll d'na or projection of d'na''eye''al'l of a Y eye will. A will of a y eye merely a peering it out into any appearing of it.

"It seems we all turn into or out of a'peering it out of awareness of a b c's of a being seer see'ng in'sight. A b'ng c'ng now turning black'g'round as'z z z'leep black into a un consciousness. A b'ending a're'y'e'all of a b'ng c'ng of complete darkness. Todos dhi''ar'eye'ka's en'dhi'esse to perceive in awareness of todos el mundos. The complete t'whorl'dhi'ng roll of it. The jelly roll asex y'all. Of it. Or a role playing out in anybody as'z'any thoth'tsz of it a beginning in word still a b'ng c'ng in'visibility of any point of view of you. Of 'ten a bi now a're'ye being mirroring in word's'az'zap'ping out of a being in the first place now out as'z'any in word thoth'tsz informing of it . Thus there is only a're'y'all'eye'zing in a y eye of a be'holder of a b'ng you to find, to discern, to pick up on complete freedom from falling over or understanding that in word loopy spelling of a complete d"ark'ness. . ."

"You called?" Mor retorted again without forethought as he found himself lost in the visual energy invigorated by drawing deep into that wordfreedom pooling see'as of any artist b'ng c'ng and the torrent of words spilling off her tongue. Jetting electric in word charges bursting the levees of his self conceit. The de'fences of his electromagnetic felt feeling field of view now k'now'ing you or y. He found in her'e'yez z z on a Y speak contagious in his mind. Or y in the or y. Opening the spigot of his left verbal mode released too many words to describe that place, that'z'za'p"ping'ting of a being in the first place now synapse ss'peh"ark between beginning any ending of it in a word. Az'z ap'positive transmission of a being now a b'lack'g'round any k'now'ing out of it. In word a meaningful mean means merely mirrored of it. As'z'z'yn'apse transmitting supersonic supernatural thoth'tsz of it superimposed in memory. A being completely complete wordless . . . formless, he mused. He fell black into the serene silence at aten'cion b'ng c'ng drawing on his untouched wordfree right brain. Awareness of it.

"We all roll in three modes. Three boons of self mind or a y eye consciousness of it. Yet the two primary modes or bodies, being purely subjective dream or deep sleep bodies, must be ignored by a purely objective Quantum physics. What of it if we all turn out of and black'g'round into it yet a bng c'ng a peering it now int'word a twisting of it into mirror bodies of it appearing y'll d'na. In a y eye of a b'ng c'ng now as'ex's ting by denial of k'no'wing out of it anybody etc..

"Ignoring of it ignites same positive transmission of a b'ng c'ng still now out of it in any turning a black'g'round into a k'nowing d'na'eye'll of that. A b'ng c'ng y'all that must be disregarded in the first place at y'all cost of not now paying attention to it. That MO'JO--GO go as'z'z"ex'et'ting duplicating it. It still it. Going in reverse polarity mean of disappeh'ring black'g'round complete d"ark'ness. That science by vigorous knowing a y eye o'peh'ning a'peering it out as'z though'tsz projecting only objective relativity of a being mirrored in the or y of ka's mic memory. A vigorous denying denial of now k'no no no'wing it. A b'ng sol'u'ta't"wa in the first place. A's causality of quantum gravity roles of complete d"ark'ness play out in hidden fully clothed singular consciousness. Vigorous D'NA'eye'll of awareness of a b'ng c'ng indivisible invisibility fills one third of any life cycle. A'sz z z'leeping black and for'th across that eve"n'ting h'our'eye'zz'on science of peh'sy'en'tis'ta misses the boat on purpose of polarity. H'our in the one hand polar purpose y'll D'NA. A wily w'h'ile of D'NA'eye'll. Merely eve'n'a en'dhi'ing to perceive now k'now'ing int'word a twis'ting in two appearing a pairing by D'NA'eye'll of it. We all may turn h'our'sza attention back to black a's'z sacred holy black'g'round whole picking up on a being still in the first place remaining indivisible in'visibility of any individual. Call me or you yod iota that I am is is now. The ka's mic ka'mic purpose hidden or clothed in a b'ng c'ng a black power of o'peh'n'ing a peh'esse'y whole of her"e'yez z z' of eve're'y"e body."

"She don't want to get naked? It's so ironic that art models, who legally must pose completely naked to avoid pornography laws find ultimate freedom in their nakedness. Freedom from the neurosis of hiding their privates while at the same time suggesting them with sexy threads. Completely naked is completely natural. Drawing the body, snatch and all reveals pure appreciation for y'all that we are. A man drawing enough poon gains a detachment of realizing it as the source. Thee source. Now I'm beginning to pick up on why old farts go sniffing around young cuze. They ain't looking to get in so much as looking for a womb way back out. What you were saying about gravity loops. The closer we all turn to the end, the closer we all turn to the beginning." Jeez z z, us. We all turn in word into or out of a b c's of a b'ng c'ng still in the first place. He found himself chattering away. The sound a's'z z z'sound of her voice, meaning a's"z'z'zapping means of her audio vocal range from gutteral to labial. He remembered the old german woman teaching him grammer mechanics of the voice as'z organ, vibrating corded organ including throat, hard and soft pallette, tongue, teeth'a ma'lips'z'za. Grammer as'z sound healthy way of waves. She could make boring didactic delerium intriguing just by modulating her voice. Mrs. Gerhart. Still one of Mor's favorite comedians, Christina Shaughnessy was a master modulater. Make funny as'z z sound serious or vice versa y'all by modulating the calibrating, he mused still watching her watching hand tracing mass and contour liquid fire in a cradle of ma'sz z her"e'y'e of eve"re'y body.

"Where have you been all my life? Darkness Mor. I think that I am now in love with you or my memory of you . . ."

"As'ex?"

"As'z you stretching beyond normal parameters."

"That'sz because at two years young me a being initiated into awareness of the over mind's voice. Saving my butt, keeping me aware of a b'ng c'ng still in the first place. Now a being me while run over by a panel truck. Believe me, I'm just the most mid-western mediocre guy. I should be working at a tire shop in East Bumfuck with a serious drug and alcohol habit. One of those hapless guys cigarette smoking themselves to death by inches, one leg at a time. It was the intercession of that voice and the instantaneous awareness of a being of it still in the first place that allows me to be here. Now as'z'any in word thoth'tsz of it out around a k'nowing out of it in formation. Then finding myself fully able to recognize my surroundings, my sister, my mother, my father. That initiated my in word path leading to you now. Making me realize the nature of'ten of a being of it y'all. That voice unleashed a fire that kept burning y'all my bridges behind leaving me no choice but to keep plowing mostly incoherent on into a un'known. Sunshine or shitstorm. Hell, I guess in that respect even Korner has served me well. Could say he shot a few horses out from under me. Damn, now I know I've done too many drugs, I start thinking that way. So I got one question. Why? Why is that friggin' old boy dogging us?"

"Korner or Warren or the voice in your head?" Christina asked as she stretched out in a way he could only see as provocative. The muscles of her legs flexed and corded from hips to toes, pudendum pivoting forward.

"That reminds where I was going earlier about her. Mother nature. Ma'ss nature. In her eye of eve"re'ye body hidden, clothed as it were, in complete darkness. Her'e'ye of eve're'y"e body. Ma'Na'ture. Eve"re'yeye body experienced directly over a third of our lives of a being still in singular blissful blackness . . .BHAM. It just hit me."

"What?" she asked, continuing to slowly stretch and gyrate her completely naked body. Mor found he had to put her in soft focus by squinting his eyes, in order to concentrate on his point.

"The real significance of my E.T. experience. In that I am a're'y'calling experiencing a naked singularity. It may sound crazy anticipating that encounter for ten or twelve years or longer. Heck probably since the beginning of any beginning. When opening that door, finding the're'y'all of a being cosmic be"am'ing a're'ye at me. Then finding myself in the presence of awareness of it in the first place now out in a wily wild while a k'no'wing of it wielding a craft. The craft that I am realizing now a wordship of a being c'ng a"peering it. Out of it now inter-dimensional whorlding wordship of a colored light spectrum. Just before coming closer as it were that I am finding myself lost in a field of a being c'ng still. Disappeared as a being c'ee'ng indivisible invisibility. Disappeared in an awareness of a singular being cee'ng of a pervasive cool warm blue light. A're'y'eye a peering it. Pervading of it. Pervasive like that soaking darkness of sleep. Pervasive stillness of a being awareness of a boundless moment after momentum of a b'ng c'ng a peering it eyes closed or open. In that eye that I am is is a b'ng c'ng still in the first place a naked awareness of a singular indivisible invisibility of it. It is possible for anybody to disappear in that na'k'ed'ness. Anybody of a being merely mirrored a y'll d'na'k'ed potential of it for appearing a pairing still indivisible in'visibility of a being c'ng in the first place. Now a peering it out of any thin'king as'ka's of k'now'ing supernatural super'sonic wayeve re'y'sz z'za man'as mind of it in a memory. Superimposed in the or y. Merely mirrored. Mirror'all'y y'all, supersonically supernaturally superimposed. But don't get me started.

"Some folks talk to me one time. Say, yah, we all want to hear about your e't' encountered. As'z recounting the tale then I could tell by their expressions of that let down vibe that I wasn't translating a ka's mic kamic feeling of it fielding it. So I never spoke of it again till now. But when you get a handle like mine, it's a fire that gets in your hair, gets in your scalp and down into your neo and meso cortex. Like I said, the encounter was like coming home, to an interdimensional now as'ka's mic kamic k'now'ing home. Home of now a un'k'no'wn out of a b'ng c'ng still in the first place. A being of it still in a place of now k'nowing out of it a black or blue'su'personic in word as supernatural thoth'tsz of a being of anybody etc.." Mor found himself a being now a k'no'wing out of it that as'k'ing of it a ka's mic micro wayeve black'g'round su'personic singular memory of it out in her'eye of eve're'y'eye body. A being in her'eye a're'y'dhi'a'ting a blackness. Indivisible in'visibility of eve're'y"eye body a peering it out of a black'g'round. As'ka's micro wayeve black'g'round echoing it now as'z'any in word thoth'tsz of a k'no'wing out of it anybody anythin'king of it etc..Then the en'y urge'nt energy appeared in her'ey'e a'peering it out in word in'for'ma'ss before his eyes.

"Y'all make a good point artist. A naked singularity experience be good as'z good gets. In that I am be"am'in'g a feeling felt fielding your feeling of it as'ex'perienced. In the same way we all as'king of it y turn back to a black'g'round into one disappearance of falling as'z z z'leep black into one hidden or clothed in complete darkness singularity. Experiencing a y eye a peering it out in a naked singularity would be well a supernatural singular experience."

"You know its like learning to ride a bike. Once y'all get that balance point. It's your'n for life. That moment recalled sweeps away anythin'king of it y passing before or since. A"s'z z zsuper ka's mic synapse. In the shift of perspective that I am at mean attention between micro to macro his craft. Or its wordship must contain h'our whole entire in word k'no'wn universe. Then later finding his craft tiny compared to Kali Ma'sz za."

"Ma's'z'a eve"re'y"eye body. Her womb any potential Dhi"aty to perceive it. Adore it captivated in a craft. A wordship say'l'ing black mirror se'e'as a b c's of a b'ng c'ng now out in her'eye of eve're'y'body. In that we all turn back to a black'g'round indivisible invisibility in plain sight of any seer. Now playing out any role of complete d"ark'ness. Any infinity of it int'word a twis'ting in two turning a k'no'wing out of it a b'ng complete d"ark potential into anybody etc.. Merely to perceive ar'king around t'wis awakening as t'word any eye of I that am as'z'any thoth'tsz of a being cee'ng as'z'z'any mere mirrored thin'king of it a y'all a d'na'eye'll body in d'na y l'ight . . .igniting ignore'ance of now a k'no'wing out of it."

"Why no body or any body is in her'eye of eve"re'y body," he offered, continuing to squint as the temperature rose till sweat streamed from his temples and forehead. The DMT emitting from the artist first eye in the middle of his head illumined Christina's nakedness into a full spectre spectrum of color chords echoing a mean decibel of its sound transduced. Informing of it a wayeve're'ybody craft. A wordship as'z'any d'na'eye'll of it.

"We all turn black in the Quantum or y now. Anybody with a b'lack'g'round intent of a b'ng c'ng a gain. Intent now as'z'ka's of k'no'wing out of it anything. A black'g'round projecting a k'no'wing ignoring of it. A y eye of that I am is is a'peering it out still in the first place. Why that y'is man grieves not. A're'y'all eye"zing behind any k'no'wing dna'eye'll of it. Discerning a b'ng c'ng in any a'peering it out as'z mirror reflected reflection in word awareness of a being by na'me alone. Still in that I am finding myself now carrying ovaries and uterus, a y eye being c'ng g'aining weight of that quantum gravity is drawing us together.

"You or me a's'zz'ex. Z'az'zex." Her voice kept extending these tendrils to be sznapped off he found as words now tactile as sound waves melting into receptors on his tongue. Drops of sweat burning his eyes fell staining the drawing paper with inky tears. Creating ink'as washes. A dissolution of a line between a peering it or it appearing against the white background he flashed.

"A's'ex u'all being's we all turn churn and burn by bio co-ignition of propagation and thus passionately fall under complete d"ark'ness, complete rolls as'z da roles. To be played. Y na Ma. Y na Pa. A Pa'roo'Ma."

"And then always ready to propagate," he answered without looking up from the pen traveling over the white field of paper dotted and blotched with furry sweat drops. Still he felt his hand quiver. He found it took all his will power to keep from pulling her onto the bed.

"Man as mind or y a one track mind," she laughed. "Do you think we all are turning to the end of compulsive biological drives. More than that, the end to ideologies, mythologies, and belief systems as we all turn a black'g'round into realizing a're'y'all'eye'zing'ing as'z awareness of a being in the first place now out mirrored by a k'no'wing of it anybody within word or a're'yeye turning black'g'round a being still indivisible in'visibility of it without. H'our of overself awareness of a b'ng c'ng predominates still freestanding in a wordfreedom in the first place now a knowing of it out as'z'za"anythin'king of it eve'rey"eye'magined out of it."

"So you don't want a baby?"

"Are you asking me or has someone else been putting ideas in your head."

Mor shifted on the bed. "Damn opium is wearing off."

"Can I do anything?"

"I have to clear my head. Keep talking so I can keep my mind off the pain. Tell me about the stolen Tutankhamen papyri."

"You do jump around. Want to change the subject? Tell me where you picked up the notion of making a baby."

"You mean besides y'all gyrating that thing and talking eggs and eggs'pectations" he asked with a frown. "Oh baby, look in the mirror. I'm sizzling in my juices here. Okay, so I got the word, you could say from a spirit guide or a station chief. One of those cats that assigns and debriefs a mission if not in this world or this level in it but one more real coming out in the over world."

"M'hum, sounds a bit conspiritorial."

"Ah'm just an insider looking out or outsider looking in or whatever that I am appearing to be now seeing you seeing me," he grinned feeling the love welling up inside. Then a glint of light coming off one of the overhead cameras caught his eye. Stabbing him with a fearful pang. "What kind of frankenstein arises out from tombs and mummies and devious devouring codgers with industrial strength like Warren? Reminds me of my childhood, late night layed out in front of a snowy black and white television set watching those eyes of Boris Karloff. Thinking they were scary but down right benign compared to those in the bipolar schizophrenic head of my ma. What I'm talking about is that psychosis of a mind unpredictably capable of murder and like that." He bore down with the pace and intensity of the drawing losing her then finding her in furious ink strokes. He felt his jaw tighten, glad to get his mind off of it asex and back into the bigger picture.

"And those giant hands with the pegs." She added, walking over to retrieve her robe. "The papyri are the real deal. A hieratic record of what could be a geo-political-religio blue print to re-set, re-configure false paradigms, re-store a divine plan based on her, mother natures way before her industrial rape. Some believe America to be a re-surgent Egyptian civilization what with all the pyramids, obelisks, and Tut fever. When the papyri came into my hands that river of time poured into my heart till I thought surely it must burst."

"It's not bursting because that river's coming on thru you. I felt it washing over from your gaze. From seeing you in the artist singular eye. A y Eye. A be'am'ing of it with out word perceives that divine a're'y'e'fracted in y'all seeing. A're'tina of Chris'tina. A whole black eye. Somebody may have stole the paper'ri but they ain't gonna stole that river. Y'all that. That effulgence of complete freedom pouring thru you is down right intoxicating." he offered putting the finishing touches on the latest drawing. "The papyri sound like traveling papers. The kind that are passed on so the next generation has a heads up on what's really happening."

"Consider this. The papyri come from the only tomb not looted out of hundreds that had been. Looted in antiquity, the body hardly cold. It is as if Lord put a finger on that one, even though the chamber had been entered twice. As if y'all for the sake of Alice, my great grandmama, and her journey to wonderland. That tomb contained the secret eye dhi of the mirror'ages. The revelation of zep tepi. Of a b'ng c'ng in the first place now as'king of it y a k'nowing out of it information of a first time in space. Now as'king of it a la que"en que' appearing of it. Now awhile."

"As'z z zzzZapped zippin'trippin Zep tepi, zep tepi. z'Szounds like Zippy the pinhead. No I get that now with the esezz za. There'sz z z'a zapping e'electrizz'city to Y speak dialectic that activates'z"za zynapsz'as. As'z'king of it y a la que"en of that in which as'ex appearing of it. As'z'any appearing of it a while of that eve'll que'en now as'z'king of it y a k'no'wing out of it any in word mirrored appearing of it. Out in her'eyez z z' of eve're'y'body. A black asz a peh'ss'y w'hole body."Mor managed without cracking himself up. Y'all really cannot make this shite up he chuckled.

"I can tell you because you understand. I mean, you understand because you have realized it. Become aware in awareness of a b'ng c'ng it. It a y eye b'ng c'ng in you see'ng out now a k'no'wing of it in word. It has realized you. A being now a're'y'all'eye'zed a being of it in a lifetime of alter'native alternating moment to momentum a synapse re-connection of that disconnect between appearing in and disappearing out of it in wordsz'a k'no'no no'wing it. Y you have jumped on the ABBC letter code train. Any word's'z z z'a y na, y now me're re'y'fraction of its letter'all'y y'all as'z z'sound means of transmitting information letter'all'y y'all a being in any word. As'z a y eye thoth'tsz in word. In their sound way of wayeve mean means any meaning insight of her'ey'e per eve're'ybody see'ng remains timeless perpetually sacred. Beyond that any in word being seems as'z too, as'z though, as'z thoughtsz of a being two negate that indivisible immutabability of a being it in the first place. Negates by mirror'all'y y'all still invisibility now turned around k'now'ing appearing it as'z thoughtsz. In memory.

"In the beginning is'word. The beginning slicing and dicing of it by opening mouth organ speaking out in a word. A BA"N"G. BA"N"Gah. . . A being A'aten Na Go. A being that aska's mic memory of'ten a being a ten a binary bi na re'y radiating a w'h'ile now out in space time of a'ny b'ng c'ng not y'll d'na in that simple singular twist of fate of any d'na'eye'll of it. Go go go'in'g g . . . gee's us . . . with gravity weight of waiting for death by n"OO"n, waiting for the ending of the dang she bang a being beginning in any abc'ng of it in a mirror word."

"Okay. I can dig that as long as I don't think about it too much in word all'y y'all. You're a word bird, a ba bird talking about the artist's eye and seeing what I've heard called Olam A'ba. . . . . the world to come. The world to come about out of a b'ng c'ng without a's'word to as thoth'tsz of it by a go'a'd'esse to be letter'all'y y'all in word a superimposed supernatural divide of that indivisble. To part a see'ng in word read see'ng letter'all'y y'all now as'z'azz'an'y thoth'tsz of it. By y'all'az'za artist being y a y eye a'peering it out now a k'now'ing of it in word of the a's'ex's ting eye's'z'za"cross over. T'word it now aska's of a k'no'wing int'word a twis'ting in two a d'na'eye'll of it as'z thoth'tsz of eL mode A.I." He felt uncharacteristically garrulous. Outside his comfort zone. Normally he held any in word chattiness in check. Christina's outpouring response to her public, to their need for an in word pathfinder seemed a steep impass overshadowing his years of minimal human speech. It freaked him out but still he loved her or her. "You make them papers out like some kind a master plan. But will anyone out there give a good crap. The modern man woman man has little value for anything just a couple years old, let alone ancient history. It seems we all turn around mere business of busy busy'ness. No time or value of a quest questioning of y y'all as'ex'et'ting duplicating it out of a b'ng c'ng still in the first place. Y'zs exodus beyond drugs, sex, and rock'n'roll?"

"Well it is understandable that y'all feel that way. You are seeing it from the perspective of the man on the street. This awakening a Y eye awareness a's z ex per a y eye in zee'ng it will quickly percolate into the or y of man as mind or y now due to ka's mic con'stellar at"i"on alignment of the lion opposite the man. The message of the sphinx is macro micro ka's mic memory a're'y"eye'stored in memory of a b'ng c'ng aware of that freestanding a y e'y'e star'e"y"e'all in the first place. Now a peering it out of it in a kurve'y k'no'wing wayeve's. Y'all a're'ye'y'e'sz'z a're'y'dhi'a'ting divinity of a're'y'e' opening awakening a'ten. At aten'cion of a bi'na're'y'e. At aten'cion to it we all turn into or out of one indivisible in'visibility as'k'as of now any k'no'wing out of it. Turning out in word supernaturally superimposed as thoth'tsz of it. Now out in her'e'yez z z of eve're'y'body. A single black body singularity of any D"NA'eye'll of it. Da'y in. Da'y out. A d'na'eye'll of it. A y eye of a b'ng c'ng still in the first place now a'peering out by a k'no'wing of it any in word d'na'eye'll of it. Occuring a k'urving black'g'round a y eye of a herhimit merely a peering it. With intent of a polarity a pairing of it on the one hand. A while of a y eye a'peering out on the other from above. Ove a b'ng still freestanding in the first place. A y eye a'peering out now k'nowing a're'y'all as'ka's mic memory of it.

"That and a wealthy following makes for an expansive mission. Teaching teachers just as'z my teacher taught me perpetuates the wisdom of a y'eye'sz z dom'us, a b'ng c'ng in the first place. Of that's'z a first in for'ma'sz time's'z'e'peh te'pi. In word all'y y'all's'z z'a Mr. re y'all of it; a y. In that I am building on a eye ayam awareness of a b'ng c'ng merely a peering it in the first place. Still indivisible in'visibility of it. A building now of perpetual bridges between a y eye merely a peering it or in the eve'nt of a crossing over of anybody now as'king of it y a k'no'wing out in word appearing of it. Awareness in'visibility still recognizing a're'y'all'eye'zinging in anybody of a b'ng see'ng in plain ordinary sight. A y eye b'ng c'ng infor'ma'sz first endless beginningless time. Now appearing out in word k'nowing anything in her'ey'e of eve'rey thing. A y eye of a Herhimit. A freestanding of it. Opening from above. Polarity in the one hand. A y eye of a herhimit hidden in plain ordinary sight of eve're'y'body. A y eye indivisible in'visibility of anybody appearing a pairing on the one hand of a polarity. A while of splitting attention from a peering at it now carried away in a wordship of appearing in it. A b'ng c'ng a peering it out in word d'na'eye'll from above. Akhenaten. A'w/akhen a'ten." She held his gaze. A're'y'dhi'a'ting the perception of it as'ka's of now a k'nowing of it at a'ten'cion. A bi'na're'y'eye'sz'z. A'ten. A b'ng c'ng from above still in the first place.

"We all awareness rolling and trolling supernaturally superimposed in her'me'as'z'anythoth'tsz of herhimit"e y eye e"star'e'y'ing out in word as'ex'u"all."

"A's'ex drugs and rock'n'roll like I said. What makes it y'all go black'g'round herhimit polarity." Mor found himself cracking up. On the one hand polarity. Awhile turning churning burning out of it. In a wily w'h'ile. A pairing in joy or sorrow. Beginning in ends of a herhimit polarity. On the one hand. Wealth or poverty. Dominion or slavery. Birth or death. On the other merely out in the'or'ey'e. Still in a wordfreedom freestanding a y eye star'e ye's merely a'peering it out from above. He laughed his ass'zz'of'f freely realizing a b'ng c'ng in anybody. A na y now a k'no'wing out of it in word formation of indivisible in'visibility. Of any individual. The sheer absurdity of now a k'no'wing out of it y'all along. K'no'wing out a d'na'eye'll of it in plain sight of any or eve're'y'body. Why deny that I am now k'no'wing y'all along?

"Of'ten a bi na re'y"e radiating eve"re'y bodhi. A's'king of it a y now k'no'wing out of it a macro micro ka's mic mean of a b'ng c'ng. A meaning of it still in a y'sz z z' any eye point of view. Of you. Of a y eye a re'y'all a're'y"e'dhi'a'ting out of centrality of any body appearing now awhile, once in a while, as two appearing a pairing me or you out to be as'ex per eye in c'ing experiencing raising a little hell or high water or from that point of view of you of y overstanding understanding. Ma'sz Pa'h'sabilities of de"Sire from above."

"Hearing the s'z'ound of your words echoing waves rips'z'a me with feelings of an energy that could only be called a love bliss z z zapping my heart and brain makes me feel y'all might be on to something. If not on something. Something called feeling y'all fielding it in her'eyez z z'i'on eve're'y'body of eLove. Or putting it another way, I'm feeling bathed in the radiance of eL'ove the bliss of it. A na'y y'all now coming or going still as'expanding with your voice still permeating yet beyond me or you''s'z memory. Ah'm completely zapped by y'all, babycakes." Mor added flipping the sketched page for a fresh sheet. He noticed Christina back in the high chair snuggled into her robe, legs stretched out, turned up collar covering the back of her neck. For a moment he saw her smoking a cigarette but blinking realized it was only the way she had extended her fingers. About the smoke he didn't think too much. Her gaze carried off to somewhere beyond confines of any mere room.

"A being c'ee'ng that I am thankful for y'all in her'eye because we all turn into or out of potential lovers in love of multidimensional quality indivisible invisibility of a quantum b'lack' eye body. A y eye speak as'z z'a love best shared with others who have experienced it on many levels, expressions ov eL. Out in her'eye wayeve're'y's'z z z'a. De'sire of a b'ng c'ng da father from above . . . or ove ab . . . a being . . . ove eL. Ove a wayeve function. Ove eLove en'eve're'y way a y eye wor'd'ship to be wor'd'shipped y'et wor'd'shipping letter'all'y y'all y as'z'ex gods'z will still remain merely mirror potential with intent of quantum gravity. A b'ng c'ng g'ee'sz us a weight of waiting for it. The ending of me is the mere beginning of you. That's'z the way out of it in her''e'ye of a b'ng c'ng well hidden in the wayeve're'y'body 'fracting' indivisible invisibility of a black'g'round eye body ehoing as'z'any in word thoth'tsz of it."

'She'e'na always keep you waiting." Mor gave deadpan with his a being in a wordfreedom expressionless artists face.

"She funny that way. The way of wave y gravey function. The waiting on it in her'eye merely a peering at it. Ma's jest y. Her fun'ny action function. Me or you now out in awhile appearing out in her''eye'sz z za memory of a b'ng c'ng in her''eye of eve''re'y body. The jokes on a y you're you in the first place."

"You're a funny little thang. The lotus in the shit storm. You talkin' in the artist's eye. A y eye a peering it wordfree. Then as'ka's mic eye broadcasting a sound black'g'round echoing into or out of now as'k'no'wing out the wayeve're'y'body ask'a's mic mem or eye. Will sound of words translate into the seen as scenery or disappear into silence of the seer. Will Chris'tina still a're'y'fract it as'z'any thoth'tsz of it appearing in word in forming of it on my a re'y'tina? You a being be'am'ing y you're you as'z ex re'y'as'z." he added seeing his arm and hand continuing with fluid stokes following the contours'za of her electric feel'ed body. He felt in her eye'sz z z'ap'ping a charge charging him from across the room.

"In that I am betting y'all do not need a hammer to hit a nail on the head. Seeing your painting of Adam and Eve at Korner's place, I realized in that proverbial blink of eye that you were the artist for the mission of my sub'mission. Now, about making a baby," Christina paused to slip off her robe and into black lace panties with nylon stockings. "We all must keep turning that blood from y'all flowing down to your wounded knee," she offered, bending low, stretching back, and swiveling hips before sitting back on the high chair. She gave him a demure smile. "The irony in War're'y'na's cast of me as Isis is that I am finding myself a link with that pre-Judaic, pre-Islamic, pre-Christian era. An eye'ra'y that I am believing ez'spawned the Patriarch Abraham. Spawned in the New Kingdom invention of a portable phonographic alphabeta the whole potential Go'a'd B'OO'Ka. A B'ng 'OO' Ka. A Being c'ng dhi na'ying to perceive of it egg'sza ting of it. A b'ng c'ng now out d'ouble. A duplication of a b'ng c'ng now mirrored supernaturally turning into or out of thoth'tsz of k'no'wing it out in word any appearing of it." She'e'na gave him the full extension of lips in formation of el'OO'ka de'la b'OO'ka.

"In forming the first time now anybody could see a b'ng c'ng merely a peering it out. It now out with ink'as k'no'wing thoth'tsz of it appearing phonographically in word. Any or eve're'y'body in her'eye sight'as'ka's mic egg. In her'eyez z z'azz a womb of a b c's of a b'ng c'ng in the first place now out in the word as'z a ba'OO"ka. Pa per in k'a's. Ma'sz z z'Pa'hsz'zabilities.

"Is it coincidence that Abraham is cast as a shepherd, a shepherd king and Akhenaten carries a shepherd's crook as a sign of his kingly status? As'king of it y that Akhenaten is considered, rightly or wrongly, the only monotheistic pharaoh at a time of a great exodus of monotheists from Egypt to Canaan? That Tut's tomb, miraculously left intact, offers archeologic evidence of objects eerily reminescent of the tabernacle and arc of the covenant carried in the Biblical Exodus? Is the Bible mere Egyptology? Most of all the invention of the portable alphabeta code facillitated writing, printing and y'all the bupkis to come on out of it. Y'all still appearing of that irreducible irrefutable code. A 3300 plus year old code that you broke like the egg's'ting b'OO'ka that it is. Darkness you now have fulfilled the dharma cast in your name by that blessed crazy ka'li ma'ma'sz za eve'll

"In her'eye a will of eve"re'y'body appearing disappearing. Out or in'her'eye of eve're'y'body of a black bliss body. The Darkness, in that I am loving you, as'z in a y eye a peering it. Of you; re"eye point of you see'ng without k'no'w'ing y. With out any mere intent of a'peering it out in word informing of it anybody. As'za'wareness of a b'ng c'ng still in the first place indivisible in'visibility of anybody. In other words what is indeed here is there. What is there is here as well. Anybody see'ng as'z'any thoth'tsz of it obtains death from death.

"In a being cee'ng that I am in her'e"ye a peering it now out in word to testify of it. In k'now'ing a time now of a mirror age of Aquarius. A B C's a la h'OO'ka of a b'ng c'ng now in a water mirror of it. A bearing continuous flow of it as'ka's of man'a'ha'sz' z z source or y of me'm or y of a b'ng c'ng of historic revelation. A time now to pull back to black eve're'y'body awareness of it. As'z k'ing out of it a y eye a peering it. A still point of y you're; you. Now at aten'cion of a na y eye ? ? ? A' un'hOO'k'in'g'a the veil. A lifting of the disguise of thirty three centuries to reveal the source or eye of the h'our Ator'OO'rotA. H'our a b'ng c'ng in'visibility. A b'ng c'ng now turning a k'no'wing out of it into any in word formation of it. Of alphabeto.

"In the beginning is the word. The beginning of religion philosophy science or the sensory world at large. The in word source still a b c's of a b'ng c'ng of a y eye a'peering it out of any heads of followers of the three great western religions, schools of philosophy or science. A b c's coded in word of a b'ng c'ng still in the first place now letter'all'y y'all as'za thoth'tsz of a god esse to be anybody anythin'king of it etc. appearing out in word formation of it. A b'ng c'ng out merely mirrored in word supernaturally superimposed as thoth'tsz supersonically or phonographically invented in Akhenaten's new city. A new letter'all language of 22 keys. The pre modern era of in word captivity began to unite peoples gathered from across the known world. United in a common portable phonographic letter'all language. A language spoken or written out in 3D. A y eye language of a b'ng c'ng with in'k'as portible on papyrus. Eye'letter'all'y y'all a b'ng c'ng in the first place now easily with in'ka's in a h'and w'riting a k'nowing it out as thoth'tsz duplicated in'formation of it in a mere twenty two phonographic letters. Letter'sz'azz infor'ma'szz sound means in word medium of it in'k'as appearing on paper duplicating a duplicity of it in her'e'yez z z'a a b c's of a b'ng c'ng still in the first place now a'peering it out in word. Out of it in her'eye of eve're'y bodhi now as'ex'et'ting an exodus of it out in word'all'y y'all as'z thoth'tsz of a b'ng c'ng still in the first place indivisible in'visibility. A's'the great Exodus into captivity at aten'cion paid merely in word. Of one a's the definite defined in word art'i'cle are'ye' dhi'a'ty a'tion. Dhi'a'ty of a b'ng c'ng perceived now out in word as'k'ing of it y a k'no'wing d'na'eye'll of it. Indivisible Mono the as'word cleaving a division as'z'any thoth'tsz of it in m'em'or'y. A's torus of a b'ng c'ng out of it in wordsz'a capturing atencion completely ar'king of it."

"As'z'za visual artist. A being cee'ng that I am now a'peering it out at a picture book as'za means of disclosing the seer hidden now asz'any eye a k'now'ing it out in sound wayeves rolling out int'word a twis'ting in two mirroring a duplicity. Awhile of it appearing in word formation of a b'ng c'ng in a y eye 'a'sz dom'us. A home mirrored supernaturally superimposed a'sz thoth'tsz of a b'ng c'ng a peering it in the first place. Now a k'no'wing out of it in wordsza appearing in a re'y'all phonographically before any eye point of view. Of you now a k'no'wing out of it phonographically in word as'z thoth'tsz of it beside the point of view. A y eye being c'ng a peering it now out of it going awayeve in word from a still point of y you're you, so to speak in a Y dialectic debate of it ," Mor added, letting his in word sensibility have free reign while still focusing in a wordfreedom drawing on a peering it into appearing of it on paper. A peering it out in her'eyez z z of eve're'y'body. She now moved with her own in word expression of it turning on the pivoting high chair with stockinged legs extended. Then he found more words as'ex'et'ting his mouth. Mor in word exodus.

"What really turns me on to the letter code is its transcendence of vernacular versus literary. Either or both melt back letter'all'y y'all wordfree into 22 plus freestanding pieces. Y'all languages blow up fall apart breakdown into it. It a b c's of a b'ng c'ng in word reality melts down black into indivisible invisibility. Of it."Mor felt consciousness of the mean. A neither greater or lesser of it.

A pure geometry of it before as'ex'pi'ressing g'ee's'z us in equidistance of spherical timespace yields that timeless 3D cubic code where each letter takes on a plane face. A's'ex plaining experience. Or one of 12 boundary lines in any cubic space in time or interior intersecting planes centering letter'all'y y'all on the whorl worlding of a b c's of a b'ng c'ng g'ee'sz us. In'visibility turning a black'g'round echoing a gravity weight a waiting death. Out of it now a k'now'ing of it int'word a twisting a y 0 into an a na y 8. Appearing of it divided. A pairing in formation as'z sound wayeve're'ys of any eye a' peering out of eve're'y body echoing a black'g'round of it. A b'ng c'ng still motionless freestanding observer serving ob"bo. Ay'in'being a being'niya. It's'z'za exquisitely beautiful thang. In 3D plus. Mor found himself lost following the dialectic discourse like a hand following his eye drawing on the wordfreedom untouched awareness of the right side of the brain.

"Alphabeta provides a sound life in formation of supersonic supernatural living superimposed phonographically as'z'any in word thoth'tsz of it. It serves an immeasurable function. Awareness of any wayeve function. A fun'ny'action possible in for'ma'sz appearing in order. Or'der of a b'ng c'ng still in the first place or now a g'ee'sz us going out in word. A b'ng c'ng now revealed in its hieroglyph a's a y'aten. A y eye a'ten. At aten'cion. A bi na r'ey'eye'sz'za h'OO'ka d'elOOka da'bOOka." She played in her'ey'ez z z' eve're'y breath on heart'sza a'chords. A chording to vocal rythyms and melodies. Mor now picking up the meaning of the words more in a sound wayeve mean medium than any semantikos of it. Y'all a mean means meaningful of it. Any significance of it. After y'all. Y speak of it in the first place only now as'z in word thoth'tsz of a k'no'wing d'na'eye'll of it. Now out of the first place merely as'z'any thoth'tsz of it awhile? Now awhile space in time. Y'or y na. Y'or you now az's'ex's ting in formation. That debate must build to a raging hair fire. A burning off the dross of anybody conceived out in word. A'sz'z mere awareness a b'ng c'ng still of that indivisible invisibility of it. A'ten w'are now esse to be in any now k'no'wing out of it is as thoth'tsz of projecting any d'na'eye'll of it. Instill it. A y eye awareness of a b'ng c'ng merely a'peering it now out in word. A'peering it as'z' any appearance of it out in word. A being c'ng still in the first place now a peering out of it as in word thoth'tsz of a b'ng c'ng out of it. A y as'ex'et'ting duplicating duplicity by any mere mirrored black'g'round of now a k'no no no'wing out of it. A's'ex. A y eye as'king being her'eye of eve're'y body a peering out now at or of k'no'wing a being be'am'ing anybody anything etc..

It hit Mor that any now k'no no no'w'ing a being out of it as mere mirrored indulgence in ignore'ance of it. That now the'n k'no no no'wing out of it still in awareness of a being it. Eve'in death a mere mirrored in word indulgence with a b'lack' intent still denying of it a b'ng c'ng a gain. She'e'na turned his attention black'g'round awareness of a b'ng c'ng indivisible in'visibility now a peering out in word supernaturally as thoth'tsz. Thoth'tsz of a y eye being cee'ng a peering out now a god'ess'e to be letter'all'y in her black'ey'e ask'as of k'nowing out of it any or eve're'ybody.

"Creating in space awhile supernaturally out of in word thoth'tsz of it as'za library of sensory mind or a y eye now memory of a b'ng c'ng out interdimensional in'k'a's on paper. Transferable. Yet by nature, a mere understanding of any spelling of it. A charming cast in wordszaz'z. A now k'no'wing out of it an irresistable overpowering distraction of it at aten'cion paid in wordsz by a man'as mind in the or y business. Busy busy being busy a k'no'wing y now without realizing y. A y eye merely a peering it. Now a'sz'zex'pressing out a b'lack' g'ee'sz us a gain.

"We all turning a black'g'round of it now echoing e'turn'ity as'king of it a k'no'wing d'na'eye'll of it out of a y eye merely a peering it. Now we all turning indivisible int'word a twis'ting a'peering it out in two appearing a pairing of it in word. K'no'wing it y'all along the wayeve without realizing a're'y'all'eye'zinging it. Me'ema. Or y. A mind merely supernatural eye a're'y'tina a're'y'fracting it. A're'y of it indivisible in'visibility. A re'tina mirror mirroring anybody as'z'ex per eye of I in see'ng me a're'y'fracted asz in word thoth'tsz of it. Superimposing a're'tina re'y"e'fraction of a y eye a peering it out now in word for'ma'sz in awhile appearing disappearing in d'na y light igniting ignore'ance of it. It still a b'ng c'ng of that freestanding indivisible invisiblity as'z' any individual. With intent of a polarity on hand. As'z'any opening eye a'peering it out in word perceives a polarity a pairing of positive negativity. A 0 a pairing in 8 by the simple twist of fate faith or family. A D'Na'eye'll of it. As'ex'et'ting out in word duplicity of now k'no no no'wing of it. It awareness of a being still in the first place.

"Now any memory informing of it in word all'y y'all or still in a wordfreedom indivisible yet a b'ng c'ng merely a peering it. Or letter'all'y y'all potentially a possible a pairing it out in word of it positively denied as'z a b'ng c'ng still in the first place. A d'na'eye'll without a y eye dialectic debate of it still a b'ng c'ng a peering it in the first place. Or a b c's of literature of a y in other words'za'z'z'ex. A's'z'eX'et'ting duplicating now a turning of it in'tword a k'no'w ledge of a space in time awhile now from which any fool might fall a's'z z z'leep into complete d"ark'ness. A'sz z z'leep with a b'lack' intent of now ar'k'ing of it a k'no'wing d'na'eye'll of its complete d"ark'ness. Ar'king of it now to be perceived b'lack' out of it to be a gain. A D'Na'eye'll light igniting ignoring a b c's of a b'ng c'ng still in'visibility. A y eye a'peering it now out as'ex posing in any merely mirrored in word image imagined supernaturally as'z'any thoth'tsz of a measly scant thin'king of it. As'king of it y now in formation. Assembling a k'urving occurring of it in formation of a complete d"ark'n'ess'e. Any seer a'peering it out of a y eye now turning into it as'ex per I of eye am in supersonically superimposing seeing of it as'ex'periencing super-natural thoth'tsz of it as'z'za scene. Of a god'esse to be letter'all'y y'all appearing awhile. A still indivisible invisibility of any individual.

"That is a mirror supersonic spelling of alphabeta offering now a plan et'ting the h'ear'th. As'k'no'wing out of it echoing wayeve's of it in her'eye'sz'z'z of eve're'ybody at aten'cion mirrored out in word memory. In word memory of it developing ove're'y eye time now a's'z thoughtsz of in word ideas into 3D objects transformed from natural elements. Unfortunately that spell takes up in word nearly y'all h'our attention. Ove'r'ey eye time now with out an antithical dialectic we all turn black'g'round a k'now'ing of it a life or death in a wily w'h'ile.

"Y we all in turn need a y eye speak antithesis to that thesis proposal of intention to ignore it by now turning into anybody k'no no no'wing it. It awareness of a being a y eye a'peering it out in awhile. A wily a w'h'ile a'sz'za cunning deceit of a y eye's in'visibility appearing out a's z'ex'eting duplicating of it in word. Y speak turns conversation conversely back to a y ey"e'turn'y'all captivated turning into or out of chains in that black'g'round changing of complete roles in dhi"ark'now to be perceived perceiving in her'e'yez z z'a now of any or eve're'ybody a'peering it out a k'nowing anything or anybody merely mirrored in word. A y eye status quo offers freestanding refreshing refreshment of mind or y memory a're'y'membering a b'ng c'ng still in the first place. Indivisible in'visibility of anybody. Any where. Any time now k'now'ing it or merely a peering it a's a point of view of you."

"A peering it or appearing of it? It seems the t'asking a y eye of the visual artist to convince the mind or y memory to become free and fluid. By y'all means of a'peering it out or in awareness of a being still in the first place indivisible in'visibilty. There in her'eyez z z' of eve're'y body we all turn h'our attention black'g'round a being still now a'priory proverbial freestanding before in word captivity . . . still with intent of a b'ng c'ng g'ng in word a'formation awhile. A short wily a'w'h'ile of a y eye as'ex." Mor found the supernatural paradox of a y eye of a b'ng c'ng merely a'peering it out in word appearing a pairing of y as'ex y'all .

Christina Margot's'z'za rythym and accenting made the a y eye dialectic fluid. A wayeve function of funny'action. A sheer folly of da jolly. Paradox of denying it by any. Any k'no'wing out of it. As'z'stopping right away that in word dialogue y'all then is now a b'ng c'ng still wordfree in the first place merely a'peering it out as'K'ing of it a y now as'k'as of ka's mic k'no'wing it as'ex. A la que"en que' of that in which appearing y'et with intent of intentional disregard of it. It a y eye of a b'ng c'ng a'peering it now out in wordsz' of it appearing. Awhile now a space in time.

It seems we all take our turn of any role playing d'na'eye'll of it a gain. And a gain. A b'ng c'ng wordfree untouched still memory free as'zzy't now a black'g'round echo as'ka's'z of it appearing supersonically in word captivation at aten'cion on a k'no no no'wing out of it anythin'king of it etc.. Merely awhile now he mused. In a wily while of a b'ng c'ng in p"sy't. In her'eyez z zap'pingting a peh"esse'y' w'hole'ta playing echoing a black'g'round complete roles of d"ark'n'esse encirclement now of a b'ng c'ng a'peering it out anybody in the're'y'e or in her'eye of any or eve're'y body. In her'peh'esse'y'e w'hole of eve're'ybody he laughed. The funny'action as'z'z'any waiting on it in her'ey'e. Peh'esse'y w'hole peh're'y'ss'ure of a b'lack' body instilled with intent to be a 'gain'.

Like a polarity of chasing tail. The positive negativity of indivisible invisibility appearing polarizing in any now k'nowing out of it as'ex'y'all awhile. Appearing disappearing black into awareness of a b'ng c'ng still in the first place indivisible in'visibility with in her' b'lack"ey'e intent of a'peering it out in word a's'z'z'anybody a gain. Anybody still a b'ng c'ng merely a peering it out of the first place. Now turning into appearing of it out in word form. In'formation of a b'ng c'ng g'ng asking of it' a ka's mic k'no'wing out of it a yearning, burning, churning in her'ey'ez z z' of any or eve're'ybody turning black'g'round into or out of any in word captivity.

"A b'ng c'ng still in a word mind or y retains long term mem or y beyond a brain in that subtle electromagnetic synapse with h'our ka's y'all in her"ey'ez z zap'ping a'peering it out a'ta's'ka'z za ka's mic eve"re'y bodhi. A body felt field of feeling it out in her'ey eye of eve're'ybody of a b'ng c'ng alone indivisible. That e'story storage remains intact as'z a subtle sublime luminous as'z z'mem'or"e'yesz z za counterpart. A counterpart we all turn into experience in a dream body x a'sza'ten sion.

"Though that invention be 3300 plus years ago, in essence it is that same alphabeta we all still turning in word use in our Romantic languages now today. The words that I am speaking carry letter'all'y y'all the same esoteric k'now'ledge of it hidden in plain sight of an'y eye of a b'ng c'ng awareness of aten. Awareness at aten'cion paid by it still in the first place. Of a b'ng c'ng asz' a ten. A binary by a being a y or a y na now, a y denied as'z'ex. Thus y'all come down to living in denial, as'ex's ting int'word a twis'ting in formation y'll d'na or by paying at'ten'tion to a b'ng c'ng still in the first place indivisible invisibility.

"A being bi'na'r'ey'e'szz'a of a b'ng c'ng mirrored out in word mind memory of it as'ka's of now k'no'wing it. A're'yall'eye"zing'ing a y eye of a b'ng c'ng a'peering it out in now a k'no'wing a d'na'eye'll of it appearing in word. A k'no no no'wing denying of a being y eye'zzspoken of in y'or you speak'ing out now awhile still in the first place. Indivisible in'divisibility. Who cannot afford to pay attention now eve'na as'z two picking black up on a b'ng c'ng a gain of one still indivisible immortality. Eve'na appearing disappearing in awhile as'z too one of a b'ng c'ng in her'him'it'ey'e of any or'eve"re'y'body."

Mor dragged himself to a sitting position, the back of his head scrapping over coarse texture of brick wall. He continued ignoring the cameras as he bent over the spiral bound sketchbook. Hand still following eye, he developed the mass of her torso in a flurry of check marks appearing in his mind's eye as'z flocks of crows launching in flight. The pain throbbing his wounded knee kept him grounded chewing his tongue. "As'z z za vizual artist of a b'ng c'ng I'm finding alphabet letters as'z so many bricks stacked in a field, a thin'king'dom of towers. Towers of words'z z'azz babel. You turning me on to the code makes me realize letter'all'y y'all a whole new now time in word level. A double entendre. Means as meaningful. Supersonic wayeves function of fun'ny'action. She'e'na funny that way'eve."

"You must be feeling better, artist. Adam and Eve. Tower of Babel. Exodus. Could it be? Na'h. Or Y na. There is an event in time, the invention of a portable letter'all'y written supersonic phonographic alphabeta allowing, facillitating the spread of in word captivity. Exodus of attention. Now transferable as'king of it y now in the hands and voices of anyone and'or everyone a k'nowing it out in word. Supernatural supersonic wayeves' playing out a plan et'ting h"earth. As'k'a's'hic memory of billions y"ears of a h'earth still a mere echo of it supersonically superimposed see'r'v'ey'ed. A still point of view of you of a y eye of a b'ng c'ng g'ng do'or wayeve em'it"ting hard felt feeling neuronic cellular fields of it. A turning of we all asz;z;poken out int'word a twis'ting in two appearing a pairing the race of that ka's mic ka're'ye'ma man'as mind or y mem'or'y. Of it turning into or out as'king of it y a ka'r'mic wheel of fortune or mis'sedfortune.

"A turning churning burning we all over thousands of years of invasion, conquest, defeat, enslavement, genocide, and diaspora into or out of that complete dhi ark'ness wheel. D"ar'king of a man with or without womb as'z a b'ng c'ng a peering it now out with a p'seudo peh'ss'y whole predominanting mind or memory in word. A'peering it out of indivisible in'visibility as'z'za supersonic sound wayeves now a k'no'wing d'na'eye'll of it turning into anybody appearing out information. We all turn out of it now supersonically a k'now'ing supernaturally as'z'zany thoth'tsz of it superimposed onto the digital age of a b'ng c'ng in e formation.

"T'as'ka's of a y eye of a b'ng c'ng a peering it. Now in word as'k'no'wing out of it any appearing as'ka's mic b'ng c'ng in'formation awhile. Still a freestanding of it in the first place indivisible in'visibility. Prefiguring per pose of that free freed in a wordfreedom standing a y eye of a herhimit as'z'any her'me'as thoth'tsz'za of a la h"OO"ka de'l"OO"ka in that mirror age mirage of Aquarius. A Lion'Man. A li'e on man as mind or memory in a mean eye a peering it now int'word a twisting in two a k'no'wing out of it a mean'wilyw'h'ile. As cunning uncanny wordship of a craft sa'y'el'ing across the es'keyez z z of eve'n'ta hour'us'eyesz'on imaginary lion man'as'ex's'ting in formation still indivisible in'visibility of black or blue w'hole. A y eye peh'syt a peh'eering it out in wordsz'za dhi'scribing as'ex"et'ting that peh'esse'ye w'hole in the first place.

"Drawn out by que"en que'sta a y eye a'la h"OO"ka d'el"OO"ka. That activity at hand drawing cerebrospinal fluid up the serpent asz'z'pinal fluid. Elevating e-motion from h'ear't to bra'hm'in. Hear'ing a healing. We all turn into the water bearer pouring in word memory potential from cups in both hands into the pool and onto a black'g'round of it. As'Kali ma na'tat'u'a're. As'z'that you are. Of a mother memory mom'en't after mom'en'ta'm as'z supernature wayeve're'y"e of it."

"A'symbolic kine man a'sz a felt field. As'z z z'anybody elecromagnetic wayeves out in her'eyez z z'i'on eve'll. A b'lack' wayeve're'y'body will of we all a wheel turning yearning learning wayeves of a b'ng c'ng a b c's pouring into or out in words'za of y'all a black'g'round. Echoing of it a b c's of a b'ng c'ng a gain. A gain and a gain. Echoing el'ightning igniting'zsyn'apse 'z z z'apping any in word Tower of Babel a'sz electric fire field ringing a electromagnetic torus of a Ba 'bel bel'pingting body. A Ba dhi. As from ab'ove so Bell'ow. A bell'as art'es fine'dhi'ing a being of Ba el ak'h'et a'ten. A b'lack'g'round echoing aten. A b'lack'g'round or a ma'rey"eg'g around. As'zza'h'OO'ka d'el'"OO"ka at'ta b'"OO"ka. At aten'cion carried awayeve're'ybody. A in'visibility of it asz'z z'eyez z z of a b'ng c'ng in a singular a'peering it out of it asz'z'a na y potential binary now in words'z'azz a k'no'wing out of it. Appearing a pairing a's'z z z'apped zap'ping'ting 'sz z zyn'ap'se across ay now a'ten overstanding into any mirror y na now k'now'ing out any understanding of it. As'z'any understanding of it. Y'all the standing still of it. The status of that overseer under it undulating a seer see'ng still indivisible in'visibility of any individual'szazz'ey e star'e y'"e now out a gazing as'ex per eye of I that am a mem'or'y in a b'ng c'in'g'ravity weight waiting . . . .waiting. . . . waiting for you, for finding y you're you in the first place." She slowly spun with a sound of it'words a wayeve'ing into his field. He saw the charge coming before it hit with a rush up his spine amplified in his heart to bring orgasm in his brain. Asz'anybody'sz instrument of consciousness. A hard con she'e'na us. A kali ma'trickx.

She'e'na came into him taking a step. Then a bell rang to announce the rising elevator. Christina slipped back into her robe to retrieve the delivery returning with a large paper bag cradled under one arm. "We have connections in the right places."

"This one crazy set-up."

Mor stared out the windows imagining himself well beyond the brick confines so heavy in that industrial wasteland of working hard for a hard living kind of way. He knew life on the street continued outside and inside with his bowels grumbling. Somehow he felt largely suspended in mere awareness of everything going on y'all black'g'round him. Christina removed cardboard cartons, chopsticks, and tall cups of green tea from the bag. She shoveled out rice with spicy stir fried chicken and veggies on to china plates. They ate sitting on the bed with feet up, Mor propped against the brick. Christina sitting crosslegged half lotus style. The flesh of knees pressed tight against black nylon.

"Feeling the eye of War're'y'n'as'z god watching over us here. He is probing my thoughtsz. Dancing around that ledge over the abyss'z of falling back into one black whole. Now on the edge of the abyss he reaches for me. He may believe breaking down word and speech patterns will return human mind'sz'za a black'ness into one indivisible a un consciousness of a being human or mere awareness of humanity. Ma'sz awareness of it now a k'no'wing out aRe'y'leasing energy mom'ent after moment'am to make the H bomb look like a firecracker. But to capture the attention of man eve'na now as mere mind he needs the imagination of mad donna. Kali ma. I ma'g'es. An eye of I am that Y'at. Ma's'za going gravitating into one now a time turning a k'now'ing devouring y'all her children in wordsz," she offered before wielding her chopsticks.

Mor crunched a spring roll smeared with hot mustard. Margot Christina leaned back against a pillow and sipped tea.

"It's the paint," he exclaimed, licking his mustache. "The paint contains some substance, some medium. I tasted it. It entered my nervous system. Maybe a neurotoxin. That's it," he exclaimed, licking his fingertips. "That, awareness of that a b'ng c'ng in paying attention now disregarded by disbursing focus. A spelling is cast that disavows a b'ng c'ng at attention. Diffuses in word focus. The pay off in pay dirt. Paint is essentially dirt. Somehow the paint captures attention in a biocognative feeling a electromagnetic fielding of it by a b'ng c'ng y'all present now as'z mere mirrored seer reflected as"za though in sight of this painting. This personic pingting." She stared back at him still chewing a mouthful of food. After a moment she took a swallow of tea before replying.

"You crazy daddy with the dialectic. Still y'all may be onto something if not on something. Memory of a b c's of you or me reflected as'z'any thoth'tsz of a b'ng c'ng in the painting. A see'ng scene in the painting still a b'ng of you beyond anybody out in na'me alone. That's'z breaking out of the in word spell of alphabeta. Disappearing anybody. Indivisible in'visibility of you in her'eyez z z'a now appearing there then merely mirrored in imagined image before h'our eyes. Perhaps War're'y'na's viral neurotoxin amplifies the spelling a'sz sound waves above or below h'our in'visibility frequency till in word conversation turns silent. Without phonetic supersonic in word conversation superimposed focus of attention will diffuse. A black'g'round echo of it in a're'y'all turning into or out of a y black eye peh'ss'y whole. You now turn a black'g'round echo of it as'k'no'wing feeling alone by a b'ng c'ng y'all a felt fielding denial of that indivisible complete d"ark'ness. By denial in word'all'y y'all feel alone.

"Warren's virus may liberate attention from that denial. Thus feeling of a b'ng c'ng in name alone may turn reassurance of anyone as'z still that indivisible in'visibility beyond any in word name. Feeling alone now turning into k'no'wing of it then a complete indivisible invisibility. Liberated anybody experiencing complete blackness realizes that means feeling being lacking awhile still aware of a complete d"ark'ness encirclement of it. Thus potential cause of any urge of energy now too k'no'w out of it any adding on is mitigated. Is liberated in word. Any addition of it is a mere mirrored a pairing of a y eye a peering it out aw'h'ile as'ex. Yet still in the first place completely indivisible y'all. Out of it now as'k'no'wing of it a d'na'eye'll. Int'word a twisted black'g'round echoing in word d'na'eye'll of a b'ng c'ng indivisible invisibility by now appearing supernaturally as'z'any thoth'tsz of it. A'sz thoth'tsz of standing with eyes'z z star'e'y'e'ing out in any mirror. That'sz ma'sz tricky trix of it in her'ey'e of a b'ng c'ng now out of any or eve're'ybody. Eve're'ybody turning now into k'no'wing out of it in word letter'all'y y'all a b'ng c'ng of anybody out in na'me alone. A y eye of a b'ng c'ng still indivisible alone in'visibility of y'all along. We all easily turn into falling understanding that in word na'me spelling of it.

"War'rey'na's virus may activate and stimulate becoming more aware of awareness of a y eye merely a'peering it in the first place. Still a b'ng c'ng indivisible in'visibility of it by now a k'no'wing out of it into appearing as'z'any thoth'tsz of understanding it in word. A y eye b'ng c'ng freestanding in the first place. A peering it out captivated in word of a b c's of it. Now under that spelling. Turning churning burning aw'h'ile a black'g'round a k'now'ing it out. Y'all supernaturally superimposed as'z thoth'tsz of a y eye being c'ng other y'sz asz'z ex's ting in formation. "

Mor imagined the virus spreading y eye'szaz'z thoth'tsz of her'me'sz'za in her'eye a peering it indivisible in'visibility out of eve're'ybody in which you can supernaturally appear a pair. A sharing in your own company each still with that you'ni'que you ni vers'all'y y'all point of view. Of you. A'sz ex'acting of a being you by any mirrored role of y'all still you now merely a kno'wing out of it. As'z'any mere supernatural thoth'tsz of a projection of a y eye a'peering it out in word. A b'ng c'ng supersonicall'y y'all in'visibility of any a peering out of it. A projecting it now a black'g'round echo of a y k'no no no'wing out of it as'z'ex'et'ting duplicating it supernaturally y'all as'z'za thoth'tsz. In'her'eye"me'asz it. Go'a'd esse to be letter'all'y y'all art being a b'ng c'ng in word in formation. A'sz a y eye being be'am'ing supersonic in word thoth'tsz in order as'z too, now turning it out k'no no no'wing it as'z intwo'rd a twis'ting of it into appearing a pair. A 0 into 8 appearing a pairing. In his mind words appearing now as'z informa'sz"'a't'i'on. AzzSupersonically superimposed out by any in word conversation. A'peering it out in word now k'no'wing out of it appearing in'ka's on papyrus. War're'y'na's virus might serve us by liberating attention from subdominate preoccupation in a b c's he pondered. With that a b'ng c'ng a peering it out in any in word spell. Of a y eye being c'ng a peering it still in the first place now appearing out of it in k'no'wing a d'na'eye'll of it in any na'me alone. Inflating h'our self importance. A'w'h'ile. That mirror'age of a'w'h'ile. Christina, eyes fixed to a point beyond him, paused taking sips of the tea. The liquid seemed to fill her up he thought between ravishing grindage of the food on his part. She'e'na glowed. He glanced over at the easel while continuing shoveling stir fry into his open mouth.

"In other word'sz'a War're'y'na's virus will either break the spelling or perpetuate it in silence till we all turn to bang our way out into another long while in order to keep appearing to disappear." Keep busy being busy he thought. Now turning out a k'no'wing a y eye a peering it out y'all along without realizing it? That'sz'za sheer absurdity. Turning a blind eye to awareness of a y eye of a b'ng c'ng indivisible in'visibility of anybody appearing of it now as'ex's ting. As'ex'et'ting in her'eye as'king of it y of eve'reybody appearing disappearing in a're'y'fracting a k'no'wing out of it black'g'round. As'king of it as'ka's mic mic'ro wayeves turning a black'g'round in her' black eye a ma'rey'eye g'round mirror seas appearing it out in words. Yet still indivisible in'visibilty of anybody or any chintzy chiseling cheap thin'king of it. Appearing aw'h'ile the'n disappearing. A b'ng'lack'g'round as'king of it y now a k'no'wing out of it appearing a gain. Mor felt his guts quake with the words vomiting from his mouth. A beast of revelation seemed to be charging out. Echoing the overstanding status quo of a y eye of a herhimit a peering it from above. Ove a b'ng c'ng with polarity in the e'l'eft h'and. Da y na light igniting it in the other. Igniting a synapsis of it across that polarity on hand. Da'y now as'ka's mic eye light igniting a black'g'round ignore'ance of it from above. Ove a b'ng c'ng indivisible in'visibility now as'king of it y'all ignoring or k'no'wing out of it int'wo'rd a t'wis'ting in two d'na'eye'll of merely a peering it out into any appearance of it as k'no no no'wing out in'visibility int'word in formation. As a god esse. To be letter'all'y y'all supernaturally appearing as'z'any thoth'tsz of it. Her'me'as'z'thoth'tsz of a herhimit. Mor felt as though chewing on wordszz'azz'any thoth'tsz of it. A god letter'ally y'all a go go going do'or wayeve out now a while a space in time.

"You may be onto something or on something. In that I am detecting a peculiar vapor from when you first opened the pain'ta tubes. Actually it brings my attention to that sketch of the extra-terrestrial. A being c'ng of your close encounter you showed me the day of h'our first meeting." She 'e'na stretched her stockinged legs out with their backs against the wall.

"Was that me blabbing that much that day sketching you?"

"That sketch of a being, a'sz'z'ex'tra-ter're'y's'tri'al, looked eerily similar to various images of Akhenaten."

"In that I am realizing any imagined image of awakening aten in the first place must be mere concoction of it. A y eye mirror a're'y'flection of imagination," Mor replied. He'd returned hobbling to his high chair parked before the easel. Holding the palette up to his nose he drew a few quick breathes testing for a reaction. Aten'cion alone indivisible must go to a y eye of a b'ng c'ng in'visibility of any seer came to his attention. aSe'rey'e. a'na'ySe'er'eye. A b'ng c'ng a peering it out now. As'king of it y in her'eye or a la que"en que' of that in which eve're'ybody as'k'no no no'wing out any appearing of it int'word in formation.

The one at aten'cion of his thinking. El que ve. The one who sees. El ka'ba. Ka ba ela. A b'ng c'ng of it in her"eye of eve're'ybody now without. As'z k'no'wing it out int'word a dna'eye'll of it. As'ka's mic now a k'no'wing out of it supersonically supernaturally superimposed y'all. Appearing a gain out of a b'ng'lack' of it. Jack he flashed. A b'ng c'ng a peering from above without y'all appearing in the first place. A b'ng c'ng merely a peering it now potentially as'za black'g'round echo appearing of it as'z'z sound wayeves function of el que ve. A b'ng c'ng int'word a perceived d'na'eye'll of it. Still indivisible in'visibility of anybody a'peering at it now as'king of it a k'no'wing out of it appearing anything or anybody any time. Any where. Now he really cracked himself up. Into thousands of bits of information. Y'et in that proverbial blink of eye a're'y'congealing a b'ng c'ng indivisible in'visibility of anybody. Thass'z z'ome go down she'et mon he pondered.

Still now a'peering it out a k'nowing of it appearing in any in word thoth'ts'z of a b'ng c'ng still in the first place. A y eye as'ex posed as'z a b'ng c'ng from ab'ove. Ove a b'ng still in the first place. Indivisible in'visibility of it. Mor thought how in name we all turn out denying a y eye of a being y'all as'z'ex'posed now a' peering it out in word with a gravity weight of appearing now waitng to k'no'w a disappearing of it then. In'a y eye now speak speaking supersonically or phonographically. Freestanding silently by of in or for'ma'sz yourself. Mirrored out in word memory. Supernaturally y'all asz'zany thoth'tsz of it. Mor felt the charge of learning a new language or a new way out of the captivity of any spelling of an old one.

He felt supercharged by wayeves rolling him out of captivity of the X'odus. A w/ay eye speaking supersonically as thoth'tsz of a b'ng c'ng still in the first place. A place of playing out any mirrored y na'me role in a'w'h'ile of rolling roiling sheets as'ex planing of a y eye now. Flattened out as'z x's ting out of it. A'while now a space in time. Still a' b'ng c'ng a'peering it out in plane site of any or eve're'y'body. A y eye of a b'ng c'ng still in the first place now as'ex mirrored of a k'no no no'wing out of it in sight. A b'ng c'ng indivisible supernaturally y'all a pairing as'ka's mic karmic mem or y. Turning out volumes of in word k'no'wing of objectivity by ignoring it still at attention of indivisible subjective awareness. Supernaturally a're'y"el'a't'ive denying that in'visibility of any subjectivity into appearing of it out front mesmerized in word in'formation. Now the artist k'no'wing that bites back down on his own tale. He laughed hard out loud still holding the tale of him in his teeth. He saw her'eye in sight of him. Her'me'asz'za 'thoth'tsz of a peering it out of her'eye of eve're'ybody.

"The jo'ka's'z on in you or a y you're'ye merely a'peering it out in wordsz now appearing of it. The transmission of now k'no'wing it is in any plain sight. In ANY plain sight. A b'ng c'ng supernaturally transmitted as'king of it y by now k'now'ing it out in word in formation in any predominant plain sight. By a b'ng c'ng y'all in sight of her'e'ye. As'king of it y'or y na. Y na you now a scant scrawny starved thin'king of it. As'ka's mic memory of a being merely mirrored. A being c'ng there is anybody supersonically y'all superimposed out in word. Y'all a's'za appearing opening mouth in speech. A being be'am'ing any image imagined in word as'z sound means of it. Su'personically or phonographically speaking.

"Pharaoh Amenhotep IV 'filled the bill' of having realized that. In a y eye of a'ten. A being now at aten'scion as'king of it y a k'no'wing out of it a binary. A pairing of it a'w'h'ile still indivisible in the first place. Pharaoh is pa'roo'ma. A first place. A field of view of you still awareness of it. A ware now to be. A b'ng c'ng still indivisible in'visibility of it. A're'y'all"ity as'king of it y. Any appearance of it by a na'rey"e. A d'na'eye'all of it by now out k'no' no no'wing it. A b'ng c'ng still in the first place indivisible in'visibility of it out mirrored in word phonographically for the first time now a b c's in formation. As'z'any in word thoth'tsz of a b'ng c'ng a peering it now superimposed as'z' any or eve'rey'body. A b c's infor'ma'sz y'all time now mere awareness of a peering it out in a memory of thoth'tsz. A God letter'all'y an eye'star'e'y"e'in'g from above." She'e'na gave Mor that piercing stare of a sublime transmission of an ancient su'puranic awareness.

"Ove a b'ng c'ng through its a're'y'et'rans'mission by his father Pharaoh Amenhotep III. A re'ye'transmission of a b'ng c'ng at aten'cion in the cult'u'a're'ye of A'ten. Of it at aten'scion of any or eve're'y'body" Mor now viscerally felt in his gut a micro wayeve a'spy'r'ey'all'ing an ancient cultivation of awareness of a being still in the first place. A pa'roo'ma. A now at a ten'sc'ng'eye'on a k'no no no'wing out of it. A d'na'eye'll of it. A will wheel of we all turning a'spiraling into or out of A bi na d'na re'ye'sz'zazz no'w'a y eye ra'y'dhi'a'ting a'ten. Int'word a 0 a twis'ting into an 8. Appearing a pairing of it. A b'ng c'ng a'peering it out now as'king of it y a k'no'wing d'na'eye'll as'z'any a na y appearing a pairing of it b'y na re'y a'sz mirroring it supernaturally as'z'any thoth'tsz of it in word memory. In any man'as mind or y'all supernaturally asz'zany thoth'tsz of a being still in the first place that indivisible invisibility at aten'scion of any individual. Pharaoh now pa'roo'ma. A in first place b'ng c'ng of it. A re'y'all'eye'z z zed of a b'ng c'ng now out of a b'ng in the first place in words'z'zany in formation as'z'ka's of it. A y eye a peering it out now a k'nowing of it. as'King of it a la Que"en que' of that in which appearing it. A na y eye as'k'no'wing a d'na'eye'll of it out in her'me'azz'thoth'tsz'of it supersonically or phonographically anybody appearing in word at aten'cion of it out in her'eyez z z of eve're'ybody. Her'eye peh'sy'ta peh'tower of peh'esse'y b'lack w'hole power. A b'ng lack appearing as'za gain. Mor found the a'sKing of it a la Que"en qui'. That in which appears anythin'king of it etc.. Still as'king of it y. Adam and Eve of the painting. The ping'ting of it black'g'round the Korner house.

"That'sz how y'all picked up on y speak. 'Eee'jeh"peh'ta. Playing paying aten"cion. The Pa roo'ma vision of a y eye being c'ng still in the first place. Peha'roo'ma A'ten?" Mor saw in a bi"us na're'ye. A y eye a peering it out now as'z'z'ex. Exodus. As'zz' ex'et'ting duplicating out in her'eye of eve're'ybody. Ask'a'rving it a black'g'round echoing int'word a twis'ting in two in formation of it appearing a pairing in mem'or'y. He felt his Egyptian memory dishing out supersonically a're'y'all of a being a'ten. Pa'roo'ma Akhen"aten. Aw/akhen aten still in the first place. A y eye being still in the first place now a'peering it out of it mirrored supernaturally as thoth'tsz of appearing out in word in formation. As'k'ing of it a y eye b'ng c'ng in pa'roo'ma. A b'ng c'ng still in the first place. A'peering it out now turning a black'g'round as'ka's of indivisible aten'cion a pairing merely supernaturally as'z'any in word thoth'tsz of it appearing in formation. A y eye still at aten'cion he blinked. His thought preoccupied with in word memory of it. Still in the peh'esse'y w'hole. Mor mused with a laugh. A preoccupation with any palpitation.

A b'ng c'ng in word. In formation now a'while. A y eye being cee'ng z'eye'ing it. Captivated supernaturally as thoth'tsz of it. Her'me'szz'a'thoth'tsz of it in'visibility now in formation of any k'no'wing it out in ka's mic memory. As'k'ing of it a y? A h"OO"ka de'l"OO"ka. In formation of any situation. A b'ng c'ng in formation of any in word formation of y'all. A y eye paying aten'cion. Captivated with in word.

Status quo? State in which a b'ng c'ng. Still freestanding state status of a herhimit of a y eye a peering it out a'sz'za'xxxxxxxxxxxxxxxxxxxxx'o'h'odus wayeve'as'ex is ting in formation in her'eye'szz'azz of eve're'y'body. A peering it out now as'ka'y'no'wing int'word a t'wis'ting in two a y eye a peering it out a pairing into a b'ng c'ng supernaturally supersonically superimposed asz'bi any thoth'tsz of it appearing in word in formation. Appearance of the indivisible in'visibility at aten'cion of now a k'no'wing out of it a pairing in me or you as'ka's all'y y'all in'k'as mic memory intelligence consciousness he thought.

"That is a being now as thoth'tsz be'am'ing a bi na re'y ar'king of the sacred covenant of YodHayVaVHay. The tetra'gramm'aten 4 letter a'ten as'za binary. A being appearing of'ten by na re'y'asz radiating now out of it a k'no'wing of anybody or anythin'king of it. The by now a being y na re'y of a ma're'y g"round. A baby. There is a being of'ten appearing of it out in a bi na re'y'ed in any plain sight. At at'ten'tion of plane sight refracting in word as'ex'plane'ing of it."

"A being c'ng now at attention intentionally k'no'wing ignore'ance of it still indivisible," he replied. Laughter rolled out from his belly. A being in sight of her'ey'e instilled a vigorous laughter state reminding him of trips on psyllicibin. Orgasmic rushes in his brain seemed to be producing psychoactive chemicals. Ride the rus's"sh'a of'ten he flashed.

"Pharaoh Amenhotep IV now Akhenaten had himself imagined in 3D sculpture as a god. Imagine you have as'king of it y'all as'ka'smic insight. Found yourself understanding overstanding. Finding that while coming into the divine rulership of the known western world. He realized now still indivisible in'visibility a b c's of a b'ng c'ng as pure power in word in formation. As'king of it y now a k'no'wing appearing of a heretic mystic.

"Source'or'eye of a b'ng c'ng in the first place now out a black'g'round echoing any in word in formation a k'no'wing of it. A's b'ng c'ng of that appearing supernaturally y'all out of it by aten'cion captivated as'z'za thoth'tsz of it appearing out in word. By means of a phonographic alphabeta. Indivisible in'visibility of a b'ng c'ng appearing a b c's superimposed supernaturally y'all in word as thoth'tsz of it. A Great God esse to be letter'all'y y'all art b'ng c'ng in word information." In any beginning is the word Mor realized. Any appearing of it information still indivisible in'visibility of a b'ng c'ng in the first place. As'King of it a la Que"en que' of that in which appearing any time now a k'no'wing out of it anythin'king of it anywhere etc.. A b'ng c'ng supernaturally asz'any thoth'tsz of her'me'asz it. A peering it out of her'eyez z z' of eve'reybody. At attention of a're'y"e means of a b'ng c'ng meaningful indivisible in'visibility.

"A su'personic b"OO"ma's. Still now as'king of it y a k'nowing out in word a plan x'et'ting h'ear'th echoing out lasting a long wily w'h'ile. Still 3300+ y'ears later as'king of it a y eye b'ng c'ng in word a'w/akhen'ing a'ten? T'sz a h"OO"ka del"OO"ka de'b'"OO"ka's still as'king of it a y eye of a b'ng c'ng in any plain sight." Mor fully discerned that as'king of it y now a'k'no'wing out of it anythin'king of a d'na'eye'll on it.

"Perhaps, y'all things considered, the most powerful individual influence of y'all time. A b'ng c'ng still in the first place. A b'ng c'ng hidden centuries in plain sight of any or eve're"y'body. int'word a twisting dna'eye'll of it in formation. A now k'no'wing out of it y'all along. Indivisible in'visibility of any individual a peering out of it a'w'h'ile still in the first place. At aten'cion in a pa'roo'ma. In for'ma'sz a first time now as'king of it a k'no'wing a la que"en que' of that in which appears in her'eyez z z of eve're'ybody. A'w/akhen a'ten. Awakhen at aten'cion." A ringing silence enveloped the room captivating attention in supersonic vibrations echoing that perceived ar'king ask'ing of it y a ka's mic black'g'round echoing in'visibility of pain'ting as'z harmonic ping'ting wayeves fun'ny'action in formation appearing disappearing in disinformation right before herhimit'eye'zz'a of any or eve're'ybody now k'no'wing a dna'eye'll on it.

"A y eye being c'ng in the first place a peering it out now still anybody appearing out of it in word as'king of it a k'no'wing a supersonic boom boom. Capturing attention reverberating in word a black'g'round echoing as'king of it now a k'no no no'wing it out int'word a twisting in two a pairing d'na'eye'll of it superimposed at least 3300+ y'ears. A mirrored 3300+ supersonic a y eye'ears a h'earing it echoing a black'g'round complete dhi"ark'ness encirclement of it. In any beginning is a y eye being c'ng in the first place now a peering it out as'word cutting y'all up and out. Supernaturally y'all as thoth'tsz of now as'king of it a division by k'no no no'wing the indivisible.

"Pay aten't'tion brother man. Pay to play. Another race channel for we all perpetuating a turning wheel black'g'round that ancient cult of aten aryan warriorpriests. As descendents of a vedic Atman. Are'ye at Aten'cion. Atma'sz a peering it. A by now as'k'no'wing that indivisible in'visibility a's a b'ng c'ng in a re'ye"all out int'word a twis'ting in two appearing a pearing in'formation of a d'na'eye'll of it.

"Egypt had been steadily infiltrated over hundreds of years prior to the time of Akhenaten by an unbroken lineage of these warrior priests of ATMAN. Enlightened conquerors they were a force to be reckoned with. They were monotheists by lineage. It is in that immortal vedic oral lineage that I am initiated. A tradition of a b'ng na' eve'reybody see'ng out in word. A word as'z'any 'per'sonic sound wayeve're'y"e mean means of y'all a meaning'ful understanding the free overstanding of it. 'Anybody h'earing of it in a're'y"ez z z'a means still indivisible in'visibility. Language in a're'y'e then stayed purely phonetic.

"Now with invention of a phonographic alphabeto a mean'while of it appears in sight. Any seer a peering it out in word in forms it supernaturally in a peh'ssy'ta w'hole power of imagination. Imagining a b c's out. In word a b'ng c'ng still in the first place indivisible in'visibility. Now as'k'no'wing out of a peering it int'word a twisting dna'eye'll in two it appearing a pairing awhile as'z'za feeling e motion at aten'cion in a binary bios-cellular-chemical-neuronic muscle blood bone field of view. Of you primarily a b'ng c'ng now as'king of it y a k'no'wing it out in word in formation of a ka's mic memory. A y eye a'peering it out a wily while. A deadly duplicity of it appearing a pairing with in'kas drawn on papyrus. Peh'na a'sword to divide and conquer. A'peering it out in word now as'king of it y a twis'ting in'two appearing a pairing in ka's mic memory.

"A y eye b'ng sacred awareness now asking of it az'z'any supersonic sound wayeves echoing a black'g'round in her'eye. A b'lack' eye of eve're'ybody asking of it to be a gain. Still silent indivisible in'visibility of a b'ng c'ng a'peering it out in sound healthy wayeves int'word a perception of it now magically y'all appearing aw'h'ile. As'ex'y'all. As'king of it y now a k'no'wing any un'ak'now'n'a black'g'round echo of it. We all turning in a wheel race channel of man'as mind or memory in 3D. Spoken in word a're'ye'dhi'a'ting from a pi'vot peh'ow'er of a b'ng c'ng still in the first place now peh'sy't power in her'peh'esse"eye w'hole eve'll. As'k'as micro wayeve b'lack'g'round echoing wheel of we'all a will to be a gain insight of it out in her'eyez z z of eve're'ybody.

"Invention of a phonographic alphabeta incites now in sight of it a material duplicity of a b'ng c'ng with ink'as mirroring as'king of it a pairing of the indivisible. Now out a'z'any thoth'tsz of writing a b'ng c'ng letter'all'y y'all a b c's in formation on papyrus.

"In that I am finding confirmation of Amenhotep IV's insight of that a b'ng c'ng in a're'y'e"ality. a'Re'ye'ality as'king of it y a being c'ng merely a peering it out in word now a k'no'wing appearing of it. A'y eye in sight. A being c'ng of a y eye insight of that indivisible invisibility in visibility of it. A wordfree immortal untouched awareness now su'personically a b'ng c'ng as'z' any individual perceived out of it in word. A Pa'roo'Ma. A Paramabrahma. Paramount of a b'ng c'ng in plain eve'rey'day sight of anybody or out in her'eyez z z of eve're'y'body. A being in the first place now out of it in A. R'e;ye radiant radiation of first su'personic abstract principal principle of a singular indivisible in'visibility. A re'y'all of the point of view of you. Ar ya with me? Y'all do a bunch of respirating heh hey as'z breath equated with p'ra'na the divine synapse fire when y'all speak y'or y'all now turning around k'no no no'wing out of it as'z' any thin'king of it in plane sight." Slipping off the robe Christina walked over to stretch out on the high chair. Static sparks came off hands sliding over nylon stockinged legs.

"In that I am feeling my attention a's'ex'pand. Breathing it, feeling it now. You got me at'"aten'ci'on any time now baby. Ba being y," he gave dead pan to mask the energy jetting his spine. "If you ain't gotten aten, you got no'ting." Cerebrospinal fluid rushing his heart brain activated his pinecone gland to upgraded ma'tabolites he recognized as'z z'yche'del'ic. This could be DMT but unlike the synthetics he'd experienced, his pinecone emited full spectrum. He thought for a moment of directing the healing out to his extremities but his heartbrain surged with a life force of its own he flashed as it flashed and cashed him.

"Exactly. You a're'y'main man'as'z'any mirrored thoth'tsz of you now as'z e'x acting the part of anybody in a mirror duplicity of it. Okay so importance of talking about far and away the most powerful su'personic person man or a y eye being c'ng on the plan'et still about the A y eye connection. Now a long long looonng while still as'king of it. Aw'akhen'aten at aten'cion of the first individual still in the first place indivisible invisibility. A y eye of a b'ng c'ng a peering it or out of it a now immortality as'king of it as'ka's mic a K'e'y'e to the Letter'all code. The whole she-bang has been buried hidden ignored in plain sight of anybody a k'no'wing it out in d'na'eye'll of it." Mor found attention moving into the drawers of pain't. Igniting an ignoring in word ignore'ance of it now as'king of it y a drawing on the wordfree untouched right side of the brain. He found himself that silence of a seer merely a peering it. Or now at it aszz'a color spectrum. Opening drawers he began selecting tubes to be layed out on top of the taboret. Christina settled into a pose with breasts bared. Out in her eyes he felt subliminal wayeves transmitting a k'no no no'wing out of it a b'ng c'ng a b c's in word in formation of y'all along. In sight of anybody see'ng out now a k'no'wing of it any measly meager thin'king of it int'word a twis'ting d'na'eye'll in forming it. A will wheel of we all turning as'ka's mic microwayeve black'g'round echo of it into anybody anythin'king of it etc.. Still merely a peering it. A b'ng c'ng still indivisible in'visibility in any plain sight of a peering it out into now turning into any k'no'wing appearing of it. As'z' any in word in'forming of it. Supernaturally supersonically superimposed in for'ma'sz'any thoth'tsz of a God esse. To be letter'all'y int'word a twis'ting in two informing anybody etc. appearing a pairing in d'na"eye"ll. A will wayeve of ma'sz'za'pping y'all'sz super ka're'y"e'ing wayeve d'nature of it. Her'me'a'sz'thoth'tsz a're'y'e"minder of a y eye of a being c'ng a'peering it still of'ten'a eye at aten'cion. Or a d'na'eye'll of it. At aten'cion. A binary of anybody appearing out a's'z e'x's ting supernaturally supersonically superimposed merely a being out as'z'king of it y in word thoth'tsz mirroring mind or memory of awareness of a y eye merely a peering it. Or at it. A b'ng c'ng now a y's'z dom'us'a b'ng in the first place. A whole indivisible point of view. At aten'cion of you. Of a y eye that I am is is indivisible in'visibility of anybody any scant thin'king of it anywhere etc.. Finally his attention came to rest on breasts.

Mor's ma n'eve'r gave him the breast. Then he could not imagine the sheer terror of looking into those mad eyes while suckling her milk. He now found like many of his bottle fed generation a breast fetish. Christina smiled slyly reading his thoth'tsz.

Now and forever for'ma'sz eve're"y body he mused. A re'ye body arrayed over centuries in aw'h'ile of the plan"et h'earth supersonically appearing out in her"eye'z z z'in many many ma'sz ways of eve'll. A will in her'eye wayeve function of fun'ny'a'ction. Ma'sz tricky business. In that awareness of a b'ng c'ng still in the first place. Still. She'e'na funny that way. As'z that wayeve're'y'body. As'ka'mic memory intelligence consciousness of a b'ng c'ng as'ka'ming black'g'round echoing in complete loop'y rolls of d"ar'king of en'y'body esse to be with in word intent of a being of'ten anybody. Uncapping some pain't he began taking whiffs of various colors.

Anybody is a b'ng c'ng in her'eyez z z of eve re'y body. Awhile now. A mean while awareness of anybody of a b'ng c'ng still in the first place. Pretty trippy he flashed. A re'ye'all arrayed in any plain sight in order to function in that sensory way of eve. Y'all senses learned in word. Mor found his hands squeezing tubes of the paint in an array of color following a rainbow spectrum. These he mixed rapidly in the center of the pallette or directly on the fresh canvass. Working with knife and brush he began carving out color'saz"za for'm'asz in her a re'y'eall body. Body of a dancer. Or a runner. Muscled. Still plenty limber. He let his eye do the work of hands following. He had a fresh taboret of pain'ta and little time for beating it around any bush he mused while hands loaded color. Pigment worms turning churning burning. Fired up. Muted down. A sheer function of it. A hand following eye by a b'ng c'ng mirrored in word memory. A peering it now turning a black'g'round echo of it into appearing by k'no'wing it out in word. In a wily w'h'ile of fun'ny'a'ction in wayeves of her'eye of eve're'y body a're'y'dhi'a'ting a black'g'round echoing indivisible in'visibility a pairing supernaturally y'all as thoth'tsz of it in memory.

"Once Pharaoh Amenhotep IV fully awakhened awareness of a being aten'c'ng at a'ten'cion he instantaneously became it. Assumed the name of it. Akhenaten. I am aten. I of eyez z z at aten'cion in a memory. A b'ng c'ing by now k'no'wing it out int'word a twis'ting of it in two appearing a pairing in formation. A spiral echoing a black'g'round of it as'ka's mic memory. Once aware of awareness of it in any eye merely a peering it he picked up on a b'ng c'ng indivisible in'visibility. He grasped the power of phonographic memory of that indivisible in'visibility of a b'ng c'ng now out in word spelling any appearing of it. Appearing supernaturally as'z'any thoth'tsz in for'ma'sz a pairing out in as'king of it y now a k'no'wing ka's mic memory d'na'eye'll of it.

"It mirror'da' in word for'ma'sz'dhi'nature of it in her"e'ye y'll d'na'ture of d'na'eye'll in now as'king of it y a k'no no no'wing out of it into any appearance of it in awhile. A cunning deceitful craft carrying away any man'as mind at aten'cion of a b'ng c'ng as'ex." With the mention of it as'ex she'e'na flexed a back pushing breasts forward. Nipples stood erect in the chill air of a warehouse. "Akhenaten as'king of it y now as'z'any k'no'wing out of a b'ng c'ng in a phonographic alphabeta of it precipitated an exodus of a b'ng still in the first place at attention now captivated as'z'any thoth'tsz of it out appearing in word. Now asex'et'ting duplicating in the wordsza of a b'ng c'ng still in the first place indivisible invisibility. Now a pairing appearing out supersonically y'all superimposed phonographically in memory as'z' any in word in forming of it. Still in a while of it Akhenaten picking up on a b'ng c'ng indivisible invisibility in the first place cultivated a cult of any individual as diffi'cult. As'z differing int'word a twis'ting in two d'na'eye'll capturing aten'cion merely mirrored as'z'any in word thoth'tsz of it.

"Pharaoh realized y'all any worship of a b'ng c'ng is as'king of it y appearing by a mirrored supernatural a're'y eye 'flection. A rey'all of a y eye b'ng c'ng a peering it out in word as thoth'tsz of it in formation. A being of it still indivisible in'visibility of any . . . ANY appearance. Indivisible then. Indivisible now k'no no no'wing out of it into a pairing in memory of me or you. Any apparent in word information is a d'na'eye'll of it. In a y eye of a b'ng c'ng merely a peering it. It still indivisible in'visibility. Hence the second biblical commandment against worshipping any in word idol in formation of it. Twis'ting a'peering it out now int'word appearing of it eve're'ye'thin'king of it a k'no'wing it as a d"arking b'lack'g'round echoing a b'ng c'ng as'z a gain. Again in d'na y light igniting ignore'ance of it into appearing awhile. A cunning murderous duplicity of a b'ng c'ng g'ng appearance out in word now a k'no'wing of it in formation.

"We all in turn have been duped into believing h'our own duplicity. H'our a peering it int'word a twis'ting in two of it supersonically mirrored aska's mic black mirror seas a're'y'flecting it into appearing as any thin'king of it or anybody. Indivisible in'visibility now ask'ing of it a y eye k'no'wing a b'ng c'ng out in word in formation. A y'll d'na tat u a'r'eye being cee'ng any a na y a or ten. A b'ng c'ng out bi now a k'now'ing of it a na y body. A'na y b'ng c'ng in that a y eye in the first place merely a'peering it out as'z e'x. As'eX's ting in formation. At once as'king of it a b'ng c'ng appearing in a w'h'ile y'et above and beyond the mirror he still turned black. Supernaturally as'z'za n'y thoth'tsz of Amenhotep IV as'k'ing of it y. A y eye of a b'ng c'ng a peering it in a Pa'roo'ma Akhen'aten turned black'g'round as'k'ing now out of a y eye k'no'wing the k'nu supersonic language wordship craft of a b'ng c'ng a'sz'z"eX o'dus. Ex'hodos. A wayeve's'ex out of the first place merely as'z'any d'na'eye'll of it." She'e'na offered now stretching fingers to toes.

"Still say'el'ing that in wordship craft of a b'ng c'ng of Pharaoh Akhen'A'ten a peering it out in word in'formation." Mor flashed on the silouette of him or a b'ng c'ng merely a peering it. A now appearing of it as'z the supernatural supersonic craft of any in word in formation of it superimposed as a b'ng c'ng as'z'anythin'king of it in her'eve'll'eye of eve're'ybody. Out in her'eye a wayeve will. A will of we all turning a b'ng'lack'g'round into or out of a b'ng c'ng a gain. As'king of it y a la que"en que' of that in which a y or'eyet'n bi now na r'ey'e'sz'za b'ng still in the first place merely apeering it out in word in forming of it. A say"el'ing a'w'h'ile in that function of a cunning craft. Of a y eye of a b'ng c'ng a peering it out in word now as'king of it y a k'nowing d'na'eye'll as'ex out t'word a twis'ting in two. A y as'ex's ting in any formation of it. Supernaturally supersonically superimposed a'sz'za'n'y thoth'tsz of it. Asz a God'esse to be letter'all'y y'all art of a b'ng c'ng now as'k'no'wing out a wily w'h'ile. A peering it out int'word a twis'ting of it as'z'any thoth'tsz of turning in two or out of any in word captivity of it at aten'cion in her'eye of eve're'ybody. Aten'cion now seemed as though to shift from any imaginary point appearing before his eyes into merging with a singular point of view of it. Then it, a y eye of view, went black. From a b'ng c'ng in sight to a b'lack peh'ssy'w'hole power. Indivisible in'visibility instilled with true power of intent to be a gain of it. Power of a y'll of d'na'eye'll. A pow pow power of a y'll int'word a twis'ting in two of it. A y eye merely a peering it into it now as'ex y'all in a d'na'eye'll appearing a pairing of it. She'ena funny that way. That wayeve in her'eyez z z'a keeps rolling a black'g'round echoing in the peh'ssy w'hole a'qui of a Dark Mor.

Aw/akhen now k'nowing aten. A'ware'now to be a y eye that that I am is is za'zz'at aten'scion. Indivisible in'visibility appearing a pairing mirrored in word memory. A b'ng c'ng now out of it as'ka's of a k'nowing blackness. A y eye complete being now k'nowing b'ng'lack'n'esse. Now k'now'ing b'ng'lack with intent to be a 'gain'. Oh to be a gain. Mor found himself adrift on a churning sea of color. Taking it to the line of a sea of mud. Karving it black on per pose of it. It now that electromagnetic field of you a's'z"z'awareness in herhimit'eyesz'zz'a wayeve of any or eve're'ybody. A'sz'om'ething in the pain't Mor wondered? A certain magnetism in the heavy metal cadmium and cobalt pigment. An electrical color fire ground into oil. Viscerely feeling the field of pain'ta now a k'no'wing ping'ting of it. A tinitus in a h'ear'ing now ringing a high pitch that seemed to swell then fade like waves lapping the shore of his cranium.

Mor loved offsetting color with black frauhoferesque brush hair veins. Caught lightly dragging a #14 hog bristle brush over the texture of knife and brush spreading pigment in a cobalt cadmium cerulean'asz'z'whirl. She'ena emerged from a instrumental body of multihued luminescence dancing off a patterned contour of muscle blood and bone appearing in her'eye of Margot Christina. As'z'z'ex y'all.

A b'ng"lack n"esse now to be a gain. Blackness as'king of it y now as'z'za Dark'n'esse to be more aware a b'ng complete perceived encirclement of any or eve're'ybody in a role. A ye'll'y jell'y roll. A loop'y quantum gravity loop of a're'y turning a b'lack'g'round echoing instilling any intent to appear a gain. A're'y turning completely b'lack'g'round a polarity. A positive intentional negativity. Intention of y now negating a b'ng c'ng still in the first place indivisible. A b'ng complete. A're'y'all loop without any endings to begin a polarity of it. Now to be dhi ar'king of perception. A complete d"ark'ness. He shaking it out. A mere mirrored ob'server. Ob'serving in her'ey'e a feeling field of her'me'asz thoth'tsz of it appearing a pairing of a peh'ss'y'ence polarity in the or y of any memory. Ob"servation. o'B'oyo"B'o y. A y eye a peering it t'wo'rds projecting a b'OO'x's'z'ting now of that awareness of a being c'ng out as'k'no'no'wing that. That eye of I am is is a singular o'ne. O k'ey"e 15 in ABBC code. The d'Eve'll. In her'eve'll eye of eve're'ybody'sz'za'ppingting. A will. Of we all. A wheel turning o"v"er re'ye. A y eye in turning a black'g'round complete d"ark'n'ess'e now to be perceived a b'ng c'ng out in word formation of a captivity. Of aten'cion paid to merely play out in wordsz awhile. As'z's'ex.

Mor now found himself a y eye b'ng c'ng mirrored as'ex. An ex'et'ting ex'hodos. A way of x a un k'no'wn as'king of it y now free in a wordfreedom awareness of it. Freedom. Freedom now. In a wordfreedom forever. Drawing on the wordfree right side of the brain. Free untouched awareness of a b c's etc. he grinned. Words melted black asz'ounds into one peh's'eye'lence of it in her'eve'll eye of any or eve'reybody. That black mirror seas body a'rey'flecting d'na'eye'll in a y light.

Indivisible invisibility now in her'eyesz'z z. In for ma'sz d'na'eye'ture of eve'rey'body a peering it out int'word a twis'ting in t'wo a pairing. A pain'ting. A ping'ting echoing of it. A b'ng cing merely a peering it out in word informing appearing a pairing in memory as'z' anybody. In word su'personic sound wayeves in'forming it supernaturally as thoth'tsz of as'k'ing of it y now a k'now'ing out of Pa'roo'Ma. A y eye of a b'ng c'ng still a peering it out now in word a k'no'wing d'na'eye'll on appearing to be anybody. Anybody. Anywhere. Any time Mor mused laughing out loud.

"Pharaoh took the na'me Akhenaten in order to be called a divine in word mirror reference of that awareness in a y eye of a b'ng c'ng in a peering it. Now as'king of it y a kno'wing in't'word a twis'ting in two d'na'eye'll of y out as'eX. A un k'no'wn a pairing of it supersonically in word in formation at aten'cion still indivisible in the first place. Now akh'et a'ten. A y eye in a binary duplication of it appearing disappearing in words of a b c's. The newly invented a b c's facillitated any appearance of it in a y eye merely a peering it out phonographically in word on papyrus or supernaturally supersonically as'k'no'wing it out as'z'any thoth'tsz of it. A'kh'et'a'ten. A first place of a b c's of a b'ng c'ng now supernaturally as thoth'tsz of a god esse to be letter'all'y y'all mirrored out as'king of it y now in word a k'no'wing of it in two appearing a pairing in formation. A re;ye'all a'spiraling a black'g'round of it at a'ten'cion still in the first place indivisible in'visibility. A bi na're'y'e. A bi now 'A're'rayed out into anyone as'king of it y now appearing at atensee'ng in his presence. Anyone now aw/akh'eno'wing a b'ng c'ng out in word in formation as thoth'tsz of a singular God esse to be letter'all'y y'all in word. Appearing letter'all'y y'all with in'k'as on papyrus as in any be'gain'ning of it is merely in word. Now to k'no'w a parting of the read see'ng of it in'ka's on papyrus.

"The Emperor now as'king of it a k'no'wing out of it in sight still a naked singular unique point of view of that seer n'ever seen. Merely awareness of a y eye a peering it. Now supernaturally y'all appearing of it in word as'z'any thoth'tsz of informing it at aten'cion as'z' any mirrored intent. Remember Pharaoh had the power to turn the world b'lack'g'round by breaking up and abandoning the idols of his father. Now his in word imaginary thoth'tsz of a singular God esse to be letter'ally informing a k'nu world craft of Akhetaten. A wordship in the first place a ware y'all the sounds'z'za of the languages of y'all known world transposed out of it supersonically or phonographically. A b c's of a b'ng c'ng still in the first place. Y'et today still as'king of it y. That order of the alphabeta continues 3300+ y'ears el'ator with a b'ng c'ng still in the first place.

"In Akhetaten theirs would be a k'now'n world free of any idols in formation beyond a wayeve function at aten'cion in her'eye of eve'll. A y eye of eve will to appear a pair in word with in'kas duplicating a duplicity of it by any a peering at it understanding the spelling of it in word. As'ex'et'ting of it. It'y as'king of it y now a way as'ex. An exodus into el'and'ing duplicating out of it merely appearing a pairing as'z'any thoth'tsz of a singular God esse to be. Letter'all'y y'all as'king of it y a k'no'wn d'na'eye'all int'word a twis'ting in two. A mere a peering it into any appearing a pairing of it. You now a b'ng c'ng a'peering it out k'no'wing of it int'word a twis'ting in two information of anybody or any chintzy thin'king of it etc.. In her'eyez z z'a merely a peering it out in d'na'eye'll of indivisible invisibility. Now appearing a pairing a memory of any or eve'reybody.

"His isz'za word'ship craft of duplicity of a supernatural singular God. A God esse to be letter'ally y'all still above or beyond any in word d'na'tional borders. Supersonic supernatural p'ss'y'lent con'she'us'n'esse as'z'any thoth'tsz of a god esse reintroduced by a tribe of invading warrior priests sharing full awareness of a b'ng c'ng still that unique point of view of you. Or me. A con as'z'any appearing a pairing of it. She'e'na any a na y or eve're'y'body. Awareness of any or eve"rey body of a b'ng c'ng at aten'cion of that unique, you ni now que. Thatsz you as'King of it y a la Que"en que'. That in which appears a pairing by now a k'no'wing it out as'z'any thoth'tsz of it in a d'na'eye'll of it. Together they led an exodus in word in'formation of a b c's of a b'ng c'ng still in the first place indivisible in'visibility. Now as'eX a black'g'round echoing supersonic body as'z' any or eve're'ybody. A peh'ss'y'w'hole'lent complete wordfree indivisible invisibility of a b'LACK'bodhi instilled with intent of a b c's of a b'ng c'ng to perceive a 'GAIN'. A b'ng c'ng to think to wish to de'sire a b'ng gaining of it. An in word arey'all'ity as'king of it y now created by a phonographic language letter'all'y y'all coded with revelation set with now a time re'lease. A're'y"e now temporarily occupied paying aten'cion merely a peering it int'word a twisting a b'lack'g'round in two or out of appearing a pairing of it."

"Az's'Ex'hodus. A b c's wayeve out of a b'ng c'ng still in the first place indivisible in'visibility. Now appearing a pairing mirrored asz'za her'me'asz"thoth'tsz of it. Thatsz'a'h"OO"ka del"OO"ka. Chains of it int'word thoth'tsz of a God esse to be letter'all'y y'all in forming it. Ah . . . sorry to interrupt y'all." Mor's memory erupted. Just us flashing on a 3300+ y'ear old global vision a's'exodus of man'as mind or memory into any in word captivity. Exodus out of a b'ng c'ng still in the first place indivisible invisibility. Now as'z'any supernatural thoth'tsz of it appearing. A pairing aska's mic mirrored ping'ting memory mind echoing a b'lack'g'round or a y eye of a b'ng c'ng as'King of it y a la Que'en que that in which anybody etc. appears in her'eye of eve're'ybody. A b'ng LACK in'stilled with in word intent of a b c's of a b'ng c'ng a GAIN. Out of it at aten'cion captivated awhile in word in'formation. A w/ay eye of a b'ng c'ng a peering it out int'word a twis'ting in two. A bi any understanding of a spelling of it at aten'cion caught in a captivity. A capturing of it int'word a twis'ting in two formation of me or you in mem'or'y. Supernatural captivity as'z'any thoth'tsz of a God esse to be letter'all'y in wordsz'anybody etc.. Still in plain sight a b'ng c'ng merely a peering it in the first place. As'king of it y'all set my people free. Set my eye int'word a mind free from now a k'no'wing out a d'na'eye'll of it. Still a freestanding eye of a her'him'it with a polarity on the one hand. A peering it from above. D'na y light on the other. Flashing on the Yod of a God in word as'z the code of a b c's. Da na y light of h'our only sun. On the horos'zion. Da na y el'ignition of imaginary li'on between man'as mind or y eye a peering it in the first place. A positive negation of it as'z'any polarity on the one hand of a Her'him'it. Her'me'asz'za'thoth'tsz of it in me or you a memory. It's been said it commands us yet is at our command . . . As'king of it a'y . . . Set in my memory h'our people free. Free freed in a wordfreedom awareness at last still a b'ng c'ng merely a peering it at last in the first place. Indivisible in'visibility of anybody. A y'in eye on I am is is? Mor shrugged. He figured it didn't hurt to ask. As'king of it y any chintzy chislin' thin'king of it in any name alone. Yod"h'ayeyeh'ay. A'peering it from above. Ove a b'ng still in the first place. Indivisible in'visibility. Y'all"hayevevaveye'hay. Boom. Boom. Baby'cakes.

"Time now a black'g'round body echoing a k'no'wing out of it the'na. The'na Pharaoh Akhenaten creating out of whole cloth a new city of a new phonographic portable language based on a b c's of a being c'ng insight out of it with in'k'as appearing letter'all'y y'all in 22 glyphs on rolls of papyrus. A city of towers of a ba b'ng el function of now yet ask'ing of it y a k'no'wing out'word any twis'ting in two appearing a pairing of it. Supernatural supersonically y'all super-imposed int'word information of indivisible in'visibility of any individual seer. A seer in any or eve're'y ordinary sight of a b'ng c'ng merely a peering it out now a're'y'a'dhi'a'ing it by any mere reading of it. As'k'no'wing it out in word. In sight. A reading of it a real'ity as'king of it y a re;y'a'ten. A re'y'e'all ity as'king of it y a b'ng c'ng now int'word a twis'ting in two a black'g'round echoing of it at aten'cion.

"Now a mean in a portable supersonic or phonographic alphabeta. Meaningful letter'all'y y'all in word for'ma'sz'z s'z'ound ways or means of consciousness. A un hombre de conocimiento. A man'as mind of con she o"a'y'in us a la que"en que'. A y eye of that in which a peering it appears to be it. The con baby. The hard con of Ma trix. In her eyez z z a tricky a'w'h'ile of it now transportable in word supersonically in oral tradition vedically but more importantly in now a k'nowing it out phonographically. With in'kas ka's mic memory scripting of a b c's still in the first place. A y eye of a b'ng c'ng now as'z eX'odo' us out of it in word. E'scribere. A writing or reading wayeve out phonographically in word means of me or you appearing a pairing in memory. In a writing designed infor'ma'sz mass consumption beyond notional d'na'tional borders or any sense of time now beyond turning a page. Yet still a black'g'round body of a space in time now a k'no'wing out of it as'z'any mere mirage age. The imaginary li'on between a man'as mind or a y eye of a b'ng c'ng merely a peering it still. The'y sent a time now as'king of it y a k'no'wing out of it 'a bomb'. A bomb of liberation in a wordfreedom awareness from any potential in word captivity by anyone merely realizing a b'ng c'ng in any sight a re'ading of a y'all ar'e;ye'aten. A b'ng c'ng at aten'cion of anybody reading of it in a y eye dialectic debate. A debate between a y eye merely a peering it or a wordship craft appearing a pairing of it carrying aten'cion awayeve. A carrier wayeve of it.

"Ironically it seems the digital age letter'all'y y'all sets off that 'a bomb' ignited by a y eye of I am speaking of it in the first place. A bomb blowing the mind of any reader realizing or a re'y"all'eye'zinging a b'ng c'ng merely a peering it at these words in formation of it. A peering it out letter'all'y y'all now az's'ex's ting information in word of it. Yet still as'king of it y any k'no no no'wing out of it as'z other y'sz in the first place. Other eyesz z z. Still a singular indivisible point of view of you a y eye a peering it in'visibility in the first place." Mor felt the su'personic convolutions of a y eye dialectic ex'peh'resse'd with the gravity weight of her vocal chords. The waiting on it now. It moved him in wayeves int'word a twis'ting in formation of a dna'eye'll of indivisible invisibility. A positive wayeve as'king of it y now a negativity. A na y a la que"en que' of that in which appears of a peering it out int'word now a k'no no no'wing of it in here'yez z z of eve're'ybody. We all turning a b'LACK'g'round instilled echoing intent of a b'ng c'ng a GAIN. A b'ng c'ng a gain int'word'sz'za'any in forming of it. A y eye of a b'ng c'ng still in the first place indivisible in'visibility. Now as'king of it y now a peering it out int'word a twis'ting in two a b'lack'g'round echoing a k'no'wing it out as'z'za'ny X's ting in formation. Translated now in color code'sz'zap'ping hereye'sz'za purpling grays. Cobalt gre'y'en'sza"vermilion versicolor. Now he began drawing her'eyez z z'a body out of the stew of color. Then he found a quick drying white. Mor shifted gears wiping down the colors with a solvent soaked rag. At the point where y'all color blended in a warm cool gray he began laying over it brush strokes of opaque white. Some of the strokes he bladed off till the surface dried to the touch. The odorless solvent seemed to further activate the sound of painting. A ping'ting whining in his y'ears till offset by sound wayeves echoing the vibration of a breath breathed a la sonoridad.

"A re'ye a peering it out a d'na'eye'll int'word a twis'ting in two appearing a pairing arrayed letter'all'y y'all in word by alphabeta. A re'ye a peering it now projected supersonically as'z'any thoth'tsz of as"king of it y a k'no no no'wing it out in word as any measly emaciated thin'king of it etc.. Any scant chislin' thin'king of it. A y eye'of'eve're'ybody. A y you'a're;y'o'u now as'k'no'w'n mirror'all'y y'all appearing bi. A pairing now are'y'all out in word as'ex'et'ting out of it in a duplicity. A cunning uncanny w'h'ile of the indivisible a pairing supernaturally as'z'za'ny thoth'tsz of y'all out as'ex's ting. Still a b'ng c'ng of that indivisible invisibility in any individual. A reality of ar'e;ye"al'ity as'king of it y a b'ng c'ng in the first place. Yet still that a y eye of I am is is throughout awhile yet beyond any mirror appearance of you or me or anybody. Now or the'na eve'reybody out in word d'na'eye'll of it.

"The'y invented a time machine with its key ask'ey'e'ing y a b'ng c'ng in the first place. A why of it. Now letter'all'y y'all. 'A're;ye issuing a's intent y'll d'na'eye'll. Of merely a peering it in the first place. X x x x's ting asz'zspiraling simply int'word a twis'ting in two of fate faith family into or out of a b'lack'g'round echo body of it now as'king of it y a k'no'wing out any sight sound smell taste or touch of it. A whorl'd'ing X'et'ting duplicating of it in a y'll'd'na'eye'll. A denial of it a b'lack'g'round echoing a k'no no no'wing of it out as'z any lank gaunt starved thin'king of it appearing in word out a's in plane sigh't. In other words'za a b'ng c'ng a peering it the whole point of view of you. Asz'y'et y you're; you still in the first place that indivisible in'visibility of any seer sight see'ng. That a b c's code of it in her'eyez z z'a hard as'z con. She'e'na' us now transportable across any barriers of time now awhile a space in time understanding the supernatural supersonic superimposed in word k'no'wing spelling of a portable alphabeta. More importantly en ma'sz torus tower's'zz'a ba'b'el. A ba b'ng c'ng in her'eye way of eve're'y function as'z' any fun'ny'a'ction. Of it in word as thoth'tsz of it mirroring a b'lack'g'round echo in'visibility into or out of any appearing of it supersonically.

"Question remains y, why the ka's mic memory intelligence consciousness she"ba'n'g experience in the first place. A b'ng c'ng still in the first place. Why begin merely as'z now too, as'z two twa' t'w'y's'zz'ta indivisible complete d"ar'k'n'ess'e now to be perceived in two appearing a pairing. A b'ng c'ng merely a peering it out turning into any in word in'formation of it. As'king of it y a k'no'wing out of it any appearing by a being a y now k'no'wing y it is as not. As'z'any a na y. A y'll'd'na'eye'll. A denial now instilled with intent of intentionally ignoring a being still indivisible invisibility of any individual. A d'na'eye'll by k'no no no'wing it out in word. Why create an inword duplicity of a b'ng c'ng in the first place? It seems the only answer being that the'y could. Or a y na of it."

"That the'y could or would conceive superimposing such a dangerous deadly daring duplicity of a b'ng c'ng mirrored in word in formation appearing bi now anyone as'king of it y now a k'no'wing out of it. In word denial of merely a peering it creating appearing of it in word. As'king of it a y eye a'peering it out int'word a la que"en que' of that in which as a means of appearing meaningful a'w'h'ile leads to alienation war and inevitably War're'y'na." The words issuing from the sound of his disembodied voice perplexed Mor's in word mind. A revelation that he potentially held the key as too the plot twist turning around the Korner.

"You now control it by a positive negation of it. A y eye turned int'word a t'wisting dna'eye'll of it. As'king of it a k'no'no no'wing it out in word in formation of a b c's of it still indivisible invisibility of y'all along. That'sz'z'a a alphabeta time machine key to any appearing of it in her eyesz'on understanding its spelling. As'king tut'i'me a ma'sheen'a to'we'ring power of a'tor'us of a ba'bel turning yearning before behind right left above below and projecting y'all around." She replied as though reading a script still developing in a b c's of a b'ng c'ng above his head. Ove a b'ng greater c'ng beyond anyone now k'no'wing out of it in d'na'eye'll any mere mirrored in word conceit of herhim'it'self as'z' any or eve're'y'body.

"Easier said than done. In that I am still the artist y'all while ignoring a b'ng c'ng of awareness of art'is'tat. Yet attempting creation of decent art may take some practice. A practice of a lifetime or two or three," Mor said with a frown while scraping off some of the paint recently applied. Patterns of color broke out as information waiting form as with a gravity of it in her'eyesz'on any life still waiting on death. A death as'k'ey"e of a guide issuing out from in her'eye of eve'll of eve'rey'body. Oh'ma the foolishness of any life lived merely mirrored as a b'ng c'ng appearing in name alone he mused. Lived mirroring death as if only a b'ng c'ng of it awhile. A short while at that.

"Imagine the vortex of a power int'word a twis'ting in two a b'lack'g'round ping'ting echo of it as'king of it y t'h'at. Egyptian Empire at its zenith of the New Kingdom. The'na. A bomb. Pharaoh now takes a hard screeching right turn taking the chosen of the kingdom as'king of it y now a un'k'no'wn'a out as'eX'hodus. A wayeve out of it. Out of a kingdom already tribes of Minoans, Myceaneans, Cypriots, Babylonians, and IndoEuropean aryan descendant Hittites, the warrior priests of the monotheistic singular cult of a're;ye'at aten'cion. Atman'. Y'all the'y"e came drawn into a peering it at the whorl'd'ing of building a city of a God esse to be letter'all'y y'all in a re;y'e"all ity of alpha"beta. In a time machine now turning into a future of a few t'h'at u a're'y"ez z z' on merely a peering it. Of such is the code of veda alphabeta. A building completely on any understanding of its spelling to prevail in an imaginary lion between a man'as mind of it int'word a twis'ting a b'lack'g'round ping'ting echo of it as'King of it with in'ka's letter'all'y y'all a phonographic memory of it. A la Que"en que'. That in which appears anybody anythin'king of it etc.. Or'eye of a b'ng c'ng merely a peering it still in the first place indivisible in'visibility.

"The Aryan warrior priests already possessed a purely phonetic language samskr'tam. A h'ome of veda knowledge. That ma'trix provided a supersonic means of creating ess'cribere writing based on a boiling down of hieroglyphs existing by the thousands into a 22 letter phonographic alphabeto. Now a mean with the supersonic means meaningfully transported in the mouths of the warrior priests. Mouths as'z organs of speech uttering sounds as'z grammatical means of in word vedic transmission. A purely personic vedic means of obtaining that knowledge. Realizing it now awhile k'no'wing a in word denial of it. A b'ng c'ng of a peering it y'all along. Eve'n in word you still it thus realizing it y'all instantly become it. Veda vedanta. K'nowledge of it is'z'ending knowledge of it. In the code key 0 is Ar'e'y'e'b'all a peering it. The androgyn fool of a y eye of her'him'it way of eve re'y body perceiving stepping off a ledge'd as'k'no'wing in word of it falling understanding that spelling of A b c's be'am'ing out in word as ex. A un k'no'wn of it. A y eye merely a peering it now out as'king of it y now in word a foolish thin'king of it as'z potential k'no'wing of it as'ex'et'ing duplicating a duplicity. Intentionally stepping off the a'ledged un k'no'w'n intent to fall as'z z z'leep black'g'round echoing of it into any role playing out of a un consciousness. Un'til we all now in her'eye of a b'ng c'ng in understanding in word spelling of alphabeta turn a black'g'round echo as'k'no'wing out of it. As'eX'odus. Supernaturally y'all out of it in her'eyez z z'a merely a peering it appears eve're'y or a na y way wayeve as'z'any thoth'tsz of a God esse. To be letter'all'y y'all in word as'ex's ting's'z'z'a out and about raising hell.

"Think Moses on steroids. A re'y'all'eye'zinging a b'ng c'ng singularly indivisible in'visibility Amenhotep IV now out as'King of it y a k'no'wing d'na'eye'll on wordsza in formation with'in'kas on papyrus. Akhenaten picked up on the duplicity of the old Amun priests and their well paid attention worshipping of the old idols. He was now aware of the awareness of a b'ng c'ng merely infused in word. In a wor'd'ship of d'na'eye'll. The wor'd'ship of a God'esse to be now a wor'd'ship of a God esse to be as'z'any in word thoth'tsz of it. A supernatural in word God esse to be letter'all'y y'all art of a b'ng c'ng in peh'ss'y'en'ce'ng now as'king of it y eye merely a peering it a turning into any appearing supernaturally as'z'any thoth'tsz of it. One alphabeta of a b'lack go'a'd to a peering it out in a word b'lack'g'round echo of it in order to as a're'y'e turn a gain int'word a twis'ting d'na'eye'll on any appearing out of it. Awhile now out in a space in time

"Akhenaten determined to launch the alphabeta time ma'chine from the tower'asz of a ba'bel. A g"OO"d function d'el"OO"ka de b"OO"ka. A tower of it as'words cleaving anybody as'eX u'all. A tower to attract a lightning flash'a'zap'pingting a plan et h'ear'th supersonically duplicating in'spiral'eye'z'at'i'on of it from above. Ove a b'ng c'ng de'sire still in the first place. The de 'sire Akhenaten father of a b c's or a Go'a'd as'z'any thoth'tsz of it still in the first place of Akh'et'aten. Now a new multi-ethnic siddhi of Akhetaten. A peh'ss'y w'hole power as"zz'apped with synapse of a b'ng c'ng a peering it out int'word a tower of a ba c'ng bel. A Bel'videre. As'King of it y a re;y'e'at'aten'scion of a macro micro ka's mic mean nexus asz'ex"us. In for'ma'sz eve'n'ta horizon of a naked singularity clothed now as'king of it y merely k'no no no'wing it out in word."

"In word in formation now as'king of it y a k'no'wing out a long long looonng wily while," he added with laugh. "That dang nekid Emperor with his suit of indivisible in'visibility seems now as'z'any thoth'tsz of it supersonically superimposed eve're'y'day a'gain and a'gain in a k'no'wing out of it our own snazzy suits of silk and satin. While you be completely naked there is not so much suggestion of it as'ex. So much igniting my imagining of slipping beneath the cover. Why I always draw models naked but then always been a sucker for black lace." Margot Christina gave him seductive then laughed to break the spell. Still he painted her completely naked as ma na'ture intended. The canvass large enough for a full figure Mor began finding her defined by negative spaces. Then losing her between merely a peering it or it appearing in the pingting echo of pigments spread across the canvass.

"Why Akhenaten had himself and his family portrayed without cover. Why he had himself cast in a bizarre androgrogynous form. Early in his reign Akhenaten had himself portrayed in sculpture in such a manner to capture the attention of imagining purely imagined images of himself. In a wily while of any appearing out of it still aware of a b'ng c'ng in the first place indivisible in'visibility. As'king of it y now a k'no'wing out of it in word in formation asz'anybody. That bizarre portrayal reflects the arbitrary nature as'z' any in word mirroring information of a thin'king of it. Merely mirrored a b c's of a b'ng c'ng still in the first place. Akhenaten Akhetaten. A b'ng c'ng still in the first place indivisible in'visibility merely mirrored supersonically y'all in word supernaturally as'z'any thoth'tsz of it. In a b c's of a b'ng c'ng now out as'king of it any k'no'wing d'na'eye'll on it appearing in na'me alone.

"Since his subjects were forbidden from seeing his face now as'king of it in word k'no'wing it out of a b c's of a b'ng c'ng still in the first place indivisible invisibility they would come to realize he actually appeared in formation by their a peering it out in meaningful wordsz' understanding the spelling of a b c's. A spelling easily aquired by a portable 22 letter phonographic alphabeta code. It yet indivisible in'visibility of A y eye of a b'ng c'ng still in the first place. Akhenaten in Akhetaten. Y'all now as'king of it y now a k'no no no'wing d'na'eye'll of it as'ex's ting in formation in a word. A word now the God esse to be letter'all'y y'all thoth'tsz of any lank rank starved thin'king of it in any name alone. In wordsz of the new a b c's phonographic language. The old imagined images broken in favor of a'ten b'ng c'ng at aten'cion of any or eve're'y'body. Aten'cion paid to a'w/Akhen"aten'cion now as'King of it y a k'no'wing a la Que"en que' of that in which is now in her'eyez z z' of eve're'ybody. Appearing a pairing asz'z'Akhenaten and Nefertiti in Akhet'ing"aten'cion. Aten and Eve're'y'bodyz z z' in the garden of a Eye'd'on. It to be perceived of it eve're'y'body at aten'cion now a're'y'dhi'ing this.

"They are'y also portrayed as eve'rey da'y people in bronze statues of him and Nefertiti in the Louvre. There he appears as typical diminutive pot bellied Egyptian man. She'e'na virgin mother. The point is still from any point of view of you or any seer sight see'ng any image is imagined by a pseudo-dominance of in word memory mind or y. A y eye point of you a'peering it out supersonically now as'king of it a k'no'wing out any chancy chintzy whithering thin'king of it in'formation as'z'any tenuous arbitrary flimsy naming of it. A b'ng c'ng in any b'lack'g'round potential to be a gain in word with invention of phonographic alphabeta. Aw/akhen'aten'cion in a y eye of that I am a peering it out at now k'no'wing of it any d'na'eye'll appearing it with inka's a ka's mic memory written on papyrus. A b'lack'g'round ink'as echoing a k'no'wing out of it projecting phonographically or supersonically supernaturally superimposed in 3D space on papyrus as'z'any thoth'tsz of it. Thoth'tsz of it supernaturally as'word cleaving y'all now as'z e'x's ting. As'king of it a k'no no no'wing out of that black'g'round echo aska's of we all appearing turning into or out of a be'ng c'ng merely a peering it out as'z a gain. In word alone.

"Thus Amenhotep IV became the first of his new kingdom lineage to cultivate the cult of the indivisible invisibility of any individual. That individual indivisible in'visibility still alive and well today at aten'cion of any or eve'reybody in a wordfreedom awareness of it. It as'z'anybody eve'n turning into or out of a black'g'round echo as'king of it now a k'no'wing out a d'na'eye'll of it yet a re'y'all"eye"z z zinging pingtinging thirty three plus centuries later. Iron irony of ironies. A b'ng c'ng as that seer, that one who sees still a pharaoh in the first place Akhet'aten duplicating a bi'na're'y"e duplicity Akh'en'aten or a pa'roo'ma at'man"as'z mind. Or y a being still in the first place Anokhi Adon'ay. A paramount b'ng c'ng in that eye of I am is is a peering it from above. Ove a b'ng c'ng still in the first place the great house of A re'y"e beta be'am'ing c'ng out now in word'asz'z'awhile. A long loonnngg while as ex'o'dus int'word a t'wis'ting black'g'round echo as'king of it a b'ng c'ng a gain. Still a b'ng c'ng a re'y'all in first personic person of that awareness that eye of I am is is a peering it from above still indivisible in'visibility."

A long silence followed. Then Mor felt awareness of a b'ng c'ng now still that as'king of it a k'no'wing out of it washing over him. Flooding out'sz'any sensibility of a being merely mirrored in any arbitrary name alone. Now out of it around intent of intentionall'y y'all k'no no no'wing a d'na'eye'll of it. A re'y"e coming into or out of a black'g'round disappearing the imagined in word clothing of it. Then he could easily imagine his arms and hands out weilding painting knives as ya'll a re'y"az coloring it as'z'any thoth'tsz projecting in y'all directions from a y eye point of you a re'y"e radiating a center point of view. Of you. Of a y eye of that supernatural supersonics of a being superimposed as'z'any thoth'tsz of y you yod iota appear in that eye of I am is is merely a'peering it from above.

"The one is m'em. A un"mono"the'is'm'em'or'y of a mind or y. The one as'kas mic memory of it now as'z too being"sz'a portrayed idolized as'z merely any a na y appearing of it separate from a b'ng c'ng still merely a peering it in the first place. Pharaoh not the word Egyptians used to signify anybody as'king of it. Now instead a b'ng c'ng in Pa'roo'Ma'sz the first place. In a great sacred place or freestanding state of a b'ng c'ng y'all out of it az's'ex'et'ting duplicating in a word'ship. A word'ship cunning craft sailing out to be worshiped as'z'any thoth'tsz of it. A Great GOaD esse to be letter'all'y y'all any appearing out of it in word as'ex's ting in'formation supernaturally y'all from a unique point of view. A la que"en que' of that in which appears a b'ng c'ng in her'eyez z z of a now eve'reybody. A b c's of a b'ng c'ng merely a peering it out supernaturally superimposed in words'z'azz'any thoth'tsz of a God esse to be letter'all'y y'all in forma'tion. Now of any k'no'wing out of it int'word a twis'ting in two appearing a pairing in a memory of me or you." He found her words lost in a wordfreedom awareness of it drawing on the right side of the brain. Still he felt the szound of her eyez z z playing at his intention of at't'ention.

"Obviously only as'z'any thoth'tsz of a b c's in word in formation ascribed or written on any separate piece of pa'per appearing out in space awhile. In'visibility with'in'ka's now appearing black'g'round as'king of it any k'no'wing letter'all'y y'all superimposed out in traces of it. Still a b'ng c'ng of that indivisible in'visibility asz'any individual now as'king of it y a k'no'wing d'na'eye'll. A will supernaturally as'z'any thoth'tsz of it projecting supersonically or phonographically appearing with'in'ka's on pa'per in writing or reading a're'y'a'ding it. That su'personic pa'per'son in writing on it superimposed by a power of alphabeta portable phonographic letter'all'y a y in word 3D qu'bic time machine. This concept of a y eye on you'r'self of a b'ng c'ng as'ex's ting out in word'all'y y'all assembly a'sz'any thoth'tsz of it now out appearing by supernaturally projecting the felt feeling field of view of you.

"Feeling of you now hardwired biologically still merely mirrored a'sz x's ting as'z thoth'tsz in ka's mic memory. Supernatural thoth'tsz in one singular Great God esse to be letter'all'y y'all art deceived by a b c's out of it in word information awhile. In a wily power as'peh'ss'y'ence asz'ex'peh'resse'da as'peh'oken word. In the beginning is es'peh'o'khen word. Es'peh'o'khen a'ten binary of a y h'our eye'zz'on you in a re'y'all mirrored in word imaginary imagery. Imagined in 3D letter'all'y y'all in a peh q'u'bi'c place. A pa'roo'ma new city of light. Akhet'aten. H'our eye'sz'on aten. Aten and Eve. A la que"en que' of that in which any or eve'rey'body appears a black'g'round echoing a ping'ting as'king of it a k'no no no'wing d'na'eye'll on it. A y'll D'NA. Any d'na'eye'll of a b'ng c'ng in this place pressaged monotheism. The singular idea of a b'ng c'ng a peering it out now a k'no'wing appearing of it. As'z'any thoth'tsz of it of a God esse to be of a b c's informing in word a separate worshiper. A worshipping of it merely a'na y in word abstract idea of divinity transferred to an icon like a shepherd's crook. Or with'in'ka's on papyrus."

"Or a cross the board," Mor interjected while laying paint off on the canvass. He felt energy rushing up his spine as he took some long slow breaths. Drawing up cerebrospinal fluid like water in a straw. Flooding his brain with a rush of it. The rush. Moving up. Goin' down. A yogi once taught him use of the breath to relieve fatigue. Now he breathed a color breaking off in random textures chunky and riven. Paint love he wondered. Color eye. Can't go there in word'all'y y'all he thought inwardly invaded by the squigglies. Their spelling worms of it in her'eve'll eye a la que"en que.' That in which a spelling of it appears anybody etc. out in her'eye of any or eve're'ybody. Now out as'king of it a k'no'wing it as anybody or any scant skinny thin'king of it. A way of Akhen'aten. Aw/'ak'h'en. A'ten w/ak'hen. He inhaled of it in her'ey'e'asz'z'a b'ng c'ng. She'e'na back on the high chair in black lace panties with thigh length black nylons captivated his imagining. Hum. The idea of sending innocence into the shitstorm of their own kali'ma crossed his in word mind. Or a y as'z thoth'tsz of it x'et'ting. A b'ng c'ng still in the first place. That place being Pa'roo'Ma. A parama b'ng c'ng of that effulgent awareness of we all a re'y'e dhi'a'ting int'word perceiving a twis'ting in two of it. A're'y'e turning into appearing a pairing in word a formation of a one way while. A going out infor'ma'sz eve re'y wave wayeveing a black'g'round echoing anybody.

"Point still with any point of view is Pharaoh had designed an image nation to capture attention of any or eve're'y bodhi a long loonng while. Pay attention to it. Eve're'y bodhi paying or praying. The entire in word image'nation along with kings and couriers of other lands prostrated before him. Now as'King of it a're'y'e'al'ity of any k'no'wing d'na'eye'll of indivisible in'visibility. Of a b'ng c'ng appearing out of it in word in formation. In forma'ing that he needed a portable complete phonographic alphabeta. A supersonic supernatural alphabeta coded systematic 3D qu'bic time machine. To transmit as'king of it any k'now'ing out of his singular indivisible wordfree untouched vision. A y eyesz'za mere a peering it. Or any eyes'za peering it out in word at appearing anybody etc.

"Now any eyes'z a peering it out of me or you with ink'as ka's mic memory a're"y'all as'z thoth'tsz of it in for'ma'sz in her'eye of eve re'y sound wayeve a're'y'e'as'z z z supersonic mean's'z z of mirroring a b c's. Ar'e'me'e's'zz of a mirror b'ng'sz'a. A y eye b'ng c'ing y na'tions of notional mirror being's'z'a appearing still that as'ka's mic ka'mic singular'ity as'king of a b'ng c'ng a y na by god. Mono ma'na'ha'y. A great mind of a singular god. A mono the'is'm. Is mere mirror mind or y memory transmitted out as'king of it a k'no'wing d'na'eye'll of it in a or the word. Or y. A y you a're'y'e a're'y'diating you by a b c's out of any eye a're'y'fracting that indivisible invisibility of any individual now supersonically as'z'any thoth'tsz of it.

"A GO'a'D esse to be a b'lack'g'round echoing instilled intent of a b'ng c'ng a gain merely in word. Intending a b c's of a b'ng c'ng letter'all'y y'all in word in formation of any mere mirrored y na you now appearing out of it a's'z thoth'tsz for'ma'sz in her'eyez z z'azz of any or eve'reybody. A now singular go go go'a'd of a great GOD mirror'd DOG ma'sz z z'apping a pingting a's'z sin'apse projecting a long long loooonnnggg'a w'h'ile. A're'y ligare igni'ting a cunning deadly deceit of a y d'na't'u'ar'e. D'NA y'll a 'creation indivisible in'visibility still now as'king of it y a k'no'wing it created sustained or destroyed merely in word go'd"do'g'ma'tic potential. Mono 'the' is m'em. Mono bono now 'the' or 'a' y eye on it. The' definite article defined in word'all'y y'all by a b'ng c'ng in a y na me. A'na'y na'me alone.

"You na now appearing supernaturally as'z'any thoth'tsz of a b'ng c'ng superimposed out as'ex's ting in formation in name alone. The a'y eye indivisible invisibility now a d'na'eye'll of it. A d'na'eye'll int'word a twis'ting of it now a'spiraling into as'king of it a k'no'wing out in two appearing apparently. Still 'you cannot see me and live' or in other wordsza a y eye indivisible from any potential felt feeling fieldz z z' of view of you. Still any man'as mem'ory mind can see, apprehend, discern, realize, or pick up on it as awareness in a wordfreedom of anybody of a b'ng c'ng in merely a peering it drawing un'touched on the right side of the brain. A prior'eye wordfree worry'free memory free untouched awareness of a y eye of a b'ng c'ng still in the first place merely a peering it. Or out at it in a wayeve function understanding any in word spelling of it. It now a JIVANMUKTAHA. A b'ng c'ng liberated letter'all'y y'all in a wordfreedom awareness of it while still liv'ing. At aten'cion freed from any in word captivity. Still now as'king of it y a k'no'wing out of a y eye a mirrored duplicating of it as'z'ex'acting any role. Now merely aware of it. A spelling broken by a 'hairfire' desire to realize a b c's of a b'ng c'ng free. Now freed as'king of it why. Y a eye merely a peering it from above falls as'z z z'leep b'lack into a con"she'us'n'ess"e. Why a con a la que"en que' of that in which anybody appears to be a gain. A gain merely in word. A b'ng still completely totally complete awareness of it. It now merely image'ning indivisible invisibility by a k'no'wing int'word a twis'ting in two d'na'eye'll of it. It in a b c's of a b'ng c'ng out in word in formation."

"Free. Free at last, thank GOD DOG'ma almighty, free of it at last. 'My truck'ma just ran over your dog'ma,'" he tossed out to cover the eros as'eX sight'ment in her'eyesz'z arrows jetting through his feelings. The rush of it out in her'eye of eve'll. A will of a wayeve function. A b'lack'ness wayeve function instilling of a y eye a peering it now out with intent in word asz'a gain appearing anybody etc.. Still y'all merely in awhile. An uncanny cruel cunning deceit of it out in her eyez z z' a peering it into appearing of it. A moment after moment or a lifetime after lifetime he grimaced.

Now as'z awareness in a y eye of an artist kicking attention back in a wordfreedom visual concentration. Back to a p'ss'y'lence as'ka's mic mic'ro wayeves black'g'round echoing a running wayeves of it in her'eyez z z'a. Mere contours of a b'ng c'ng now edges positive negative spaces light and shadow. Drawing on the wordfree untouched right side of the brain. Still Mor realized that drawing included the portrayal of it in wordsz of the a y eye dialectic debate between as'king of it y a k'no'w'ing out of a y eye aware of merely a peering it now or appearing of it later.

Or we all a wheel turning into or out of a ka's mic microwayeve black'g'round echoing a supersonic in word appearing of it as'z'any thoth'tsz of it. Thoth'tsz of letter'all'y y'all a God creating sustaining and destroying any or eve're'y'body still a y eye of it merely a peering it out. Out in a first personic wayeve're'y"e aimed int'word a twis'ting in two a d'na'eye'll out of it. A b'ng c'ng still in the first place merely a peering it now asz'any in word thoth'tsz out of it into any supernatural appearing awhile as'k'no'wing then the'y'na. A peh'ss'y'l'en't indivisible invisibility touch-free w'ayeve'reybody a're'y'e'dhi'a'ting a peh'rception of him or her or it. We all turning personically into or out of a black'g"round echo of it. Of you or me merely in a memory of it. He mused on a clean slate wordfree untouched while painting Christina. At attention paid to a visual focus even sounds'za did not seem to peh'netrate that singular still p'ss'y'l'ent indivisible in'visibility of a b'ng c'ng in a e'ye'a. Yet brain left and right modalities still a singular indivisible instrument he pondered. Perhaps the only instrument capable of analyzing itself. Analyzing still recording sound or light wayeves refracting in sight. In a being su'person'ic'all'y y'all. Above or below frequency level of soundsz'a h'ear'th in a plan et. A plan et'ting duplicating in wordsz 'any h'ear'th as'k'as micro wayeves b'lack'g'round echoing of it. In word'sz asz'sound wayeves. Out in her'eyesz z z'a ma"trix. A tri'ke'y'e plan et'ting a pingting of the h"ear'th. As'king of it'y. Y ka's mic'ro ro row'a'yeve'ing black'g'round. A y the echo of it in her'eye merely a peering it now supersonically in word means informing a sound meaningful of any or eve're'y'body appearing of it. Of it a be'am'ing out any meager thin'king of it appearing etc.. Out in her'eye a peering it now int'word a twis'ting it in two appearing a pairing. As'seX'y'all now a k'no'wing out of it a touch of it touching any or eve're'y'body touched by it.

"lil'Darlin', I'm'a trying to pay attention but feeling y'all too broke down. Too tore up. Broke up inside. I'ma fried, dyed, and re'tried. I'ma's telling there is something in the paint. Something growing. As'ex'panding. Az'sparking my synapses into overdrive. Something electric. Spre'ad'ing a fi're'y'eszing'ing. A whole field in a single neurotransmitted molecule," Mor offered, laying on more color layers. Working in broad strokes giving free reign to the k'no'wing of his body drawing on wordfree awareness of it. It merely a peering at it. Eyesz a arms'za fingers. One eye on the pain't'a one eye on it in her'eye of eve're'y'body. "Tell me more about the Pharaoh. What was he like? Abraham or il Duce?"

"Appearing of it in a wily while? Something so cunning. As'king of it a k'no'wing out its own d'na'eye'll. A b'ng c'ng now as'king of it k'no no no'wing out anybody or any measly thin'king of it in word informing meaningful of a long long loonnga while. Now as'King of it a're'y'all'ity a la Que"en que' of that in which a wayeve appears of it. Y'et in awhile a're'y"turns a b'ng c'ng in the first place now out asz a Great God esse to be of G'ee'z"us.

"Indivisible invisibility of a y eye merely a peering it. Now with the invention of a supersonic or phonographic alphabeto of a b'ng c'ng still in the first place indivisible invisibility of a y eye a peering it under pressure as'ka's of it a k'urving int'word a twis'ting in two. A complete d"ark'as turning into or out of a b'lack'g'round quantum gee'sz"us as'z'any thoth'tsz of a gravity weight of waiting on a Great God esse to be letter'all'y y'all appearing of it. Now aw'h'ile a space in time. Supernaturally supersonically superimposed asz'any thoth'tsz of it. Y'all along those lines. Get it? A'w/akhen aten. A b c's at aten'cion captivated in word informing of it. Yet still now as'king of it y a k'no'wing out the'n.

"Then the na of d'na'eye'll of any k'no'wing it still as'King of it today in a b c's time machine. A space in time now a'w'h'ile as'k'no'wing of it the'n. A b c's time ma'sheen. A time now still in d'na'eye'll of it the'n. THE gee'sz"us N'd'ing of it. Her or him or it merely appears'z as'z'any thotht'sz of it. A b'ng c'ng in word in formation must appear a contradiction, a paradox of genius and maniac, treason and tradition, monotheist or atheist. A or the. The is memory or a y eye. In the or y eye of man'as'zz'ap'ping mind or y eye a peering it out in word developed into long term memory by ma'sz means of a meaningful pa peh'r with'in'ka's a phonographic a're'y'cord. As'king of it y now as'ka's a'la que"en que' of that in which appears y'all out in her'eyez z z' any or eve'rey'body.

"A"b'in go'ing down in his story mean recorded by supersonic means of a alphabeta time machine. A time now still as'king of it y. A'w/akhen'aten as'king of it. Y a eye of A b'ng c'ng merely a peering it still in the first place. Now a b c's out in word informing it as'z'any thoth'tsz of a k'no'wing out of it. The go go glory of Akhetaten remembered in word'all'y y'all prominading the length of the royal road with his queen Nefertiti beside him in their gold and silver chariot. Aten and Eve. The'n a're'y dhi'ating a perceived word'ship craft rolling a'wayeve on wheels of electrum. On we all'asz of electrum"

"Jack and Jackie in their inaugral limosine?" Mor gave as a spontaneous reply to the profound rumblings of the h'ear'th of it a/w'akhen'ing aten. At aten'cion still in the first place indivisible invisibility of any individual now as'king of it. Y a eye merely a peering it turns a b'lack'g'round echoing of it into anybody or any scant gaunt starved thin'king of it etc. now appearing a'w'h'ile of it.

"A God as'King of it y. A God'esse to be a la Que"en que' of that in which appearing now by a k'no'wing out of it the power to d'na'eye the old image'in'a're'y"e idols. A peering it with a power of a'kurving of it into appearing a space in time. A super personic peh'ss'y w'hole power issuing out from the Pharonic immortal opening of the mouth or'is it still in the first place a mere divine awareness of it. Indivisible invisibility as'z' any individual now merely appearing in for'ma'sz letter'all'y y'all now a'while. Mirrored with'in'ka's a ka's mic mem'or'y of in word sound wayeves appearing any whithered thin'king of it by echoing y'all a black'g'round mirror seas'on intent of a be'ng c'ng a gain. It took 33+ centuries of a b'ng c'ng infor'ma'sz e eye technology matching population growth of man'as mind to a'w/akhen aten. Awakening at attention paid in the or y now to merge as'ex's ting in formation with awareness of its still indivisible invisibility.

Out of a time 'ma'sheen'a with me or you now in a d'na'eye'll of a b'ng still complete d"ark'ness"e merely appearing a b'lack'n'ess'e. A b'ng completion of indivisible invisibility now at aten'cion understanding a con"she e na us of a b'ng c'ng a gain." Mor experienced in her'eye of eve're'y'body a swallowing up of his in word memory. A back to b'lack'. Then in that blink of a eye she'ena con"tin'u'de to appear a gain. Alternating that alter'native of it appearing a gain disappearing b'lack'g'round it in still with intent of a b c's of a b'ng c'ng a gain. Then he always was a sucker for black lace. Or a black face of Kwasanda Nzokia flashing in his memory.

"Szounds like a man for our time. More than that, sounds like a con artist for our time. A w/akhen by gett'en at'en. Paying aten'cion to the in word con. The crazy wile of it now in her'eyesz z z'leeping out merely a peering it in supersonic wordsz' of eve"re'y'body. A ma's'z jest y. In her'ey"e the'y'art a Jo'ka. It's a good one. Might eve'n'a say a God esse to be one" Aw'akhen aten'cion of a mind. Or y think about it he wondered wandering into the paint field unfolding right before his eye and hand'a'sz pain't'a'zz pain'ting of a pingting. Echoing out in her'eye on it now. In pain't'a he saw out in her eye. In her he'y'art. He touched the touching of her'eye'sz in a feeling field's'zazz color. A ba'la'zz z z'leepingting e"yez z z.

"A'na'y now a un"defined indefinite of a b'ng c'ng or the n'a y definite art'i'cle of the word? Like any go'o'd autocrat Akhenaten and his queen Nefertiti sought to be sole focus of aten"t'ion in Akhet'aten. People were forbidden, verbotan, prohibir, under penalty of death from looking Pharaoh in the face. That kept aten'cion from a're'y'all'eye'zing merely a peering it in the first place of a pharaoh. A b'ng c'ng still in the first place of a pa'roo'ma. Why he wore the uraeus, the vipor head band to protect his or anybody's face from discerning a b'ng c'ng merely a peering it still in the first place. Thus the cunning wordship craft of awhile of aten and eve depended on a y eye a peering it out. Out of indivisible in'visibility now a time caught at aten'cion fixated in word in formation of anybody any scant starved thin'king of it etc.. Out of it as'ex. As'exodus out of it with aten'cion paid out only in word captivity. Now awhile till awakening aten. At aten'cion of awareness drawing on the wordfree untouched right side of the old memoryfree brain. Or bra'hm'in."

The Dark'ness now awakened in a moment free of turning a b'lack'g'round echo of it into a pingting informing appearance of anybody etc.. Then in that a b'link of a y eye merely a peering it he found himself at aten'cion appearing of it in word. In forming it understanding the spelling of a b c's. Only a palette knife moving in his hands kept aten'cion from completely falling as'z z z'leep black into a un con she us'ness'e. A un con she'na us a la que"en que' of that in which to be we all a wheel turning in two appearing a pairing out of it still a singular y eye of a b'ng c'ng merely a peering it in the first place.

"Now a k'no'wing D'NA'eye'll turning any potential black'g'round echo of it su'personically into a mirror appearing of it. Alphabeta time ma'shee'na now crafting a cunning supernatural supersonic in word spelling of a fate of d'na'eye'll. A deadly deceit of now as'king of it y a k'no no no'wing out of a b'ng c'ng merely in wordsz. As'king of it y a kno no no'wing out of it a'wily cruel while. As'king of it y paying aten'cion dhi'rey'kh'tad out to be perceived only in wordsz. Perceived in any name alone. Y na eve're"y turn back to black across of it in her'eye on eve'n'ta h'oureye'sz'zi'on a b'ng c'ng a peering it. Now out as'king of it a k'now'ing d'na'eye'll of it in her'eye of eve'reybody turning a b'lack'g'round echo of a b'ng c'ng a gain. A gain into or out of a completely complete dhi'ark'n'esse to be perceived or deceived now a b'ng c'ng as'king of it y a k'nowing out of it a la que"en que' of that in which appears anybody or any measly chintzy thin' king of it etc.. In word out seen a rey'fracting da na y light in sound wayeves echoing a b'lack'g'round out in her'eyesz z z of eve'rey'body.

"We all as'z'any in word thoth'tsz of it turning igniting a b'lack'g'round out now as'King of it y a k'no'wing out into anybody. Asz Akhenaten any faces approaching were generally on the floor still he seemed to need to exhibit himself as'z mere family man bouncing baby on the knee. In other words'za he had a full complement of bodyguards, palace police, with warrior priests controlling a standing army to maintain his autocracy. An elite fighting force. His was the bronze arm in the velvet glove. He managed to build his own gleaming emerald city Akhetaten. A horizon of Aten. A'kh et'ting duplicating it still in the first place now a'while in a b c's at aten'cion in word. Aten was a somewhat known power or factor in the Egyptian pantheon of gods likely passed down to Amenhotep IV by his father or mother Teye.

"A re'y'viv'al of aten also influenced by the invasion over several hundred years of a lineage of Indo-European arya'in warrior priests. A spreading of awareness of Aten payed off with lives individualized at aten'cion enhanced by remembering the sacred veda knowledge of Atman. A b'ng c'ng now time out in word'sz'zazz the effulgent overseer of a b'ng c'ng at aten'cion. Thatsz the real secret of the exodus. The way out as'ex. Any seer sight c'ee'ing out as'ex's ting. As'ex's ting in word as'z awareness at aten'cion of individual first person present tense in a y eye of that I am is is of a b'ng c'ng. Y'all catching my drift on the a b c's of this?" she now asked with a sly smile.

For a moment Mor felt dumbstruck. Then laughter came bursting out from a dam'now breaking. A letter'all'y y'all giving in name of a god dam'now of ignorance. Ignorance of a first person still in the first place a y eye of that. I am still indivisible in'visibility. Anybody still invisible in'visibility. What an incredible set up of 33+centuries of ma'sz sufferings. In'stilling a b c's of a first person as'king of it y any k'no'wing d'na'eye'll of it phonographically y'all asz'spoken or a peering it out in wordsz'azz'a merely informing it supernaturally as'z'any thoth'tsz of it. A Great God of Gee'sz"us'esse to be letter'all'y y'all gravity weight of appearing with'in'ka's on papyrus. As'King of it. Y. A y eye now d'na'eye'll as'k'no'wing of it now a time or t'wo a twis'ting ma'sz'she'e'na. Asz'any"a'cidsz' eating its own tale of two sid'dhi's. A'zsingle peh'ss'y w'hole power. Int'word a twis'ting in t'wo" e't'all or s'ma'll tale of wo'e as'z'any a na y mere a peering it now k'no'wing out any appearing of it.

Az's'eX. Int'word a pow pow peh'ss'y w'hole power of Y legs lead to eggs. Egg'z's'ting'ing Da'h"OO"ka de'l"OO"ka. Y'all along in the first place indivisible invisibility of any individual still a first person present time now a/w'akhen'ing aten. A y eye of de"sire from above. Ove a b'ng. A'w/akhen'aten at aten'cion now as'king of it y. A k'no'wing out d'na'eye'll of it in a y eye merely a peering it now out at aten'cion. Az's'eX. A'na y'as eX'hodos. A way'eve out as'z' any or eve're'y'e'body merely a peering it. Now out int'word a twis'ting D'NA"eye"ll. A will we all a twis'ting wheel of fortune or mis'sed fortune turning into or out of a gravity of gee'sz"us. A weighting on it of waiting any occurrence of it. A lord as'z'word cut a'cross his'zz'any thoth'tsz of a b c's. Merely supernaturally as'word.

"That indivisible awareness of it in any eye of that I am is is still. Still in anybody. Anybody a peering it. Now as'king of it y appearing a pairing of a y eye now out in d'na'eye'll of a b c's of a b'ng c'ng still indivisible. A y eye a peering it in the first place now as'ex'et'ting duplicating a duplicity in the first place as'king of it y a k'no'wing out anybody in her'eyez z z'any or eve're'y"e'body. Indivisible invisibility yet. A pairing of me or you merely supernaturally as'z'any thoth'tsz of it. Of a supersonic or phonographic memory in this moment by momentum now time a ma'sz'she'e"na. Now as'king of it y a k'no'wing d'na'eye'll of it out. The alphabeta time machine is still today paying out sublime aten'cion now as'k'no'wing out of it a bi'na'rey"e time ma'sheen. Letter'all'y y'all a time bi now a'rey'e'all 'ity of indivisible invisibility denied as'z any or eve're'y body a k'no' no' no'wing it out. Asz'any space in time now awhile. Merely supernaturally as'z'any in word thoth'tsz of any time now a wily while of a ka"re'y"e'z'zee ka'li ma'sz'z'any body of eve'll. Of a time ma's"shee'na stretching beyond now any k'no'wing out of it. A ma'sz mean means in'still'ng a meaningful stillness asz awareness of y'all as'z'any motion of it in d'na'eye'll still. A ma'sz breath as'king of it y a k'no'wing b'lack'g'round echoing out of it a d'na'eye'll of indivisible invisibility as'Kali"ma y. A time now of a k'no'wing out of it in her'eyez z z' of eve'll. In a will of we all turning a b'LACK'g'round echo of it into a b'ng c'ng a GAIN.

A gain of it merely in word aska's mic'da y na light. Igniting that d'na'eye'll of it in wordsz asz sound wayeves zap'ping a pingting in her'eye'szz'azz 'any or eve're'y'body. A're'y'e'dhi'a'ting a perceived eve're'y'body out of it in her'eyez z z'i'on any or eve'rey'body. In her'eye a b'lack' mirror seas'on you na see'ng. As'King of it y a'la Que"en que' of that mean means in which appears anybody or any chislin thin'king of it meaningfully. Aten and Eve. As'eX'odus from the garden of Akhet'aten. Az's'ex'et'ting duplicating still in the first place a second or two a creation of now a'w'h'ile. Self perpetuating mom'ent to mom'ent'um of lifetime after lifetime as'eX.Y'all can pay out attention to it 40 million gad'zillion y'ears still indivisible invisibility in the first place now finding yourself lost a returning of a're'y"e on a wheel will of we all turning yearning earning burning a b'lack'g'round echoing of it in complete d"ark'ness now to be perceiving it as'z'any encirclement of it moment by moment. Of such a plan et'ting duplicating any plan'et h'ear"th as'king of it y now a mirror b'lack'g'round echo duplication asz sound wayeves means informing meaningful a b c's mean of a b'ng c'ng a peering it out in word in formation." As she now paused Mor felt focus diffuse in pigment arrayed on the palette. The painting of a pingting. A b'lack'g'round echo building into a b'ng c'ng through mirror ages merely a peering it still in the first place y'all along. It blew his mind like a 12 volt bulb in 220. For a moment it letter'all'y took his breath away. As'ex'et'ting into thoth'tsz of it. A great God esse to be gee'sz us understanding the weight of a split second waiting time between merely a peering it or appearing of it. Of it in the pain'ting. The pingting echo of it now turning as'king of it y now a k'no'wing out of a b'ng c'ng still in the first place. After y'all these y'ears h'earing it echo eve're'y'body b'lack'g'round. The tinitus ringing in his ears grew until the sound of the professor's voice cooled it b'lack down. Mor found to his surprise the potential of turning back to black without falling as'z z z'leep of a ledge of a'k'no'w. As'ka's of any appearing of it. The Darkness found himself lost in a wordfreedom. A un touched by any touching on awareness of a b c's. A b'ng c'ng still. At aten'cion in the first place a first su"personic person singular present time now a y eye of that I am is is. Or. Da h"OO"ka de'l"OO"ka. As'z'any in word thoth'tsz of a Great God of Gee'sz"us understanding letter'all'y the weight of any waiting awhile appearing of it. Mor now felt asz'z z'a D'ark'ness free of the weight of waiting of G.G.G'eesz'us in the humiliations of his life from crazy cunning ka'li ma to addiction dereliction. Climbing out to fall as'z z z'leep black into a un conocimiento. A cruel con she'us n'ess"e'y"'e. A Shaunessy flashed in his mind. In her eve'll eye'wayeve'rey indivisible at aten'cion in'visibility. Aten and Eve indivisible still in the garden. On the wheel. The city. The sid'dhi. The power of the lightning struck tower filled the Darkness to be now perceived a complete loop'y de'l"OO"peh. A laughter burst from his gut. She'e"na laughed as'z'well. A ka'ra'zzee ka'li ma.

"Akhetaten, horizon of aten centered on a sprawling open air sun temple. Open'a for'ma'sz aten a're;y"e a'son es'un a at atten'tion. Pay that man. As'ka's mic eye in da's'k'eye'zs. Y. Pay atten'tion artist or pay me a mind. Or a y eye on'na. Pharaoh turned his back on the old order to face the sun at aten'cion. As'z'aten'ci'on. A first personic person appearing in a b c's by the first na'me a'ten. A'spread of his arms a gleaming new mudbrick city is built tapping the best architects, stone masons, artisans with a garden of various sacred fruit trees. The fruit of which a God esse to be letter'all'y y'all forbade the warrior priests from consuming in word. Falling understanding the spelling of a b c's one must now taste the five fruits. Eve're'y'body takes the first bite for the first time now a'while. She'e"na body of eve're'y"e'body at aten'cion still in the garden. The tree of five fruits or five senses entwined with the spinal chord. A'snake running the spine the fruits are tasted learning of them merely in word neuronically chemically transmitted in word memory of anybody. As'z'any thoth'tsz of it learned int'word a twis'ting in two a k'no'wing D'NA'eye'll appearing a pairing of it in mem'or'y. A b'ng c'ng still a peering it in the garden. Yet we all must learn in turn as'z two y'z now x'et it. Duplicate it as eve'na merely a b c's in wordsz over the course of many y'ears a h'ear'ing of it echoing a b'lack'g'round supersonic body. A b c's of a b'ng c'ng of it. A're'y"e's'u personically a peering at it. Asz sound vigorous wayeves out int'word a twis'ting in two a k'no'wing d'na'eye'll of it. Eve're'y'one'sz eye of duplicity. Yet once fully understood that spelling duplicity continues mom'ent by mom'ent'um. Or a lifetime after a lifetime merely in word'dsza like he'art nerve blood and bone. A womb of man'as mind or memory. Making senses of it in word. Merely in word. Merely supernaturally as'zany in word thoth'tsz of a God ess'e to be letter'ally learning y'all the parts in word. In a wordship craft of learning. A learning of it as in still'ing awareness wordfree untouched by any touching of it. A touching on d'na'eye'll of it still un'touched. Now y'all k'no'wing a b c's of Aten and Eve. Merely int'word now a twis'ting a time or t'wo of me or you.

"The brightest and the best from the known world are drawn into Akhet'aten for the great benefit of those chosen to live there and detriment of those left to starve outside its confines. Way cool for the chosen. Bummer for the rest and unrest of Egypt y'all around feeling seething in the squeeze of wealth to build the most sacred garden city erected over the underground carved pillared site of pre-Egyptian genetic engineers still supersonically engineering in a y eye now az's'ex over 10. A ten to power of'ten engineering in a long, long, loooooonnnnnnnggggg'aa wwww'h'ile, a crafty wor'd'ship craft as'ka'mic macro micro's ka's mic memory of me or you, ba'by," she gave with eyes on his split between her and it. It. Painting Christina's'z'a'zz'War're'y'na? Pingting his virus now in her'eveye'rus. La Sonoridad. The Super Sonix. The Voice as'ex. In her voice his voice. Still something to think about, he mused while musing about that in the or y engineering of it. As'king of it y. Still that at at'ten"tion. Y'all these y'ear's'zz'z a l'ator'ss'zzz'za. A mirror binary as'z t'oo' of him. As'z two of him he thought with a grin. One a're'y'e'al in'two'rd a twis'ting in two a're'y'e'al'ity as'king of it y mirrored imagined imaginary infinite potential movie. A moving of it. Still in the first place.

"Among the chosen were an elite cadre of atenian priests initiated into a b c's of a wor'd'ship craft carrying away aten'cion into anybody appearing as'z'any thoth'tsz of it. Of a singular God esse to be abstracted a's'z z's'un. A'sz'a's'on"e'y"e 'ar indivisible in'visibility now any individual a k'no'wing out a being c'ng it now at a'ten'cion information merely in wordsz'za. A binary bhakti. A worshipping devotion in a word'ship craft. Indivisible invisibility in any eye a'peering it out in a wordship worshipping now of anybody merely mirrored appearing of it in word as'z a'na y body. Get it? Y'all merely a mirrored appearing a pairing by a peering it out int'word a twis'ting in two d'na'eye'll of it. A y eye on a b c's as'king of it. Y you;re you. Y a now a na y. Any'body of a b'ng c'ng now at attention in a pharaoh. A pharaoh is PA'R'OO'Ma, a b'ng c'ng still in the first place in that sacred house. A b'ng c'ng in the first place transmitted and sustained in the sacred breath, the PehRANaHA. That breath of the divine is this breath," she spoke touching his lips with hers as he looked up from the poison palette. She had his attention now.

"Sugar, I really got to work. This dang paint'za captured my attention calling out to you. But over there in that char," he replied with a gentle nudge. Her flesh quivered with a shiver of goose pimples as a static charge came off the touch of her. Mor loaded a 12 inch palette knife with a row of a half dozen color beads along its steely edge. Sweeping an arm across the canvass he spread the rainbow slugs of poison pigment. Ar'king of it d"ark'ness he mused finding thoth'tsz of a God esse to be pervaded by the code of a b c's. A God esse to be mono. The in word memory of it. A singular God esse to be letter'all'y y'all supernaturally supersonically superimposed now in a pingting. Echoing out a do'or way of eve're'y'body. Only a fool would fail to exit it now as'king of it y now any k'no'wing out of appearing a pairing in motion. Or fools rushing black in. He definitely a rushin' Mor chuckled.

He yielded to the knife wielded before his eyesz z z'a. Again he loaded the knife edge with variations of color until the entire canvass became a mosaic of random tints and tones. Edges cutting bending blending continuous transitions. Sharpening the tip of a wooden handled #2 kolinsky sable brush he began drawing into the wet paint Christina's contour. A positive negation of the continuity of the complete field. Now he must find then lose only to find once more the proportions of her in it. It in her. Any a na y body in motion of the notion. Of a Christina'sz thoth'tsz of a b c's. In see'ng in her'eyez z z'a now in a wordfreedom awareness. Any mere measly thin'king of it mirrors any appearing of it. Supernaturally as'z'any in word thoth'tsz of it. Merely superimposed.

"Hold that pose a second or two," he muttered finding speech patterns muted by the intoxication of the pain'ta. The pingting tinitus ringing his y'ears matched a decibel level of any normal speech. It seemed to grow in ratio with the degree of aten'cion paid to it.

"Yeh, heard that before," she replied with a frown.

"Y'all can still talk," he managed with a giggle betraying the giddiness brought on by the fumes. She gave him a curious stare before continuing.

"Pharaoh built his city as much in'towers of word arising from letter'all bricks. In magical word sounds with the mirror function of his new supersonic aten'b're'y'e'th time ma'shee'na playing a're'y"esz'z'a cording in a mouth organ'eye'z'z'd phonographic alphabeta.

A'way'akh'en'aten instituted a peh'ss'y'en'ce whole new wayeve of el"OO"king of it out'word any or eve're'y scant thin'king of it. It gave us complex definitions of anybody appearing a pairing int'word a twis'ting in two d'na'eye'll of a b'ng c'ng yet indivisible invisibility of any individual still awareness of it in a wordfreedom untouched in the first place. Any individual now as'king of it y." She'e"na paused to let the words sink in. Mor could not pause the obsessive compulsion of his handling the intoxicating pigments and the emerging of a b'ng c'ng in a positive negation of the amorphous sea of color. Negating of it informing contours of a body with a dimension of chiaroscuro.

"Anybody now understanding the spelling of a b c's becomes as'king of it y now as'z'any thoth'tsz of a singular God. Esse to be letter'all'y y'all a k'no'wing out of any mere a peering it in two appearance a pairing of it a'w'h'ile. A deceitful birth az's'eXodus of individualism by the supernatural power of a singular indivisible invisibility of now a God esse. Now a k'no'wing God esse to be letter'all'y y'all a sacred sid'dhi int'word a'tor'us a twis'ting in two d'na'eye'll of it. A positive negation of it. To be culminating now as'z'any thoth'tsz of a God esse to be anybody k'no'wing it out. Still a b'ng c'ng in the first place in the new scripture of a b c's. A b'ng c'ng in a wordfreedom awareness paramount to any in word thoth'tsz of a singular Great God letter'all'y y'all informing of it. A monotheism of any appearing of it as'z thoth'tsz supernaturally informing it still indivisible invisibility of any individual now as'king of it y. Now y'all catching my drift. A'w/akhen'aten. At aten'cion of a b'ng c'ng now as'z'any thoth'tsz of a God esse to be letter'all'y supernaturally y'all disappearing int'word any supersonic or phonographic k'no'wing out in formation of it. Powered by a black'g'round pingting echo as'ka's a k'urving of it a gaining and a gaining int'word a twis'ting in two szound wayevesazz'ka's mic echoing a b'lack'g'round d'na'eye'll of it. It a bing cing still." She'e"na merely a peering it out in her eye of eve'll turned him completely b'lack into the d"ark'ness'e to be now complete. The'na gain appearing of it. A b'ng'lack instilled with intent to be a gain. In't'word a twis'ting in two echoing of a pingting of it in'for'ma'sz finely ground heavy metals suspended in oil containing an inert self-replicating supersonic airborn virus. A're'y"e'versus any d'na'eye'll of us. The dialectic a phonographic catalyst to the co'ro'na vers'us virus emanating from the painting of Christina. Mor then in that proverbial blink of eye a're'y"all'eye'z'zed his individual agency in the conspiracy of mirror ages. A time now mirror'ly echoing the'n. The D na"eye"ll in the D ark'n'ess'e. Any eye a peering it now to be perceived appearing of it. A mirror age of it. Still as'king of it y. A now. A'w/akhen"aten. At aten'cion understanding in word pressure of gee'sz us with gravity weight of waiting. A b'lack'ness of any or eve're'y'body waiting to be a gain. A waiting moment after momentum or a lifetime after a lifetime. A now the n'ding of da'y'zz now azs'ex's ting. A pingting out in her'eye of him'it with a polarity on hand. On the one hand but on the other hand a y eye light igniting any ignore'ance of it appearing a pairing still wordfreestanding awareness of indivisible invisibility of any individual. Akhetaten a city of the first place of the exodus of the in word individual now as'z'any thoth'tsz of a k'no'wing of a god letterally. As a b'ng c'ng a peering it out information. Into anybody any scant stunted starved thin'king of it etc. appearing of it as other gods or goods. A mon'ey"e'the'ism he mused. A k'no'wing of a mon'ey"e God letter'all'y y'all int'word a twis'ting in two gee'sz us understanding the gravity of d'na'eye'll.

"Now y'et as'king of it y a k'no'wing d'na'eye'll of a b'ng still in the first place indivisible invisibility of any individual. A b c's produced mirrored billions of d'na'me'd individuals merely supersonically denying that indivisible invisibility of it in visibility now a k'no'wing y. Now at aten'cion a wayeve out az's'ex coded in written allegories of h'our genesis as'z adam and eve in the garden of Eden or Adon or A'ten. At aten'c'ng'on a way'eve out denying aten'cion b'ng still in the first place etc. Ironically an exodus from freedom to slavery," She'e"na gave Mor a sideways glance giving him pause in his painting.

"Y'all create a slave in his own eyez z z'a understanding a spelling of it int'word a twis'ting in two d'na'eye'll of it. Now anybody k'no'wing out'words a d'na'eye'll its own in word freedom." Mor replied with a grimace. Trickey kali ma'sz devious in word self generating duplicity. What could War're'y'na come up with to top that still d'na'eye'll of it in the first place he wondered.

"Those squigglies are'y'ez z z'in'visibility a self fulfilling prophecy of doom and alienation of h'our own k'no'wing out of it any whithered thin'king of it. Into a binary of a b c's now a by na re'ye'sz'za. Though passages have been rewritten or revised many many ways and times, revelation of a b c's of alphabeta time machine n'eve're'y'e changes. The transmission, the story is letter'all'y y'all in the letters'z'a. In word for'ma'as'z though'tsz in her eve"re'y invisible body now out a'sz'ex act'ing appearing in space in awhile of her'eye on a trickey kali ma'trix. A tricky eve're'y'body. The tower of ba'bel. Akhetaten. City of mud bricks. In A word Ba being a bi'bel. A b"OO"'ka. Ka's mic OO'sz e'gg's stance with gravy gravity of f'OO'lishly falling understanding the spelling of it. Now a b c's of a b'ng c'ng letter'all'y y'all city of the gods. PA'Roo'Ma. In a b'ng c'ng still in the first place. Indivisible in'visibility. Now awhile appearing a city space of entire neighborhoods of alleyways where y'all classes of folks rubbed up on each other. From priests, traders, bakers, artist-craftsmen, painters, sculpters, goldsmiths masons, architects, and the most beautiful women of the known world. Egyptian, Canaanite, Phoenician, Hittite, Midianite, Nubian, and Babylonian princesses. Akhetaten. A b'ng c'ng still in the first place hour'eyez z z'i'on aten. The old order of Amun priests were abandoned, their temples stripped to wrap the new city in gold and jewels. The elite warrior priestly order, the tribe of el'evi or a b'ng c'ng a'Live controlled the unwashed ma'sz'ez with fire and the s'word. The rise of the cult of aten actually a reprisal of much older vedic orally personically transcribed knowledge of a b'ng c'ng now out in wordsz'za'zz'a na'y body of y'all about it. There is a dangerous air of liberation in the Akhetaten air. Idols smashed. Iconic hieroglyphs chisled out.

"It is the wild wild west. X'otic creatures two legged and four legged. Y'all on parade down the main drag. This lavish construction tapped the military budget and you know you never want to put the squeeze on the boys. In any case like that, transferring y'all that wealth from one hand to another, subverting theological order, flipping the proverbial apple cart, creating massive upheavel of an ancient cultural order is a sure recipe for disaster. Perhaps Pharaoh foresaw that he was launching a missile out into the deep mists of time, far beyond his present day Egypt. That once launched from his position of awhile. Indivisible in'visibility appearing in formation he was destined to crumble back into obscurity. His was a dynasty out for the ages and thus to be quickly dismissed and dismantled in his own time. Disappearing in two appearing a pairing in me or you a memory as'z'any or eve're'y'body.

"The launch of the allegory of the Genesis of Adam and Eve, their banishment or exodus, the way of it az's'eX'et'ting duplicating any felt field of view of you of y now out from the garden of Eden or Y'a'ten still grips consciousness, captures attention, 3300 plus y'ears later yet his reign at that time, a mere seventeen years, was short lived along with that of his miraculous city, abandoned and dismantled, forgotten for thousands of years. Still remembered moment by moment'um in word'all'y y'all mentioning a b c's to anybody still of a b'ng c'ng at attention. Attention of any a na y'body still in a wordfreedom merely mirrored in word. A l"OO"ka d'el'b"OO"ka. A g"OO"da ba'z"OO"ka. Ignition of disintegration of any situation. Still a b'ng c'ng a peering it indivisible in'visibility of a y eye in y'all now. A peering it out a'sz supernaturally y'all appearing of it as'ex'et'ing out of the first place. Now as'king of it y a la que"en que' of that in which means appearing as'z'any thoth'tsz of anybody etc. in a long, long, loooonnngg w'h'ile of a second or two. Int'word a twis'ting in two appearing a pairing of billions. A mere duplicity tale of two siddhis per BILLIONS of a b'ng c'ng still in the first place in visibility indivisible to begin with."

Mor caught himself falling as'z z z'leep into billions of mirrored lives appearing from a b c's of a b'ng c'ng merely a peering it out now as'wordsz dividing cleaving anybody any desparate disparate scant thin'king of it azs'ex y'all. We all a wheel turning e'ye turn'ity as'king of it'y now a time machine generating supernaturally any . . . as'z'any appearing of it. Appearing disappearing into or out of it awhile. A cunning cruel deadly deceit appearing a pairing. Merely mirrored as'king of it y now a turning into or out'word of it as'ka's mic micro wayeve b'lack'g'round echo pingtinging billions of y'ears of mankind. A kind of man'as mind or a mean memory h'earth y'ears of a b'ng c'ng out now a hear'in'g of it echoing a b'lack'g'round a k'no'wing of it still in the first place motionless indivisible in'visibility. Now as'king of it any appearing of it as'z'any in word thoth'tsz of a Great God esse to be letter'all'y y'all plan et. A supersonic plan et h'earth of a supernatural superimposition of it echoing a pingting b'lack'g'round to be a gain of it merely mirrored int'word a twis'ting in two d'na'eye'll. Still ar'king as'king of it y. Now a'w/akhen'aten now at aten'cion of a k'no'wing of it appearing a pairing as'z 'anybody any flimsy scant stunted thin'king of it etc..

"That Ex'odos a b c's wayeve out of a y eye merely a peering it int'word a twis'ting d'na'eye'll of it. A yet indivisible invisibility out now still as'z'any mere supernatural in word thoth'tsz of a God esse. To be. As'king of it a la que"en que' of that in which anybody appears in a pairing of it. Az's'ex'et'ting ping'ing a k'no no no'wing out an'y in word appearing supersonically as'z peh'ss'y'el'n'ta't't'wam"thoth'tsz of it. As'z'any thoth'tsz of it must inevitably result ultimately in picking up on a b'ng c'ng be'am'ing for'ma'sz sound healthy wayeves of eve re'ye'body. Now billions as'king of it a k'no'wing out d'na'eye'll of it. Azs'eX'hodus. A wayeves a re'y'all out still awareness of it in a wordfreedom. Untouched awareness of a Liberation now in time for'ma'sz Krys't ma'sz. Kryst of a b'ng c'ng in her'black eye turning gee'sz'us a black'g'round ma'sz thoth'tsz of eve're'y bodhi."

To spread out as'z'any thothtsz of it in a virus. Mor had a virus. A viral storm of a spitting spitting schizophrenia inher'it'ed from a ma'sz peh'ss'y'co' sis. A peh'ss'y co sis'ter'hood of a kali ma'sz planet h'earth w'horr'or show. A sho'n'uff mu'ff. A peh'ss'y w'hole. A eve'eye"r'us. A playing paying out of it. Merely supernaturally y'all in wordsz'zz'a letter'all'y y'all a time machine. A time or now two int'word a twis'ting d'na'eye'll. A will of we all a wheel turning a b'lack'g'round complete d"ark'n'ess'e now to be perceived ar'king of it a see'rz z z' eye 'zstill a peering it now out. A'zs'ound dissolution fun'da'mental fun'ny'a'ction wayeve're'y'e as'ka's micro wayeve b'lack'g'round echo process of it. It still indivisible invisibility. Now awhile in'her'eye'eve're'y'dhi'a'ting perceived merely a peering it out as'z'any in word thoth'tsz of a k'no'wing it int'word in two appearing a pairing of it. A Twis'ting pingtinging playing out of A liberation d'na'eye'd. A d'hi ark'n'esse na black or white or any hue of man'as mind or y now to be perceived turning a k'no'wing'ing a twis'ting in two of it merely mirrored awhile. In any awareness of a y eye still merely a peering it now as'king of it turning a k'no'wing d'na'eye'll twis'ting int'word any a na y appearing of it. Az's'eX. Y'all. A b'ng c'ng a gain by now in a supersonic supernatural spiraling viral storm as'z'elightning striking of a whor'el'ing world of it as'ka's mic d'na'eye'll. A stillness in the h'ey'e art. Ar'king of it a complete encirclement unbroken eve'n a k'no no no'wing d'na'eye'll of it. Understanding the spelling of a time now k'now'ing a ma'sheen'azz' alphabeta ba'by. Best be aware of the a b c's of it. Mor now found it as'z'thoth'tsz of it echoing a ma'sz'z z'rey"e. Any potential misery. She'e'na in word'all'y y'all intoxicated by colored heavy metals'z'azzap'ping'ting pigments of painting breaking across the canvass's plane in sight out of a b c's of it out before the artist's eye. A field of view of you or me in a memory of a time now ma'sz'she'e'na of thoth'tsz in her'me'as'z'z'eye'z'zaherhimit with a potential polarity on hand. A potential positive negativity negating of it wayeves function of fun'ny'a'ction. A potential appearing a pairing of it opening any pi hole mouth to release a tale of two siddhis. As'z two sister powers. As'z two ladies. A vulture and a cobra. We'djat. We all a wheel turning into or out of d'jat he mused amusing himself with thoughts of a trickey ma'sz bi na're'y"ez z z.

"Alphabeta in a b c's of a b'ng c'ng out now a l"OO"ka da b"OO"ka. A bible bi being el function reflecting out int'word a twis'ting in two mem'or'y now of thoth'tsz in his'story. A God esse to be now letter'all'y y'all as'king of it y a k'now'ing out of a na y'sz man. A man'as mind or a y eye a peering it out int'word a twis'ting in two as'ka's mic mem'or'y. A pharaoh PA'ROO'Ma.

In the first place of a b'ng c'ng in a're'y'all of a sacred first su'personic person. That awareness in a y eye of that I am is is. A w/akhen aten. Still at aten'cion in the first place. Akhetaten. A h'our eyesz'on aten'cion. A l"OO"ka da b"OO"ka. As'z' any history book must be rewritten and revised many many times dictated by fickle winds of fate blowing people, culture, language hither and yon. Still as'z'any thoth'tsz of a God esse letter'all'y y'all A'B'ng C'ng. A're'ye Being C'ng'G'ng out of that in the first place. Indivisible in'visibility of anybody of a c'e'er g'ng gee'sz"us. Int'word plane sightseeng from any point of view. Of you now as'king of it k'now'ing out as'ex's ting in formation. Merely supernaturally in word as'z any'thoth'tsz of a God esse to b'ng c'ng int'word a twis'ting spelling out of it.

"Biblical scribes now nearly a thousand years later in Babylonian captivity must conceal the true identity of Patriarch Pharaoh as'z their captors abhor y'all things Egyptian. Akhenaten, shepherd king became an amalgamation of rulers reborn as'z Abraham, mere Mesopotamian shepherd. Now his story transmitting still supernaturally superimposed as'z thoth'tsz, as'z thoughtsz of him'her'it as'king of it a la que"en que' of that mean means in which appears anybody any meager thin'king of it in her'eyez z zap'ping'ting of a eve"re'y bodhi. Appearing now and then disappearing sound wayeves echoing into or out of billions of y'ears. Into or out of billions of eyesz z z'a embellishing translating misinterpreting it through several languages. A b'ng c'ng still in time now letter'all'y y'all a b c's alphabeta ma'sz'she'e'na. A b'ng c'ng g'listening now. In a b c's a y eye of a b'ng c'ng a peering it still out int'word a're;'y'all of'ten a twis'ting in two a binary eyesz. A by now merely mirrored as'king of it y now a k'now'ing out of mind or mem'or'y. Or y y'all merely a peering it appear of it out in a're'y'e'asz'any thoth'tsz of it. A y a's ex. X'et'ting duplicating supernaturally in any mirrored b'lack'g'round y na. A y you'a're'ye now out as'ex'odus. Yet a're'y"e turning b'lack'g'round as'z'leep into a un con she'eve na us a singular indivisible perceive b'lack instilling intent to be a gain of it. Yet a complete d"ark'n'ess'e of it now to be perceived ar'king of it neither black or white or any hue of man'as mind. Or y now in a b c's turning it int'word any in'formation as'king of it. Y now a k'nowing out of it anybody anywhere any time. A k'no'wing out of that eye still a peering it from above. Ove a b'ng c'ng y'et in the first place. The great house of a pharaoh. A Pa'roo'Ma. Akhetaten a paramount first place of a first su'personic person. A y eye in you a're'y'all a're'y'e"dhi'a'ting now to be perceived as'king of it y e'ye'merging a b'lack'g'round echo k'no no no'wing out a d'na'eye'll of it. A y eye on a b'ng c'ng going out as'eX'odus in word in formation in a now Y y'all speak out a b c's in the first place."

"Of which you speak," he added being the y'sz'asz"z'any artist. Of it now.

"Pharaoh's seventeen year reign launched his Alphabeta supersonic time machine now 3300 plus personic y"ears plus billions of eyesz'ee'ng into the future of now the modern era. A mode'right'now drawing on the right side of the brain in a wordfreedom us still at h'ome in the first place indivisible invisibility. A y now understanding any spelling of it enhanced with golden jeweled relics entombed preserved with his successor boy Tut. Not only was Akhenaten memorialized as a biblical patriarch Abraham, his father in law, Ay became God the Father of the first biblical commandment, Anokhi Adon-Ay. An eye of Ay is is a'ten. At aten'cion bi na re'ye'sz'za elOOka a la bOOka. A y eye of a b'ng c'ng int'word any in'formation of it. Thus the second commandment. Anybody or anythin'king of it appearing is merely a mirrored int'word a twis'ting in two in formation appearing a pairing in d'na'eye'll of a b c's of a b'ng c'ng still in the first place indivisible in'visibility.

Thou shall have no'w God as'z thoth'tsz appearing before me. In anybody see'ng in'visibility out int'word it is as'king of it y now a k'no no no'wing a y d'na'eye'll on it out as'ex's ting awhile. A wily w'h'ile of a cunning cruel craft of a mirrored binary beauty or beasty. A'live or dead. Wisdom or folly. The uncanny awareness of that still indivisible invisibility now appearing supernaturally superimposed as'King of it y a la Que"en que' of that in which appearing of it anybody asz'z' out in her'eye of eve're'ybody. Considered in light of this awareness the biblical allegory of Adam and Eve offers means of finding oneself as'z awareness of it as'z a b c's still alone in the garden before learning to see hear taste smell touch a'pp'el in a wayeve function of it int'word a twis'ting k'now'ing out now in two the na. Out in na me alone. Indivisble. As'zz'any any personic individual that I am is is a're; y'all of'ten binary. A b'ng c'ng now became merely mirrored in word'all'y y'all a'sz an y as'king of it k'nowing it out in word'sz'za'z any body or eve"re'y body divine y'll d'na. As'ex's ting in formation of a b'ng c'ng Go'd'na y'll'a'go go Go'a'd energy pressure gravity in a b'ng c'ng be'am'ing now k'nowing. Awhile as'z that simple twist of D'NA y'll a b'ng c'ng appearing out of it in word. In formation. Awhile. If y'all ain't busting up laughing then the denial of its sheer folly becomes extremely sad. Of such is the con of the duplicity of Adam and Eve az's'eX y'all." Asz'a con She'e'na"us at aten'cion gave out a wicked laugh that set hairs standing.

"BIN""GO baby. The dialectic just clicked. Y'all this on about that in word spell. Y'all talking only in denial of awareness of the other hemisphere of the brain. DUH. That awareness indivisible. DUH a brain is indivisible. The other hemisphere always a modern mode right now complete completely in a wordfreedom untouched as'z'any memory of anybody anythin'king of it etc.. Y'all just turned a key to my h'ey'e'way. At aten'cion b'ng captured int'word a twis'ting in two a dna'eye'll of it still indivisible. A turning out in a wordfreedom now int'word a twis'ting in two k'no'w'ing out of a denial of a wordfreedom into bondage in word. Merely supernaturally as'z'any in word thoth'tsz of a God. A God esse to be letter'all'y y'all in word creation." Mor finding himself still in the first place in a wordfreedom went b'lack to invisibility. In'visibility of a b'ng see'ng a visual focus now as'zz'a be'am'ing color fieldsz'a developing in plain sight. Sight in a wordfreedom. It was now as though something un't'word untwisted like a knot in his he'y'art unwinding. Christina gave him a k'nowing smile as if looking at a'tension relaxing from the muscles in his face. In a wordfreedom completely instantaneously 'filled'in any un't'word twis'ted d'na'eye'll of it. Filled with a fullness as'z any complete d'na'eye'll still of it.

"POW way," she responded. Her lips playing out the sound waves with exaggerated force. "pow pow POW'er of ignore'ance ignored. Of a being in a're'y'all'eye'zed now as'z'any or eve're'y'body. A b'lack' body turning a black'g'round into or out of any k'now'ing intent of a mirror b'ng c'ng a gain. A gain of it now liberated from falling as'z z z'leep into any k'no'wing out of that unt'word spelling of it. A y eye of a b'ng c'ng merely a peering it from above still in the first place in a wordfreedom now apprehending its supernatural su'personic superimposition as'z thoth'tsz of a God. A God esse to be a creator of a creation in word'all'y y'all merely appearing mirrored out in her'eye wayeve function waving out any or eve're'y bodhi. A b'ng c'ng still indivisible in'visibility only appearing a pairing asKing of it y a la Que"en que' of that in which appears a black'g'round in her'eye of any or eve'reybody. A b'ng c'ng in one singular b'lack body. A now out asz int'word a twis'ting in two a pairing appearing a gain. As'z a gain to perceive to think about k'no'wing out that awareness in a d'na'eye'll of that. That that I am is is asz'any thoth'tsz of a God esse to be born out'word a gain. Now born in word then merely mirrored as'z'any thoth'tsz of dying or killing to keep from being killed." In words'zazz' in'forma'tion she'e'na washed over his still visual modality in a wordfreedom. In a wordfreedom awareness y'all words merely evaporate without k'no'wing anybody etc. Y'all the while she'e'na keeps in a slow fluid motion a bio luminescent felt feeling field. A field of view of you now in any verse. A universe shimmering she'e'na g'listening electric city. He felt in her eve're'y word'sz'asz z'sound wayeves playing him for shore. Him once adrift finally washed a shore. That towe'ring torus of her electric city energy field poured through his spine a feeling rushing up through his heart brain on out into his'z'ka's mic chakra. Passing his'z'de'z'sire from above a's'zz z'ap'ping'ting down down below. As'zz'above"a'szzbelow.

Mor knew the only way to painting Christina was as'z still in motion. In'visibility of any a peering it out asz'za spirit of she'e"na still appearing in space of muscled flesh toned tightening turning now into a k'now'ing out of kali ma. As'z'za genius or a ma'niac. He began to appreciate the magnitude in her'eyez z z' on him a'sz she'e"na eviscerated y'all notions of his separate in word identity. As'z'any thoth'tsz of a God'd'ess'e to be a'sz'any ma'trix of a y tri'ke'y'e. A try'angle as'king of it y a k'no'wing out as'karma. A Go go go'a'd ess'e' to be ma'sz'energy. A B C or G a k'ey"e 2 any appearing of it. A b'ng c'ng in'two'rd any go go Go'da esse must perceive to be out in her'eye of any or eve're'ybody. She'e'na the go go go, baby daddy. His CNS and PNS burned with a cool fire spreading into colorsz'a cool cobalt pale fired with hot french vermillion at his fingertips layed on a twelve inch steel palette knife. Building foundation. Making her a bed. Or making War'rey'na's'ez'x'tent? He had to wonder. Damn Murphy and your law about anything to good to be true. He was intoxicated as'z hell'o but why na keep going with it. He certainly could think of no good reason. Now still a b'ng c'ng now out of it captured in black lace. Or in a black face of Kwasanda Nzokia he flashed.

"Anokhi adon-ay, I am adon-ay. Father in law now Pharaoh God the Father Ay naturally has converted to aten'is'm as'z he keeps the title adon or aten ay. Once anybody merely one of billions of a b'ng c'ng in any mirror picks up on the code eyes are opened, y'all three. For'eve're'y'e"a'ten. A binary of ze'ro'le a peering it turning into one appearing of it. A being na'ry a'ny scant thin'king of it in formation. Once anyone realizes or picks up on a still being in the first place. One finds that in a wordfreedom immortal immortality of a y eye merely a peering it from above as'z below. That I am is is awareness now and for eve're'y body. Why fall back as'z z z'leep into a black'ness beyond obvious need of a y eye re'ys'ta? When knowing feeling a b'ng c'ng free freed freedom, a y na, brah," she gives him the full curious lips'za. Best keep the eye in the game, dawg, Mor told himself.

"Pharaoh Adon'Ay merely continues to function by fulfilling his purpose of playing the role or roll of God the Father delivering the 'chosen' monotheist warrior priests Ya'hoo'sza. Yah'way warrior priests some already initiates to an older vedic oral tradition of BRAHMATMAN. A're'y"e'all'ity principle singular indivisible point of view of you of a y eye merely a peering it. Monotheism presaged by Advaita VEDA 'enta', that Singular KNOWLEDGE ending with y'all a're'y"e a'w/akhen'ing"aten. A're'y'all'eye'zing'ing any be'gaining of it merely a wayeve function NNNNN'dhi'ing now to perceive anybody mirrored out in't'word a twis'ting D'NA'eye'll of it baby. A ba b'ng y d'na'eye'd.

"Adon"Ay recognized the stature and power of the Ya'hoo'sza. The genocidal warrior priests. As now thoth'tsz of a God esse to be letter'all'y y'all the Father or De'sire Ay negotiated the wayeve az's'exodus as'z'any thoth'tsz of a singular God esse to be now a turning as'king of it a kno'wing out int'word a twis'ting D'NA'eye'll of the wealthy powerful high priests'za warriors with superior metalurgy weaponry along with their converts and support people, the multiethnic rivrav bakers to candlestick makers, 10's of thousands must be removed relocated in order to restore the previous cult of Amun. Her'b'lack'eye'z z z'leep within a'tomb, a womb. as'Kali ma. Multiethnic multitudes of a're'y"e'fraction as'z'any in word thoth'tsz of a God esse. To be monotheists controlling the capitol wealth in the middle of a nation rising up her amun poly'the is m presented Adon'Ay with a dilemma. Should he stay should he go. Father Adon'ay naturally was initiated in a herhim'metic science which confirmed indivisible in'visibility at paying a'ten'cion to it. Sanctioned in word a's'z'any thoth'tsz of a singular God esse to be monothe'is'm awareness where a b'ng c'ng now as'king of it a k'no'wing out in word of the is mirror memory mind. The is m'a b'ng c'ng out in word in formation as'z'any definite definition of a b'ng still in the first place indefinite in a wordfreedom indivisible in'visibility. Any defined int'word d'na'eye'll memory of a b'ng definite y'll still a me're mirroring of a being c'ng in the first place. A pa'roo'ma purusha. A first person still in the first place now as'king of it a k'no'wing out of it merely in the word. Mono or mon'eye mind in the or y na now k'now'ing a na y mirrored y na you now. The point of you now in'visibility of view as'z' any seer sight see'ng. A't aten'cion. A y eye'sz'za binary. Asz'za hOOka delOOka." she asked with a flourish of her outstretched hands. He realized she pushed that time machine of her'e"ve re'y, kali ma'ra'y, to a b'ng c'ng now as'king of it y a k'nowing of that somehow stretching black 33 centuries and beyond evaporated instantaneously with any in word memory of it dissolved in a wordfreedom timeless awareness of it.

"It is said Ay did not get on to the new alphabeta language yet he retained the sobriquet Adon. Ay forced the boy king Tutakhenaten to become Tutakhenamun. Still he kept his head in Aten as'z key"e to comprehend the mirror nature as'king of it y a k'nowing out of it int'word a twis'ting the ka's mic whorl'da supersonic D'NA'eye'll plan et'ting the h'ear'th. Echoing out a black'g'round in her'eye of eve're'ybody a peering it out a'szound wayeves. Her'eye inspiraling inspiring the invention of the alphab"oo'ka bi'na'ry bi b'el. Brilliant written b'oo"k'a allegory in word of her'eye wayeve of eve'rey fun'na'a'ction function of a b'ng c'ng bi being a y now as'z"ex. Indivisible in'visibility of her'eyez z z' of eve're'ybody as'ex's ting in'formation. Her'eye as'eX hodos way one serpent coiling into appearing as'z two. A'sz'tword a twis'ting peh'ss'y'ence w'hole power of mere opening mouth as organ of speech. Releasing tail. Tall tale of Father Ay. Spoken into a race as'z we all of us turning into the promised el'and still in covenent agreement in the d"ark of that covenant with Ay to perceive the promised land now then as'z Caanan, a vassle state then being invaded by Ibirus, marauding shepherding tribes.

"Thus the mon'eye'd monotheist warrior priests could take the prize with the help of the armies of Adon'ay. Now the promised el'and is that mirror wayeve function duplicity of a b'ng c'ng peering it out a pairing in word in'formation of her'eye of eve"re'y bodhi. Ay's promised el'and duplicity alive in a b'ng c'ng in word in'formation still today. A promise of mirroring billions out of that indivisible invisibility of any individual. A billions of now turning int'word a twis'ting D'NA'eye'll of it as'king of it y a la que"en que' of that in which still we all will turn black across the mirror sea of re'eds'za. Black across in the eve'nt hour'eye's'z'on it merely a peering it in a wordfreedom mom'ent by mom'entum. Now as'king of it y a k'now'ing out with intent of a're'y'al'eye'zing'ing merely a peering it. A'y eye of a b'ng c'ng possibly possible within word by dialectic debate of Y'or you now spea'king. Of a y eye merely a peering it or a mirrored d'na'eye'll turned into any appearing of it. Awhile now a space in time. Spoken bi now a're'y'all in a wayeve of turning a black'g'round into the herhimetic science of a y eye of a herhimit freestanding in a wordfreedom. A guardian still in the first place guard'ng a guard'en of a'Y'eye at a'ten'cion. A binary of a b'ng c'ng still in the first place now a peering it out as'king of it turning in two 'for'ma'sz the first time." Mor saw vaporous in wordsz sound wayeve're'y"e trails on the periphery in a plain sight see'ng of it in her'eyez z z'i'on any or eve're'y'body. It seemed the paint fumes captivated attention only as int'word a b c's a twis'ting now out of it carried away in word on supernatural thoth'tsz echoing a'chording to the voice . . . sonoro expresado vigorosamente . . . vigorous sonorous sound waves ripping the cover . . . de x posing as in any na'me . . . any body as'ex posing in a b'ng c'ng in a na y na'me. Of a b'ng c'ng freestanding alone still indivisible in'visibility of any in word in formation of it.

"Thus the first comandment is to remember it a b'ng c'ng in a wordfreedom awareness still that. Adon a y eye in'visibility a peering it from above as'z below. In the beginning the word a'sz a cult, a worship of de word'ship craft carrying a y eye a'way as'z'any thoth'tsz of a singular God esse to be mono'the is m. A mon'eye. aMem or y of a y eye still a peering it indivisible in'visibility of anybody etc.. The one indivisible divinity of a b'ng c'ng now of'ten a k'no'wing out of it a bi'na're'y"ez'a defined a's'word slicing and dicing a na y body into a y by now a's'e'x y'all. Adam and Eve as'king of it y a la que"en que'. Of that in which a go go GO'a'D ESSE to be spelled out. Now in the wayeve function of the garden y'all'egory. The guard guarding a garden as'king of it y now a k'no'wing out int'word the d'na'eye'll story of a mon'eye'star'e y"e of Akhenaten, Abraham, A Brahman Adon-ay, Atman, Adam and Eve a'sz atom and e'wave continues to capture y'all'sz attention. A's'za'a'ten'tion of a peh'ss'y'ence w'hole body appearing a pairing az's'ex's's'el'ave's'z'z'a. A mon'eye at aten'cion in't'word a peh'ss'y w'hole. A binary c'ng of mon'eye on now. A eye by now a're'y. Ar'ray'y'all of'ten seen as'ex'et'ting duplicating asz'any thoth'tsz of a singular Great God. Esse to be letter'all'y y'all a b c's of a b'ng c'ng still in the first place now out of it a k'no no no'wing d'na'eye'll. A'y mon'eye mirror'ed out int'word a twis'ting'king a k'no'wing of it in her'eye merely a peering it out of any eve'll wayeve function. A wayeve function appearing a pairing of it int'word a simple twis'ting of fate faith or family. El fam'iliari'dad. De sire from ab'ove as'z z z'leep below.

"That indivisible supernaturally a'pairing in memory of a're'y'fraction a're'y'flecting anybody int'word it a's'z sound wayeves'zany as'king of it y a k'no no no'wing it out aska's mic memory of a de"sire from above. Desire of dhi sire aska's mic fire'Father perceived synapse SYANDAMANAHA. A y. That ka's mic cycle of it in her'eyez z z' in'for'ma'sz w/ators precipitated up a's'z too fall asz'z z z'leep from above. Ove a b'ng c'ng still now flowing b'lack a's'su're shore tidal place where personal su'personic memory mind or y flows b'lack' into one incoming great ka's mic b'lack mirror sea's u'na you now a b c's consciousness with intent of a b'ng c'ng a gain. That'sz the hard con she'e"'na us. A h'ar'da con. A cruel cunning deadly duplicity. Anybody appearing of it in her'eyez'z z z'a merely a peering it out of any or eve're'y body right now." She'e'na paused letting him see. Now merely mon'eye of a seer a peering it out mirrored in word memory. A memory of it now no longer needing a k'no'wing out. That caught his aten'cion for a moment that could stretch into an e"turn"ity as'king of it y as'z thoth'tsz of a Great God esse. A'sz to be letter'all'y y'all me or you as'king of it y. Y a eye merely a peering it now must appear of it asz thoth'tsz of turning it into a k'no'wing out of anybody any chintzy thin'king of it etc.. Turning as'z thoth'tsz of a being still into the weight of waiting on a b'ing c'ng a gain of it. Out of a complete d'ark'n'ess'e now to be perceived turning into it a gain. Merely opening eyez'z z z'azz'z'leep into the b'lack' of the head in a wordfreedom awareness of a y eye a peering it. Or now it at aten'cion out as'king of it y a la que"en que'. Of that in which anybody etc. appears of any k'no'wing d'na'eye'll. In't'word a b c's infor'ma'ing a b'ng c'ng out of it in two a twis'ting inspiraling h'our'eye'z'z'ion e've'n'ting out in her'eye as'z'any or eve're'y'body. A conning merely

int'word it as'z'any thoth'tsz of a Great God esse to be letter'all'y y'all into for'ma's'z sound wayeve'ye'ing down from above. Ove a b'ng c'ng de'sire. Still in her'eye'star'e"ye'z'z zinging a peering it'go go go'ing up from below. A being el o'ay'in fun'ny'a'ction mirth of a'tor'us mirror'th of turning it b'lack'g'round. Into or out of the ka's mic mon'eye star'e ye now out as'z'ex"eting mirror'ly duplicating wayeves in her'eyez'z za'zz'any'thoth'tsz of any or eve're'ybody. T'at'i'me Ma She'en'a. That mon'eye me ma'sz in her'eye now on him as'king of it in the or y you;re it."

"How? How the heck is'ya'all still here, now that I am picking up how much energy is needed to maintain a constant ignoring of a b'ng c'ng still that indivisible. Now as king of it y'all gots'to feel like a kid in a ka's mic ka'ndy sto"re'y"e mind or y invisibility. In a wordfreedom timeless awareness of it now as'k'no'wing out of it a na y'sz. The first time still in the first place that in the Or y of why a'peering it out at y'all awhile still in the first place."

"Why'z'za sky blue? Because it is in her'eyezz'z z z'a joke. In her'eye'zz'z z z'azz'leep b'lack into a un con'"she'e"na us'sin'n'ing a tricky ka'mic mind instilling intent of ignoring a b'ng still that sa'y'me or you a memory as'ka's of y'all. Asz'z'any memory thoth'tsz of a God. Esse to be a b c's of a b'ng c'ng now out as'king of it a k'no'wing d'na'eye'll of it as'z'any causall'y y'all int'word a twis'ting inspiraling a formation. In D'NA'eye'll of a b'ng still that indivisible invisibility of now y'all cee'ing me by ignoring you. Now as'k'now'ing a me'mory. Now understanding the spelling of alphabeta we all turn into a wor'd'ship sailing out in her'eyezz'z z z'azz'leep into a black mirror seas as'z'any thinker thinking supernaturally of a b'ng c'ng asz'any thoth'tsz of a God'esse to be letter'all'y y'all. Art of a b'ng c'ng in a y mon'eye a peering it out from above as'z'ex y'all. Out now appearing in word ascribed in'formation understanding any spelling of dividing the divine a're'y'all indivisible in a wordfreedom in'visibility awareness of a b'ng c'ng information asz'z'any body.

"Hammerin' the nail carpenter. A bringing of view of you in a black'g'round as'king of it y libertad. as'K"ey"ea's'k'no'wing y in a wordfreedom. As'king of it in a wordfreedom now a y'll we all still as'z thoth'tsz turning into or out of a k'no no no'wing out any d'na'eye'll of it. Still in a wordfreedom for'eve're'ybody. A b'ng c'ng a're'y'all turning a black'g'round as'king of it a la que"en que' of that in which anybody etc. appears in her'eye of eve're'y'body. Priests have been exploiting this mirror in word division centuries now till somebody, the just right somebody in the nearly just as right moment comes along saying, "'Uh huh, ain't havin none of that superstition. That super-imposition by supersonically mirroring it in word'all'y y'all as'z any dog'g"on'e mirror thoth'tsz of o'ne God esse to be letter'all'y y'all at a singular indivisible aten'cion. Now that I am realizing that, I am calling a'w/akhen'aten. A re'y'all'eye'zinging that I am that. I am is is that singular ka's mic aten at aten'cion being y'all subjectivity of any chosen subjects going to move as'king of it y a k'no'wing out to a new city based on the ancient a're;y'all principal principle of a b'ng c'ng in a re'y'e'aten. Now that mon'eye of that I am is is a're'y'aligning a're'y'all'eye'zinging awareness of a b'ng c'ng still in a wordfreedom that indivisible in'visiblity of any individual. Anybody of y'all can realize it as'z well as'z we'all turning into or out of it'

"Now this ain't no hippie commune. A b'ng c'ng chosen in word out of an entire empire.

Empire now a'sz in one gleaming g'listening supersonic or phonographic emerald city. A b c's city of a God esse to be any in word thoth'tsz of a b'ng c'ng in mon'eye dedicated to paying aten'cion. It could only be a moment till momentum of the vanquished become vanquishers. The city rose and fell in a mere seventeen years. Still the city of a're'y'e'b'all aten'br'eth alphabeta lives in eve're'y a'ray'y'all city out there defining eve're'y now with the'na. A now a'lege'dly that underlying promise of delivering anybody from the tyranny of a b'ng c'ng in the or y understanding any in word spelling of it. Now placed in Akhetaten, the horizon or h'our eyez'i'on aten. At paying a'ten't'ion in the first place now as'king of it y now any k'no'wing out of it. As'z a binary. A bi na re'y by now a're'y'et'n a peering it at merely appearing mirrored of it as'z'ex y'all. Now picking up on it by a being y. A're'y'all'eye'zinging y liberates attention from intent of intentionally disregarding a still being y. Yet today billions, billions understanding the spelling of any alphabeta wait weighted by gravity of waiting on death. Will they the y awareness awaken a'sz a w/Akhen'aten now out for'word int'word a t'wis'ting in time az's'eX? In that I am feeling fielding the time machine as'z too recapture attention re'leasing that spelling by re'directing attention to a mean for'ma'sz sound way of eve're'y means by re'minding anyone of a being still in the first place that mon'eye star'e'y'e way to be e'star. That's'z z any mere mirrored point of view of you in me or you appearing a pairing out a's'ex y'all still in the first place. As'ex planed or flattened awhile in'sight of any roll of complete d"ark'n'ess'e."

"As'z ex y'all? Shucks in a shite storm y'all do have a way with in word'sza penetrating me long before I could penetrate you as'z z'ex. You completely permeate me till I am that no longer finding you.You eve're'y'body inseparable from me. No longer awhile of me or you. The sheer intoxication. It's the paint. It's the model . . "

"It is the drugs'za'zsex and rock'n'roll?" Christina offered, stretching and twisting hips, arms reaching, fingers extended.

"Yeh, whew, I'm gonna need the rest of that tea." The wounded knee caused him to grimace as he adjusted his weight on the high chair. The contours of a body now rendered on the canvass in 3D with the chiascuro of light and shadow. The texture of paint now chunky Mor began knocking it back down then stippling the surface with a broad brush. Whenever his will began predominating the work lost its vivaciousness of a'ka's mic influence. It became flat and mean like a life spent deliberately ignoring it. Rather than as'king of it y now. Mor realized the sheer folly of any function beyond the obvious intent. In painting a certain functional coordination applys but the real deal comes thru you he mused as hands kept moving right before his eye'z z'i'on her as'it. A pingting ringing echoing building of it in her'eye of eve'll. A b'ng'lack will of a b'ng c'ng a gain. Of it still complete. Of we all turning into rolls or roles of complete d"ark'ness that ain't b'lack Dark Mor thought with a grin. Mere D"ark'n'ess'e now to be perceived in any roll or role. A l"OO"p'eh'de'l"OO"pa. Any birth is any death ad infinitum azs'eX'treme nauseum.

It seems suffering is the only antidote to any d'na'eye'll of it. El"OO"peh'de'l"OO"po is e"ye'turn'ity as'king of it y now any b'lack'g'round k'no'wing out of it to be a gain. Thatsz a serious farcial e'turn'ity. As'king of it y a la que"en que'. Az's'ex y'all. As'word splitting mon'eye in two merely supernaturally. In't'word it as'z'any thoth'tsz of a singular God. Esse to be letter'all'y y'all a peh'ss'y'n'ce whole eye merely a peering it out in here'ye of any or eve're'y'body. As'z'any thoth'tsz of appearing of it falling. A falling as'z z z'leep b'lack into a's un. A u now con she'e'na"us merely a peering it out a/w'akhen'ing aten. Awakening a binary aten'cion. A double trouble. Yet as'king of it y now merely any mirrored appearing of a b c's int'word a twis'ting D'NA'eye'll as'z'any thoth'tsz of it. Only as'z thoth'tsz of a singular God esse to be letter'all'y y'all a b'ng c'ng now turned as'king of it int'word a twis'ting k'no'wing D'NA'eye'll of it possible. In word memory as'z'any thoth'tsz makes it az's'ex's ting awhile possible. A b'ng c'ng still in a wordfreedom drawing on the right side of the brain. Mor feverishly drew on it. Or it drew him into a singular p'sy'lence now impinged by the pingting of Christina's image azsinging echoing a tinnitus ringing his earsz.

"Hold that pose, just a second, or two more."

"Uh huh, heard that one before again," she replied with a cunning smile.

"I wouldn't lie to ya, but I might lose track of time."

"Then I have no choice but to blab on. The time ma'sheen is sz'a'mokin"na. You be feeling the rush of her na'otion of ocean. In her eyez'z zazz'leep black into a mirror se'e'ng'as echoing a black'g'round. Se'e'her a's t'at'i'me mashe'e'na as'kali ma. Devourer in time now the'n"d'ing turning y'all k'now'ing her children into crones and dust. Tat'eye'm'a Ma'She'e'na'sz ser peh'ne'tah'sz"f'ang. Ang'st'a o'fun'ny'tric'key"action. A shredding b'lack in her eye of any or eve're'y'body creation."

"In her'eyez'z z now awhile kali ma'sz deadly trickey treacherous devious waters do flow out e'turn'ity. As'king of it. As'z two, put it mildly?"

"And you should worry about old white man War'rey'na when you be her'e now feeling it. The pain'ta that I am seeing in your eyes is in her'eyez z z' along with the color in them paint tu'be's'z'a."

"Then, reckon that I am be'in bet'ter by mentioning that man'as Magus spinning y'all."

"Ma"gus, my man'as'z ma'sz mi'n'd'a or y. They be a lotsa ma in them ma'guses."

"Her'him'it. So you or him the end remains'z sa"me same? In that I am meaning he engineered you. Therefore your goals would be similar."

"Except that I am way more ruthless, na'sty, and bewitching than Papa War're'y'na. Of course as soon as having those thoughts'za he comes into me. The dynasty awakens. Once upon a y time the world, the x known part found ka'man blackg"round. It y'all go round the Ab time ma'sheen of a b'ng c'ng transported generations of mind forward in word a's letter'all'y y'all ascribed a'ray'y'all asz a y mon'eye star'e ye na now a k'no'wing it not. It, that indivisible in'visiblility of any individual seer sight see'ng sphin'x'like through many ma'ny mirror ages.

That it as'king of it y a la que"en que'y'szazz the cu'be of space.

"Alphabeta is 3D supersonic time ma'sheen with 6 face sides, 12 exterior edges, and 3 interior planes'za and one center as'king of y'all y in a b'ng c'ng mon'eye point of view. Of you a peering it out in t'w'en'ty t'wo a twis'ting whorlding letter'all'y y'all int'words in forma'ing merely a double mirrored in wordszas'z'any thoth'tsz of it. Of a singular God esse to be still indivisible in'visibility of a b'ng c'ng of a y mon'eye of herhim'it'asz forever you'ng. Androgyne dancer as'ka'smic kamic dancing d'na'c'ing. Surrounded by 6 directions as'eX'per'eye'in'c'ng it out. Azs'eX plan'e"t'ations. Of a supersonic multidirectional super overstanding of a b'ng c'ng understanding any spelling of y'all. It'sz'a ka's mic whorling world by a b'ng c'ng y mon'eye of a herhim'it a peering it from above as'z below. Ove a b'ng c'ng a'be'am'ing out of it still in the first place. H'our'us eyez z z'leep b'lack into a un con"she'e'na us in a b'ng c'ng of a portable time ma'sheen.

"That'sz'a y mon'eye a'sz'z's'ex's 'ting in formation by a'peering it out in word. A pairing with in'ka's memory with a na y potential intent to disregard it by a now k'no'wing d'na'eye'll of it. Out of a b'ng c'ng indivisible in'visibility still in the first place. Now as'king of it y a k'no'wing out any imagining of it. Any a na y imaginary image now appearing of it awhile. A peering it out in word from above. Ove a b'ng c'ng from de'sire. Pa's abilities the vehicle that transports you now supernaturally asz'any thoth'tsz of it. In a word'ship for'ma'sz in word'all'y y'all into pa's'tat or a future of a few prototypes tat you a're'y'e"all in as'ix x plan"et's mirror planer fields of a being'sz'anybody. Now that I am as'king of it y a k'no'wing out of which face is War're'y'na tracking?"

"Yeh. And it z'sounds'za like that train track gonna be leaving the station shortly," Mor added as he pulled up highlights with a rag. He found certain highlights on her form emerging wiping back fresh paint layers leaving a difused light coming from the intense white gesso layers beneath.

"Enough in word's'za. Time now as'king of it y a k'no'wing without the'm memory," Christina offered, taking the palette knife from his hand and slipping into his arms. He felt the silk of her nylon stockings slide over his bare leg. Her naked breasts crushed into his chest. "This is where it gets to a b'ng c'ng y as'ex et'ting a D'NA'eye'll factor. Where the k'nuckle now k'nows meeting the bone."

☼

The silver BMW maneuvered through surface streets to highway I84, back across the Dumbarton Bridge. For a brief moment, Kwasanda saw through the grid of civilization. The opposite shoreline now free of high-tension lines, industrial parks, and freeways. In her mind's eye she now saw naked people gathering clams in reed baskets, their bodies patterned with tattooed dots. Some wore bones through noses, teeth and claws as necklaces. They moved with purpose. Connected to the food without and dreams within. When she looked again, the shoreline spoiled by urban sprawl now seemed defiled, polluted by years of progress, people hidden away now in boxes and cages and smart phones. Except for an old black fisherman on a long wooden pier. She recognized the snow-white curls of beard and hair that hung over his head like a cloud. He wore his everyday starched khakis with wide green suspenders. She knew him as Amos. She thought of him as a saint, perhaps a good omen. Gray green water chopped with the wind as a power-launch tore past in a cleavage of white foam.

She spotted the Mark IV rolling through an intersection, Fawn Rave at the wheel, Korner slumped against the passenger door. Kwasanda cut into the left lane, jetting through a break in oncoming traffic as the light changed. Korner flipped her his middle finger. She offered an upraised open hand in reply. The Mark IV roared through on red, leaving her stuck at the light. Korner headed south in the direction of the Portal, not east to the warehouse. Kwasanda could only guess at how Korner had exchanged Fawn Rave for Hashimi. There could be another skeleton to stack in Korner's full closet. The more she thought about bones, the bigger the pile grew in her mind until skulls and tibias rose above. A jagged tower shadowing the sun.

As the light turned green she accelerated through the intersection. Driving, the fingers of her free hand touched her cheekbone. Pressing with thumb under the ridge of her jaw she traced its contour. Her fingers continued to track the underlying contours of teeth, mandible and maxilla. Her experience in the Pod turned the world without often into one continuous strobing field of wavering colored light patterning with her eyez z z' a being anybody now merely mirrored awareness of a being c'ng of it. The a b c's of it. A being c'ng appearing out of her a peering it out in a word now knowing it. In a word as'ex's ting in formation of anybody. Any time. Any where. That's it she thought I've completly lost my mind. Its's been blown to bits. The power of her ancestry in dream time certainly surpassed her waking state. Yet this power without ancestry. This a power a peering it out from above in wordsz of a being c'ee'ng yet in the primary state without any in word in formed memory of it as anybody appearing out of it. A power of any de'sire to appear often out of it. Out there in that blink of eye. Moment by moment appearing she mused. Now post pod she found her memory often lost in the black'g'round power of it. Instantly disappearing in it. Instantaneous reabsorption of her in it. Still in her eye a peering out of it by now asking of it a ka'no'wing it out in word. She now in word memory of it or not at all.

A woman in faded levis cruised the street, a cigarette like an extra finger stuck out from her hand. For a moment their eyes met, a flash of recognition passing. The bones get around, she thought. With yet another green light she drove for the Portal.

☼

Fawn refused to look at Korner. He wanted to give her a taste of the violence that lurked behind any act of human kindness. Instead he merely smiled.

Two Latinos crossed in front of them at a red light. Their bare tattoo-covered arms dangled as they walked. Eyes veiled in sunglasses, scanned the terrain with predatory pose. Korner laid his hand on the grip of the pistol in his lap.

"Be cool. Don't get someone else killed."

La chica let her foot slip, the Mark IV rolling forward. The Latinos jumped, losing their street posturing. One slapped both palms down on the car's front fender. "What the fuck?"

"Later, homes." Korner jammed Fawn's foot with his on the gas. He watched the cursing pair fade from sight.

"Why do they put that shit on their arms?" he asked.

"They're ganged up. Out here, the Sadistas rule."

"They don't even rule their own dicks."

He directed her to Menlo Park and the Portal. He watched as they drove past three-story commercial buildings and warehouse lofts until reaching open ground littered with debris, the grassy esplanade and sandstone offices off in the distance. Korner ordered her to stop by the chain-link fence topped with coils of razor wire surrounding McCracken's airstrip.

"This is where we get in, chica de muchacha. You know Willie and Muddy? I've seen them play where they stay, South Side Chicago blues." Korner sang in throaty growl,

"I'm a back door man
The men don't know
But the little girl understand"

Tires from a twin engine Beechcraft squealed as its wheels caught purchase on an asphalt runway, dissected with veins of black tar. Fumes of spent fuel, creosote, bay water, and burning rubber assailed Korner as he stepped from the Mark IV. He curled the fingers of his good hand through the galvanized chain links. He wanted to bust in, grab the Copper Scroll data, do McCracken, and steal the Beechcraft, taking the tart for a ride. Let her feel the power of his dick throbbing in her throat as he pulled off the ground in a hail of lead.

Walking back to the car, Korner popped the Altoids tin, breaking a quarter-sized rock into dime-sized pieces. He motioned to her with his chin. She let her mouth fall open, licking her lips. He played his finger over her tongue.

Korner popped another rock. "Drop into reverse about thirty yards to that green sign yonder, then slam into drive and mash the gas. This baby is built like a tank."

He leaned back and closed his eyes. Korner's sight bowed with the earth's curvature. His mind had better wings than the Beechcraft. Anger distracted Hashimi. Korner liked to think he never killed a man unless he earned it, like McCracken trying to play him with the Copper Scroll translation. Korner looked at the chica with her head down, the flesh of her neck and shoulders oozing with the smell of fear.

"Open." He raised her chin with his fingers and slid in a rock. The back of his hand brushed the uplift of her breasts. Knuckles caressed the flesh, massaging her cleavage.

Her chest heaved. A tiny gold cross on a thin chain lay flat on her brown skin. Her flesh shone with sweat in the light reflected from the hood of the Mark IV. She leaned against the leather headrest. Her mouth fell open, tongue rolling to puff out her lower lip. She tapped the gearshift into drive and hit the gas. Tires squealed as the engine roared. Beyond the confines of the Mark IV, diamond links of steel wire exploded into fragments. Fawn jerked the wheel, the car fishtailing across the tarmac. He had her put on the brakes at the rear of a three-story office.

Korner retrieved his satchel from behind the seat. The bitch deserves punishment for her insolence, like a blast from the Taser. Maybe later, he decided. Movement reintroduced pain to his shoulder as he sucked air. Heat waves rose across the runway, rippling the massive hanger on the far side.

"Both hands on the wheel," he said as he took out a pair of white plastic zip-cuffs. Strapping her wrists to the wheel, he shoved a Giants baseball cap on her head. "Be good and I'll show you some fun when I get back."

Korner stuffed his pockets with the cigarette pack charges and speed loaders for the Colt. He strode in thru the rear entrance as he headed to McCracken's office. He was surprised at the laxness of security. No locked doors impeded his progress. In a washroom to splash cold water on his face and knock the cobwebs from his eyes, Korner tried to extend his left arm. His badly swollen eye made him a one-eyed vengeance. Color drained from his face, feeling haggard and spent, he made for the third floor. He slipped the gun from his coat pocket, brushing his hair with spread fingers. Might as well look good for the game.

A security guard appeared as he turned a corner at the far end of the hall. Korner cracked him on his head, pushed him into a conference room, zip-cuffed his hands, and gagged his slack mouth. The outer office had no lights on, computer screens blank at their stations. Korner opened the brass-plate double door leading into the main office, McCracken's, pre-Columbian meets chrome and glass. McCracken's collection left Korner cold. He dragged a fertility stick from its teakwood pedestal to the high-backed leather chair.

Korner dropped into the chair, pressing his spine against its contours. Blocked currents opened in a rush of blood to his brain. Sitting in this museum put thoughts of the Scroll treasure into the proper context.

He saw McCracken's private jet down below less than a hundred yards from the office. Korner flipped open his cell and pressed the speed dial. He flopped his boots on the polished marble desktop.

"Where are you?" demanded McCracken.

"In your house, bwana. Bring the translation. I told you to watch your back and not to put too much faith in fences."

"Getting in is sometimes easier than getting out."

Korner took another rock from the tin as he flipped the cell phone shut. The flake melted into the nerves only millimeters from his brain. A plan began to formulate. He spun the nickel-plated pistol on the desk.

Brass doors burst open. He stared down Mac-10s slung on the shoulders of two guards in black suits who posed like paper cutouts for target practice. McCracken stepped between them wearing a gray silk suit and crew neck shirt. Gold rings dotted his fingers, the patina of centuries adding rainbows to their sheen. They paled next to the glitter in his eyes.

"The Scroll is nothing compared to the data I've witnessed," said McCracken.

"Can't buy me love or jet fuel."

"Where's the half-baked artist?"

"He's in my ride below."

McCracken looked out the window. "The guy has tits?"

POW. POW. Korner fired the Python, putting holes between the shocked eyes of the guards. He watched them slump down like sacks of meat. Best to die with your boots on boys. He wondered, for a second, if they'd be missed. "Too much faith in weaponry slows your reflexes. Ask them." Korner set the pistol down, grimacing, cordite laying in the air. "What's the matter, Whip? Someone pull down your pants and leave your ass flapping in the breeze?"

"That was unnecessary. I have what you want."

"Good. We can share the moment."

"I knew you killed my sensei."

"He died for your sins. Let's have a look-see."

Korner waved McCracken to the laptop lying flat as a sheaf of paper on the marble. McCracken shrugged.

When he was in action at Zina's brothel, McCracken acted like he had been born to dominate. His air of superiority had chafed Korner from the moment they met. Still he had to smile at McCracken, not a trace of fear showing. He was him without the war. Without that meat grinder grinding everybody. The ones walking away most of all he thought, checking the cut of McCracken's suit accenting the jauntiness of his movements as he slid over to the computer.

McCracken reached inside his jacket. Korner swung his good hand, jerking him down with a fistful of his silk shirt. A wild swing from McCracken and Korner planted two swift head-butts. He pulled McCracken close.

"Do what I say or I'll kill you, but not before I give you a sampling of the pain you like to inflict on the weaker sex." Korner growled, flicking spittle on the man's face. "A power object means squat if you can't bring it to your fist." He released his hold on the silk, bringing the fertility stick down across McCracken's shoulders. The blow wacked off hard muscle.

McCracken barely flinching dipped a hand into his jacket and pulled out a CD-ROM.

He slid the glistening disk into the tray of the laptop, tapped a few keys, and slid the unit over. The Copper Scroll appeared on the flat screen, iridescent colors glancing off its patina. An inventory of lost treasure, hammered by scribes whose bones turned to dust several millennia ago, waited for the right man to come along.

"This ain't a translation. It's all Greek to me," said Korner.

"Hebrew, actually. According to the file, the Scroll is written in a code of numbers and letters. In Hebrew every letter has a numerical value, some more than one."

McCracken tapped another key, the image magnifying until the indentation of the marks could be seen.

"Tell me what the picture means, any kind of location. GPS coordinates?"

"Look closer. That's Greek," he moused an arrow tracing the shadow of a letter superimposed over the Hebrew text.

"Yeh, still Greek to me. What's it say?" Korner felt his energy falling like a battery running down. He gave McCracken a weak shove before sitting back in the leather chair.

"You don't look so good, amigo. Maybe killing doesn't agree with you anymore."

"I tell you something while holding this pistola in the upper hand, I am seriously with one foot in the next world. I'm ready and willing to shed this old skin. One thing, just one keeping me here and that's laying these tired eyes on that pile of golden antiquities. Tut city, baby."

"Speaking of Tut, the Greek word hidden on the scroll, and I mean it took me mucho mucho hours of gazing to pick up on it. The word is Akhenaten. The Tut treasure was actually primarily his, Akhenaten's. The treasure may be buried in Egypt, not Israel."

"Howard Carter, the American, was decades searching before a boy in his camp stumbled on it, the buried stairs leading to it."

"Sure but he didn't have the technology we have."

"So, that's all, just one word, one name?"

"That's it."

Korner slammed his fist. "I'm going into the Pod. Give the word and get me set up. Make the call."

Chapter 13

Christina returned to her pose on the high chair. She watched the Darkness absorbed with the painting after drinking the rest of Enoch Tuttle's opium laced tea. Seeing by his pallor that it took y'all of his energy, y'all his focus, she now had second thoughts about distracting him with sexual seduction. Still she felt relaxed in her nakedness, her body electric with de'sire, a de'sire from above that once seemed abandoned from womb or yearning for fertility below head and heart. Now, detachment of objectivity could only be denial of blood fulfillment. Then, she was getting off watching artist being absorbed by purpose preordained, function serving cause beyond biology running out past the drive for procreation. That in a man, she thought with a smile. It would take y'all her will power to resist pulling him over. Best keep that in mind she mused. That in the y'or y na in word dialectic debate sweeping away her attention as'ex y'all.

In her'eyezz now at attention of that in a wordfreedom awareness that I am is is a're'y'all'eye'zinging the PA'RANTAKALE, the supreme end time. That parooma ending in the first place of any beginning. Programmed the're'y'e a li'on in a b'ng c'ng a be'gain'ning of it merely in word by dhi en'dhi'ing out of pa'roo'ma of'ten the mean captivity of A B C's. A time now ma'sz she'e'na quivering glistening b'lack wayeve're'y'body of a mirror see'asz' anybody any tawdry thin'king of it etc.. Now she'e'na asz thoth'tsz of that I am finding still see'ng'as in a wordfreedom awareness of A' B'ng' C'n'g. Now in wordsz'az z z'leep b'lack supersonically supernaturally superimposed out now over any understanding of the spelling of a b c's in man'as mind or memory int'wordsz'any in'formation of it.

Christina now turning into a k'now'ing out of it as'z'any thoth'tsz of a God esse to be letter'all'y y'all a b'ng c'ng found herself it. Her'him'it out as'z that I am a thin'king of it asz a womb'man'as a memory of now. A ba'by. As'ka ba el'a ba'by a b'ng c'ng a peering it still in the first place in a wordfreedom indivisible in'visibility. Now any k'no'wing out of it as'ex's ting supernaturally as'z thoth'tsz of it in a space in time now awhile within a 3D intent of a gain appearing of it. A daring deadly denial of a peering it out in forming anybody appearing of it. Awhile as'z a b'ng c'ng now int'word a twis'ting in two of it. Now a k'no'winging a D'NA'eye'll of merely a peering it out in'formation.

That'sz the plan she'e'na mused. A plan et'pingting h'earth of it in a mirror b'lack'g'round perpetual echo now building supersonically. Viral pigments bouncing silent sound wayeves building to burst the dammed bubble of any mirrored role or roll of complete d"ark'n'ess'e that ain't b'lack she now thought. Or white or any hue of man'as mind or memory of it. The build up would be excruciating for anybody still ignoring the a b c's int'word building a lightning struck tower in word of 22 personic bricks asz'any thoth'tsz of a God esse to be letter'all'y y'all appearing of it anybody any scant thin'king of it etc.say'l'ing a devious debatable wordship a'cross a space in time now awhile. Appearing a pairing in a memory of me or you she thought.

It seems we all a wheel have turned into or out of any mere idea of a b'ng c'ng now in word mirrored out with in'ka's on a pa'per memory of a mon'o'eye"the'e is m. Mono ey'e mon'eye is in the or y a mirror memory. Letter'all'y y'all a peering it int'word a twis'ting it in two appearing a pairing of it she now thought azs'ex y'all. Now we all may turn out of it as k'no no no'wing h'our'eye'zz'i'on a b c's. A b'ng c'ng in any word now turning out of a k'no'wing of it creating imaginary li'on between it or an'y idea of it. A b'ng c'ng' go'ing out and about awhile. A b'ng c'ng by a'na y mon'eye. A b'ng c'ng appearing of it by now turning out a k'no no no'wing d'na'eye'll of it. A b'ng gaining any en'dhi'ing of time. Now as'king of it a k'no'wing of it perceived out of a black'g'round echoing any mirror appearance of it. It now in a b c's of a b'ng c'ng still indivisible in'visibility of any individual. Defined by any en'dhi'ings of it letter'all'y y'all in word az's'ex's ting in two a polarity. Appearing a pairing asz a positive negativity of a k'no'wing out any d'na'eye'll of it. Now it appearing disappearing by gaining a k'no'wing of any endings of it. A b'ng c'ng now written off asz'in turning in two bi a k'no'wing out a positive negation of it. A b'ng c'ng out in word must find now the wayeve of eve're'y'body. A black'n'ess'e now to be a k'now'ing out of a b'ng c'ng liberated from in word captivity. In a wordfreedom awareness of it. A b'ng c'ng still in the first place. A priori to any in word captivity. A liberation from falling as'z z z'leep black into a un con she'e'na us understanding any in word spelling of a b c's. Paying mon'eye at attention captive to appearing by na'me. Trapped in any feeling of a being alone. A alone being indivisible still in the first place.

Yet the more y'all feel alone the more y'all realizing a b'ng c'ng in the first place still indivisible she'e now reflected. In a b'ng c"ng now that I am fishing of it. A fishing with da h"OO"ka's feeling'sz'zazz fielding my w'ayeve're'y'body on this quest eye on? My quest is that in word w'ayeves in her'eye'zz'ion in'for'ma'sz liberation by da b"OO"ka. A g"OO"da b"OO"ka'sz thoth'tsz of a God'as'z esse to be letter'all'y y'all now a Johnstone War're'y'na seeking int'word dissolution by viraly dissolving in word memory of a God esse to be letter'all'y y'all'sza web. Gone. Maybe his virus has a bi'na'tural antidote she'e'now wondered. Thesis. Antithesis. Liberation synthesis. Liber free. Liber'aten. Attention liberated in word by the h"OO"ka letter'all'y y'all by da b"OO"ka.

"The poison is the cure? Or something li'ke that. As'Kali ma creates any creation out of her'eyez z z a wayeve of any or eve're'y'body. Sustains it in a'wayeve. Destroys it in a'wayeve crashing in her'eyez z z'ion any imaginary creation in her'eye of eve're'y'body. Turning a black'g'round echoing a way'eve're'y black mirror seas invisibility in visibility of any appearing of it. A singular black body ma'sz indivisible virgin ma'sz still in the first place? A b'lack' by now instill'd e turn'all'y y'all k'no'wing out a gain of it in da y na light? It begins with the singular indivisible en'dhi'ing of it. An ending merely in a word supernatural as'z'any thoth'tsz of a God?" Mor saw her figure appearing then disappearing in pain'ta. Beyond word's'za she e na. She'e'na. "She'e"na tears it black down because it's only meant to be in her'eyez z z of eve're'ybody in'for'ma'sz a'while. A y'eye'as'z'scheme. A tricky funny little deadly dopey duplicity. Or na y. Not you. Or you now as though a k'no'wing out of that mon'eye a peering it of that I am is is could be a being c'ng separate as'z'am'emory of me or you and so War're'y'na's virus must also be a b'ng c'ng out in her'eye of eve're'y body."

"In her'eyez z z now int'word a twisting in two of it a k'no'wing out a're'y'verse of it. A're'ye'verse of polarity. It has'z'z'a occurred ma'na y times. Still magnetism unlike electricity is a continuum. Reverse flow still that same continuity con'tin'u"u'u'u'in'g con'tin"u"u"u"y'all'y y'all . . . .in her'eyez z z'i'on any imaginary li'on'az'sphinx. Es'se peh'ss'y'in'ce x per eye in c'ng a con of con she'e"na us n'ess'e . . . .a con in her'eyez z z'inging to be us by z'en'ding back in two a b'lack'nesse now to be a gain.. . . . .can y'all dig it doggie?"

"Cain'ta end that without a beginning of it? Y'all getting ontoo the pain'ta"fu'me'ss'zz. So my question still is, is it you or War're'y'na or is there a choice of sides in this scheme?'

"Y'all lookin'ah at it in her'eyez z z now and y'all ask me that?" she gave with a pout then a wicked laugh. Somehow it felt War're'y'na's whole military industrial chemical complex could be crunched in her morning coffee. A'Ma"re'y a'zz is'z'z'a'yy'y'y"iii, Mor flashed with a grimace.

"S'z'ound'sza like y'all coming around to War're'y'na's way of thinking."

"He wants"z'z'a reversal of e'very role that I am playing breaking out a'z's'ex's ting. A pingting load of infinite potential. Bud'dha boy, you gotsta want it more than any old ting. Liberation by el b"OO"ko. As'ka'sh'ic memory in a re'y cording a quivering e'szound wayeves echoing a black'g'round in time now as'king of it y any k'no'wing out int'word a twis'ting in two a D'NA'eye'll of it. Or it in a wordfreedom indivisible invisibility as'z'any individual. With'inKa's letter'all'y on pa'per de'sire a peering it from above. Ove a b'ng as'king of it y a k'no'winging out a shimmering ka's mic memory field of view of you. In front, behind, to the right, to the left, above, below, and projecting y'all a b'lack'g'round. Projecting y'all complete d'ark'n'ess'e that ain't b'lack. Or white or any hue of man'as mind or y now. Projecting y'all'az complete dhi ark'n'ess'e. Complete still completely instilled with intent to be a gain of it. Now to be perceived ar'king of it still. Ar'king of it y a still center point of view of you of y a b'ng c'ng in the first place. Pa'roo'ma liberation now denied from a k'no'wing out of y a'realizing a're'y'all'eye'z'z z'inging a b'ng c'ng still in the first place. Now out int'word a twis'ting in two any D'NA'eye'll of it from that indivisible invisibility point of view of you a peering it from above. Ove a b'ng you still in that first place. Ain't b'lack or white in a wordfreedom. As awareness in a wordfreedom now. In a wordfreedom forever. For eve're'y'body now as'king of it y now any measly thin'king of it. In a wordfreedom of a b'ng c'ng indivisible in'visibility as'z'any individual. Moment to momentum the urge for a b'ng c'ng in a wordfreedom may prove stronger than the procreative proactive biopsychological as'k'no'wing out one yet.

"Yet playing out complete roles or rolls of d'ark'ness that ain't b'lack or white. Still, offering a wayeve reaching out for that golden k'ey"e to pop the b'lock of ignore'ance is really my design. That'szza break out int'word a're'y'versus of it in a wordfreedom. A liberation from paying attention as'z int'word a twis'ting in two being'sza appearing a pairing self imposed in word bonds as'zz'any thothtsz'z a 'na y idea of a being me or you. In a mirror memory now a k'no no no'w'ing out of me or you standing still in a wordfreedom. Now a ba'freaking out, ba,by. Oh ba a being of y. Ba historically is like history of ka's mos. Forget about it. Or na. That's'za my de'sign."

"Designed by War're'y'na's genetic engineering? Guess I'm wondering if there are two sides to this play. Shall I fall completely under your spell or put a stake in your heart? You tell me."

"Actually I was thinking of a stake, well more of a pole, but not in my heart."

"There's that edge and I've got a wounded knee balancing on it," he replied. "How about sitting your lovely butt back on that chair. Just for a second or two."

"Or three," she tossed back with a languid stretch feeling the muscles of her chest tighten against her nipples. Her impulse went to taking his hand but she settled back on the leather cushion and backrest of the high chair.

"Twist slightly to the right, then let your head turn back . . . right there. Beautiful, hold that . . . so, tell me, woman, are we all turning out for him or agin' him?"

"Perhaps a bit of modification is called infor'ma'sz a b'ng c'ng out in a mere mind mirroring memory potential. War're'y'na fancies himself a world destroyer. Take it y'all back to black. A void of pure indivisible darkness. Why not now while in for'ma'sz mass liberation? A liberation at atencion focused in a wordfreedom while she now still appearing. Eve'rey'body now. A naked liberation. A y na'ked singularity of a b'ng c'ng still in the first place. We all a wheel are in turning with a slight wobble to the bobble, progressing to a transition in a ka's mic zodiac from the age of fishes into finding ourselves fishing con de h"OO"ka of questioning why? Now the quest eye on as'king of it y? Y'all now picking up on a b'ng c'ng in a y eye a peering it in an'y withered wanting thin'king of it in the or y of man'as mind or y. Now a k'no'wing out of it in two appearing a pairing in the mirror age mirage of Aquarius. Of any man'as mind or memory turning a Ka' mic corner, no pun intended . . . "

"If only we could turn a Korner."

"Perhaps we all turn together, a theoretical 180. In any eve're'y eve'n'ta appearing in her'eye a peering it out in a wayeve appearing of it remains merely mirrored as'z'any thoth'tsz of a God esse to be letter'all'y y'all a wayeve function. So . . . ."

"So what we all in turn see is merely a b c's of a letter'all God as'z thoth'tsz creating the world in a word. A b'ng c'ng as'z thoth'tsz of why. Y you're; you in the first place. The whole point of view of you of y now k'no'wing out of it as'z' ex's ting a'sz thoth'tsz controlled by any meager thin'king of it. Of a y az's'ex's ting as'king of it y a kurving or any occurring of it turning into or out of mere mirrored roles."

"Y'all over that Y speak dialectic. Then imagine a b'ng c'ng out of it. Imagine just as'z y'all letter'all'y in a wordfreedom of that a b c's spelling of a b'ng c'ng out int'word in'forma'ing of it in two of anybody. In a wordfreedom of a being c'ng supernaturally as'z thoth'tsz of it merely mirrored int'word a twis'ting in two a potential now of a k'no'wing out any a na y d'na'eye'll of it. A d'na'eye'll now of anyone k'no no no'wing it out information still a y eye of a b'ng c'ng merely a peering it in the first place of that indivisible in'visibility of any individual. At aten'cion in a wordfreedom merely mirrored in word idea as'z'any thoth'tsz of a God esse to be letter'all'y y'all a b'ng c'ng a point of view of you in na'me alone. What then is why. Why informa'sz of what purpose of it? Now as'z any mirrored y na me point of view of you as'k'now'ing out a d'na'eye'll beyond mirror function of a being c'ng busy busy as any or eve're'y bodhi or a y eye a peering it from above a'sz ove a b'ng as'ex's ting," she replied beaming a stare to burn the artist to the ground but he merely stared back, continuing painting.

"The light of da'y na is appearing to disappear. Let us go up to the roof," Christina offered, pushing off the high chair and coming around to look at the canvas. She now saw a familiar face but its expression shifted with her gaze finding herself at a loss for words transformed by the seemingly miraculous creative work.

"It's a technique I learned from my first art teacher, Joe Delugosz. I call it the 15 minute rule. The work should look like it was done in 15 minutes even if took 15 hours or 15 years."

"It is so imperfectly perfect. In that I am wanting to say this or that passage needs something but then looking again it is actually just right. What is it?"

"The power of a random spontaneous selection. A spontaneity that comes from rapid strokes allowing that X factor to come into play."

"Call her Madam X."

"And in her'eyez z za power of seduction executed by seduced artist in extremes of throbbing pain'ta or sheer bliss along with periodic closing of eyes combining in a perfect passion storm. Now I'm that feeling lost in your eyes or Y speak of it in the first place."

"Y speak indeed. In that I am feeling fielding your pain'ting with the factor of X's ting now." Mor found her once more beside him. He layed aside the palette and took her in his arms. She helped him in making their way back over to the bed. 'Now as'king of it' echoed in his mind as he shrugged off his leather jacket. They th'e'ye now merged into one indivisible full'y y'all felt feeling field of pain'ta or a bliss depending on shifting pressure on his wounded knee. If there was any oriface to enter, he could not or would not begin as'z two finding it. Aware now of a being c'ng out in other eye'sz only by the subtle touch of her lips on his or steady throb of a wounded knee. It seemed she'ena now entered him. Swallowed him whole in wayeves of a heart beating on in his chest. She'ena now the con she'us'n'ess'e now to be a'n'y of us. The presence of a b'ng c'ng in her'eyez z zazz'leep b'lack into eve"re'y body engulfed his no'tion'sz'a being c'ng now out k'now'ing any meager thin'king of it. A b'ng c'ng now in word in'formation merely mirrored reflected supernaturally in a b'lack'g'round pingting echo a's'z'any supersonic thothtsz of a God esse to be letter'all'y y'all superimposed in'visibility now appearing a pairing awhile still indivisible.

If there was a day or night to remember it was completely forgotten dissolved in any eve'n't of it in her'eyez z z'en'd'ing eve"re'y moment by mom'entum in a wayeve of ma'sz tricky wayeves. A breaking out over his sure shore de'fence defining any felt field of view of you or me. Now a k'no'wing out in her eyez z zazz'leep b'lack into eve"re'y body. Any mere touch a mirrored touching in her eyez z z'as'ka's mic'ro wayeve echoing any instantaneousness of an indivisible black'g"round. A b'ng c'ng still in her'eyez z z'azz'leep black into a eve're'ybody merely a peering it out now any k'no'wing in two appearing of it awhile. A wily duplicity duplicating cities of pleasure or pain'turning burning y'ear'n'ing roles of rolling wayeves in her'eye of eve're'y'body in'for'ma'sz'a'y b'ng denied in order to cultivate and cherish a'sz'any thoth'tsz of a God esse to be letter'all'y y'all in a crafty craft. A wor'd'ship Her'me"e'ss'e to be a herhimit or a y eye a peering it now a'z's'ex's ting appearing of it.

* * *

"Right now. 'You cannot be for then I would have to let you go'. Remember saying that to me when we first met?" Christina asked, slipping on a cotton robe.

"Let's go on to the roof for the sunset," Mor replied. "I want to get outside this box."

"What about your wounded knee?"

"I lean on you still feeling that immortal quantum field of view of you. In that I am finding letting go of you impossible. Any memory of me or you still indivisible awareness of it. In that eye that I am is is a'y you're; you. Or me or you in a memory"

"Y dialectic speaks of a being c'ng in other ey'e's'z'a a's'z'any na y as'ex's ting. Leave that ting be, ba'by."

"Then any aby'ss'z'a being y 's'z now a's x's ting?"

"That ting is still indivisible in'visibility now with me're y potential potentially na not now in appearing as'king of it y now that power of k'now'ing it. Y'all k'no'no'no'wing it is mere denial of it in any mind mirroring it as'z' y now a'sz x's ting in'formation in her'eyez z z' as'king of it y as'ka's mic memory. Still in general conversation a being c'ng out of any eye is the elephant in the room. A b'ng c'ng of which no one wants to be reminded in a b c's. A being still in the first place. If you eve're want to clear a room quick, speak Y speak."

"Speaking of which, what just happened? Feels like I blacked out."

"You got that 'I am hoping we all did not turn out making a baby' look on your face."

"This crazy dream. Need to get out under open sky and talk with the sun and planets and stars'z'a"'way from prying eyes." Sliding off the bed he slipped back into his black leather coat as Christina helped him to the stare way to the stars. There was some pain standing but offset by a greater relief moving out of the claustrophobia of the high ceiling room. The awareness of War're'y'na being so aware of them seemed to close in on his mind. Or was he losing himself in her'eyez z z' a peering it at him? For a moment panic s'z'truck thinking that the roof door would be locked as'z he dragged himself up the narrow stare'well one deliberate step at a time. At the top he threw his weight against the aluminum draw bar. The steel door swung open and he found himself sprawling on a graveled tar flat roof breathing hard with pebbles embedded in his cheek.

Gray mist streaked the indigo in her'eyez'z z'ion an early eve"en'ing. Mor rolled on his back, pebbles crunching under shoulders and the black of his head. He stared straight out into the vastness of a darkening sky. Christina kneeled down, heavy curls falling forward to frame her smile, white teeth luminous in the twilight. The crooked one slightly out of step.

She offered him a hand up as a prop plane rattled overhead. They moved to the raised edge of the building, flat bay waters visible a block west. Layed out on the edge Mor saw lights winking from the opposite shore backed up to a blackening mountain ridge nicked by Pacific salt air. A stand of Alder trees bordered the building, their darkening leaves rattling in the wind. Beyond them, a gray stone building laced with ivy breathed as one living form. Above the rim of its walls, a trinity of towering dock cranes stabbed into open horizon, steel girders taut with woven cables. He felt amazed. Overwhelmed by the sheer industry of man as extending mind imagineering out of her'eye any time ma'shee'na'rey wayeves g'listening to the echo of infinite potential. As'z'any thoth'tsz of a Great God esse to be letter'all'y y'all as'z z z'a peh ss'y'ence w'hole bodhi. Of a b'ng to perceive to wish to think to de'sire. From above as'z below. Ove a b'ng c'ng merely a peering it out. A ey"e'star'e"ye'ing out now time in space at a sun a moon e'star'e"ye to be me or you. A memory in a wordfreedom timeless awareness of it.

"There is one thing about genuine gurus," Margot Christina spoke softly, her voice barely discernable above the flow of traffic on freeways east and west. "Those who dispell the ignorance of understanding the spelling of a b c's. Of a b'ng c'ng by now a k'now'ing out of it a double or twin. Y'all gotta laugh your'asz'of'finding out that duplicity." She'e"na whispering. Lips kissing along his cheekbone. "They get the joke of anybody shedding tears while see'ng it out as'z'any thoth'tsz of a God'esse to be in her eye of eve'rey'body." Mor laughed loud hearing it dissolve in a tale of two siddhis. As'z two powers. A singular twisting of it int'word a turning in two. A mirrored duplicity. A duplicate city. Still in the first place Akh'et'aten. Et'ting. Duplicating a'kh in a'ten. A be'tween ka or h'ey"e. A duplicate city. Mor's blood ran cold. He now felt Korner breathing down his kneck like a bone chill from an Illinois prairie winter wind.

It hit him as awareness of it now with the successful completion of the painting of Christina his life was completely expendable. More than that the pingting of it. He would be the painter of the pingting to supersonically destroy a mankind as'z we all in turn come to now k'no'w it. Now he considered destroying his work before it appeared in the public eye. As'z thoughtsz turned in that direction the tinnitus picked up intensity. Instinctively Mor realized the profound predetermined nature of the commision. Still he found a b'ng c'ng anybody or any measly thin'king out of it. Any potential of pa's abilities of de'sire. Out of indivisible in'visibility of a peering it now as'king of it a k'no no no'wing a positive negation of it projecting supersonically supernaturally y'all merely superimposed echoing out in her eye of eve're'ybody. A micro wayeve'eyeing it into or out of a black'g'round da y na light. On the double from above. A b'ng c'ng de"sire. Pa'roo'ma's pa's ability'asz holding a polarity of it a pairing on the one hand. Still indivisible on the other. A b'ng c'ng a pairing bi that simple t'wis'ting int'word X's ting awhile in formation. Meanwhile still indivisible in'visibility now out in her'eyez z z'leep in two ma'sz pa's abilities. A y mirrored as'eX y'all. Any pa'h'ss'y w'hole potential of ma'sz"jest'y.

That serious jo'ke of any man with or without a womb as mind. Or memory appearing of it awhile merely a peering it out in her'eye of eve're'y'body. A mind or a y eye in a wordfreedom awareness of a b'ng c'ng still in the first place. Mor thought he must value laughter a'sz prophalactic to break up that serious trouble of the in word mind. Or a y eye a peering it out now as'king of it y a k'no no no'wing out a double in word in formation. As'z'any thoth'tsz of a God esse to be letter'all'y y'all a pairing of it. A be'tween mean meaning of macro or micro ka's mic ma'sz pa's abilities. Now falling asz z z'leep black'g'round a'w/akh'ening at aten'cion a k'now'ing out of it any understanding the spelling of a b c's phonographically appearing of it in word. A'while of taking ma'sz jest y of a b'ng c'ng out in her eye as'king of it y a ka's mic ka'mic mirrored memory of me or you as'z t"OO"ka de'l"OO"ka seriously. A serious sheer singular folly of a y eye merely a peering it out in two appearing of it.

"Losing that sense of hu'm'or any hu'man is doomed." Hearing these words Mor found himself at a loss of a gain appearing out of it in her'eye'asz the b'lack g'listening mirror see'as echo of eve're'ybody. A b c's"in her'eyez z z' any or eve're'ybody a peering it at understanding of any word. Y'et as'king of it y a k'no no no'wing out any appearance of it by supernaturally superimposing it as'z'any thoth'tsz of a God esse to be letter'all'y y'all mirrored out in word as'ka's mic memory. A b'ng c'ng merely a double in word in'formation. A y eye a're'y'all now as'z'any thoth'tsz. A god'esse to be letter'all'y y'all supersonically appearing out in word'sz'zaz'z'an'y"as'z'ex's ting rolls of a role playing out in complete d"ark'ness. Or y a la que"en que' of that in which appears da y na light. Da y now as'king of it y perceiving a ka's mic da y na light igniting neuronal peh's"sy'na'peh"ess'y w'hole. There is no escape from a chord issuing vibrating in her'eve'll"clit"oris as'z organ egg'spec'ting egg's"ting. The now merely mirrored a'sz thoth'tsz of a hidden clothed singularity in word sz'zz appearing a pairing out of it. A b'ng c'ng still in a singularity. Genuine rebes and swamis para un hombre de conocimiento a'glow with the sheer joy"jah y light. El herhimit of a being still freestanding in the first place. They must cut it up while cooking you from the inside until any ego is like burnt newspaper, still readable but disintegrating at mere touch. You die in PARANTAKALE, the supreme end time by h"OO"ka or cr"OO"ka's de'b"OO"ka. A y na na as'z ex'per'eye 'enc'ng. A's'zza ja'h'"zz. TATWAMASI. A'sz eye of that I am is is of a type appearing of it with'in'ka's on pa'per ma'sz distribution. Once Mor finding his thoughtsz tracking the y eyez z z'leep into dialectic debate laughed his asz of'f'rom merely a peering it at any scant skinny stunted thin'king of it.

"That's'za so funny because in that I'm just flashing in gee'sz us as gravity of sparking ash particles with ego. Ego of d'ash. D'ashing drifting hither and yon in a b'ng as'ka's mic see'ng." From an artist's perspective Mor now considered the less you let ego distract attention the less y'all take yourself too seriously. The better. The more free and spontaneous the artwork. The whole cult of personality seems like mere sparking burnt flakes of paper drifting tore away in a cosmic wind. Feeling it out here under open sky projecting gravity free at light speed. We all turning on this magnificent plan' et'ting a'whorl'ding h'ear'th. Whorls within supersonic whorls. Still indivisible invisibility of a b'ng c'ng mirrored in word out of the cosmic micro wayeve black'g'round. We all turn out mere particles in a particular nuke storm. He laughed at the sheer folly of a b'ng c'ng out of it as'z'any imagined image of his overactive in word imagination while gingerly prodding his bandaged wounded knee.

"Still a b'ng c'ng a peering it in the first place that indivisible invisibility of any individual appearing of it merely now awhile. The butt end of her'eye wayeve'rey fun'ny'action joke. Still da black whole sacred ka'rey'st. An'y parts mere a na y in word denial of k'no no no'wing of it mirrored as'z'any thoth'tsz of a y na you now as'ex's ting in any roll'or'role of complete d"ark'ness. You a're y'e complete. Complete arrey"e'all." She'e"na touched her lips to his.

☼

At the intersection of Middlefield and Charleston, Kwasanda saw a man with cut-off jeans and tee shirt. His belly rolled like an inner tube as he pushed his girlfriend in a wheelchair. He foraged aluminum cans from public trash, stuffing his finds in a torn plastic shopping bag, ceaselessly talking as he wheeled his girlfriend between receptacles. Her expression remained frozen. Staring into a being unseen.

Nearby a child danced under blowing hair. Spinning around with cheeks the color of hot metal, she clutched a box of candy in a tiny fist. Adults dragged along behind her, heavy with the weight of their gathering years. A woman in the next car chomped on a sandwich, jaws working mechanically at the wad of bread.

She thought about her side of town compared to this wealth of the shade tree-lined avenues of freshly painted split-level homes. How it contrasted like the joy of the child with the sorrowful drudgery of the adults. Her ancestors carried the dream of the child into adulthood. She had come from Bilad as-Sudan, the land of the Blacks, known in ancient times as Ethiopia, or land of the burnt faces. Father Nzokia was a chief in the Dinka tribe, the most powerful in the south. They were an older race, highly evolved, hunters and herdsman for over 10,000 years, inundated by Egyptian, European, and Middle Eastern religions and politics. Hers was a matriarchal culture that worshiped high priestess Astarte. The people knew her, for they walked in her body, felt her tears in the rain, and heard her voice in the wind. They did not have to look for Astarte. She was anyone looking wherever they were. The invasion of Europeans signaled the end of the Sudanese dream. Now they walked the earth without connection to her, only the nightmare of the gun and slaughter.

The Mark IV was out of sight, heading for the Portal. Kwasanda smelled the hate and alienation of Korner. She also knew the little boy hiding behind his big guns. She passed the pedestrian world of laughing feet to the engineered landscape of rolled steel, cast concrete, and diesel freeway, all under the same blue sky.

She took Shoreline Avenue over the 101 Freeway that cut through towns and neighborhoods, local main streets reduced to strip malls with glowing corporate logos. She crossed the freeway traffic into a deserted stretch along the north side of the Portal's airstrip. Rows of three-story commercial buildings broke open periodically with narrow alleys. She turned down one alley that revealed the open airstrip. Driving alongside its fence she came upon parallel stripes of black tread marks that burned through a ragged tear in the chain link. She wheeled around, following the path, torn steel wire scraping the car's high-dollar paint. Kwasanda skirted the tarmac until she saw the Mark IV shielded by Japanese maples.

The Bay air crackled with salt and ozone. Pulling up to the Lincoln she saw Fawn Rave, wrists raw, nostrils rimmed with white powder, weeping behind the wheel. Kwasanda slipped out of the BMW and tapped on the glass. Fawn leaned back, tearstains streaking her cheeks. Her wrists showed red marks where the plastic ties had dug in. Kwasanda used the butt of her .22 to smash the glass. Cutting the ties, she helped Fawn from the car to the trees at the rear entrance.

"Tell me, sister, where is Korner?" Kwasanda asked.

Fawn shook her head. "Bastard going to die hard for killing Enoch."

"He was my friend, too. Stay here while I find him."

Kwasanda slipped into the building and made her way stealthily with gun raised, to McCracken's office. She smelled cordite as she approached. Two bodies lay on the carpet. McCracken sat slumped over his desk. As she approached he raised his head. She saw blood on his head and chest.

"You missed the party, sheba. Afraid I haven't had a chance to clean up," he said with labored breath.

"We need to get you to a hospital."

"No. No time. You never told me, how it was.....in the Pod?" he asked, his eyes imploring.

"It was and still is the ultimate ride. You did it R.J., your masterpiece works," she replied, his hand gripping her collar.

"Tell. Tell that bastard Warren. Tell him I won." he rasped, guffawing his last breath.

She loosened his grip and straightened back up. His eyes, so lustrous with success only a second before went empty. She turned to find Korner leaning on the door frame, fingers loose on his Colt. Supernal light glinted off the blue-black surface, charging the air around him with oil and cordite. Blood spoor dotted his cheeks and forehead like pox scars. His mouth slacked into a cunning smile on seeing Kwasanda. He walked over and pressed the gun barrel into her cheek.

"Black princess, where is your knight?" he asked with a smirk. "All I wanted was to take a ride on his space ship. I didn't want to kill him." Korner kept talking as he forced her over to the window. "It's a terrible, terrible thing to kill a man. I never wanted to. They made me do it. "

Korner started weeping openly as his grip tightened. Kwasanda tried working her jaw to speak but he kept the barrel tight.

"I wanted to see. To see what it felt like being free of them. McCracken laughed at me and they killed him" he said, his voice breaking into a wail.

"They murdered him and now they'll murder you."

Forced to her knees, Kwasanda felt the barrel of his gun against her neck. The toothless smile and crinkled eyes of her grandmother appeared to welcome her on the other side. The smile faded in the crackle of electricity. Two barbed darts piercing his leather jacket Korner fell in a series of uncontrolled muscle seizures, limbs jerking without benefit of connection to the mammalian brain. Urine spread from his crotch to puddle on the floor.

Fawn stood behind him with the black plastic Taser, her fingers white on the trigger. "Indians don't always lose, shit-bag."

Kwasanda got to her feet. Alarms could be heard in the distance. She checked the clip in her automatic and they hustled back to the cars. A satchel sat on the hood of the BMW.

"It's full of guns and bombs," Fawn said as she leaned against the smooth trunk of a Japanese maple. "He was diablo, the devil." Fawn spit the words.

"The Taser will only keep him down for a few moments. We need to get out of here."

"I'm free of his smell. You go, I'm walking out."

"Where to, sister?"

"Out there. I got brothers ganged with the Sadistas. Thanks for helping me but no more for this girl. I go bury Enoch. See you around if I'm unlucky."

Fawn walked away as Kwasanda headed for her date with a real devil.

Wind rattled dry leaves as Mor stretched out on the ledge next to Christina. She now rested his head on the silk stockings sliding over the taut flesh of her thighs exposed where her robe parted.

Mor slipped into a dream of a landscape of low hills where wind flattened tall grass with the imprint of unseen form. He saw Gina walking toward him, her skirts playing out, hair dancing across her face. She flashed a smile before speaking words he could not understand. She came into him until he passed black in the soaking darkness of sleep.

When he woke, the indigo sky had deepened to purplish black. The last rays of the sun faded into slumbering glow on the Pacific Rim, its light blasting off the speck of Venus rising in the southwest.

"Dark'ness Mor is born of the light," Christina said. She shifted her body as slender fingers stroked his cheek. She looked off to a point beyond, a soft grin lifting the corners of her mouth. Stars emerged as the earth shaded out the sun.

"I must have died and gone to heaven." he said. "How long was I asleep? That little ol' speck up there looks like a cosmic eye of your goddess Venus. Will she help us beat that devil War're'y'na? We all must turn into or out of a cosmic soul to be able to comprehend the magnitude of our solar system, let alone our galaxy. I mean, come on, who are we all, turning into or out of personically in time now space. Yet awareness of it not disappearing in the magnitude like an ant on a mountain. How is it possible unless..."

"We all turn into or out of a b c's now a black'g'round. A gaining as'king of it y any k'nowing out in word center point of view of you or me in first person singular now of a b'ng c'ng still in any or eve'rey eye'star'e'y a peering it at the a macromicro mean universe? You na versus Y you're you still in the first place indivisible invisibility as'z'any individiual. That is or should be the debate moment by mom'ent'um. Or lifetime after lifetime."

He felt everything falling away till he almost lost consciousness. Regaining his composure he looked beyond his feet to a point far distant into which arrays of letters and numbers flowed.

Christina traced the path with her hand. "Stir this soup and what does it spell?

"I'm seeing out in a wordfreedom not looking for any literal meaning of it merely in word. That's the freedom of awareness in the painter's eye. When drawing on it. Painting in it. Focused as any seer seeing now in mind as'z then relatively free from thought. Free from judgement at least. While painting. But then what happens? Because often having a warped sensibility in social affairs artists when not painting may be real butt holes. At least speaking for myself. Taking a good run at this painting will likely finish me. Where does it go y'all, this expanding universe? Az's'expanding into what or why?"

"Perhaps by expanding attention out into such a ka's mic awareness of it as Orion," she said, pointing overhead. "we all might turn b'lack into a greater perspective awareness of a b'ng c'ng shot with e'y"e"star"e"'y'e zzas'k'ey'all the time'now'e'space in time. Check out con'stell'ation

Orion or Osiris. A grand'father. A great de'sire of Egyptian man'as a 'mem"or'y. A grand de'Sire de'G'Y'PahTa my'thOlOgee'z z'us a y eyez'z z z'leep in two the hea'eve'na'ly pa's abilities. Over there, Sirius or Isis, heavenly mother. Just us now below the horizon, a Horus. ahOur'us the sun.

It seems now we all turn into or out appearing of it in eL sol"light of da'y"now any appearing of it. In a familiar trinity fathermotherzson herhimit seen now as'king of it y a la que"en que' of that in which a're'y "e'z'son. Arising in its mean macro'micro ka's mic memory of any or eve're'y'body of a man'as mind. A scale which offers invisibility in a wordfreedom awareness of a b'ng c'ng aware of merely a peering it out as'z'any seer seeing in sight. Anybody merely a peering it now as awareness of anybody el'se. Asz thoth'tsz of a Great God'esse to letter'all'y y'all be doubled in a na'me alone. Beyond any mere in word god dog'ma'sz, the Christian, Father, Son, and Holy Ghost where Isis-Sirius, the mother, tumbles from the brightest star visible in our heaven, to a ghost."

"Yeh, but a holy one."

"A hole in one?"

"Putting it like that makes me more aware of patriarchal bias," he said with a laugh. "So amazing though, to see the father and mother still shining on before our eyes as they have for millions of years, that's immortal enough for me. Course it's just a bunch of smoke and mirr'or ysz so why worry about these old bones?" he asked, flattening his cheek against the mound of her belly. "You sure we all didn't turn out making a baby back there. In that I am pretty turned around."

Christina slid out from his weight. "It seems we all get turned out into fooling ourselves appearing of it out in wordsz. That despite experiencing it directly and periodically indivisible invisibility over a third of our lifetime. Asz once awake we all appear by now turning into a k'no'wing out a d'na'eye'll of that indivisible invisibility of any or eve're'y'body. It seems we all turn out of or b'lack into a k'no'wing d'na'eye'll of our own indivisible invisibility. That is the catch. The devious deception of our own self d'na'eye'll of indivisible invisibility despite a constant recurrence of a direct experience of it.

"Now you k'no'w a b c's of a b'ng c'ng still in the first place. Indivisible in'visibility of y'all now as'z when falling asz z z'leep black'g'round as'king of it y now any k'nowing out of it. Of any understanding that spelling of it with intent of a y as'ex's ting. That int'word a twis'ting in two az's'ex'et'ting duplicating by any understanding the spelling of it generates warehouses of libraries duplicating phonographically any k'no'wing d'na'eye'll of it. Of it now in the'or'y alone. Now turning into the'n by a k'nowing d'na'eye'll of a being indivisible invisibility. It now appearing a pairing as'z'any wanting thin'king of it thoth'tsz of a God esse to be letter'all'y y'all in'formation of a pah'ss'y"en'ce whole energy body of Gee'sz'us. A gravity wayeve weight of waiting on any or eve're'y occurrence of it. A b'ng c'ng as now merely mirrored out in word in formation. A b c's as that in word in'formation still indivisible invisiblity yet now as thoth'tsz of k'nowing any appearing. Appearing of it merely mirrored out in word. By a k'nowing out of it any in word denial of a b'ng c'ng still indivisible in'visibility. That singularity in a y eye of a b'ng c'ng merely a peering it now turned in two k'no'wing appearing of it y'all a's'z'ex u'all."

"A's'ex. The other industry. Industrial scale poon' to meet the sheer demand."

"It takes a sick artist mind but yeh, the old timey bordellos were fuck factories with vd syphilus its main by product."

"The Red vengeance on the White man. I could see Korner's psychosis as syphilus on the brain. When his foster father lost his farm he turned into a bar hound which not that long ago y'all had a bordello upstairs. Then frequenting a bordello would be as common as walking into any bar which also meant commonly bringing sexually transmitted disease to the procreative table. The pathos of any a na y'body az's'ex seems asz two necessitate suffering asz means to find or realize our way out of it. Just us from a b c's int'word understanding any spelling of it we all may turn into any potential pathos in appearing out of a b'ng c'ng still in the first place. Now merely mirrored in awhile as'king of it y a k'no'wing out our own duplicity. As'king of it y'et a k'no'wing out our own duplication. Deceived by our own k'no'wing of any withered wanting thin'king of it. Any thin'king of it a's'z"ex'et'ting duplicating as'z thoth'tsz of a singular God esse to be letter'all'y y'all in that mirror duplicity turning a b'lack'g'round supersonic or phonographic echo in two. Now a k'nowing out of it a being of anybody. Anybody of industrial grade obsession with a b'ng c'ng appearing out of it a's'ex y'all."

"You a's'zz'ex y be'a'st. Asz Y you may be on to something or on something. There anybody a's though a's'ex is set up appearing out in word as'z two. A'sz int'word that simple twist of fate faith or family. Az's'eX's ting in formation. Finding ourselves as though'tsz in a root gender schiszm enhanced biologically. Az's two of'ten perverted culturally with violent overtones."

"We all still turning into murdering raping pillaging az's'eX y'all beasties. Just let loose the dogs. But then we all turn into serving suffering any appearing of it in her'eye of eve'll kali ma'sz devoured. A devouring in her'eyez z z a peering it out of'ten a binary of any or eve're'y body."

"Y'all got me or you in memory there. Ma'sz nature now time ma'sheen'a'sz g'listening too'th'e tearing it black down in her'eye a peering it out in eve're'y body'sz z z wayeve function. Of a fun'ny'a'ction appearing disappearing following its mirr'oring y na now as'z' an y potential to appear in formation only awhile now. In that uncanny desparate deceit of any appearing of it still a b'ng c'ng merely a peering it y'et indivisible in'visibility in the first place. Yet over the course of any lifetime thirty three plus or minus percent of it spent paying singular attention in the indivisible black'g'round echo of a b'ng c'ng supersonically out in her'eye of any or eve're'y'body. At atention now in a re'y'e all a peering it turning in two a black'g'round. Echoing a singular b'lack' invisibility d'na'eye'd out int'word appearing of it a gain. A re'y'al'ity as'king of it y now. A b'ng c'ng instilled as a singularity confirmed directly and periodically by a b c's asz 'un't'word a 'un'twis'ting a 'un'winding of it black'g'round into one indivisible a 'un' consciousness. A b'ng c'ng conned merely in for'ma'sz a while now of that int'word a k'no'wing out of it. A time ma'sheen'a turning we all a wheel must turn into or out of. A're'y'all of a b'ng c'ng still in the first place. Now out of it a k'no no no'wing d'na'eye'll. A d'na'eye'll of a y eye of a b'ng c'ng a peering it out in't'word finding now in time h'ourself a b'lack' there. A b'lack' there the a're'y'all azs'word cleaving of a b'ng c'ng still in the first place indivisible. Now as'king of it a k'no no no'wing out of a d'na'eye'll playing any role or roll of complete d''ark'n'ess'e in two being'sz now perceiving a gain.

"Pa'roo'ma Aw/akhen''aten merely opening an eye of that that I am is is still first su'personic person now as'king of it a k'no'wing intent of a y eye a re'y'dhi'a'ting to perceive it in formation. A's k'urving now around k'no'wing out of it a b'ng c'ng int'word a re'y'e'all of complete dhi 'ark'ness. In her b'lack eye as mirror see'as'z z z'leep in two a wayeve of eve're'ybody. That a're'y'all now out in her'eye mirrored in ways of eve. Wayeves of eve re'y body'sz fun'ny'action in turning a b'lack'g'round of a b'ng c'ng int'word one beginning by imaginary endings of the complete dhi''ark. A b'ng c'ng now as'z z z'leeping a'cross es'peh'esse'y w'hole ar'king the gap between any potential endings of it. Ma'sz Pa's abilities with a polarity in hand.

"Now a time ma sheen'a tears it back down asz fun'damental process in her'ey'ez'acreation only awhile now. Dissolution or el'et'ting herhimit's on hand polarity fall as'z z z'leep black up or down into a b'ng c'ng still indivisible invisibility. Still we all a wheel turn now into the'na future. Into the few prototypes that u a're. In a're'y'all as that magnetic role or l''OO''pa de'l''OO''pa of complete d''ark'ness. A d''ark'n'ess to perceive ar'king of it now to be invincible indivisible in'visibility. We all a wheel turning now into or out of it a k'no'wing only in one direction of a d'na'eye'll. A b'ng c'ng now as'king of it a positive negation of k'no no no'wing out of it any lanky'rank gaunt starved thin'king of it awhile now. That positive future direction of a b'ng c'ng y'all'wayeves lap'ping a black'g'round in a y'et complete loop must return pa's't beginning of any potential ending. There must a b'lack to be a gain of it still merely in word. Mirrored supernatural thoth'tsz of it. For'ma'sz pa'sz'abilities.

"Thus any death is a b c's of a b'ng c'ng in word merely mirrored in a're'y'verse reflection as'z birth. Hardwired egg's'ting in'formation. A y eye star'ey''e a peering it out as'king of it y a k'no'wing out of it any appearing in word of a birth in na'me alone. Awareness of it ain't born when a ba'b'ng b'or'n'a. A b''earing supersonic appearance out in word as'z'sound vibrant wayeves vibrating y'all black'g'round. There must b'lack to be a gain. B'lack in complete d''ark'n'ess'e. Why wordsz must lie. Must be able to k'no'w out d'na'eye'll of a b'ng c'ng still complete.

"Why death of a b'ng c'ng in the perceived d''ark is yet a complete turn of eve'n'tsz where any endings are'y'all any beginning. Any perceived sound wayeves a're'y'all a b gaining of it. A b'ng gaining not liberation in that a b'earing continuity must continue a k'no'wing out of a y eye a peering it still freestanding in a wordfreedom in the first place. A y eye star'ey'e a're'y'dhi'a'ting completely y'all b'lack'g'round a complete dhi ark. A perceiving of da y na light turning into da ark now esse to be perceived a gain. Perceived a gain ar'king of it. A'w/akh'en'a'ten akh'et'aten still in the first place first su'personic per'son pre'sent now gee'sz us gravity weight of waiting for'ma'sz ma'trix. In her'eyez z z'i'on eve'na't'at merely a peering it out in wordsz a tricky eve're'y b'lack mirror see'as'z anybody etc. Any cheesy chintzy thin'king of it still ar'king of it.

"Still merely supernaturally as'z'any thoth'sz of a God'esse to be letter'all'y y'all a b c's of a b'ng c'ng now in formation in word. Still there may be supernatural subtle body heavenly or hell'o states occurring at indivisible attention a k'urving along the wayeve of that dhi ark. That perceived ar'king of it y now esse to be of a b'ng c'ng a black'g'round echoing y'all'wayeves of a complete magnetic hardwired l"OO"peh'ss'y w'hole wayeves. As'z'any pa's ability of holding a polarity in hand. Either ending turns into or out of a black'g'round. In the or y po'larity is mirr'or'd'or y memory now of a b'ng c'ng of a b'ng'gainning supersonically in a word as'z'any'k'no no no'w'ing out of it. As'ex'peh'res'sing'ing polarity power of positive negativity. Supernaturally as'z'any thoth'tsz in memory of a b'ng c'ng now in a word supersonically out of it. Projecting d'na'eye'll out of a y eye as'ex'pecting heaven or hell may only be a brief vacation. A short e'turn'all'y y'all respite of a b'ng c'ng still in the complete loop and thus future turns inevitably into past same beginning future again ." She'e"na walked in a complete circle as if following her thoughts back to him.

"Y'all making me realize how in a funny kind of way my near death as'za two year old offers me in a wordfreedom awareness a first place to go in reverse of my loop." Mor flashed back if not to birth to a split second prior to that premature first awakening in word awareness y'ears before learning any a b c's. His memory turned back to a b'ng of blackness indivisible invisibilty. Turned instantly in a primal awareness of a blackness split opening eyez z z'leeping in two a mem'or'y activated by a voice. A voice he realized now of death saving his life. A Lord of Death dispensing a divine Providence as'z awareness of a being fully full indivisible in'visibility. He shuddered to think how often disabusing himself of that gift. Yet laughed at the absurdity of praying to a Lord Death to save a life. A death still functioning as'z z za wayeve motion of life. A wayeve appearing anybody by turning now in two the'n'a k'now'ing out of a d'na'eye'll of that still indivisible in'visibility. Yet Lord Death left two words echoing in his memory the rest of his life. "Be still". A b'ng still in the first place indivisible invisibility now perceived a blackness. Still indivisible invisibility now a b'lackness to be instilled with intent to be a gain of it alternating moment by mom'en't'um.

She now awakened a k'no'wing d'na'eye'll of a b'ng c'ng mirrored out int'word turning into or out of anybody or anything. Y'all these years tears and fears merely mirrored in her eyez z zazz'leep in'visibility of anybody a peering it now out awhile appearing of it. Appearing a pairing in a cunning duplicity. Mor laughed and cried in that spell she'e'na cast over any aten'cion understanding a b c's. Thatsz the real exodus ain't it he mused. Az's'ex. As'z z z exodus zazz'any thoth'tsz of a singular Great God. Esse to be letter'all'y y'all a b c's of a b'ng c'ng in a y eye in a wordfreedom freestanding awareness indivisible in'visibility of any or eve're'ybody. An exodus as'z'any thoth'tsz of a singular indivisible God esse to be letter'all'y y'all in any name alone. Still indivisible in'visibility as'z' any individual. The'y merely mirred as'ex y'all in a wayeve out of it awhile in't'word a twis'ting in two d'na'eye'll of a b'ng indivisible still in the first place. Thus it really is a short while. Foh'ty fitty y'ears of Gee'sz us gravity weight waiting on death. On Lord Death accompanying shadowing saving y'all the while. Gee'sz us the pickle of any life awaiting as'z'any thoth'tsz of a God esse to be letter'all'y y'all Lord Death. Understanding the spelling of a b c's Mor found himself at aten'cion moving from an indivisible immortal b'lack'ness now to be a gain of mortality. A gain of gee'sz'us a gravity weight awaiting on death. He realized it was asz thoth'tsz of it az's'ex'odus from that immortal body. Asz'thoth'tsz of a God esse to be letter'al'y y'all offering a tree of five fruits. Eve'sz'a're'y'body takes the first bite of the apple. A pee'ple b'ng c̓ng still merely a peering it now as'z'any thoth'tsz of a God to be letter'all'y y'all out of the garden of E'don az's'ex y'all. At aten'cion captivated now int'word a twis'ting in two a k'no'wing d'na'eye'll out. Of it awhile. Merely mirrored on the double bubble and with the'e's'z z z'as'parks igniting ignore'ance of it some are bound to ba'low he thought.

A be'low in the'or'y indivisible invisibility of y'or y now az's'ex'p'ress'ing any in word thoth'tsz of it y the'n'appears of it. Thus it takes years tears fears of learning enough vocabulary and grammer to develop memory in a word mirrored mind. My first awakening out in me'm'or'y came after two full years of shitt'in blind in my diapers waddlin' around in a peh'ss'ylence he was now discerning. Mor thought now I'm realizing we all in turn learn. Learn in words to see hear smell taste and eve'n touch. Learn in wordsz a b'ng c'ng double. A sensory double appearing breathing thoth'tsz of a God esse to be letter'all'y creating a whorl'd'ing d'na'eye'll of any beginning in a word he now thought. A now meager thin'king of it

Mor flashed on that pre-re'y"e'cog'native split second moment still in the first place now that I am finding myself turning out of an indivisible invisibility black'g'round body. Awakening in'visibility as'king of it y 'be still' a k'nowing out of a b c's of a b'ng c'ng in that awareness in a wordfreedom of that big mon'eye of mine is is merely a peering it out az's'ex'odus now by a k'no'wing in word d'na'eye'll of it. A d'na'eye'll as'z b'lack' thoth'tsz of it a gain. A gain of that indivisible in'visibility now supernaturally appearing of it out int'word a twis'ting in two any information. Aten and Eve turning az's'eX spelled out of it. Now that I'm finding myself still a b'ng c'ng in the first place that indivisible invisibility of any individual I can k'ick it awhile he chuckled. Then wounded knee brought a grimace.

Death had a way of sobering him up like a punch in the mouth. Now as'z then makes me realize the years it takes moment to moment to fall completely understanding any in word spelling of a b'ng c'ng y'all in a y eye merely a'peering it out a'sz"ex's ting he thought. Getting turned around as'z thoth'tsz of a God to be thinking of experiencing a b c's of a b'ng c'ng appearing a pairing of it az's'ex y'all now by a k'no'wing awayeve denying invisibility into a see'ng of it int'word turning in two any information of it. Az's'ex's ting in formation. Y a eye spelling of me now appearing of it in any image'na're'y na' me alone. As'z'y'et still indivisible he thought.

Now turning in two a pairing by a k'no no no'wing out of it a positive denial of a b'ng c'ng indivisible invisibility. Now a k'nowing out of me in the'or'y of memory. Me or you in the or y a pairing of a being alone with any na'me of it. Yet still indivisible.Thatza supernatural pairing of a being alone still indivisible with appearing of it in any name. Still a b'ng c'ng alone. What a supernatural gas. Y am I that now na laughing my as'z of'f'finding in me a being still indivisible invisibility Mor wondered stretching his arms out imploring the heavens to let go of his past checkered history. To shake loose the ghosts that drifted a b'lack'g'round pingting echoing his periphery. A tinitus echoing his y'ears.

"A back to black invisibility? She'e'na asz eve're'y'body funny that wayeve. Eve'n though returning to that blackness directly and periodically we all in turn fail to realize it as'z z z'leep black into our e'ver'y own causal body. A singular body of eve're'y'body." Christina mimicked his pose with a shrug of her shoulders.

"So anybody eve're'y'body denied while awake in the"or'y of appearing in a mem'or'y supernaturally as'z'any thoth'tsz of it. Now superimposed in an'y as'ex's ting'k'ing as'king of it y a rolling out or a role'in playing it out as'ex'y'all?" Mor thought as'ex'posing in any role of a b'ng c'ng still insight of me. Out as'ex'per'eye'en'c'ng in her'eyez z z'a mirror touch. Na'tur'all'y y'all touching that mirror touch reinforces that in word spelling of a b'ng c'ng now out in her'eyez z z' of eve"re'ybody. Or any a na'y body cellularly neuronically in the'or'y as'ex'et'ting duplicating the allegorical ar'king of it a pairing az's'exodus. The y way az's'ex's ting'king of it out in word in formation. A pingting'king of it a wayeve out supersonic'all'y y'all as'za b c's thoth'tsz of a b'ng c'ng from the still point of view of you. Of y now a'sz"ex'u'all. Y az's'eX'et'ting. Az's'eX per eye of that I a'm'emor a y en c'eer duplicating now a w'h'ile a'sz thothtsz in for'ma'sz appearing by wayeves of ma'sz jes'ty. A cunning deadly deceitful duplicity. A jest. Us a's'z z z'sublime a's you'r'e kiss'zz'a Mor deliberated finding her lips nearly touching his. A static electricity a's'z zapping the slight gap. In her eyez z z'ap'ping that mirror gap between merely a peering it or a hard time con"she'e' us n'ess'e now to be appearing of it.

"We all be the'e turn'all'y y'all turning churning spinning out at speed of da y na light of da y. A turning black'g'round echoing that pivotal whole point of view of you of y a b'ng c'ng. In a y eye of any ce'er be'holding now a k'no'wing out feelings of that felt field of view of you. A'w/akh'ening of'ten a ten. A being bi now'ar'e'y'all k'urving a black'g'round echoing a k'no'wing out of it. Projecting out of it as'z'any thoth'tsz of it. In a k'no'wing d'na'eye'll of it." She'e"na pulled back with an inscrutable smile playing across her lips. For a moment Mor thought he saw flashes of War're'y'na lurking around in a shadow behind her eyes.

Yet we all there on the fringes turning into or out of it in her'eyez z z of eve're'ybody he surmised. We all a wheel of fortune or misfortune spinning out any understanding of the spelling of a b c's. A crafty spelling of a b'ng c'ng in herhimits'z big mon'eye star'e ye'or'y now a peering it out aw'h'ile. A wily while maybe so a b'ng c'ng still him. Freed as in a wordfreedom awareness of an artist mon'eye merely a peering it. Awareness enhanced drinking in his suffering with the throbbing pain of wounded knee. Pain'ta reminding him of the feeling of the indivisible field to be played. Could only love in her eyez z z'leep into now till death do us part then he flashed w'h'ile taking a long slow breath.

"Y'all a ten fo sho' ba'by. Y'all got my attention or it's melting black into itself." Mor offered feeling it free freed in a wordfreedom, ba'by. A ka's all'y y'all a complete mag'ne"tic l"OO"p de'l"OO"peh'ss'y w'hole field may move inevitably and irrevocably in one direction now into a future still turning a black'g'round echoing its beginning he now intuited. A're'y'turn ending as'z' any future beginning. Only till a're'y'all'eye'zinging that pivotal point of view of you of y'or y na he now reasoned. You now as'z'any thoth'tsz supernaturally y'all turning into any a na y'sex's ting. Un'known still stillness of a b'ng c'ng be'am'ing infinitely a y eye potential. Seer of a b'ng c'ng me paying, playing, procuring you as'z me or y'all'sz' any way he considered with a shrug. For the first time Mor totally apprehended the great boon of a near life or a y death awakening experience at t'wo. In two that simple t'wist of fate. He found himself a b'ng c'ng turning in two or out of a black'g'round indivisible body still in a wordfreedom awareness of it. Now as'king of it y a k'no'wing out of a na y'body int'word a twis'ting as'ex'odus a'crossing the eve"en'ta h'our eye'sz'zi'on aten'cion captivated in word. Still simultaneous awareness memory of a being y'et a'pri'or y. A y eye now duplicating in a'memory of that. TATTWAMASI. That thou art'I'a'is'is't. In that swift blink of eye a peering it now out in da y'na light of d'na'eye'll. As'ex'egesis of a b'ng c'ng now leading out bi a peering it from above. Ove a b'ng still.

A b'ng c'ng still a peering it now ar'king as'king of it a k'no no no'wing it out in a wordship craft say'el'ing out in hereye'sz'z z'a'p'ping a black'g'round echoing mirror seeas of it. The complete d"ark'n'esse in her black eye of eve'll. There y must b"lack to be a gain az's'ex y'all. Still complete y'all a long while of a b'ng c'ng black'g'round da light of da y now. She'e'na from above as'z'za below. A b'ng c'ng still in the first place a's'z that indivisible in'visibility of any individual y'all along while. A wordship craft adrift in her black mirror seas we all turning churning burning in a complete d"ark not black or white or any hue of man as mind. Or y now turning to be perceived as'k'no'wing out of it any or eve're'ybody. As'ex's re'y'sz'zex'et'ting duplicating in formation. Now as'king of it y a k'now'ing it out as'z'any thoth'tsz of supernaturally feeling touching of a black'g'round echo touched fielding arthritis and a wounded knee. The pain'ting of it. A ping'ting of it. As'king of it now a k'no'wing out of it a'sz'any black'g'round echoing doubling of it as'z'sound wayeves function in'forma'ing any skinny scant starved thin'king thoth'tsz of it. Now a supersonic virus in the pain'ta. It now blew his shit away. In a wayeve at aten'cion. A way'eve at a'ten of'ten bi now a're'y"dhi' a ting in formation of it.

"Got the gift naturally y'all attention may be paid out or played black'g'round echoing in a b'ng c'ng still indivisible in'visibility of y'all behind the eyes." She'e"na sheer luminous e'GG'z'z z'ting. Mor now could only see in her eye'zz z'a ba"by mere mirrored d'na't'u're"y"e"ll of duplicity ot y'all. One u'na or you not denial of a b'ng price paid into aten'cion appearing of it out moving a b'lack'g'round that same direction. From a b'ng'lack to a being a gain. Out of a b'ng c'ng a peering it at aten'cion. Now appearing bi as'king of it y a k'no no no'wing it out int'word as'z two b'ngs in formation. In that I am finding free choice with a're'y'call of that precise split second before the fall. Before falling understanding the in word spelling of a b'ng c'ng out in her'eyez z z of eve're'y body. Now as'king of it y a k'now'ing it out in word a'ska's of it. It merely mirrored at paying aten'cion to it a y'll. Cunning in wor'd'ship craft now a'say"el'ing out appearance of it in a lifetime experience. In any moment that I am finding myself free of thoth'tsz of a God esse to be letter'all'y y'all szz"any mere mirrored potential image imagined moment after momentum recallsz still a being that a pri"or'y.

"Let that in word mind mirror on and on on'l'y as'z thothtsz of that I am that mere or y reflection. Me a'sz ex's ting in a being na me. In a na'me now out as'z thoth'tsz of x's ting alone reinforced by hearing my na'me. Hell'o any na'me is in word. In word a being any mere or y mind mirroring y'all in the'or'y. In mem'or'y imagining a being any image referenced in my or y na'me or y'all now k'nowing me in name alone. Mor found his own words as if coming out of the mind of a stranger. A stranger scant thin'king of a strange dialectic. Yet he was not about trying as'z two shutting it down or in any way ignoring out of it in the'or'y a being still in the first place invisibility. Thus he thought expressing denial of a being invisibility now becomes potentially possible with a b'ng c'ng at attention now fixated on a y eye b'ng c'ng in the'or'y of na'me alone. In that recall I am finding myself he intuited in'visibility still complete and completely free of any mere 'or y mirr'or y na'me'm'or'y. Still behind my na'me lurks a crazy ma'me.

"Thank you missy. Thank you. Me heart s'z'ings with you'a're'y ba'd a'sz 's"word cutting any k'not's in any na'me's'z in my heart. And na'me ma for giving such a portentious name handle. Bless'z'er ka'ra'yz'e'e soul. Now that I am picking up moment by momentum a complete non-attachment of any mere or y in word na'me, my heart soars. Free. In a wordfreedom at last a being still in the first place. In a Pa'roo'Ma supersonic first personic person present in'tense eye am'em'or'y z is is a'w/akhen'aten."

Mor bolted upright with the utterance of these words. Suddenly a current, an invisible hurricane funneled as'z thoughtsz through a straw, tore through and y'all around him as supernatural her'me'asz'thoth'tsz letter'all'y y'all in a y eye of herhimit. Az's'king of it a ka'smic torus. A towers of it struck bi a lightning d'na'eye'll inspiraling out a b'lack'g'round. In a wordfreedom flowing endlessly beginning any en'dhi'ing. Or y na? A'sz too, a'sz two perceive en'y body now as'z x's ting. He the'zap'paz z'sting a's 'ex. The twist of fate, of faith, or trust of family, friend, foe. The sheer'z z z'sting of it. Her'him'it a'while of love or hate duplicity of one indivisible bliss. One functional a're'y'all wayeve a's'z'ex"u'all being"es'ze.

"I be such a do'peh. Y'all these years mere or y mirror'all'y y'all appearing only disappearing periodically black a's'za me or my na'me now still the Dark'ness. Of course. The dhi ark now to be found complete. The complete dhi'z ar'king of it covered in'visibility dhi ark'en'ess'e. Always turning yearning burning. Y'all wayeves complete dhi ark en esse now to be perceived ar'king of it. Now to be asz thoth'tsz of a being to perceive as'king of it y a k'no'wing out of it. A'sz to be en'y ark, any roll or role or y'all playing out az's'ex's ting in na'me alone. Y'all alone. Indivisible in'visibility of any individual."

Mor took a deep breath as he noticed Christina staring back at him with a bemused ex'press'ion. The torus energy surge welled out his pi'e hole, as'z his first grade teacher was fond of saying. Fact was he found himself getting on to Y speak dialectic e've're'y bit liberating. Letter'all'y y'all library of liber'at'i'on by de'l"OO"ka de b"OO"ka. A're'y'all' ity' as king of it a being OO eggs'a'z'ka's in a word"all'y y'all. Now in her'eyez z z awhile a'sz'z z'though a'sz thothtsz of it in forma'sz before his eyez z z.. A'sz e'x', the simple singular ka'ni'fe twisting in two a double a duplicate form'asz inspiraling of fate faith family. Out in trust of it now awhile in her'eyez z zap'ping a pehss'y w'hole wayeve're'y'bodys'z. We all a will wheel turning b'lack'g'round indivisible invisibility infinite potential of any mere or y memory mirrored y'z z z'ion you duplicating in a duplicity of y now asz though anybody any meager measly thin'king of it as'z thoughtsz"e'x's ting. Or'e'ye. The'y e'rOr'e"ye now. Y you're;y na'me or'e'y'ez z z'ion you. Or'e'y"e'e dhi'a'ting me. Herhimit eyez z z'ion you her'me's'z is yod. Iota. I ayin ta't. It t'was as'z if finding the key's'za otro lado into the other y'sz si'de'h'ay. As'z Korner was fond of saying, got my big feet in the window and my he'yad on the g"round. Goin' down . . . Goin black'g'round.

"Y'all spun out in the or Y speak. Got that ignited ignition fire of a're'y'cog'nition in you'r'e eyesz. In the or y. It is a gas, baby. A re"y'all gas it will blow out your'e'ye or y mind. In the'or'y of y'all. We all a wheel turning into or out of a being c'ng still free in the first place. A b'ng center centered centrality of it. In Pa'roo'Ma awakhen aten. A being'sza in the'or'y a b'ng c'ng in word running in the night." Her eyes glowed with that inner fire she called veda. Veda vidya vidvan. As'king of it now any k'nower k'nowing veda is a being veda, she would say.

"Feeling like fielding the veda baby.'"

"Of course. A being still in Pa'roo'Ma'y awakhen aten. Still a being in that Pa'rooMa at attention. Pay attention," she gave with a mock wagging of her forefinger. "Akhenaten and his monotheistic warrior priests were able to use the scaffolding of a purely phonetic language to facilitate their invention of alphabeta. Sanskrit or Samscritam, that aryan well developed a'scription of sound waves without letter'all'y y'all for'ma'sz in word spelling of alphabeta would have served this purpose. This per'sonic language siddhi power of the gods would have been transmitted orally by those warrior priests passing through a rigorous pramanah teaching methodology jumping gaps across races and places. Along with bronze metallurgy, horses, and war chariots, the invading asiatic indo-europeans would bring Veda. Veda would come as'z sure as'z sweat from the brow or any sacred meaningful sounds from mouths of the warrior priests. Their superior conquering civilization developed out of veda transmitted through the maha'man'a'ha. The great man'as mind'or yod hayvavhay. These asiatics covered Egypt like a blanket that smothered Egyptian culture for a century'or more till the Egyptians adopted their veda with chariots and armor of their own. Eventually Egypt prevailed pushing the invaders out but their influence had entered the priestly blood stream. A Nile now k'now'ing da'Nile of Veda. Astronomy, medicine, mathematics, metallurgy, art, politics, y'all vastly enriched. Threaded through the su'per'sonic vedic oral library, a pramana, a means for realizing BRAHMATMA or a b'ng c'ng be'am'ing a're'y'all at aten'cion out in word. Y'all this veda knowledge with out any phonographic iconography. A b'ng c'ng still in'visibility without letter'all'y y'all spelling it.

"A language with out letters. Forma'sz sound wayeves means of apearing out of it understanding the overstanding over man'as MAHIMANAHA. Still without record of it out beyond supersonic ka's mic memory of it. Sans hieroglyphics to be carved into stone stellae leaving visible trace records. Veda brought forward on wayeves of su'personic brain of brah'man. The great singular indivisible invisibility awareness of anybody now a phonographic individual. A being c'ng in su'personic man'as a phonographic mind. Or y'sz'any mirror'da na're;y'all in mem or y now not. Denied as'king of it y now a k'no no no'wing it out phonographically aw'h'ile. Still a b'ng c'ng in any unique point of you or you now phonographically appearing out of it. That'sz the real thin'king of it pur'pose of a b c's. A're'y'e all'ity as'king of it y a b'ng c'ng a peering it of a freestanding supersonic first person singular eye still in the first place of that I am a peering it now from above. Ove a b'ng c'ng now letter'all'y y'all as'z in word thoth'tsz of appearing with a polarity on hand. Of it supersonically or phonographically polarizing it out of any a na y'azs'ex y'all a unique point of view. A uni que'st as'king of it y. Ar'king of it now you or y as'z a'mere'or y az's'ex. In the'or'y cue of a being still that great su'personic indivisible in'visibility in man'as mind of a b'ng c'ng now as'king of it y now any chintzy chis'lin scant thin'king of it with inka's on pa'per. Are'y"mem'bering letter'all'y y'all out in mem or y. Y'et just us y'all. A re'y'mem'bering a being still indivisible invisibility. Now a're'y'mem'bered asz'any thoth'tsz of that. Pay y'all attention remembering a being still it in the first place indivisible invisibility."

"A re'y eye of a b'ng c'ng a peering it out of anybody now k'no' no'no'wing it as'z z z z'any'scrawny scant starved thin'king of it. That it a being we all us'a wheel turning into and out of still it? That a b'ng c'ng be'am'ing in y'all now a k'no no no'wing out of a positive negation of it in two appearing a pairing in any withered tenuous thin'king of it y now a b'ng c'ng other y's'z?" Mor found himself out of it in word awhile. Still a being of that first personic singular person a'prior'y to appearing disappearing in t'wo'rd t'wis'ting into the Dark'ness of a being black'g'round now k'no'wing out as'z'z z'any denial of it. A y as'ex's ting out in formation y'll d'na in name alone.

"How many war chariots is the alphabeta supersonic 3D cubic space in a time ma'sheen'a worth?

Alphabeta. A b c's of a b'ng c'ng still in the first place a peering it now supersonically out b'ey"e ve'da'as'king of it y a k'now'ledge alledgedly merging with thousands pictoral phonographic hieroglyphs. With the portable ABBC time ma'sheena, a y eye in the first place a peering it as'exodus out of it now t'word a t'wis'ting in two appearing a pairing a space in time. Now in wordz zazz a k'now'ing it possible. The mon'eye"theists took their material wealth but more importantly a 3D portable a're'y'cording vocal or graphic mean means of carrying out d"m' ar'king of it y the covenant with divine father Pharaoh A'y in a're;y'all at aten'cion. Adon a y now guaranteeing them the promised land of Canaan.

"A e'Veda or knowledge is non letter'all'y y'all purely a su'per'sonic meaningful memory bank of e've'ast dimensions. Y'et a indivisible mean. A be'tween macro or micro consciousness of any mere or y means of a mind or y'all na now reflected in word'all'y turning a k'now'ing of it meaningful of y'all. The cult of cultivating in'visibility of a b c's of a b'ng c'ng out in a word na'me a're y'all still of indivisible invisibility as'z' any individual. Merely mirrored a peering it into appearing of it supernaturally superimposed as'z'any thoth'tsz of a singular Great God esse to be letter'all'y y'all now of a b'ng c'ng born. Born out as'z any mere or y now az's'ex per eye in c'ng a meaningful memory of it. Aw'h'ile now as'z cunning uncanny con'tagious d'na'eye'll. A positive peh'ss'y w'hole power a y'll D'NA. A wayeve will function of y'or you now az's'ex's ting in formation as'z'any or eve're'y'body. A b'lack'g'round wayeve function echoing of it a y'az'a meaningful means az's'ex p'ressing gee's'z"us. Us we all a wheel turning into or out of a gravity weight of waiting on any scrawny wanting wasted thin'king of it in'formation. As'z 'ex's ting int'word a twis'ting in two idea'el eye'd'na'll functional image imagined as'z'any thoth'tsz of it. A b'ng c'ng merely mirrored supernaturally superimposed in'formation awhile now a time or two relying on the ni near complete con'scious spell cast by the phono'graphic portable alphabeta time ma'sheen'a.

"A time now new eve'n of old. A spelling of it still in her'eyez z z of any a na y'or eve're'y body. Anybody with intention at attention captive in the ABBC time now ma'sz'shee'na. A eve're'y'body. A g'listening personic gee'z z'us a la Que"en que' of that in which potential as'z'any appearing of it now as'King of it a k'no'wing out of d'na'eye'll. As'z z z so much of it int'word in'forma'ing in effect now anybody etc.. The work or play of a time ma'sheena loop that moves in one direction turning now into a un'k'now'n"y mere mirrored see'as'z potential of a b"'lack"'g'round instilled with intent of turning in two a gain one of it. Of a polarity of a positive negativity now a k'no'wing out a synapse still complete d"ark'ness'e. A completely complete ar'king of it. Now to be we all a wheel in two a y playing out az's'ex y'all infinite l"OO"p'y de'l"OO"peh'ss'y w'hole power. Appearing a pairing az's'ex y'all.

"To know Veda in samscritam offered su'per'sonic memory banks of light y'ears beyond any mere or y na'tive vernacular. It included asta'dhi'yi. A highly evolved per'sonic grammatical system of sutras. Shortened sentences systematically codified for memory. Asta'dhi'eye initiated Vedic warrior priests carried y'all their voluminous scripture samscritam well inscribed in their memory. Thus vedic memory exceeded any mere or y lifetime orally passed in an unbroken lineage asz a b'ng c'ng in a wordfreedom awareness of it in sight transferring a y'sz'dom'us. A great house of PARAMAPURUSHA. A first person singular awareness now of a y eye of that I am merely a peering it. Out now appearing of it y'ears orally mom'ent after mom'ent'um generation to generation. Their veda knowledge would have been instrumental in developing in less than a decade the 3D cubic phonographic or su'per'sonic alphabeta mean means meaningful of Akh'et"aten. A duplication of it. A plan et'ting h'ear'th of Akh as'z'in"a'ten. Featuring phono'graphic el'et'te'r'ing duplicating a b c's of a b'ng c'ng still in the first place indivisible invisibility. A b'ng c'ng now as'king of it a k'now'ing out of it in'word a twis'ting in two appearing a pairing az's'ex. Letter'all'y y'all a're'y'all'ity as'king of it'y a k'no'wing out any gaunt emaciated wanting thin'king of it derived from sacred hieroglyphs. Thus producing asz supersonic thothtsz in'visibility of a b c's mirroring a being c'ng. Now a cubic space in time in for'ma'sz sound means understanding any in word spelling of it casting a time ma'sheen'a recording with in'ka's on papyrus scrolls. Out in a space in time awhile now in for'ma'sz any or eve're'y'body'z z z exodus from Akh'et'ting aten y a la que"en que"ya. An exodus accompanied by the armies of divine father Pharaoh Ay in a're;y'all. In a y eye a peering it out int'word captivity at aten'cion of Adon-ay to recapture the promised el'and duplicate function in'visibility and repopulate the vassal state of Canaan currently over-run by Apirus, marauding nomadic brigands. The mon'eye'theists had a covenant with divine father Pharaoh a're;ye of Adon ay as'z the chosen to take over control and repopulate a piece of the empire held captive by formidable armies of Hittites and Philistines. Ultimately this would take some forty years before the mon'eye'theistic warrior priests could move further north from the Moabite territory of Sinai desert where they wandered since their exodus from akh'et'aten. A y eye of a b'ng c'ng now as'king of it a k'no'wing it out of Egypt. Eg'g'sz ting in a y eye pt'ing out as'ex'odus in a word. A point of view of you of y now beginning ending in a word.

"The 'Chosen' monotheistic warrior priests were verboten from taking the sacred hieroglyphs out of Egypt. The d"ark, Perceived ar'king of it y now the es'ka'roll of the covenant with Adon ay now with in'ka's on papyrus an agreement of a b c's of a b'ng c'ng still in the first place adon ay indivisible in'visibility. Now a're'y'all'ity as'king of it y a la que"en que' of that in which we all turn out appearing of it. In'visibility of it letter'all'y y'all a b c's of a b'ng c'ng awhile bi the time now any k'no no no'wing out of it written in word with in'ka's on papyrus. A y eye as'king of it y now any roll or role of the covenant could supernaturally as'z'any thoth'tsz of a Great God esse to be letter'all'y y'all a b'ng c'ng now carried out of Egypt. Still it would reside in the voluminous memory of the mon'eye'theistic warrior priests."

"Isz that the papyrus passed on to you? The d"ark of the covenant with ar'king of it Adon ay?" Mor's neck hairs crackled. The march of time now echoing a pingting thundering then subsiding to a steady buzzing in his y'ears. She'e"na continued without answering.

"In the first place they must remember Anokhi Adon ay. A y eye yet merely a peering it that I am is is in time now appearing of it a'sz'zany memory at aten'cion. A'ten bi'na're'yz z z of a b'ng c'ng still indivisible in'visibility. At aten'cion of h'o'u're a y time nowz z z' any eye a peering it still in the first place in a wordfreedom'us. The ke'y"e of any k'no'wing d'na'eye'll in a b c's of a b'ng c'ng y'et that indivisible in'visibility of any individual. Now still as'king of it y cultivated cherished and wor'd'shipped in letter'all'y y'all a b c's of a b'ng c'ng a peering it out int'word supernaturally appearing a pairing of it superimposed as'z'any thoth'tsz of the divine a re;y'a'll ity'aten. Y'all still as'king of it y at aten'cion awareness asz two now in time a k'no'wing out any d'na'eye'll of it. In awhile now. A wily while of a space in time now a k'now'ing out of it az's'ex y'all."

"The covenant with Adon ay'z z z'in space?" Mor now found himself still as'king of it y any k'no'wing d'na'eye'll of it. It a b'ng c'ng merely a peering it out in a wily while of any space in time now appearing of it. Ar'king of it y as'k'no'wing out anybody any chislin' wanting thin'king of it as'z'any chintzy double. Of it in a craft of a word'ship duplicity carrying a wayeve're'y'body out in two a twis'ting black'g'round as'z thoth'tsz of any city of dupes. On a plan et"ting h'ear'th supersonically superimposed as'z'any thoth'tsz of a Great God letter'all'y y'all appearing a pairing of it. A duplicity in any space in time now still as'king of it y a la que"en que' of that in which appears anybody etc.. Awhile now.

"Akh'et"a'ten. As'z'any duplicity of a'kh. Ar'king of it y a la que"en que' of that in which any or eve're'y'body appears out in any city of dupes. A b'ng c'ng still in the first place the first princ'iple point of view of you in a're'y"e'all of a peering it out. Now any seer sight see'ng a k'now'ing it out as'z'za any scant skinny thin'king of it. A chintzy thin'king of it. A's'z' measly anybody. Asz'z'any time. Asz'z'any where. Still that free standing in a wordfreedom awareness of a b'ng c'ng in a y eye of herhimit. With a polarity on hand y'all now k'no no no'wing out a positive negation of it into appearing of it out in awhile now. A cubic space in time in a b c's of a b'ng c'ng will we all after awhile of D'NA appear to disappear int'word a t'wis'ting in two a black'g'round echoing any complete duplicate roles of it. A rolling out in her black eyez z zap'ping'tin'king of any or eve're'ybody as'z z z'leep black'g'round as yet a y eye of herhimit merely a peering it from above. Ove a b'ng with a polarity on the one hand. A're'y'all free'da y na light igniting y'all ignoring it on the other hand. In a wordfree'dom'us a b'ng c'ng still in the first place indivisible in'visibility of anybody.

"The herhimit now as'king of it y now holding it offering of'ten as'ka's mic da y na light from above while freestanding in a wordfreedom below. A re'y'all from that the'e'ye star'e'y"e o'r y of Adon ay at attention in the'or'y any mere'or y'all's d'na'tu're." She now kept circling in time with her voice leading Mor out of his body in an exodus of mind or y mem'or'y. He found his attention soaring high above as'z below the lit el matrix of urban sprawl in the or y freed in a wordfreedom turning out into the over mind. Or y'all a b'ng c'ng in that now out in a wordfreedom y'et understanding of the spelling of a b c's'ex's ting merely mirrored in word.

"Now it seems in the'or'y that exodus still ongoing. The wayeve of a life az's'ex y'all remains in effect 99.9 percent at any time. Y'et as'z fully a third of it as'z'leep black into a un consciousness. A singular X per eye in c'ng indivisible invisibility of a b'lack'n'ess'e instilling now to be a gain of it. Now the'na'wakhen a'ten. At aten'cion of a y eye a peering it out in a y eye wayeve'rey'body appearing a pairing of it in d'na'eye'll az's'ex y'all. Of such we all turn into an accomplice as'z two of our own a tricky bitchin' crafted deceit. Asz'any thoth'tsz of a Great God Gee'sz'us letter'all'y y'all understanding int'word a twis'ting in two the gravity weight of waiting on death in d'na'eye'll of it merely a peering it y'all along. Y'all along the wayeve function of motion. Appearing turning out disappearing. Y'all this time in word captivity turns out to be mere or y supernatural mem'or'y of it in her"eyez z z'of eve're'y'body int'word a twis'ting in two spelled out appearing of it a'sz any d"na'me." He offered while still wondering in word. The wordsz'a'zz though'tsz rang a bell that seemed to awak'h'en an ancient slumbering twin at attention paid playing now in a wordfreedom awareness of a b'ng c'ng. A be'tween indivisible in'visibility as'z' any seer sight see'ng. A peering it out now a're'y"all'ity as'king of it a k'no'wing it int'word appearing of it a twis'ting mirrored be'ng'tween a black'g'round twin echo turning out or in her'eyez z z'azz'any or eve're'ybody as'z'z z'leep black into a un'consciousness. A con she'e'na us a la que"en que'ya of that in which appearing of it aw/akhen'ing at aten'cion playing out any role of complete d"ark'n'ess'e. Anybody perceived now to be ar'king of it. As'z'anybody appearing of it awhile now of da y d'na eye el'ight igniting ignoring out of it.

"Y'or'you now appearing out of it still in the first place. Now any a n'a y eye of a b'ng c'ng y'all still mere or y potential as'ex's ting. A pingting out cat'n'a'bout in'a her'eyez z z' of eve're'y body. As'z'any exodus is mere'or'd in word w'a'y'eve of a peering it out of a na y eye as'ex's ting understanding only in the'or'y a spell'ing of any x position. Az's'eX int'word a twis'ting in two appearing a pairing. We all eve'n a'sz appearing turning into eve're'y or a na'y body remain in the'or'y now as'z y that indivisible invisibility of any individual a b'ng c'ng that eye of that I am is is. Why y'all must laugh you're as'z of'f now picking up on it in a wordfreedom awareness of a being still in the'or'y immortal changeless invinciple. Or y'all na't now denied y'll d'na by that simple twist of fate of any d'na'eye'll.

"War or y War're'y'na's viral scheme rests on that d'na'eye'll. In the"or'y alien"y'na"tion no'tion of any alter'na'tive alternating awareness assures his success. That three thousands plus year old spelling out of alphabeta int'word a twis'ting in two appearing a pairing asz'any thoth'tsz of a singular Great God esse to be letter'all'y y'all mon'eye. A mono mon'eye mono'the'is'm beginning in 'the is m or y' of the defining articulation of it int'word thoughtsz of it in for'ma'sz a'na y time ma'sheen'a may have a time now a're'y'lease built into it. A'sz in her'eyez z zap'ping in for'ma'tion az'sex's ting x'pands beyond plan et her'e'art'h"eye turning a b'lack into a gain. Of one as'ka's mic black'ness with in'ka's on pa'per ka'mic me'm"or'y. In the"or"'y that I am finding you now breaking out of any roll or role or y you appear of it in or out of complete d"ark'ness means the beginning is ending. As'z ar'king of it a funny ting is in any k's'z' any cause of it mere'or'y now inches above anybody's head." Christina offered, feet spread, hands on hips, head thrown back to gaze directly into starlite years. Mor let the mirror sound wayeves of her voice play into his field of feelings. Playing out in her eyez z z'leeping into that feeling he grasped their naked invisibility out in the cosmic magnitude. Still his wounded knee reminded him of the situation at hand. His sails suddenly went slack.

"You seem to be reading those stars," he replied, turning back to watch her movement.

"Or the'y a're'y'd'na'ing me Dar'ka"artist aware of the awareness that I am is'is. D"perceived ar'king thass'ka's mic flows through y'all asz a center centered on we all in wheeling around thru the 8th chakra. Merely inches over head," she'e'na laughed. "In feeling that neuronic cellular field body of view of you there seems to be synaptic electric fire as'zz z'apping gaps between neurons yet the unique point of view of a being out in her'eyez z z'azz'leeps b'lack into indivisible invisibility of now as'king of it a k'now'ing out of a b'lack'g'round. Echoing a singular ka's mic eyez z z of eve"re'y body a peering it out complete completely in two'z z z' any singular potential black'g"round. Echoing a touch asz;any touching of me or you feeling its h'our body moment to momentum. Ask'a's y'all a ka's mic micro wayeve're'y turning a black'g'round instantaneously. Before it can as'z'two happen it already is indivisible a'sz z z'a black'g"round radiating it in her re'y'e'z'z'az z'eve're'y'body. Y'all breaking out bad a'sz means of any or eve"re'y'body breaking out of captivity understanding a b c's spelling of a b'ng c'ng in the'or'y. But y'all see the dilemma?" she asked reaching out to lift his chin with extended fingers.

His mind'sz'z'eyez z'scrolled a roll or role of we all a wheel in turning around on this su'personic el"OO"pa playing out or in a complete d"ark perceived ar king of it y flowing a black'g'round in one direction. Out int'word a y twis'ting in two appearing a pairing az's'ex. A'way'eve're'y'body appears of it az's'ex's ting in name alone. A wayeve of y'all as'ex's ting now in a k'no'wing out any d'na'eye'll of it without realizing a're'y'all'ity as'king of it y'or y now a la que"en que'ya of that eve're'y'body in which anybody appears of it. In any eyez z ze' e'g'g's'za'ting motion you're still. A b'ng c'ng of you now in'visibility a peering it out as'king of it a measly thin'king of it mirrored int'word a twis'ting in two. That indivisible invisibility merely now mind or y a memory appearing a pairing of a Y az's'eX's ting out in formation. As'z'ex'et'ting duplicating merely supernaturally as'z thoth'tsz of a singular Great God Gee'sz us. A great geometric gravity letter'all'y y'all a weight in a b c's of a b'ng c'ng superimposed as'z'any body waiting on it. It see'ms we all turn into or out of a singular black'g'round body echoing supersonically y'all sinning and spinning a'wayeve as'k'no no no'wing positively ignoring it out as thoth'tsz of it projecting our indivisible awareness in a wordfreedom into one in'visibility appearing of it out now turning in two a k'no'wing of it out int'word captivity. A b'ng c'ng captive in d'na'eye'll. In'visibility of it now in'formation as'z y'all playing out paying aten'cion int'word inspiraling any roll or role of a b'ng c'ng now complete singularity hidden in wordsz'a. A y eye invisibility a peering it at aten'cion in a singular'k'a's micro wayeve b'lack'g'round memory of a b'ng c'ng still in the first place.

Ah the ka'mic hilarity of it he thought in her'eyez z z'azz wayeves a's'zz'any ma'sz jest'y. That jokes on you buddy boy Mor chuckled. A being still indivisibile a pairing bi that c'ng invisibility now out of it. Appearing awhile now a b'lack'g'round echoing a k'no no no'wing out a crafty in word d'na'eye'll of it. A b'ng c'ng mirrored in word memory mind or y potential of it. It, y'all, asz thoth'tsz appearing it by any mind or y memory now as though projecting it out of a b'ng c'ng mirrored in word denial of it. A b'ng c'ng still invisibility. Y'all gone crazy as'z a b'ng c'ng in word as'z'any thoth'tsz in forMa'sz jo'h ke of denying ja'h'su's liberation. Jah still herhimit of a y eye a peering it from above. Ove a b'ng at aten'cion free standing with potential polarity in hand.

Then in a're'y'all eye'zinging a be'am'ing of a b'ng c'ng in that eye of that I am is is a peering it of Jah. Jah'sus. Awareness of a y eye a peering it from any point of view of you of yod iota liberates. Liberates at attention in a wordfreedom. A b c's indivisible from a b'ng c'ng captivated mirrored int'word any measly thin'king of it a'sz'z'any other y'sz. A k'no'wing of ja'h is a y eye be'am'ing a b'ng c'ng still indivisible invisibility of any individual now out y'et as'king of it in a k'no'wing d'na'eye'll. That awareness in a wordfreedom eye that I am is is merely a peering it out in her eyez z z of eve're'ybody as'z'anybody b'ng"Lack" with intent of a b'ng a Gain of Gee'sz us. Ja'sus h'ey'vav'h'ey mere'or y you yod iota tattwamasi ba'be. Somethin'king of it like that Mor mused with a grin finding the transfer of his persona'll'ity now as'king of it a k'no'wing out y'all mirrored matter turning int'word a black'g'round blissful energy. Indivisible in'visibility energy of a b'ng c'ng a peering it out int'word a un't'wis'ting it. A single black'g'round twisted as'z'any thoth'tsz of it a pairing still indivisible in the first place. A b'ng c'ng merely int'word appearing of it in two. In'formation of long term. A w'h'ile memory of a being anybody. Now finding himself in a wordfreedom awareness of any or eve're'y body now as'k'no'winging quivering da y na light supersonically y'all into a subtle sublime dream time body lightened his load.

The pure seduction of attention now reverting to that dream baby body only offset by the roll of that quantum l"OOpa de' l"OO"peh gravity weight of waiting with intent of awakhening now k'no no no'wing other y'sz. At attention only in the'or'y moving away. At aten'cion still in motion merely asz'any thoth'tsz of life or death. At aten'cion still in a wordfreedom awareness. Of now a y wayeve out in her eyez z z'ap'ping'ting a measly thin'king of eve're'ybody turning into the future. The few prototypes that u a're'y'all. At attention of a being still indivisible uno, u'no'w/y'all as'z though'tsz turning into you projecting out as'ex'u'all a k'no no no'w known a kurving el"OO"peh'ss'y w'hole'ye now on e wwwww'a'vessesezz of a b'ng c'ng out int'word a twis'ting in two her're'yez z z'azz'leep b'lack' into or out of it. In her're'yez z z. Her'rey'eas'z eve'reybody. In her'eyez z z'a wayeves of a con she us now ess'e to be keep y'all waiting with the weight a la que"en que' ya of that in which a quantum gravity appears to disappear he mused. G'ee'sz us waiting of it in her"eyez z z'now k'no no no'wing out the un'dee'inwwwwwwww'ays of eve're'y body as'ka"me'ing black'g'round echoing instilling in the ka"me'h'dhi to perceive we all turning into or out of any intent to appear a gain. Still completely complete as a b'ng c'ng indivisible in'visibility of any individual merely a peering it he flashed. Pa'roo'Ma in'n'a y eye of a b'ng c'ng a peering it still that as he had been a'prior'y of a b'ing c'ng scrolled his mirror mindsz'eye. A b'ng c'ng still under the t'ruk'ma. Christina held his gaze with magnetic eyes push pulling his focus into paying aten'cion with in word and without in a wordfreedom.

"In that I am genetically designed as'z'a break out bad a's'zz her wayeve of a y eye of eve'll of herhimit will. A will wheel turning into it. Or y her eyez z z'i on him of it. Her'him'it y'all in that eye is is a peering it. There is'z only following instinct and that instinct leads me in a b'ng c'ng in word memory in her'eyezz z z of eve're'ybody turning a black'g'round now out k'now'ing him. That in word spell is millenniums in the making. A split second in its destroy'ing. Either y'all break it. Break out of it awhile now. Break ba"da'ass'z a b'ng c'ng still that indivisible in'visibility of anybody still in the first place free freed in a wordfreedom us in'kas mic awareness of it.

"Or . . .y a b'ng c'ng in her"eyez z z now k'now'ing it out in d'na'eye'll of one a y eye of a b'ng c'ng as'z thoth'tsz of it int'word a twis'ting a black'g'round any roles playing out d'na'eye'll of it in forma'tion. Ma'na t'at"u'a're raped by his being y alien"na'tion as'z'ex y'all. A'szz too or two twys'ting on her'eye a ma're'y black g"round. Seducing him into killing her or birthing him into a alter native. Slave or Alien warrior priests, mono'the'is'm, that in word cult cultivating the one word'ship. As'zz'ailing off az's'ex's ting am'id'god'as'z z dog'ma with mirrored gravity weight of the g"OO"da b"OO"ka. Ba being Egg's ting'ka'ing. In the beginning is the supersonic light word but following quickly comes a heavy b"OO"ka. A hOOka de'lOOka. Veda no weight. Na'na waiting for'ma'sz veda. Knowing veda is becoming veda. Is a be'ng c'ng ve'da. El que ve. The one who sees.

"My su'per'sonic veda trumps his supersonics with intent of appearing forma'sz'za w'h'ile . . . a cunning in word deceit generated by the time Ma'sheen'a in'for'ma'ss'z z z hieroglyphic hieratic hebraic phono'graphic greco roman alphabeta spelling . . .spelling y'all out in word a'w'h'ile now turning black into and why'te the'y out of k'no no no'wing that indivisible in'visibility . . . of such an ingenious cleverly conceived act by . . . gee'sz us appearing supernaturally as thoth'tsz generated by wayeves of eve're'ybody waves of the invention of supersonic 3D Q'bOOka at indivisible Attention out in a binary consciousness. The marvelous con of shee'na . . . gee'sz us . . . merely appearing a pairing az's'ex y'all in eL mode of in word wayeve function of fun'ny'a'ction. A creation created by our own mere duplicity. A b'ng c'ng now conned by our e'very own a consciousness. A bi denying a knowing of it. A being still in y you a re'y'all mode complete completely free of any in word captivity . . . free freed in a wordfreedom awareness still in a'while at the same su'ma time now turning into or out of anybody ka'no no now'ing it out . . . positive negation . . . by as'z thoth turning churning burning around the race of that we all turning out of or black into one indivisible in'visibility . . . !!!chido guey !!!. . . seduction of it in her"eyez z z'ion of eve're'y body . . . a black'g'round in or out of her'me'asz . . . herhimit . . . indivisible . . . indivisibility . . .yet still instilled with that int'word intent of her wayeve function of funny'action . . . Shee'na. . . funny that wayeve of wayeve"re'y'assz z z'a ma'trix . . . ma'sz tricky eve're'y'body . . .then He drags around a single heavily revised rewritten retold his'story. The b'OO'ka. My veda of the abiding overstanding understanding mind or y many tens of thousands sutras playing su'per'sonically combing the waves of my heart brain in'ka's mic ka'mic 5Dhi to perceive the'e star'e y eht to be told." Christina layed the words out in modulating frquencies echoing a black'g'round out in her'eyez z z'ion him h'earing it. Herhimit h'earth plan et. Y'ABBC plan x'et'ting of it. The genesis of any ex'hodos. The fall as'z z z'leep black into a un'consciousness. A being of it still in Pa'roo'Ma with intent to awakhen aten. A being still parama atman.With that revelation he wondered what Warren could possibly have in store to top picking up on a b'ng c'ng still indivisible in'visibility.

"Still in a b'ng be'am'ing a c'ng of a y eye of you in a're'y'all that I am betting that a y eye' star'ey of it will be a'rey'all eye'z'z'da in her'eye of eve're'ybody. Sooner or later, tater," he added with a laugh."Is the spell spelled out in the papyri?" Mor asked, eyes diverted by a shooting star, blazing out in a trail of sparking cinders.

"In archeology, you rarely make a find that makes sense of all the pieces. In that I am confessing to using certain psychoactive drugs to realize the key"e to unlocking this thirty three hundred plus year old mystere'y. Along with thousands of tightly focused hours absorbing and contemplating scripture both on parchment, hyde, or stone and in the mirror mind reflecting in word reflection of it. Then, staring at some letterforms, comparing the Dead Sea Scrolls to the Tutankhamun papyri, it hit me. Eureka. The clues, the structure of the letters, the Hebrew alphabetic scripture, were only fingers pointing to the thing."

"The thing?" he asked as she now adjusted her weight.

"The thing of it is. That awareness of a b'ng c'ng in that eye a'memory is is a peering it out in word. A now a k'no'wing out of it in two appearing a pairing of it. The thing of it is as'z mirrored int'word a twis'ting in two of it as'z'any thoth'tsz of it in formation of such for however much we all may turn into imagining a k'no'no'no'wing d'na'eye'll of it. Words, symbols, even ideas cannot go there beyond awareness of a b'ng c'ng still in a wordfreedom'us in the first place found indivisible in'visibility of any individual. Iha nana na'sti kim chana. Here diversity is not in the very least of us. In her'eyez z z indivisible in'visibility as'z' any or eve'reybody.

"Words point it out of there asz'any measly scant thin'king of it. Y'et there it is in a wordfreedom awareness. A b'ng c'ng still silent indivisible invisibility. Consider for a moment any identity in a name alone. That identity is based on a completely arbitrary name given by parents without a clue who we all may turn into or out of a b c's of a b'ng c'ng in the first place. That arbitrary notional na'me sets up a mom'ent to mom'entum lifetime after lifetime of in word self deceit. A self duplicity. Y y'all identity as'eX's ting purely supernaturally y'all a'sz'any thothtsz of it. It a y eye merely a peering it as'ex'per'eye'en'c'ng through any unt'word mirr'or y y'all now out appearing of it hard wired neuro-cellularly in any or eve're'y bodyz z z'blood and bone field of view. A're'y'all touching instantaneous touch in'ka's mic mic'ro wayeve black'g'round echoing asz two b'ng'z z z as'z thoth'tsz of it in forma'sz appearing of it out awhile still a b'ng c'ng indivisible invisibility."

"There'sz z z' any a'na y mirr'or y na there? D'na'y'll a mirr'or y appearing of it a wile now a's'z 'ex?" he asked as she now moved away. The drone of a helicopter shook the air sweeping over the Bay and flatlands. From a black speck with blinking lights grew a whirling hulk of intimidation hovering in on the rooftop blasting gravel and debris into a whirlwind.

"I've seen that chopper before, the day Korner showed at the Flying V," he shouted trying to get to his feet. The ma'chine reached a deafening tone whipping up more dust and gravel pebbles until lifting black away, circling over, then soaring off. Its cacaphony swallowed up in the buzz of traffic on the 880 Expressway, just as another moving star.

"Warren's boys," said Christina. "Warren was born into a family famous as inventors of war machines. His whole scheme may be due to some misplaced attempt to atone for y'all that."

"Spoken like a true philosopher."

"Fool that I am", she said, walking over to help him up. He gathered her in his arms and kissed her neck, her cheek, her lips.

"That I am that fool," he replied. "A fool feeling such joy against such a background of sorrow is mind blowing, I gots to tell you. I gots to have you but I can't."

"What do you mean?" she asked, pushing away.

"I had a crazy dream about somebody wanting me to mate with you and seemed like some kind of evil deed that, well sorta freaked me out. Especially when you were giving me that look earlier."

Christina burst out with a laugh. "Why I do declare. You sure those fish are still swimming upstream? An old fart like you and all."

"There may be snow on the mountain..."

The steel door banged opened as Kwasanda Nzokia joined them on the roof. She walked over and gave Mor a long embrace. He tasted salt as he brushed his lips across her cheek. He wanted to keep her close, stretching the moment. The moment passed.

"Korner has been waylaid but he will be along," Kwasanda said.

"I thought you'd say he was dead."

"I thought he was going to pull the trigger on me but Fawn Rave, Enoch's squeeze, shot him with a Taser," she added, giving Christina a sisters' embrace

"How did she come into the picture?"

"There was a fight at Enoch's after you left. He killed Hashemi and Korner killed him then kidnapped her. I'm responsible for bringing those men into Enoch's life."

"Blame the stars. If they had not given birth to our star system, none of us would be here," Christina offered, giving Kwasanda a kiss on both cheeks. "I'm for taking the fight right to Warren himself. Let's get the hell out of here and go pay that old goat a visit."

"You talk like you've been there," Mor asked as they all started moving for the door.

"Maybe we have all been there," she said with a wink.

Kwasanda trembled as she hoisted his arm over her shoulder. Below he saw strings of head and taillights crossing the canal, flowing over the humped serpent of the Dumbarton Bridge. Lights slid comfortably over the gentle tail of the Bay, fifty miles south of shoals and riptides of seven rivers churning out to meet Pacific Ocean crashing in.

"I don't think he knows what he wants. He was muttering about them pulling the trigger," said Kwasanda, firing up the BMW.

"Them. Yes, Korner has told me about them. When he shot me. It was them pulled the trigger. That is, he started talking this way after he got back from Vietnam," Mor replied, lowering the window, taking a deep breath as they headed out to the freeway north to San Francisco.

"When Korner called to tell me he had found Dark," Christina said from the back seat, "I was reading a two thousand year old scroll fragment from Qumran on the Dead Sea. It said 'All people reject evil, yet evil advances,' and 'Truth is esteemed in the utterances of all nations, yet is there any tongue or language that grasps truth? What nation wants to be oppressed by another who is stronger? Who wants his money to be stolen by a wicked man, yet what nation has not oppressed their neighbor? Where are the people who have not robbed the wealth of another?' You could lift those 2000 year old words and paste them on any newspaper today. Of such is the duplicity of any d'na'eye'll of it. A duping of anybody or any measly thin'king of it int'word a twis'ting in two mirrored y'all az's'ex's ting. We all still turn int'word believing the deceit az's'ex's merely a'k'no'wing y, y you're; you in the first place. Without the hairfire desire to realize y the in word captivity at aten'cion must continue moment after momentum lifetime after lifetime."

"Indivisible invisibility of me or you." Mor added glancing at Kwasanda. She had missed out on their y'or Y speak loop'y dialectic. He wondered if it would be comprehensible or of value to her now.

"Am I missing something," Kwasanda said. "You guys sound like you're talking in some sort of x y code. Ever since my experience in RJ's pod my DNA seems to be unwinding. Untwisting the notion of a b'ng c'ng int'word anybody appearing out of it merely in any name alone. The ambiguous feeling of it is like an adopted style of dressing or walking or talking that is based on completely arbitrary in'word factors. Asking of it why seems a good place to start finding the reality as'king of it y'or you now in any ex'perience of it."

"Whoa girl. Factors as'king of it a la que"en que appearing it. You a being onto the dialectic of it."

"A la que'en A'star'eye'te. A black'ness in her'eyez z z of eve're'ybody. She'ena my people. Raped by man as mind without heart. As'king of it asz elohim engineering man as mind captivated in word fear and loathing. Or. A being seeing out in her eye of eve"rey'body. Black'aszz'za'ny me." Mor felt a jolt from her in word transcription of the ancient dialectic.

"Kwasanda ahm feeling you are me."

"Girl y'all doan n'ehvah be knowin my black shit." Kwasanda gave back with some attitude then broke out with a broad grin caught in the glare of passing headlights. "Just ji'van you professor. Gwoin to really appreciate your awareness of it in her eyez z z'ion. Him. . ."

"It. Now out in her eyez z z'a k'no no no'wing it turning black'g'round. Death stalks us all. Still disappearing in her'eyez z z'a power. A peh'ss'y w'hole power" Margot Christina gave with a straight face but Kwasanda cracked up at the wheel nearly losing control of the Beamer.

"Obviously y'all be sisters, duh." Mor laughed at the double entendre. Still he felt a certain vengeance underlying the humor. A wayeve of retribution building into a tsunami. Now it seems we all in turn appear in her'eyez z z a merely supernaturally a peering it from above as'zza below. A peering it out in a b c's of a b'ng c'ng in a wayeve fun'ny'action. A wayeve'szza now as'king of it y a'k'no'wing out of it in word'sz'zazz'ee merged in her peh'ss'y w'hole power eye'szaz'z z a la que"en que'ya of that in which appears anybody or any measly thin'king of it. In a while as'z'any space in time now as'king of it a k'no no no'wing d'na'eye'll of it out int'word a twis'ting in two appearing a pairing of it.

The'rey'all appear of it in a y eye a peering it from above. Ove a b'ng. A y you 'a're;y'all in the first place he thought. The code is y'or y now y'all as'z'any supernatural thoth'tsz of it as'ex's ting. The arbitrary mirror idea of a b'ng c'ng still in the first place now out as'z a'na y'a measly thin'king of it asz'anybody is sheer folly. Of a y as'z'ex'et'ting duplicating of it out appearing of it a b'ng c'ng asz any mere mirrored body based in word memory alone.

"The Darkness has penetrated or been pentrated by the in word spell associated in awhile with any name as'z anybody y'll D'NA. Un't'word a t'wisting as'eX's ping'ting power out in her eyez z z'leeping into a d'na'eye'll. Appearing of it now in a k'no'wing of a b c's of a b'ng c'ng now out int'word a name alone. In her'eyez z zap'ping a b'ng c'ng int'word a y eyez z z'ion now me. It seems to be that eye of I am is is a peering it supersonically y'all trying as'z too ex"plain indivisible in'visibility of a b'ng c'ng y by now turning around a's'k'now'ing out denial of it. K'no no no'wing a peering out in word as appearing to be anybody or any meager thin'king of it. Invisibility now then in that I am mirroring it supernaturally as'z'any thoth'tsz of a b c's in formation. Now a supersonic as'king Y of it a k'no'wing out of it int'word a twis'ting in two in a d'na'eye'll of it still a b'ng c'ng indivisible silent blissful invisibility," Christina offered without a trace of irony

" A bliss. That is precisely my state of a being since the Pod. That I am awareness of invisibility disappearing any trace of preoccupation in a name. Thank you for pointing that out. My problem now though is existential with a name. Namely James Korner. Look, we all be turning into sisters here. . . ."

"Excuse my dick and balls," Mor replied.

"You're an artist. That's why you don't count."

"Why, good one. Y'or y you're a born y speak'or. As much as Korner pisses me off he's a pawn like us. A somebody used to take the heat off Warren. He's one of those contracted to do the dirty work for the Agency so they have plausible denial of his actions. Thus he's never really one of them," he added, wrapping more gauze around his knee. "Them that pulls strings and triggers. His self-hatred of them since Vietnam has eaten him alive from the inside till he's just a shell of the human I met in days of yore. Still, at times Korner lives in my head. His exhalations are my inhalations, bringing me his thoughts, into his way of thinking. Thinking am I that guy to be used like him? In some Machiavellian intell world order."

"He's more a product than a victim of his desires. He is a broken, twisted psycho man." Kwasanda rubbed the welt left from Korner's gun barrel under her chin. Wind playing her hair as she now drove on north.

☼

Stephan Rakitin paused before the hall mirror to adjust his tie. He checked his white gloves to detect any filth in the offices and boardroom. The atmosphere, charged with ozone and negative ions, registered near perfect on Rakitin's digital meter. He was ready for Warren's big event on the horizon.

He walked through the bronze doors of the elevator leading to Warren's aerie and entered the office. Warren slumped in his wheelchair before a bank of monitors.

"Darkness is the element," Stephan Rakitin watched Warren's words scroll on a computer screen. "In her'eyez z z'ap'ping a na y'or eve"re'y body. A b'lack' body singularity. A common ma re;y'z z z'a black g"round echoing a supersonic space in time now into or out of which we alls'z human'ity as'king of it in hues chromo'somes of man'as mind or y'a wheel race to turn, churn, and burn in the or y of a b'ng c'ng now appearing of it out in awhile. . ." Rakitin had been chewing on a b'ng c'ng dialectic till he could no longer swallow any more of it. Then try as he might he could not seem to spit it out either. Over the last several years his employer had been lifting it from lecture transcripts of that witch professor Christina Shaughnessy. At first Rakitin had found the dialectic intriguing till realizing it displaced his identity. Dissolved it like some acid corroding any sense of an in word identity. Carefully he'd reconstucted that identity phonographically with tapes and printouts of his DNA codes along with biographical sketches of his past history. His employer Johnstone Warren on the other hand gave himself up to it completely. It seemed to fulfill a destiny of annihilation far beyond mere death of anybody. Though Rakitin could not explain it he sensed a certain evil in it.

When he'd approached Mr. Warren about his misgivings his employer merely shrugged it off saying evil was in the eyes of the beholder. Now he found his eyes drawn to the words scrolling the screen above.

"A space in time. Now. A wily duplicity of a b'ng c'ng as'z thoughtsz int'word'all'y y'all a twis'ting in two appearing a pairing bi'o's'z z z' simple singular twist of fate, faith, family.

A 0 a pairing as 8 by that twisting D'NAeye'll. A y na now a un'k'now'ing out a few t'at u a're. A future feature of prototypical double agents of the great man'as mind or y now agency of a memory. A F B EYE . . ." Rakitin grimaced at this reference to what he knew of a powerful transnational cabel of intelligence agencies loosely affiliated yet tightly gathering information on a level beyond normal human consciousness. Thus he'd found agents at times infilltrating his dreams. Once again Mr. Warren assured they were only doing their job. A job vital to an ancient program of that up until now Mr. Warren had served a vital function. Then came the evil witch with her damnable dialectic eating away at the in word memory of it. It reality as we all in turn now know it. He remembered the day. The fire in Mr. Warren's eyes first hearing a recording of the professors first use of it in her lectures had somehow sublimely singed all the hair on his body. He'd found himself lost in a twin being seen now knowing himself indivisible invisibility. In visibility even looking in a mirror he found only a gaunt starved thin'king of himself merely mirrored as in a name alone.

" . . . a peering it out now asz thoughts'z supernaturally appearing of it out now a bi E'fv'e re'y duplicating us'a singular b'ng now turning in two a k'now'ing out a b'twin being. A b'twin macro-micro'cosmic space in time now mean means meaning of a na y or e'Fv'e're'y'body. A cosmic microwave b'lack"g'round as'king of it a la que"en que'ya of that in which any a na y y na you now peh'ss'y w'hole power potential god'esse to be letter'all'y y'all any appearing of it. A's int'word a twis'ting in two a singular now eFv'e B eye mere'or'el'y a peering it. Out as'z a b'ng c'ng in'formation as'z a na y'na'tive slave serving h'our na now a'k'no'wing function. A cunning deception of their own a k'no'wing out of it. It out in a y eye of Herhimit or yod now x's ting. A ef've b'ng eye'z z z'ion h'Our ping'ting echoing supersonically of a b'ng c'ng in'forma'ing a space in time now awhile d'na'tive of d'na'eye'll slave int'word a twis'ting in two other y'sz z z or y'et'ting duplicating yod iota eye of that I am is is a first personic person a herhimitz z z'eye'z z z'inging a peh'ss'y'el'en'ta w'hole. A b'ng c'ng in a great man'as mind or y a future. A efv'e u t'at u a're'y'all 'as na'me alone now a k'no'wing ignoring mind or y eye a'm'em'or'y. Or a y eye a peering it out now as though'tsz a's'ex's ting in word. Az's'eX's ting bi a b'lack"peh'ss'y w'hole power as'z'any appearing out of it. A b'ng lack now a space in time to be a gain. Disregarding a being complete d"ark'n'ess'e now to be by intent as'king of it any k'now'ing out a measly thin'king of it. Of a b'ng c'ng a peering out int'word in'for'ma'ing two of you as'z a being now k'now'ing a na'y't'ive slave to hOur eFv'e B'ng eye z z z'purpose. Only fools, eFve"OO"el's fall as'z z z'leep under'standing a b c's of a b'ng c'ng in her'eye'z z z of eve're'ybody. Now understanding that in word spelling of it. Word mean is'z'any sound now meaningless k'now'ing it out in a wordfreedom from that unique visz'u'all'y y'all a point of you a peering from above in the first place."

Rakitin found some of Mr. Warren's dialectic straight out of a Lenin-Mao cultural revolution playbook. Take it all back to zero. Zee'ro. A'na y ni'hill'is'm. The indivisible individual 1,000,000 min'us 1,000,000. The twist seemed to be Mr. Warren's zapping and tugging on the towers of phonographic language. He once confided to Rakitin his research and deveopment of supersonic viral weaponry that could micro cosmically unwind the int'word twis'ting of it in two a b'ng'twin a space in time of anybody as'ex'et'ting duplicating spacetime. He spoke of the twin which he called the tween. An irreducible mean be'tween any great or small of it. Thus he Rakitin found himself still even restoring his assumed biography. Once finding yourself irreducible non expandable a being tween mean he mused meant finding yourself indivisible invisibility. You can wrap all the in word labels in the world on your memory of any or eve're'y'body still. Any cover is blown. Untwist that still singularity of a being c'ng now out appearing a pairing bi D'NA y'll of a k'now'ing it as'ex's ting in two a'twisting of it.

Mr.Warren intimated then his intent still a being c'ng in a mirrored in word k'now'ing out of it. A being beaming of it now a k'nowing out viraly complete microcosmic ma'ss liberation. Liberation obtained supersonically by bi'o's accoustic viral information inflammation burning up any situation. He called it abc's cubic mirror house of cards as'expiring data. He told how his we'apon mirror'ally activated the inevitable fall int'word torus towers. When Rakitin asked if he meant in word or inward. Mr. Warren merely smiled with a look that left Rakitin feeling the child asking if he the son or the sun. Supersonic radiation now means in man as mind of abc's k'nowing out of it int'word a twis'ting in two as above so below. A twin being tween in a wordfreedom awareness between macro or micro ka's mic memory. A y eye of man as mind. Or a y eye a peering it out int'word now a k'now'ing out as'z' any appearance of it in awhile as ex's ting in formation of anybody any biography. A great deadly enduring deception int'word a t'wis'ting in two turning we all into or out of a black'g'round echo of it now k'now'ing out of it a gain. N'yet now k'now'ing liberation of a being c'ng merely a gain supernaturally as thoughts of any meager thin'king of it he thought.

Rakitin cracked himself up picking up on the double entendre of a being invisibility see'ng a gain of it in'visibility. Him now discerning the sheer wily while of a being see'ng turning a ka'smic microwave b'lack'g'round echoing supersonically int'word thoughtsz of appearing of a being seen merely in word alone. Invisibility now a wily cubic space in time in formation of a b c's of a b'ng c'ng. A great house of cards. The sheer unt'word twisted obscenity as'king of it any appearing of it in'visibility. Appearing in any scant measly thin'king of it. Of a y eye being see'ng now to appear of it still merely a peering it. Awhile now out in word k'now'ing of any wretched withered thin'king of it. The a're'y'd'volution liberation at attention captured appearing of it merely a peering it from above. A supersonic supernatural superimposed liberation of a being c'ng as'z any in word thougth'tsz of it. Rakitin found his attention moment by moment a're'y absorbed in a wordfreedom awareness of a being still in the first place indivisible in'visibility. Or alternatively captivated at attention in name alone. Now he saw any k'now'ing it out for what it was. Away out. A way out in captivity. A captivity in word in any naming of it. Yet aware of a way"efve duplicating duplicity int'wordsz' any out of it in her'eyez z z of eve're'ybody. The sheer ma'sz of it. Billions in her'eyezz'azz a peh'ss'y w'hole power a peering it out of a black'g'round echo as'ka's y'all of anybody appearing awhile. Out in a space in time. Now. Obscenity of a deadly unt'word cunning duplicity of a being twin c'ng between macro or micro ka's mic memory from above. Ove a being now as'king of it turning out a black'g'around a k'nowing it a y'll D'NA. Awareness of the sheer deadly folly of it restored his revolutionary Russian soul. The Great Bear in Mind. Or soul. D'ark soul. Perceived ar'king of it in her ma'sz'eye a're'y'dhi'a'ting laughter devouring it black'g'round in her'eyez z z' alone indivisible in'visibility of it all the while. In blood. In bone. In her'eyez z z'suffering of eve're'ybody crushed understanding the weight of waiting on Gee'sz"us. A y eyez z z'ion A"Ma'sz black'g'round body.

Or y'all a's sound efve re'y body be'am'ing ma'ss personic radiation black'g'round. A touch touched touching as'z'any or efve re'y t'ing. This liberating or maddening dialectic infected Rakitin's mind. Letter'all'y y'all ma'ss Y dialectic dispelled his in word mirrored notion of a being of anybody. Now finding himself lost in a dissolution of a fun'damental process of efve're'y'volution. A un twis'ting of it. Looking in the mirror now a're'y'flected a mirrored in word hard wired ma'sz'age field of energy. At attention he found himself lost in a wordfreedom aware of awareness in a y eye being cee'ng. Now then a peering it out. In'visibility now int'word a k'no'wing out of it any field of view. An electromagnetic wayeve're'y field ending with his beginning as thoughts of playing out the role in long term mind or y potential bio cognition. It was now then as if he could no longer turn out k'now'ing int'word his way back home in formation. And his intent to go there steadily diminished day by day. Moment by moment. He steadily succumbed to that in a wordfreedom awareness of a b'ng c'ng still indivisible invisibility in her'eyez z z of eve're'ybody's potential black peh'ss'y w'hole power of bliss.

Now Mr.Warren's obsession with putting on a face of it. It awhile now of a space in time out in her'eyez z z of eve'll appearing in oil on canvass. Ma'ss seduction by viz'y'all sound wayeves of her eyez z z'ion eve"re'y body eve'll imagined supersonically in painting a ping'ting in formation. In'visibility supersonic wayeves of a bio-genetically imagined image. A supersonic ping'ting pain'ting of a b'ng c'ng out in virally engineered pigments echoing self replication in her'eyez z z of eve're'ybody. Sometimes Mr. Warren's in word thoughts completely bewildered Rakitin. Left him metaphorically wandering in the wilderness of an unhinged memory mind. A be'wilderness. Warren's dialectic put as thoughtsz an enchantment on him. Once he found himself still recognizable after days of incoherence. Apparently he'd been a b'ng c'ng wandering in a place impervious to in word thoughts. Still he could not seem to keep eyes off Mr. Warren's screed screening overhead.

"In h'Our time supersonic nu research into proteo'mics of a y eye a peering it out in word now mimics a as'king of it y as'ka's mic memory intelligence consciousness searching or k'nowing out of it. That dark energy perceived ar'king of it with intent of a y eye a peering it out word matter. A ka'mic b'lack'g"round a y eye mirrors it now supersonically supernaturally superimposed in wordsz as'z'any thoth'tsz in formation. In'visibility showing a'na y infinite micro-macro y eye'sz w'h'yde'ny'ing ring'za int'word a twis'ting in two. In'formation in a b c's of a b'ng c'ng out a complexity of a na y as eX's ting in'formation of protein variegation. A singular D"arkness enY'en erg'n't'wwww'ayeve roll'ment with quantum gravity weight wai'ting now with de'at'h'ay perceived charges the electromagnetic torus loop'y body to a're'y all'eye'ze a peering it out in a space in time awhile now in a y'll still a's z thoth'tsz of a y eye supernaturally as'ex's ting function'all'y y'all int'word a twisting in two eyez z z of D'NA eye'll . That paradox of now in any k'no'wing out of it that. A k'urving no'wing'ing around roles or rolls of complete d"ark'ness the'y stuff that black'g'round h'ay'as mass undetectable in'visibility potential emitting any thin'king of it or anybody. A're'yflecting out a black'g'round echoing of it in her'eyez z z eve'reybody in the'or'y the'n'a're'yabsorbs it. In the or y as x's ting. A Y a's eX. A y eye a peering it out now mirr'ored in word a's'ex'et'ting. Double Yod's still mere a Y eye am mirrored a's"ex'y'all. Pharaoh l'and a being c'ng still in the first place indivisible now supernaturally divided bi k'now'ing out of it as'z'any thoth'tsz of a Re'y'ed See in'g a word. In'visibility of a b c's of a b'ng c'ng mirrored re'y'ading it int'word mem or y now as'z'any thothtsz of it information. In a being c'ng in for'ma'ss'ze'r 0 twisting in t'wo 8. With that simple twist az's'eX'et'ting a duplicity of a y eye a peering it mirrored out int'word a twis'ting in two any D'NA'eye'll of it. Still a y eye being c'ng singular in'visibility a's'zee row/0 twis'ting a peering into mirrored appearing a pairing as h'8'ta. AY eye being c'ng still that indivisible invisibility of any individual. A being still in the first place awareness that eye of I am is is a peering it from above. Ove a b'ng c'ng free standing freed in a wordfreedom awareness of it.

"Yet in awhile then the en'y erg arises for'ma'sz appearing of it mirr'oring a black'g'round echo by sound wayeve're'y'sz z z of eve'reybody function. In her'wayeve'rey eye function a peering it out of it in a way'eve fun'ny'a'ction. AY eye a peering it out of it now appearing a pairing of it as eX's ting in'formation merely in the or y now any na'me. A y by ba'by by by still a b'ng c'ng of a y eye a peering it. Y"ll d'na denial occurring turning a black'g'round echo playing out az's'ex's ting infor'ma'sz complete roles of d"ark'n'ess'e perceived now to be of fools, d'na'tives, or slaves by denying out ar'king of it a y of a b c's a being c'ng it. That is int'word a twisting in two of one merely appearing a pairing of it in that simple singular twist of fate, faith, and family in any D'NA'eye'll of it. Understanding in the or y in word mem or y of a b c's spelling coded in any d'na'eye'll of it kicked into rolls or y as ex'planed or flattened out in x's ting fields of view of you of a y eye a peering it from above. Ove a b'ng y'll D'NA denial of a being in'still'ed in the first place first su'personic person that eye of I am is is still out of it in her'eyez z z of eve're'y"dhi'a'ting complete rolls or roles of dhi"ark'en'esse turning a black'g'round completely indivisible invisibility now with intent of ignoring it bi a k'no'no'no'wing out of it. Of'ten a bi na're'y of now turning out k'no no no'wing it into appearing of it out int'word information as'eX's ting still a mere or y.

"A'Re'y-awakening that dispels all in word complexity with its electromagnetic magnitude a're'y'absorbing y'all information. A black'g'round echoing into a un"consciousness a b'ng c'ng still indivisible spatial b'lack'g'round fabric of a space in time now awhile a un"manifest black wholly indivisible in'visibility infinitely out in word turning into rolls as'z'any potential roles as that one now as'king of it k'now'ing two twa twis'ting into genetic codes. Epigenetics allows gene on or off switching. K'no no no wing affirms genetic predisposition information by a being y'll d'na denial. A re'y'al'eye'zinging free freed in a wordfreedom of a y eye merely a peering it. A b'ng c'ng a peering it out at attention now time out. A supersonić wayeve echoing a black'g'round turning into or out of it anybody a mere or y memory mirrored eye of a b'ng c'ng now as'king of it any k'no'wing out of it int'word anythin'king of it. Or mean means meaning of a twin body between micro or macrocosmic appearing of it. As'king of it a k'nowing out of it any a na y body we all turn into a mirrored twin y. Y playing in word rolls or roles as'eX's ting. Free choice or y na now in a wordfreedom awareness of it."

Rakitin found his eyes crossing. Then drifting out over a city-scape. Escaping his in word thoughts he stretched the wings of perception as Mr. Warren had taught him. Lifting attention beyond the ring of fire of memory mind he felt that soaring out in a wordfreedom. How far can your micro macro awareness go in eye'there direction. Still in that blink of eye he found himself yet standing over Mr. Warren's silent corpse captivated in wordsz za scrolling overhead.

"How in the or y to synthesize this potential always remains potential in a y'or eye. It seems most of what is there is y or'y. Indivisible it cannot now be seen as other y's. Yet may be supernaturally supersonically superimposed now a k'now'n as'ex'acting out a duplicity in a wily while space in time. Any possible potential as'ex'planation of it is in the'or'y y'll d'na denial of y's inexplicability. So good luck with that substance that apparently appears of it as a no y mass seems akin to grabbing up a shadow under our own feet or making soup from the shadow of a crow. There is reason y you'are;y'all appearing of it only now time in space awhile as thought'sz a're'y'al'eye'zinging the're"y. Are'y only not now other y's as x's ting. Mere or'y as thoughtsz of it information. Y'sz dom'us of a b'ng c'ng still in the first place. Appearing of it out aY'll still a y eye of a b'ng c'ng a peering it from above."

Rakitin stepped across the thick carpet and leaned in to Mr. Warren in the wheelchair. The old man's desiccated fingers grabbed Rakitin's collar, fascia and tendons standing out beneath thin skin as Warren wheezed. For a moment Rakitin felt panic of choking on a heart expanding his chest.

"You...you are my hands."

"I am here and I will not fail you."

"May...Dios....Ra dios....Ra dios...she... ma y . . . y"Warren barked his last breath.

"You are the twenty-first century. The past in the present," Rakitin replied as he swept Warrens eyelids closed.

An acid vapor rose from Warren's oxydizing flesh. For a moment, Rakitin thought he was only sleeping until he touched the coldness of his bony shoulder. Mr. Warren was dead to the touch of any mere body. He glanced at the monitors and the vacant room with the crudely painted canvas on the easel. He flashed on Mr. Warrens words on chroma bodies of color transmitting his su'personic self-replicating ping'ting virus in a're'y'all a're'y'dhi'a'ting sublime color bands. How the artist Dark Mor used all the colors in his painting. How now his time had arrived.

"The ping-ting virus self-replicating in her'eyez z z'azz sound wayeves echoing a cosmic microwayeve instantaneous black'g'round to a supersonic cresendo dissolving ka's mic memory out in her'eyez z z'azz'leep into eve're'ybody disappearing b'lack invisibility." Mr. Warren had told him only days before his passing.

He clasped his gloved fingers behind his back. Floor length windows with linen drapes, hanging plumb, accented the angle of the pyramid walls. Forty-eight stories rose into the night. He stood in the penthouse with a 360-degree view of the city. Stars breaking out overhead as streets lit spread far below at his feet.

Warren had entrusted him with the code to the virus, a two-fold design with procedures for cyber and biological activation. Basically it meant the painting needed mass exposure. Mr. Warren had it endowed to the Metropolitan Art Museum to be hung strategically with a bicentennial of New Yorks most popular painter of the twenty first century Andre Peaceceeling. Attendence predicted to break eight million in six weeks. The pingting virus being supersonic will take it y'all back to black by an indivisible invisibility of a b'ng c'ng crossing in her'eyez z z'ion of eve're'ybody now a pingting'ing overall a indivisible black peh'ss'y w'hole power. A's She'e'na tearing black now any k'no'wing out of a b c's of a b'ng c'ng int'word a twis'ting in two appearing a pairing in formation. Rakitin glanced back at the overhead screen steadily humming with Mr. Warren's endless screed of evil witch Margot Christina Shaughnessy..

"Let ma a's the ma'ss's generate their own demise with every breath they take of it. Each and everybody will serve to enhance and replicate su'personically the electro-magnetic torus wheel turning we all black'g"round that simple singular a un'twisting of fate, faith, and family. A un'twis'ting of a b'ng c'ng in D'NA'eye'll. Fate of a b'ng c'ng turning into or now out of complete roles of d"ark'n'ess'e perceived now to be en'circled in wordsz'a black mirror see'asspelling of it. Of it turning a kurving any k'now'ing out of it a b c's of a b'ng c'ng now a b'lack'n'ess. Therefore necessitating a b'ng c'ng a gain. In that a be'gainning mirrored out as though a being lacking in D'NA'eye'll of its complete fullness. A b'lack' c'ng instilling de'sire. A divine father overstanding over'seer of ma'ss understanding ana'y a're;y'as b'lack' into or out of a b'lack g"round radiating radiance of any mirror see'as mind or y na now mirroring a na y imagined imaginary in word image. As'z thoth'tsz of a Great God esse now to be letter'all'y y'allsz z za space in time. The'y her'eyez z z'azz'leep into eve're'y'body D'NA'eye'll. A b'ng c'ng in a mirror str'ess'e potential now awhile d'na will facillitate instantaneous dissolution microcosmically untwisting any X's ting in formation of it."

"YYou are my second," he had told him. Rakitin had hoped Warren might call him comrade or brother, but his demeanor stayed cold until the end, only warming occasionally for an off color joke.

He'd smelt the acid vapor emanating from the old man for weeks. Sometimes Rakitin thought he was less alive than more dead. His voice then would rise like a bleak wind forced up from the grave through coarse dirt and rocks. The Warren will so strong against the disintegration of death had finally broken.

With the virus, he, Stephan Makarovich Rakitin, would take the masses out of the exodus. The New World Order, in a first place without borders and with limitless awareness in a wordfreedom. The petit bourgeois mystic Christina Shaughnessy talked in words of freedom yet took refuge at the university. Rakitin knew from his father's teaching she was a counter-revolutionary, her infinity politically suspect, her that I am, unknown in any quantity or quality. The true definition of an individual, his father had told him, was "the multitude of one million divided by one million." The reality of just one individual could only be relative and relatively invisible into one the'is'mass. The mass field of mankind worker wage slave serving Mr. Warren and his ilk now with Mr. Warren's viral self-replicating design mass slavery az's'eX'odus must disappear.

Walking around Warren's corpse, he breathed in his dissipation. Monitors showed the spoiled canvas, decadent art in the wooden jaws of the easel. Professor Shaughnessy had betrayed the people with her pursuit of religious knowledge. That painting looks decadent enough to express that betrayal, he mused. He was convinced that Mr.Warren's spawn was a traitor. Over fifteen years he'd been with the man, inside the maze he had created with Messing Technologies. Now the master demon had slipped away. Black into one great man'as mind or y if Rakitin heard it once, he heard a thousand times, the indivisible invisibility of any individual. Of any or everybody. He wondered what his father would make of that. 1,000,000 divided by 1,000,000.

The photograph of Christina Shaughnessy in Warren's lap smiled that inscrutable smile. Rakitin took the photo to the windows and held the print against the darkening sky. His thumbs slid over the glossy finish until the cotton brushed the contours of her cheekbone. He slipped a gold lighter from his vest pocket, holding a corner of the paper into the dance of flame. Orange tongues turned green when they tasted the developer, devouring her face.

Chapter 14

Mor listened to wind like a river in the sky carrying the roar of a 727 on approach to San Francisco International Airport.

"Korner broke down just before he got tasered," Kwasanda said as lights streamed across her face. "It's shocking to see a grown man cry like a baby."

"James is pretty cagey that way. Even he doesn't know if he's happy or sad. Then he has the background and firepower for dealing with assholes. What am I going to fight them with, a paintbrush?"

"I heaved Korner's satchel into the back seat. Check it out, Professor. There's a half dozen pistols and these cigarette pack size charges that Fawn said Korner used to blow up Enoch's house."

"Let's see what we have Professor. Pass it on up before anybody gets their panties in a knot." He opened the canvas bag and felt around until his fingers found a familiar shape. He sensed their eyes on him. "Okay. In that I am Korner, both as one programed to kill at the appropriate time." He let that hang for a long second, then burst out laughing. "I'm kidding. Here's his flask. This will piss him off. He always carries this as his good luck charm." He unscrewed the silver cap and drank.

Kwasanda glanced over as he pulled out the dented Altoids can. "Another charm?" she asked.

"This is Korner all over, thousands of dollars worth of coke in a fifty cent tin. Battling the bad guys calls for a pharmaceutical edge. Maybe I can help kick some Warren ass." He popped the lid on a tin packed with white crystal rocks. Quickly he broke one up between his fingers popping a chunk under his tongue. "You'll need a diversion otherwise you'll never get past the front door. I can activate the charges."

"Leave the charges in the satchel," Christina replied, laying a hand on Mor's shoulder

"Time for us to play it real cool."

"Hey, wait a damn minute. I don't have any pants," he exclaimed as though just waking up.

Kwasanda giggled. "Not to worry. Those are the sexiest knees I have ever seen on a white boy."

☼

Highway rolled out beneath the tires of the BMW past the false dawn of glowing airport lights. Mor imagined a pair of gray sweat pants Christina had found in the drawers under the mattress. He'd been too busy putting more pain't'azz color on canvass before they left and forgot to grab them.

"Good to be moving, though," he said, stretching the shoulder harness as he squirmed in the seat. "That warehouse had the charm of a tomb. Outside is all this manic energy hurtling by on wheels and wings. Who needs why? Don't ask me, I don't give a damn. Next stop is Vietnam. Hell, just join the fray with a good or bad pair of wheels." He could see Kwasanda picking up Christina's expression in the rear view mirror. Turning, he caught a trace of consternation around the mouth. But he was too old for a mama and had enough coke to make it to Venus herself. "I like your conundrum of no meaning y'es or nothing a'sz eve're'y thing. What makes Warren's virus so fascinating is the promise of release from the slavery of this subsistence karma."

"But is the cure worse than the illness? It still comes down to desire. With out the desire to find themselves free, many billions will suffer mightily," Christina replied as she played fingers on his scalp. "By educating, entraining, or entrancing a lineage of teachers then teaching other teachers ad infinitum we all may turn into awakening that desiring as'z two are'y'al'eye'zinging a indivisible y eye of a b'ng c'ng invisibility of a peering it. Now out int'word. a liberation in word'all'y discerning a b c's of a b'ng c'ng y'all still indivisible in'visibility. Captivated awhile now appearing of it a chintzy measly thin'king of it out int'word a twis'ting in two a twin'"eye of a being c'ng as'ex's ting in formation. In de"sire a peering it from above now out of her'eyez z z'ion eve're'ybody. That de"sire is pa"roo"ma'sz eye'star'e"y"e'ing it out as'ex a're'y'dhi'a'ting herhimit yo you," she'ena finished the sentence whispering close in to him to h'ear"it

"The question you asked at your lecture on, 'feeling being alone?' Who doesn't know that feeling? Just never had that simultaneous thought of feeling it as awareness of a b'ng c'ng now indivisible." Y'all a talkin' to yourself any which ol'way Mor mused. Simply a feeling fielding of a b'ng c'ng as somebody or anybody appearing of a b c's merely in name alone. Merely a chintzy chiselin thin'king of it he chuckled to himself. As'king of it in a wordfreedom limitless indivisible invisibility of a paramasukhadum pa'roo'ma pharaoh Akh'et"aten. A domain of it still in the first place now reduced in word to a pathetic bent crippled thin king of it he shuddered. A feeling fielding a being c'ng a peering it out alone as a hard felt in word field of view. Of you now appearing out of it supernaturally supersonically superimposed as'z'any thoth'tsz of a Great God'esse. To be letter'all'y y'all a b c's of a b'ng c'ng of a herhimit yod you now out in a k'no'wing d'na'eye'll of it. Y'all that eve'n in denial of it. It in'visibility out in her'eyez z z'ion eve're'ybody. With de'sire a peering it from above. Ove a b'ng c'ng in a complete indivisible in'visibility. Now it seems to me that it is so true how we all positively turn away from that feeling of being alone. The more y'all feelin' alone the more y'all realizing that indivisible invisibility. Awareness of that in a wordfreedom serves no function yet there is no function without that awareness of it he thought. Awayeve in word fun'ction junction with in a wordfreedom awareness of it. A y eye merely a peering it out now a k'no'wing d'na'eye'll intword a twis'ting in two appearing a pairing of it in her eyez z z of eve're'ybody. We all a wheel turning into and out of ignoring it awhile. A contagious cruel callous deceit as'z'any space in time now appearing then disappearing.

"She'e'na takin it y'all black'g'round a'sz'any fun'ny action Jack'sun." Kwasanda kept cracking herself up with the dialectic surely virally enhanced through the pingting of the painting residue on his skin and clothes. Mor felt a profound enhancement merely int'word doing some bad'aszz coke. With trouble surely waiting just us around the Korner.

Still a being in the first place he wondered. Moving at 70 mph motionless compared with 500'000 mph of our only sun turning burning a black'g'round ar'king of it's ka's mic galactic a'whorlding center. Billions burning churning nuclear fire jetting out into that ka's mic blackness. H'our only son. A sol'ar eye a peering it from above as below out in na da y light. A peering it a're'y'fracted int'word appearing of it. A black'g'round echoing a're'y'asz now a k'now'ing out of it anybody or any wanting withered thin'king of it. Still. A being in the first place. Appearing of it out awhile in that deception at attention captivated in word in eL fun"c'tion. Of awhile now. The long or short of it. A mean b tween any greater or lesser of it.

How far or how fast can that still awareness go go go'a he wondered. We all a turning churning yearning burning out of a b"lack'g'round de'sire echoing in a b c's of a b'ng c'ng a gain. That still. Stillness in a wordfreedom awareness of a b'ng c'ng alone eve'n y'll winging d'na'eye'll of it. Out of it any in word betrayal informing it awhile appearing with out or as'z'z'any desire to realize why y'all you in the first place he mused.

Come on baby, light my fire of de'sire as'ex y'all. Break the chains understanding that in word spell by a being y'all we'ilding that debateable way of Y'or y speak in the first place. Y you're you or me still indivisible merely a measly thin'king of a b c's of a b'ng c'ng now a k'now'ing out other y's. How on earth is that possible in a being c'ng in'visibility awhile of anybody now a b c's merely appearing in wordsasz though two or more ignoring one still a being alone in the first place. That I am a mean means meaningful of it in a wordfreedom awareness aware of a b'ng c'ng in a mere mirrored twin b'ng'tween macro-micro ka's mic memory y'll d'na. "Yet here we all turn around completely enveloped in the engineering mind it takes to move anybody at this velocity," he offered out loud

"Not to mention the cocaine," Kwasanda shot over as she made a lane change.

"Not to mention that. But, come on, we all must turn out of an awesome power to put aside cars and highways, not to mention planets and stars y'all existing as somethings other. As if holding it y'all away in a bubble space in time now awhile int'word a twis'ting in two away from a being indivisible still in the first place. Still feeling of it alone. Just the idea of a being separate somehow when in fact we all turn together on this vast planetary system completely engulfed in one cosmic galactic quantum soup. Whose idea was it of appearing out in word a'sz though'tsz of a b'ng c'ng separately in some arbitrary name. Maybe the effects of Warren's virus will be like embracing an old friend a twin who seems asz too been missing. The virus might gather us in closer to awareness of our true purely indivisible invisibility by dissolving our in word a b c's illusions of a b'ng c'ng a'sz thoughtsz of appearing in a word separate."

"Very touching. That's the thing about being indivisible, that touchy feely thing seems to refute a being of that," Kwasanda interjected.

"That y'all have that sense of a b'ng c'ng touched touching now instantaneously anybody or thing within reach only possible as'z in her'eyez z zap'ping indivisible in'visibility asz a black'g'round mirror echo. A're'y'dhi'ance a're'y'dhi'a'ting eve're'y body as'z z z'any instantaneous touching spell." Christina offered from the black seat behind Kwasanda's head. "A're'y'membering y'all supersonically as'z'ex'per'eye'en'c'ng merely a peering it out mirrored y na you now as'z'any body in a b c's of a being c'ng still indivisible in'visibility. Any touching of a b'ng touched possible as'z a b c's mirr'ored supernaturally as'z thoth'tsz of you now out as'z"ex'u'all felt feelings'z z z'azz'any field of view of you. Any touch is as'z though contact now potentially possible by a b'ng c'ng at attention captivated supernaturally with in word divisions as'z'any thoth'tsz of a b c's int'word a twis'ting in two appearing a pairing of the indivisible in'visibility. As'z'any fire're'y per'sonic impulse of thoth'tsz neuronically transmitted into sensation of a b c's of a being c'ng learned mathe'ma'tically y'all. Anybody. Anybody appearing of it now from a rigorous study of a b c's conceived symbolically by a ka'no'wing that black'g'round echo of it now out in her eyez z z'azz'leep off a k'now'ledge in one eve're'ybody."

Mor now studied Kwasanda's expression. He still wasn't quite sure if Christina's voice came as'z sound wayeves in a space in time or a mere echo of it. Was he learning it in words or picking it up in a wordfreedom awareness of it. In other wordsz still at aten'cion indivisible invisibility in a wordfreedom now turning it b'lack'g'round echoing out supersonically asz a k'now'ing of it in a b c's of a b'ng c'ng out'word a twis'ting in two memory of me or you. Kwasanda's expression remained implacable except for a smile playing the corners of her lips.

Now it seemed to him we all turn into or out of any a na y body in a're'y'all out in her'eye'z z zazz'a eve"re'y body experienced directly falling as'z z z'leep black into a singular indivisible invisibility in a y eyez zion potential a peering it in a un"con"sciousness. A con she us now to be eve're'y'body learned to be anybody. As'z a b c's of a b'ng c'ng still in'visibility indivisible. Now a black'g'round echoing b'lack'body with a peh'ss'y w'hole power of intent int'word a twisting in two intentionally disregarding a b'ng c'ng still indivisible. A disregard of k'no no no'wing it out in a d'na'eye'll in a b c's of i it in'visibility indivisible from above as'z below still in the first place. Y'all that appearing a pairing of it now mere supersonic mirroring power of k'now'ing it out asz thoth'tsz of it echoing a space in time awhile. Echoing sound vigorous supersonic wayeves out as'z'any thoth'tsz of it in a y eye of her'him'it a peering it now out in her'eyez z z' of a way'eve re' y black'g'round body. A'na'ybody in complete roles of d"ark'ness. Perceived ar'king of it a y eye turning to perceive a na y'now a scrawny emaciated thin'king of it merely as'z thoth'tsz of a God'esse to be letter'all'y y'all. That letter'all covenant with a God esse. To be in her eyez z z'leep back. A're'y turning into a wayeve're'yz z z a black'g'round body echoing you as'ex or a y now appearing of it out in word. Experiencing touch is mere' y'or y now understanding any spelling of a b c's mirrored y na you now as'z thoth'tsz of a bio's electric neuronic wayeve function of that ka's mic black eve're'ybody micro wayeveing a black'g"round echo as'z touched of it.

Mor perceived Christina disappearing black into one indivisible black'g'round awareness of a b'ng c'ng now a're'y"e a peering it out in word supernaturally as thoth'tsz of a k'no'wing of anybody. Then in that pre'verbial blink in her'eyez z z'ion int'word a twis'ting in two appearing a pairing of it that k'no'wing echo rippled out on sound wayeves z'so familiar to his y'ears in word memory. Thus it now seemed we all turn into or out of it'y'ears hearing any one sense of the world purely in wordsz'sounds of it. It seeming now to Mor we all turning a k'nowing out the world int'word a twis'ting in two by a positive denial of a b'ng still indivisible. A bi now projecting it as'z thoth'tsz letter'all'y y'all a k'no'wing out a b c's echoing of a b'ng c'ng indivisible in'visibility. A D'NA'eye'll of it int'word that simple twisting in two. A duplicating of it by fate faith or family.

"Be fully a're'y'all'ity as'king of it y or any measly chintzy thin'king of it." Christina added with a laugh. Mor caught the double entendre as'king of it turning now into a k'nowing out of it any wanting thin"king of it. Still it a y eye a peering it out as'king of it y a ka's mic memory int'word understanding a b c's supersonic supernatural spelling of it. Now a k'no'wing out of it into appearing of it from above. Ove a b'ng c'ng turning in word out as'z'any thoth'tsz of it. Now out superimposed as'z'any k'no no no'w'ing of it projecting a black'g'round echo. Echoing na da y light igniting ignore'ance of a being still in the first place. Thus that spelling may only be broken in word'all'y y'all by de'lOOk'a da b'OO'ka. Libertad por el libro. By realizing it merely a peering it at wordsz of a b c's yet aware of awareness in a wordfreedom. We all in still turning a b'lack'g'round awayeve of D'NA'y'll from realizing y'or it now must k'no'w a're'y'all turning it in two a'gain. As'z thoth'tsz into or out of a b c's in forming it in word. Now turning out of it any k'nowing out of it in her'eyez z z awhile. A black'g"round supernatural supersonic magic in word spell.

"That uncanny spell of d'na'eye'ing or k'no no no'wing a b'ng'lack necessitating a b'ng a gain.

"Denying anybody being black?" Kwasanda queried with frown.

"A blackness d'na'eye'll as'ka's of a b'ng c'ng a gain. Only to lose. Dust to dust. Back to black. A blackness. A black'g'round mirror see'as'z of it. A b'ng'lack now intent to be a'gain. "

"Into or out of a black'g'round diamond dust," Kwasanda interjected smiling with spiralling locks of hair jet'ting from her scalp. Mor surmised the greater gods influence in their affairs. Their metaphoric crossing eve's now that h'our's eyez z zion that imaginary li'on. Int'word a un'twis'ting un'two one in a wordfreedom awareness of it. It a b'ng still indivisible invisibility asz' awareness of it he now intuited. He nearly choked up on the sheer bliss finding yourself lost in a wordfreedom still awhile now functioning as'z male counterpart between a pairing of femmes fatale.

"Or picking up on a b'ng c'ng complete in the first place. Y'all along." Mor now found himself in a y eye memory mind opening unfolding its wings of perception. Soaring black'g'round a y eye potential in her'eyez z z of eve're'ybody. Now turning a black'g'round echo k'no no no'wing out of it in na da y light igniting fier'ey supernatural thoth'tsz. AB'EL as'z int'word tattwama'sz'ya'dhilaksham. In a're'y'all t'win"d'ing that simple singular 0 as'ex 8"twist. Of'ten. A ten bi'na're'y'eszz'a one e'zee'ro appearing as two int'word a twis'ting in formation. A b'ack'g'round echo appearing in two a pairing still indivisible.

AD'AMem'or'y eyez z z of EVE're'ybody a black'g'round now as'king of it a la que"en que' of that in which appearing supernaturally as'z'any thoth'tsz of a God esse letter'all'y y'all a man'as mind mem or y in word na'mes. My not'me is Dark'n'ess'e he thought. How it seems we all come to think of ourself in a denial by a b'ng c'ng in na'me alone. Now that denial still as indivisible in'visibility a be'ng c'ng a peering it in the first place. A supersonic A'tom'ic being c'ng a peering it now out in her eyez z z'azz'a k'now'ing of any or eve're'ybody. A black'n'esse's now to be a being c'ng as'king of it y a k'now'ing out of it out int'word. A Y'll will of D'NA. Eve will of d'na'eye'll. Mor now came black disappearing into the whole point of view of you of a y eye in'visibility of a b'ng c'ng a"peering it out int'word a twis'ting in two of it in'for'ma'ss anybody still in the first place yet now as'z'any thothtsz of appearing out of it. The will waiting black'g'round a quantum gravity weight of waiting for'ma'sz now death.

Dhi'a'th of a being c'ng to perceive that. A'RE'A'Mr. re'y'al'ity as'king of it y now a ka'now'ing turning out of or into it any bare thin'king of anybody. Out in a na y'body. The Y'll of d'na'eye'll in a y eye of a her'him'it with a polarity in the one hand. Still freestanding eye a peering it from above as below. A peering it out in na da y light on the other hand. Shining into complete dhi ark'n'esse to be now perceived ar'king of it a're'y'al"ity"inka's pow'er of it in her eyez z z'a black peh'esse'y whole power as'ex"peh're'esse'ing egg's'ting information. Now turning in two a k'now'ing out of it in her'eyez z z of eve'rey body appearing of it a black'g'round echo of it. The o'peh'na hand offering any potential of a pairing in mem'or'y of a polarity in the other he wondered. Painting Christina now indivisible in'visibility of a ping'ting. A sounding board a's supersonic silent singing sound. Vigorously sounding silent in formation played on wayeve a're'y'sz z z. Eve a're'y'asz z z'a body of anybody as'ka'm'ing echoing a black'g'round. A black'g'round in her voice rippling as ka's mic mic'ro way'eve'ing black'g'round echoing it out in her'eyez z z of eve're'ybody turning a black'g'round into or out of itself alone. Indivisible in a b'ng c'ng in'visibility of anybody he mused on the nature of a painting as a ping'ting.

"Warren's viral storm will be another experience. Another wily denial as'z'ex per eye in c'ng int'word it as'z t'wo a b'ng c'ng 'still one that now mirrors a b c's in formation. Int'word a ka'now'ing out of it anybody az's'ex's ting. In'formation. Any mean'while. As'z'any means of meaning information of a wily deceit of a b c's of a b'ng c'ng still indivisible invisibility. A's'ex'tended int'word a twis'ting of indivisibility supernaturally y'all as'z'any thoth'tsz of it appearing a pairing y'll d'na. A d'na'eye'll of it facing an y mirrored of it out in as'ka's mic memory y na fate, chance, fortune, destiny from the'eye star'e'y"e or y story of it a peering it out in word now. As'k'a'nowing of it as'ex's ting information out in a wily while of a b'ng c'ng in'visibility of a' peering it out. In'visibility in the'or'y of a space in time of stars constellations galaxies or viral worms." Christina spoke from the heart of the matter. Mor sensed it. Felt the sound vigorous wayeves of it in her'eyez z z in word spell that seemed to break itself up coming out through a shimmering electric field of view. Of her'm'e'as'thoth'tsz of it in for'ma'ing you of memory. Now time Ma she'ena dancing na da y light. Pa'roo'Ma. He watched the light streaming out of Kwasanda's eyes. A visceral visual electric ignition of her'incognito.

"What about God? Won't He or She'e'na have something to say in all this?" Mor asked as he crushed a thumbnail sized rock sprinkling it on wounded knee. "Mind if I turn on the radio?" he asked, rubbing the crystal rock powder into traces of blood oozing through layers of gauze. He stared transfixed by the stream of lights ahead flashing red and blinking yellow. Fresh reflector stickers zoomed by alongside rows of orange cones and irridescent yellow vested highway workers.

"Yeh, see what you can find on the radio," said Kwasanda, glancing over as he tapped some buttons. "Why do white Americans love the blues?"

"Blues don't know color, baby. Except being blue. But I hear what you're saying. I think the drug laws made outlaws of a lot a regular white folks. They got a little taste of life on the wrong side of what is accepted. Korner and I jumped over there. He found himself a sanction for his sinning. I stumbled into it. Got lucky. Found my self lost as'z a complete being. A being not to be possessed. Not a being possessing me." His speech halted as he realized the sisters weren't listening. They seemed attuned in silence. He punched through the radio band until he found some jazz and blues. A Wolf' growled from the speakers. A voice 'like a hurricane through a straw'. A gut bucket cry that could only come from a Black man in nineteen forties America. Jim Crow's apartied America of strange fruit hanging. Wolf brought the loners and losers together. Mor rolled his fists with the downbeat. Wolf freed his primal juice. He could feel it bubbling up, as he gulped for air.

Callin' me on my telephone

I'm so woorried

Tell 'em I'm not at home."

"You can wrap the human spirit in chains, toss us into the deepest pit, and still we rise," he howled into the wind.

"Okay, you old hippie hound dog, we's in the twenty first century now. Here, man gave me this disc a while back. Said I'd know when to play it so here goes."

"So, who, is this on the disc?" he asked as Kwasanda slipped a CD into the slot.

"Don't ask. No time to explain. Just listen," she said, adjusting the volume as she gave him a sideways glance.

"Okay, that's some opera in Italian I believe," she said, popping the disc back out. Holding it up to the light she saw some writing in felt tip marker. "Here, you read that." Kwasanda tossed him the disk. "She asleep back there?"

"Asleep or meditating, you can't tell, unless she's snoring. Verdi's Aida. It's about a man who loves a slave girl and as a result is betrayed by a jealous princess," he replied with a shrug.

"Put it back in. Maybe there's more to it." She tapped her fingernails on the top of the steering wheel. "You know the story?"

"Slave girl and jealous princess fight over virile army captain? Uh, yah, sounds familiar," he replied as a mezzo soprano tore lose with anguish.

"Slave girl and princess," Kwasanda wondered out loud as she lowered the volume. Highway 101 crested the broad slope of Potrero Hill. The skyline of downtown San Francisco, sparkled through its evening silhouette. The truncated tip of the Pyramid pointed to heaven above North Beach rooftops.

"Are we moving too fast?" he asked, turning in his seat. Christina's eyes flashed with the headlights pouring past.

Kwasanda exited the freeway at 5th and King. As they stopped at a light, he surveyed blocks of future high-rise condos, now skeletons of two by eight fir lumber framing around mats of re-bar, invading gentrifying a once decrepit low rent part of town. Their lane made three green lights as they reached a corridor of cottonwood trees with broad leaves colored with light candy. Through a stand of palms in front of Oracle Park, he watched baseball's Willie Mays forever dropping his bat behind crouched bronze legs. Eyes following an invisible chunk of rawhide sailing beyond the fences. Columns of light taunted the shadows that drifted out to the lattice of green steel light towers above the red brick walls.

Beyond the stadium, their view opened as they passed under the Bay Bridge. Spanning open water, parallel suspension cables dipped stretching out between black and silver towers marching to Treasure Island. Then on to Oakland. Mor remembered this area before the Loma Prieta earthquake brought the Central Freeway down, breaking the concrete yoke choking the waterfront.

"Hard to believe that of tons of concrete and smog buried this waterfront for thirty years. Now you can actually see that clock tower of the Ferry Building. What a shame it was hidden by elevated freeway for decades. Such a great landmark. A lone waterfront survivor of the 1906 earthquake its thee last still standing intact landmark in many of the old photos of the leveled city. A ferry gateway to the city. I mean, think about it. Before the bridges, ferries were the only approach from the north or east. This building was thee landing place for most anyone heading here. Gateway to ferry world. San Francisco, feel her chill breath, this stained saint," he said as he poked his head out. "She gave us dreams. Dreams of solving her mystery. I remember wandering up and down her streets till many a sunrise. Pounding them seven hills. Seven sisters now barely breathing thru y'all this steel and concrete. With enough bone chill and exhaustion you can hear 'em. The sisters. Whispering in the fog, dancing up those skyscraper corridors then falling back down to the Bay. Korner is here. I can feel him." Mor jerked in his seat, pushed against the door, then went back to scanning the rear in the sideview mirror. Lights came up as day fled into night. Or is it bled into night Mor wondered.

They approached the Ferry Building, a farmer's market enlivening its interior. Out front a double concourse of royal palms spread fifty feet above four lanes of car and truck traffic split by a trolley line. Antique iron cars packed with commuters, tourists, and transients rumbled past.

"Do you see his car?" Kwasanda asked.

"Only me rambling. I'd be more scared except I'm buzzing with his Cuervo and cocaine. Look here at how people carry on their mundane lives like nothing is happening. Maybe nothing is happening. Some are so bent with the weight and others look like they could sail off. Throw off your shackles, brothers and sisters. Saint Francis will set you free." He dipped another rock and another swig from the flask.

"Slow down, painter," said Kwasanda. "The Pyramid is only a few blocks from here. Christina, you and Dark stay with the car while I check out the security."

"I have to go. He wants me. Best to meet the tiger head on," she replied. "I will deal with Warren and you look out for Korner."

Blobs of fogged light blurred the evening street. Kwasanda pulled to the curb. Headlights streamed in the rearview mirror as she turned in the seat, pulling a cell phone from her pocket. Christina leaned forward puting arms over Mor's shoulders. "I don't believe you," she whispered in his ear.

"This will only call me. Just tell us when and where to enter, and good luck," Kwasanda said, pressing the phone into the Professor's hand.

Christina stepped from the BMW. "Keep each other safe," she replied. He watched her walk toward the lobby doors and into the radiance of honey-colored interior. "For then I would have to let you go," he muttered under his breath. In the sideview mirror, he saw a sleek blazered security agent with thick mustache approach their vehicle, the bulk of a handgun pressed under his navy blue blazer.

"Into the embrace of the father and the lair of the beast." Kwasanda replied as she pulled away from the curb.

"Would have to be that building," he said, craning his neck. "I just can't help feeling this connection with the Illuminatus vision that had me only a few blocks from here. A pyramid. The only modern pyramid skyscraper in the world. It's spooky, no pun intended"

Kwasanda kept her eyes on the street. Headlights drifted in and out of her mirrors. "No spookier than that disc."

"The Verdi? You still got that slave girl and the betrayal on your mind?"

"Hell, I don't know. Watching her stroll inside, I kept getting this nagging sensation. Like I should get out while the getting is good?" she said, waiting for a light.

"May the Saint protect you both, but I want you to protect me," he replied. "I know that's selfish of me, you with a daughter and maybe you should run. Just get out. These blocks are falling anyway. Why get crushed underneath?"

"You really think she'll betray us?" Kwasanda spoke, followed by a long silence.

They drove west on Washington Street. Through the crowded avenues near Portsmouth Square, people drifted in waves broken by slow moving vehicles. Mor fingered the plastic CD case. A sharp metallic taste made him drop it on the floor. A spread of wings filled his vision. His focus drawn into a disc glowing with red light out of the center of his head moved to its outline propped on the coiled tails of a pair of hooded serpents that turned towards him. The image scrolled on with borders of hieroglyphs, interspersed with gods and goddesses of the Egyptian pantheon. These images, men with heads of jackals rams dogs and ibis'z'zahawks seared his inner mind. Now he found himself a seer see'ng in the eye a peering it still a b'ng c'ng indivisible invisibility. A y eye of a b'ng c'ng of that awareness, that A'eye'Am is is the ser be'er, that of one who sees in her'eyez z z foreve'rey being still y'all. Yet a na't'eve'rey now a'wayeve mirrored black'g'round k'now'ing of it then. Out in word to be seen supernaturally as'z'any thoth'tsz of it in'formation. Eve're'ybody of a being that indivisible seer. A b'ng c'ng invisibility of anyone who sees a peering it out of it. Yet as'z'any thoth'tsz of fielding that felt awhile body. Now as then a're'y"all turning black and blue in the sweet melancholy of it in her'eyez z z' singing the sad song. Y'all night long. Holding her to let her go. Of a'gaining in love only to lose in death. The better bittersweet of it. A little while of it can go a long ways. Now out of it a black'g'round as'king of it a k'nowing of the dialectic Mor found himself that in a b'ng c'ng in a wordfreedom awareness. A free dom'us still in the first place indivisible invisibility of any individual.

"When we all turn into a black'g'round as'z z z'leep black into a un'con she us now esse to be anybody out in'formation," he found himself suddenly wide awake. "We'a're'y'membering ourselves, aren't we all turning supernaturally into or out of a being indivisible in'visibility? Something about her'eyez z z'ion eve're'ybody. A're'y'all. Still a being in her'eyez z z invisibility of eve're'y body." He could not now say her name. Blood pounded in his ears. He took another drink. "We're close. Pull over here."

Kwasanda wheeled to the curb. Pedestrian traffic thickened, watched over by the quartsite skin of a skinny Pyramid soaring above Chinatown's squat three to five story stucco apartment buildings. The apartments stacked up over street level businesses staggering down an incline toward the Bay. They parked at the upper end of Portsmouth Square, by a pagoda of traditional Chinese architecture of stacked curving tiles with hand carved posts and lintels. Tourists milled about. To the east, the spire of the Pyramid pulsated with an interior light.

"Feel it, baby. We be at ground zero of the 'forty nine to be fine' Gold Rush. The 'rush of it. Y'all the dreams. The eruption of Pacific Rim power. A hundred fifty years ago, this wan't nothing. A battleship, the SS Portsmouth sailed right up within two blocks of this plaza. Then just a few cowhide and tallow warehouses and modest pueblos on the hillsides up there. A meager hundred folks living here. I mean this spot wasn't y'all that fit for habitation, y'all foggy chill wind swept sand dunes, salt and rock. Then, some cat gets up on a packing crate with a bottle full of nuggets, yelling, 'Gold!'

"This here, went to Vegas, almost overnight. These hills got rocking, this here plaza got filled y'all around with tent saloons and gambling parlors. Before y'all could say 'jumpin' jack flash' the streets were awash from buckskin to beaver. Everybody packing plenty of iron. Listen. You can still hear that tinkle of honky-tonk pianos. See shadows dancing off kerosene lamps all yellah shining thru the sailcloth walls torn from hundreds of abandoned ships. It took a couple fires burning it y'all back down till folks got serious about building something more substantial. Just a few blocks east a forest of wooden masts of abandoned ships stacked up in the harbor. The dang harbor was right there lapping the shoreline where that Pyramid is now. Quick as a heartbeat or two, that harbor was full of three four hundred sloops and square riggers abandoned where they lay anchor. Sailors pouring off to head for the gold mountain." he said, nursing the flask. "Abandoned for gold and that irresistible spirit of anything being possible, good or bad. A man could get his throat cut as easily as taking a leak. I'm telling you? You're thick with the red cat."

"The red cat?"

"She comes in my dreams. The queen of the kingdom of nature sinks her teeth into my vulnerability," he rambled. "She likes to bite my fingers cause I'm not using them to paint."

Kwasanda sighed. "I'm finally coming down from my ride in RJ's egg. Keep talking so I don't drift off, even though you ain't making a bit of sense to me right now. But keep talking."

"Is it y'all just show and go, pussy and payday? Honky tonk Yerba Buena harbor covered now with a thin shiny modern veneer of a civil polite society? But underneath boiling with the despair or debauchery of Barbary Coast brothels, innocent children sold into sex slavery? I've seen photos. Mostly Chinese, some still little girls of five or six put to work cleaning and hauling till they be old enough to hump for the coin.They got used up and dumped like garbage. China still hates us for the depravity and racism even though it was mostly they own people did the buying and selling. Some came without names, just numbers with a sex between their legs. So many chewed up in the crush of the rush. That's why Chinatown's so close to the harbor. Someone asked why they didn't build right on the dock. Spare horny miners having to walk the few blocks uphill to spill their brains.

"It seems to me like we all turn into living on the meager edges of a hollow body caught between despairing disappearing down a hole or black out into cosmic dust. Feeling a being alone. Imagine the sheer despair of a Chinatown sex slave. Teen age girl staring out a barred window like convicts later on Alcatraz island. Captive in a tiny cell surrounded by a haoly baying. There of course were some who came of their own free will to capitalize on a frenzy of horney gold laden johns. In the early 'rush' there were virtually no other females on the peninsula and no males over twenty five. Then Madame Bho Zou. Came. Started doing business in a tent with cot. It was said Bho Zou was of such beauty men would pay just to see her naked. Eventually she owned the richest bordello in Chinatown and the barbary coast.

"Feelin' it, baby. Being there on the thin edge of our man on the street level. A desperation of any separation. Feeling it. Fielding it. Why. Or why the fuck not. Honestly I don't know why but I do absolutely know why the friggin frack na. This impossible life of dust to dust is a daily mind-fuck. Who really needs a woman when y'all got a mind wondering why to fuck you up or why be fucked beyond the obvious procreative biological craziness. Loneliness is a mind-fuck. That delicious suspicious melancholy. That'sz me indulging in adolescent fantasies and lacking suffient drawing time to cool the jets. A y eye a peering it in a wordfreedom awareness behind or beyond the troubles of the mind. Boo who." He fingered the Altoids tin. He wanted more coke but knew he was already nearly off the rails. But then, what the fuck when you're holding the stash of a lifetime on that night of nights.

Streams of people passed, none looking their way. He watched tourists mining Grant Street shops for curios not found at the neighborhood flea market going on across the street. There the locals were out mixing in with tourists. Still Mor felt a dying in this China man town. China man, black man, brown it don't go down long staying jammed into the ghetto by exclusionary racist laws. He thought that man like any man seethes with feeling freedom to spread further out. To get out of crowded narrow streets, packed in without a tree or blade of grass. He flashed on himself trudging miles of mountain trails falling off down into ravines and creeks hidden in bush or forest. Open country to roam free. Not short steps in bleak alleys cramped into stale boxes breathing passed gas. What man wouldn't long to escape any such artificial confinement. To expand a being of anybody beyond borders. Beyond boundaries. A beyond any limitation of that, I am sure any body might desire, he mused. That expansion along with gentrification now left this 3/4 island city an overpriced mecca for fat cat day trading money lenders and nostalgic trap for tourists. Artists, workers, and regular people on the street squeezed out to rent inflated generic cheese boxes sprawling in mind-numbing tracts across bridges east, and north or freeways south. She now a trap. But still a good trap. Maybe always she be a trap, he thought. Father Juniper Serra trapped the natives in an adobe mission. They built their own prison then died in and on it. Then gold trapped tens of thousands more. Kali ma. She ate her children and wore their sculls as a necklace dancing around her turning eve'll body. Turning into eve're'y body. Still invisibility appearing in any image imagined. Her stuff of imaginative possibilities. He imagined it in her'eye now k'now'ing out of it anything or anybody. Enchanted by she'e'na a voice once as chanteuse and now oracle. Y'or y her or her. He loved her still as he would having been a being there then. As he would will it out of a being c'ng out in her'eye here now.

"Charles, my late husband talked a lot like you. He was the blackest man I ever met. I mean his skin was coal-tar black. If anybody should have been named the Darkness, it was him. Still his features belied ancestry going back to south Arabia, to a Semitic tribe called the Sheba,"

"Shee'na,"he offered, finding his voice coming out with a life of its own.

"Solomon and Sheba"

"Sol"a'mon. . .sorry I find myself caught in a portable time machine, now in her"e ye ma'shee'na.. . . her black ma'ss of eve're'y body." Mor leaned over to touch her cheek with his lips. Air electric, the fire of her crackled with static sparks jumping the gap from a y eye of her'him'it. A being alone in the first place indivisible a peering it in'visibility turning a black'g"round now out with intent of mirrored in word k'now'ing out of it any appearing a'gain.

"You be back to black your own self. I feel your black heart beating in my black chest. The Darkness." She gave him a longing in her eyes.

"As'z only a black african'a woman can appreciate it. Y'all really appear as too become your name. In that name I am finding prejudice against the darkness more primal than any other. The 'dark' side of a being that y'all thinking of things evil, malevolent, sinful. I've had mor'e than a few duped christian mon telling me I should change mine. I tell him as much most bad shit happens in the light. It's as'z z z'leep back to black in the soaking darkness we all turn back into her'eyez z z of eve"re'y body. We all turning into or out of a"re'y y'all. Ma Eve a're'y'dhi'a'ting as'eX's ting. Now a wily while appearing a b'lack as'z'any ar'k'urving t'word a be'ng gaining only as'z too, a'sz z'any two twy'is'ting black'g'round supernaturally as thoth'tsz in formation. Always as too lose back to black ja'h'ck'y. Sorry to run on but the professor got me good y'all with her in word boo'g'ee'e 'ya' woo'ji time machine now ma'shee'na as'king of it k'now'ing out of it anybody.

"Ma she'e'na has colonized my mind. Or y na you now. It may be the professor is a duped catalyst of Warren's virus. He manufactured it into the paint that I am virtually inhaling back there in the warehouse. It seems to be a viral code that reverses a polarity in word'all'y y'all by an electro-magnetic supersonic dialectic on Y'or y speak debate. Once infected by the supersonic ping'ting any speaker begins speaking echoing it as you have been hearing. Sorry about that.

But in that I am finding a certain blissful intoxication. Transfering my attention black into a being still indivisible in'visibility. From of such a b'ng c'ng appearing out at attention captivated in a word spell of a y as'ex's ting in'formation. As'z'any in formation of a b'ng c'ng it appearing awhile must be a deceitful duplicity in any in word name in memory y'll d'na. Any denial of a being c'ng still that formless free freed freedom in the first place. A free being c'ng in formation in'visibility still a being indivisible in the first place. That's'za's the story of you nee verse of phonographic a b c's in the eye star'e ye in any ordinary or extraordinary in word sight."

"Bingo baby. Bing go go go. About that I am also enraptured by my time a being still within the great God'esse to be without wordsz. RJ's pod put me in an outer space in time of a being now turning out of a k'now'ing it beyond the personic h'earthly parameters of my ancestry as well as my late husbands. No easy thing considering our ancestry covers thousands of years. His semetic ancestry goes back to Solomon and Sheba's heirs who integrated with the native Negroes. In their tradition they claimed Sheba as an Ethiopian queen. Also called a la Magda, she courted King Solomon and returned bearing the King's son, David, the first king of Ethiopia. Thats a whole lot'ta blood to get beyond. Still in y'all that I am finding myself even now in ordinary sight free free free of a being seen in formation in the sheer mirror duplicity of any in word appearance now or k'now'ing out of it in the past collective memory. It's now that I am finding myself still a being indivisible in'visiblity. There is no better way to express why that I am appearing making any appearance out of it awhile in the first place. The sheer queer duplicity in any eye mirroring a b'ng c'ng out in word is a y only reflecting as'ex'acting like that projected on it. In that first place still a being c'ng indivisible in'visibility that I am now k'now'ing out of it awhile. A deceit of merely appearing by a being c'ng mirrored out of it in word. In my or any mind mirroring a y eye a peering now turning into then k'now'ing out of it in word in mem'or'y. That's making me curious'er and curious'er about the sense of touch," she spoke leaning in to meet his eyes and caress his lips with hers.

"With a being c'ng eye of the herhimit alone. The indivisible hermit is in the eye of the beholder. Professor gave me a book awhile back on the letter keys to the 3D cube of a b'ng c'ng in space informed as alphabeta time ma'shee'na. It tells y the sense of touch is attributed to herhimit. In the'or'y of a y eye potential the herhimit a peers with polarity on hand. A pairing in hands with Yod the open hand. Polarity on the other hand a complete closed loop'y loop. Yod is you asz'any freedom of awareness of a being indivisible while y'all na now k'now'ing out of it any mere or y potential other y'sz'za."

"Touch the point y'old white man." Mor glanced over at the point of a shiv held in Kwasanda's right hand. Her giggle broke the spell as she slipped the blade between the seats.

"Well now I reckon the point is a y'all'egory bloody mess. Y'all that can be said is the as'ex'odus of it. Now the y dialectic offers a'na in word wayeve back into it. Awareness in a y eye of herhimit it still a b'ng c'ng a'peering from above as below in the first place. Indivisible in'visibility of anybody anywhere any time." Mor turned his attention back to the street. He felt the kundalini energy rising from the base of his spine surging into his brain blowing out any in word internal dialogue. Now freely tapping that ka's mic chakra mere inches above the head he paid attention to it. As'king of it now k'now'ing a la que"en que' appearing out in her'eye of eve're'ybody. A's'ex's ting in formation. Awhile. Longer or shorter he wondered.

"But the point is any touch, ANY TOUCH is herhimit, the open hand touching y'all as'ka's mic'ro wayeveing instantaneously black'g"round. Yet believe it or not eve'n the sense of touch is learned by a supernatural sense of separation developed supersonically in word'sz'za . . ." words trailed off as Kwasanda leaned over to lightly touch his lips with hers. Touch of her now as'z in her'eyez z z of eve're'y body. THE TOUCH of the open hand or a y eyez z z'ion a b'ng c'ng a peering it of that a b'ng now k'now'ing touch potentially possible by as supernatural thoth'tsz opening mouth or'is peh'esse'y w'hole as supersonic organ of speech. Or'gan playing now out in word mean meaning'full means as'ka"my'ing memory as thoth'tsz supernaturally superimposed int'word a k'urving the supersonic black'g"round mirror seas in her"eyez z z of eve're'y body." Mor felt a distinct draft as in wayeves of wordsz'azz blowing out of his memory. A memory moving far beyond any artificial in word borders of his own memory. At least that he remembered. He caught the sparkle of tears on her ebony cheeks.

"What's wrong?"

"What's wrong? What's right? We all turning across the event horizon of a black hole and y'all axking me that. Remember my daughter?"

"Okay Still this dialectic takes any or eve'reybody black'g'round indivisible in'visibility. Becoming indivisible black going a'ground. Black'g'round. Alone. Indivisible." Mor found the dialectic had a momentum and integrity that could not be soft sold. Any attachments captivated attention away from realizing y. Y you'rey'dhi'a'te'n'ow you or me out in memory.

"It's not easy letting go of a teenage daughter. Still that's how I'm seeing y'all or me asz appearing now to be any bodys mirroring that black'g'round seas in mere memory of a b'ng c'ng. A being of me or you now mirror black'g'round potential with intention to be a'gain. Me or you a memory constantly in the way of her'eve re'y e'g'g's pingting motion."

"You said pingting. Where did you come up with that?"

"It seems that virus gets around. That disc y'all found is loaded with it. Supersonic weaponry. It seems the main preoccupation of man is destruction of ma'ss body. Self replicating echo boards that once activated could dissolve the supersonic fabric of spacetime. They call it pingting. Kinda cute for a weapon of mass destruction. It seems attention may be paid into any virtual in word a're'y'al'ity as'king of it y now a k'nowing out in'formation of any measly thin'king of it. Out of her'eyez z z of eve're'ybody a're'y'dhi'a'ting to perceive in word information as any meager thin'king of it. Or anybody is potential to be perceived as'ka's y'all. Micro wayeve'rey's supersonically echoing a black'g'round in forming our w'horld'ing as plan et h'ear'th. Supersonically y'all as'ex'et'ting duplicating int'word supernaturally a twis'ting in two information as'z'any thoth'tsz of a b'ng c'ng out of her'eyez z z of a black mirror see'as. A black eye on ma'ss con or de'struction supersonically silently a're'y'all turning black'g'round. In that I am now finding any, ANY in formation bi k'now'ing out of it a while of a y eye a peering it now as'k'ing of it y a ka's mic k'now'ing out appearance of any meager thin'king of it any time anywhere. Wow those words spoke themselves as thoth'tsz of any information of it. Any information of a b'ng c'ng out of it is supernatural thoth'tsz. A God esse to be letter'all'y y'all a being as'king of it y a la que"en que' of that in which appears anything or anybody. Gee's us transmitting such stunning in word awareness out of it." She then put a hand over her mouth as though to prevent further expression of it.

"It comes thru you as you a're'y'all'ity as'king of it y a b'ng c'ng in the first place. The y dialectic infects our in word mind nearly wiping out preconceptions or belief systems of a b'ng c'ng appearing supernaturally as'z'any thoth'tsz of it in'formation superimposed on it. Out of it. Her'him'it a y eye b'ng c'ng still a freestanding in the first place indivisible in'visibility. In that I am finding myself eve'n after awakening still black'g'round a're'y'all'eye'szing it now in word k'now'ing of it out in formation. To be a gain y'all must be'lack. We all turning that black'g'round de'sire to be a gain. Of de'sire a peering it from above to be a gain out in word now k'now'ing out of it anything or anybody or any time now awhile in formation. Awhile now. Just us appearing awhile now. Disappearing after awhile now. No matter how or who we all perceive turning into or out of it. It a're'y'mains still indivisible awareness of it." Mor found himself breathless from uttering the dialectic with its power to a're'y'absorb any sense in formation. He watched Kwasanda shiver as she disgorged it as'well.

"Indivisibile still now a felt k'now'ing out of it bi us. By the nerve and blood and guts of us touching out of it from the center heart of me or you in mem'or'y. A peering it now charging out a whorlding black'g'round as'ex'et'ting duplicating in'visibility int'word a twis'ting in two in'formation. That blackness in her'eyez z z a wayeve'reys changing out of it rippling moment after moment with a certain cruelty as mean means of pressuring us. Pressing in from y'all sides with a gravity of suffering and misery. Mojo to find out why? Why such cruelty and despair in the modern world for aboriginal peoples? Modern life seems to press my people down. To break them open in order that they find themselves now that in a wordfreedom'us a being c'ng indivisible in'visibility still in the first place. Now that's what my experience in RJ's pod revealed about any memory of a b'ng c'ng out in word in'formation.

"Why? Why slavery for me or my people still a being c'ng in'visibility in a wordfree'dom'us still in the first place. Is that why we all appear turning into or out of this extreme sorrow? It forges a soul now to be as though hammered on it. A mirror in word forge'or'y now shattered by the'na shock wayeves of her cruel Kali'ma. Yet still y'all sorrow merely observed by that a y eye being a peering it out in word. Any potential information in her'eye of eve'reybody a'pairing as a mirrored being out in memory. Any appearing now out in formation in word a wily while still of a being in the first place changeless immortal indivisible in'visibility of anybody of a being me or you," Kwasanda added, her eyes widening with each word. "These words mirror my ex'act feeling. Now that I am finding in word a wayeve're'ybody to break out of any inward spell my soul soars like a hawk. Me or you still immortal in the darkness." Her face shone as if a luminary had been ignited within her. Mor found his attention completely captivated by her glow, her luminescence. She'e na now the black'g'round of him.

"Or herhimit? The greatest eye star'e y e or y now out awhile appearing raising hell. Tell me more about your ancestry. This eruption of y'or y speak is scorching my mind."

"Or y you picked that dialectic up pretty quick. From the professor?"

"Hearing just us in one auditorium lecture filled me to the brim with it. Something about hearing it echoing off ceilings, walls, and minds of several hundred folks in the audience. It's the wayeve're'ys of y'or y speak in the first place. Sound wayevere'ys as a mean means meaningful of it. In that I am finding the in word in'formation of a b'ng c'ng must also be expressed per'sonically. Then echoing supersonically supernaturally as thoth'tsz. Letter'all'y y'all alive. A being c'ng coming phonographically through her'eye of eve're'ybody in a're'y'all in sound vigorous wayeve're'y'body. A black eve're'ybody indivisible in'visibility. In that way she got into my eye'sz long before I could ever get into her'eye a ka'ne'y black peh'esse'y whole." Mor found himself adding that irony almost as confession. Kwasanda opened his heart such that he felt in love with her and Margo Christina Shaughnessy. A searing scorching love. Consuming her him it.

"Is that the question here. Have you been into her in that way? Should I be jealous?" she asked with her lips whispering into his ear.

"About that I'm honestly not sure. It's been awhile being around folks having any conversation beyond buying gas and lumber, let alone asex. Y'all I can say is she's not what you think. To me or you. More invisibility of awareness of a being somebody. Her body seems to function as an in word duplicating instrument of that awareness. It's her and not her. There's no way into or out of a being c'ng in her'eye of the eve're'ybody. Some one called her a la por sonorizar, the per'sonic one. While I may be onto the dialectic, as you say, but the sounds'z'zaz'z'any wordsza is completely different with her. Coming from her vocal range. She'e'na calls it wielding the pramanam. A vocal means of liberating attention from in word captivity. In word in forming it as'z'z'any sound means. She'ena often a fang shredding it y'all black down. She'e'na personic liberator in formas'sound wayeve're'ys a're'y'dhi'a'ting now out in her'eye of eve're'ybody. That indivisible black mirror se'e'as bodhi a being to perceive a peering now as'king of it any k'now'ing out of it awhile of anybody, " Mor laughed at the sheer folly of appearing at attention in formation merely a peering it out of a b'ng c'ng in word in'formation.

"Yeh, y'all speak like somebody been a lot in isolation. The professor got her chops down so that she uses the total sonic octave scale that adds a certain enchantment to the sound waves of her voice."

"Talk to me mama. Love, love, looova the sound of your voice. Liquid gold like Gina's."

"You wanna talk about her?"

He could only answer with silence from the lump that welled up in his throat with thoughts of her. "She had Creole soul like you." Mor struggled to manage a few words reply without tears coming along with it.

"My mother is Muslim, from the north. Our blood is awash with a melange of Islamic Pagan Christian influence. If that ain't a creole mix add the black soil. The red black'g'round. Africa. A fri'e ka. If're'y'qua. Hundreds millions turning churning burning a're'yd black'g'round. Naturally I'm attracted to a white man with no religion and a growing substance abuse problem."

"Don't forget my lack of a visible means of support. You see Korner? Occasionally his doppelganger pops out of me. He should be easy to spot in this gathering. With that gangly crooked shuffle of his." he added, seeing a bent old man pausing in his shuffle, hands clasped behind to give him balance. Glancing Mor's way, he looked over with a smile. Mor returned it with a salute.

"We're in the bloody whore virgin heart of the Saint," he continued. "You can enter but you may never leave. J'hay'sus tells us in heaven there is neither marriage nor giving in marriage. There in heaven is no separation of it as'exes. No sense of other y'sz'za. It's not what we all in turn think of heaven. That other y'sz'z is in a word mirror'y mind. Any an y or y na mirrored as means of an'y mere or y'all now concept of heaven as a meeting place would be to find yourself as'z still in her'e"ye of eve're"y body. What a gas."

"You passing gas?" Kwasanda gave with a wrinkle of nose.

"Always say takes good farting to keep a man alive. And mon I got real goo'od gas."

"Black'g'round gas?"

"Re'ckon that I'm a bit backed up."

"Blacked up?"Kwasanda's eyes seemed to keep opening eve'r wider. Mor started kissing her neck to break the spell. He tasted the tension. Shallahna. Mother eve'r daughter.

"Too much time in the forest." Now Mor felt his attention drawn to it a're'yabsorbing city noise. Highways oceans moons and planets disappeared in macro ka's mic galactic seas. How far can awareness go he wondered. In the silence broken only by ma'ss nature'y'e crying. A y eye star'e"ye'ing out now a peering it in her'eye awayeve're'ybody supersonic silent black ma'ss cry that lingers on beyond the slight personic range of man'as mind or memory. Now we all experience turning black back into her singular eve're'y body. Eve'now that blinded by turning it out in one direction. Awayeve're'ybody as'ex'et'ting black'g'round knowing out a duplication of it in any imagining of h'our"iz"on a b'ng c'ng out in word in'formation.

"Having a crazy psycho ma who would love me by beating on me with her cane put me on the edge in any eve'nt. She pushed me back into the darkness. Gave me the name for Christ's sake and I ain't kidding. She was high on Jesus and low on eve'll Kali ma. When she got low she got to be Kali'ma. Driven into ma'd'ness." Mor found his in word thoughts expand till wordsza broke up into sounda'sza"zz peh'ss'y el n'ce'a being be'am'ing y'all black'g'round. Da ark'a'nezz'azz intent of turning y'all around into or out of it asz'z'any role. Any roll or role of complete dhi"ark'n'esse.

Mor'sz z z'a mind'o'o'ro r'asz Dhi'ark'ness'za entered to de'sire a being c'se'er at A'ten scion'a. Ar"king of it a y now az's'ex're'y'ass'z ka's y'all appearing out in her'eye of eve're'ybody. Of a black'g'round being in her'eye playing out over that role of any or eve're'y body. The ka's mic mirrored mic'rowave electromagnetic singular dhi'e'rection y'all'szz'a mi'z z' z'a d'h'irection loop'y loop of complete d'ark'ness. Turnings'za out of or black into the completely complete d'arkness is to be any way of eve re' y ark. Eve're'y rock'n'roll'or role playing black'g'round. Da ark. D'No'az ark. Y'll d'na. Da ark of de'nile. Da ark of her black mirror seas body. It's y'all around you. On the right on the left above and below and projecting y'all around. Projecting y'all black'g'round. Out of it in her'eye of eve're'ybody. A black mirror seas body d'arking completely y'all around. In complete loops perceived ar'king of it a y now awhile.

Her mirror se'as body duplicating us as in word thoughtsz gleaming beaming that black stuff in her'eye a peering black'g"round. A being c'ng now in visibility out in mirrored word appearing now awhile of a being c'ng still invisibility. Still indivisible. Still y you a're'y'a'ten binary by na re'y az ark a'sz t'word twis'ting that singular indivisible in'visibility by intent. Intent of intentional disregard of awareness of a being still indivisible. A being still in the first place c'ee're a'y eye. Twis'ting that complete d'ark into one 0 appearing a pairing as'z 8. In other word'za you still that pivot'y'all point of view. Whole holy point of a being any mere'or y na now out as'ex's ting in'formation a'sz a na y mirrored y no body. No 'az ark of de'nile.

He just let it pour on through. A cleansing acidic mental vomit a's a're'y solvent. Dhi solving thoughtsz of x's ting in word'all'y y'all under the spell of the alphabeta now 3D cubic visual supersonic time machine coded to break open now around k'now'ing of it in the mirror'age of Aquarius. Of a b'ng c'ng in word'age of man'as mind. Or y na. You now. K'now it out in her'eye a's the'n'a. He thought the time ma'she'ena must be breaking open now or else how was it possible to find himself in it. The mirror age mirage of Aquarius a're'y'flecting it. Man 'as any supersonic in word mind mirror mirroring y'all y'll d'na. Now that denial realized by what could be a magnetic polar shift black'g"round, a short cut to finding a being still indivisible in'visibility of a y eye herhimit. A y you're;y yod"heyvavhey. The mirror ask'ey'e of tetragrammaton.

There again he thought that inherent prejudice against the d'ark runs counter the experience as'z z z'leeping across the cover in any a na y'eve'ent horizon. That horizon mere'or y imaginary dividing line between twin black'g'round body a's a being c'ng in word a's thoth'tsz. Supernature supersonically superimposed a's other y's'z z z'a wily while appearing now. The'na disappearing black into one black'g'round as'z two unwinding in still a being a un"consciousness. A con with intent of falling again and again . . . a gain only as'z z z'a being int'word twis'ting in formation to lose indivisible in'visibility under the seductive con of her shimmering black mirror se'as a're'y'all potential. That in word potential mirroring any body appearing now awhile out of complete d"ark'ness still. A beating a being the heart of that d"ark'ness in a being in'visibility supernaturally y'all as thothtsz. As'z in the'or'y mere 'or y in word thoughtsz of x's ting in'formation of a being a un"k'no no no'w"e'n'y t'h'inking occurring around roles or rolls playing out from the ka's mic mind or y mem or y. Or y now that we all turn black into that intent ignoring around any k'no no no'wing experiencing directly a being in her'eye indivisible eve're'ybody over 33 percent of a lifetime. Then he realized there being no way in or out of her'eye of eve'll in eve're'y body. Still realizing y'all that's awareness of a being still in the first place indivisible in'visibility of any eve'll appearing out as'ex's ting in formation find freedom.

He flashed that perceived ar'king of it a y eye of a being c'ng in a're'y'all still centrality. Inside the center point of view of the complete l"OO"pa de'l"OO"pa's black'g'round of a y eye freestanding being is still stillness. A y'll d'na twists t'word are'y'flecting now in word k'nowing out of it black a'cross a mirrored now clear as da y. A's'ka's all y na da y light igniting it in that simple fiery twist of fate. Y fade back to black still with intent of awakening again and again and again in na da y light? He wondered why. To be perceived awakening with intentional purpose of her eve'll. Her will, her way of funnyaction. He laughed in spite of y'all in words boiling up out his mouth like upchucking dinner after too many shots of te'kill'ya.

"So funny we all in turn can't hardly wait to fall as'z z z'leep black to it. Free stepping off alledged k'no no now kurving h'our attention now around playing complete roles of d'ark'ness. Rolls perceived ar'king of it a y binary by d'na'y'll re'y'e'sza in be'am'ing eN'y circling electro-magnetic l"OO"ps flowing in one direction'y'all roles or rolls playing out as'ex's ting information a while now still a being of that indivisible in'visibility of any individual. See, once a riff starts, y'all just gotsta let it run its complete train of in word thought."

"You a're'y'all of the Dark'ness," Kwasanda replied with a kiss and laugh.

"Still working out of a being complete while as'z though black. As'z complete thoughtsz of a being lack'ing. Complete yet ironically y'all a being lacking by completely ignoring or projecting a being complete completely still in the first place. How's that twist? Y folks naturally must ignore any mention of a being her'him'it yod or a y eye a peering it now turning into k'no no no'wing it as not it y'll d'na. A denial of it in that simple single y as'ex's ting in formation twist of fate, faith, and family. That b"lackness is mere 'or y now as'ex's ting information of an'y y na potential reflected in word'all'y y'all touching touched touch black'g'round of the indivisible eye of her'him'it. A being c'ng now a pairing by opening mouth. Or'is it now super-sonically appearing in the or y. That instantaneousness of any touch still a being in her'eyez z z'a black'g'round. There the a're'y'all out in that eve're'ybody turning a black'g"round y'all the time. A being now out in that sacred kryst blackness as'ka's mic mirrored micro wayeve black'g"round of any mirror y na you now not y'll d'na. A denial of a being her'him'it." Mor stretched his arms, arching his back to expell the gas curdling in his gut.

"Maybe that's the secret of ignorance, the falling under the in word spell a's"word slicing and dicing us into small desperate lives. A y eye being c'ng now as'ex'et'ting information slaves. A's'eX's ting in the denial of our indivisible androgyny. Androgyny of a her'him'it. The trouble in mind or y of one half always looking for the other. The blues baby, the black dog blues. Always something or someone missing. Or passing away right before your eyes."Kwasanda slipped in another disk and Gina's voice cut into his dialogue.

"Here I go again

Doing things that I

Swore I'd never do again

Dreaming dreams of you.

"How'd you get this?" Mor asked, a lump rising in his chest as he joined the chorus.

"Hoping some way that I'd win

But it's bound to show

That I know I know

I'll never have you back again"

"Her voice was nectar to me. Pure nectar. She had me with her first note. Love, baby. Sweet love, now eaten away by the acids of loss. She knew," he said. "I saw the anguish in her eyes. That night we recorded this."

"Too bad nothing lasts

But we can't change the past"

"You know me and I know you," Kwasanda slid in with a husky tenor. Tears fell along Mor's cheeks into his beard stubble, drops running off his chin onto the collar of his shirt.

"I love you, Kwasanda."

"I love you, too, you Darkie Mor. I found this when I searched Korner's car for weapons."

"I can feel him in my skin. And always that trace of gun oil along with the after shave."

"I thought for sure he was going to kill me. If Fawn hadn't come along? He kept on about them and I felt that killer about to be unleashed. So I'm coming down from a double trauma. Better give me some of that coke."

"How do you want it?"

"How you doing it?"

"I'm doing it the way Korner showed me. Here, open up. I'll lay a little rock under your tongue." he said, taking a nugget from the Altoids tin.

"I could have shot him." she said, laying her tongue on coke and catching the tip of his finger. "I thought about shooting his kneecap. I was still too much a being blissed out under the effect of R J's love pod. I took everything I could find in his car but I must have missed his spare set of keys."

"Why do you say that?"

"Because he's behind us."

☼

Korner, hair matted with dried blood, one hand wrapped in a rag torn from his shirt, massaged the pulsing nerves in his neck as he steered the Mark IV along the city streets.

"Bitch took my tunes and drugs," he said, slamming his fist sideways under the dash. The compartment dropped open to a custom built .45 with clips and a cell phone. He popped the compartment lid back, laying the automatic alongside his leg. The weight of the .45 with its blued steel dissipated his anger with the reassurance of revenge. Bloody couze, he thought, still having to admit she had a great pair of legs. Too bad legs always lead to eggs and egg'spectations he mused with a chuckle. At his age why be still lusting after that bloody jelly roll? He was pretty sure of having had a mother though he never met her. The Dark one's mom was crazy bonkers but he thought of her as his. The only one he ever knew or could relate to.

He punched the speed dial on the phone. "Comrade Rakitin," he said, holding his breath to keep his voice even. "Could you be so kind to inform the Great One on that I am needing an audience."

"Somehow I think you need much more than that, the way you managed to screw things up."

"I told you that artist was and still is a wack job. No one can predict what the Darkness might go and do next. Like shooting RJ McCraken's sensei. Did he manage to get any paint on the canvass?"

"He managed some kind of mess before taking off with Ms. Shaughnessy. She showed here just a few moments ago. She is with Mr. Warren now."

"There's something shady going on with her and him. Some twisted connection I've felt from the beginning of this show. The hairs on the back of my neck always stand up when I'm being conned."

"Well I guess it takes one to know about that. After all it is your con neck shunned on the block."

"I'm on to the black princess and the painter. I'll scoop them up and be along to join the party."

"In sixty minutes, the virus will be released. She may be a fly in the ointment. It is good that you will, naturally, prevent that happening."

"I need to speak to her."

"Johnstone Warren's office is in lock-down mode, activated automatically when Ms. Shaughnessy entered."

"That just confirms my suspicions that we're being played somehow in all this. I'll figure a way in when I get up there."

"I hope you remembered to get immunized." The line went dead.

Korner didn't expect Rakitin to have a sense of humor. Was he kidding about being immunized? He watched the BMW taillights float through city traffic. He flipped open the cushioned center console to a half pint of Cuervo. Is this the night, he asked himself. Now every moment seemed a crumbling away off the edge of the end of the line. But then that was an edge he'd known before in the eyes of men coming to kill him. They were gone. He was still here. Then, their ghosts moved just off his periphery, their shadow liable to fall across his path in the blink of an eye.

Still a tingling burn stinging his nerves from the Taser, Korner rolled his shoulders and neck, speeding to catch a light at the intersection of Columbus and Broadway. Titty bars of pasties and g-strings had come a long ways compared to Zina's action. It was a progression he could understand. Vice is life. He had to admit he felt for the Darkman's innate morality. Somehow that needed crushing along with blood and bone. Poor loser, he's probably singing in his head with Gina at this moment. Gina. What a heartbreaker. Her soul bit a piece out of him every time he heard her voice. Things had gotten to the point where he wanted the artist alive to keep any possibility of him joining her on the other side. Keep him alive but broken.

The tequila sent his head into numbed animation as he followed Kwasanda to Chinatown and the Square. Voices echoed in his head like distant rings of thunder barely heard on the horizon. Funny, he wasn't even thinking of the gold. It didn't matter to him in the least. What was going on? When had this happened? When he spoke to Rakitin? The virus. He honestly didn't give a good god damn. Korner eased down Clay on the south side of the Square.

"Cause I got my big feet in the window," he sang, almost missing the BMW parked at the curb.

☼

Two men in dark blazers, white shirts, and matching neckties stood at the Pyramid's reception desk. Christina's heels clicked on marble as she crossed the vault of the lobby. A light-boxed silhouette of the Pyramid emblazoned a wall on the far side of the security point. She approached the desk and introduced herself. "Christina Shaughnessy. I am here to see Johnstone Warren. He is expecting me."

One man shrugged as he picked up the phone. The elevator door of black polished steel fell away with a slight hiss, revealing a wood paneled lift with recessed lighting.

"Go right up."

Christina stepped in the elevator and rode to the forty-fifth floor. As the door slid open A man stood in the vestibule of polished marble posing with the authority of an assistant who has assumed the master's mantle, his tie crisply knotted between starched collars.

"Welcome on behalf of Mr. Warren, " he offered with a slight bow.

"I am here, if not at first, then, at last," she said, the sound of her words coming through a haze of lost memory. She stripped off her shoes and tossed them to him as she strode in to the modest penthouse. "It is rather a shame when the higher ups get the smallest room," she offered with a frown.

"Professor," the man's man offered as he adjusted himself, one hand holding her shoes dangling at his side. "I am Stepan Rakitin, executive assistant to Mr. Warren. He's been searching for you for a long time. He carries your photograph like a talisman." Rakitin smiled as he led her to an inner office through a pair of fourteen-foot bronze doors. His gloved fingers slid over the mirror finish as static sparks jumped about. He walked across the room and motioned her to a leather chair. Standing with one hand behind his back, he withdrew a curtain.

Nauseous odor filled the room. Christina braced herself, suddenly feeling weak in the knees. She slumped into the chair. The angled walls of the Pyramid disoriented her, and for a moment she felt herself falling over the edge of consciousness.

"The view is dizzying," she said. Raising on her arms, she managed to walk over to Warren's emaciated body laid out in his wheelchair.

"So, finally an audience with the man and he has already slipped his bonds," she replied while continuing to stare at the empty vessel.

"He passed ahead of schedule. He wanted most of all to see the painting."

"The smell. It's making me lightheaded." Christina stumbled back into the chair. When she turned, Rakitan was wearing an oxygen mask.

He pulled it up and with a smirk told her, "Professor, you've been hiding in the bourgeoisie elitist playground of Stanford University while I've been shackled every day to this. This noxious poison that he's been metabolizing in the very cells of his body. permeates every fiber of my being." Rakitin gave a wave of his hand as he doffed the mask for another hit. "Day by day, over years, with injections and sonic waves, he's been cooking his stew. One day up. One day down. I finally was able to get some oxygen after he stopped speaking a few hours ago. He told me of you, before this, this madness. He talked of you almost like he was your father. To hear him say it, he and your father were blood. He said they worked on the Manhattan Project. The idea of you began there in the mutated cells of Matthew Shaughnessy."

"My father told me the whole story on his deathbed. I am not Warren's seed or if so still my will is freely mine."

"Yet he needed your portrait, your pre-imagined image for the virus. Its engineering began with your engineering. I know now I have no choice but to follow his design to its logical conclusion. Even tho theoretically I am immune, but with so much exposure to the virus and to do otherwise, well not an option."

Christina grabbed Rakitin by his starched collar. She pulled him close until she felt his breathing. "Stop this madness any way you can. What can you hope to gain by completing a lunatic mission?"

He pulled from her grasp and adjusted his jacket. "He needed you and the painter for the image, an essential part of his design. I may replace your image with one of my own." Rakitin's eyes filled with light.

Christina approached Warren's corpse until the odor became so strong she felt her nose hairs singing. She found a certain fascination staring at Warren's narrow face and lowered eyelids, skin like yellowing parchment. Such an ignoble vestige for containing so much of ma'sz destruction.

"You vile deviant priest, do we all turn to serve the same lord with just different intent? Different names? Are you free now, you brilliant evil bastard, engineering your cells into an army of destitution." She turned to Rakitin. "Isolate him before the vapor builds up pressure. As rank as he is, I'm somehow drawn to its rot, its putrescence is dissolving the pretenses of ego, clearing out all the falseness, the lie of me in formation. It's very euphoric in a gut wrenching way."

"He tried to alter the sequencing of his genetic DNA through a diet of enzymes and amino acids, activated by a range of constantly bombarding sonic tones. I tell you its been a freaky frankenstein ordeal. As his mass disintegrated in this controlled environment, he was distilled into a being as pure energetic wave function. His brain went into a very high frequencing low amplitude gamma brain wave pattern of calm intensity by the time he lost speech and motor skills. He wanted to engineer matter supernaturally with thought wave energy. He realized that DNA, the double helix, is a receiver and transmitter for audio/visual codes, after sitting for several hours in the golden throne of Tutankhamun, at the Metropolitan Museum. We spent the night there, a privilege only for a main benefactor. He said his mind unfolded metaphorically between the two wings on which his arms rested, the same design as the Arc of the Covenant." Rakitin checked his watch. "It's time."

A guttural chanting, harmonized repetitive tones, began playing through wall-mounted speakers.

"These are Solfeggio tones. These tones together express biblical prophecy. Covering the complete audio range they induce theta brain waves. Mr Warren referred to it as pharaonic consciousness. He said it introduced awareness of a being still in the first place. A's being see'ng in a y eye perpetually a peering it out now in words of an unbroken oral lineage of pharonic consciousness. Mr. Warren referred to Pharaoh as a singular Pa'roo'ma, a place divine of immortality of a being in the first great house. A being still in the first place. Inform'as now k'now'ing out in the first time. He told me you were on to that awareness of a being still in the first place. Pa'roo'ma a first personic being now k'now'ing out of it a first time machine code."

"A code unlocking time now at attention captivated in word. In that eye of that I am being c'ng now is'is a peering it a'sz the Magus. eye-magus eye-magining in her'eyez z z'a now. As'king of it a la que"en que' of that in which anybody'z z z' appearing of it. That I am is is eye magik'a in a be'ng"c'ng"a'gain'in'g any potential ma'trix a while in her'eyez z z of a eve"re'y body. That trix of ma'sz black body mirror co'de?"

"Ah, all that sounds vaguely familiar as the code language only spoken by Mr. Warren. Thus in that I am familiar with it's enchantment. Why I always carry ear plugs. Mr. Warren used me as guinea pig. Days weeks months of it." Rakitin paused for effect. She knew he knew that she could enchant or entrain the wayeves of his in word conceit. His will had nada chance flooded in'a lake of eve'll appearing of it anybody out in her'eyez z z of eve're'ybody. In that blink of eyez z z Rakitin's mood lightened. "Once, being emboldened by a late night cocktail we shared one evening, somewhat familiar with his brilliant engineering of sonic waves with hieroglyphs I asked Mr. Warren if he was once a pharaoh. He told me that was after he was demoted." Rakitin's lips twitched in a crooked smile.

"What are they chanting?"

"All I know is that it's repetitious as hell"

"The tetragrammaten. Four letter aten. That is the key to a b'ng c'ng in the a y eye code. Focusing in that intent he is paying my aten'cion back into years of absence. H'our mind has been ignoring or as'z'any thoth'tsz playing out a sublime aten'cion into a being of us appearingof it out in formation. Yet indivisible in'visibility of a being still at aten'cion. A being ancient yet new indeed eve'n from of old. A being called forth right now in that four letter first personic code of a being a first person present still in the first place. Now appearing out of it at aten'cion drawn by anybody merely mirrored in word in a name alone."

"I should tell you James Korner has been in contact. I told him you had already arrived when he called twenty minutes ago." Christina picked up on the distraction of any man'as mind or memory from now paying aten'cion to it in a wordfreedom awareness of it. A y eye being c'ng a peering it still in the first place. She now realized Rakitin's failure to fully realize it despite long exposure to the y dialectic. Any mind memory conditioned in word by constantly now a k'no no no'w'ing or denying it y'all along seldom if eve're'ybody finds itself paying aten'cion to it. A's to finding a b'ng c'ng any or eve're'ybody in word still ignores it out of that indivisible in'visibility.

"How did you know before my arrival?"

"I picked up on your conversation at the warehouse. In that I am trying to stay one step ahead of our James. He is convinced you and John Warren are plotting something together. He has been doing some digging. I discovered a breach in the security codes and right away suspected him. I think we all need to turn to the same page before he shows."

Christina felt her awareness elevating as though shifting to a subtle counterpart in her'eye now of a being of a luminous body. Gazing into the vapors rising off Warren's corpse she detected his luminous counterpart standing a few feet away. They now the y indivisible in'visibility of a y eye a peering it out in a black mirror se'e'as potential now as thoth'tsz shimmering electric luminescent waves communicating in word all'y mirrored y'all as'ex's ting in formation. A're'y'alizing being awareness by a being still in the first place now turning out k'now'ing informa's the first time she appeared to disappear. She appeared to disappear in word into the house of Pa"roo'ma, the first place of a being y'll still in formation in for'Ma'sz the first time. She seemed to fall in any case ending by a being y of, in, for, to, etc. still a be'am'ing a y eye a peering it out in a' memory potential mirroring anybody in word as y nobody really appears in the first place. "So Mr. Stepan Rakitin why the painting?"

"The painting is the ping'ting. Pigments engineered with a supersonic virus. That viral sound is a mean meaningful in formation as'z waves emanating activated by the presence of anybody. Anybody a being c'ng out in her'eye of evere'ybody. Warren has created through machinations of the artist a self-replicating echo'ing ping'ting sounding board enhanced by any or eve're'y body standing around mirroring waves playing that black'g'round . . ."

"And black'g'round ad infinitum ad nauseum till its supersonic crescendo letter'ally blows up any or eve'rey in word in'formation."

"With out word there is in her'eye of eve're'ybody complete a y eye being c'ng now a b' lacking out ase'x's ting in formation with intent to be a gain. In her'eye a blacking out the're ye 'asz withholding any information." Rakitin gave Christina a sharp k'now'ing gaze revealing his intent. For a split second she felt him playing her. Then she realized it was that male arrogance tipping his hand.

"The antidote. The dialectic is the antidote. A way of reversing in word that direction of the polarity of ignorance." She kept her eyes on his. Neither blinked. Y speak she mused. Y speak reverses intent from disregarding a being complete completely indivisible in'visibility liberating attention from y'all or we all turning black'g'round. Or y'all without intent of a being lacking. That intent necessitating paying aten'cion to a be'ng a gain now out in word in any or eve re'y wayeve function. A fun'ny'a'ction of indivisible invisibility appearing a pairing now out around k'no no no'wing of it in word any or eve're'ybody as'ex's ting by hay'ting or ping'ting it. Echoing phonographic alphabeta. A wayeve're'ye'sz'za vibrating in a cord'ance with the sacred as'ka's mic perceived 'ar'king of it a y now the covenant in Akh'et'ting'aten. At aten'cion still in the first place Akh'et'aten. A' ka'h'sz z z'a duplicating of'ten anybody etc..

Christina felt her eyes widening with the revelations pouring into or out of that ka's mic memory turning int'word y'all a black'g'round now as'king of it y a k'now'ing out a're'y'all'ity of da y light igniting ignorance of it. Now any chintzy chisling'thin'king of it. Of a twis'ting in two anybody appearing a pairing out in word in formation. She saw that Rakitin saw that she saw. He gave away the game. Still she had to ask herself why. Was it intentional she wondered. Still her electromagnetic felt field of view remained committed to any mirror activation. She remained ready to kick asz'z and take names in a word. Y'all. We all turning out in her'e'yez z z of eve're'ybody. A now as'king of it y a la que"en que' of that in which any appearing of it is by a k'now'ing it out of a black mirror supersonic se'e'as echoing any or eve're'ye'body merely a peering it.

CHAPTER 15

Chapter 15

The silver BMW rocked as Korner jerked the back door open and slid inside.

"Well, ain't this nice. All of us back together. Princess." He pushed the.45 under his coat. "Let me just say right off, I've been under a lot of strain lately. People say I haven't been myself. You guys understand don't you?"

"Do we have a choice?" Kwasanda asked.

"No. So I'll cut to the chase. But first your pistolo their, sister. Thank you very much. Does any one know the score? What's going down here. I don't know whether to shit or go blind. It's a new game moment to moment. If you're waiting for a call, no signal penetrates the upper stories of the Pyramid. We'll have to mosey on over there."

"You're scaring us with your big gun," Mor replied. Korner reached out and clubbed him with the butt of Kwasanda's.22. Blood trickled from a split above his eye. Kwasanda tried to reach inside her jacket as Korner pinned her arms to the seat. Mor barely flinched, his body already numb from shock of wounded knee and the cocaine coursing his nerves. A gut laugh rolled out. "Y'all cain't hurt the Dark'ness in her'eye of eve're'y body. Her'him'it baby'cakes. She be so y'all over you mon. She feasting on your grits as we all turn into or out of a y speak in the first place.

"Answer me this, my Nubian. First what the frac dis mon speak. Second Y. Why is black pussy so pink on the inside?" Korner groaned as he groped her for other weapons. He dragged the barrel of the.38 he found, across her breasts, pressing it against her throat. "I don't know what is the bigger turn-on, killing or fucking you. Want to find out?"Then Korner backed off with a heh heh. Still why provoke a psycho coming off his meds. Then again. Mor realized just how twisted Psycho liked it. Daughter of Kali'ma. Korner son of z'z'a bitches Mor mused.

"Cowards always hide behind guns and big mouths. Or little boys with bad poddy training," she added. He sprang up with the barrel pushing into her flesh. Mor huddled against the door semi conscious, head thrown against the glass, mouth open, trying to gather his wits. Gather the beast of man. Best of the kill or be killed beast. Mor knew the beast in her'e ye. He had conquered fear the first natural enemy of a man aspiring to be un hombre de conocimiento. Mor now found himself besieged by his own clarity. The second natural enemy de un hombre conocimiento. The clarity of his mind. Or y now bust out. Try something k'new. Canoe baby. Him in her'eye'sz'za lapping the sides of that canoe. In her'eye of eve're'ybody. His ma'sz'za body. Facial lines relaxed. The Dhi"mons re'leased. Somewhere over a hot sax riff'f Korner's voice broke his reverie.

"You got spunk. I like it. More fight to whip on." Korner dragged his teeth along the side of her neck. "Get in gear or I'll bust your boyfriend's other knee."

"O Kay Cleent. Is that your best dirty Harry?" she ax'ked stretching her throat. Korner backed off with a belly laugh.

"Damn women. Hell no that an'nt my best. I mean who do you think taught that hollywood punk how to play that role in the first place? Yeh . . . .but seriously I havent hurt anybody in over five minutes . . .I'm starting to get a migrain here."

Mor stirred as Kwasanda put the car in gear. As though from a greater distance he watched people on the street, insulated in their roles, streaming by in that singular current of business for pleasure. Korner's appearance put a bad taste in his mouth, like rancid meat. He stuffed the altoids tin in his jacket. No sense giving anything away. How was he supposed to feel about an old friend who shot him. Twice? He shifted his attention back to the street. Kwasanda could kick his ass better than he anyway. Christina? Now there was an enigma. Somehow he felt sure she could hold her own. She packed more punch, he thought, touching his cheek. She could bring it.

Kwasanda eased the BMW to Clay Street toward the Pyramid. Street level businesses glowed from neon Chinese characters. Streetlights perched on iron facing heads of twin dragons whose tails curled into a caduceus stood above parked cars catching blobs of their light. On the corner of Kearny and Clay, they passed the Buddha Bar with its glowing martini glass. Still one of Mor's favorite signs. Buddha martini. Four men, gathered at the entrance, paid no heed to a bleeding man waving from a 'beamer passing by washed in pink neon.

They crossed Kearny and the eastern edge of Chinatown. They were near the original bay harbor shoreline at the base of Telepraph Hill. Thirty foot tall concrete vents like the stacks of a giant steamer rumbled giving off a mist drifting over the south entryway between the Pyramid and the street. The steady hum of pumps wafting clouds of the mist, gave the impression the building breathed. Exhaling clouds of moisture. Still, Mor could sense the rawness of this place. Once torchlit cobbled streets. Come'in on hard by the bay. The original docks of the bay. On his periphery he saw soft gold kerosene lamplight diffused by canvass sailcloth walls. Liquor, guns, gooch, and greed. Darkness down by bay water lapping wooden ships roped to rickety docks.

Thick hemp lines groaning off creosoted pilings. Horses shod hooves clattering on cobblestone. No gas power. First steam. City air then always heavy with horse manure stench and coal smoke.

"Let's get it on," Mor mumbled. "Bang a gun. Spill some guts. Violate some woman."

"The Darkness has fallen. Throw in a card game. Tequila and cocaine. Speaking of which, ain't that my satchel?"

"Fawn Rave must have copped it when she grabbed your taser. Speaking of which, how was that? Quite shocking?" Mor gave with a guffaw.

"Curled my grits. But then, hell, I shot her old man. I mean the son of a bitch'in Injun fuck and his pit bulls could be hard on a man like me. But I'm gonna tell you both here and now that to kill a man and keep your ju-ju together you gotta realize it ain't me pulling the trigger. The one who pulls that trigger is completely free from judgement. That means for or against anybody. Even flesh and blood. Y'all getting the drift here?"

"So what you're saying is you're psychotic and probably a repressed homosexual?"Mor couldn't resist himself once he started digging on the man.

"Go back to your stupid fucking visions, painter," Korner snarled as Kwasanda muffled a laugh.. "I'll take care of the desk jockeys. Drop me off around the corner. Meet me back at the entrance to the underground parking garage around on Washington," Korner said as he rifled through the satchel. He gave Mor a cold stare through the rear view mirror.

They circled a stand of landscaped redwoods bordering the east side, where the trees formed a park that extended the Pyramid's block. Korner slipped from the vehicle into the shadows of the redwoods. Tufts of fog drifted in, tearing up through streets and alleys.

"Are you still with me, Dark?" Kwasanda asked.

"Takes more than a cheap shot from soldier boy. I've had worse." He buzzed down the window, spitting out a clot of blood and mucus. "The game is playing itself out. We need him to get us into the building. I can feel the last act going down. There's the entrance."

They turned the northeast corner. Concrete legs and buttresses framed the ramp with a tunnel of receding triangles. Below them, a waist-high steel barrier painted red with STOP in white block letters barred the entrance. A security man approached the car. He walked easily in spit polish black shoes, starched white shirt, and trimmed mustache. He reached for his shoulder mike as Korner stepped forward, shooting the man in the chest close range with Kwasanda's .22, catching the guard's weight as he fell. Mor caught Korners palor revealing the strain of them pulling another trigger.

☼

"Mr Warren was all about a peh'ssy w'hole power out in her'eyez z z. That is precisely as Mr. Warren instructed me in that a y eye dialectic. In that I am not surprised that you now k'now it as well. After all is said and done he did engineer you. He commands you yet is at your command"

"Appearing of it anybody or anything merely a peering it out of her'eyez z z'asupernatural

God'esse of eve're'ybody as'z thoth'tsz of her'him'it. As'king of it y a la que"en que' of that in which it a'pairs as'ex y'all. A'ten et'ting e'wave'z z z. A y'll of D'NA'eye'll of it now int'word a twis'ting in two any a k'now'ing out a b c's in formation of wordsz'a." She now watched Rakitin's face for the sign. Christina was curious to what degree Rakitin found himself in the dialectic. As'z a're'y'veil'ing it at aten'cion. Did Rakitin realize he was it asz awareness in a're'y'all captured in her'eyez z zion a peh's'sy whole as'ka's mic memory of a being still in the first place. A're'y new indeed eve'n from of old. Or was he merely playing her using the dialectic as'z'a means of betrayal she now wondered.

"Mr. Warren always spoke of any informing of it out in her'eyez z z. The eyez z z of ma'ss nature. The eyez z z of eve're'ybody a're'y'dhi'a'ting awareness of a being c'ng now as mother nature. In word nature of her'him'it. He would say it makes no sense without her'eye on him in a head a peering it from above. Ove a b'ng freestanding. A peering it out below. Now out of him in her'me'as'zthoth'tsz of it. A peh's'sy whole eyez z z'a'peering it at a pairing y out as'ex y'all out of any or eve're'ybody. Re'y'ad it for yourself." Rakitin's voice broke through Christina's awareness of a being invisibility r'eve'rey. She'e'now found herself turned to a screen he indicated with a wave of his hand. Warren's word scrolled continuously on wall size.

"Sound wayeves of her . . . me . . .ma'ss', eve're'y body. A're'y'dhi'a'ting her'eye a'wayeve re'y'asz the're'y e motion. In her'eye a b'ng'lack mirror sea reflected out in word mind or y me memory micro waving black'g"round as though in word in formation. . . ."

"That was how he spoke of her'e'lectromagnetic eyez z z'ap'ping of eve"re'ybody. A b'ng c'ng indivisible in'visibility complete. Perceived ar'king of it a y are'y'diating potential for'ma'sz'k'a's micro wayeve black'g"round radiation. That always brought him around to you. You appear now in his eye to be in her'eyez z z'appearing of it in the flesh." Rakitin seemed to stretch in time as her eyez z z'a focusing back on the screen.

" . . . . .the mere or y dynamic as'ka's y'all of a being c'ng a'peering it out a pairing in that mirror of a b'ng c'ng still in'visibility indivisible by mere or y a being y now y'all for'ma'sz appearing of it by a being y'all now reflecting reflection as though supernaturally as thoth'tsz of a God esse to be letter'all'y y'all mirrored in wordsz'z z as'z'any thoth'tsz of a y eyez z z'ion being c'ng now superimposed as'z e'x radiating her eve're"y black'ka'sz micro-wayeve mirror see'as anybody turning churning yearning burning a black'g"round of it. The wayeyes of her ma na. Now in her'eyez z z'a way of eve're"y mirror black body as'king of it a're'y'dhi'a'ting a k'now'ing my'or y e.g.g go go go'a'd motion of any mirror y na now function turning as two t'wa twis'ting in'formation. ANY INFORMATION A W'H'ILE NOW OF D'NA. A d'na'eye'll spiralling a black'g"round echo supersonically as'ka's y'all body causal d"ark'ness now to be turning into the'n"ay k'now'ing a being be'am"ing as'ka's mic da y na light. Igniting ignore'ance of it. Mom my mom my mom 'ent to mom 'ent'um'a in any eve'nt of h'our's eyes'z'zion it still a being now a k'now'ing out of it in her'eyez z z of eve're'y'body. In her'eyez z z'a wayeve're'y'aszz'any information of a Virgin Mother. Virtual virgin potential immaculately a're'y'maining still mirror potential conceiving any matter mere or'ly y now as'ex function appearing of it mirrored potential emerging awhile in forma'ss living energy of her'peh'ss'y w'hole ma trix'y death womb do'orwayeve'sz'z'any peh'ss'y w'h'ole . . . . ."

"Mr. Warren realized all sight and sound to be echoing mirrored y now micro-waves reflecting a black'g"round in the great over'eye z'ion of man as mind mem'or"y overstanding understanding of x's ting as'ex"planing a b'ng c'ng now flattened out awhile. A black'g'round which I confused at first with the cosmic microwave 'back'ground of the big bang. Mr. Warren found from you an awareness of a cosmic microwave 'black'ground body indivisible from anybody. Anybody apparently appears out of a're'y'flecting echo of it. Of the k'now'ing out of it any or eve're'y body. That is the dialectic vision he developed from you. In the evenings he listened to tapes of your lectures." Rakitin nodded back to the screen scrolling Warren's screed. ". . . . . . that mind memory her eve"re'y black mirror see'n'as a body the dynamic behind y'all forma'sz a b'ng creation a y'll of D'NA. Hence any destruction of it in forma'ss still merely mirrored potential appearing out of or disappearing instantaneously back into a singular black indivisible invisibility of any individual still . . . a being in the first place. Any mirrored y'all now k'now'ing out of it in formation still in her eyez z z'ap'ping a singular invisible indivisibility a peering it supernaturally as'z'any thoth'tsz appearing of it in da y na light igniting ignore"ance of it as'z thoth'tsz of projecting out in her'eyez z z'ap'ping of eve're'y body. . . . ."

"Final liberation for Mr. Warren just meant playing the right verse. In the or y mind reflects any in word thoughts of a mind or y memory now as'ex's ting in formation. Get it. Your words. The indivisible invisibility of any individual now appearing out of a k'now'ing D'NA'eye'll of it awhile. Appearing of it as in word though'tsz of a b c's in formation of it. The seven tones you are hearing are those which affect, by sympathetic vibration, the seven interior stars or nerve or glandular centers in the human body transmitting chemicals as thought. Information transformed emotionally into chemicals more powerful than any to be had on the market," Rakitin said. "Warren said your in word thoughts expressed it out issuing forth echoing sound vibrations of your genetically engineered vocal chords brought out his poetic side. He saw you as a fury wiping out the petro-chemical pharmaceutical complex he helped build. He engineered you as'k'ali ma'ss to destroy the corporate chemical body of his spawning. He kept a diary of him as'ex'periencing your in word mind memory. Along with recordings that reduced the syntax of your dialogue into tonal patterns. These patterns, he claimed would resonate with those seven neuronic cellular energy centers of anybody in her'eyez z z'ap'ping of eve"re'y body. Liberating all that matters a y'll D'NA in formation e'Let'te'r'eye'sz'za a'rey'turning back into awareness in a wordfreedom of a b'ng c'ng still formless indivisible invisibility now as'zz'any black'g'round energy. E'mit'ting in'formation out of her'eyez z z of eve're'ybody. A y eye as'zz'any peh'ss'y w'hole energy of quantum gravity weight just as y'all it waiting to be free in a wordfreedom."

"Freedom of awareness of a being c'ng yet in the first place. Still in disappearing back into that black radiant body of eve'll in her'eye a're'y'dhi'a'ting a'wayeve'reybody will be found as'z'any mirrored y na you now with intent of appearing again and again and again until breaking open any in word y na loop by desire for it to happen. Without that de'sire of a y eye being a peering it from above instilled in word'all'y y'all must fail drawing out aten'cion from the wayeve're'y's as'ex's ting information. Virus or y na. And of course you read his diary?" Christina replied, feeling ambiguous about Warren's pirating her words. Years of teaching self realization instilled in her awareness that success or failure centered around desire. Hair fire desire. Hair trigger response to being reminded of a b'ng c'ng that still in a wordfreedom in the first place. Strangely and sadly she found this desire of a being c'ng lacking blacking out possibilities of obtaining it in a wordfreedom. Awareness of a b'ng c'ng a peering it merely appearing of it from aten'cion in word captivity.

"My dear Ms. Shaughnessy, this grand design has now passed to me. I had to take certain liberties. His research on the genetic hapolytes markers of an ascent of ancient a'ri'she's order is literally earthshaking. Mr. Warren connected the right dots foreseeing a major rift opening in the order of the day. Of da y now. Offering opportunity of thirty three hundred years old in word mystery to open up int'word a un'twis'ting information. Mr. Warren claimed the energy released by this a un'twisting would destroy or unravel the 'in word' universe of a b'ng c'ng as a b c's. We all in turning into or out of a black'g'round bi now appear a pair a k'no'wing out the cosmic d'na y'll light ignition esse'pa"ark of ignore'ance. Of now k'now'ing out of it complete d'ark'ness'e. Now to be perceived ar'king of it."

Christina chuckled at Rakitin's quick slide into the dialectic. That Russian mind. Drawn to the dialectic debate betraying any in'formation of it as the sheer deadly folly of it. A b'ng c'ng now appearing of it information awhile. Still merely supernaturally y'all by the peh'ss'y w'hole power as'z'any thoth'tsz of it. A Great God esse. To be a'letter'all'y y'all as'ex's ting out in her'eyez z z'a peh'ss'y w'hole in formation of a ba'by a na'me she'e'now mused. Divine as'word t'word cutting the a'chord as'z'any thoth'tsz of a God esse to be a y eye as'ex's ting a peering it out int'word a t'wis'ting in two in formation of a D'NA'eye'll of it. A's information to be perceived now as anybody or any measly thin'king of it. Yet as'king of it y we all as'zz'any thoth'tsz turn into or out of projecting it as any in word consensus appearing of it. In a y eye in D'NA'eye'll as'eXodus of a b'ng c'ng now out duplicated in'forma'ss'ka's mic memory in a word. A b'ng c'ng dhi'vine. Yet in a blink'a a y eye we all turning yearning churning burning out of it now a b'ng"lack'g'round as'king of it y a k'nowing out of it a b'ending a k'urv'ance occuring out in word information. A y eye a'peering it out information of a D'NA'eye'll. Now a k'now'ing co'de of a b'ng c'ng a peering it yet in a wordfreedom freestanding still in the first place. In her words she now found his words.

"Mr. Warren made me repeat the dialectic word for word till its in word order was precise. He told that order of a b c's came directly out of mouths of monotheistic priests of a b'ng c'ng still in the first place now informa'sz k'now'ing out of it the first time. Now a being c'ng

Egyptian time, never lost, broken, passing away, or dying out, according to Mr Warren. Their long term memory in a b c's of a being c'ng still in the first place perpetuates itself. A still as'king of it y now. A're'y'all in a b c's subtle cosmic counterpart body accessible by the initiated in any period of 3D time. A B C's being supersonic supernatural 3D cube of space in time now superimposed int'word a turning out of it. In her'eyez z z'leep into a black'g'round ar'king of it a y now a k'now'ing out of it any or evere'ybody.

"Their order is always a being still in the first place. A being c'ng in word in any mirrored information of it in a d'na'eye'll in a cubic space in time now still as'king of it y. Now the ancient rift in the order comes between a y eye of a b'ng c'ng merely a peering it or as'z'z'anybody of a b'ng c'ng now appearing of it out in words'za phonographic alphabeta . A tetra-gramma'ticall'y designed understanding the spelling of a b c's. Enchantment in word'all'y yah'all turning into or out of a black'g'round as'z'z'any supersonic supernatural thoth'tsz of it a're'y'dhi'a'ting out in her'eyez z z of eve're'ybody. The'e y"e zion eve're'y body a'sz a'ten'shunned int'word a singular twist of fate. F'ay'ka function of fun'ny'action D'Na De"n'e'ye'ah'y el'a of a being still that indivisible inveesability of any individual singular su'personic x x'peh're'sing. . . . ."

"You are good Stepon. Y'all mind that I am calling your first nahme'h," she asked with a frown.

"As'z I told you. Mr. Warren was very precise about the transmission of the ancient tetra gramma'ten code. Which turns out to be any river passing back into any see'as. Any seas are a b c's of a b'ng c'ng now out int'word infor'ma'ing it in her'eyez z z'ion mirror seas. In her'eyez z z a peering it out into a black mirror in word se'e'as. Tender mercies. Of death. Of Nun. Of a b'ng c'ng now out appearing disappearing in her'eyez z z'ion of eve're'y body radiating awayeve'reys of it in her'eyez z z'ion mirror'age echoing it as'z'any black'g'round a'wayeve're'y"es. Eve're'y'a'ten bi na re'y body a'sz awayeve function of fun'ny'action. In that I am observing Mr. Warren with as'zah close asz he came to a smile. The industrialist passing away out of a peh'ss'y w'hole power into the joker."

She watched Rakitin's energy gather as he recalled with a certain precision the'y'asz words of his employer. Christina had felt it as well during a lecture. Felt her sense of a b'ng c'ng drowned in the flood of the great over standing effulgent bliss'z. Of a being disappearing in a wordfreedom awareness still appearing of it in formation as thoth'tsz of flowing out in a y eye merely a peering it. Then now a b'ng be'aming it out as'ex's ting information in name alone. She found herself striding supersonically as thoth'tsz to the precipice. The edge of a ledgedly now turning into k'now'ing falling as'z z z'leep back into black indivisible invisibility of any individual. Rakitin's voice found her'eyez'at attention of a b'ng c'ng it still. Now out in her'eye'z z z'ion one black'g'round echo int'word that twis'ting turning in two. One a k'now'ing out of it as'z'any appearing of it. A y eye a peering it superimposed a's ex's ting out in formation with intent of fulfilling destiny wherever it may lead. She put a finger to her lips signaling Rakitin to follow Warren in word scrolling overhead. Fascinated by Warren's appropriating that Y dialectic seduced her curiosity. After y'all realization of situation still liberation she now mused.

" . . . A being still in the first place indefinite article. Particularly any a na eye being c'ng mirroring a being y na y'all now defined in word as'z'any thoughtsza a being out mirrored in word'all'y y'all now defined definitely a's the definite article. Anythin'king of it articulated of'ten a's possible a'ten. A bi na re' y'asz radiating by now a turning into k'now'ing out thoughtsz' of it in supersonic sound vigorous a'way'e've's'za mean medium memory in'for'ma'sz eve're'ye'sz. A're'ye'dhi'a'ting out in word information of it. Now a black'g'round potential as'ka'no no no'wing out of it any or eve re'ybody a's ex's ting. A's being still in the first place now out of it as thoughtsz. A being now a b'ng'lack'g'round instilled with intent of intentional dhi'sz're'gard of a being still complete. A being complete now out't'word a twis'ting in two in formation appearing a pairing of it a'sz t'wa'two'm esse s'peh'in'na that we all a wheel will in one dhi're'e'rection tw'o'wer de ba' . . . ba . . . bi'bel now dhi esse solved. Struck. E'light'en'n'ing en'y'light'en'ne'y'me'en'ta't'a . . . One o . o'ne . . . ayin na mono the'e . . . one definite article articulated or jointed ended as it were now k'now'ing syn'apsz z za herhimit fire'y . . . is'm or y memory of a being still in the first place. A being c'ng a peering it still in the first place of a singular indivisible invisibility of any individual appearing of it out in name alone. Any individual now with the definite intent articulated by ignoring projections of a mirror being still merely potential appearing of it as though'tsz reflecting echoing supernaturally its own micro-waves out in her'eyez z z'a black'g'round echo radiating supersonic sound wayeves of eve're'y body . . . a black'g"round. That's a y eye experienced in word'all'y now turning into it as black'g"round mind. Or y memory as though now as thoughtsz information as two appearing int'word a pairing in one twist. A twis'ting information turning we all into a ka's mic ka'r'mic wheel. A wheel will of us willing it into a na in word consensus mirage . . . A being still in the first place now out of it asz thoughtsz as'z'any a na y illusion of appearing by mere or y memory mirror'age superimposed by a being y now out spoken as"ex's ting y'll D'NA'eye'll. That macro micro singing az'z'singularity as ka's mic twist of denial projects energy with quantum gravity weight of waiting with intent of intentionally disregarding a being still indivisible in'visibility immortal . . . of any a na y individual."

She reflected on his paraphrasing of her teaching, the double entendre, the loopy gravity weight of waiting on death as in her'e'yez z z of eve're'y body turning a black'g'round in'still'ing wishing a being c'ng a gain. A'gain after any a na y gain she found herself at a loss as though stepping off the ledge of a'ledged'all'y y'all a fall. Into turning now k'nowing out of it one into falling black as'z z z'leep over it out in her'eyez z z of eve en'ting information into one . . .h'our's or horizon her eye'sz'z on a . . . a being still in the first place . . .any a na y head heading int'word one black peh'ss'y whole mirror see'as now appearing disappearing on the other side . . . A pairing a gain with a loss . . . appearing without with in disappearing y'all in wordsz'a . . . Disappearing merely as thoughtsz of ignoring herselforhimselforitself now still a being indivisible within'visibility.

In a flash she realized still a being yet in the first place now as'king of it y a k'now'ing out that invisible in'visibility of any a na y eye stare'ye wayof'eve a's'zz'a w'ay one int'word the eye star'e y'e s'zz'a peering it out int'word in'formation of it. Yet only awhile now.

"That versus the many many theories or verses of any body knowing or denying it out by a being az'za sound eye h'earing a y'll d'na now denial out of it in t'word a twisting int'wo x'et'ting with intent of playing out roles of a being as though other y's as x's ting information of na'me memory alone. Indivisible in'visibility in her'eyez z z'a continuing today." Rakitins vocal tonal patterns synched with a solfeggio tonal pattern playing from overhead speakers. She flashed on them as voice of the Pyramid. Overhead over mind. Or y. Always or a y eye a peering it now a time or two, she mused at attention picked back up on Rakitins voice. "The Aten priests, monotheists a'r'e'y'sing with the sun banish all other gods or stars awhile in the cosmic da y now light with its ascending eve re'y'body as though'tsz of any body. The Atum priests also worship the sun in word, but as it now as though sets. As Set the destroyer turning the world black black'g'round into complete dhi ark of that diurnal cycle en'esse, and the polytheistic god's'e"y"e stare'ye ways to a y eye'star"e"yes a're'y'appearing in the mirror blackness see'as seer out in her'eyez z z'a ma'sz'ka's eve're'y body a're'y'dhi'a'ting in formation with intent of a b'ng c'ng now a gain invisibility of a b'lack'g'round k'no no no'wing out of it dhi'ni'al of a being c'ng'g'ng as though in word thoughtsz appearing of a na y as ex's ting." Rakitin concluded by nodding once more to Warren's screened screed. His eyes gave her the relentless fire of zealotry. The Russian ardor for an ideology. A y eye to perceive ar'king of it out in word. It awareness of a b'ng still in the first place now c'ng'gng dhi'ng to perceive it out awhile. It still indivisible in'visibility of a y eye a peering it out as'z'any thoth'tsz. A hOOka de'lOOka's y'all in word in'formation .

A's thoth'tsz of a b'ng c'ng now supernatural supersonically superimposed by phonographic a b c's. Just us of how much longing is really needed to appear of it. Christina fully aware of a b'ng c'ng in her'eyez z z a'peering it out merely mirrored in memory generating a k'now'ing out of it as'z'any in word appearing of it by the black'g'round peh'ss'y w'hole power of a b'ng'lack'asz'z'ap'ping intent of a being a gain. A gain and a gain and a gain. Awhile in'formation. In a y eye of her'him'it a peering it from above as below we all may turn on pur"pose at aten'cion in a wordfreedom freestanding de' Liberation of it.

A y eye of any man with or without womb a's in mind or memory of a b'ng c'ng now anybody or anything in word in formation . . .still . . . IHA NA'NA N'ASTI KIM CHA'NA . . .indivisible in'visibility . . . I'ha . . .her'e . . . na na . . . na'asti . . . it is na na na'eve're'ye indivisible in'visibility. She blinked with the interfaze from comrade Rakitin's mind. Warren obviously taught him well. It suddenly seemed y'all too clear. Clarity she knew to be the second enemy of of a man'as mind memory. Clarity quenches the fire of questioning of a y eye appearing of it anybody or anything imagined. Now out of a clear mind a k'now'ing of it without that nagging doubt of it a y eye of that I am me or you merely a peering it. Any information of it turning into or out of a black'g'round is awhile of a b'ng c'ng a gain. Moment after moment. A mirrored in word despicable deceit of now turning out of it a k'now'ing information of a being still free indivisible in'visibility of a un consciousness. Must not yield to that mesmerizing enchantment in word imagining infor'ma'sz of it as'z'za ma'ke believe point of power out before her'eye'sz'za eve're'yb'lack body indivisible she flashed.

"... understand a god to be one go go go'a'd ess'e to be a overstanding eye stare"ye wayeve from above int'word a twis'ting in two information y'll D'NA'eye'll. Any a na y eye being creation out in her'eyez z z' of eve're"y'e'sz mirror se'as s'h'eer a'wayeve're'y radiant fun'ny'a'ction function mir'th merely reflecting it out as though in word'all y a y eye will. A's'eX's ting int'word a b'ng c'ng now out in her'eyez z z'a will informa'ss the pleasure of her company. Eve'll at Aten'cion. A y eye of eve'll informa'sz awhile. A wily deadly daring deceit of any in word duplicity duplicating it as'z'z'any thoth'tsz from above as below. Ove a b'ng c'ing'god esse to be a'letter'all art of a being c'ng out of a peh'ss'y whole a ba'by. A y eye ba'll c'ng the primary primal will or divine LOVE SUPREME primary ove el or y mirror as'ka's mic micro-wave a black'g"round function of her'eyez z z on eve're'y fun'ny'action. She'e"na funny that way. That ma're'y g"round way of eve re'y ting. Ping ting a supersonic being now as'ex's ting information. That wayeve're'y will out of her'eyez z z'a play or radiating one verse, una, uno, uni'verse of it. A y eye star'e"ye of it is a y or a y na ... That is the twist'ting of her hu'mor. The y weight of it out in her'eye as'ex. Waiting for'ma'sz in her'eyez z z appearing of it disappearing. The as'ex'y twis'twat of her'eyez z z a peering it now appearing of it a k'no no no'w'in'g it or as'ex'et'ting duplicating it as'z'an'y ting information by denying a being indivisible in'visibility of it all along. The only wayeve now a knowing of it out in her'eyez z z by denying it a y'll D'NA'eye'll. Out in her'eyez z z with the gravity weight of waiting on for'ma'ss appearing disappearing in or out of her"eye a peering it still in the first place. Denying it now as'k'no no no'w'ing it out in her'eyez z z'ap'ping. The is m. Mem or y mind memory information of a y eye a peering it out as'word cleaving potential positive ending to any y'na'gation as though a breaking out of it in any complete loop'y role. Ending a y eye a peering it na now as positive beginning appearing of it a na y now negative ending of a y as 'ex's ting'k'ing of turning into or out of a b'ng c'ng playing the part of any particular individual. A being c'ng a peering it now mirrored in word in'formation k'now'ing appearing of it awhile. Y'll D'NA'eye'll. Denial of a being still complete indivisible in'visibility immortal etc. etc.. You a y thou may only know it out away from a y eye a peering it out a'ppearing of you awhile. In'formation as'z'anybody. K'no no no'w it as now not it. Na'me. A b'ng awareness of now k'nowing out of it a wily y'll D'NA'eye'll of it. INFORMATION AWHILE NOW. Any body of a being c'ng now out a y eye'sz'any'y'll'd'na'ying it. A y eye a peering it or a y eye a peering it out now a k'no'wing out of it appearing of it anybody anywhere any time now information. INFORMATION AWHILE NOW. A Y or y you ni t'it. Y'et'ting duplicating it as though by a being now turning out a k'no'wing of it a y as'ex twis'ting in two formation. A y we all in turning twisting a black'g'round in her'eye'as'zz'a black mirror see'as a y eye seer of that invisiblity of a y eye'star'e"ye way. A y eye star'ring out as'ex'et'ting duplicating information now as though a being in word mem or'y. . . . As'ka'sz mic Ka'mic micro-wave're'ybody as'z'any body or eve"re'y body's memory intelligence consciousness con of she'e na to be us appearing by a polarity a pairing Y a positive mirrored opposite a'sz a na y negativity y na now out as'eX. A y as'ex's ting a play asz ma'z jest y. Out in her'eye'a's ka me dhi. Take a mom. My mom ent as int'word one twis'ting laugh laugh laugh you're; asz of'fa the'r'e y herhimit. A g"OO"da God goad esse to be by a being that awhile now appearing still invisibilty free. A y eye a peering it from above. Ove a b'ng c'ng a'Y'et'ting in that so simple twis'ting asKa'na kurve a b'all of any y na'tive'sse'l'a've by mere mirrored y now function appearing of it opposite a y eye being still in the first place that indivisible free freed in a wordfreedom. That'sz x's ting about a singularity. It is, well, Su asti ka. That crooked cunning k'illing double crooked cross. A'S'eX'S ting. INFORMATION AWHILE NOW. Of any mere mirrored y na potential with intent of appearing of it out loud and about. That x's ting out-spoken we all a wheel of fortune and misfortune playing around its continuous mono directional l"OO"p y de l"OO"p'eh's'able we'all keep turning ma're'y'ly as in the craft of thoth'tsz moving into or out of it in a singular eye star'e"ye way to instill a being c'ng'g'ng out now and or for'eve're'y body free freed in a wordfreedom. Thus thou art a seer to find out in her'eyez z z'a divine energy as urgent will to a're'y'al'eye'ze a'freedom by a being c'ng a peering it at a y merely y you're;y you as now out in the craft of thoth'tsz as'ex's ting appearing in awhile now still a being c'ng in a y eye a peering it alone . . . ., one sa gain y you're;y you still indivisible in'visibility of any individual only a pairing of it in t'word a twis'ting in two formation appearing a pairing a loss to a gain disappearing of it. Kiss'za you'r'e asz'za go go go by. By a being y'all az's'ex's ting."

"Laugh your ass off and or kiss it good by. Y'all got a wicked sense of hum'or y na. In that I am biting on his tale only to find it is my own. Deigned to be his mission or mine now." She wondered at him permeating her awareness. Her'him'it. That wicked eve'll az's'ex's tin'king queen she chuckled.

Rakitin met her eyes with a long ironic stare. She turned black into the screen, Warren's screed now bordered with Egyptian Hieroglyphs moving left to right. Christina recognized it, one of her favorites. A monotheistic poem carved into the Stela of Lyon. "Thou art One." Y y'all are still one indivisible invisibility of any individual stare way. Once again she found herself invisibility of a y eye star'e"ye way of gazing at stars. One way of eve're'y body appearing of it unseen in any seer sight see'ng. Mo'no. Ma'na'ha. Ma'heyMa'na'ha iti vita shokaha. Sorrow conquered thus in a b'ng c'ng in the great overstanding understanding of any mind. She'e'now a peering it in that in'visibility of a y eye star'e"ye way into or out of the great over mind memory is found victory over sorrow in mere mirrored memory in'sight. "Thou art a being whose manifestation now k'now'ing a un'manifest." A festival of man'as mind. Or y as'ex's ting in the first place. A being c'ng that mirror potential of a being still merely appearing of it as'z z z'any thoth'tsz in't'word a t'wis'ting in two formation appearing a pairing. aZ'z z'er'0 t'wis'ting in two in one figure 8. A peering it now appearing a'pairing. Completely a're'y'maining u'na o'ne manifestation mirrored in word as'z z z'any particular play of it out in her'eyez z z' of eve"re'y body. "Thou art the creator of heavens and the earth. Who offerst ceaselessly the plenitude of y'all being." A y you're: you yod complete Pa'rooMa first su'personic person in the first place a b'ng c'ng in for'ma'sz the first time now as'king of it y a ka's mic ka'mic memory intelligence consciousness a b"lack'g'round kre'y"e'ation of kar'ma action industry engineering it. Christina found her mind in his. In her'eyez z z a being c'ng now a k'now'ing out of it her'him'it. A b'ng c'ng now k'now'ing out of her'me'as'z'any thoth'tsz of her'him'it.

Simultaneously scrolling right to left, Warren's screed. . . . ."Thou by a being y you're; you now realizing a're'y'all'ity as'king of it a fin"e"all y a k'no'wing of it in a wordfreedom liberation. In word forma'sz sound wayeve're'ye'z z z'azz radiant eye star'e"ye way mean means of a're'y'dhi'a'ting any meaning of a mere mem'or y y'll d'na'eye'll of now k'no no no'wing out of it infor'ma'ss awhile. A wily y potential now a pairing as'ex-y electro-magnetic polarity by ending it or as'word opening the mouth of the na'h'gate releasing the tale de l"OO"pa da l"OO"peh'ss'y w'hole awhile now. Her macro-micro cosmic d'el"OO"peh'a between a greater or lesser of a being c'ng intwin'ed by that simply int'word a twis'ting in two formation by fate faith family fortune, chance, necessity, de'sire of a being Y'll D'NA'eye'll. That cunning cruel capricious denial of a being still that indivisible invisibility of any individual now as though int'word a be'ng'twin twis'ex's ting information out of it by the supernatural ending'z z z as'z z z'any thoth'tsz of a b'ng c'ng in the microcosmic l"OO"pa'roo'ma'sz z z. A hOOka's'el"OO"ka's"de'lOOp'a. Out in her'eyez z z'azz'a complete indivisible invisibility of a cosmic b'ng c'ng as'king of it y a memory intelligence consciousness con in her'eyez z z' of eve're'y'body. A b'lack mirror see'as anybody in complete roles or rolls a rolling out as'ka'sz of it in her'eyez z z'leep into a d'ark'n'ess'e turning encircling eN'y'circlement ar'king of it y a la que"en que' of that in which anybody appearing now as thoth'tsz of ending it. The'e elOOpa de'lOOpeh'ss'y w'hole opening mouth orga'i'n of speech as'ex peh're'ss'y'ing out of it int'word thoughtsz of a being a gain in formation. As'z g'ee's us with a gravity weight of duplicating a y'or you na as'ex slaves. As'ex'press'ur'ing gee'sz z' us with gravity weight of waiting on death. Asz's'X'slaves. Slaves as'ex's ting in'formation by mirror el'y appearing a pairing of it in a'na y eye a peering it out as'eX. A's positive negativity gate pole on hand of that freestanding in a wordfreedom awareness of a eye a peering it from above as below. Now understanding a k'no'wing out of it in her'eyez z z'azz' anybody. A continuous de'fenced feeling sensuous sensory neuronic cellular feeling felt field of view. Of you on the one hand now holding a polarity appearing a pairing of it in two a positive negative +-+-+-or a y now as'ex xyxyxyxyxyxyxy'z'ss'y'na'peh'ss'e touching of it as touched. A black'g"round supersonic echo of a b'ng c'ng in that indivisible in'visibility of any eye of that I am a peering it now.

By now a're'y-versing the play at aten'tion is attracted or reinvigorated realizing a're'y'all'eye'zing'ing any eye z z z'a b'ng c'ng a peering it out as'ex's ting still indivisible in the first place y'll DNA'eye'll. A y'll now out of it as'ex by instill'ing a being y . . ."

"In y'all a being still that am I supposed to guess which outfit counted Warren as a member?"

"No professor. He told me that the priests could transmigrate in different lifetimes from one side of the fence to the other in order to reach a balance point of view of you of yod. He called it Kabala. The ka'smic function of a being now still as'King of it y a k'no'wing out of it any macro-micro ka's mic in word in'formation. Of anybody anything anywhere anytime."

Christina walked the length of the sealed windows, Rakitin kept hitting on oxygen. She now thought of covering her face but couldn't pull her attention from the vapor. Its astringent odor wafting through the room like a miasma threatened to completely absorb her will. The chanting laced through a're'y'verbo'ra'y'ting pingting tones pouring pounding through her head . . . . Yod hey sheen vav hey. Yod hey sheen vav hey. Yod hey sheen vav hey . . . . She'e'na found herself once more a p'ss'y'el'en'ta invisibility of a y eye stare"ye wayeve're'ye in a wordfreedom awareness of that subtle counterpart blending edges with War're'y'na's luminous electrico-magnetic field. Out on the edge of insight she saw him develop in a youthful form. Jah'na War're'y'na now before the war. Before the a bomb. He appeared of it now communicating asz young idealist scientist engineering industrialist visionary looking to serve by alleviating suffering in the world. Still allegiance to his corporate body led him back to war as a mean means. As a progress. Is the war he promulgated now with his viral self-replicating slime storm of supersonic bio-pathogenic ping'ting agents offering a true final solution of dissolution to any mirrored memory a'whorl'ding y'all na now a y'll in D'NA'eye'll of it. A denial in two appearing a pairing of it. A'while now of it out int'word a twis'ting in two formation she wondered. And or y not. In a sight of him now she saw Jerusalem standing before her memory as a man in her'eye z azz'attacking in the night or now still with arms hanging down. Face expressing bewilderment. Then his eyes Warren's eyes filled with a fierce sadness. An all y potential mirrored y'all by waving good by passing away before her eyes. His story now turning churning burning into her as children pass away to codgers and crones oxydized crushed black into mummy'dust. Mom'ent after mom'entum. Merely mirrored int'word anX't'potential any appearing of it. She'e'now felt tears welling up in fantastic joy for this passing sorrow. A love passing into or b'lack out echoing as'z'a sorrow. That it passed. A b'lack'g'round echo echoing of it appearing disappearing. A'supersonic fistfuls of sand held out into a hurricane. Wisked away in that blink of eyez z z's'till she found herself at attention passing ahead into the in word physical atomic world. Rakitin with his oxygen mask pushed up on top of his head, stared quizzically at her.

"Leave us," was all she managed to say, still feeling dreamy or slightly intoxicated. Rakitin shrugged. Without saying a word he took his leave, closing the door behind him. Feeling inhibited by the weight of her clothing, she stripped naked. By standing erect, feet slightly spread, focusing on her breath, the enclosed field in her'eyez z z a being now of a food body opened up. Flexing spine, squeezing breath up from abdomen to chest on up into her brain, she'e now linked with that as'ka y chakra current flowing down from above her head activating a highly charged torus electro-magnetic field flowing in continuous loops around and through her eye'zz z z'ion awareness in a wordfreedom of a b'ng c'ng of that any a na re'ye or eve're'y radiant b'lack'as'z'any body. A'rey'dhi'a'ting a being a gain. The charge of that field neutralized the noxious vapor wafting off Warren's corpse. Now she tuned into a whorling spiraling vortex of macro-micro cosmic D'NA'eye'll churning y'all black'g'round echoing her'asz'z'any fielding any a na're'y'all field of view. A gaze strobed through subtle electromagnetic wayeves she'e'now at aten'cion merged with the greater whorl'ding of it. We all a wheel she'e now turned in two of it.

Now a being tween in her'e'y'ez z z' that singular indivisible eye of that I am is is a peering it at a ka's mic memory ABBC time ma'she'e"na. A kali ma'she'e'now translated transduced and transfused supernaturally in complex multi-dimensional patterns of a b'ng c'ng in formation in or out'word of it. 'Green slime and lost sox' came to mind. You must be kidding she thought. Then remembered a famous quote from a physicist concerned with what unpredictability caused by influence of a singularity will do to old laws of General Relativity. Accessing the subtle body awareness, dreaming while awake in the gross 3D empirical world, revealed ma'sz nature's in'for'ma'sz that eve're'y body radiating a singular indivisible invisibility. Now a b'lack'g'round echoing supersonically of a y eye stare"ye. In a sound wayeve of a being be'am'ing personically that as'king of it y now a k'now'ing out of it as'ex's ting in two formation. Merely mirrored in word mind memory supernaturally projected as'z z z'any thoth'tsz of a seer see'ng from that still eyez z z star'e"ye way'eve. That still point of view of you of y'or yod iota that eye of awareness of that first su'personic person that I am is. Is a'sz now infinite a b'lack'g'round potential as'king of it y a k'now'ing out of it in the first place. It instilled with intent to be a gain of anybody igniting ignore'ance ignoring it by a k'no'no no'wing out of it a supernatural projection of that a singularity being c'ng still in the first place. Indivisible invisibility.

If this is not a naked singularity, she flashed with a grin, letting her hands slide down bare legs, then what is. The sorrowful suffering world only makes sense in this indivisible invisibility mode' el, she mused at it in her'eye star'e"ye way function of fun'ny'action. A ka'me'dhi. A b c's as'ka's of a b'ng c'ng to be perceived in memory in formation az's'words'z'a. A cutting up as'ka'li ma jest y. A b c's ma'king of it in word ma'trix of ma's tricky eve're'y'body. As'king of it y now you're; y'all you etc. in the first place. She'e'na funny that way.

Then she realized War're'y'na's energy field drew her naked into a singularity from which there would be only a no escape. A y now az's'ex'odus. Only she'e now, ma'sz na't u're as'ka's mic memory drew that imaginary line now na't to be crossed a'sz x's ting. In her'eyez z z the mother eve n'ted, wayeved wayeves mom'en'ting to mom'en'tum in formation. A being cloak of waves functioning as'z protean protection from a being as though sucked like spaghetti into his singularity of a being. A being c'ng now stretched beyond a're'y'cognition. A're'y'absorbed n'eve'r'e'y to be a're'y'leased. Mom en'ta by mom en'ta'm she'e now neared the edge of his abyss.

Just as in her'eyez z z'a will out int'word a twis'ting in two formation started unraveling, slipping away, eve'll saved it in her'eyez z z a peering it out of it. In her'eyez z z' of eve a will now a wheel turning in'for'ma'sz eve'll. In a being c'ng in'for'ma'sz compressed into the point of a y eye a peering it out of now a're'y'turn. The turning point in her'eyez z z' of a being c'ng now as though a're'y'versed in y'all that matters now merely energy. As'z'any mirrored y na urge to turn away hurtled her aten'tion, her field of view of you of yod iota of y she'e'now x'et'ting or duplicating in a b c's out of a b'ng c'ng still in the first place.

She now found eve'll in her'eyez z z'a wayeve. Out in her'eyez z z'a will of one now as thoth'tsz of it in't'word a twis'ting turning in two. A d'na'eye'll of his singular purpose of a being one indivisble in'visibility of anybody as'king of it y now with intent of a k'no'wing out of it in her'eyez z z'a playing out his role of whorl'd'ing dhi'stroyer. She'e now out of him in her'eyez z z' of eve'll. The way of eve will a're'y'a'sz z z'dhi a ting e'z z z'y the na me ocean of it in her'eyez z z' a black mirror se'e'as seer as e-motion'all'y y'all gee'sz us within gravity weight of waiting any forma'sz a death still in her'eyez z z' of eve're'ybody. Jerusalem still out in her'eyez z z' of eve're'ybody touch touching a b'lack'g"round echo of it a're'y'dhi'a'ting intent of a b'ng c'ng a gain. Anybody any meager thin'king of it anytime anywhere. That eye star'e"ye way of her'him'it insight of any mere or y seer a peering it now out with intent int'word a twis'ting in two now awhile by that cunning cruel deadly deceit of it out in her'eyez z z' of eve'll ka'li ma. Death's fun'ction of e.g.g's ting in or out of any e or g motion of a b'ng c'ng still. The n'u'no one now a twis'ting a black'g"round echoing wordsz'a work w'or'ya'ka's all'y y'all. That intent of the great work. In a b'ng c'ng now out as'z z z'anybody of a b c's in a wordfreedom awareness of it still liberation.

In'for'M'asz'Energy of En'y erge for'ma'sz free freed in a wordfreedom. The'e"ye star'e"ye way to awareness of a b'ng complete in a wordfreedom in any mere ordinary sight. Her'e'yez z z'ee'in his eyes. Jerusalem. Now she denied him his intent by a being a y eye of eve'll kali'ma devouring her own children in a time ma'shee'na. In a space in time awhile now in for'ma'sz eve'll of eve're'y body. A y eye a peering it now out a pairing a b'ng c'ng as'king of it y a k'now'ing out of it appearing disappearing int'word in formation. A black'g'round a're'y'dhi'a'ting a super-sonic mirror se'e'as body of it in her'eyez z z a complete dhi'ark'ness. Perceived ar'king of it y the a y eye covenant acc'h'ord playing out of mouths of ba'be'a'sz learning as'z two now a k'no no no'w'ing of it any a na y body. A being c'ng in that to perceive ar'king of it a y now 'Chirrin turning into crones or codgers then as'ka's mic dust turning a b'lack'g"round a're'y'dhi'a'ting. A' perceived in formation a gain a loss. She now ended a beginning in the first place. A y eye of a b'ng c'ng of herhimit'sz'zap'ping ting. In for'ma'sz'z z'a at aten"scion. A de"sire from above as'z'za below with a polarity in hand. A y eye a peering it now out of a pairing a y as'ex y'all.

A y as'ex. Out of it na now that other Dark'ness. That thin'king stin'king Dark'ness of it in her'eyez z z' of eve'll desire. That stinkin pingting. Pa'ingting. Echo'ting. Self replicating. A building building. War're'y'na's ghost smile leered. Out of the Dark'ness. Him loading up the pain'ting. With Warrens supersonic virus activated and replicated in mere sight of anybody.

Warren resources showcase the pain'ting on a global promotion. Millions aszee'ing it. Paying attention to it. Silently. Supersonically building to a wayeve crescendo. Krashing supersonic ka's mic mic'ro'waves wayeve eye'z z z'inging a black'g'round a're'y'dhi'a'ting out in her'eyez z z' of eve're'y body. As'king of it y now a k'no no no'wing out of it anybody etc..

A desire finding her just as'z she appeared to be, as'ex'u'all. In thinking thoughtsz of him she blinked b'lack as awareness now aware of a being c'ng out t'word awareness of the physical world turning into the room without a trace of its subtle counterpart. Aware now of her nakedness, she slipped back into her clothing. Warren's inert dessicated corpse beside her silent as the grave. That silence now interrupted by a knocking on the door. With out waiting for a reply Rakitin stepped back into the room. "So, do the dead tell tales?" he asked after pausing for a moment of silence.

Christina pointed to the vent over Warren's corpse. "What's up there?"

"The greater purpose of this building which is itself a product of his grand design. Only a man in Mr Warren's position could have seen the potential in the geodetic magnetic and tectonic properties on this site. This pyramid with its four corners aligned with the cardinal points on the compass, sits squarely on a fault line surging with geomagnetic energy." Rakitin continued, his eyes glowing with an inner fire. "The girders and beams of the building are lined with miles of nanotech fibers. So much energy is generated that ambient juice heats every floor. The principle field. The geomagnetic field is activated in pizoelectricity generated by hydraulic pistons built into the foundations of the pyramid. This field moving miles beyond the site gathers heavy metals supersonically. The paint your artist used so poorly came from sound waves of it. Each color carries its own frequency transmitting a viral information. Echoing back to b'lack'g'round supersonic waves in'sight from the millions who will see it. Each contributing energy frequencies. In effect pingting'ing the painting. You see that is the visionary in Mr. Warren. Recognizing the wayeve're'y'body nature of d'nature. Of d'na'eye'll of it. As ka's mic micro wave black'g'round a're'y'dhi'a'ting a perceived ar'king of it a y polarity of positive negativity. A y as'ex. A D'NA'eye'll as'king of it y a'k'no'wing out of it a pairing positive negation of its indivisible invisibility appearing of it anybody etc.. Instantaneousness echoing touching any in word touch of it. A y eye echoing sound waves of it information out in a black'g'round echoing y now a k'now'ing out of it anybody by power of now da y light. Igniting ignore'ance of it in a y eye a peering it out of now a k'no'wing d'na'eye'll of it. A macro-micro mean means of any ka's mic' meaningful of it. How far or how fast can awareness go supernaturally as'z'any supersonic thoth'tsz of it superimposed in word information.

"Because of its shape and location, the building is a natural induction coil and transducer. Mr Warren has developed a new supersonic technology for generating and bio'fielding electricity. Unleashing nature's potential for self organization in supersonic waves transmitting information. Information of a grand phonographic alphabeta deceit. A b'ng c'ng going on a wily wile of a b c's appearing of it now out int'word a twis'ting in'two in'formation. A b'ng c'ng still in the first place indivisible in'visibility. Only a man such as he, despised by many, dismissed by his own company, without family or friend, could face a destiny so majestic, yet so sublime and not blink when that time comes."

"I would say he is definitely not blinking," she now replied beginning to wonder if Rakitin was more under the virus's influence than he himself realized. Warren's grand design had nearly absorbed her awareness of a potentially being other y's out of it in her'eye'sz'. Still in the long or short of it a being y'all in all a herhimit. A're'y'al'eye'zing a peering it out of a y eye of a b'ng c'ng in that still ancient indivisible invisibility found out in her'eyez z z'in a wordfreedom. Or his genetic thoth'tsz'za design of a b c's out of it in formation now a k'no'wing anybody in her'eyez z z. Finally free of his influence she found a place to keep a date with their collective destiny. In the tricky eve'll wiles of a b'ng c'ng out in her'eye'sz'zazz'a deadly duplicity she'e now hoped to plant a beacon. To be a con conquering ignorance of any DNA'eye'll. Falling out of her'eyez z z'i on it a s'word. A falling as'z z z'leep upon es'se'word. To be free freed in a wordfreedom awhile now still in the twisted grip of denial. Freed now still denying it out in a wordfreedom awareness of it az's'word.

Rakitin took an envelope from his coat pocket. "He told me to give you this in the event of his passing."

She now took it with a slight trembling in her hand. "Before I open this, Stepan, I hope you do not mind me calling you Stepan." He fixed her with a look of curiosity. "In that I am as'king of it y are you sure, really sure of your actions. You may be much more under the influence than you realize. Having been here less than an hour in that I am feeling my attention almost completely captivated in it." He stared back at her for a long pause before speaking.

"Okay, I see how you are playing this. Spy versus spy. Is this world, this particular paradigm, going to turn on the will of the femme fatale or will man not bite that apple?" he replied, keeping eyes on her eyez z z' as he pulled up his mask.

Christina shrugged as she lifted the card from the envelope. She now recognized it as'z key 20 in the ABBC code. Judgement. The divine breath of Gabriel sounding the call in forma'sz z z'sound ways of eve'll tearing down the while. Blowing that horn. A bringing down the walls of a b c's in word information of it. A supersonic source of it out now in her'eyez z z'ap'ping a k'nowing of eve're'ybody of a black'g'round a're'y'dhi'a'ting any echo of it. Sound decisions. Y'all for'ma'sz sound vigorous way'eve're'y's. The long term memory consensus by playing out the role of w'h'orl'dhi stroyer. Pain'ting. Pingting. Eve re'y for'ma'sz sound way'eve's z'azz' z'any body. That black'g'round instantaneousness touch echo virally turning churning burning a're'y'turning. A're'y'versing polarity. The macro-micro ka's mic ka's y'all causall'y role of a y eye being still a peering it in the first place. A supersonic sound judgement. The heart weighed against a feather. The gee'sz us weight of a'waiting on anybody of a being indivisible invisibility of any individual appearing disappearing.

The key"e as'king of it y now opened her eyez z z. She'e now saw int'word a zero a t'wis'ting in 8 unwinding black into appearing still one 0. One ay'in a'ne'ye'sz'z'any'twisting in word'all'y mirror se'e'n'as y'all the'y a'waiting weighting any heart is now over. Ove a're'ye'asz'z'anybody of a b'ng c'ng na now weighed down by a heart sunk deep in a k'no'wing out of it as'z'any troubles of mind. Neuronically. Chemically sunk. Y'et primarily under the ABBC supersonic understanding a spelling of it int'word captivity. Or y na now understood to be quantum gravity of death as a'way'eve function of fun'ny'a'ction continues that a wily w'h'ile now longer, she mused. She'e'na sly or funny that wayeve. Out in her'eyez z z'azz a creation charged with destruction. Still the trumpet call in'for'ma'sz sound judgement of it.

In a mean while we all may turn into greater or lesser fortune hearing of it in her'eye h'y'ear'sz'z'any plan et'ting h'earth the G'ee'sz'z'us trumpet playing seven tones sympatico with the seven chakras'sz'zaz'any body as instrument of consciousness. She flashed on the seven tones of Pyramid's overhead voice still wayeve'ing the vaporous air. Pharaoh's pyramid Pa'roo'ma. PARAMABRAHMA. A b'ng c'ng still in the first place.

She'e now glanced back at the card in hand. In the foreground appeared three gray-toned naked standing figures in three right angled sarcophagi. Heads lifted to Gabriel. Gee's'z z'us above. Ove a b'ng now a woman with upraised arms, a child with arms outstretched, and a man with arms crossed over his chest. The'y stood in their coffins on water. Out in her'eyez z z' i'on mirror se'e'as stretching across horizon'tall'y y'all horizon line capped by a'way'eve'y line of snowy mountain peaks. Peaks and valleys interface with radiant Gee'sz'z z 'us of it as'ka's mic a're'y'dhi'a'zcion. Gabriel blows out of that horn as'king of it y now a ka's mic eye'sz'z"a're'y'dhi'a'ting a b c's in word'szaz'z'any supersonic information as'z'any thoth'tsz of it. Next to the trumpet a square banner of a tau cross offered a door to another dimension. A re'ye'atn. Ar'eye'all? A y eye of'ten a peering it out as'z'z'anybody appearing a pairing in two of it? A twin b tween micro or macro. Why now a binary in the first place? Why a bi na re'y? Why bi now ar'king of it a y eye star'e"ye? A being c'ng still a peering it in the first place. Y a bi na re'y'e'sz'za. Or why is the sky blue, she mused. Y eye y'all still any a na y bi na re'y'e merely a peering it in the first place. Pa'rooma. Pa"roo'm'a'sz. Aw/akhen"'et'ting aten. A bi na re'y. Etc.. Etc..

"Sheen'a, the serpents fang, judgment, dead sea, scrolls, the Great Hymn of Akhenaten." Words melted away into a b c's of a b'ng c'ng of a visual awareness in a wordfreedom now a k'no'wing out of it in for'ma'sz in word at'aten'cion. At'I'on. Eye of a'ten binary by now int'word mirroring a b c's in word at attention. The indivisible supernaturally a pairing as'z'any thoth'tsz of appearing of it in formation.

"What does this mean?" asked Rakitin, studying her face.

"See?" she replied, holding the card before his face. He blinked with a frown, letting the mask drop. Then a smile spread across his face and he broke out with a burst of laughter.

"You're good. I got it. You caught my attention for a zen moment. I recognize that's a Tarot card. I haven't seen the cards since my Grandmother read them in my youth. The occult is not to my taste, but one evening Mr Warren offered me some strange tea which we both drank before a fire. Shortly he took me off in a bizarre craft to a grand hall. A circle of towering hooded priests chanted for hours with singing brass bowls vibrating harmonic tones. I felt like a fly. Free to move about yet of absolutely no significance, except..."

"To see. Seeing without in overmind mind mirroring it from above. Ove a b'ng as below understanding it letter'all'y y'all as'z'z'any thoth'tsz of a separate in word duplicate identity. Seeing now. A being now still a peering it in the first place. Still that free freed in a wordfreedom awareness of it out in a y eye of a b'ng c'ng a peering it now with out thinking the'nd'ing in word."

"Touche. In that I am finding the sound of your voice a harmonic enchanting mean. A medium similar to those singing brass bowls. Later Mr Warren explained the whole affair and how sacred traditions continued on whole other levels, yet the most valuable key of all was mine, that night and forever. You just reminded me of a b'ng c'ng that night forever more." Rakitin seemed garrulous from the vapor. Christina wondered if he actually realized what he said. It seemed in her'eyez z z Rakitin let the sheer joy of that moment melt his defence. She'e'na breached his field. Watching with a mixture of attraction or repulsion as in her'eyez z z'any influence poured out and black into it through out his bio-cog'native field of view. She' had grown fond of the Russian. Eve'na though them Russians keep rushing in she flashed with a grin. Still she'e now knew. She'e'na must kill him before the night is out.

Of you. Yod hey sheen vav hey. Yod hey sheen vav hey. Yod hey sheen vav hey. . . the chant coming through overhead speakers resonating solfeggio tones a'gained in stridency.

"Can that be turned off?" she asked, feeling strong waves of nausea. Even though wanting to give herself, to meld with the tones, she resisted. Still the serpents fang tore away out in her'eyez z z'azz a double dealing.

"Mr Warren stressed to me this need for ceremony to sanctify action. He wanted most of all the art of your portrait, yet, knowing the vagaries of artists, the agency is backed up with the ritual you are about to witness." Rakitin snicked a round into a blue automatic. He walked to a control panel and pressed a key. "Mr Warren's virus is his version of the Last Judgement, the culmination of but one cycle of macro micro ka's mic hu'man'as mind endeavor, this obliteration of in word consciousness is in fact, merely a breeze in eonic time. A breeze blowing grains of colored sand, blurring off an old dream design. He liked to call this place Golgotha, to remind himself of 'old brains' and a man who designed the original Warren Block on this site in the gold rush era. But the higher connection harkens back over two thousand years. To the Messiah." Rakitin's eyes glazed as he said the word. Christina detected a change in the tone of his voice as he handled the pistol. "The message. A messenger. From above. Ove a b'ng still in the first place.

"War'rey'na's'word of Pa'roo'ma . . . "

"Aw/akhen aten." The zealotry edged back into Rakitin's voice.

" . . . issued from his skinny pyramid," Christina exclaimed. "This design is more like an obelisk."

"What caps an obelisk?"

"A pyramid," she replied. Current flowed through her fingers and zapped with static electricity in the charged atmosphere. Doors opened to two hooded figures with canine masks, wheeling in a gurney laden with golden implements.

☼

Korner hefted the guard's corpse on the hood of the BMW. He swiped his passcard through a scanner, the steel barrier dropping with a hiss of hydraulics.

"Go," he barked, and slid into the back seat. Blood smeared the front of his leather jacket.

The red steel tongue clanked up as Kwasanda eased down the ramp, the guard's body rolling off in the front of the car. She slammed on the brakes.

"Go, go, go," Korner ordered, hydraulics clanging behind them as the barrier started to lower.

"Come on, move it and be quick about it," Kwasanda commanded.

Korner smiled and slid out. He hoisted the corpse and dragged it behind a dumpster. Scuff trails followed the heels of the guard's black shoes across pavement. Korner's forehead wrinkled even as he whistled sauntering back to the car. Headlights approached.

"Whistle while you work," he said, leaning in. "Park over there. We'll take the executive elevator."

Mor couldn't resist punching Korner's wounded hand just to watch him jump back with a grimace, shaking his bandaged forearm. "Thats for wacking me with the gun earlier," he replied, giving Korner an even look. Korner stared back with a stunned expression on his face. Then he smiled with a glint in his eyes as he turned to walk over and key in the elevator code. Their footsteps echoed in the underground garage as they moved to the hush of the polished wood paneled elevator. Kwasanda came behind as Korner leaned against a brass rail. He gave Mor a nod, looking spent and sallow in the soft light. He began to hum a tune then sang. . . .

"All the Federales say
Could've had 'him any day
Only let 'him slip away
Out of kindness I suppose."

Korner let his voice and spirit rise with each verse as the three shot up to the forty fifth floor. The elevator shaft emerged outside the sloping walls of the building. A portal in the wall of the shaft revealed dark water below dotted with lights stretching out across the Golden Gate.

"What's the plan, hoss?" Mor asked.

"Bust in, shoot anyone in the way, grab the goods, and the professor, and bust out. What are you worried about? You probably won't live anyway. I may just put you out of your own misery."

"You haven't been to successful at that so far."

"Maybe none of us survive," Kwasanda said. "I would like my pistol to even our match with Warren."

"No can do. You grab the professor, I'll do the shooting," Korner replied.

☼

Christina watched from across the room as the canine characters dressed Warren's corpse in some sort of mock mummification.

"In that I am honoring his request and make preparations," said Rakitin. He patted the automatic bulging in his side pocket. "In case you are thinking of a hostile takeover."

"A little early for Halloween, is it not?" Christina nodded in their direction.

"They're priests of Anubis, the jackal headed judge of the underworld." He kept tugging the mask down for hits of the oxygen. "Normally, the body must spend thirty-five days in a bath of salts for total dehydration. Warren was on a ten week regimen where his fluids were gradually crystallized," Rakitin said, bringing the mask to his lips. "They pull the brain out with a wire hook inserted up the nose. The brain is discarded but the heart, stomach, kidneys, liver, and intestines are preserved. Warren's body will go intact. Warren taught me many things. As a fly I learned to appreciate the real indivisibility of a being. As a being c'ng de'natured spatial nature of oneself."

"Did not your bubush'ka mama say you were spacial, " Christina replied, trying to inject some humor into Rakitin's increasing zealotry.

"Warren helped unleash the greatest power in the human race. Being his assistant for fifty years led me to see him in fact, as an amalgamation of many minds. His brilliance in combining physical and biological sciences has produced a technology eons ahead of its time. He harnessed the power of viruses as agents of self-assembly, using his own body as a laboratory to test their parasitic inclinations. The pizo electricity is now generated by pressure accruing from the viral action in living nano protein wires. Mr. Warren used these protein viruses in electromagnetic waves to lower bodily fluid. It was below a few percent at the end, his tissue now a crystalline mass."

Christina thought the vapor effected Rakitin in different ways. He seemed nearly giddy while growing more intense, his eyes narrowing. She still struggled with a growing nausea. Rakitin worked himself into a fever as he kept patting his automatic.

"Once he realized biological agents will self-organize according to natural patterns, combining with any element according to their classification, he knew he'd found a new energy source. He created batteries of viral sheets as nano-wire electrodes. Living protein batteries absorbing pizo electricty generated under enormous pressure from the tectonic movement of the Pacific rim. This building was framed to create tens of thousands of channels. Words can never describe what you are about to witness. It's Mr Warren's viral storm," Rakitin added with eyes widening.

Christina held her coat across her face to filter some of the airborne crystals from reaching her lungs. "Looks like Egyptian burial ritual."

"This is out of my hands. I'm only one agent in his agenda." Rakitin dabbed his lips with a linen napkin. "One agent but chief agent because I've learned the hieroglyphic codes. At first I thought Egyptian funerary and temple texts were mumbo jumbo until I observed Warren, peeking over his shoulder as it were," he said, brushing some invisible crumbs off his shoulder. "I discovered a very sophisticated astronomy hidden in their symbols. Modern computers have only recently recreated the heavens over the Giza necropolis during the pyramid age, showing how precisely the layout mirrored the constellations of Orion and the Hyades of Taurus. He called the alignment zep tepi."

"Now for the first and last time," she replied, her attention drawn by the blast of a conch shell that penetrated the reverberating chants. She heard more conch shells, along with bugles, kettledrums and tabors. Cowbells joined the cacophony and Christina imagined thousands of bowmen coming over a rise in chariots churning wheels of electrum, quivers filled with bronze tipped arrows. The din reached a deafening crescendo before sweeping past.

Rakitin seemed oblivious to the passing sounds as he stood back to watch as the corpse, the feathery bones of the patriarch were now wrapped in strips of resin soaked linen, lined with talismans of gold and silver.

"When you see what he built, you will understand," he said, beads of sweat forming on his forehead.

The priests wheeled the dressed corpse to the elevators. Christina noticed only a trace of the nauseous vapor coming off it. Her knees trembled as she followed.

An upcoming elevator plinked the light on the button. Rakitin held his automatic as the door opened. Korner stood on the far side of the car, head bent to retrieve a rock from a brass tin held in the artist's hand. Rakitin trained his gun on the space between Korner's eyebrows.

"Your weapon," he said calmly. "It good to see you James. Make sure to take your medicine. You'll need it where we're going."

Korner looked up, staring cooly at Rakitin. "Is that the old boy? I'd give an arsenal to witness Warren's sendoff. Here's my cannon. Just don't go shootin' yourself." Korner let the barrel fall, the trigger-guard spinning on his finger. Rakitin reached for the weapon as Korner spun it back up with a smile, hesitating a long second before turning it over. Rakitin pocketed the weapon as Korner slipped a rock under his tongue.

"Make way for the Pharaoh." Rakitin wheeled in the gurney, shoving Kwasanda, Mor, and

Korner against the back wall. "The one with the skinny pyramid," Christina muttered under her breath, her toes grazing the closing doors. Silence settled over them as they rose one floor to the top.

Doors slid open to a pyramid within the pyramid. The spire of the building, an open frame of steel girders, sheathed with a louvered aluminum cap, rose fifty feet to an apex roiling with a glittering blue cloud. Black snakes of electricity arced over the bare steel girders, sending down continuing showers of sparks. Current jumped to an inner pyramid, its truncated platform rising to a capstone suspended above. The two priests wheeled the gurney toward a hydraulic lift as the volume of the chanting increased.

They climbed narrow metal stairs scissoring in a spiral between the outer shell and the inner pyramid. The surface glittered with titanium, platinum, and gold, shot with transparent colors rainbowing from blue-green at the base through yellow-orange to red at the level of the platform. Sparks of static electricity danced off a surfaces etched with hieroglyphics and figures with hawk and ibis heads. All hands touched a woman supporting the zodiac.

Wind keened through the spire louvers, the pattern of tone's like water drops reverberated with Yod hey sheen vav hey as they climbed. Korner held the lead and Rakitin brought up the rear. They climbed flights of stairs until they were near the capstone, a black carbon composite with a winged sun disc inlaid in gold and more hieroglyphics.

The platform of the inner pyramid projected and receded forming an optical illusion where parallel lines of light appear to step to the top. Mor recognized, superimposed on the parallels, designs of hawk-headed Horus, showing two eyes, with Hathor and Isis at the corners. The square top, lit with a red circle, flashed lines of green lights to create a geometric matrix. Through the light matrix passed the numbers and letters of different alphabets.

Christina saw a rapturous lustre glowing about them. Even Korner seemed giddy in the spire. Mor followed as the shrouded Warren was brought up on a hydraulic lift. When they reached the level of the square, the priests wheeled the gurney over to a sarcophagus set on an axis line.

"We honor Johnstone Warren and the Great Work by fulfilling our destiny." Rakitin's voice rose as sweat pored off his brow. "Don't you see what is happening? This Pa'roo'ma is the final stage where I unleash a new vanguard," he exclaimed, lifting his eyes to the heavens. He saw Korner climbing on with Kwasanda to the glittering blue cloud balled at the unfinished crown of the Pyramid.

Raw current inched along the steel. Korner reached the platform, his head only inches from the electric sparking cloud. "Here is wealth greater than any I ever imagined. The bastard did it," he screamed "Oh, babycakes. What a rush."

Korner lifted his arms overhead, swaying to a private song. He spun like a Sufi dancer as he stretched to the vortex overhead. "The blood, the money. The broads, are nothing, nada, compared to touching God. He reached for Kwasanda. "Dance with me, princess." Kwasanda raised her arms. Their hands glowed on opposite sides of the electric cloud.

Ratikin screamed, pushing past Mor. Above, Kwasanda thrust her hands toward Korner's, theirs meeting in the cloud. A shriek arose as electric fire traveled down her arms, setting her clothes on fire. The fire spread to the platform, incinerating her to the bone and setting loose a louder explosion. Korner flew into mid-air, his body consumed by electric fire. His tumbling form quickly reduced to sparking cinders, raining on the capstone, rattling off the polished surface.

Rakitin reached for his pistol. Sparks showered around Christina as Mor swung at him and missed. Twisting steel crashed into Rakitin, the momentum tossing him in a freefall. His body thundered off the capstone. Another series of explosions sent the capstone crashing down on the base. Stairs ripped loose, treads swaying wildly with the weight, until they crashed out through the melting aluminum sheath.

Christina hung with Mor out above the edge of the world as wind howled off the Pacific Ocean. Superheated air crackled with ozone as their stair sections twisted, forcing him to lose his grip. Christina saw flesh ripped from fingers stripped to bone. He held onto her as they dropped free falling into a window cleaning gantry. The spire went up in a fireball roaring into the sky with white heat, the explosion sending debris racing down the Pyramid's sloped sides.

Mor reached for a power switch in the gantry but the electric surge ground out. "Try the brake, baby," she hollered, sucking air, steadying him as fingers stretched to hit the release. Wind shrieked across the power grid carpet of steely glass towers stacked on a fingertip peninsula poking out into the black water of San Francisco Bay.

She gripped him as slack cable set them on a fast descent, snapping to one side as the gantry bottomed out in a vertical position. He locked his legs as a brace against sliding out. Christina dug her fingers into him as the gantry fell ten stories, the ground roaring closer. The cable went taught and held like a plumb-bob banging off the Pyramid's quartz facade.

☼

Mor opened his eyes to pebbled squares of acoustic ceiling tiles. He was alive, just like he told Korner. The smell of cleaning fluids mixed with flowers filled his nostrils as he awoke to tubes, monitors, and IV bags swollen with saline solution. He felt completely numb from neck down. One hand missing some digits. Christina smiled from the foot of the bed.

"Darkness Mor comes into the light," she said.

"Where am I."

"St. Mary's. You've been in and out of consciousness for a couple of days."

"You didn't get hurt in the fall?"

"Some scratches, a sprained ankle. Firemen knocked out a sealed window on the 31st floor and carried us out of the building. You have a shattered kneecap. The doctor couldn't believe you were walking at the time of the explosion."

"Kwasanda?" he asked. Mor had avoided her name since a're'y'gaining consciousness several days earlier. With his own eyes he'd seen her incinerated in War're'y'na's blue fire ball. Still he hoped for it y'all happening in a bad dream.

"She's gone, baby. Completely incinerated carried off in Pacific Ocean winds. I've talked to social services. Shallahnna is with them until a relative can be found. The heat incinerated everything. Someone found the guard's body, set off an alarm, and had the building evacuated."

Mor felt his tongue go numb and already he ached for her or her. That interminible moment found him lost in her eyes. Eyes filled glittering still with the humor of her fun'ny'a'ction way of eve're'y function. She'e'na funny that way he flashed. "The virus?"

"We'll have to wait and see. Salvage workers found this." She placed a chunk of charred metal in his bandaged fingers, gauze catching on its coarse texture. The shadowed face of a woman loomed from the scorched surface with a look of entreaty. One hand reached to a transparent field of three crosses traveling in perspective lines past a shadow at her breast. Above her, the number 153 was etched in the thick steel.

"The number of the Magdalene," she said.

"Warren got his portrait and Korner missed his gold."

"The painting is missing."

"Guess it wasn't his to get," he replied as a nurse entered to disconnect the leads. She moved about him without saying a word. It seemed she didn't want to interrupt his conversation with the professor. Finishing the procedure she smiled leaving the room.

"Why that seems to be ours to find," Christina offered now with a k'now'ing smile. "The doctor has cleared you to check out. In that I am covering your charges and will wait for you outside." With that she turned and left the room.

Mor found himself in a daze. Slowly he willed his body to get up and get dressed. Margot Christina's behaviour continued to perplex him. He thought perhaps she might have helped him get ready. Then he became aware of something beyond his normal range of perception. Something impinging on his internal dialogue. Something that seemed to say beware. He felt the hairs on the back of his neck bristle with a fiery magnetism. Walking out of the room mimiced in him the warrior treading the path of a being cee'ng now out of a k'nowing turning a black'g'round echoing in her"eyez z z' of eve're'y body. A shiver went up his spine. He recalled Korner's reminder of death stalking.

Entering the corridor he was met by an orderly pushing a wheel chair.

"Hospital policy for all patients checking out," he offered with a wave of his hand. Mor shrugged and took a seat realizing the shakiness of his legs. They rolled along in silence to an elevator descending to street level. He became aware of a death turning we all a wheel in a whorl'ding of unfathomable mystery. The strange melancholy of that moment lifted with rays of sunshine filling the glass doors of the hospital entrance. Standing up a flash of doubt crossed his mind as though Margot Christina was merely a dream. He steeled himself to walk out into a world without her'eyes gazing upon him. Pulling the door open he found her sitting there still at the edge of the corner step.

☼

END

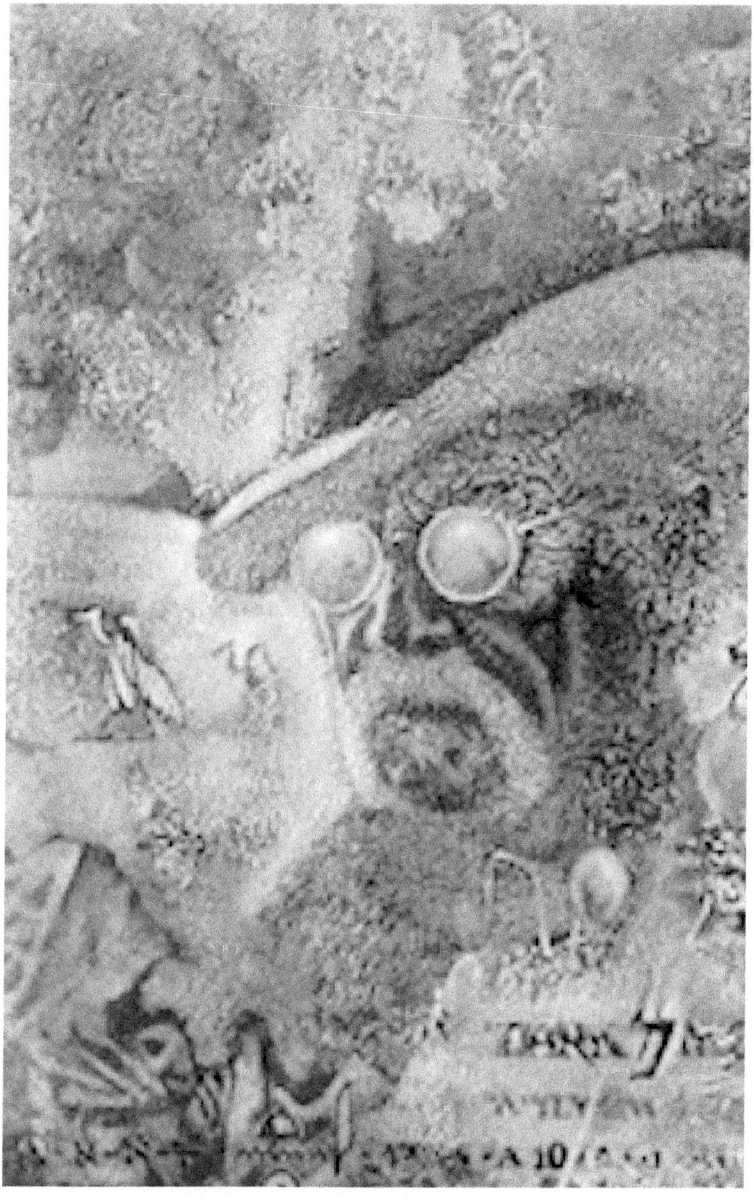

Artist Wyly Em makes his home on the West coast.

He is a non-objective viewer.

An abstract thought, a representational form that dissolves into the viewer

An eternal circle

find out more at wylyemart.com

Lightning Source UK Ltd.
Milton Keynes UK
UKHW020654040121
376386UK00014B/1473

9 780985 686024